D1321540

The Lies *of* Locke Lamora

BOOK ONE *of the*
Gentleman Bastard Sequence

SCOTT LYNCH

First published in Great Britain in 2006 by
Gollancz
An imprint of the Orion Publishing Group
Orion House, 5 Upper St Martin's Lane,
London WC2H 9EA
An Hachette UK Company

This edition published in Great Britain in 2011 by Gollancz

A CIP catalogue record for this book
is available from the British Library

Typeset at The Spartan Press Ltd,
Lymington, Hants

Printed and bound by CPI Group Ltd,
Croydon, CRO 4YY

The Orion Publishing Group's policy is to use papers that
are natural, renewable and recyclable products and made
from wood grown in sustainable forests. The logging and
manufacturing processes are expected to conform to the
environmental regulations of the country of origin.

www.scottlynch.us
www.orionbooks.co.uk

For Jenny, this little world that was blessed
To have you peeking over my shoulder while it took shape —
Love always.

INTRODUCTION

I was deeply upset when I first read Scott Lynch's *The Lies of Locke Lamora*. But not because it was bad. Oh no. Far worse. Because it was very good, and my first book was coming out within a couple of months of it, from the same publisher. And I am a venomously ambitious sociopath.

My deep hatred for Scott is made worse because I think he and I come from similar places – no, not Wisconsin – we are similar in our takes on fantasy. We both grew up during the 80s boom in commercial fantasy, both played a lot of role playing games (Lynch actually wrote a few supplements himself), and both felt the need for a new formula to apply to the tropes of a genre that some might say had become slightly stale. Perhaps even a little mouldy in places . . .

Lynch's is a style of fantasy that takes its lead more from the smelly moral ambiguity and freebooting fun of Fritz Leiber, and from the gritty realism and lethal unpredictability of George R. R. Martin, than it does from the more stately tradition of Tolkien and his legions of imitators. This is not high fantasy, it is proudly and unapologetically low – no elves, no dwarves, precious little magic and what there is is decidedly unpleasant, but plenty of squalid backstreets, swearing and corruption. Few magic swords but a lot of dirty knives in the back. His villains can be exceedingly unpleasant, his heroes scarcely less so. In fact he takes as his central characters some of the most unappealing people you'll find – thieves, tricksters, self-serving liars – and still manages to make us like them.

A lot of that appeal springs from the wit. *The Lies of Locke Lamora* isn't slapstick, but it is light on its feet, ducking and weaving like its con-man hero, never letting the reader know quite what to expect next, occasionally blindsiding them with a blow that really stings. There's nothing stodgy here, none of that self-regarding pomposity that big fantasy can sometimes be guilty of.

But perhaps the best thing about Lynch's creation is the setting itself. The city of Camorr is built around, inside, and on top of a much more ancient city made from alien glass, a beautiful and mysterious architecture which shows through, and contrasts with, the ugly crust of human buildings on top and the often filthy lifestyles of the villains living in them. It's a wonderfully simple idea, takes minimal time and effort to explain to the reader, requires no map and no glossary, but immediately gives a unique feel to pretty much every location in the book and allows for some great, vivid, descriptive writing. The city truly becomes a character in its own right and one with which the people in the novel all have their own relationship. A fascinating, beautiful, and alien setting created without interrupting the flow of the story? That's my idea of great world-building.

It seems to me that Scott Lynch is at the forefront (well, just behind me) of a new wave of fantasists combining the length, detail and scale of epic fantasy with a wit, moral ambiguity and edgy unpredictability that owes far more to the tradition of Sword and Sorcery. But Lynch has an eye for setting, a knack for dialogue and a sheer exuberance which is all his own.

Bastard.

Joe Abercrombie

Joe Abercrombie (www.joeabercrombie.com) is the *Sunday Times* bestselling author of The First Law trilogy (THE BLADE ITSELF, BEFORE THEY ARE HANGED and LAST ARGUMENT OF KINGS) and THE HEROES.

Joe has donated his fee for this introduction to Shelter

www.shelter.org.uk

PROLOGUE

The boy who stole too much

I

At the height of the long wet summer of the Seventy-Seventh Year of Sendovani, the Thiefmaker of Camorr paid a sudden and unannounced visit to the Eyeless Priest at the Temple of Perelandro, desperately hoping to sell him the Lamora boy.

'Have I got a deal for you!' the Thiefmaker began, perhaps inauspiciously.

'Another deal like Calo and Galdo, maybe?' said the Eyeless Priest. 'I've still got my hands full training those giggling idiots out of every bad habit they picked up from you and replacing them with the bad habits I need.'

'Now, Chains.' The Thiefmaker shrugged. 'I told you they were shit-flinging little monkeys when we made the deal, and it was good enough for you at the—'

'Or maybe another deal like Sabetha?' The priest's richer, deeper voice chased the Thiefmaker's objection right back down his throat. 'I'm sure you recall charging me everything but my dead mother's kneecaps for her. I should've paid you in copper and watched you spring a rupture trying to haul it all away.'

'Ahhhhhh, but she was special, and this boy, this boy, he's special too,' said the Thiefmaker. 'Everything you asked me to look for after I sold you Calo and Galdo. Everything you liked so much about Sabetha! He's Camorri, but a mongrel. Therin and Vadran blood. He's got larceny in his heart, sure as the sea's full of fish piss. And I can even let you have him at a . . . a discount.'

The Eyeless Priest spent a long moment mulling this. 'You'll pardon me,' he finally said, 'if experience suggests that I would be wise to meet unexpected generosity from you by arming myself and putting my back against a wall.'

The Thiefmaker tried to let a vaguely sincere expression scurry onto his face, where it froze in evident discomfort. His shrug was theatrically casual. 'There are, ah, problems with the boy, yes. But the problems are unique to his situation in my care. Were he under yours, I'm sure they would, ahhhh, vanish.'

'Oh. Oh. You have a *magic* boy. Why didn't you say so?' The priest scratched his forehead beneath the white silk blindfold that covered his eyes. '*Magnificent*. I'll plant him in the fucking ground and grow a vine to an enchanted land beyond the clouds.'

'Ahhhhh! Ah ah ah, I've tasted that flavour of sarcasm from you before, Chains.' The Thiefmaker gave an arthritic mock bow. 'Is it really so hard to say that you're interested?'

The Eyeless Priest spat. 'Suppose Calo, Galdo and Sabetha might be able to use a new playmate, or at least a punching bag. *Suppose* I'm willing to spend about three coppers and a bowl of piss for an unlooked-for mystery boy. What's the boy's problem?'

'His problem,' said the Thiefmaker, 'is that if I can't sell him to you, I'm going to have to slit his throat and throw him in the bay. And I'm going to have to do it *tonight*.'

2

On the night the Lamora boy had come to live under the Thief-maker's care, the old graveyard on Shades' Hill had been full of children, standing at silent attention and waiting for their new brothers and sisters to be led down into the mausoleums.

The Thiefmaker's wards all carried candles; their cold blue light shone through the silver curtains of river mist as street lamps might glimmer through a smoke-grimed window. A chain of ghostlight wound its way down from the hilltop, through the stone markers and ceremonial paths, down to the wide glass bridge over the Coalsmoke canal, half-visible in the bloodwarm fog that seeped up from Camorr's wet bones on summer nights.

'Come now my loves, my jewels, my newlyfounds, keep the pace,' whispered the Thiefmaker as he nudged the last of the thirty or so Catchfire orphans over the Coalsmoke bridge. 'These lights are just your new friends, come to guide your way up my hill. Move now, my treasures. There's darkness wasting, and we have so much to talk about.'

In rare moments of vain reflection, the Thiefmaker thought of himself as an artist. A sculptor, to be precise, with orphans as his clay and the old graveyard on Shades' Hill as his studio.

Eighty-eight thousand souls generated a certain steady volume of waste; this waste included a constant trickle of lost, useless and abandoned children. Slavers got some of them, to be sure – hauling them off to Tal Verarr or the Jeremite islands. Slavery was technically illegal in Camorr, but the act of enslavement itself was winked at if there was no one left to speak for the victim.

So, slavers got some, and plain stupidity took a few more. Starvation and the diseases it brought were also common ways to go for those that lacked the courage or the skill to pluck a living from the city around them. And then, of course, those with courage but no skill often wound up swinging from the Black Bridge in front of the Palace of Patience. The Duke's magistrates disposed of little thieves with the same rope they used on bigger ones, though they did see to it that the little ones went over the side of the bridge with weights tied to their ankles to help them hang properly.

Any orphans left after dicing with all of those colourful possibilities were swept up by the Thiefmaker's own crew, brought in one at a time or in small groups to hear his soothing voice and eat a hot meal. Soon enough they would learn what sort of life awaited them beneath the graveyard that was the heart of his realm, where seven score cast-off children bent the knee to a single bent old man.

'Quick-step, my lovelies, my new sons and daughters; follow the line of lights and step to the top. We're almost home, almost fed. Out of the rain and the mist and the stinking heat.'

Plagues were a time of special opportunity for the Thiefmaker, and the Catchfire orphans had crawled away from his very favourite sort: Black Whisper. It fell on the Catchfire district from points unknown, and the quarantine had gone up (death by clothyard shaft for anyone trying to cross a canal or escape on a boat) in time to save the rest of the city from everything but unease and paranoia. Black Whisper meant a miserable death for anyone over the age of eleven or twelve (as near as physikers could figure, for the plague was not content to reap by overly firm rules) and a few days of harmless swollen eyes and red cheeks for anyone younger.

3

By the fifth day of the quarantine there were no more screams and no more attempted canal crossings, and so Catchfire evaded the namesake fate that had befallen it so many times before in years of pestilence. By the eleventh day, when the quarantine was lifted and the Duke's ghouls went in to survey the mess, perhaps one in eight of the four hundred children previously living there had survived the wait. They had already formed gangs for mutual protection and learned certain cruel necessities of life without adults.

The Thiefmaker was waiting as they were coralled and led out from the sinister silence of their old neighbourhood.

He paid good silver for the best thirty, and even more good silver for the silence of the ghouls and constables he relieved of the children. Then he led them, dazed and hollow-cheeked and smelling like hell, into the darkness and the steambath mists of the Camorri night, towards the old graveyard on Shades' Hill.

The Lamora boy was the youngest and smallest of the lot, five or six years old, nothing but jutting bones under skin rich with dirt and hollow angles. The Thiefmaker hadn't even chosen him; Lamora had simply crept away with the others as though he belonged. The Thiefmaker was not unaware of this, but he'd lived the sort of life in which even a single free plague orphan was a windfall not to be overlooked.

It was the summer of the Seventy-Seventh year of Gandolo, Father of Opportunities, Lord of Coin and Commerce. The Thiefmaker padded through the shrouded night, shepherding his ragged line of children.

In just two years he would be all but begging Father Chains the Eyeless Priest to take the Lamora boy off his hands, and sharpening his knives in case the priest refused.

3

The Eyeless Priest scratched his grey-stubbled throat. 'No shit?'

'None whatsoever.' The Thiefmaker reached down the front of a doublet that was several years past merely shabby and pulled out a leather pouch on a fine leather cord; the pouch was dyed the rust-red of dried blood. 'Already went to the big man and got permission. I'll do the boy ear-to-ear and send him for teeth lessons.'

'Gods. It's a sob story after all.' For an Eyeless Priest, the fingers he jabbed into the Thiefmaker's sternum struck swift and sure. 'Find some other lackwit to shackle with the chains of your conscience.'

'Conscience can go piss up a chimney, Chains. I'm talking avarice, yours and mine. I can't keep the boy and I'm offering you a unique opportunity, a genuine bargain.'

'If the boy's too unruly to keep, why can't you just pound some wisdom into him and let him ripen to a proper age of sale?'

'Out of the question, Chains. Limited options. I can't just slap him around because I can't let any of the other little shits know what he's, ahhh, done. If any of them had the slightest inclination to pull what he's pulled . . . gods! I'd never be able to control them again. I can either kill him quick, or sell him quicker. No profit versus a paltry sum. So guess which one I prefer?'

'The boy's done something you can't even mention in front of the others?' Chains massaged his forehead above the blindfold and sighed. 'Shit. This sounds like something I might actually be interested in hearing.'

4

An old Camorri proverb has it that the only constant in the soul of man is inconstancy; anything and everything can pass out of fashion, even something as utilitarian as a hill stuffed full of corpses.

Shades' Hill was the first graveyard of quality in Camorr's history, ideally situated to keep the bones of the formerly well-fed above the salty grasp of the Iron Sea. Yet over time the balance of power shifted in the families of vault-carvers and morticians and professional pallbearers; fewer and fewer of the quality were interred on Shades' Hill, as the nearby Hill of Whispers offered more room for larger and gaudier monuments with commensurately higher commissions. Wars, plagues and intrigues ensured that the number of living families with monuments to tend on Shades' Hill dropped steadily over the decades. Eventually, the only regular visitors were the priests and priestesses of Aza Guilla, who sleep in tombs during their apprenticeships, and the homeless orphans that squatted in the dust and darkness of the ill-tended burial vaults.

The Thiefmaker (though of course he wasn't known as such just yet) had wound up sharing one of these vaults at the low point of his life, when he was nothing but a miserable curiosity – a pickpocket with nine broken fingers.

At first, his relationship with the Shades' Hill orphans was half-bullying and half-pleading; some vestigial need for an authority figure kept them from killing him in his sleep. For his part, he grudgingly began to explain to them some of the tricks of his trade.

As his fingers slowly mended (after a fashion, for most of them would forever resemble twice-broken twigs), he began to impart more and more of his crooked wisdom to the dirty children that dodged the rain and the city watch with him. Their numbers increased, as did their income, and they began to make more room for themselves in the wet stone chambers of the old graveyard.

In time, the brittle-boned pickpocket became the Thiefmaker; Shades' Hill became his kingdom.

The Lamora boy and his fellow Catchfire orphans entered this kingdom some twenty years after its founding; what they saw that night was a graveyard no deeper than the dirt piled above the old tombs. A great network of tunnels and galleries had been dug between the major vaults, their hard-packed walls threaded with supports like the ribs of long-dead wooden dragons. The previous occupants had all been quietly disinterred and dropped into the bay. Shades' Hill was now an ant-mound of orphan thieves.

Down the black mouth of the topmost mausoleum the Catchfire orphans went, down the wood-ribbed tunnel lit by the flickering silver fire of cool alchemical globes, with greasy tendrils of mist chasing at their ankles. Shades' Hill orphans watched them from every nook and warren, their eyes cold but curious. The thick tunnel air was saturated with the smells of night soil and stale bodies – an odour the Catchfire orphans soon multiplied with their own presence.

'In! In!' cried the Thiefmaker, rubbing his hands together. 'My home, your home, and welcome to it! Here we all have one thing in common – no mothers and no fathers. Alas for that, but now you'll have as many sisters and brothers as you can need, and dry earth over your head! A place . . . a family.'

A train of Shades' Hill orphans swept down the tunnel in his wake, snuffing their eerie blue candles as they went, until only the silver radiance of the wall-globes remained to light the way.

At the heart of the Thiefmaker's realm was a vast warm hollow with a packed dirt floor, perhaps twice the height of a tall man, thirty yards wide and long. A single high-backed chair of oiled black witchwood stood against the far wall; this the Thiefmaker eased himself into with a grateful sigh.

Dozens of grotty blankets were set out on the floor, covered with food – bowls of bony chicken marinated in cheap almond wine, soft thresher-fish tails wrapped in bacon and soaked in vinegar, and brown bread flavoured with sausage grease. There were also salted peas and lentils as well as bowls of past-ripe tomatoes and pears. Poor stuff, but in a quantity and variety most of the Catchfire orphans had never seen before. Their attack on the meal was immediate and uncoordinated; the Thiefmaker smiled indulgently.

'I'm not stupid enough to get between you and a decent meal, my dears. So eat your fill; eat more than your fill. Make up for lost time. We'll talk after.'

As the Catchfire orphans stuffed their faces, Shades' Hill orphans crowded in around them, watching and saying nothing. Soon the chamber was packed and the air grew staler still. The feasting continued until there was literally nothing left; the survivors of the Black Whisper sucked the last vinegar and grease from their fingers and then turned their eyes warily to the Thiefmaker and his minions. The Thiefmaker held up three crooked fingers, as though on cue.

'Business!' he cried. 'Three items of business.'

'First,' he said, 'you're here because I *paid* for you. I paid extra to get to you before anyone *else* could. I can assure you that every single one of your little friends that I didn't pay for has gone to the slavers. There's nothing else to be done with orphans. No place to keep you, nobody to take you in. The watch sells your sort for wine money, my dears; watch-sergeants neglect to mention you in their reports, and watch-captains neglect to give a shit.

'And,' he continued, 'now that the Catchfire quarantine's lifted,

7

every slaver and would-be slaver in Camorr is going to be *very excited* and *very alert*. You're free to get up and leave this hill any time you see fit – with my confident assurance that you'll soon be sucking cocks or chained to an oar for the rest of your life.

'This leads me to my second point. All of my *friends* you see around you,' he gestured to the Shades' Hill orphans lined up against the walls, 'can leave whenever they please, and mostly go wherever they please, because they are under my protection. I know,' he said with a long and solemn face, 'that I am nothing especially formidable considered as an individual; do not be misled. I have powerful friends, my dears. What I offer is security by virtue of those friends. Should anyone, a slaver, for example, dare to set a hand on one of my Shades' Hill boys or girls, well, the consequences would be immediate and gratifyingly, ahhh, *merciless*.'

When none of his newcomers seemed appropriately enthusiastic, the Thiefmaker cleared his throat. 'I'd have the miserable fucking bastards killed. Savvy?'

They were indeed.

'Which brings us neatly to my third item of interest, namely, all of you. This little family always needs new brothers and sisters, and you may consider yourselves invited, *encouraged*, no less, to, ahhh, condescend to offer us the pleasure of your *intimate and permanent* acquaintance. Make this hill your home, myself your master, and these fine boys and girls your trusted siblings. You'll be fed, sheltered and protected. Or you can leave right now and end up as fresh fruit in some whorehouse in Jerem. Any takers?'

None of the newcomers said anything.

'I knew I could count on you, my dear Catchfire jewels.' The Thiefmaker spread his arms wide and smiled, revealing a half-moon of teeth brown as swampwater. 'But, of course, there must be responsibilities. There must be give and take, like for like. Food doesn't sprout from my arsehole. Chamber pots don't empty themselves. Catch my meaning?'

There were hesitant nods from about half the Catchfire orphans.

'The rules are simple! You'll learn them all in good time. For now, let's keep it like this. Anybody who eats, works. Anyone who works, eats. Which brings us to work, my fourth— Oh, dear. Children, children. Do an absent-minded old man the favour of imagining that he held up four fingers. This is my fourth important point.

'Now, we've got our chores here on the hill, but we've got chores elsewhere that also need doing. Other jobs . . . delicate jobs, unusual jobs. Fun and interesting jobs. All about the city, some by day and some by night. They will require courage, deftness and, ahhh, discretion. We would so *love* to have your assistance with these . . . special tasks.'

He pointed to the one boy he hadn't paid for, the small hanger-on, now staring up at him with hard, sullen eyes above a mouth still plastered with tomato innards.

'You, surplus boy, thirty-first of thirty. What say you? Are you the helpful sort? Are you willing to assist your new brothers and sisters with their interesting work?'

The boy mulled this over for a few seconds.

'You mean,' he said in a high thin voice, 'that you want us to steal things.'

The old man stared down at the little boy for a very long time while a number of the Shades' Hill orphans giggled behind their hands.

'Yes,' the Thiefmaker said at last, nodding slowly. 'I might just mean that, though you have a very, ahhh, *uncompromising* view of a certain exercise of personal initiative that we prefer to frame in more artfully indeterminate terms. Not that I expect that to mean anything to you. What's your name, boy?'

'Lamora.'

'Your parents must have been misers, to give you nothing but a surname. What *else* did they call you?'

The boy seemed to think very deeply about this.

'I'm called Locke,' he finally said. 'After my father.'

'Very good. Rolls right off the tongue, it does. Well, Locke-after-your-father Lamora, you come here and have a word with me. The rest of you, shuffle off. Your brothers and sisters will show you where you'll be sleeping tonight. They'll also show you where to empty this and where to put that – chores, if you savvy. Just to tidy this hall up for now, but there'll be more jobs for you in the days to come. I promise it will all make sense by the time you find out what they call me in the world beyond our little hill.'

Locke moved to stand beside the Thiefmaker where he sat on his high-backed throne; the throng of newcomers rose and milled about until larger, older Shades' Hill orphans began collaring them and issuing simple instructions. Soon enough, Locke and the master of Shades' Hill were as alone as they could hope to be.

'My boy,' the Thiefmaker said, 'I'm used to having to train a certain reticence out of my new sons and daughters when they first arrive in Shades' Hill. Do you know what *reticence* is?'

The Lamora boy shook his head. His greasy dust-brown bangs were plastered down atop his round little face, and the tomato stains around his mouth had grown drier and more unseemly. The Thiefmaker dabbed delicately at these stains with one cuff of his tattered blue coat; the boy didn't flinch.

'It means they've been told that stealing things is bad, and I need to work around that until they get used to the idea, savvy? Well, you don't seem to suffer from any such reticence, so you and I might just get along. Stolen before, have you?'

The boy nodded.

'Before the plague, even?'

Another nod.

'Thought so. My dear, dear boy . . . you didn't, ahhh, lose your parents to the plague, now, did you?'

The boy looked down at his feet and barely shook his head.

'So you've already been looking after yourself, for some time. It's nothing to be ashamed of, now. It might even secure you a place of some respect here, if only I can find a means to put you to the test . . .'

By way of response, the Lamora boy reached under his rags and held something out to the Thiefmaker. Two small leather purses fell into the old man's open palm – cheap things, stiff and stained, with frayed cords around their necks.

'Where did you get these, then?'

'The watchmen,' Locke whispered. 'Some of the watchmen picked us up and carried us.'

The Thiefmaker jerked back as though an asp had just sunk its fangs into his hand, and stared down at the purses with disbelief. 'You lifted these from the fucking city watch? From the yellowjackets?'

Locke nodded, more enthusiastically. 'They picked us up and *carried* us.'

'Gods,' the Thiefmaker whispered. 'Oh, gods. You may have just fucked us all superbly, Locke-after-your-father Lamora. Quite superbly indeed.'

5

'He broke the Secret Peace the first night I had him, the cheeky little bastard.' The Thiefmaker was now seated more comfortably in the rooftop garden of the Eyeless Priest's temple, with a tarred leather cup of wine in his hands. It was the sourest sort of second-hand near-vinegar, but it was another sign that genuine negotiations might yet break out. 'Never happened before, nor since.'

'Someone taught him to charm a coat, but didn't tell him that the yellowjackets were strictly off-limits.' Father Chains pursed his lips. 'Very curious, that. Very curious indeed. Our dear Capa Barsavi would so love to meet such an individual.'

'I never found out who it was. The boy claimed he'd just taught himself, but that's crap. Five-year-olds play with dead fish and horse turds, Chains. They don't invent the finer points of soft-touching and purse-cutting on a whim.'

'What did you do about the purses?'

'I flew back to Catchfire watch station and kissed arses and boots until my lips were black. Explained to the watch-captain in question that one of the newcomers didn't understand how things worked in Camorr, that I was returning the purses with interest, begging their magnanimous apologies and all the gracious etcetera etcetera.'

'And they accepted?'

'Money makes a man mirthful, Chains. I stuffed those purses full to bursting with silver. Then I gave every man in the squad drink money for five or six nights and we all agreed they would hoist a few to the health of Capa Barsavi, who *surely* needn't be, ahhh, troubled by something as inconsequential as his loyal Thiefmaker fucking up and letting a five-year-old breach the bloody Peace.'

'So,' the Eyeless Priest said, 'that was just the very first night of your association with my *very own* windfall mystery bargain boy.'

'I'm gratified that you're starting to take a possessive bent to the little cuss, Chains, because it only gets more colourful. I don't know quite how to put it. I've got kids that *enjoy* stealing. I've got kids that don't think about stealing one way or another, and I've got kids that just tolerate stealing because they know they've got nothing else to do. But nobody, and I mean *nobody*, has ever been hungry for it like this boy. If he had a bloody gash across his throat and a physiker was trying to sew it up, Lamora would steal the needle and thread and die laughing. He . . . steals *too much*.'

'Steals too much,' the Eyeless Priest mused. 'Steals too much. Of all the complaints I never thought I'd hear from a man who trains little thieves for a living.'

'Laugh now,' the Thiefmaker said, 'here's the kicker.'

6

Months passed. Parthis became Festal became Aurim and the misty squalls of summer gave way to the harder, driving rains of winter. The Seventy-Seventh Year of Gandolo became the Seventy-Seventh year of Morgante, the City Father, Lord of Noose and Trowel.

Eight of the thirty-one Catchfire orphans, somewhat less than adept at the Thiefmaker's *delicate* and *interesting* tasks, swung from the Black Bridge before the Palace of Patience. So it went; the survivors were too preoccupied with their own delicate and interesting tasks to care.

The society of Shades' Hill, as Locke soon discovered, was firmly divided into two tribes, Streets and Windows. The latter was a smaller, more exclusive group that did all of its earning after sunset. They crept across roofs and down chimneys, picked locks and slid through barred embrasures, and would steal everything from coins and jewellery to blocks of lard in untended pantries.

The boys and girls of Streets, on the other hand, prowled Camorr's alleys and cobbles and canal bridges by day, working in teams. Older and more experienced children (clutchers) worked at the actual pockets and purses and merchant stalls, while the younger and less capable (teasers) arranged distractions – crying for nonexistent mothers, or feigning illness, or rushing madly around crying 'Stop! Thief!' in every direction while the clutchers made off with their prizes.

Each orphan was shaken down by an older or larger child after returning to the graveyard from any visit outside; anything stolen or gathered was passed through the hierarchy of bruisers and bullies until it reached the Thiefmaker, who ticked off names on an eerily accurate mental list as the day's catch came in. Those that produced got to eat; those that didn't got to practise twice as hard that evening.

Night after night the Thiefmaker would parade around the warrens of Shades' Hill laden down with money-pouches, silk handkerchiefs, necklaces, metal coat-buttons and a dozen other sorts of oddments that were worth clutching. His wards would strike at him from concealment or by feigned accident; those that he spotted or felt in the act were immediately punished. The Thiefmaker preferred not to beat the losers of these training games; rather, they were forced to drink from a flask of unalloyed ginger oil while their peers gathered round and chanted derisively. Camorri ginger oil is rough stuff, not entirely incomparable (as the Thiefmaker himself opined) to swallowing the smouldering ashes of Poison Oak.

Those that wouldn't open their mouths had it poured into their noses while older children held them upside-down. This never had to happen twice to anyone.

In time, even those with ginger-scalded tongues and swollen throats learned the rudiments of coat-teasing and 'borrowing' from the wares of unwary merchants. The Thiefmaker enthusiastically instructed them in the architecture of doublets, waistcoats, frock coats and belt-pouches, keeping up with all the latest fashions as they came off the docks. His wards learned what could be cut away, what could be torn away, and what must be teased out with deft fingers.

'The point, my loves, is not to hump the subject's leg like a dog or clutch their hand like a lost babe. Half a second of actual contact with the subject is often too long, too long by far.' The Thiefmaker mimed a noose going around his neck and let his tongue bulge out past his teeth. 'You will live or die by three sacred rules. First, always ensure that the subject is nicely distracted, either by your teasers or by some convenient bit of unrelated bum-fuckery, like a fight or a house fire. House fires are *marvellous* for our purposes; cherish them. Second, minimise, and I damn well mean *minimise*, contact with the subject even when they are distracted.' He released himself from his invisible noose and grinned slyly. 'Lastly, once you've done your business, clear the vicinity even if the subject is as dumb as a box of hammers. What did I teach you?'

'Clutch once, then run,' his students chanted. 'Clutch twice, get hung!'

New orphans came in by ones and twos; older children seemed to leave the hill every few weeks with little ceremony. Locke presumed that this was evidence of some category of discipline well beyond ginger oil, but he never asked, as he was too low in the hill's pecking order to risk it or trust the answers he would get.

As for his own training, Locke went to Streets the day after he arrived, and was immediately thrown in with the teasers (punitively, he suspected). By the end of his second month his skills had secured him elevation to the ranks of the clutchers. This was considered a step up in social status, but Lamora alone in the entire hill seemed to prefer working with the teasers long after he was entitled to stop.

He was sullen and friendless inside the hill, but at teasing he was a natural artist; it brought him to life. He perfected the use of over-chewed orange pulp as a substitute for vomit; where other teasers would simply clutch their stomachs and moan, Locke would season his performances by spewing a mouthful of warm white and orange slop at the feet of his intended audience (or, if he was in a particularly perverse mood, all over their dress-hems or leggings).

Another favourite device of his was a long dry twig concealed in one leg of his breeches and tied to his ankle. By rapidly going down to his knees he could snap this twig with an audible noise; this, followed by a piercing wail, was an effective magnet for attention and sympathy, especially in the immediate vicinity of a wagon wheel. When he'd teased the crowd long enough, he would be rescued from further attention by the arrival of several other teasers, who would loudly announce that they were 'dragging him home to mother' so he could see a physiker. His ability to walk would be miraculously recovered just as soon as he was hauled around a corner.

In fact, he worked up a repertoire of artful teases so rapidly that

14

the Thiefmaker had cause to take him aside for a second private conversation (this after Locke arranged the inconvenient public collapse of a young lady's skirt and bodice with a few swift strokes of a finger-knife).

'Look here, Locke-after-your-father Lamora,' the Thiefmaker said, 'no ginger oil this time, I assure you, but I would *greatly* prefer your teases to veer sharply from the entertaining and back to the practical.'

Locke merely stared up at him and shuffled his feet.

'I shall speak plainly, then. The other teasers are going out day after day to watch *you*, not to do their bloody jobs. I'm not feeding my own private theatre troupe. Get my crew of happy little jack-offs back to their own teasing, and quit being such a celebrity with your own.'

For a time after that, everything was serene.

Then, barely six months after he arrived at the hill, Locke accidentally burned down the Elderglass Vine tavern and precipitated a quarantine riot that very nearly wiped the Narrows from the map of Camorr.

The Narrows was a valley of warrens and hovels at the northern-most tip of the bad part of the city; kidney-shaped and something like a vast amphitheatre, the island's heart was forty-odd feet beneath its outer edges. Leaning rows of tenement houses and windowless shops jutted from the tiers of this great seething bowl; wall collapsed against wall and alley folded upon mist-silvered alley so that no level of the Narrows could be traversed by more than two men walking abreast.

The Elderglass Vine crouched over the cobblestones of the road that passed west and crossed, via a stone bridge, from the Narrows into the green depths of the Mara Camorrazza. It was a sagging three-storey beast of weather-warped wood, with rickety stairs inside and out that maimed at least a patron a week (indeed, there was a lively pool going as to which of the regulars would be the next to crack his skull). It was a haunt of pipe-smokers and Gaze addicts, who would squeeze the precious drops of their drug onto their eyeballs in public, and lie there shuddering with visions while strangers went through their belongings or used them as tables.

The Seventy-Seventh Year of Morgante had just arrived when

Locke Lamora burst into the common room of the Elderglass Vine, sobbing and sniffling with gusto, his face showing the red cheeks, bleeding lips and bruised eyes that were characteristic of Black Whisper.

'Please, sir,' he whispered to a horrified bouncer while dice-throwers, bartenders, whores and thieves stopped to stare. 'Please. Mother and Father are sick; I don't know what's wrong with them. I'm the only one who can move – you must,' – sniff – 'help! Please, sir . . .'

At least, that's what would have been heard had the bouncer not triggered a headlong exodus from the Elderglass Vine by scream-ing 'Whisper! Black Whisper!' at the top of his lungs. No boy of Locke's size could have survived the ensuing orgy of shoving and panic had not the badge of illness on his face been better than any shield. Dice clattered to tabletops and cards fluttered down like falling leaves; tin mugs and tarred leather ale-jacks spattered cheap liquor as they hit the floor. Tables were overturned, knives and clubs were pulled to prod others into flight, and Gazers were trampled as an undisciplined wave of human detritus surged out every door save that in which Locke stood, pleading uselessly (or so it seemed) to screams and turned backs.

When the tavern had cleared of everyone but a few moaning (or motionless) Gazers, Locke's companions stole in behind him: a dozen of the fastest teasers and clutchers in Streets, specially invited by Lamora for this expedition. They spread out among the fallen tables and behind the battered bar, plucking wildly at anything valuable. Here a handful of discarded coins, here a good knife, here a set of whalebone dice with tiny garnet chips for markers. From the pantry, baskets of coarse but serviceable bread and salted butter in grease-paper, and a dozen bottles of wine. Half a minute was all Locke allowed them, counting in his head while he rubbed his make-up from his face; by the end of the count, he motioned his associates back out into the night.

Riot-drums were already beating to summon the watch, and above their rhythm could be heard the first faint flutings of pipes, the bone-chilling sound that called out the Duke's ghouls – the Quarantine Guard.

The participants in Locke's smash-and-grab adventure threaded their way through the growing crowds of confused and panicked

Narrows-dwellers, and scuttled home indirectly through the Mara Camorrazza or the Coalsmoke district.

They returned with the largest haul of goods and food in the memory of the Shades' Hill orphans, and a larger pile of copper half-barons than Locke had hoped for (he hadn't known that men who played at dice or cards kept money out in plain view, for in Shades' Hill such games were the exclusive domain of the oldest and most popular orphans, and he was neither).

For a few hours, the Thiefmaker was merely bemused.

That night, panicked drunks set fire to the Elderglass Vine, and hundreds tried to flee the Narrows when the city watch was unable to locate the boy who'd first triggered the panic. Riot-drums beat until dawn, bridges were blocked, and Duke Nicovante's archers took to the canals around the Narrows in flat-bottomed boats, with arrows to last all night and then some.

The next morning found the Thiefmaker once again in private conversation with his littlest plague orphan.

'The problem with you, Locke-*fucking*-Lamora, is that you are not *circumspect*. Do you know what *circumspect* means?'

Locke shook his head.

'Let me put it like this. That tavern had an owner. That owner worked for Capa Barsavi, the big man himself, just like I do. Now, that tavern-owner paid the Capa, just like I do, to avoid *accidents*. Thanks to you, he's had one hell of an accident, even though he was paying his money and didn't have an accident forthcoming. So, if you follow me, inciting a pack of drunk fucking animals to burn that place to the ground with a fake plague scare was the opposite of a *circumspect* means of operation. So now can you venture a guess as to what the word means?'

Locke knew a good time to nod vigorously when he heard it.

'Unlike the last time you tried to send me to an early grave, this one I can't buy my way out of, and thank the gods I don't need to, because the mess is huge. The yellowjackets clubbed down two hundred people last night before they all figured out that nobody had the Whisper; the Duke called out his fucking regulars and was about to give the Narrows a good scrubbing with fire-oil. Now, the only reason, and I mean the *only* reason, that you're not floating in a shark's stomach with a very surprised expression on your face is that the Elderglass Vine is just a pile of ashes; nobody knows

17

anything was stolen from it *before* it became that pile of ashes. Nobody except us.

'So, we're *all* going to agree that nobody in this hill knows anything about what happened, and *you* are going to re-learn some of that reticence I talked about when you first arrived here. You remember reticence, right?'

Locke nodded.

'I just want little things from you, Lamora. I want nice, neat little jobs. I want a purse here, a sausage there. I want you to swallow your ambition, shit it out like a bad meal, and be a *circumspect* little teaser for about the next million years. Can you do that for me? Don't rob any more yellowjackets, don't burn any more taverns, don't start any more fucking riots. Just pretend to be a coarse-witted little cutpurse like your brothers and sisters. Clear?'

Again, Locke nodded, doing his best to look rueful.

'Good. And now,' the Thiefmaker said as he produced his nearly full flask of ginger oil, 'we're going to engage in some, ahhh, *reinforcement* of my admonishments.'

And, for a time (once Locke recovered his powers of speech and unlaboured breathing), everything was serene.

But the Seventy-Seventh Year of Morgante became the Seventy-Seventh Year of Sendovani, and though Locke succeeded in hiding his actions from the Thiefmaker for a time, on one more specific occasion he failed spectacularly to be circumspect.

When the Thiefmaker realised what the boy had done, he went to see the Capa of Camorr and secured permission for one little death. Only as an afterthought did he go to see the Eyeless Priest, intent not on mercy but on one last chance for a slim profit.

7

The sky was a fading red and nothing remained of the day save for a line of molten gold slowly lowering on the western horizon. Locke Lamora trailed in the long shadow of the Thiefmaker, who was leading him to the Temple of Perelandro to be sold. At long last Locke had discovered where the older children had been disappearing to.

A great glass arch led from the north-west base of Shades' Hill to the eastern edge of the long, vast Temple District. At the apex of this bridge the Thiefmaker paused and stared, north, across the lightless houses of the Quiet, across the mist-wreathed waters of the rushing Angevine, to the shaded manors and tree-lined white stone boulevards of the Alcegrante islands, laid out in opulence beneath the impossible height of the Five Towers.

The Five were the most prominent Elderglass structures in a city thick with the arcane substance; the smallest and least magnificent, Dawncatcher, was a mere eighty feet wide and four hundred feet tall. The true colour of each smooth tower was mingled now with the sinking furnace-light of sunset, and the weblike net of cables and cargo baskets that threaded the tower tops was barely visible against the carmine sky.

'We'll wait here a moment, boy,' said the Thiefmaker with uncharacteristic wistfulness in his voice. 'Here on my bridge. So few come to Shades' Hill this way, it might as well be mine.'

The Duke's Wind that blew in from the Iron Sea by day had turned; the night, as always, would be ruled by the muggy Hangman's Wind that blew from land to sea, thick with the scents of farm fields and rotting marshes.

'I'm getting rid of you, you know.' The Thiefmaker added after a moment, 'Not, ahhh, fooling. Goodbye, forever. It's a pity you're missing something . . . common sense, perhaps.'

Locke said nothing, instead staring up at the vast glass towers as the sky behind them drained of colour; the blue-white stars brightened and the last rays of the sun vanished in the west like a great eye closing.

As the first hint of true darkness seemed to fall over the city a new light rose faint and glimmering to push it back; this light gleamed within the Elderglass of the Five Towers themselves, and within the translucent glass of the bridge on which they were standing. It waxed with every passing breath, gaining strength until it bathed the city with the fey half-light of an overcast day.

The hour of Falselight had come.

From the heights of the Five Towers to the obsidian smoothness of the vast glass breakwaters to the artificial reefs beneath the slate-coloured waves, Falselight radiated from every surface and every shard of Elderglass in Camorr, from every speck of the alien material left so long before by the creatures that had first shaped the city. Every night, as the west finally swallowed the sun, the glass bridges would become threads of firefly light; the glass towers and glass avenues and the strange glass sculpture-gardens would shimmer wanly with violet and azure and orange and pearl-white, and the moons and stars would fade to grey.

This was what passed for twilight in Camorr – the end of work for the last daylight labourers, the calling of the night-watches and the sealing of the landward gates; an hour of supernatural radiance that would soon enough give way to true night.

'Let's be about our business,' the Thiefmaker said, and the two of them headed down into the Temple District, walking on soft alien light.

8

Falselight was the last hour during which the temples of Camorr traditionally remained open, and the Eyeless Priest at the House of Perelandro was wasting none of the time still left to fill the copper money-kettle sitting before him on the steps of his decrepit temple.

'Orphans!' He bellowed in a voice that would have been at home on a battlefield, 'Are we not all orphaned, sooner or later? Alas for those torn from the mother's bosom, barely past infancy!'

A pair of slender young boys, presumably orphans, were seated on either side of the money-kettle, wearing hooded white robes. The eldritch glow of Falselight seemed to inflame the hollow blackness of their staring eyes as they watched men and women hurrying about their business on the squares and avenues of the gods.

'Alas,' the priest continued, 'for those cast out by cruel fate to a wicked world that has no place for them, a world that has no use for them. Slaves is what it makes of them! Slaves, or worse, *playthings* for the lusts of the wicked and the ungodly, forcing them into half-lives of unspeakable degeneracy, beside which mere slavery would be a blessing!'

Locke marvelled, for he had never seen a stage performance or heard a trained orator. Here was scorn that could boil standing water from stone; here was remonstrance that made his pulse race with excited shame, though he was himself an orphan. He wanted to hear the big-voiced man yell at him some more.

So great was the fame of Father Chains, the Eyeless Priest, that even Locke Lamora had heard of him; a man of late-middle years with a chest as broad as a scrivener's desk and a beard that clung to his craggy face like a pad of scrubbing wool. A thick white blindfold covered his forehead and his eyes, a white cotton vestment hung to his bare ankles and a pair of black iron manacles encircled his wrists. Heavy steel chains led from these manacles, back up the steps of the temple and through the open doors to the interior; Locke could see that as Father Chains gestured to his listeners, these chains were nearly taut. He was approaching the very limit of his freedom.

For thirteen years, popular lore had it, Father Chains had never set foot beyond the steps of his temple. As a measure of his devotion to Perelandro, Father of Mercies, Lord of the Overlooked, he had chained himself to the walls of his inner sanctuary with iron manacles that had neither locks nor keys, and paid a physiker to pluck out his eyes while a crowd watched.

'The Lord of the Overlooked keeps vigil on every son and daughter of the dead, on that point I can assure you! Blessed in his eyes are those, unbound by the duties of blood, who render aid and comfort to the motherless and the fatherless . . .'

Though he was known to be blind as well as blindfolded, Locke could have sworn that Father Chains' head turned towards himself and the Thiefmaker as they approached across the square.

'. . . out of the undoubted goodness of their hearts, they nourish and protect the children of Camorr; not with cold-souled avarice, but with selfless kindness! Truly blessed,' he hissed with fervour, 'are the protectors of Camorr's *gentle, needful* orphans.'

As the Thiefmaker reached the steps of the temple and started up, he was careful to slap his heels against the stones to announce his presence.

'Someone approaches,' Father Chains said, 'two someones, or so say my ears!'

'I've brought you the boy we discussed, Father,' the Thiefmaker announced loudly enough for several passersby to hear, should they be listening. 'I've prepared him as well as I could for the, ahhhh, tests of apprenticeship and initiation.'

The priest stumbled across the steps towards Locke, dragging his clattering chains behind him. The hooded boys guarding the money-kettle spared him a brief glance, but said nothing.

'Have you, then?' Father Chains' hand shot out with alarming accuracy and his calloused fingers spidered themselves over Locke's forehead, cheeks, nose and chin. 'A small boy, it seems, a very small boy. Though not without a certain measure of character, I venture, in the malnourished curves of his sad orphan's face.'

'His name,' said the Thiefmaker, 'is Locke Lamora, and I wager the Order of Perelandro will find many uses for his, ahhhh, unusual degree of personal initiative.'

'Better still,' the priest rumbled, 'that he were sincere, penitent, honest and inclined to discipline. But I have no doubt that his time in your affectionate care has instilled those qualities in him by example.' He clapped his hands together three times. 'My boys, our day's business is done; gather the offerings of the good people of Camorr, and let's show our prospective initiate into the temple.'

The Thiefmaker gave Locke a brief squeeze on the shoulder, then pushed him quite enthusiastically up the steps towards the Eyeless Priest. As the white-robed boys carried the jangling copper bowl past him, the Thiefmaker tossed a small leather purse into it, spread his arms wide and bowed with his characteristic serpentine theatricality. The last Locke saw of him, he was moving rapidly across the Temple District with his crooked arms and bony shoulders rolling gaily; the strut of a man set free.

9

The sanctuary of the Temple of Perelandro was a musty stone chamber with several puddles of standing water; the mould-eaten tapestries on the walls were rapidly devolving into their component threads. It was lit only by the pastel glare of Falselight and the half-hearted efforts of a frosted white alchemical globe, perched precariously in a fixture just above the steel plate that chained the Eyeless Priest to the sanctuary wall. Locke saw a curtained doorway on the back wall, and nothing else.

'Calo, Galdo,' said Father Chains, 'be good lads and see to the doors, will you?'

The two robed boys set down the copper kettle and moved to one of the tapestries. Working together, they swept it aside and pulled at a concealed device; some great mechanism creaked in the sanctuary walls, and the twin doors leading out to the temple steps began to draw inward. When they finished sliding together with the scrape of stone against stone, the alchemical globe suddenly flared into brighter luminescence.

'Now,' said the Eyeless Priest as he knelt, letting a great deal of slack chain gather in little steel mounds about him, 'come over here, Locke Lamora, and let's see if you have any of the gifts necessary to become an initiate of this temple.'

With Father Chains on his knees, Locke and he were roughly forehead to forehead. In response to Chains' beckoning hands, Locke stepped close and waited. The priest wrinkled his nose.

'I see that your former master remains less than fastidious about the pungency of his wards; no matter. That will soon be rectified. For now, simply give me your hands, like so.' Chains firmly but gently guided Locke's small hands until the boy's palms rested over Chains' blindfold. 'Now . . . merely close your eyes and concentrate . . . concentrate. Let whatever virtuous thoughts you have within you bubble to the surface – let the warmth of your generous spirit flow forth from your innocent hands . . . Ah, yes, like that . . .'

Locke was half-alarmed and half-amused, but the lines of Father Chains' weathered face drew downward, and his mouth soon hung open in beatific anticipation.

'Ahhhhhhh,' the priest whispered, his voice thick with emotion, 'yes, yes, you do have some talent . . . some power . . . I can feel it . . . It might almost be . . . a *miracle*!'

At that, Chains jerked his head back, and Locke jumped in the opposite direction. His chains clanking, the priest lifted manacled hands to his blindfold and yanked it off with a flourish. Locke recoiled, unsure of what eyeless sockets might look like, but the priest's eyes were quite normal – in fact, Chains squinted in pain and rubbed them several times, wincing at the glare of the alchemical globe.

'Ahhhh-ha-ha-ha!' he cried, finally holding out his hands towards Locke. 'I'm healed! I'm healed! I can *SEE ONCE MORE!*'

Locke stared, gaping like a slackwit for the second time that night, unsure of what to say. Behind him, the two hooded boys started to giggle, and Locke's eyebrows bent inward in suspicion.

'You're not . . . really blind,' he said.

'And you're clearly not stupid!' Chains cried, leaping up with a glee that brought wet-sounding pops from his kneecaps. He waved his manacled hands like a bird trying to take flight. 'Calo! Galdo! Get these damn things off my wrists so we can count our daily blessings!'

The two hooded boys hurried over and did something to the manacles that Locke couldn't quite follow; they slid open and fell to the floor with a jarring clatter. Chains gingerly rubbed the skin that had been beneath them; it was as white as the meat of a fresh fish.

'You're not . . . really a priest!' Locke added, while the older man caressed some colour back into his forearms.

'Oh no,' Chains said. 'No, I am a priest. Just not a priest of, um, Perelandro. Nor are my initiates initiates of Perelandro. Nor will you be an initiate of Perelandro. Locke Lamora, say hello to Calo and Galdo Sanza.'

The white-robed boys swept back their hoods and Locke saw that they were twins; perhaps a year or two older than himself, and far sturdier-looking. They had the olive skin and black hair of the true Camorri; their identical long, hook-ended noses, however, were something of an anomaly. Smiling, they joined hands and bowed in unison from the waist.

'Um, hi,' Locke said. 'Which of you is . . . which?'

'Today, I am Galdo,' said the one on Locke's left.

'Tomorrow, I will probably be Galdo,' said the other one.

'Or perhaps we'll both want to be Calo,' added the one that had first spoken.

'In time,' Father Chains interrupted, 'you'll learn to tell them apart by the number of dents I've kicked in their respective arses; one of them always manages to be ahead of the other, somehow.' He stood behind Locke and placed both of his wide, heavy hands on Locke's shoulders. 'Idiots, this is Locke Lamora. As you can see, I've just bought him from your old benefactor, the master of Shades' Hill.'

'We remember you,' said presumed-Galdo.

'A Catchfire orphan,' said presumed-Calo.

'Father Chains bought us just after you arrived,' they said in unison, grinning.

24

'Knock that bullshit off,' Father Chains said, his voice somehow regal. 'You two have just volunteered to cook dinner. Pears and sausage in oil, and a double portion for your new little brother. Get. Locke and I will deal with the kettle.'

Sneering and gesturing rudely as they went, the twins ran for the curtained door and vanished behind it. Locke could hear their footsteps trailing away down some sort of staircase, and then Father Chains motioned for him to sit beside the copper money-kettle.

'Sit, boy. Let's have a few words about what's going on here.' Chains eased himself back down to the damp floor, crossing his legs and settling a thoughtful stare on Locke. 'Your former master said you could do simple sums. Is this true?'

'Yes, master.'

'Don't call me "master". Makes my balls shrivel and my teeth crack. Just call me Father Chains. And while you're sitting there, let's see you tip that kettle and count all the money in there.'

Locke tried to pull the kettle over on one side, straining, seeing now why Calo and Galdo preferred to share the burden. Chains gave the kettle a push on the base and its contents finally spilled out on the floor beside Locke. 'Makes it much harder to snatch, having it weigh that much,' Chains said.

'How can you . . . how can you pretend to be a priest?' Locke asked, while he sorted full copper coins and clipped copper bits into little piles. 'Don't you fear the gods? The wrath of Perelandro?'

'Of course I do,' Chains replied, running his fingers through his round, ragged beard. 'I fear them very much. Like I said, I'm a priest, just not a priest of Perelandro. I'm an initiated servant of the Nameless Thirteenth, the Thiefwatcher, the Crooked Warden, the Benefactor, Father of Necessary Pretexts.'

'But . . . there are only the Twelve.'

'It's funny just how many people are sadly misinformed on that point, my dear boy. Imagine, if you will, that the Twelve *happen* to have something of a black-sheep younger brother, whose exclusive dominion *happens* to be thieves like you and I. Though the Twelve won't allow his Name to be spoken or heard, they have some lingering affection for his merry brand of fuckery. Thus, crooked old posers such as myself aren't blasted with lightning or pecked apart by crows for squatting in the temple of a more respectable god like Perelandro.'

'You're a priest of this . . . Thirteenth?'

'Indeed. A priest of thieves, and a thieving priest. As Calo and Galdo will be, some day, and as you might be, provided you're worth even the pittance I paid for you.'

'But . . .' Locke reached out and plucked the Thiefmaker's purse (a pouch of rust-red leather) from the piles of copper and passed it to Chains. 'If you paid for me, why did my old master leave an offering?'

'Ah. Rest assured that I *did* pay for you, and you were cheap, and this is no offering.' Chains untied the little pouch and let its contents drop into his hand – a single white shark's tooth, as long as Locke's thumb. Chains waved it at the boy. 'Have you ever seen one of these before?'

'No . . . What is it?'

'It's a death-mark. The tooth of the wolf shark is the personal sigil of Capa Barsavi – your former master's boss. My boss and your boss, for that matter. It means that you're such a *sullen, thick-skulled little fuck-up* that your former master actually went to the Capa and got permission to kill you.'

Chains grinned, as though he were imparting nothing more than a ribald joke. Locke shivered.

'Does that give you a moment of pause, my boy? Good. Stare at this thing, Locke. Take a good, hard look. It means your death is paid for. I bought this from your former master when I got you at a bargain price. It means that if Duke Nicovante himself adopted you tomorrow and proclaimed you his heir, I could still crack your skull open and nail you to a post, and nobody in the city would lift a fucking finger.'

Chains deftly shoved the tooth back into the red pouch, then hung it around Locke's neck by its slender cord. 'You're going to wear that,' the older man said, 'until I deem you worthy to remove it, or until I make use of the power it gives me and . . . so!' He slashed two fingers across the air in front of Locke's throat. 'Hide it under your clothes, and keep it next to your skin at all times to remind you just how close, how *very* close, you came to getting your throat slit tonight. If your former master were one shade less

26

greedy than he is vindictive, I don't doubt you'd be floating in the bay.'

'What did I do?'

Chains did something with his eyes that made the boy feel smaller just for having tried to protest; Locke squirmed and fiddled with the death-mark pouch.

'Please, boy. Let's not start out with either of us insulting the other's intelligence. There are only three people in life you can never fool – pawnbrokers, whores, and your mother. Since your mother's dead, I've taken her place. Hence, I'm bullshit-proof.' Chains' voice grew serious. 'You know perfectly well why your former master would have cause to be displeased with you.'

'He said I wasn't . . . circumspect.'

'Circumspect,' Chains repeated. 'That's a good word. And no, you're not. He told me everything.'

Locke looked up from his little piles of coins, his eyes wide and near-watering. 'Everything?'

'Quite. Everything.' Chains stared the boy down for a long, difficult moment, then sighed. 'What did the good citizens of Camorr give to the cause of Perelandro today?'

'Twenty-seven copper barons, I think.'

'Hmmm. Just over four silver solons, then. A slow day. But it beats every other form of theft I ever met.'

'You steal this money from Perelandro too?'

'Of course I do, boy. I mentioned that I was a thief, didn't I? Not the sort of thief you're used to. Better. The entire city of Camorr is full of idiots running round and getting hung, all because they think that stealing is something you do with your *hands*.' Father Chains spat.

'Um . . . what do you steal with, Father Chains?'

The bearded priest tapped two fingers against the side of his head, then grinned widely and tapped his fingers against his teeth. 'Brains and a big mouth, my boy, brains and a big mouth. I planted my arse here thirteen years ago and the pious suckers of Camorr have been feeding me coins ever since. Plus I'm famous from Emberlain to Tal Verrar, but mostly I'm in it for the cold coinage.'

'Isn't it uncomfortable?' Locke asked, looking around at the sad innards of the temple. 'Living here, never going out?'

'This shabby little back-stage is no more the full extent of my

27

temple than your old home was really a graveyard.' Chains chuckled. 'We're a different sort of thief here, Lamora. Deception and misdirection are our tools; we don't believe in hard work when a false face and a good line of bullshit can do so much more.'

'Then . . . you're like . . . teasers.'

'Perhaps, in the sense that a barrel of fire-oil is akin to a pinch of red pepper. And that's why I paid for you, my boy, though you lack the good sense the gods gave a carrot. You lie like a floor-tapestry. You're more crooked than an acrobat's spine. I could really make something of you, if I decided I could trust you.'

His searching eyes rested once more on Locke, and the boy guessed that he was supposed to say something.

'I'd like that,' he whispered. 'What do I do?'

'You can start by talking. I want to hear about what you did at Shades' Hill; the shit you pulled to get your former master angry at you.'

'But . . . you said you already knew everything.'

'I do. But I want to hear it from you, plain and clear, and I want it right the first time, with no backtracking or parts left out. If you try to conceal anything that I know you should be mentioning, I'll have no choice but to consider you a worthless waste of my trust – and you're already wearing my response around your neck.'

'Where,' Locke asked with only a slight catch in his voice, 'do I start?'

'We can begin with your most recent transgressions. There's one law that the brothers and sisters of Shades' Hill must never break, but your former master told me that you broke it twice and thought you were clever enough to get away with it.'

Locke's cheeks turned bright red, and he stared down at his fingers.

'Tell me, Locke. The Thiefmaker said you arranged the murders of two other Shades' Hill boys, and that he didn't pick up on your involvement until the second was already done.' Chains steepled his fingers before his face and gazed calmly at the boy with the death-mark around his neck. 'I want to know why you killed them, and I want to know how you killed them, and I want to hear it from your own lips. *Right now.*'

BOOK I
AMBITION

Why, I can smile, and murder whiles I smile
And cry 'Content' to that which grieves my heart,
And wet my cheeks with artificial tears,
And frame my face to all occasions.

Shakespeare, *Henry VI, Part 3*

CHAPTER ONE

The Don Salvara Game

I

Locke Lamora's rule of thumb was this – a good confidence game took three months to plan, three weeks to rehearse, and three seconds to win or lose the victim's trust forever. This time around, he planned to spend those three seconds getting strangled.

Locke was on his knees, and Calo, standing behind him, had a hemp rope coiled three times around his neck. The rough stuff looked impressive, and it would leave Locke's throat a very credible shade of red. No genuine Camorri assassin old enough to waddle in a straight line would garrotte with anything but silk or wire, of course (the better to crease the victim's windpipe), Locke reflected. Yet if Don Lorenzo Salvara could tell a fake strangling from the real thing in the blink of an eye at thirty paces, they'd badly misjudged the man they planned to rob and the whole game would be shot anyway.

'Can you see him yet? Or Bug's signal?' Locke hissed his question as lightly as he could, then made a few impressive gurgling sounds.

'No signal. No Don Salvara. Can you breathe?'

'Fine, just fine,' Locke whispered, 'but shake me some more, really shake me. That's the part that convinces.'

They were in the dead-end alley beside the old Temple of Fortunate Waters; the temple's prayer waterfalls could be heard gushing somewhere behind the high plaster wall. Locke clutched once again at the harmless coils of rope circling his neck and spared a glance at the horse staring at him from just a few paces away, laden down with a rich-looking cargo of merchant's packs. The poor dumb animal was Gentled; there was neither curiosity nor fear behind the milk-white shells of its unblinking eyes. It wouldn't have cared even had the strangling been real.

31

Precious seconds passed; the sun was high and bright in a sky scalded free of clouds, and the grime of the alley clung like wet cement to the legs of Locke's breeches. Nearby, Jean Tannen lay in the same muck while Galdo (mostly) pretended to kick his ribs in. He'd been merrily kicking away for at least a minute, just as long as his twin brother had been strangling Locke.

Don Salvara was supposed to pass the mouth of the alley at any second and, ideally, rush to rescue Locke and Jean from their 'assailants'; at this rate, he would end up rescuing them from boredom.

'Gods,' Calo whispered, bending his mouth to Locke's ear as though he might be hissing some demand, 'where the hell is that damn Salvara? And where's Bug? We can't keep this shit up all day; other people *do* walk by the mouth of this damned alley!'

'Keep strangling me,' Locke whispered. 'Just think of twenty thousand full crowns and keep strangling me. I can choke all day if I have to.'

2

Everything had gone beautifully that morning in the run-up to the game itself, even allowing for the natural prickliness of a young thief finally allowed a part in his first big score.

'Of course I know where I'm bloody well supposed to be when the action starts,' Bug whined. 'I've spent more time perched up on that temple roof than I did in my mother's gods-damned womb!'

Jean Tannen let his right hand trail in the warm water of the canal while he took another bite of the sour marsh apple held in his left. The forward gunwale of the flat-bottomed barge was a choice spot for relaxation in the watered-wine light of early morning, allowing all sixteen stone of Jean's frame to sprawl comfortably – keg belly, heavy arms, bandy legs and all. The only other person (and the one doing all of the work) in the empty barge was Bug, a lanky mop-headed twelve-year-old braced against the steering pole at the stern.

'Your mother was in an understandable hurry to get rid of you, Bug.' Jean's voice was soft and even and wildly incongruous – he spoke like a teacher of music or a copier of scrolls. 'We're not. So indulge me once more with proof of your penetrating comprehension of our game.'

'Dammit,' Bug replied, giving the barge another push against the gentle current of the seaward-flowing canal. 'You and Locke and Calo and Galdo are down in the alley between Fortunate Waters and the gardens for the Temple of Nara, right? I'm up on the roof of the temple across the way.'

'Go on,' Jean said around a mouthful of marsh apple. 'Where's Don Salvara?'

Other barges, heavily laden with everything from ale casks to bleating cows, were slipping past the two of them on the clay-coloured water of the canal. Bug was poling them north along Camorr's main commercial waterway, the Via Camorrazza, toward the Shifting Market, and the city was lurching into life around them.

The leaning grey tenements of water-slick stone were spitting their inhabitants out into the sunlight and the rising summer warmth. The month was Parthis, meaning that the night-sweat of condensation already boiling off the buildings as a soupy mist would be greatly missed by the cloudless white heat of early afternoon.

'He's coming out of the Temple of Fortunate Waters, like he does every Penance Day right around noon. He's got two horses and one man with him, if we're lucky.'

'A curious ritual,' Jean said. 'Why would he do a thing like that?'

'Deathbed promise to his mother.' Bug drove his pole down into the canal, struggled against it for a moment, and managed to shove them along once more. 'She kept the Vadran religion after she married the old Don Salvara. So he leaves an offering at the Vadran temple once a week and gets home as fast as he can so nobody pays too much attention to him. Dammit, Jean, I already know this shit. Why would I be here if you didn't trust me? And why am *I* the one who gets to push this stupid barge all the way to the market?'

'Oh, you can stop poling the barge any time you can beat me hand-to-hand three falls out of five.' Jean grinned, showing two rows of crooked brawler's teeth in a face that looked as though someone had set it on an anvil and tried to pound it into a more pleasing shape. 'Besides, you're an apprentice in a proud trade, learning under the finest and most demanding masters it has to offer. Getting all the shit work is excellent for your moral education.'

'You haven't given me any bloody moral education.'

'Yes. Well, that's probably because Locke and I have been dodging our own for so many years now. As for why we're going over the plan again, let me remind you that one good screw-up will make the fate of those poor bastards look sunny in comparison to what we'll get.'

Jean pointed at one of the city's slop-wagons, halted on a canalside boulevard to receive a long dark stream of night soil from the upper window of a public alehouse. These wagons were crewed by petty criminals whose offences were too meagre to justify continual incarceration in the Palace of Patience; shackled to their wagons and huddled in the alleged protection of long leather ponchos, they were let out each morning to enjoy what sun they could when they weren't cursing the dubious accuracy with which several thousand Camorri emptied their chamber pots.

'I won't screw it up, Jean.' Bug shook his thoughts like an empty coin purse, searching desperately for something to say that would make him sound as calm and assured as he imagined Jean and all the older Gentlemen Bastards always were – but the mouth of most twelve-year-olds far outpaces the mind. 'I just won't. I bloody *won't*; I promise.'

'Good lad,' Jean said. 'Glad to hear it. But just what is it that you won't screw up?'

Bug sighed. 'I make the signal when Salvara's on his way out of the Temple of Fortunate Waters. I keep an eye out for anyone else trying to walk past the alley, especially the city watch. If anybody tries it, I jump down from the temple roof with a longsword and cut their bloody heads off where they stand.'

'You what?'

'I said I distract them any way I can. You going deaf, Jean?'

A line of tall counting houses slid past on their left, each displaying lacquered woodwork, silk awnings, marble façades, and other ostentatious touches along the waterfront. There were deep roots of money and power sunk into that row of three- and four-storey buildings: Coin-Kisser's Row, the oldest and goldest financial district on the continent. The place was as steeped in influence and elaborate rituals as the glass heights of the Five Towers, in which the Duke and the Grand Families sequestered themselves from the city they ruled.

'Move us up against the bank just under the bridges, Bug.' Jean gestured vaguely with his apple. 'His nibs will be waiting to come aboard.'

Two Elderglass arches bridged the Via Camorrazza right in the middle of Coin-Kisser's Row, a high and narrow catbridge for foot traffic and a lower, wider one for wagons. The seamless brilliance of the alien glass looked like nothing so much as liquid diamond, gently arched by giant hands and left to harden over the canal. On the right bank was the Fauria, a crowded island of multi-tiered stone apartments and rooftop gardens. Wooden wheels churned white against the stone embankment, drawing canal water up into a network of troughs and viaducts that criss-crossed over the Fauria's streets at every level.

Bug slid the barge over to a rickety quay just beneath the catbridge; from the faint and slender shadow of this arch a man jumped down to the quay, dressed (as Bug and Jean were) in oil-stained leather breeches and a rough cotton shirt. His next nonchalant leap took him into the barge, which barely rocked at his arrival.

'Salutations to you, Master Jean Tannen, and profuse congratulations on the fortuitous timing of your arrival!' said the newcomer.

'Felicitations to you in respect of the superlative grace of your entry into our very humble boat, Master Lamora.' Jean punctuated this statement by popping the remains of his apple into his mouth, stem and all, and producing a wet crunching noise.

'Creeping shits, man.' Locke Lamora stuck out his tongue. 'Must you do that? You know the black alchemists make fish poison from the seeds of those damn things.'

'Lucky me,' said Jean after swallowing the last bit of masticated pulp, 'not being a fish.'

Locke was a medium man in every respect – medium height, medium build, medium-dark hair cropped short above a face that was neither handsome nor memorable. He looked like a proper Therin, though perhaps a bit less olive and ruddy than Jean or Bug; in another light he might have passed for a very tanned Vadran. His bright grey eyes alone had any sense of distinction; he was a

35

man the gods might have shaped deliberately to be overlooked. He settled down against the left-hand gunwale and crossed his legs.

'Hello to you as well, Bug! I knew we could count on you to take pity on your elders and let them rest in the sun while you do the hard work with the pole.'

'Jean's a lazy old bastard is what it is,' Bug said. 'And if I don't pole the barge he'll knock my teeth out the back of my head.'

'Jean is the gentlest soul in Camorr, and you wound him with your accusations,' said Locke. 'Now he'll be up all night crying.'

'I would have been up all night anyway,' Jean added, 'crying from the ache of rheumatism and lighting candles to ward off evil vapours.'

'Which is not to say that our bones don't creak by day, my cruel apprentice.' Locke massaged his kneecaps. 'We're at least twice your age, which is prodigious for our profession.'

'The Daughters of Aza Guilla have tried to perform a corpse-blessing on me six times this week,' said Jean. 'You're lucky Locke and I are still spry enough to take you with us when we run a game.'

To anyone beyond hearing range, Locke and Jean and Bug might have looked like the crew of a for-hire barge, slacking their way towards a cargo pick-up at the junction of the Via Camorrazza and the Angevine River. As Bug poled them closer and closer to the Shifting Market, the water was getting thicker with such barges, and with sleek black cockleshell boats, and with battered water-craft of every description, not all of them doing a good job of staying afloat or under control.

'Speaking of our game,' said Locke, 'how is our eager young apprentice's understanding of his place in the scheme of things?'

'I've been reciting it to Jean all morning,' said Bug.

'And . . . the conclusion is?'

'I've got it down cold!' Bug heaved at the pole with all of his strength, driving them between a pair of high-walled floating gardens with inches to spare on either side. The scents of jasmine and oranges drifted down over them as their barge slipped beneath the protruding branches of one of the gardens; a wary attendant peeked over one garden-boat's wall, staff in hand to fend them off if necessary. The big barges were probably hauling transplants to some noble's orchard upriver.

'Down cold, and I won't screw it up! I promise! I know my place and I know the signals and I won't screw it up!'

3

Calo was shaking Locke with real vigour, and Locke's performance as his victim was a virtuoso one, but still the moments dragged by. They were all trapped in their pantomime, like figures out of the richly inventive hells of Therin theology; a pair of thieves destined to spend all eternity stuck in an alley, mugging victims that never passed out or gave up their money.

'Are you as alarmed as I am?' Calo whispered.

'Just stay in character,' Locke hissed. 'You can pray and strangle at the same time.'

There was a high-pitched scream from their right, echoing across the cobbles and walls of the Temple District. It was followed by shouts and the creaking tread of men in battle harness – but these sounds moved away from the mouth of the alley, not towards it.

'That sounded like Bug,' said Locke.

'I hope he's just arranging a distraction,' said Calo, his grip on the rope momentarily slackening. At that instant a dark shape darted across the gap of sky between the alley's high walls, its fluttering shadow briefly falling over them as it passed.

'Now what the hell was that, then?' Calo asked.

Off to their right, someone screamed again.

4

Bug had poled himself, Locke and Jean from the Via Camorrazza into the Shifting Market right on schedule, just as the vast Elderglass wind chime atop Westwatch tower was allowed to catch the breeze blowing in from the sea and ring out the eleventh hour of the morning.

The Shifting Market was a lake of relatively placid water at the very heart of Camorr, perhaps half a mile in circumference, protected from the rushing flow of the Angevine and the surrounding canals by a series of stone breakwaters. The only real current in the market was human-made, as hundreds upon hundreds of floating merchants slowly and warily followed one another counter-clockwise in their boats, jostling for prized positions against the flat-topped breakwaters, crowded with buyers and sightseers on foot.

City watchmen in their mustard-yellow tabards commanded sleek black cutters, each rowed by a dozen shackled prisoners from the Palace of Patience, using long poles and harsh language to maintain several rough channels through the drifting chaos of the market. Through these channels passed the pleasure barges of the nobility, and heavily laden freight barges, and empty ones like that containing the three Gentlemen Bastards, who shopped with their eyes as they sliced through a sea of hope and avarice.

In just a few lengths of Bug's poling, they passed a family of trinket dealers in ill-kept brown cockleshells, a spice merchant with his wares on a triangular rack in the middle of an awkward circular raft of the sort called a *vertola*, and a Canal Tree bobbing and swaying on the leather-bladder pontoon raft that supported its roots. These roots trailed in the water, drinking up the piss and effluvia of the busy city; the canopy of rustling emerald leaves cast thousands of punctuated shadows down on the Gentlemen Bastards as they passed, along with the perfume of citrus. The tree (an alchemical hybrid that grew both limes and lemons) was tended by a middle-aged woman and three small children, who scuttled around in the branches throwing down fruit in response to orders from passing boats.

Above the watercraft of the Shifting Market rose a field of flags and pennants and billowing silk standards, all competing through gaudy colours and symbols to impress their messages on watchful buyers. There were flags adorned with the crude outlines of fish or fowl or both; flags adorned with ale mugs and wine bottles and loaves of bread, boots and trousers and threaded tailors' needles, fruits and kitchen instruments and carpenter's tools and a hundred other goods and services. Here and there, small clusters of chicken-flagged boats or shoe-flagged rafts were locked in close combat, their owners loudly proclaiming the superiority of their respective goods or implying the bastardy of one another's children, while the watch-boats stood off at a mindful distance, in case anyone should sink or commence a boarding action.

'It's a pain sometimes, this pretending to be poor.' Locke gazed around in reverie, the sort Bug would have been indulging in if the boy hadn't been concentrating on avoiding collision. A barge packed with dozens of yowling housecats in wooden-slat cages cut their wake, flagged with a blue pennant on which an artfully rendered dead mouse bled rich scarlet threads through a gaping hole in its throat. 'There's just something about this place. I could almost convince myself that I really did have a pressing need for a pound of fish, some bowstrings, some old shoes and a new shovel.'

'Fortunately for our credibility,' said Jean, 'we're coming up to the next major landmark on our way to a fat pile of Don Salvara's money.' He pointed past the north-eastern breakwater of the market, beyond which a row of prosperous-looking waterfront inns and taverns stood between the market and the Temple District.

'Right as always, Jean. Greed before imagination. Keep us on track.' Locke added an enthusiastic but superfluous finger to the direction Jean was already pointing. 'Bug! Get us out onto the river, then veer right. One of the twins is going to be waiting for us at the Tumblehome, third inn down on the south bank.'

Bug pushed them north, straining to reach the bottom of the market's basin (which was easily half again as deep as the surrounding canals) with each thrust. They evaded overzealous purveyors of grapefruits and sausage rolls and alchemical light-sticks, and Locke and Jean amused themselves with a favourite game, trying to spot the little pickpockets among the crowds on the breakwaters. The inattention of Camorr's busy thousands still managed to feed the doddering old Thiefmaker in his dank warren under Shades' Hill, nearly twenty years since Locke or Jean had last set foot inside the place.

Once they escaped from the market and onto the river itself, Bug and Jean wordlessly switched places. The fast waters of the Angevine would be better matched against Jean's muscle, and Bug would need to rest his arms for his part in the game to come. As Bug collapsed in Jean's former place at the bow, Locke produced a cinnamon-lemon apparently from thin air and tossed it to the boy. Bug ate it in six bites, oily dry skin and all, masticating the reddish-yellow pulp as grotesquely as possible between his bright but crooked teeth. He grinned.

'They don't make fish poison from those things, right?'

'No,' Locke said. 'They only make fish poison from things that Jean eats.'

Jean harrumphed. 'A little fish poison puts hair on your chest. Excepting if you're a fish.'

Jean kept them nearly against the southern bank of the Angevine, clear of the depths where the pole couldn't reach. Shafts of hot, pearl-white light flashed down on them as Eldgerglass bridges passed directly between their barge and the still-rising sun. The river was two hundred yards wide, sweating its wetness up into the air along with the smell of fish and silt.

To the north, rippling under the heat haze, were the orderly slopes of the Alcegrante islands, home to the city's minor nobility. It was a place of walled gardens, elaborate water sculptures and white stone villas, well off-limits to anyone dressed as Locke and Jean and Bug were. With the sun approaching its zenith, the vast shadows of the Five Towers had withdrawn into the Upper City, and were currently nothing more than a rosy stained-glass glow that spilled just over the northern edges of the Alcegrante.

'Gods, I love this place,' Locke said, drumming his fingers against his thighs. 'Sometimes I think this whole city was put here simply because the gods must adore crime. Pickpockets rob the common folk, merchants rob anyone they can dupe, Capa Barsavi robs the robbers *and* the common folk, the lesser nobles rob nearly everyone, and Duke Nicovante occasionally runs off with his army and robs the shit out of Tal Verarr or Jerem, *not to mention* what he does to his own nobles and his common folk.'

'So that makes us robbers of robbers,' said Bug, 'who pretend to be robbers working for a robber of other robbers.'

'Yes, we do sort of screw the pretty picture up, don't we?' Locke thought for a few seconds, clicking his tongue against the insides of his cheeks. 'Think of what we do as, ah, a sort of secret tax on nobles with more money than prudence. Hey! Here we are.'

Beneath the Tumblehome Inn was a wide and well-kept quay with half a dozen mooring posts, none of them currently occupied. The smooth grey embankment was about ten feet high here; broad stone steps led up to street level, as did a cobbled ramp for cargo and horses. Calo Sanza was waiting for them at the edge of the quay, dressed only slightly better than his fellows, with a Gentled horse standing placidly behind him. Locke waved.

'What's the news?' Locke cried. Jean's poling was skilled and graceful; the quay was twenty yards away, then ten, and then they were sliding up alongside it with a gentle scraping noise.

'Galdo got all the stuff packed into the room – it's the Bowsprit Suite on the first floor,' Calo whispered in response, bending down to Locke and Bug as he picked up the barge's mooring rope.

Calo had dark liquor-coloured skin and hair like an inky slice of night; the tautness of the flesh around his dark eyes was broken only by a fine network of laugh lines (though anyone who knew the Sanza twins would more readily describe them as mischief lines). An improbably sharp and hooked nose preceded his good looks like a dagger held at guard position.

Once he had made the barge fast to a mooring post, Calo tossed a heavy iron key to Locke, a key attached to a long tassel of braided red and black silk. At a quality rooming house like the Tumble-home, each private suite's door was guarded by a clockwork lock-box (removable only by some cunning means known to the owners) that could be swapped out from a niche in the door. Each rented room received a random new box and its attendant key; with hundreds of such identical-looking boxes stored behind the po-lished counter in the reception hall, the inn could pretty much guarantee that copying keys for later break-ins was a practical waste of a thief's time.

This courtesy would also give Locke and Jean guaranteed privacy for the rapid transformation that was about to take place.

'Wonderful!' Locke leaped up onto the quay as spryly as he had entered the boat; Jean passed the steering pole back to Bug, then made the barge shudder with his own leap. 'Let's go on in and fetch out our guests from Emberlain.'

As Locke and Jean padded up the steps towards the Tumble-home, Calo motioned for Bug to give him a hand with the horse. The white-eyed creature was utterly without fear or personal initiative, but that same lack of self-preservation instincts might lead it to damage the barge very easily. After a few minutes of careful pushing and pulling, they had it positioned in the centre of the barge, as calm as a statue that just happened to have lungs.

41

'Lovely creature,' said Calo. 'I've named him Impediment. You could use him as a table. Or a flying buttress.'

'Gentled animals give me the bloody creeps.'

'I don't disagree,' said Calo. 'But tenderfoots and softies prefer Gentled packhorses, and that's our master merchant of Emberlain in a nutshell.'

Several more minutes passed, and Calo and Bug stood in amiable silence under the punishing sun, looking the part of an unremarkable barge crew waiting to receive a passenger of consequence from the bosom of the Tumblehome Inn. Soon enough, that passenger descended the stairs and coughed twice to get their attention.

It was Locke, of course, but changed. His hair was slicked back with rose oil, the bones of his face seemed to shadow slightly deeper hollows in his cheeks, and his eyes were half-concealed behind a pair of optics, rimmed with black pearl and flashing silver in the sun.

He was now dressed in a tightly buttoned black coat in the Emberlain style, almost form-fitted from his shoulders down to his ribs, then flaring out widely at the waist. Two black leather belts with polished silver buckles circled his stomach; three ruffled layers of black silk cravats poured out of his collar and fluttered in the hot breeze. He wore embroidered grey hose over thick-heeled sharkskin shoes with black ribbon tongues that sprang outward, somewhat ludicrously, and hung over his feet with the drooping curl of hothouse flowers. Sweat was already beading on his forehead like little diamonds – Camorr's summer did not reward the intrusion of fashions from a more northerly climate.

'My name,' said Locke Lamora, 'is *Lukas Fehrwight*.' The voice was clipped and precise, scrubbed of Locke's natural inflections – he layered the hint of a harsh Vadran accent atop a slight mangling of his native Camorri dialect like a barkeep mixing liquors. 'I am wearing clothes that will be full of sweat in several minutes. I am dumb enough to walk around Camorr without a blade of any sort. Also,' he said with a hint of ponderous regret, 'I am entirely *fictional*.'

'I'm very sorry to hear that, Master Fehrwight,' said Calo, 'but at least we've got your boat and your horse ready for your grand excursion.'

Locke stepped carefully down towards the edge of the barge, swaying at the hips like a man newly off a ship and not yet used to surfaces that didn't tilt beneath his feet. His spine was arrow-straight, his movements nearly prissy. He wore the mannerisms of Lukas Fehrwight like a set of invisible clothes.

'My attendant will be along any moment,' Locke/Fehrwight said as he/they stepped aboard the barge, 'his name is *Graumann*, and he too suffers from a slight case of being imaginary.'

'Merciful gods,' said Calo, 'it must be catching.'

Down the cobbled ramp came Jean, treading heavily under the weight of one hundred and twenty pounds of creaking horse's harness, the embroidered leather packs crammed full of goods and strapped tightly shut. Jean now wore a white silk shirt, straining tight against his belly and already translucent in places with sweat, under an open black vest and a white neckerchief. His hair was parted in the middle and held in stasis by some thick black oil; never picturesque, it now resembled two pads of wool arched over his forehead like a tenement roof.

'We're behind schedule, Graumann.' Locke clasped his hands behind his back. 'Do hurry up and let the poor horse do its job.'

Jean heaved his mess over the Gentled horse's back, to no visible reaction from the animal. He then bent down and fastened the harness securely under the horse's stomach. Bug passed the steering pole to Calo, then slipped the barge's rope from the mooring post, and they were off once again.

'Wouldn't it be damned amusing,' said Calo, 'if Don Salvara picked today to dodge out on his little ritual.'

'Don't worry,' said Locke, briefly dropping the voice if not the posture of Lukas Fehrwight. 'He's quite devoted to his mother's memory. A conscience can be as good as a water-clock when it comes to keeping some appointments.'

'From your lips to the gods' ears.' Calo worked the pole with cheerful ease. 'And no skin off my balls if you're wrong. You're the one wearing a ten-pound black felt coat in the middle of Parthis.'

They made headway up the Angevine and came abreast of the western edge of the Temple District on their right, passing beneath a wide glass arch as they did so. Standing atop the middle of this bridge some fifty feet above the water was a lean, dark-haired man with looks and a nose to match Calo's.

43

As Calo poled the barge underneath the arch, Galdo Sanza casually let a half-eaten red apple fall from his hands. The fruit hit the water with a quiet little splash just a yard or two behind his brother.

'Salvara's at the temple!' Bug said.

'Sublime.' Locke spread his hands and grinned. 'Didn't I tell you he suffered from an impeccable sense of maternal devotion?'

'I'm so pleased that you only choose victims of the highest moral quality,' said Calo. 'The wrong sort might set a bad example for Bug.'

At a public dock jutting from the north-western shore of the Temple District, just under the heights of the city's vast new House of Iono (Father of Storms, Lord of the Grasping Waters), Jean tied them up in record time and led Impediment, looking every bit the part of a wealthy merchant's packhorse, up off the barge.

Locke followed with Fehrwright's nervous dignity on full display; all the banter was now banked down like coals under a cookfire. Bug darted off into the crowds, eager to take up his watch position over the alley junction where Don Salvara's ambitions would soon be sorely tempted. Calo spotted Galdo just stepping off the glass bridge, and casually moved towards him. Each twin was unconsciously fingering the weapons concealed beneath their baggy shirts.

By the time the Sanza brothers fell into step beside one another and began moving towards the rendezvous at the Temple of Fortunate Waters, Locke and Jean were already a block away, approaching from another direction. The game was afoot.

For the fourth time in as many years the Gentlemen Bastards were drawing a bead on one of the most powerful men in the city of Camorr. They were setting up a meeting that might eventually divest Don Lorenzo Salvara of nearly half his worldly wealth, and now it was up to the Don to be punctual.

5

Bug was in a perfect position to spot the reinforced foot patrol before anyone else did, which was according to the plan. The foot patrol itself was also in the plan, after a fashion. It meant the plan was blown.

'You're going to be top-eyes on this game, Bug.' Locke had explained the task several times, and Jean had followed up with relentless quizzing. 'We're deliberately making first touch on Salvara on the most deserted street in the Temple District. A spotter on the ground would be obvious a mile away, but a boy two storeys up is another matter.'

'What am I spotting for?'

'Whatever shows up. Duke Nicovante and the Nightglass Company. The King of the Seven Marrows. A little old lady with a dung-wagon. If we get interlopers, you just make the signal. Maybe you can distract common folk. If it's the watch, well – we can either play innocent or run like hell.'

And here were six men in mustard-yellow tabards and well-oiled fighting harness, with batons and blades clattering ominously against their doubled waistbelts, strolling up from the south just a few dozen paces away from the Temple of Fortunate Waters. Their path would take them right past the mouth of the all-important alley; even if Bug warned the others in time for them to hide Calo's rope, Locke and Jean would still be covered in mud and the twins would still be (purposely) dressed like stage-show bandits, complete with neckerchiefs over their faces. No chance to play innocent; if Bug gave the signal, it was run-like-hell time.

Bug thought as fast as he ever had in his life, while his heart beat so rapidly it felt like someone was fluttering the pages of a book against his lungs. He had to force himself to stay cool, stay observant, look for an opening. Catalogue! He needed to catalogue his options.

His options stank. Twelve years old, crouched twenty feet up in the periphery of the wildly overgrown rooftop garden of a disused temple, with no long-range weapons and no other suitable distractions available. Don Salvara was still paying his respects to his mother's gods within the Temple of Fortunate Waters; the only people in sight were his fellow Gentlemen Bastards and the sweat-soaked patrol about to ruin their day.

Wait.

Twenty feet down and six feet to Bug's right, against the wall of the crumbling structure on which he squatted, there was a rubbish pile. It looked like mould-eaten burlap sacks and a mixed assortment of brown muck.

The prudent thing to do would be to signal the others and let them scurry; Calo and Galdo were old hands at playing hard-to-get with the yellowjackets, and they could just come back and restart the game again next week. Maybe. Maybe a screwed-up game today would alarm someone, and lead to more foot patrols in the coming weeks. Maybe word would get around that the Temple District wasn't as quiet as it should be. Maybe Capa Barsavi, beset by problems as he was, would take an interest in the unauthorised disturbance, and turn his own screws. And then Don Salvara's money might as well be on the bloody moons, for all that the Gentlemen Bastards could get their hands on it.

No, prudence was out. Bug had to *win*. The presence of that rubbish pile made a great and glorious stupidity very possible.

He was in the air before another thought crossed his mind. Arms out, falling backwards, staring up into the hot near-noon sky with the confident assurance of all twelve of his years that death and injury were things reserved solely for people that weren't Bug. He screamed as he fell, in wild exaltation, just to be sure that he had the foot patrol's unwavering attention.

He could feel the great vast shadow of the ground looming up beneath him, in the last half-second of his fall, and at that instant his eyes caught a dark shape cutting through the air just above the Temple of Fortunate Waters. A sleek and beautiful shape, heavy – a bird? A gull of some sort? Camorr had no other birds that size, certainly none that moved like crossbow bolts, and . . .

Impact with the semi-yielding surface of the rubbish heap walloped the air out of his lungs with a wet *hoooosh* sound, and snapped his head forward. Sharp chin bounced off slender chest; his teeth punched bloody holes in his tongue and the warm taste of salt filled his mouth. He screamed again, reflexively, and spat blood. His view of the sky spun first left then right, as though the world were trying on strange new angles for his approval.

Booted feet running on cobblestones; the creak and rattle of weapons in harness. A ruddy middle-aged face with two drooping sweat-slicked moustaches inserted itself between Bug and the sky.

'Perelandro's balls, boy!' The watchman looked as bewildered as he did worried. 'What the hell were you doing, screwing around up there? You're lucky you landed where you did.'

There were enthusiastic murmurs of agreement from the

yellow-jacketed squad crowding in behind the first man; Bug could smell their sweat and their harness-oil, as well as the aroma of the stuff that had broken his fall. Well, when you jumped into a random pile of brown glop in Camorr, you knew going in that it wouldn't smell like rosewater. Bug shook his head to clear the white sparks dancing behind his eyes, and twitched his legs to be sure they would serve. Nothing appeared to be broken, thank the gods. He would re-evaluate his own claims to immortality when all of this was over.

'Watch-sergeant,' Bug hissed thickly, letting more blood spill out over his lips (damn, his tongue burned with pain), 'watch-sergeant . . .'

'Yes?' The man's eyes were going wider. 'Can you move your arms and legs, boy? What can you feel?'

Bug reached up with his hands, casually, not entirely feigning shakiness, and clutched at the watch-sergeant's harness as though to steady himself.

'Watch-sergeant,' Bug said a few seconds later, 'your purse is much lighter than it should be. Out whoring last night, were we?'

He shook the little leather pouch just under the watch-sergeant's dark moustaches, and the larcenous part of his soul (which was, let us be honest, its majority) glowed warmly at the sheer befuddlement that blossomed in the man's eyes. For a split second the pain of Bug's imperfect landing in the rubbish heap was forgotten. Then his other hand came up, as if by magic, and his Orphan's Twist hit the watch-sergeant right between the eyes.

An Orphan's Twist, or 'little red keeper', was a weighted sack like a miniature cosh, kept hidden in clothes (but never against naked skin). It was traditionally packed full of ground shavings from a dozen of Camorr's more popular hot peppers, and a few nasty cast-offs from certain black alchemists' shops. No use against a real threat, but just the thing for another street urchin. Or a certain sort of adult with wandering hands.

Or an unprotected face, at spitting distance.

Bug was already rolling to his left, so the spray of fine rust-coloured powder that erupted from his Twist missed him by inches. The watch-sergeant was not so lucky; it was a solid hit, scattering the hellish-hot stuff up his nose, down his mouth, and straight into his eyes. He choked out a string of truly amazing wet

47

bellows, and fell backwards clawing at his cheeks. Bug was already up and moving with the giddy elasticity of youth; even his bitterly aching tongue was temporarily forgotten in the all-consuming need to run like hell.

Now he definitely had the foot patrol's undivided attention. They were shouting and leaping after him, as his little feet pounded the cobbles and he sucked in deep stinging gulps of humid air. He'd done his part to keep the game alive. It could now go on without him while he gave the Duke's constables their afternoon exercise.

A particularly fast-thinking watchman fumbled his whistle into his mouth and blew it raggedly while still running – three short bursts, a pause, then three more. *Watchman down.* Oh, shit. That would bring every yellowjacket in half the city at a dead run, weapons out. That would bring *crossbows.* It was suddenly deadly important that Bug slip the squad at his heels before other squads started sending spotters up onto roofs. His anticipation of a merry chase vanished; he had perhaps a minute and a half to get to one of his usual cosy-holes and pull a vanish.

Suddenly, his tongue hurt very badly indeed.

6

Don Lorenzo Salvara stepped out of the temple portico into the stark bright dampness of high Camorri noon, little imagining the education a certain boy thief was receiving in the concept of *too clever by half* just across the district. The trilling of watch-whistles sounded faintly. Salvara narrowed his eyes and peered with some curiosity at the distant figure of a lone city watchman, stumbling across the cobbles and occasionally bouncing off walls, clutching his head as though afraid it was going to float off his neck and up into the sky.

'Can you believe it, m'lord?' Conté had already brought the horses around from the temple's unobtrusive little stabling grotto. 'Drunk as a baby in a beer barrel, and not a heartbeat past noon. Fucking pissant lot of softies, these new goldenrods.' Conté was a sun-wrinkled man of middle years with the waistline of a professional dancer and the arms of a professional oarsman. The manner in which he served the young Don was obvious even without a glance at the pair of thigh-length stilettos hanging from his crossed leather belts.

'Hardly up to your old standards, eh?' The Don, on the other hand, was a well-favoured young man of the classic Camorri blood, black-haired, with skin like shadowed honey. His face was heavy and soft with curves, though his body was slender, and only his eyes gave any hint that he wasn't a polite young collegium undergraduate masquerading as a noble. Behind his fashionable rimless optics, the Don had eyes like an impatient archer hungry for targets. Conté snorted.

'In my day, at least we knew that getting shit-faced was an indoor hobby.' Conté passed the Don the reins of his mount, a sleek grey mare little bigger than a pony, well-trained but certainly not Gentled. Just the thing for short trots around a city still more friendly to boats (or acrobats, as Doña Salvara often complained) than to horses. The stumbling watchman vanished around a distant corner, vaguely in the direction of the urgent whistling. As it seemed to be coming no closer, Salvara shrugged inwardly and led his horse out into the street.

Here the day's second curiosity burst upon them in all of its glory. As the Don and his man turned to their right, they gained a full view of the high-walled alley beside the Temple of Fortunate Waters – and in this alley two finely-dressed men were clearly getting their lives walloped out of them by a pair of bravos.

Salvara froze and stared in wonder – masked thugs in the Temple District? Masked thugs strangling a man dressed all in black, in the tight, heavy, miserably inappropriate fashion of a *Vadran*? Merciful Twelve. A Gentled packhorse was simply standing there taking it all in.

After a handful of seconds lost to sheer amazement, the Don let his own horse's reins go and ran towards the mouth of the alley. He didn't need to glance sideways to know that Conté was barely a stride behind him, knives out.

'You!' The Don's voice was reasonably confident, though high with excitement. 'Unhand these men and stand clear!'

The closest footpad snapped his head round; his dark eyes widened above his improvised mask when he saw the Don and

49

Conté approaching. The thug shifted his red-faced victim so that the man's body was between himself and the would-be interlopers.

'No need to trouble yourself with this business, my *lord*,' the footpad said. 'Just a bit of a disagreement. Private matter.'

'Perhaps you should have conducted it somewhere less public.'

The footpad managed a truly exasperated look. 'What, the Duke give you this alley to be your estate? Take another step and I break this poor bastard's neck.'

'You just do that.' Don Salvara settled his hand suggestively on the pommel of his basket-hilted rapier. 'My man and I appear to command the only way out of this alley. I'm sure you'll still feel quite pleased at having killed that man when you've got three feet of steel in your own throat.'

The first footpad didn't release his hold on the coiled loops of rope that were holding up his barely conscious victim, but he began to back off warily towards the dead end, dragging the black-clad man clumsily with him. His fellow thug stood away from the prone form of the man he'd been savagely kicking. A meaningful look flashed between the two masked bandits.

'My friends, do *not* be stupid.' Salvara slid his rapier halfway out of its scabbard; sunlight blazed white on finest Camorri steel, and Conté crouched forward on the balls of his feet, shifting to the predatory stance of a knife-fighter born and trained.

Without another word, the first footpad flung his victim straight at Conté and the Don. While the unfortunate black-clad fellow gasped and clutched at his rescuers, the two masked thugs bolted for the wall at the rear of the alley. Conté sidestepped the heaving, shuddering Vadran and dashed after them, but the assailants were spry as well as cunning. A slim rope hung down the wall, barely visible, knotted at regular intervals. The two thugs scrambled up this and all but dived over the top of the wall; Conté and his blades were two seconds too late. The weighted far end of the rope flew back over the wall and landed with a splat in the crusted muck at his feet.

'Fucking useless slugabed bastards!' The Don's man slid his stilettos back into his belt with easy familiarity and bent down to the heavyset body lying unmoving in the alley muck. The eerie white stare of the Gentled packhorse seemed to follow him as he pressed fingers to the fat man's neck, seeking a pulse. 'Watchmen stumbling drunk in broad daylight, and look what happens in the bloody *Temple District* while they screw around . . .'

'Oh, thank the Marrows,' choked out the black-clad man as he uncoiled the rope from his neck and flung it to the ground. Don Salvara could now see that his clothes were very fine, despite their spattering of muck and their unseasonable weight – excellently cut, form-tailored and ornamented with expensive subtlety rather than opulent flash. 'Thank the Salt and thank the Sweet. Thank the Hands Beneath the Waters those bastards attacked us right beside this place of power, where the currents brought you to our aid.'

The man's Therin was precise, though heavily accented, and his voice was unsurprisingly hoarse. He massaged his abraded throat, blinked, and began to pat the muck around him with his free hand as though looking for something.

'I believe I can help you again,' said Don Salvara in his best Vadran, which was as precise and as heavily accented as the stranger's Therin, in the opposite direction. Salvara picked a pair of pearl-rimmed optics out of the muck (noting their light weight and sturdy construction – a superior and very expensive pair indeed) and wiped them off on the sleeve of his own loose scarlet coat before handing them to the man.

'And you speak Vadran!' The stranger spoke his own tongue now, with what seemed perfect fluency to Salvara's ears. The black-clad man slid the optics back over his eyes and blinked up at his rescuer. 'A complete miracle now, far more than I have any right to pray for. Oh! Graumann!'

The black-clad Vadran scrambled unsteadily to his feet and stumbled over to his companion. Conté had managed to roll the portly stranger over in the slime; he now lay on his back with his great muck-slick chest rising and falling steadily.

'He lives, obviously.' Conté slid his hands along the poor fellow's ribcage and stomach. 'I don't believe he has anything broken or ruptured, though he'll likely be green with bruises for weeks. Green as pondwater, then black as night, or I don't know shit from custard tarts.'

The slender, well-dressed Vadran let out a long sigh of relief. 'Custard tarts. Indeed. The Marrows are most generous. Graumann is my attendant, my secretary, my diligent right hand. Alas, he has no skill at arms, but then I am myself plainly embarrassed in that regard.' The stranger spoke Therin now, and he turned to stare at Don Salvara with wide eyes. 'Just as plainly I do you discourtesy, for you must be one of the Dons of Camorr.' He bowed low, lower even than etiquette would require of a landed foreigner greeting a peer of the Serene Duchy of Camorr, almost until he was in danger of pitching forward on his chin.

'I am Lukas Fehrwight, servant to the House of bel Auster, of the canton of Emberlain and the Kingdom of the Seven Marrows. I am entirely at your service and grateful beyond words for what you have done for me today.'

'I am Lorenzo, Don Salvara, and this is my man Conté, and it is we who are entirely at your service, without obligation.' The Don bowed at exactly the correct angle, with his right hand held out as an invitation to shake. 'I am in a sense responsible for Camorr's hospitality, and what befell you here was not hospitality. It was upon my honour to come to your aid.'

Fehrwight grasped the Don's proffered arm just above the wrist and shook, with the Don holding his forearm in the same place. If Fehrwight's grasp was weak, the Don was willing to charitably ascribe it to his near-strangling. Fehrwight then lowered his own forehead until it gently touched the back of the Don's hand, and their physical courtesies were settled. 'Yet I beg to differ; you have here a sworn man, quite competent by his looks. You could have satisfied honour by sending him to our aid, yet you came yourself, ready to fight. From where I stood, it seemed he ran to keep up with you. I assure you, my viewpoint for this affair was uncomfortable but excellent.'

The Don waved his hand gently as though words could be swatted out of the air. 'I'm just sorry they got away, Master Fehrwight. It is unlikely that I can give you true justice. For that, Camorr again apologises.'

Fehrwight knelt down beside Graumann and brushed the big man's sweat-slick dark hair back from his forehead. 'Justice? I am lucky to be alive. I was blessed with a safe journey here and, with your aid, I am alive to continue my mission, and that is justice enough.' The slender man looked up at Salvara again. 'Are you not Don Salvara of the Nacozza Vineyards? Is not the Doña Sofia your wife, the famous botanical alchemist?'

'I have that honour, and I have that pleasure,' said the Don. 'And do you not serve *the* House of bel Auster? Do you not deal with the, ah . . .'

'Yes, oh yes, I serve *that* House of bel Auster; my business is the sale and transport of the substance you're thinking of. It is curious, so very curious. The Marrows toy with me; the Hands Beneath must wish me to drop dead of sheer wonder. That you should save my life here, that you should speak Vadran, that we should share a common business interest . . . it is uncanny.'

'I, too, find it extraordinary, but hardly displeasing.' Don Salvara gazed around the alley thoughtfully. 'My mother was Vadran, which is why I speak the tongue enthusiastically, if poorly. Were you followed here? That rope over the wall bespeaks preparation, and the Temple District . . . well, it's usually as safe as the Duke's own reading-room.'

'We arrived this morning,' said Fehrwright, 'and after we secured our rooms – at the Inn of the Tumblehome, you know of it, I'm sure – we came straight here to give thanks and drown the offerings for our safe passage from Emberlain. I did not see where those men came from.' Fehrwright mused for a moment. 'Though I believe that one of them threw that rope over the wall after knocking Graumann down. They were cautious, but not waiting in ambush for us.'

Salvara grunted, and turned his attention to the blank stare of the Gentled horse. 'Curious. Do you always bring horses and goods to the temple to make your offerings? If those packs are as full as they look, I can see why thugs might have been tempted.'

'Ordinarily, such things would be under lock and key at our inn.' Fehrwright gave Graumann two friendly pats on the shoulder and rose again. 'But for this cargo, for this mission, I fear I must keep them with me at all times. And I fear that must have made us a tempting target. It is a conundrum.' Fehrwright scratched his chin slowly, several times. 'I am in your debt already, Don Lorenzo, and hesitant to ask aid of you once again. Yet this relates to the mission I am charged with, for my time in Camorr. As you are a Don, do you know of a certain Don Jacobo?'

Don Salvara's eyes fixed firmly on Fehrwright; one corner of his mouth turned infinitesimally downward. 'Yes,' he said, and nothing more, after the silence had stretched a few moments.

'This Don Jacobo . . . it is said that he is a man of wealth. Extreme wealth, even for a Don.'

'That is . . . true.'

'It is said that he is adventurous. Bold, even. That he has . . . how do you say it, an eye for strange opportunities. A toleration of risk.'

'That is one way of describing his character, perhaps.'

Fehrwight licked his lips. 'Don Lorenzo . . . it is important . . . if these things are true, would you, could you – through your status as a peer of Camorr – assist me in securing an appointment with Don Jacobo? I am ashamed to ask, but I would be more ashamed to forswear my mission for the House of bel Auster.'

Don Salvara smiled without the slightest hint of humour, and turned his head for several seconds as though to gaze down at Graumann, lying quietly in the muck. Conté had stood up and was staring directly at his Don, eyes wide.

'Master Fehrwight,' said the Don at last, 'are you not aware that Paleri Jacobo is perhaps my greatest living enemy? That the two of us have fought to the blood, twice, and only on the orders of Duke Nicovante himself do we not settle our affair for all time?'

'Oh,' said Fehrwight, with the tone and facial expression of a man who has just dropped a torch in a hogshead cask of lamp oil. 'How awkward. How stupid of me. I have done business in Camorr several times, but I did not . . . I have insulted you. I have asked too much.'

'Hardly.' Salvara's tone grew warm again; he began to drum the fingers of his right hand against the hilt of his rapier. 'But you're here on a mission for the House of bel Auster. You carry a cargo that you refuse to let out of your sight. You clearly have your plan fixed upon Don Jacobo in some fashion, though . . . you still need to gain a formal audience with him. So, to be clear, he doesn't know you're here, or that you plan on seeking him out, does he?'

'I . . . that is . . . I fear to say too much of my business . . .'

'Yet your business here is plain,' said Don Salvara, now positively cheerful, 'and have you not repeatedly stated that you are indebted to me, Master Fehrwight? Despite my assurances to the contrary, have you not refused those assurances? Do you withdraw your promise of obligation *now*?'

'I . . . with the best will in the world, my lord . . . damn.'

Fehrwright shook. 'I am ashamed, Don Lorenzo. I must now either forswear my obligation to the man who saved my life or forswear my promise to the House of bel Auster to keep its business as private as possible.'

'You must do neither,' said the Don, 'and perhaps I can aid you directly in the pursuit of your master's business. Do you not see? If Don Jacobo does not know of your presence here, what obligation do you have to him? Clearly, you are set here upon business. A plan, a scheme, a proposal of some sort. You're here to *initiate* something, or else you'd have your connections already in place. Don't be angry with yourself; this is all plain logic. Is it not true?'

Fehrwright looked down and nodded reluctantly.

'Then here it is! Although I am not as wealthy as Don Jacobo, I am a man of substantial means; and we are in complementary lines of business, are we not? Attend me tomorrow, on my barge, at the Shifting Revel. Make your proposal to *me*; let us discuss it thoroughly.' There was a wicked gleam in Don Salvara's eyes; it could be seen despite the brightness of the sun overhead. 'As you are indebted to me, repay this obligation by agreeing only to attend. Then, free of obligation, let us discuss business to our mutual advantage. Do you not see that I have a vested interest in taking whatever opportunity you present away from Jacobo, even if he never learns of it? *Especially* if he never learns of it, so he will never need to be angry with you? And am I not bold enough for your tastes? I swear your face grows longer as though by sorcery. What's wrong?'

'It is not you, Don Lorenzo. It is merely that the Hands Beneath are suddenly unfailingly generous once again. We have a saying – that undeserved good fortune always conceals a snare.'

'Don't worry, Master Fehrwright. If it's really business that you want to discuss, never doubt that there will be hard work and bitter troubles enough waiting for us down the road. Are we in agreement, then? Will you dine with me tomorrow morning, and take in the Shifting Revel, and discuss your proposal with me?'

Fehrwright swallowed, looked Don Salvara in the eyes, and nodded firmly. 'There is great sense in what you propose. And perhaps great opportunity for both of us. I will accept your hospitality, and I will tell you everything. Tomorrow, as you say. It cannot come soon enough for me.'

'It has been my pleasure to make your acquaintance, Master Fehrwight.' Don Salvara inclined his head to Fehrwight. 'May we help your friend up out of the muck, and see you to your inn to ensure you have no further difficulties?'

'Your company would be most pleasing, if only you would wait and look after poor Graumann and our cargo long enough for me to finish my offering within the temple.' Locke removed a small leather pack from the horse's jumble of goods and containers. 'The offering will be more substantial than I had planned. But then my masters understand that prayers of thanks are an unavoidable expense in our line of business.'

7

The journey back to the Tumblehome was slow, with Jean putting on an excellent show of misery, grogginess and confusion. If the sight of two mud-splattered, overdressed outlanders and three horses escorted by a Don struck anyone as unusual, they kept their comments to themselves and reserved their stares for Don Salvara's back. Along the way, they passed Calo, now walking about casually in the plain garb of a labourer. He flashed rapid and subtle hand signals. With no sign of Bug, he would take up position at one of their prearranged rendezvous sites. And he would pray.

'Lukas! Surely it can't be! I say, Lukas Fehrwight!'

As Calo vanished into the crowd, Galdo appeared just as suddenly, dressed in the bright silks and cottons of a prosperous Camorri merchant; his slashed and ruffled coat alone was probably worth as much as the barge the Gentlemen Bastards had poled up the river that morning. There was nothing now about him to remind the Don or his man of the alley cut-throats; unmasked, with his hair slicked back under a small round cap, Galdo was the very picture of physical and fiscal respectability. He twirled a little lacquered cane and stepped towards Don Lorenzo's odd little party, smiling broadly.

'Why – Evante!' Locke-as-Fehrwight stopped and stared in mock astonishment, then held out a hand for a vigorous shake from the newcomer. 'What a . . . what a pleasant surprise!'

'Quite, Lukas, quite – but what the hell's happened to you? And to you, Graumann? You look as though you just lost a fight!'

'Ah, we did.' Locke looked down and rubbed his eyes. 'Evante, it has been a very peculiar morning. Grau and I might not even be alive if not for our rather extraordinary guide here.' Pulling Galdo to him, Locke held a hand out towards the Don. 'My lord Salvara, may I introduce to you Evante Eccari, a solicitor of your Razona district? Evante, this is Don Lorenzo Salvara. Of the Nacozza Vineyards, if you still pay attention to those properties.'

'Twelve!' Galdo swept his hat off and bowed deeply at the waist. 'A Don. I should have recognised you immediately, m'lord. A thousand pardons. Evante Eccari, entirely at your service.'

'A pleasure, Master Eccari.' Don Salvara bowed correctly but casually, then stepped forward to shake the newcomer's hand; this signalled his permission to deduct any superfluous bowing and scraping from the conversation. 'You, ah, you know Master Fehrwright, then?'

'Lukas and I go well back, m'lord.' Without turning his back on Don Salvara, he fussily brushed a bit of dried muck from the shoulders of Locke's black coat. 'I work out of Meraggio's, mostly, handling customs and licence work for our friends in the north. Lukas is one of bel Auster's best and brightest.'

'Hardly.' Locke coughed and smiled shyly. 'Evante takes all the more interesting laws and regulations of your duchy, and reduces them to plain Therin. He was my salvation on several previous ventures. I seem to have a talent for finding snares in Camorr, and a talent for finding good Camorri to slip me out of them.'

'Few clients would describe what I do in such generous terms. But what's this mud, and these bruises? You said something of a fight?'

'Yes. Your city has some very, ah, enterprising thieves. Don Salvara and his man have just driven a pair of them off. I fear Graumann and I were getting the worst of the affair.'

Galdo stepped over to Jean and gave him a friendly pat on the back; Jean's wince was fantastic theatre. 'Twelve Gods! My compliments, m'lord Salvara. Lukas is what you might call a good vintage, even if he's not wise enough to take off those silly winter wools. I'm most deeply obliged to you for what you've done, and I'm at—'

'Hardly, sir, hardly.' Don Salvara held up one hand, palm out, and hitched the other in his sword-belt. 'I did what my position demanded, no more. And I have too many promises of obligation being thrown at me already this afternoon.'

Don Lorenzo and 'Master Eccari' fenced pleasantries for a few moments thereafter; Galdo eventually let himself be skewered with the politest possible version of 'Thanks, but piss off.'

'Well,' he said at last. 'This has been a wonderful surprise, but I'm afraid I have a client waiting, and clearly, m'lord Salvara, you and Lukas have business that I shouldn't intrude upon. With your permission . . . ?'

'Of course, of course. A pleasure, Master Eccari.'

'Entirely mine, I assure you, m'lord. Lukas, if you get a spare hour, you know where to find me. And should my poor skills be of any use to your affairs, you know I'll come running . . .'

'Of course, Evante.' Locke grasped Galdo's right hand in both of his and shook enthusiastically. 'I suspect we may have need of you sooner rather than later.' He laid a finger alongside his nose; Galdo nodded, and then there was a general exchange of bows and handshakes and the other courtesies of disentanglement. As Galdo hurried away, he left a few hand signals in his wake, disguised as adjustments to his hat.

I know nothing about Bug. Going to look around.

Don Salvara stared thoughtfully after him for a few seconds, then turned back to Locke as the party resumed its journey towards the Tumblehome. They made small talk for a while. Locke had little trouble, as Fehrwight, letting his pleasure at seeing 'Eccari' slip; soon he was projecting a very real downcast mood, which he claimed to be an incipient headache from the attempted strangling. Don Salvara and Conté left the two Gentlemen Bastards in front of the Tumblehome's street-side citrus gardens, with admonitions to rest soundly that night and let all business wait for the morrow.

No sooner were Locke and Jean safely alone in their suite (the harness full of 'precious' goods thrown back over Jean's shoulders) than they were exploding out of their muddy finery and donning new disguises so they could hurry off to their own rendezvous points to wait for word of Bug, if any was forthcoming.

This time, the swift dark shape that flitted silently from rooftop to rooftop in their wake went entirely unnoticed.

8

Fading Falselight. The Hangman's Wind and the swampwater mist glued clothes to skin and rapidly congealed Calo and Galdo's tobacco smoke around them, half-cloaking them in a cataract of greyness. The twins sat, hooded and sweating, in the locked doorway of a fairly well-kept pawnshop on the northern tip of the Old Citadel district. The shop was shuttered and barred for the evening; the keeper's family was obviously drinking something with a merry kick two floors above them.

'It was a good first touch,' said Calo.

'It was, wasn't it?'

'Our best yet. Hard to work all those disguises, what with us being the handsome ones.'

'I confess that I wasn't aware we shared that complication.'

'Now, now, don't be hard on yourself. Physically, you're quite my match. It's my scholarly gifts you lack. And my easy fearlessness. And my gift for women.'

'If you mean the ease with which you drop coins when you're off a-cunting, you're right. You're a one-man charity ball for the whores of Camorr, you are.'

'Now that,' said Calo, 'was genuinely unkind.'

'You're right.' The twins smoked in silence for a few seconds. 'I'm sorry. Some of the savour's out of it tonight. The little bastard has my stomach twisted in knots. You saw . . .'

'Extra foot patrols. Yeah. Agitated, too. Heard the whistles. I'm real curious about what he did and why he did it.'

'He must've had his reasons. If it really was a good first touch, he gave it to us. I hope he's well enough for us to beat the piss out of him.'

Stray shapes hurried past in the backlit mist; there was very little Elderglass on the Old Citadel island, so most of the dying glow poured through from a distance. The sound of a horse's hooves on cobbles was coming from the south, and getting louder.

At that moment Locke was no doubt skulking near the Palace of

Patience, eyeballing the patrols coming and going across the Black Bridge, making sure that they carried no small, familiar prisoners. Or small, familiar bodies. Jean would be off at another rendezvous point, pacing and cracking his knuckles. Bug would never return straight to the Temple of Perelandro, nor would he go near the Tumblehome. The older Gentlemen Bastards would sit their vigils for him out in the city and the steam.

Wooden wheels clattered and an annoyed animal whinnied; the sound of the horse-drawn cart came to a creaking halt not twenty feet from the Sanza brothers, shrouded in the mist. 'Avendando?' A loud but uncertain voice spoke the name. Calo and Galdo leapt to their feet as one, 'Avendando' was their private recognition signal for an unplanned rendezvous.

'Here!' Calo cried, dropping his thin cigarette and forgetting to step on it. A man materialised out of the mist, bald and bearded, with the heavy arms of a working artisan and the rounded middle of moderate prosperity.

'I dunno exactly how this works,' the man said, 'but, ah, if one of you is Avendando, I was told I'd have ten solons for delivering this here cask to this, ah, doorway.' He jerked a thumb over his shoulder towards the cart.

'Cask. Indeed.' Galdo fumbled with a coin-purse, heart racing. 'What's, ahhh, in this cask?'

'Ain't wine,' said the stranger. 'Ain't a very polite lad, neither. But ten silvers is what he promised.'

'Of course.' Galdo counted rapidly, slapping bright silver discs down into the man's open palm. 'Ten for the cask. One more for forgetting all about this, hmmm?'

'Holy hell, my memory must be cacked out, because I can't remember what you're paying me for.'

'Good man.' Galdo slipped his purse back under his nightcloak and ran to help Calo, who had mounted the cart and was standing over a wooden cask of moderate size. The cork stopper that would ordinarily be set into the top of the barrel was gone, leaving a small dark air hole. Calo rapped sharply on the cask three times; three faint taps came right back. With grins on their faces the Sanza twins muscled the cask down off the cart and nodded farewell to the driver. The man remounted his cart and soon vanished into the night, whistling, his pockets jingling with more than twenty times the value of the empty cask.

'Well,' Calo said when they'd rolled the cask back to the shelter of their doorway, 'this vintage is probably a little young and rough for decanting.'

'Put it in the cellar for fifty or sixty years?'

'I was thinking we might just pour it in the river.'

'Really?' Galdo drummed his fingers on the cask. 'What's the river ever done to deserve that?'

There was a series of noises from inside the cask that sounded vaguely like some sort of protest. Calo and Galdo leaned down by the air hole together.

'Now, Bug,' Calo began, 'I'm sure you have a perfectly good explanation for why you're in there, and why we're out here worrying ourselves sick over you.'

'It's a magnificent explanation, really.' Bug's voice was hoarse and echoed faintly 'You're going to love it. But, um, first tell me how the game went.'

'It was a thing of beauty,' said Galdo.

'Three weeks, tops, and we're going to own this Don down to his wife's last set of silk smallclothes,' added Calo.

The boy groaned with obvious relief. 'Great. Well, ahhh, what happened was, there was this pack of yellowjackets heading right for you. What I did pissed them off pretty fierce, so, I ran for this cooper's that I know in Old Citadel. He does business with some of the wine places upriver, so he's got this yard of barrels just sitting around. Well, I just sort of invited myself in, jumped in one, and told him that if I could stay there until he delivered me here after Falselight, there'd be eight solons in it for him.'

'Eight?' Calo scratched his chin. 'The cheeky bastard just asked for ten, and got eleven.'

'Yeah, well, that's okay.' Bug coughed. 'I got bored sitting around the cask yard so I lifted his purse. Had about two solons' worth of copper in it. So we got some back.'

'I was going to say something sympathetic about you lying around inside a cask for half the day,' said Galdo, 'but that was a damn silly thing to do.'

'Oh, come on!' Bug sounded genuinely stung. 'He thought I was in the cask the whole time, so why would he suspect me? And you just gave him a load of money, so why would he suspect you? It's perfect! Locke would appreciate it.'

'Bug,' Calo said, 'Locke is our brother and our love for him has no bounds. But the four most fatal words in the Therin language are "Locke would appreciate it."'

'Rivalled only by "Locke taught me a new trick,"' added Galdo.

'The only person who gets away with Locke Lamora games . . .'

'. . . is Locke . . .'

'. . . because we think the gods are saving him up for a really big death. Something with knives and hot irons . . .'

'. . . and fifty thousand cheering spectators.'

The brothers cleared their throats in unison.

'Well,' Bug said finally, 'I did it and I got away with it. Can we go home now?'

'Home,' Calo mused. 'Sure. Locke and Jean are going to sob over you like grandmothers when they find out you're alive, so let's not keep them waiting.'

'No need to get out; your legs are probably cramped up,' said Galdo.

'They are!' Bug squeaked. 'But you two really don't need to carry me all that way . . .'

'You've never been more right about anything in your entire life, Bug!' Galdo took up position at one side of the cask and nodded at Calo; whistling in unison, the brothers began rolling the cask along the cobbles, steering for the Temple District, not necessarily by the fastest or smoothest route available.

Interlude:
Locke Explains

'It was an accident,' Locke said at last. 'They were both accidents.'

'Excuse me? I must not have heard you.' Father Chains' eyes narrowed in the faint red glow of Locke's tiny ceramic lamp. 'I could have sworn you just said, "Toss me over the parapet, I'm a useless little cuss and I'm ready to die at this very moment."'

Chains had moved their conversation up to the roof of the temple, where they sat comfortably beneath high parapets meant to be threaded with decorative plants. The long-lost hanging gardens of the House of Perelandro were a small but important aspect of the sacrificial tragedy of the Eyeless Priest; one more bit of stage-setting to draw sympathy, measured in coins.

The clouds had roiled in overhead, palely reflecting the parti-coloured glimmers of night-lit Camorr, obscuring the moons and the stars. The Hangman's Wind was little more than a damp pressure that nudged the sluggish air around Chains and Locke as the boy struggled to clarify himself.

'No! No, I meant to hurt them. But that's all. Hurt them. I didn't know . . . I didn't know those things would happen to them.'

'Well . . . that I can almost believe.' Chains tapped the index finger of his right hand against his left palm, the Camorri market-place gesture for *Get on with it*. 'So take me all the way. That "almost" is a major problem for you. Make me understand, starting with the first boy.'

'Veslin,' Locke whispered. 'And Gregor, but Veslin first.'

'Veslin,' Chains agreed. 'Veslin indeed. Poor soul, got a super-fluous orifice carved into his neck by none other than your old master. The Thiefmaker had to buy one of those lovely sharks' teeth from the Capa, and that one got *used*. So . . . why?'

'In the hill, some of the older boys and girls stopped going out to work.' Locke wove his fingers tightly together and stared down at them as though they might sprout answers. 'They would just take things when we came back each day. Shake us down. Make our reports to the master for us, leave things out sometimes.'

Chains nodded. 'Privileges of age, size, and arse-kissing. If you survive this conversation, you'll find that it's just the same in most of the big gangs. *Most*.'

'And there was one boy. Veslin. He'd do more. He'd kick us, punch us, take our clothes. Make us do things. Lots of times he'd *lie* to the master about what we'd brought in. He'd give some of our things to the older girls in Windows, and all of us in Streets would get less food, especially the teasers.' Locke's small hands pulled apart and curled slowly into fists as he spoke. 'And if we tried to tell the master, he laughed, he just laughed, like he knew about it and thought it was funny! And after we told, Veslin would . . . Veslin would just get worse!'

Chains nodded, then tapped his index finger against his palm once more.

'I thought about it. I thought about it a lot. None of us could fight him, he was too big. None of us had any big friends in the hill. And if we ganged up on Veslin, his big friends would all come after us.

'Veslin went out each day with some of his friends. We saw them while we were working; they wouldn't mess with our jobs, but they would watch us, you know? And Veslin would say things.' Locke's thin-lipped scowl would have been comical on a less dirty, less emaciated, less hollow-eyed boy; as it was, he looked like a slender wall-gargoyle, working himself up for a pounce. 'Say things when we came back. About how we were clumsy or lazy, and not taking enough. And he would push us more, and hit us more, and cheat us more. I thought and I thought and I thought about what to do.'

'And the idea,' said Chains, 'the fateful idea. It was all yours?'

'Yes.' The boy nodded vigorously. 'All mine. I was alone when I had the idea. I saw some yellowjackets on patrol, and I thought . . . I thought . . . about their sticks, and their swords, and I thought, what if *they* beat up Veslin, what if *they* had some reason not to like him?'

Locke paused for breath. 'And I thought more, but I couldn't work it. I didn't know how. So then I thought, what if they weren't angry with Veslin? What if I used them as an excuse to make the *master* angry with Veslin?'

Chains nodded sagely. 'And where did you get the white iron coin?'

Locke sighed. 'Streets. All of us who didn't like Veslin stole extra. We watched and we clutched and we worked hard. It took weeks. It took *forever*! I wanted white iron. I finally got one from a fat man dressed all in black. Black wool. Funny coats and ties.'

'A Vadran.' Chains seemed bemused. 'Probably a merchant come down to do some business. Too proud to dress for the weather at first, and sometimes too cheap to see a tailor in town. So, you got a white iron coin. A full crown.'

'Everyone wanted to see it. Everyone wanted to touch it. I let them, then I made them be quiet. I made them promise not to talk about it. I told them it was how we were going to get Veslin.'

'So what did you do with your coin?'

'Put it in a purse, a little leather purse. The kind we clutched all the time. And hid it out in the city so it wouldn't get taken from us. A place we knew about, where nobody big could get to. And I made sure that Veslin and his friends were out of the hill, and I got the coin, and I went back in early one day. I gave up coppers and bread to the older girls on the door, but the coin was in my shoe.' Here Locke paused and fiddled with his little lamp, making the red glow waver on his face.

'I put it in Veslin's room. The one where he and Gregor slept, one of the nice dry tombs. Centre of the hill. I found a loose stone and hid the purse there, and when I was sure nobody had seen me, I asked to see the master. I said that some of us had seen Veslin at one of the yellowjacket places in the Narrows. Forts, stations. You know. That he'd taken money from them. That he'd shown it to us, and said that if we told on him he'd sell us to the yellowjackets.'

'Amazing.' Chains scratched his beard. 'You know you don't mumble and stutter quite so much when you're explaining how you fucked someone over?'

Locke blinked, then turned his chin up and stared hard at Chains. The older man laughed. 'Wasn't a criticism, son. I didn't mean to dam the flow. Keep the story coming. How did you know your old master would take offence at this? Did the yellowjackets ever offer you or your friends money?'

'No,' Locke said. 'No, but I knew the master gave *them* money. For favours, for information. We saw him putting coins in purses, sometimes. So I figured, maybe I could work it the other way.'

'Ah.' Chains reached within the folds of his robe and withdrew a flat leather wallet the colour of baked bricks in the light of Locke's lamp. From this he withdrew a scrap of paper onto which he shook a dark powder from another corner of the wallet. He rapidly folded the paper end over end until it was a tight cylinder, and with courtly grace he lit one end by holding it in the flame of Locke's lamp. Soon he was sending ghostly grey swirls of smoke up to join the ghostly grey clouds; the stuff smelled like burning pine tar.

'Forgive me,' Chains said, shifting to his right so his direct exhalations would miss the boy by a few feet. 'Two smokes a night is all I let myself have; the rough stuff before dinner, and the smooth stuff after. Makes everything taste better.'

'So I'm staying for dinner?'

'Oh-ho. My cheeky little opportunist. Let's say the situation remains fluid. You go ahead and finish your story. You tipped your old master that Veslin was working as an auxiliary member of the famed Camorr constabulary. He must have thrown quite a fit.'

'He said he'd kill me if I was lying.' Locke scuttled to his own right, even farther from the smoke. 'But I said he'd hidden the coin in his room. His and Gregor's. So . . . he tore it apart. I hid the coin real well, but he found it. He was supposed to.'

'Mmmm. What did you expect to happen then?'

'I didn't know they'd get killed!' Chains couldn't hear any real grief in that soft and passionate little voice, but there seemed to be real puzzlement, real aggravation. 'I wanted him to beat Veslin. I thought maybe he'd do him up in front of all of us. We ate together, most nights. The whole hill. Fuck-ups had to do tricks, or serve and clean everything, or get held down for caning. Drink ginger oil. I thought he'd get those things. Maybe all those things.'

'Well.' Chains held an inhalation of smoke for a particularly long moment, as though the tobacco could fill him with insight, and looked away from Locke. When he finally exhaled, he did so in little puffs, forming wobbly crescents that fluttered a few feet and faded into the general haze. He harrumphed and turned back to the boy. 'Well, you certainly learned the value of good intentions, didn't you? Caned. Serving and cleaning. Heh. Poor Veslin got served and cleaned, all right. How did your old master do it?'

'He was gone for a few hours, and when he came back, he waited. In Veslin's room. When Veslin and Gregor came back that night, there were older boys nearby. So they couldn't go anywhere. And then . . . the master just killed them. Both. Cut Veslin's throat, and . . . some of the others said, he looked at Gregor for a while and he didn't say anything, and then he just . . .' Locke made the same sort of jabbing motion with two fingers that Chains had made at him earlier. 'He did Gregor, too.'

'Of course he did! Poor Gregor. Gregor Foss, wasn't it? One of those lucky little orphans old enough to remember his last name, not unlike yourself. Of course your old master did him, too. He and Veslin were best friends, right? Two draughts from the same bottle. It was an elementary assumption that one would know that the other was hiding a fortune under a stone.' Chains sighed and rubbed his eyes. 'Elementary. So, now that you've told your part, would you like me to point out where you fucked everything up? And to let you know why most of your little friends in Streets that helped you pluck that white iron coin are going to be dead before morning?'

CHAPTER TWO

Second Touch at the Teeth Show

I

Idler's Day, the eleventh hour of the morning, at the Shifting Revel. The sun was once again the baleful white of a diamond in a fire, burning an arc across the empty sky and pouring down heat that could be felt against the skin. Locke stood beneath the silk awning on Don Salvara's pleasure barge, dressed in the clothes and mannerisms of Lukas Fehrwight, and stared out at the gathering Revel.

There was a troupe of rope dancers perched atop a platform boat to his left; four of them, standing in a diamond pattern about fifteen feet apart. Great lengths of brightly-coloured silk rope stretched among the dancers, around their arms and chests and necks – it seemed that each dancer was working four or five strands simultaneously. These strands formed an ever-shifting cat's cradle between the dancers, and suspended in this web by clever hitches were all manner of small objects: swords, knives, overcoats, boots, glass statuettes, sparkling knick-knacks. All these objects were slowly but gradually moving in various directions as the dancers twirled arms and shifted hips, slipping old knots loose and forming newer, tighter ones with impossibly smooth gestures.

It was a minor wonder on a busy river of wonders, not the least of which was Don and Doña Salvara's barge. While many nobles hauled trees to and from their orchards on the water, Locke's hosts were the first to go one step further; their pleasure barge was a permanent floating orchard in miniature. Perhaps fifty paces long and twenty wide, it was a double-hulled wooden rectangle stuffed with soil to support a dozen oak and olive trees. Their trunks were a uniform night-black, and their rustling cascades of leaves were an unnatural emerald, bright as lacquer – an outward testimony to the subtle science of alchemical botany.

Wide circular stairs criss-crossed with patches of leafy shade wound up several of these trees, leading to the Don's silk-topped observation box, comfortably perched within the branches to give the occupants an unobstructed forward view. On each side of this supremely ostentatious sliver of floating forest were twenty hired rowers, seated on outrigger-like structures that kept the top-heavy central portion of the yacht from plunging sideways.

The box could easily hold twenty; this morning it held only Locke and Jean, the Don and the Doña, and the ever-watchful Conté, currently tending a liquor cabinet so elaborate it might have been mistaken for an apothecary's lab. Locke returned his gaze to the rope dancers, feeling a strange kinship with them. They weren't the only ones with ample opportunity to screw up a delicate public act this morning.

'Master Fehrwight, your *clothes!*' Doña Sofia Salvara shared the forward rail of the observation box with him, her hands scant inches from his. 'You would look so very fine in one of your Emberlain winters, but why must you suffer them in our summer? You shall sweat yourself as red as a rose! Might you not take something off?'

'I . . . my lady, I am, I assure you . . . most comfortable.' Thirteen gods, she was actually *flirting* with him. And the little smile that crept on and off her husband's face told Locke that the Salvaras had planned this in advance. A little close feminine attention to fluster the awkward master merchant; perfectly staged and perfectly common. A game before the game, so to speak. 'I find that whatever discomfort these clothes bring me in your . . . very interesting climate only serves to . . . to goad me. Into concentrating. Keeps me alert, you see. A better, ah, man of business.'

Jean, standing a few paces behind the two of them, bit his tongue. Throwing blondes at Locke Lamora was not unlike throwing lettuce at sharks, and the Doña Sofia was *very* blonde; one of those gorgeous Therin rarities with skin like burnt amber and hair the colour of almond butter. Her eyes were deep and steady, her curves artfully not concealed by a dark orange summer dress with a cream-white underskirt barely showing at the hem. Well, it was just the Salvaras' luck to run up against a thief with the most peculiar damned taste in women. Jean could admire the Doña for them both; his limited role today (and his 'injuries') would give him little else to do.

'Our Master Fehrwight is made of unusually stern stuff, my dear.' Don Lorenzo lounged against a far corner of the forward rail, dressed in loose white silks and an orange vest matching his wife's dress. His white neckerchiefs hung rakishly loose, and only the bottom clasp of his vest was fastened. 'Yesterday he took the beating of a lifetime, today he wears enough wool for five men and dares the sun to do its worst. I must say, I'm more and more pleased with myself that I've kept you out of Jacobo's grasp, Lukas.'

Locke acknowledged the smiling Don with a slight bow and an agreeably awkward smile of his own.

'Do at least have something to drink, Master Fehrwight.' Doña Sofia's hand briefly settled over Locke's, long enough for him to feel the assorted calluses and chemical burns no manicure could conceal. She was a true alchemical botanist, then; this barge was her direct handiwork as well as her general design. A formidable talent – by implication, a calculating woman. Lorenzo was obviously the more impulsive one, and if he was wise he'd weigh his wife's opinion before agreeing to any of Lukas Fehrwight's proposals. Locke therefore favoured her with a shy smile and an awkward cough; let her think she was getting to him.

'A drink would be very pleasing,' he said, 'but, ah, I fear that you shall have no reassurance for my condition, kind Doña Sofia. I have done much business in your city; I know how drinking is done here, when men and women speak of business.'

' "Morning's for sweat, and night's for regret," ' Don Salvara said as he stepped from the rail and gestured to his servant. 'Conté, I do believe Master Fehrwight has just requested nothing less than a Ginger Scald.'

Conté moved adroitly to fill this request, first selecting a tall crystal wine flute, into which he poured two fingers of purest Camorri ginger oil, the colour of scorched cinnamon. To this he added a sizeable splash of milky pear brandy, followed by a transparent heavy liquor called *ajento*, which was actually a cooking wine flavoured with radishes. When this cocktail was mixed, Conté wrapped a wet towel around the fingers of his left hand and reached for a covered brazier smouldering to the side of the liquor cabinet. He withdrew a slender metal rod, glowing orange-red at the tip, and plunged it into the cocktail; there was an audible hiss and a small puff of spicy steam. Once the rod was stanched, Conté stirred the drink briskly and precisely three times, then presented it to Locke on a thin silver plate.

Locke had practised this ritual many times over the years, but when the cold burn of the Ginger Scald hit his lips (limning every tiny crack with stinging heat, and outlining every crevice between teeth and gums in exquisite pain, even before it went to work on tongue and throat), he was never able to fully hold back the memories of Shades' Hill: of the Thiefmaker's admonitions, of a liquid fire that seemed to creep up his sinuses and burn behind his eyes until he wanted to tear them out. Expressing discomfort at his first sip of the drink was much easier than feigning interest in the Doña.

'Incomparable,' he coughed, and then, with quick jerky motions, he loosened his black neckcloths just the slightest bit; the Salvaras smirked charmingly together. 'I'm reminded again why I have such success selling gentler liquors to you people.'

2

Once per month there was no trading done in the Shifting Market. Every fourth Idler's Day the merchants stayed clear of the great sheltered circle abutting the Angevine River; instead, they drifted or anchored nearby while half the city came out to see the Shifting Revel.

Camorr had never possessed a great stone or Elderglass amphitheatre, and had fallen instead into the curious custom of rebuilding its spectator circle anew at each Revel. Huge multi-storeyed observation barges were towed out and anchored firmly against the stone breakwaters surrounding the Shifting Market, looking like floating slices cut from the heart of a great stadium. Each barge was operated by a rival family or merchant combine and decked in unique livery; they competed fiercely with one another to fill their seats, and brawls between the habitual customers of particularly beloved barges were not unknown.

When properly aligned, these barges formed an arc about

71

halfway around the circumference of the Floating Market; a channel was left clear for boats entering and leaving the centre of the calm water, and the rest of the periphery was reserved for the pleasure barges of the nobility. A good hundred or so could be counted on at any Revel, and half again as many for major festivals, such as this one; scant few weeks remained until the midsummer-mark and the Day of Changes.

Even before the entertainments began the Shifting Revel was its own spectacle, a great tide of rich and poor, floating and on foot, jostling for position in a traditional contest richly loved for its lack of rules. The yellowjackets were always out in force, but more to prevent hard words and fisticuffs from escalating than to prevent disturbances altogether. The Revel was a citywide debauch, a rowdy public service the Duke was happy to underwrite from his treasury. There were few things like a good Revel to pull the fangs from any unrest before it had time to fester.

Feeling the fire of the approaching noon despite the silk awning over their heads, Locke and his hosts compounded their situation by drinking Ginger Scalds as they stared out across the rippling heat haze at thousands of Camorri packing the commoner barges. Conté had prepared identical drinks for his lord and lady (though with a touch less ginger oil, perhaps), which 'Graumann' had served them, as Camorri etiquette dictated in these situations. Locke's glass was half empty; the liquor was a ball of expanding warmth in his stomach and a vivid memory in his throat.

'Business,' he said at last. 'You have both been . . . so kind to Grau and myself. I agreed to repay this kindness by revealing my business here in Camorr. So let us speak of it, if that would please you.'

'You have never had a more eager audience in your life, Master Fehrwight.' The Don's hired rowers were bringing them into the Shifting Revel proper, and they were closing on dozens of more traditional pleasure barges, some of them crammed with dozens or hundreds of guests. The Don's eyes were alive with greedy curiosity. 'Tell on.'

'The Kingdom of the Seven Marrows is coming apart at the seams.' Locke sighed. 'This is no secret.'

The Don and the Doña nonchalantly sipped their drinks, saying nothing.

'The Canton of Emberlain is peripheral to the major conflict. But the Graf von Emberlain and the Black Table are both working, in different, ah, directions, to place it in the way of substantial harm.'

'The Black Table?' asked the Don.

'I beg pardon.' Locke took the tiniest sip of his drink and let new fire trickle under his tongue. 'The Black Table is what we call the council of Emberlain's most powerful merchants. My masters of the House of bel Auster are among them. In every respect save the military and the matter of taxes, they run the Canton of Emberlain. And they are tired of the Graf, and tired of the Trade Guilds in the other six cantons of the Marrows. Tired of limitations. Emberlain grows rich on new means of speculation and enterprise. The Black Table sees the old Guilds as a weight around their neck.'

'Curious,' said the Doña, 'that you say "their" and not "our". Is this significant?'

'To a point.' Another sip of the drink; a second of feigned nervousness. 'The House of bel Auster agrees that the Guilds have outlasted their usefulness; that the trade practices of centuries past should not be set in stone by Guild law. We do *not* necessarily agree,' he sipped the drink yet again, and scratched the back of his head, 'that, ah, the Graf von Emberlain should be deposed while he is out of the canton with most of his army, showing his flag on behalf of his cousins in Parlay and Somnay.'

'Holy Twelve.' Don Salvara shook his head as though to clear it of what he'd just heard. 'They can't be serious. Emberlain is . . . smaller than Camorr! Exposed to the sea on two sides. Impossible to defend.'

'And yet the preparations are underway. Emberlain's banks and merchant houses do *four times* the yearly business of the next-richest canton in the Marrows. The Black Table fixates upon this. Gold should certainly be considered potential power; the Black Table errs by imagining it to be direct power, in and of itself.' He finished his drink in one long, deliberate draught. 'In two months, civil war will have broken out anyway. The succession is a mess. The Stradas and the Dvorims, the Razuls and the Strigs . . . they are all sharpening knives and parading men. Yet as we speak, the merchants of Emberlain are moving to arrest the remaining nobility while the Graf is away. To claim the navy. To raise a levy of "free citizens". To hire mercenaries. In short, they will now attempt to secede from the Marrows. It is unavoidable.'

'And what, specifically, does this have to do with you coming here?' The Doña's knuckles were white around her wine flute; she grasped the full significance of Fehrwight's story. A fight larger than anything seen in centuries, civil war across the north mixed with possible economic disaster.

'It is the opinion of my masters, the House of bel Auster, that rats in the hold have little chance to take the wheel of a ship that is about to run aground. But those same rats may very easily *abandon the ship*.'

3

In the centre of the Shifting Revel a great many tall iron cages had been sunk into the water. Some of these served to support wooden slats on which performers, victims, fighters and attendants could stand; a few particularly heavy cages restrained dark shapes that circled ominously under the translucent grey water. Platform boats were rowed around at a steady clip, showing off rope dancers, knife throwers, acrobats, jugglers, strongmen and other curiosities; the excited shouts of barkers with long brass speaking trumpets echoed flatly off the water.

First up at any Revel were the Penance Bouts, where petty offenders from the Palace of Patience could volunteer for mismatched combat in exchange for reduced sentences or slightly improved living conditions. At present, a hugely muscled *nichavezzo* ('punishing hand'), one of the Duke's own household guard, was handing out the beatings. The soldier was armoured in black leather, with a gleaming steel breastplate and a steel helmet crested with the freshly-severed fin of a giant flying fish. Scales and spines scintillated as the soldier stepped back and forth under the bright sun, striking out seemingly at leisure with an iron-shod staff.

The *nichavezzo* stood on a platform that was small but rock-steady; a series of circular wooden flats surrounded him, separated by an arm's-length span of water. These wobbly, unstable platforms were occupied by about two dozen slender, grimy prisoners, each armed with a small wooden cudgel. A concerted rush might

74

have overwhelmed their armoured tormentor, but this lot seemed to lack the temperament for cooperation. Approaching the *nichavezzo* singly or in little groups, they were being dropped, one after another, with skull-rattling blows. Little boats circled to fish out unconscious prisoners before they slipped under the water forever. The Duke, in his mercy, did not allow Penance Bouts to be deliberately lethal.

'Mmmm.' Locke held his empty wine flute out for just a second; Conté plucked it out of his fingers with the grace of a swordsman disarming an opponent. When the Don's manservant stepped toward the liquor cabinet, Locke cleared his throat. 'No need to refill that particular glass just yet, Conté. Too kind, too kind. But with your permission, my lord and lady Salvara, I should like to offer a pair of gifts. One as a matter of simple hospitality. The other as a . . . Well, you'll see. Graumann?'

Locke snapped his fingers and Jean nodded. The heavyset man moved over to a wooden table just beside the liquor cabinet and picked up two heavy leather satchels, each of which had iron-reinforced corners and small iron locks sewn into its cover. Jean set these down where the Salvaras could easily see them, and then stepped back so Locke could unseal the satchels with a delicate key of carved ivory. From the first satchel he withdrew a cask of pale aromatic wood, perhaps one foot in height and half that in diameter, which he then held out for Don Salvara's examination. A plain black brand on the surface of the cask read:

BRANDVIN AUSTERSHALIN 502

Don Lorenzo's breath hissed in between his teeth; perhaps his nostrils even flared, though Locke kept the face of Lukas Fehrwight politely neutral. 'Twelve Gods, a 502. Lukas, if I seemed to be chiding you earlier for your refusal to part with your goods, please accept my deepest—'

'Oh, unnecessary, unnecessary.' Locke held up a hand and mimicked the Don's gesture for shooing words down out of the air. 'For your bold intervention on my behalf, Don Salvara, and for your excellent hospitality this morning, fair Doña, please accept this minor ornament for your cellars.'

'Minor!' The Don took the cask and cradled it as though it were an infant not five minutes born. 'I . . . I have a 506 and a pair of

504s. I don't know of anyone in Camorr who has a 502, except probably the Duke.'

'Well,' said Locke, 'my masters have kept a few on hand, ever since the word got out that it was a particularly good blend. We use them to . . . break the ice in matters of grave business importance.' In truth, that cask represented an investment of nearly eight hundred full crowns and a sea-trip up the coast to Ashmere, where Locke and Jean had contrived to win it from an eccentric minor noble in a rigged card game. Most of the money had actually gone to evade or buy off the assassins the old man had later sent after his property; the 502 vintage had become almost too precious to drink.

'What a grand gesture, Master Fehrwight!' Doña Sofia slipped a hand through the crook of her husband's elbow and gave him a possessive grin. 'Lorenzo, love, you should try to rescue strangers from Emberlain more often. They're so charming!'

Locke coughed and shuffled his feet. 'Ahh, hardly, my lady. Now, Don Salvara—'

'Please, do call me Lorenzo.'

'Ah, Don Lorenzo, what I have to show you next relates rather directly to my reason for coming here.' From the second satchel he drew out a similar cask, but this one was marked only with a stylised 'A' within a circle of vines.

'This,' said Locke, 'is a sample drawn from last year's distillation. The 559.'

Don Salvara dropped the cask of 502.

The Doña, with girlish agility, shot out her right foot to hook the cask in mid-air and let it down to the deck with a slight thump rather than a splintering crash. Unbalanced, she did manage to drop her Ginger Scald; the glass vanished over the side and was soon twenty feet underwater. The Salvaras steadied one another and the Don picked his cask of 502 back up, his hands shaking.

'Lukas,' he said, 'surely . . . surely you must be *kidding*.'

Locke didn't find it particularly easy to eat lunch while watching a dozen swimming men being pulled apart by a Jereshti devilfish, but he decided that his master merchant of Emberlain had probably seen worse, in his many imaginary sea-voyages, and he kept his true feelings far from his face.

Noon was well past; the Penance Bouts were over, and the Revel-masters had moved on to the Judicial Forfeitures. This was a polite way of saying that the men in the water were murderers, rapists, slavers, arsonists and so forth selected to be colourfully executed for the amusement of the Revel crowds. Technically speaking, they were armed and would receive lesser sentences if they could somehow contrive to slay whatever beast they were matched against, but the beasts were always as nasty as their weapons were laughable, so mostly they were just executed.

The devilfish's tentacles were twelve feet long, the same length as its undulating grey-and-black-striped body. The creature was confined within a sixty-foot circle of cages and platforms, along with a number of screaming, flailing, water-treading men – most of whom had long since dropped their slender little daggers into the water. Nervous guards armed with crossbows and pikes patrolled the platforms, shoving prisoners back into the water if they tried to scramble out. Occasionally, the devilfish would roll over in the churning red waters and Locke would catch a glimpse of one lidless black eye the size of a soup bowl, not unlike the one currently held in his hands.

'More, Master Fehrwight?' Conté hovered nearby with the silver tureen of chilled soup cradled in his hands; white-fleshed Iron Sea prawns floated in a heavy red tomato base seasoned with peppers and onions. Don and Doña Salvara were a peculiar sort of droll.

'No, Conté, most kind, but I'm well satisfied for the time being.' Locke set his soup bowl down beside the broached cask of '559' (actually a bottle of lowly fifty-crown 550 liberally mixed with the roughest overpriced rum Jean had been able to get his hands on) and took a sip of the amber liquor from his snifter. Even mixed with crap, the counterfeit was delicious. Graumann stood attentively behind Locke's hosts, seated opposite him at the intimate little table of oiled silverwood. Doña Sofia toyed unselfconsciously with a subtlety of gelled orange slices, paper-thin and arranged in whorls to form edible tulip blossoms. Don Lorenzo stared down at the snifter of brandy in his hands, his eyes still wide.

'It just seems almost . . . sacrilegious!' Despite this sentiment, the Don took a deep gulp of the stuff, satisfaction well evident in the lines of his face. In the distance behind him, something that might have been a severed torso flew up into the air and came back down with a splash; the crowd roared approval.

Austershalin brandy was famously aged for a minimum of seven years after distillation and blending; it was impossible for outsiders to get their hands on a cask any sooner than that. The House of bel Auster's factors were forbidden even to speak of the batches that were not yet on sale; the location of the vintner's aging-houses was a secret reportedly guarded by assassination when necessary. Don Lorenzo had been struck stupid when Locke had casually offered up a cask of 559; he had nearly thrown up when Locke had just as casually opened the seal and suggested they share it with lunch.

'It is.' Locke chuckled. 'The brandy *is* the religion of my house; we tread so carefully around it.' No longer smiling, he drew a quick finger across his throat. 'It's possible we're the only people in history to have an unaged sample with a lunch of soup. I thought you might enjoy it.'

'I am!' The Don swirled the liquor in his glass and stared closely at it, as though hypnotised by the soft caramel-coloured translucence. 'And I'm dead curious about what sort of scheme you've got up your sleeve, Lukas.'

'Well.' Locke swirled his own drink theatrically. 'There have been three invasions of Emberlain in the past two hundred and fifty years. Let's be frank; the succession rites of the Kingdom of the Marrows usually involve armies and blood before they involve blessings and banquets. When the Grafs quarrel, the Austershalin mountains are our only landward barrier, and the site of heavy fighting. This fighting inevitably spills down the eastern slopes of the mountains, right through the vineyards of the House of bel Auster. This time it will be the same. The Black Table draws it down upon us! Thousands of men and horses coming over the passes. Trampling the vineyards. Sacking everything in sight. It might even be worse, now that we have fire-oil. Our vineyards could be ashes half a year from now.'

78

'You can't exactly pack your vineyards up and take them with you if you . . . jump ship,' said Don Lorenzo.

'No.' Locke sighed. 'It's the Austershalin soils, in part, that make Austershalin brandy. If we lose those vineyards, it will be just as it was before – an interruption in growth and distillation. Ten, twenty, maybe even thirty years. Or more. And it gets worse. Our position is terrible. The Graf can't let Emberlain's ports and revenue go if the Marrows are coming to civil war. He and his allies will storm the place as fast as possible. They'll likely put the Black Table to the sword, impound their goods and properties, confiscate their funds. The House of bel Auster won't be spared.

'At the moment, the Black Table is acting quietly but firmly. Grau and I sailed five days ago, just twelve hours before we knew the port would be sealed off. No Emberlain-flagged ships are being allowed out; they're all being docked and secured for "repairs" or "quarantine". Nobles still loyal to the Graf are under house arrest by now, their guards disarmed. Our funds, in various lending houses of Emberlain, have been temporarily frozen. All the Black Table merchant houses have consented to do this to one another, a gesture of "goodwill". It makes it impossible for any house to flee en masse, with its gold and its goods. Currently, Grau and I are operating on our local credit, established at Meraggio's years ago. My house . . . well, we simply didn't keep our funds outside Emberlain. Just a bit here and there for emergencies.'

Locke watched the Salvaras very closely for their reaction; his news from Emberlain was as fresh and specific as possible, but the Don might have sources of intelligence the Gentlemen Bastards hadn't spotted in their weeks of surveillance and preparation. The parts about the Black Table and the impending civil war were solid, educated speculation; the part about a sudden port closure and house arrests was pure homespun bullshit. In Locke's estimation the real mess in Emberlain wouldn't start for a few months. If the Don was wise to this, Conté might be trying to pin him to the table with his daggers in just a few seconds. And then Jean would pull out the hatchets he had concealed down the back of his vest, and everyone in the little group beneath the silk awning would get very, very uncomfortable – a blown game was never pretty.

But the Salvaras said nothing; they merely continued to stare at him with eyes that plainly invited him to go on. Emboldened, he continued: 'This situation is unbearable. We will neither be hostages to a cause that we barely profess, nor victims for the Graf's vengeance upon his inevitable return. We choose a . . . somewhat risky alternative. One that would require substantial aid from a noble of Camorr. You, Don Salvara, if it is within your means.'

The Don and his wife had clasped hands under the table; he waved his free hand at Locke excitedly.

'We can surrender our funds. By taking no steps to secure them, we buy ourselves more time to act. And we are quite confident that replacing those funds will merely be a matter of time and effort. We can even abandon' – Locke gritted his teeth – 'our vineyards. We will completely burn them ourselves, leaving nothing to anyone else. After all, we enhance the soil ourselves, alchemically. The natural soil is just a beginning. And the secret of that enhancement is kept only in the hearts of our Planting Masters.'

'The Austershalin Process,' Sofia breathed, betrayed by her own rising excitement.

'Of course, you've heard of it. Well, there are only three Planting Masters at any given time. And the process is complex enough to defy soil examination, even by someone with talents such as yours, my lady. Many of the compounds our alchemists use are inert, and intended only to confuse the matter. So that's that.

'The one thing we *cannot* abandon is our stock of ageing blends – the last six years, batched in their casks. And certain rare vintages and special experiments. We store the Austershalin in thirty-two-gallon casks; there are nearly six thousand such casks in our possession. We have to get them out of Emberlain. We have to do it in the next few weeks, before the Black Table imposes harsher control measures and before the Graf begins laying siege to his canton. And now our ships are under guard, and all of our funds are untouchable.'

'You want . . . you want to get all of these casks out of Emberlain? All of them?' The Don actually gulped.

'As many as possible,' said Locke.

'And for this you would involve us how?' Doña Sofia was fidgeting.

'Emberlain-flagged ships can no longer leave port, nor enter if they wish to escape again. But a small flotilla of *Camorr*-flagged

ships, with Camorri crews, financed by a Camorri noble . . .'
Locke set his glass of brandy down and spread both his hands in
the air.

'You wish me to provide . . . a naval expedition?'

'Two or three of your larger galleons should do it. We're
looking at a thousand tons of cargo, casks and brandy alike.
Minimal crew, say fifty or sixty men a ship. We can take our pick
of the docks and get sober, trustworthy captains. Six or seven days
bearing north, plus however long it takes to scratch the crews and
ships together. I guess perhaps a week. Do you concur?'

'A week . . . yes, but . . . you're asking me to finance *all* of this?'

'In exchange for a most handsome recompense, I assure you.'

'Provided everything goes well, yes, and we'll come to the matter
of recompense in a moment. But just the rapid acqusition of two
galleons, good captains, and very reliable crews . . .'

'Plus,' said Locke, 'something to stick in the hold for the trip
north. Cheap grain, dried cheese, low-grade fresh fruit. Nothing
special. But Emberlain will shortly be under siege; the Black Table
will be happy to have a cache of extra supplies offloaded. Emberlain's position is too tenuous to fail to respect the sovereign
neutrality of Camorr; that's what my masters are counting on to
get the ships in and out. But added insurance cannot hurt.'

'Yes,' said Don Lorenzo, tugging on his lower lip. 'Two
galleons, crews, officers, cheap cargo. A small crew of mercenaries,
ten or twelve a ship. There are always some hanging around this
time of year. I'd want a hard core of armed men on each ship to
discourage . . . complications.'

Locke nodded.

'How exactly would we go about . . . removing the casks from
your ageing-houses and transporting them to the docks?'

'A very simple ruse,' said Locke. 'We maintain several breweries
and storehouses for small beer; it's a sideline, a sort of hobby for
some of our Blending Masters. Our beer is stored in casks, and the
location of these warehouses is public knowledge. Slowly, carefully, while Grau and I sailed south, my masters have been moving
casks of Austershalin brandy to the beer warehouses and relabell-
ing them. They will continue to do so while we prepare here, and
until our ships appear in the harbour of Emberlain.'

'So you won't be loading brandy in secret.' Doña Sofia clapped her hands together. 'As far as anyone knows, you'll be loading beer in the open!'

'Exactly, my lady. Even a large export of beer won't be anywhere near as suspicious as a movement of the unaged brandy. It'll be looked on as a commercial coup; we'll be the first to dodge the interdict on Emberlain-flagged vessels; we'll bring in a pile of supplies for the coming siege and a fine apparent profit for ourselves. Then, once we've got all the brandy loaded, we'll put out to sea, bringing sixty or seventy bel Auster family and employees to form the nucleus of our new business operations in Camorr. Discovery after that will be immaterial.'

'All of this to be thrown together on short notice.' Don Lorenzo was deep in thought. 'Fifteen thousand crowns, I'd say. Perhaps twenty.'

'I concur, my lord. Count on an additional five thousand or so for bribes and other arrangements.' Locke shrugged. 'Certain men are going to have to look the other way for us to do our job when we reach Emberlain, warehouse ruse or no.'

'Twenty-five thousand crowns, then. Damn.' Lorenzo downed the last of the brandy in his glass, set it down, and folded his hands together on the table before him. 'You're asking me for more than half of my fortune. I like you, Lukas, but now it's time to discuss the other side of the proposal.'

'Of course.' Lukas stopped to offer the Don another dash of the counterfeit 'unaged'; the Don began to wave him off, but his taste buds prevailed over his better judgement, and he held out his glass. Doña Sofia did so as well, and Jean hurried over to pass her glass between her and Locke. When he'd served the Salvaras, Locke poured a companionably large amount into his own snifter. 'First, you have to understand what the House of bel Auster is and is not offering.

'You will never have the Austershalin Process. It will continue to be passed down verbally, and strictly within the house. We can offer you no properties as collateral or in payment; we expect to forfeit them upon fleeing Emberlain. Re-securing the vineyards at a future date is our own problem.

'Any effort on your part to pry into the Austershalin Process, to suborn any bel Auster men or women, will be regarded as an absolute breach of trust.' Locke sipped brandy. 'I have no idea what specific penalties we could levy to express our displeasure. But it *would* be fully expressed. I am instructed to be entirely clear on this point.'

'And so you are.' Doña Sofia placed one hand on her husband's left shoulder. 'But these limitations are not yet an offer.'

'Forgive me, gracious Doña Sofia, for speaking to you so. But you must understand – this is the most important thing the House of bel Auster has ever contemplated. Grau and I hold the future of our combine in our rather vulnerable hands. At this moment, I *can't* speak to you just as Lukas Fehrwright. I am the House of bel Auster. You have to understand that some things are not on the table, not even by the most remote implication.'

The Salvaras nodded, Sofia just a bit more slowly than Lorenzo.

'Now. Consider the situation. War is coming to Emberlain. Our vineyards and our properties are as good as lost. As I have said, without those vineyards there will be no Austershalin actually produced for only the Marrows know how long. Ten years? A generation? Even when we have the vineyards back, the soil will need years to recover. This is the way it has been, three times before. For many, many years to come the only new Austershalin available is going to come from whatever portion of those six thousand casks we can move out of Emberlain, like thieves in the night. Imagine the *demand*. The price escalation.'

The Don's lips moved unconsciously as he calculated; Doña Sofia stared off into the distance, her brow furrowed. Austershalin brandy was the finest and most sought-after liquor known; even the alchemical wines of Tal Verrar, in a hundred bewitching varieties, were not as expensive. A single half-gallon bottle of the youngest available Austershalin was thirty full crowns at retail; the price went up sharply with age. With a surprise shortage, and a fixed supply, and no new crop of Austershalin grapes in sight?

'Fuck*damn*,' said Conté, totally unable to help himself when the sums involved vanished over his mental horizon. 'Beg pardon, Doña Sofia.'

'You should.' She drained her snifter in one quick un-ladylike gulp. 'Your calculations are off. This merits a triple fuckdamn at the very least.'

'The House of bel Auster,' Locke continued, 'wishes to establish a partnership with you, based in Camorr, to store and market

Austershalin brandy during our . . . interregnum. In exchange for your assistance in transporting it from Emberlain in our moment of extreme need, we are prepared to offer you fifty per cent of the proceeds from the sale of anything you transport for us. Again, consider the situation, and the price of Austershalin during a shortage. You could recoup your initial investment ten times over in the first year. Give us five years, or ten . . .'

'Yes.' Don Lorenzo fiddled with his optics. 'But, Lukas, pardon me. Somehow, sitting here discussing the possible destruction of your house and a move to a city half a thousand miles to the south, you don't sound . . . entirely displeased.'

Locke used a particularly endearing wry smile he'd once practised before a mirror-glass for weeks. 'When my masters grasped the essence of their current situation, some of them suggested we should have engineered an artificial shortage years ago. As it is, we are determined that we can turn a painful setback into a glorious return. Those six thousand casks, sold at shortage prices over a number of years . . . We could return to Emberlain with a fortune that eclipses everything we'd be leaving behind. And as for your own situation . . .'

'We're not talking about hundreds of thousands of crowns.' Doña Sofia returned from her thoughtful trance. 'We're talking about millions. Even split between us.'

'Very possibly,' said Locke, 'my masters are also prepared to grant one other compensation, upon our successful return to Emberlain and the restoration of the Austershalin vineyards. We offer your family a permanent stake in all bel Auster operations thereafter; certainly nothing close to a controlling interest, but something respectable. A ten-to-fifteen per cent share. You would be the first and, we hope, the only foreigners ever offered such an interest.'

There was a pause. 'That's . . . a very attractive offer.' Don Salvara spoke at last. 'And to think all this was going to fall into Jacobo's lap simply by default. By the gods, Lukas, if we ever cross paths with those thieves again, I'm going to thank them for arranging our introduction.'

'Well,' Locke chuckled, 'I for my part can let bygones be bygones. Graumann might feel somewhat differently. And the fact remains that while I sense we may be shaking hands very soon, we still have to assemble our ships, sail north to Emberlain, and snatch up our prize. The situation is like a damaged cargo rope unravelling down to a single thread.' He saluted the Salvaras with his brandy snifter. 'It *will* snap.'

Out on the water, the devilfish was victorious, and the guards rewarded it for its service by filling it with poisoned crossbow bolts. Boathooks and chains were used to haul the carcass out of the centre of the Shifting Revel; there was just no putting a creature like that back into the box once it had served its purpose. The monster's red blood mixed with that of its victims and slowly settled in a broad, dark cloud. Even this had a deliberate part to play in what was to come next.

5

Scholars of the Therin Collegium, from their comfortable position well inland, could tell you that the wolf sharks of the Iron Sea are beautiful and fascinating creatures; their bodies more packed with muscle than any bull, their abrasive hide streaked with every colour from old-copper green to stormcloud black. Anyone actually working the waterfront in Camorr and on the nearby coast could tell you that wolf sharks are big aggressive bastards that like to *jump*.

Carefully caged, starved, and maddened by blood, wolf sharks are the key to the customary highlight of the Shifting Revel. Other cities have gladiatorial games; other cities pit men against animals. But only in Camorr can you see a specially armed gladiator (a *contrarequialla*) battle a live, leaping shark, and in Camorr only women are allowed by tradition to be *contrarequialla*.

This is the Teeth Show.

6

Locke couldn't tell if the four women were truly beautiful, but they were undeniably striking. They were all dark-skinned Camorri with muscles like farm girls, imposing even at a distance, and they wore next to nothing – tight black cotton shifts across their chests, wrestler's loincloths and thin leather gloves. Their black hair was pulled back under the traditional red bandannas and threaded with brass and silver bangles that caught the sunlight in chains of white flashes. The purpose of these bangles was a matter of argument. Some claimed that they confused the poor eyesight of the sharks, while just as many claimed that their glare helped the monsters better sight their prey.

Each *contrarequialla* carried two weapons, a short javelin in one hand and a special axe in the other. These axes had grips enclosed by full handguards, making them difficult to lose; they were double-headed, with the expected curved blade on one side and a long, sturdy pick-head on the other. A skilled fighter usually tried to slash a shark's fins and tail to nothing before making a kill; few but the very best could kill with anything but the spike. Wolf shark skin could be like tree bark.

Locke stared at the grim women and felt his usual melancholy admiration. They were, to his eyes, as mad as they were courageous.

'I know that's Cicilia de Ricura there, on the far left.' Don Lorenzo was pointing the women out for Lukas Fehrwight's benefit, taking a break from more than an hour of rapid negotiations. 'She's decent. And beside her is Aganesse, who carries her javelin but never, ever uses it. The other two, well, they must be new. At least new to the Revel.'

'It's so unfortunate,' said the Doña, 'that the Berangias sisters aren't out there today for you to see, Master Fehrwight. They're the best.'

'Probably the best there ever has been.' Don Salvara squinted to cut some of the glare rising off the water and tried to estimate the size of the sharks, barely visible as shadows within their cages. 'Or ever will be. But they haven't been at the Revel for the past few months.'

Locke nodded and chewed on the inside of one of his cheeks. As Locke Lamora, *garrista* of the Gentlemen Bastards, and respectable sneak thief, he knew the Berangias twins personally and he knew *exactly* where they'd been for those past few months.

Out on the water, the first fighter was taking her position. *Contrarequialla* fought across a series of stepping platforms, each about two feet wide and raised half a foot out off the water. These platforms were set out in a square grid, four or five feet apart, leaving plenty of room for the opposition to swim between them. The women would have to hop between these platforms at a rapid pace to strike out at the sharks while dodging leaps in return; a slip into the water was usually the end of the contest.

Beyond the line of shark cages (opened by chain pulleys connected to a barge well beyond the periphery of any possible shark activity) there was a little boat, crewed by (extremely well-paid) volunteer rowers and carrying the three traditional observers of any Teeth Show. First, there was a priest of Iono in his sea-green robes fringed with silver. Beside him there was a black-robed, silver-masked priestess of Aza Guilla, Lady of the Long Silence, goddess of death. Lastly, there was a physiker, whose presence had always struck Locke as an extremely optimistic gesture.

'Camorr!' The young woman, apparently Cicilia de Ricura, raised her weapons into the air over her head. The heavy murmur of the crowd subsided, leaving only the noise of water lapping against boats and breakwaters. Fifteen thousand watchers held their collective breath. 'I dedicate this death to Duke Nicovante, our lord and patron!' Such was the traditional phrasing of the *contrarequialla*'s salute; 'this death' could conveniently refer to either participant in the battle.

To a great flourish of trumpets and the cheer of the crowd, the boatmen outside the circle of cages loosed the afternoon's first shark. The ten-foot fish, already blood-mad, shot forth from imprisonment and began to circle the stepping-platforms, its ominous grey fin slicing the water with a churning wake. Cicilia balanced on one foot and bent down to slap the water with the heel of the other, screaming oaths and challenges. The shark took the bait; in a few seconds it was in among the platforms, stocky body whipping back and forth like a toothy pendulum.

'This one doesn't like to waste time!' Don Salvara actually wrung his hands together. 'I bet it's an early leaper.'

Barely had these words escaped his mouth than the shark rocketed up out of the water in a fountain of silver-shining spray, hurling itself at the crouching fighter. The shark's leap was not a high one; Cicilia avoided it by jumping right, to the next platform over. In mid-air she let her javelin go with a back-handed cast; the shaft sunk into the shark's flank and quivered there for a split second before the streamlined mass of hungry muscle splashed back down into the water. Crowd reaction was mixed; the cast had displayed remarkable agility but minimal power. Cicilia's shark was likely only further angered, and her javelin wasted.

'Oh, poor decision.' The Doña clicked her tongue. 'This girl needs to learn some patience. We'll see if her new friend gives her the chance.'

Thrashing, spraying pink-foamed water left and right, the shark manoeuvred for another attack, chasing Cicilia's shadow on the water. She hopped lively from platform to platform, axe reversed so the spike was facing outward.

'Master Fehrwight.' Don Lorenzo removed his optics and played with them while he watched the fight; apparently, they weren't necessary for use at long distances. 'I can accept your terms, but you have to appreciate that my portion of the initial risk is quite heavy, especially relative to my total available funds. My request, therefore, is that the split of revenues from our Austershalin sales be adjusted to fifty-five, forty-five, in my favour.'

Locke pretended to ponder while Cicilia pumped her arms and leaped for dear life, the eager grey fin slashing through the water just behind her feet. 'I'm authorised to make such a concession on behalf of my masters. In return . . . I would fix your family's ownership interest in the re-secured Austershalin vineyards at five per cent.'

'Done!' The Don smiled. 'I will fund two large galleons, crew and officers, necessary bribes and arrangements, and a cargo to take north with us. I'll oversee one galleon; you the other. Mercenary crews of my choosing to be placed aboard each vessel for added security. Conté will travel with you; your Graumann can stay at my side. Any expenditures that bring our budget over twenty-five thousand Camorri crowns are to be made solely at my discretion.'

The shark leaped and missed again; Cicilia performed a brief one-armed handstand on her platform, waving her axe. The audience roared while the shark rolled over gracelessly in the water and came back for another pass.

'Agreed,' said Locke. 'Signed identical copies of our contract to be kept by each of us; one additional copy in Therin to be kept with a mutually agreeable neutral solicitor, to be opened and examined by them within the month should one of us have . . . an accident while fetching the casks. One additional copy in Vadran to be signed and placed into the care of an agent known to me, for eventual delivery to my masters. I shall require a bonded scribe at the Tumblehome this evening, and a promissory note for five thousand crowns, to be drawn at Meraggio's tomorrow so I can get to work immediately.'

'And that is all that remains?'

'Quite everything,' said Locke.

The Don was silent for several seconds. 'The hell with it. I agree. Let's clasp hands and take our chances.'

Out on the water, Cicilia paused and hefted her axe, timing a blow as the shark approached her platform on her right, undulating, moving too slow for a high leap. Just as Cicilia shifted her weight to bring the spike down, the shark jackknifed in the water beside her, squeezing its body into a "U" shape, and drove itself straight down. This manoeuvre flicked its tail into the air, catching the *contrarequialla* just under her knees. Screaming more in shock than in pain, Cicilia de Ricura fell backwards into the water.

It was all over a few seconds after that; the shark came up biting and must have taken her by one or both legs. They turned over and over in the water a few times – Locke caught glimpses of the frantic woman's form alternating with the dark rough hide of the shark; white then grey, white then grey. In moments the pink foam was dark red once more, and the two struggling shadows were sinking into the depths beneath the platforms. Half the crowd roared lusty approval; the rest bowed their heads in a respectful silence that would last just until the next young woman entered the ring of red water.

'Gods!' Doña Sofia stared at the spreading stain on the water; the surviving fighters stood with their heads lowered and the priests were gesturing some sort of mutual blessing. 'Unbelievable! Taken in so fast, by such a simple trick. Well, my father used to say that one moment of misjudgement at the Revel is worth ten at any other time.'

Locke bowed deeply to her, taking one hand and kissing it. 'I doubt him not at all, Doña Sofia. Not at all.'

Smiling amiably, he bowed to her once more, then turned to shake hands with her husband.

Interlude:
Locke Stays for Dinner

I

'What?' Locke nearly jumped to his feet. 'What are you talking about?'

'My boy,' said Chains, 'my intermittently brilliant little boy, your world has such small horizons. You can see clearly enough to pull a fast one on someone but you *can't* see past that, past the immediate consequences. Until you learn to think ahead of the repercussions, you are putting yourself and everyone around you in danger. You can't help being young, but it's past time that you stopped being stupid. So listen carefully.

'Your first mistake was – taking coin from the watch isn't a beating offence. It's a *killing* offence. Are we clear on that? Here in Camorr the watch takes *our* coin, and never the other way round. This rule is set in stone and there are no exceptions, no matter what kind of thief you are or what your intentions are. It's death. It's a throat-slashing, shark-feeding, off-to-meet-the-gods offence, clear?'

Locke nodded.

'So when you set Veslin up, you *really* set him up. But you compounded this mistake when you used a white iron coin. You know how much a full crown is worth, exactly?'

'Lots.'

'Ha. "Lots" isn't "exactly". You don't speak Therin, or you don't really know?'

'I guess I don't really know.'

'Well, if everything's butter and nobody's been shaving the damn thing, that little piece of shiny white iron was worth forty silver solons. You see? Two hundred and forty coppers. Your eyes are wide. That means you can think that big, that you understand?'

'Yes. Wow.'

'Yes, wow. Let me put it in perspective. A yellowjacket, one of our selfless and infinitely dutiful city watchmen, might make that much for two months of daily duty. And watchmen are well paid, for common folk, and they sure as blessed shit do *not* get paid in white iron.'

'Oh.'

'So not only was Veslin taking money, he was taking too much money. A full crown! Morgante wept. You can buy a death for much less, yours included.'

'Um . . . how much did you pay for my . . .' Locke tapped his chest, where the death-mark still hung beneath his shirt.

'I don't mean to prick your rather substantial opinion of youself, but I'm still not sure if it was two coppers wisely spent.' At the boy's expression, Chains barked out a rich and genuine laugh, but his voice grew serious once again. 'Keep guessing, boy. But the point remains. You can get good, hard people to do serious work for less. You could buy five or six major pieces of business, if you know what I mean. So, when you stuck a white iron coin in Veslin's things . . .'

'It was too much money . . . for anything . . . simple?'

'Dead on. *Far* too much money for information or errands. Nobody in their right mind gives a fucking graveyard urchin a full crown. Unless . . . that urchin is being paid to do something big. Kill your old master, for example. Smoke out all of Shades' Hill and everyone in it. So if the poor Thiefmaker was upset to discover that Veslin was on the take, you can imagine how he felt when he saw how much money was involved.'

Locke nodded furiously.

'Ahhhhh, so. Two mistakes. Your third mistake was involving Gregor. Was Gregor *supposed* to get hit with the ugly stick?'

'I didn't like him, but no. I just wanted Veslin. Maybe I wanted Gregor to get a little, but not as much as Veslin.'

'Just so. You had a target, and you had a twist to play on that target, but you didn't control the situation. Your game for Veslin spilled over and Gregor Foss got the knife, too.'

'That's what I said, isn't it? I already admitted it!'

'Angry now? My, yes, you *would* be . . . angry that you fucked up. Angry that you're not as clever as you think you are. Angry that the gods gave lots of other people the same sort of brain they gave Locke Lamora. Quite the pisser, isn't it?'

Locke blew his little lamp out with one quick breath, then flung it in an arc, as high over the parapet as his slender arm could throw. The crash of its landing was lost in the murmur of the busy Camorri night. The boy crossed his arms defensively.

'Well, it certainly is nice to be free from the threat of that lamp, my boy.' Chains drew a last breath of smoke, then rubbed his dwindling sheaf of tobacco out against the roof stones. 'Was it informing for the Duke? Plotting to murder us?'

Locke said nothing, teeth clenched and lower lip protruding. Petulance, the natural non-verbal language of the very young. Chains snorted.

'I do believe everything you've told me, Locke, because I had a long talk with your former master before I took you off his hands. Like I said, he told me everything. He told me about your last and biggest mistake. The one that tipped him off and got you sent here. Can you guess what it might have been?'

Locke shook his head.

'Can't or won't?'

'I really don't know.' Locke looked down. 'I hadn't actually . . . thought about it.'

'You showed other kids in Streets the white iron coin, didn't you? You had them help you look for it. You let some of them know what it might be used for. And you ordered them not to talk about it . . . but what did you, ah, back that order up with?'

Locke's eyes widened; his pout returned but his petulance evaporated. 'They . . . they hated Veslin too. They wanted to see him get it.'

'Of course. Maybe that was enough for one day. But what about later? After Veslin was dead, and Gregor was dead, and your master'd had a chance to cool down some and reflect on the situation. What if he started asking questions about a certain Lamora boy? What if he took some of your little boon companions from Streets and asked them nicely if Locke Lamora had been up to anything . . . unusual? Even for him?'

'Oh.' The boy winced. 'Oh.'

'Oh-ho-ho!' Chains reached out and slapped the boy on the shoulder. 'Enlightenment! When it comes, it comes like a brick to the head, doesn't it?'

'I guess.'

'So,' said Chains, 'now you see where everything went wrong. How many boys and girls are in that little hill, Locke? A hundred? Hundred and twenty? More? How many do you really think your old master could handle, if they turned on him? One or two, no problem. But four? Eight? All of them?'

'We, um . . . I guess we never . . . thought about it.'

'Because he doesn't rule his graveyard by logic, boy, he rules it by fear. Fear of him keeps the older sprats in line. Fear of them keeps little shits like you in line. Anything that undermines that fear is a threat to his position. Enter Locke Lamora waving the idiot flag and thinking himself *so* much cleverer than the rest of the world!'

'I really . . . I don't . . . think I'm cleverer than the rest of the world.'

'You did until three minutes ago. Listen. I'm a *garrista*. It means I run a gang, even if it's just a small one. Your old master is a *garrista*, too, the *garrista* of Shades' Hill. And when you mess with a leader's ability to rule his gang, out come the knives. How long do you think the Thiefmaker could control Shades' Hill if word got around of how you played him so sweetly? How you jerked him around like a kitten on a chain? He would never have real control over his orphans ever again; they'd push and push until it finally came to blood.'

'And that's why he got rid of me? But what about Streets? What about the ones that helped me get Veslin?'

'Good questions. Easily answered. Your old master takes orphans in off the streets and keeps them for a few years; usually he's through with them by the time they're twelve or thirteen. He teaches them the basics: how to sneak-thief and speak the cant and mix with the Right People; how to get along in a gang and how to dodge the noose. When he's through with them, he sells them to the bigger gangs, the real gangs. You see? He takes orders. Maybe the Grey Faces need a second-storey girl. Maybe the Arsenal Boys want a mean little bruiser. It's a great advantage to the gangs; it brings them suitable new recruits that don't need to have their hands held.'

'That I know. That's why . . . he sold me to you.'

'Yes. Because you're a very special case. You have profitable skills, even if your aim so far has been terrible. But your little friends in Streets? Did they have your gifts? They were just regular little coat-charmers, simple little teasers. They weren't ripe. Nobody would give a penny for them except slavers, and your old master has one sad old scrap of real conscience – he wouldn't sell one of you to the crimpers for all the coin in Camorr.'

'So . . . like you said. He had to . . . do something to all of us that knew about the coin. All of us that could . . . figure it out or tell about it. And I was the only one he could sell.'

'Correct. And as for the others, well . . .' Chains shrugged. 'It'll be quick. Two, three weeks from now, nobody'll even remember their names. You know how it goes in the hill.'

'I got them killed.'

'Yes.' Chains didn't soften his voice. 'You really did. As surely as you tried to hurt Veslin, you killed Gregor and four or five of your little comrades into the bargain.'

'Shit.'

'Do you see now what consequences really are? Why you have to move slowly, think ahead, control the situation? Why you need to settle down and wait for time to give you sense to match your talent for mischief? We have years to work together, Locke. Years for you and my other little hellions to practise quietly. And that has to be the rule, if you want to stay here: no games, no cons, no scams, no *anything* except when and where I tell you. When someone like you pushes the world, the world pushes back. Other people are likely to get hurt. Am I clear?'

Locke nodded.

'Now.' Chains snapped his shoulders back and rolled his head from side to side; there was a series of snaps and cracks from somewhere inside him. 'Ahhh. Do you know what a death-offering is?'

'No.'

'It's something we do, for the Benefactor. Not just those of us who are initiates of the Thirteenth. Something all of us crooks do for one another, all the Right People of Camorr. When we lose someone we care about, we get something valuable and we throw it away. For real, you understand. Into the sea, into a fire, something like that. We do this to help our friends on their way to what comes next. Clear so far?'

'Yeah, but my old master—'

'Oh, he does it, trust me. He's a real miser and he always does it in private, but he does it for each and every one of you he loses. Figures he wouldn't tell you about it. But here's the thing – there's a rule that has to be followed with the offering. It can't be given willingly, you understand? It can't be something you already have. It has to be something you go out and steal from someone else, special, without their permission or their, ah, complicity. Get me? It has to be genuine theft.'

'Uh, sure.'

Father Chains cracked his knuckles. 'You're going to make a death-offering for every single boy or girl you got killed, Locke. One for Veslin, one for Gregor. One for each of your little friends in Streets. I'm sure I'll know the count in just a day or two.'

'But I . . . They weren't—'

'Of course they were your friends, Locke. They were your very good friends. Because they're going to teach you that when you kill someone, there are consequences. It's one thing to kill in a duel, to kill in self-defence, to kill for vengeance. It's another thing entirely to kill simply because you are careless. Those deaths are going to hang over your head until you're so careful you make the saints of Perelandro weep. Your death-offering will be a thousand full crowns per head. All of it properly stolen by your own hand.'

'But I . . . what? A thousand crowns? Each? A *thousand*?'

'You can take that death-mark off your neck when you offer up the last coin of it, and not a moment sooner.'

'That's impossible! It'll take . . . forever!'

'It'll take years. But we're thieves, not murderers, here in my temple. And the price of your life with me is that you must show respect for the dead. Those boys and girls are your victims, Locke. Get that through your head. This is something you owe them, before the gods. Something you must swear to by blood before you can stay. Are you willing to do so?'

Locke seemed to think for a few seconds. Then he shook his head as though to clear it, and nodded.

'Then hold out your left hand.'

As Locke did so, Chains produced a slender blackened-steel stiletto from within his robe and drew it across his own left palm; then, holding Locke's outstretched hand firmly, he scratched a shallow, stinging cut between the boy's thumb and index finger. They shook hands firmly, until their palms were thick with mingled blood.

'Then you're a Gentleman Bastard, like the rest of us. I'm your *garrista* and you're my *pezon*, my little soldier. I have your oath in blood to do what I've told you to do? To make the offerings for the souls of the people you've wronged?'

'I'll do it,' Locke said.

'Good. That means you can stay for dinner. Let's get down off this roof.'

2

Behind the curtained door at the rear of the sanctuary there was a grimy hall leading to several grimy rooms; moisture and mould and poverty were on abundant display. There were cells with sleeping pallets, lit by oiled-paper lamps that gave off a light the colour of cheap ale. Scrolls and bound books were scattered on the pallets; robes in questionable states of cleanliness hung from wall hooks.

'This is a necessary nonsense.' Chains gestured to and fro as he led Locke into the room closest to the curtained door, as though showing off a palace. 'Occasionally, we play host to a tutor or a travelling priest of Perelandro's order, and they have to see what they expect to see.'

Chains' own sleeping pallet (for Locke saw that the wall-manacles in the other room could surely reach none of the other sleeping chambers back here) was set atop a block of solid stone, a sort of heavy shelf jutting from the wall. Chains reached under the stale blankets, turned something that made a metallic clacking noise, and lifted his bed up as though it were a coffin lid; the blankets turned out to be on some sort of wooden panel with hinges set into the stone. An inviting golden light spilled from within the stone block, along with the spicy smells of high-class Camorri cooking. Locke knew that aroma only from the way it drifted out of the Alcegrante district or down from certain inns and houses.

'In you go!' Chains gestured once again, and Locke peeked over the lip of the stone block. A sturdy wooden ladder led down a square shaft just slightly wider than Chains' shoulders; it ended about twenty feet below, on a polished wood floor. 'Don't gawk, climb!'

Locke obeyed. The rungs of the ladder were wide and rough and very narrowly spaced; he had no trouble moving down it, and when he stepped off he was in a tall passage that might have been torn out of the Duke's own tower. The floor was indeed polished wood; long straight golden-brown boards that creaked pleasantly beneath his feet. The arched ceiling and the walls were entirely covered with a thick milky-golden glass that shone faintly, like a rainy season sun peeking out from behind heavy clouds. The illumination came from everywhere and nowhere; the wall scintillated. With a series of thumps and grunts and jingles (for Locke saw that he now carried the day's donated coins in a small burlap sack) Chains came down and hopped to the floor beside him. He gave a quick tug on a rope tied to the ladder, and the false bed-pallet fell back down and locked itself above.

'There. Isn't this much nicer?'

'Yeah.' Locke ran one hand down the flawless surface of one of the walls. The glass was noticeably cooler than the air. 'It's Elderglass, isn't it?'

'Sure as hell isn't plaster.' Chains shooed Locke along the passage to the left, where it turned a corner. 'The whole temple cellar is surrounded by the stuff. Sealed in it. The temple above was actually built to settle into it, hundreds of years ago. There's not a break in it, as far as I can tell, except for one or two little tunnels that lead out to other interesting places. It's flood-tight, never lets in a drop from below even when the water's waist-deep in the streets. And it keeps out rats and roaches and suckle-spiders and all that crap, so long as we mind our comings and goings.'

The clatter of metal pans and the low giggle of the Sanza brothers reached them from around the corner just before they turned it, into a comfortably appointed kitchen with tall wooden cabinets and a long witchwood table surrounded by high-backed chairs. Locke actually rubbed his eyes when he saw their black velvet cushions and the varnished gold leaf that gilded their every surface.

Calo and Galdo were working at a brick cooking shelf, shuffling pans and banging knives over a huge white alchemical hearthslab. Locke had seen smaller blocks of this stone, which gave off a smokeless heat when water was splashed over it, but this one must have weighed as much as Father Chains. As Locke watched, Calo (Galdo?) held a pan in the air and poured water from a glass pitcher onto the sizzling slab; the great uprush of steam carried a deep bouquet of sweet cooking smells and Locke felt saliva spilling down the back of his mouth.

In the air over the witchwood table, a striking chandelier blazed; Locke would, in later years, come to recognise it as an armillary sphere, fashioned entirely from glass with an axis of solid gold. At its heart shone an alchemical globe with the white-bronze light of the sun; surrounding this were the concentric glass rings that marked the orbits and processions of the world and all her celestial cousins, including the three moons; at the outermost edges were a hundred dangling stars that looked like spatters of molten glass somehow frozen at the very instant of their outward explosions. The light ran and glimmered and burned along every facet of the chandelier, yet there was something wrong about it; it was as if the Elderglass ceilings and walls were somehow drawing the light *out* of the alchemical sun; leavening it, weakening it, redistributing it along the full length and breadth of all the Elderglass in this uncanny cellar.

'Welcome to our real home, our little temple to the Benefactor.' Chains tossed his bag of coins down on the table. 'Our patron has always sort of danced upon the notion that austerity and piety go hand in hand; down here, we show our appreciation for things by *appreciating*, if you get me. Boys! Look who survived his interview!'

'We never doubted,' said one twin.

'For even a second,' said the other.

'But now can we hear what he did to get himself kicked out of Shades' Hill?' The question, spoken in near-perfect unison, had the ring of repeated ritual.

'When you're older.' Chains raised his eyebrows at Locke and shook his head, ensuring the boy could see the gesture clearly. '*Much* older. Locke, I don't expect that you know how to set a table . . . ?'

When Locke shook his head, Chains led him over to a tall cabinet just to the left of the cooking hearth. Inside were stacks of white porcelain plates; Chains held one up so Locke could see the hand-painted heraldic design (a mailed fist clutching an arrow and a grapevine) and the bright gilding on the rim.

'Borrowed,' said Chains, 'on a rather permanent basis from Doña Isabella Manechezzo, the old dowager aunt of our own

Duke Nicovante. She died childless and rarely gave parties, so it wasn't as though she was *using* them all. You see how some of our acts that might seem purely cruel and larcenous to outsiders are actually sort of convenient, if you look at them in the right way? That's the hand of the Benefactor at work, or so we like to think. It's not as though we could tell the difference if he didn't want us to.'

Chains handed the plate to Locke (who clutched at it with greatly exaggerated care and peered very closely at the gold rim) and ran his right hand lovingly over the surface of the witchwood table. 'Now this, this used to be the property of Marius Cordo, a master merchant of Tal Verrar. He had it in the great cabin of a triple-decker galley. Huge! Eighty-six oars. I was a bit upset with him, so I lifted it, his chairs, his carpets and tapestries, and all of his clothes. Right off the ship. I left his money; I was making a point. I dumped everything but the table into the Sea of Brass.'

'And that!' Chains lifted a finger in the direction of the celestial chandelier. 'That was being shipped overland from Ashmere in a guarded wagon convoy for the old Don Leviana. Somehow, in transit, it transformed itself into a box of straw.' Chains took three more plates out of the cabinet and set them in Locke's arms. 'Damn, I was fairly good back when I actually worked for a living.'

'Urk,' said Locke, under the weight of the fine dinnerware.

'Oh, yeah.' Chains gestured to the chair at the head of the table. 'Put one there for me. One for yourself on my left. Two for Calo and Galdo on my right. If you were my servant, what I'd tell you to lay out is a casual setting. Can you say that for me?'

'A casual setting.'

'Right. This is how the high and mighty eat when it's just close blood and maybe a friend or two.' Chains let the set of his eyes and the tone of his voice suggest that he expected this lesson to be retained, and he began to introduce Locke to the intricacies of glasses, linen napkins and silver eating utensils.

'What kind of knife is this?' Locke held a rounded buttering utensil up for Chains' inspection. 'It's all wrong. You couldn't kill *anyone* with this.'

'Well, not very easily, I'll grant you that, my boy.' Chains guided Locke in the placement of the butter knife, and assorted small dishes and bowls. 'But when the quality get together to dine, it's impolite to knock anybody off with anything but poison. That thing is for scooping butter, not slicing windpipes.'

'This is a lot of trouble to go to just to eat.'

'Well, in Shades' Hill you may be able to eat cold bacon and dirt pies off one another's arses for all your old master cares. But now you're a Gentleman Bastard, emphasis on the Gentleman. You're going to learn how to eat like this, and how to serve people who eat like this.'

'Why?'

'Because, Locke Lamora, some day you're going to dine with barons and counts and dukes. You're going to dine with merchants and admirals and generals and ladies of every sort! And when you do . . .' Chains put two fingers under Locke's chin and tilted the boy's head up so they were eye to eye. 'When you do, those poor idiots won't have any idea that they're really dining with a thief.'

3

'Now, isn't this lovely?'

Chains raised an empty glass and saluted his three young wards at the splendidly furnished table. Steaming brass bowls and heavy crockware held the results of Calo and Galdo's efforts at the cooking hearth. Locke, seated on an extra cushion to raise his elbows just above the tabletop, stared at the food and the furnishings with wide eyes. He was bewildered at how quickly he had escaped his old life and fallen into this new one with strangely pleasant crazy people.

Chains lifted a bottle of something he'd called alchemical wine; the stuff was viscous and dark, like quicksilver. When he pulled the loosened cork, the air was filled with the scent of juniper; for a brief moment it overwhelmed the spicy aroma of the main dishes. Chains poured a good measure of the stuff into the empty glass, and in the bright light the wine ran like molten silver. Chains raised the glass to a level with his eyes.

'A glass poured to air for the one who sits with us unseen; the patron and protector, the Crooked Warden, the Father of Necessary Pretexts.'

'Thanks for deep pockets poorly guarded,' said the Sanza

brothers in unison, and Locke was caught off guard by the seriousness of their intonation.

'Thanks for watchmen asleep at their posts,' said Chains.

'Thanks for the city to nurture us and the night to hide us,' was the response.

'Thanks for friends to help spend the loot!' Chains brought the half-filled glass down and set it in the middle of the table. He took up another, smaller glass; into this he poured just a finger of the liquid silver. 'A glass poured to air for an absent friend. We wish Sabetha well and pray for her safe return.'

'Maybe we could have her back a little less crazy, though,' said one of the Sanzas, whom Locke mentally labelled Calo for convenience.

'And humble.' Galdo nodded after he'd said this. 'Humble would be really great.'

'The brothers Sanza wish Sabetha well.' Chains held the little glass of liquor rock steady and eyed the twins. 'And they pray for her safe return.'

'Yes! Wish her well!'

'Safe return, that would be really great.'

'Who's Sabetha?' Locke spoke quietly, directing his enquiry to Chains.

'An ornament to our little gang. Our only young woman, currently away on . . . educational business.' Chains set her glass down beside the one poured to the Benefactor, and plucked up Locke's glass in exchange. 'Another special deal from your old master. Gifted, my boy, gifted like you are with a preternatural talent for the vexation of others.'

'That's us he's talking about,' said Calo.

'Pretty soon it'll mean you, too.' Galdo smiled.

'Pipe down, twitlings.' Chains poured a splash of the quicksilver wine into Locke's glass and handed it back to him. 'One more toast and prayer. To Locke Lamora, our new brother. My new *pezon*. We wish him well. We welcome him warmly. And for him, we pray, wisdom.'

With graceful motions, he poured wine for Calo and Galdo, and then a nearly full glass for himself. Chains and the Sanzas raised their glasses; Locke quickly copied them. Silver sparkled under gold.

'Welcome to the Gentlemen Bastards!' Chains tapped his glass gently against Locke's, producing a ringing sound that sweetly hung in the air before fading.

'You should've picked death!' said Galdo.

'He did offer you death as a choice, right?' Calo spoke as he and his brother tapped their own glasses together, then reached across the table in unison to touch Locke's.

'Laugh it up, boys.' Soon all the knocking about with glasses was finished and Chains led the way with a quick sip of his wine. 'Ahhh. Mark my words, if this poor little creature lives a year you two will be his dancing monkeys. He'll throw you grapes whenever he wants to see a trick. Go ahead and have a drink, Locke.'

Locke raised the glass; the silvery surface showed him a vivid but wobbly reflection of his own face and the brightly lit room around him; the wine's bouquet was a haze of juniper and anise that tickled his nose. He put the tiny image of himself to his lips and drank. The slightly cool liquor seemed to go two ways at once as he swallowed; a line of tickling warmth ran straight down his throat while icy tendrils reached upward, sliding across the roof of his mouth and into his sinuses. His eyes bulged; he coughed and ran a hand over his suddenly numb lips.

'It's mirror wine, from Tal Verrar. Good stuff. Now go ahead and eat something or it'll pop your skull open.'

Calo and Galdo whisked damp cloths off serving platters and bowls, revealing the full extent of the meal for the first time. There were indeed sausages, neatly sliced and fried in oil with quartered pears. There were split red peppers stuffed with almond paste and spinach; dumplings of thin bread folded over chicken, fried until the bread was as translucent as paper; cold black beans in wine and mustard sauce. The Sanza brothers were suddenly scooping portions of this and that onto Locke's plate too fast for him to track.

Working awkwardly with a two-pronged silver fork and one of the rounded knives he'd previously scorned, Locke began to shovel things into his mouth; the flavours seemed to burst gloriously, haphazardly. The chicken dumplings were spiced with ginger and ground orange peels. The wine sauce in the bean salad warmed his tongue; the sharp fumes of mustard burned his throat. He found himself gulping wine to put out each new fire as it arose.

To his surprise, the Sanza twins didn't partake once they'd

served him; they sat with their hands folded, watching Chains. When the older man seemed assured that Locke was eating, he turned to Calo.

'You're a Vadran noble. Let's say you're a Liege-Graf from one of the less important Marrows. You're at a dinner party in Tal Verrar; an equal number of men and women, with assigned seating. The party is just entering the dining hall; your assigned lady is beside you as you enter, conversing with you. What do you do?'

'At a Vadran dinner party, I would hold her chair out for her without invitation.' Calo didn't smile. 'But Verrari ladies will stand beside a chair to show they want it pulled out. It's impolite to presume. So I'd let her make the first move.'

'Very good. Now.' Chains pointed to the second Sanza with one hand as he began adding food to his plate with the other. 'What's seventeen multiplied by nineteen?'

Galdo closed his eyes in concentration for a few seconds. 'Um . . . three hundred and twenty-three.'

'Correct. What's the difference between a Vadran nautical league and a Therin nautical league?'

'Ah . . . the Vadran league is a hundred and . . . fifty yards longer.'

'Very good. That's that, then. Go ahead and eat.'

As the Sanza brothers began to indecorously struggle for possession of certain serving dishes, Chains turned to Locke, whose plate was already half empty. 'After you've been here a few days, I'm going to start asking questions about what you've learned, Locke. If you want to eat you'll be expected to learn.'

'What am I going to learn? Other than setting tables?'

'Everything!' Chains looked very pleased with himself. 'Everything, my boy. How to fight, how to steal, how to lie with a straight face. How to cook meals like this! How to disguise yourself. How to speak like a noble, how to scribe like a priest, how to skulk like a half-wit.'

'Calo already knows that one,' said Galdo.

'Agh moo agh na mugh baaa,' said Calo around a mouthful of food.

'Remember what I said, when I told you we didn't work like other thieves work? We're a new sort of thief here, Locke. What we are is actors. False-facers. I sit here and pretend to be a priest of

Perelandro; for years now people have been throwing money at me. How do you think I paid for the contents of this little fairy-burrow, this food? I'm three and fifty; nobody my age can steal around rooftops and charm locks. I'm better paid for being blind than I ever was for being quick and clever. And now I'm too slow and too round to pass for anything really interesting.'

Chains finished off the contents of his glass and poured another.

'But you. You and Calo and Galdo and Sabetha . . . you four will have every advantage I didn't. Your education will be thorough and vigorous. I'll refine my notions, my techniques. When I'm finished, the things you four will pull . . . well, they'll make my little scam with this temple look simple and unambitious.'

'That sounds nice,' said Locke, who was feeling the wine; a warm haze of charitable contentment was descending over him and smothering the tension and worry that were second nature to a Shades' Hill orphan. 'What do we do first?'

'Well, tonight, if you're not busy throwing up the first decent meal you've ever had, Calo and Galdo will draw you a bath. Once you're less aromatic company, you can sleep in. Tomorrow, we'll get you an acolyte's robe and you can sit the steps with us, taking coins. Tomorrow night . . .' Chains scratched at his beard while he took a sip from his glass. 'I take you to meet the big man. Capa Barsavi. He's ever so curious to get a look at you.'

CHAPTER THREE

Imaginary Men

I

For the second time in two days Don Lorenzo Salvara found his life interrupted by masked and hooded strangers in an unexpected place. This time it was just after midnight, and they were waiting for him in his study.

'Close the door,' said the shorter intruder. His voice was all Camorr, rough and smoky and clearly accustomed to being obeyed. 'Have a seat, m'lord, and don't bother calling for your man. Your man is indisposed.'

'Who the hell are you?' Salvara's sword hand curled reflexively; his belt held no scabbard. He slid the door closed behind him but made no move to sit at his writing desk. 'How did you get in here?'

The intruder who'd first spoken reached up and pulled down the black cloth that covered his nose and mouth. His face was lean and angular; his hair black, his dark moustache thin and immaculately trimmed. A white scar arced across the man's right cheekbone. He reached into the folds of his well-cut black cloak and pulled out a black leather wallet, which he flipped open so the Don could see its contents – a small crest of gold set inside an intricate design of frosted glass.

'Gods.' Don Salvara fell into his chair, nervously, without further hesitation. 'You're Midnighters.'

'Just so.' The man folded his wallet and put it back in his cloak. The silent intruder, still masked and hooded, moved casually around to stand just a few feet behind Don Lorenzo, between him and the door. 'We apologise for the intrusion. But our business here is extremely sensitive.'

'Have I . . . have I somehow offended His Grace?'

'Not to my knowledge, m'lord Salvara. In fact, you might say we're here to help prevent you from doing so.'

'I . . . I, ah, well. Ah, what did you say you did to Conté?'

'Just gave him a little something to help him sleep, is all. We know he's loyal and we know he's dangerous. We didn't want any . . . misunderstandings.'

The man standing at the door punctuated this statement by stepping forward, reaching round Don Salvara, and gently setting Conté's matching fighting knives down on the desktop.

'I see. I trust that he'll be well.' Don Salvara drummed his fingers on his writing desk and stared at the scarred intruder. 'I should be very displeased otherwise.'

'He is completely unharmed, I give you my word as a Duke's man.'

'I shall hold that sufficient. For the time being.'

The scarred man sighed and rubbed his eyes with two gloved fingers. 'There's no need for us to start out like this, m'lord. I apologise for the abruptness of our appearance and the manner of our intrusion, but I believe you'll find that your welfare is paramount in our master's eyes. I'm instructed to ask – did you enjoy yourself at the Revel today?'

'Yes . . .' Don Salvara spoke carefully, as though to a solicitor or a court recorder. 'I suppose that would be an accurate assessment.'

'Good, good. You had company, didn't you?'

'The Doña Sofia was with me.'

'I refer to someone else. Not one of His Grace's subjects. Not Camorri.'

'Ah. The merchant. A merchant named Lukas Ferhwight, from Emberlain.'

'From Emberlain. Of course.' The scarred man folded his arms and looked around the Don's study; he stared for a moment at a pair of small glass portraits of the old Don and Doña Salvara, set in a frame decked with black velvet funeral ribbons. 'Well. That man is no more a merchant of Emberlain than you or I, m'lord Salvara. He's a fraud. A sham.'

'I . . .' Don Salvara nearly jumped to his feet, but remembered the man standing behind him and seemed to think better of it. 'I don't see how that could be possible. He—'

'Beg pardon, m'lord.' The scarred man smiled, gruesomely and artificially, as a man without children might smile when trying to comfort an upset babe. 'But let me ask you – have you ever heard of the man they call the Thorn of Camorr?'

2

'I only steal because my dear old family needs the money to live!'

Locke Lamora made this proclamation with his wine glass held high; he and the other Gentlemen Bastards were seated at the old witchwood table in the opulent burrow beneath the House of Perelandro; Calo and Galdo on his right, Jean and Bug on his left. A huge spread of food was set before them and the celestial chandelier swung overhead with its familiar golden light. The others began to jeer.

'Liar!' they chorused.

'I only steal because this wicked world won't let me work an honest trade!' Calo cried, hoisting his own glass.

'LIAR!'

'I only steal because I have to support my poor lazy twin brother, whose indolence broke our mother's heart!' Galdo elbowed Calo as he made this announcement.

'LIAR!'

'I only steal,' said Jean, 'because I've temporarily fallen in with bad company.'

'LIAR!'

At last the ritual came to Bug; the boy raised his glass a bit shakily and yelled, 'I only steal because it's heaps of fucking fun!'

'*BASTARD!*'

With a general clamour of whooping and hollering the five thieves banged glasses together; light glittered on crystal and shone through the misty green depths of Verrari mint wine. The four men drained their glasses in one go and slammed them back down on the tabletop. Bug, already a bit cross-eyed, handled his somewhat more delicately.

'Gentlemen, I hold in my hands the first fruits of all our long weeks of study and suffering.' Locke held up a rolled parchment embossed with ribbons and the blue wax seal of a member of the lesser nobility of Camorr. 'A letter of credit for five thousand full crowns, to be drawn tomorrow against Don Salvara's funds at

Meraggio's. And, I daresay, the first score our youngest member has ever helped us to bring in.'

'Barrel boy!' The Sanza brothers hollered in unison; a moment later a small almond-crusted bread roll arced from between their seats, hit Bug right between the eyes, and plopped down onto his empty plate. Bug tore it in half and responded in kind, aiming well despite his wobbliness. Locke continued speaking as Calo scowled and rubbed crumbs out of his eyes.

'Second touch this afternoon was easy. But we wouldn't have gotten so far, so fast, if not for Bug's quick action yesterday. What a stupid, reckless, idiotic, ridiculous damn thing to do! I haven't the words to express my admiration.' Locke had managed to work a bit of wine-bottle legerdemain while speaking; the empty glasses were suddenly full. 'To Bug! The new bane of the Camorr city watch!'

When the cheering and the guzzling from this toast had subsided and Bug had been smacked upon the back often enough to turn the contents of his skull sideways, Locke produced a single large glass, set it in the middle of the table, and filled it slowly.

'Just one thing more before we can eat.' He held the glass up as the others fell silent. 'A glass poured to air for an absent friend. We miss old Chains terribly and we wish his soul peace. May the Crooked Warden ever stand watch and bless his crooked servant. He was a good and penitent man, in the manner of our kind.'

Gently, Locke set the glass in the centre of the table and covered it with a small black cloth. 'He would have been very proud of you, Bug.'

'I do hope so.' The boy stared at the covered glass in the middle of the opulent glassware and gilded crockery. 'I wish I could have met him.'

'You would have been a restful project for his old age.' Jean kissed the back of his own left hand, the benedictory gesture of the Nameless Thirteenth's priesthood. 'A very welcome respite from what he endured raising the four of us!'

'Jean's being generous. He and I were saints. It's the Sanza brothers that kept the poor old bastard up late praying six nights out of seven.' Locke reached out toward one cloth-covered platter. 'Let's eat.'

'Praying that you and Jean would grow up quick and handsome

like the two of us, you mean!' Galdo's hand darted out and caught Locke's at the wrist. 'Aren't you forgetting something?'

'Am I?'

Calo, Galdo and Jean met this question with a coordinated stare. Bug looked sheepish and gazed up at the chandelier.

'Gods damn it.' Locke slid out of his gilded chair and went to a side cupboard; when he returned to the table he had a tiny sampling-glass in his hand, little more than a thimble for liquor. Into this he let slip the smallest dash of mint wine. He didn't hold this glass up, but pushed it into the centre of the table beside the glass under the black cloth.

'A glass poured in air for an absent *someone*. I don't know where she is at the moment and I pray you all choke, save Bug, thanks very fucking much.'

'Hardly a graceful blessing, especially for a priest.' Calo kissed the back of his own left hand and waved it over the tiny glass. 'She was one of us even before you were, *garrista*.'

'You know what I *do* pray?' Locke set his hands on the edge of the table; his knuckles rapidly turned white. 'That maybe someday one of *you* finds out what love is when it travels farther up than the buttons of your trousers.'

'It takes two to break a heart.' Galdo gently placed his left hand over Locke's right. 'I don't recall her fucking things up without your able assistance.'

'And I daresay,' said Calo, 'that it would be a tremendous relief to us all if you would just have the courtesy to go out and get yourself wenched. Long and hard. Gods, do three at once! It's not as though we don't have the funds.'

'I'll have you know my patience for this topic was exhausted long before—' Locke's voice was rising to a shout when Jean grabbed him firmly by his left bicep; Jean's fist wrapped easily all the way around Locke's arm.

'She was our good friend, Locke. Was and still is. You owe her something a bit more godly than that.'

Jean reached out for the wine bottle, then filled the little glass to its brim. He raised it into the light and took his other hand off Locke's arm. 'A glass poured to air for an absent friend. We wish Sabetha well. For ourselves, we pray brotherhood.'

Locke stared at him for a second that seemed like minutes, then let out a long sigh. 'I'm sorry. I didn't mean to ruin the occasion. That was a poor toast and I . . . repent it. I should have thought better of my responsibilities.'

'I'm sorry, too.' Galdo grinned sheepishly. 'We don't blame you for the way you feel. We know she was . . . she was . . . *her*.'

'Well, I'm not sorry about the wenching bit.' Calo shrugged in mock apology. 'I'm fucking serious, man. Dip your wick. Drop your anchor. Go see a lady about a sheath for a dagger. You'll feel better.'

'Isn't it obvious that I'm just ecstatic right now? I don't need to feel *better*; you and I still have work to do this evening! For the love of the Crooked Warden, can we please just kill this subject and throw its gods-damned corpse in the bay?'

'Sorry,' Calo said after a few seconds and a well-aimed glare from Jean. 'Sorry. Look, you know we mean well. We're both sorry if we push. But she's in Parlay and we're in Camorr, and it's obvious you— '

Calo would have said something else, but an almond roll bounced off the bridge of his nose and he flinched in surprise. Another roll hit Galdo in the forehead; one arced into Jean's lap, and Locke managed to throw up a hand in time to swat down the one intended for him.

'Honestly!' Bug clutched still more rolls in his outstretched hands and he pointed them like loaded crossbows. 'Is this what I get to look forward to when I grow up? I thought we were celebrating being richer and cleverer than everyone else!'

Locke looked at the boy for just a moment, then reached out and took the full sampling-glass from Jean, a smile breaking out as he did so. 'Bug's right. Let's cut the shit and have dinner.' He raised the glass as high as he could toward the light of the chandelier. 'To us – richer and cleverer than everyone else!'

'RICHER AND CLEVERER THAN EVERYONE ELSE!' came the echoing chorus.

'We toast absent friends who helped to bring us to where we are now. We do miss them.' Locke set the little glass to his lips and took a minuscule sip before he set it back down.

'And we love them still,' he said quietly.

3

'The Thorn of Camorr . . . is a particularly ridiculous rumour that floats around the dining parlour when some of the more excitable Dons don't water their wine quite thoroughly enough.'

'The Thorn of Camorr,' said the scarred man pleasantly, 'walked off your pleasure barge earlier this evening with a signed note for five thousand of your white iron crowns.'

'Who? Lukas Fehrwight?'

'None other.'

'Lukas Fehrwight is a *Vadran*. My mother was Vadran; I know the tongue! Lukas is Old Emberlain all the way through. He covers himself in wool and flinches back six feet any time a woman blinks at him!' Don Lorenzo pulled his optics off in irritation and set them on his desk. 'The man would bet the lives of his own children against the price he could get for barrels of herring guts on any given morning. I've dealt with his kind too many times to count. That man is no Camorri, and he is no mythical thief!'

'My lord. You are four and twenty, yes?'

'For the time being. Is that quite relevant?'

'You have no doubt known many merchants in the years since your mother and father passed away, may they have the peace of the Long Silence. Many merchants, and many of them Vadrans, correct?'

'Quite correct.'

'And if a man, a very clever man, wished you to think him a merchant . . . well, what would he dress up and present himself as? A fisherman? A mercenary archer?'

'I don't grasp your meaning.'

'I mean, m'lord Salvara, that your own expectations have been used against you. You have a keen sense for men of business, surely. You've grown your family fortune several times over in your brief time handling it. Therefore, a man who wished to snare you in some scheme could do nothing wiser than to act the consummate man of business. To deliberately manifest all of your expectations. To show you exactly what you expected and desired to see.'

'It seems to me that if I accept your argument,' the Don said slowly, 'then the self-evident truth of any legitimate thing could be taken as grounds for its falseness. I say Lukas Fehrwight is a merchant of Emberlain because he shows the signs of being so; you say those same signs are what prove him counterfeit. I need more sensible evidence than this.'

'Let me digress, then, m'lord, and ask another question.' The scarred man drew his hands within the black folds of his cloak and stared down at the young nobleman. 'If you were a thief who preyed exclusively on the nobility of our Duchy of Camorr, how would you hide your actions?'

'Exclusively? Your Thorn of Camorr again. There can't be any such thief. There are arrangements . . . the Secret Peace. Other thieves would take care of the matter as soon as any man dared breach the Peace.'

'And if our thief could evade capture? If our thief could conceal his identity from his fellows?'

'If. If. They say the Thorn of Camorr steals from the rich' – Don Salvara placed a hand on his own chest – 'and gives every last copper to the poor. But have you heard of any bags of gold being dumped in the street in Catchfire lately? Any charcoal-burners or knackers suddenly walking around in silk waistcoats and embroidered boots? Please. The Thorn is a commoner's ale-tale. Master swordsman, romancer of ladies, a ghost who walks through walls. Ridiculous.'

'Your doors are locked and all your windows are barred, yet here we are in your study, m'lord.'

'Granted. But you're men of flesh and blood.'

'So it's said. We're getting off the subject. Our thief, m'lord, would trust you and your peers to keep his activities concealed *for* him. Hypothetically speaking, if Lukas Fehrwight were the Thorn of Camorr, and you knew that he had strolled off with a small fortune from your coffers, what would you do? Would you rouse the watch? Cry for aid openly in the court of His Grace? Speak of the matter in front of Don Paleri Jacobo?'

'I . . . I . . . that's an interesting point. I wonder—'

'Would you want the entire city to know that you'd been taken in? That you'd been tricked? Would men of business ever trust your judgement again? Would your reputation ever truly recover?'

'I suppose it would be a very . . . difficult thing.'

The scarred man's right hand reappeared, gloveless and pale

against the darkness of the cloak, one finger pointing outward. 'Her ladyship the Doña Rosalina de Marre lost ten thousand crowns four years ago, in exchange for titles to upriver orchards that don't exist.' A second finger curled outward. 'Don and Doña Feluccia lost twice as much two years ago. They thought they were financing a coup in Talisham that would have made the city a family estate.

'Last year,' the scarred man said as a third finger unfolded, 'Don Javarriz paid fifteen thousand full crowns to a soothsayer who claimed to be able to restore the old man's firstborn son to life.' The man's little finger snapped out, and he waved his extended hand at Don Lorenzo. 'Now, we have the Don and Doña Salvara involved in a secret business deal that is both tempting and convenient. Tell me, have you ever heard of the troubles of the lords and ladies I have named?'

'No.'

'Doña de Marre visits your wife in her garden twice weekly. They discuss alchemical botany together. You've played cards with the sons of Don Javarriz many times. And yet this is all a surprise to you?'

'Yes, quite, I assure you!'

'It was a surprise to His Grace, as well. My master has spent two years attempting to follow the slender threads of evidence connecting these crimes, m'lord. A fortune the size of your own vanished into thin air and it took ducal orders to pry open the lips of the wronged parties. Because their pride compelled their silence.'

Don Lorenzo stared at the surface of his desk for a long moment.

'Fehrwight has a suite at the Tumblehome. He has a man-servant, superior clothes, hundred-crown optics. He has . . . proprietary secrets of the House of bel Auster.' Don Salvara looked up at the scarred man as though presenting a difficult problem to a demanding tutor. 'Things that no thief could have.'

'Would fine clothes be beyond the means of a man with more than forty *thousand* stolen crowns at his command? And his cask of unaged brandy – how would you or I or any other man outside the House of bel Auster know what it should look like? Or what it should taste like? It's a simple fraud.'

'He was recognised on the street by a solicitor, one of the Razona lawscribes who sticks to the walls at Meraggio's!'

'Of course he was, because he began building the identity of Lukas Fehrwright long ago, probably before he ever met Doña de Marre. He has a very real account at Meraggio's, opened with real money five years ago. He has every outward flourish that a man in his position should bear, but Lukas Fehrwright is a ghost. A lie. A stage role performed for a very select private audience. I have tracked this man for years.'

'We are sensible people, Sofia and I. Surely . . . surely we would have seen something out of place.'

'Out of place? The entire affair has been out of place! M'lord Salvara, I implore you, hear me carefully. You are a financier of fine liquors. You say a prayer to your mother's shade each week at a Vadran temple. What a fascinating coincidence that you should chance upon a needy Vadran who happens to be a dealer in the same field, eh?'

'Where else but the Temple of Fortunate Waters would a Vadran pray while visiting Camorr?'

'Nowhere, of course. But look at the coincidences piling heavily upon one another. A Vadran liquor merchant, in need of rescue, and he just so happens to be on his way to visit Don Jacobo? Your blood enemy? A man that everyone knows you would crush by any means if the Duke hadn't forbidden you?'

'Were you . . . observing us when I first met him?'

'Yes, very carefully. We saw you and your man approach that alley to rescue a man you thought to be in danger. We—'

'*Thought?* He was being strangled!'

'Was he? The men in those masks were his accomplices, m'lord. The fight was staged. It was a means to introduce you to the imaginary merchant and his imaginary opportunity. Everything you value was used to bait the trap! Your sympathies for Vadrans, your sense of duty, your courage, your interest in fine liquors, your desire to best Don Jacobo. And can it be a coincidence that Fehrwright's scheme must be secret? That it runs on an extremely short and demanding schedule? That it just happens to feed your every known ambition?'

The Don stared at the far wall of his study, tapping his fingers against his desk in a gradually increasing tempo. 'This is quite a shock,' he said at last, in a small voice without any fight left in it.

'Forgive me for that, my lord Salvara. The truth is unfortunate. Of course the Thorn of Camorr isn't ten feet tall. Of course he can't walk through walls. But he is a very real thief; he is posing as a Vadran named Lukas Fehrwright, and he *does* have five thousand crowns of your money, with an eye for twenty thousand more.'

'I must send someone to Meraggio's, so he can't exchange my note in the morning,' said Don Lorenzo.

'Respectfully, my lord, you must do nothing of the sort. My instructions are clear. We don't just want the Thorn, we want his accomplices. His contacts. His sources of information. His entire network of thieves and spies. We have him in the open now, and we can follow him as he goes about his business. One hint that his game is unmasked, and he will bolt. The opportunity we have may never present itself again. His Grace Duke Nicovante is quite adamant that everyone involved in these crimes must be identified and taken. Towards that end, your absolute cooperation is requested and required, in the Duke's name.'

'What am I to do, then?'

'Continue to act as though you are entirely taken in by Fehrwright's story. Let him exchange the note. Let him taste some success. And when he returns to you asking for more money . . .'

'Yes?'

'Why, give it to him, my lord. Give him everything he asks.'

4

Once the dinner dishes were cleared away, and a tipsy Bug was given the task of setting them a-sparkle with warm water and white sand ('Excellent for your moral education!' Jean had cried as he'd heaped up the porcelain and crystal), Locke and Calo withdrew to the burrow's Wardrobe to begin preparations for the third and most critical touch of the Don Salvara game.

The Elderglass cellar beneath the House of Perelandro was divided into three areas: one of them was the kitchen, another was split into sleeping quarters with wooden partitions, and the third was referred to as the Wardrobe.

Long clothes-racks stretched across every wall of the Wardrobe, holding hundreds of pieces of costuming organised by origin, by season, by cut and by size and social class. There were sackcloth robes, labourer's tunics and butcher's aprons with dried blood-stains. There were cloaks of winter weight and summer weight, cheaply woven and finely tailored, unadorned or decorated with everything up to precious metal trim and peacock feathers. There were robes and accessories for most of the Therin priestly orders – Perelandro, Morgante, Nara, Sendovani, Iono, and so forth. There were silk blouses and cunningly armoured doublets, gloves and ties and cravats, enough canes and walking sticks to outfit a mercenary company of hobbled old men.

Chains had started this collection more than twenty years before, and his students had added to it with the wealth gained from years of schemes. Very little worn by the Gentlemen Bastards went to waste; even the foulest-smelling sweat-soaked summer garments were washed and dusted with alchemical pomanders and hung carefully. They could always be fouled up again, if needed.

A man-height looking glass dominated the heart of the Ward-robe; another, much smaller glass hung from a sort of pulley system on the ceiling, so that it could be moved around and positioned as necessary. Locke stood before the larger mirror dressed in matching doublet and breeches of midnight velvet; his hose was the scarlet of blood in sunset waters and his simple Camorri tie was a near match.

'Is this bloody melodrama really such a good idea?' Calo was dressed quite similarly, though his hose and his accents were grey; he pulled his tunic sleeves back above his elbows and fastened them there with black pearl clips.

'It's a fine idea,' Locke said, adjusting his tie. 'We're Mid-nighters. We're full of ourselves. What sort of self-respecting spy would break into a manor house in darkest night wearing green, or orange, or white?'

'The sort that walked up and knocked at the door would.'

'I appreciate that, but I still don't want to change the plan. Don Salvara's had a busy day. He'll be wide open for a nice shock at the end of it. Can't shock him quite the same in lavender and carmine.'

'Well, certainly not in the way you're thinking, no.'

'This doublet's damned uncomfortable in the back,' Locke muttered. 'Jean! Jeeeeaaaaaaan!'

'What is it?' came an echoing return shout a long moment later.

'Why, I just love to say your name! Get in here!'

Jean ambled into the Wardrobe a moment later, a glass of brandy in one hand and a battered book in the other.

'I thought Graumann had the night off for this bit,' he said.

'He does.' Locke gestured impatiently at the back of his doublet. 'I need the services of Camorr's ugliest seamstress.'

'Galdo's helping Bug wash up.'

'Grab your needles, glass-eyes.'

Jean's eyebrows drew down above his reading optics, but he set down his book and his glass and opened a small wooden chest set against one of the Wardrobe walls.

'What're you reading?' Calo had added a tiny silver and amethyst clip to the centre of his tie and was examining himself in the small glass, approvingly.

'Kimlarthen,' Jean replied, working black thread through a white bone needle and trying not to prick his fingers.

'The Korish romances?' Locke snorted. 'Sentimental crap. Never knew you had a taste for fairy stories.'

'They happen to be culturally significant records of the Therin Throne centuries,' Jean said as he stepped behind Locke, seam ripper in one hand and threaded needle in the other. 'Plus at least three knights get their heads torn completely off by the Beast of Vuazzo.'

'Illustrated manuscript, by chance?'

'Not the good parts, no.' Jean fiddled with the back of the doublet as delicately as he had ever charmed a lock or a victim's coat pocket.

'Oh, just let it out. I don't care how it looks; it'll be hidden by the back of my cloak anyway. We can pretty it up later.'

'We?' Jean snorted as he loosened the doublet with a few strategic rips and slashes. 'Me, more like. You mend clothes like dogs write poetry.'

'And I readily admit it. Oh, gods, much better. Now there's room to hide the sigil-wallet and a few surprises, just in case.'

'It feels odd to be letting something out for you, rather than taking it in.' Jean arranged his tools as he'd found them in the

117

sewing-chest and closed it back up. 'Do mind your training; we wouldn't want you gaining half a pound.'

'Well, most of me *is* brain-weight.' Locke folded his own tunic sleeves back and pinned them up as Calo had.

'You're one third bad intentions, one third pure avarice, and one eighth sawdust. What's left, I'll credit, must be brains.'

'Well, since you're here, and you're such an expert on my poor self, why don't you pull out the masque box and help me with my face?'

Jean paused for a sip from his brandy glass before pulling out a tall, battered wooden box inset with many dozens of small drawers. 'What do we want to do first, your hair? You're going black, right?'

'As pitch. I should only have to be this fellow two or three times.'

Jean twirled a white cloth around the shoulders of Locke's doublet and fastened it in front with a tiny bone clasp. He then opened a poultice jar and smeared his fingers with the contents, a firm dark gel that smelled richly of citrus. 'Hmm. Looks like charcoal and smells like oranges. I'll never fathom Jessaline's sense of humour.'

Locke smiled as Jean began to knead the stuff into his dirty-blonde hair. 'Even a black apothecary needs to stay amused somehow. Remember that beef-scented knockout candle she gave us, to deal with Don Feluccia's damn guard dog?'

'Very droll, that.' Calo frowned as he made further minute adjustments to his own finery. 'Stray cats running from every corner of Camorr at the scent. Dropping in their tracks until the street was full of little bodies. Wind shifting all over the place, and all of us running around trying to stay ahead of the smoke . . .'

'Not our finest moment,' said Jean. His job was already nearly finished; the stuff seemed to sink into Locke's hair, imparting a natural-looking shade of deep Camorri black, with only the slightest sheen. But many men in Camorr used slick substances to hold or perfume their hair; this would hardly be noteworthy.

Jean wiped his fingers on Locke's white neck-towel, then dipped a scrap of cloth into another poultice jar containing a pearly gel. This stuff, when applied to his fingers, cleared the residue of hair dye away as though the black gel was evaporating into thin air. Jean dabbed the cloth at Locke's temples and neck, erasing the faint smudges and drips left over from the colouring process.

'Scar?' Jean asked when he was finished.

'Please.' Locke ran his little finger across the line of his right cheekbone. 'Slash right across there if you would.'

Jean withdrew a slender wooden tube with a chalky white tip from the masque box and drew a short line on Locke's face with it, just as Locke had indicated. Locke flinched as the stuff sizzled for a second or two; in the blink of an eye the white line hardened into a raised, pale arc of pseudo-skin, perfectly mimicking a scar.

Bug appeared through the Wardrobe door at that instant, his cheeks a bit ruddier than usual. In one hand he held a black leather folding-wallet, slightly larger than that which a gentleman would ordinarily carry. 'Kitchen's clean. Galdo said you'd forget this if I didn't bring it in and throw it at you.'

'Please don't take him literally.' Locke held out a hand for the wallet while Jean removed the white cloth from his shoulders, satisfied that the hair dye was dry. 'Break that thing and I'll roll you to Emberlain in a barrel. Personally.'

The sigil inside the wallet, an intricate confection of gold and crystal and frosted glass, was by far the most expensive prop of the whole game; even the 502 cask of Austershalin had been cheaper. The sigil had been crafted in Talisham, four days' ride down the coast to the south; no Camorri counterfeiter, regardless of skill, could be trusted to be quiet or comfortable about mimicking the badge of the Duke's own secret police.

A stylised spider over the royal seal of the Serene Duchy; none of the Gentlemen Bastards had ever seen one, but Locke was confident that few of the lesser nobility had, either. The rough description of the dreaded sigil was whispered by the Right People of Camorr, and from that description a best-guess forgery had been put together.

'Durant the Gimp says that the Spider's just bullshit,' said Bug as he handed over the wallet. All three older Gentlemen Bastards in the room looked at him sharply.

'If you put Durant's brains in a thimble full of water,' said Jean, 'they'd look like a ship lost in the middle of the sea.'

'The Midnighters are real, Bug.' Locke patted his hair gingerly and found that his hands came away clean. 'If you're ever found breaching the Peace, you'd better pray the Capa gets to you before they do. Barsavi's the soul of mercy compared to the man that runs the Palace of Patience.'

'I know the Midnighters are real,' said Bug. 'I just said there's some that say the *Spider* is bullshit.'

'Oh, he exists. Jean, pick out a moustache for me. Something that goes with this hair.' Locke ran a finger over the smooth skin around his lips, shaved just after dinner. 'There's a man behind the Midnighters. Jean and I have spent years trying to figure out which of the Duke's court it must be, but all the leads go nowhere in the end.'

'Even Galdo and I are stumped,' added Calo. 'So you know we're dealing with a devil of singular subtlety.'

'How can you be sure, though?'

'Let me put it like this, Bug.' Locke paused while Jean held up a false moustache; Locke shook his head and Jean went back to digging in the masque box. 'When Capa Barsavi does for someone, we hear about it, right? We have connections, and the word gets passed. The Capa *wants* people to know his reasons – it avoids future trouble, makes an example.'

'And when the Duke does for someone himself,' said Calo, 'there's always signs. Yellowjackets, Nightglass soldiers, writs, trials, proclamations.'

'But when the Spider puts the finger on someone . . .' Locke gave a brief nod of approval to the second moustache Jean held up for consideration. 'When it's the Spider, the poor bastard in question falls right off the face of the world. And Capa Barsavi doesn't say a thing. Do you understand? He pretends that *nothing has happened*. So when you grasp that Barsavi doesn't fear the Duke . . . looks down on him quite a bit, actually . . . well, it follows that there's someone out there who *does* make him wet his breeches.'

'Oh. You mean other than the Grey King?'

Calo snorted. 'This Grey King mess will be over in a few months, Bug. One lone madman against three thousand knives, all answering to Barsavi – the Grey King is a walking corpse. The Spider isn't so easily got rid of.'

'Which,' said Locke, 'is exactly why we're hoping to see Don Salvara jump six feet in the air when he finds us waiting in his study. Because the bluebloods are no more comfortable with surprise visits from Midnighters than we are.'

'I hate to interrupt,' said Jean, 'but did you shave this time? Ah. Good.' With a small stick he applied a glistening smear of transparent paste to Locke's upper lip; Locke wrinkled his nose in disgust. With a few quick finger motions Jean placed the false moustache and pressed it home; in a second or two it was set there as firmly as if it had grown naturally.

'This gum is made from the inner hide of a wolf shark,' Jean explained for Bug's sake, 'and last time we used it, we forgot to pick up some of the dissolving spirit . . .'

'And I had to get rid of the moustache in a hurry,' said Locke.

'And damned if he didn't scream when Jean did the honours,' said Calo.

'Like a Sanza brother in an empty whorehouse!' Locke made a rude gesture at Calo; Calo mimed aiming and loosing a crossbow at him in return.

'Scar, moustache, hair; are we done here?' Jean packed the last of the disguise implements away in the masque box.

'That should do it, yes.' Locke stared at his reflection in the large mirror for a moment, and when he spoke next his voice had altered; subtly deeper, slightly rougher. His intonation was the bored humourlessness of a watch-sergeant dressing down a petty offender for the thousandth time in his career. 'Let's go tell a man he's got himself a problem with some thieves.'

5

'So,' said Don Lorenzo Salvara, 'you wish me to continue deliberately granting promissory notes to a man that you describe as the most capable thief in Camorr.'

'Respectfully, m'lord Salvara, that's what you would have done anyway, even without our intervention.'

When Locke spoke, there was no hint of Lukas Fehrwight in his voice or in his mannerisms; there was no trace of the Vadran merchant's restrained energy or stuffy dignity. This new creation had the fictional backing of the Duke's incontrovertible writ; he was the sort of man who could and would tease a Don while invading the sanctity of that Don's home. Such audacity could never be faked – Locke had to feel it, summon it from somewhere inside, cloak himself in arrogance as though it were an old familiar garment. Locke Lamora became a shadow in his own mind – he was a Midnighter, an officer in the Duke's silent constabulary. Locke's complicated lies were this new man's simple truth.

'The sums discussed could . . . easily total half my available holdings.'

'Then give our friend Fehrwright half your fortune, m'lord. Choke the Thorn on exactly what he desires. Promissory notes will tie him down, keep him moving back and forth between counting houses.'

'Counting houses that will throw my very real money after this phantom, you mean.'

'Yes. In the service of the Duke, no less. Take heart, m'lord Salvara. His Grace is entirely capable of compensating you for any loss you incur while aiding us in the capture of this man. In my opinion, though, the Thorn will have time to neither spend it nor move it very far, so your stolen money should be recovered before that even becomes necessary. You must also consider the aspects of the situation that are not strictly financial.'

'Meaning?'

'His Grace's gratitude for your assistance in bringing this matter to our desired outcome,' said Locke, 'balanced against his certain displeasure if any *reluctance* on your part should alert our thief to the net drawing tight around him.'

'Ah.' Don Salvara picked his optics up and re-settled them on his nose. 'With that I can hardly argue.'

'I will not be able to speak to you in public. No uniformed member of the Camorr watch will approach you for any reason related to this affair. If I speak to you at all, it must be at night, in secret.'

'Am I to tell Conté to keep refreshments at hand for men coming in through the windows? Shall I tell the Doña Sofia to send any Midnighters to my study if they should pop out of her wardrobe closet?'

'I give you my word any future appearances will be less alarming, my lord. My instructions were to impress upon you the seriousness of the situation and the full extent of our ability to . . . bypass obstacles. I assure you, I have no personal desire to anatagonise you any further. Re-securing your fortune will be the capstone to many years of hard work on my part.'

'And the Doña Sofia? Has your master dictated a part for her in this . . . counter-charade?'

'Your wife is a most extraordinary woman. By all means, inform her of our involvement. Tell her the truth about Lukas Fehrwight. Enlist her very capable aid in our endeavour. However,' Locke said, grinning malignantly, 'I do believe that I shall regretfully leave you the task of explaining this to her on your own, my lord.'

6

On the landward side of Camorr, armed men pace the old stone walls of the city, ever-vigilant for signs of bandits or hostile armies in the field. On the seaward side, watchtowers and war-galleys serve the same purpose.

At the guard stations on the periphery of the Alcegrante district, the city watch stands ready to protect the city's lesser nobility from the annoyance of having to see or smell any of their actual subjects against their wishes.

Locke and Calo crossed the Angevine just before midnight on the broad glass bridge called the Eldren Arch. This ornately carved span connected the western Alcegrante with the lush semi-public gardens of Twosilver Green, another spot where the insufficiently well-heeled were discouraged from lingering, often with whips and batons.

Tall cylinders of ruby-coloured glass shed alchemical light onto the wispy threads of mist that curled and wavered below the knees of their horses; the centre of the bridge was fifty feet above the water and the usual night fog reached no higher. The red lamps swayed gently within their black iron frames as the muggy Hangman's Wind spun them, and the two Gentlemen Bastards rode down into the Alcegrante with that eerie light surrounding them like a bloody aura.

'Hold there! State your name and business!'

At the point where the bridge met the Angevine's north shore there was a low wooden shack with oil-paper windows through which a pale white glow emanated. A single figure stood beside it, his yellow tabard turned to orange in the light of the bridge lamps. The speaker's words might have been bold but his voice was young and a little uncertain.

Locke smiled; the Alcegrante guard shacks always held two yellowjackets, but at this one the more senior had clearly sent his less-hardened partner out into the fog to do the actual work. So much the better – Locke pulled his precious sigil-wallet out of his black cloak as his horse cantered down beside the guard station.

'My name is immaterial.' Locke flipped the wallet open to allow the round-faced young city watchman a glimpse of the sigil. 'My business is that of His Grace, Duke Nicovante.'

'I . . . I see, sir.'

'I never came this way. We did not speak. Be sure that your fellow watchman understands this as well.'

The yellowjacket bowed and took a quick step back, as though afraid to stay too close. Locke smiled. Black-cloaked riders on black horses, looming out of darkness and mist . . . It was easy to laugh at such conceits in full daylight. But night had a way of lending weight to phantasms.

If Coin-Kisser's Row was where Camorr's money was put to use, the Alcegrante district was where it was put to rest. It was four connected islands, each a sort of tiered hill sloping up to the base of the plateau that held the Five Towers. Old money and new money mingled crazy-quilt fashion here in mazes of manor houses and private gardens. Here the merchants and money changers and shipbrokers looked down comfortably on the rest of the city; here the lesser nobility looked up covetously at the towers of the Five Families that ruled all.

Carriages clattered past from time to time, their black lacquered wood cabins trailing bobbing lanterns and banners proclaiming the arms of whoever travelled within. Some of these were guarded by teams of armed outriders in slashed doublets and polished breast-plates, this year's fashion for rented thugs. A few teams of horses wore harnesses spotted with miniature alchemical lights; these appeared at a distance looking like chains of fireflies bobbing in the mist.

Don Salvara's manor was a four-storey pillared rectangle, several centuries old and sagging a bit under the weight of its years, for it had been built entirely by human hands. It was a sort of island unto itself at the heart of the Isla Durona, westernmost neighbourhood of the Alcegrante, surrounded on all sides by a twelve-foot stone wall and enclosed by thick gardens. It shared no party walls with neighbouring manors. Amber lights burned behind the barred windows on the third floor.

Locke and Calo quietly dismounted in the alley adjacent to the manor's northern wall. Several long nights of careful reconnaissance by Locke and Bug had revealed the easiest routes over the alley wall and up the side of the Salvara manor. Dressed as they were, hidden by mist and darkness, they would be effectively invisible as soon as they could hop the outer wall and get off the street.

A moment of fortunate stillness fell upon them as Calo tied the horses to a weathered wooden post beside the garden wall; not a soul was in sight. Calo stroked his horse's thin mane.

'Hoist a glass or two in memory of us if we don't come back, love.'

Locke put his back against the base of the wall and cupped his hands. Calo set a foot in this makeshift stirrup and leapt upward, propelled by the mingled strength of his legs and Locke's arms. When he'd hoisted himself quietly and carefully atop the wall, he reached back down with both arms to hoist Locke up – the Sanza twin was as wiry as Locke was slender, and the operation went smoothly. In seconds they were both down in the wet, fragrant darkness of the garden, crouched motionless, listening.

The doors on the ground floor were all secured from within by intricate clockwork failsafes and steel bars – they simply could not be picked. But the rooftop . . . Well, those that weren't yet important enough to live with the constant threat of assassination often placed an inordinate degree of faith in high walls.

The two thieves went up the north face of the manor house, slowly and carefully, wedging hands and feet firmly into chinks in the warm, slick stone. The first and second floors were dark and quiet; the lights on the third floor were on the opposite side of the building. Hearts hammering with excitement, they hauled themselves up until they were just beneath the parapet of the roof, where they paused for a long interval, straining to catch any sound from within the manor that would hint at discovery.

The moons were stuffed away behind gauzy grey clouds; on their left the city was an arc of blurred jewel-lights shining through mist, and above them the impossible heights of the Five Towers stood like black shadows before the sky. The threads of light that burned on their parapets and in their windows enhanced rather than reduced their aura of menace; staring up at them from near the ground was a sure recipe for vertigo.

Locke was the first over the parapet; peering intently by the faint light falling from above, he planted his feet on a white-tiled pathway in the centre of the roof and kept them there. He was surrounded by the dark shapes of bushes, blossoms, small trees and vines – the roof was rich with the scent of vegetation and night soil. The street-level garden was a mundane affair, if well tended; this was the Doña Sofia's private botanical preserve.

Most alchemical botanists, in Locke's experience, were enthusiasts of bizarre poisons. He made sure his hood and cloak were cinched tight around him, and pulled his black neck-cloth up over his lower face.

Soft-stepping along the white path, Locke and Calo threaded their way through Sofia's garden more carefully than if they had been walking between streams of lamp oil with their cloaks on fire. At the garden's centre was a roof hatch with a simple tumbler-lock. Calo listened carefully at the door for two minutes with his favourite picks in his hands, then charmed the lock in less than ten seconds.

The fourth floor: Doña Sofia's workshop, a place where the two intruders wanted even less to stumble or linger than they had in her garden. Quiet as guilty husbands coming home from a late night of drinking, they stole through the dark rooms of laboratory apparatus and potted plants, scampering for the narrow stone stairs that led down to a side passage on the third floor.

The operations of the Salvara household were well known to the Gentlemen Bastards; the Don and Doña kept their private chambers on the third floor, across the hall from the Don's study. The second floor was the solar, a reception and dining hall that went mostly disused when the couple had no friends over to entertain. The first floor held the kitchen, several parlours, and the servants' quarters. In addition to Conté, the Salvaras kept a pair of middle-aged house-keepers, a cook, and a young boy who served as messenger and scullion. All of them would be asleep on the first floor; none of them posed even a fraction of the threat that Conté did.

This was the part of the scheme that couldn't be planned with any precision – they had to locate the old soldier and deal with him before they could have their intended conversation with Don Salvara.

Footsteps echoed from somewhere else on the floor; Locke, in the lead, crouched low and peeked round the left-hand corner. It turned out he was looking down the long passage that divided the third floor in half lengthwise; Don Salvara had left the door to his study open and was vanishing into the bedchamber. That door he closed firmly behind him – and a moment later the sound of a metal lock echoed down the hall.

'Serendipity,' whispered Locke, 'I suspect he'll be busy for quite some time in there. Light's still on in his study, so we know he's coming back out . . . Let's get the hard part over with.'

Locke and Calo slipped down the hallway, sweating now, but barely letting their heavy cloaks flutter as they moved. The long passage was tastefully decorated with hanging tapestries and shallow wall sconces in which tiny glow-glasses shed no more light than that of smouldering coals. Behind the heavy door to the Salvaras' chambers, someone laughed.

The stairwell at the far end of the passage was wide and circular; steps of white marble inset with mosaic-tile maps of Camorr spiralled down into the solar. Here Calo grabbed Locke by one sleeve, put a finger to his lips, and jerked his head downward.

'Listen,' he murmured.

Clang, clang . . . footsteps . . . *clang, clang.*

This sequence of noises was repeated several times, growing slightly louder each time. Locke grinned at Calo. Someone was pacing the solar, methodically checking the locks and the iron bars guarding each window. At this time of night there was only one man in the house who'd be doing such a thing.

Calo knelt beside the balustrade, just to the left of the top of the staircase. Anyone coming up the spiral stairs would have to pass directly beneath this position. He reached inside his cloak and took out a folded leather sack and a length of narrow-gauge rope woven from black silk; he then began to thread the silk line through and around the sack in some arcane fashion that Locke couldn't follow. Locke knelt just behind Calo and kept one eye on the long passage they'd come down – a reappearance of the Don was hardly likely yet, but the Benefactor was said to make colourful examples of incautious thieves.

Conté's light, steady footsteps echoed on the staircase beneath them.

In a fair fight the Don's man would almost certainly paint the walls with Locke and Calo's blood, so it stood to reason that this fight would have to be as unfair as possible. The moment the top of Conté's bald head appeared beneath him, Calo reached out between the balustrade posts and let his crimper's hood drop.

A crimper's hood, for those who've never had the occasion to be kidnapped and sold into slavery in one of the cities on the Iron Sea, looks a bit like a tent as it flutters quickly downward, borne by weights sewn into its bottom edges. Air pushes its flaps outward just before it drops down around its target's head and settles on his shoulders. Conté gave a startled jerk as Calo yanked the black silk cord, instantly cinching the hood closed around his neck.

Anyone with any real presence of mind could probably reach up and fumble such a hood loose in a matter of seconds, which is why the interior is inevitably painted with large amounts of some sweet-scented fuming narcotic, purchased from a black apothecary. Knowing the nature of the man they were attempting to subdue, Locke and Calo had spent nearly thirty crowns on the stuff Conté was breathing just now, and Locke fervently wished him much joy of it.

One panic-breath inside the airtight hood; that would be enough to drop any ordinary person in his or her tracks. But as Locke flew down the stairs to catch Conté's body, he saw that the man was still somehow upright, clawing at the hood – disoriented and weakened, most definitely, but still awake. A quick rap on the solar plexus – that would open his mouth and speed the drug on its way. Locke stepped in to deliver the blow, wrapping one hand around Conte's neck just beneath the crimper's hood. This nearly blew the entire game.

Conté's arms flashed up and broke Locke's lackadaisical

choke-hold before it even began; the man's left arm snaked out to entangle Locke's right, and then Conté punched him – once, twice, three times; vicious jabs in his own stomach and solar plexus. With his guts an exploding constellation of pain, Locke sank down against his would-be victim, struggling for balance. Conté brought his right knee up in a blow that should have knocked Locke's teeth out of his ears at high speed, but the drug was finally, thankfully smothering the old soldier's will to be ornery. The knee barely grazed Locke's chin; instead, the booted foot attached to it caught him in the groin and knocked him backwards. His head bounced against the hard marble of the stairs, somewhat cushioned by the cloth of his hood; Locke lay there, gasping for breath, still hanging awkwardly by one of the hooded man's arms.

Calo appeared at that instant, having dropped the line that cinched his crimper's hood and dashed down the staircase. He slipped one foot behind Conté's increasingly wobbly legs and pushed the man down the stairs, holding him by the front of his doublet to keep the fall relatively quiet. Once Conté was head down and prone, Calo punched him mercilessly between the legs – once, then again when the man's legs twitched feebly, and then again, which yielded no response. The hood had finally done its work. With Conté temporarily disposed of, Calo turned to Locke and tried to help him to a sitting position, but Locke waved him off.

'What sort of state are you in?' Calo whispered.

'As though I'm with child, and the little bastard is trying to cut his way out with an axe.' Chest heaving, Locke tore his black mask down off his face, lest he vomit inside it and create an unconcealable mess.

While Locke gulped deep breaths and tried to control his shuddering, Calo crouched back down beside Conté and tore the hood off, briskly waving away the sickly-sweet aroma of the leather bag's contents. He carefully folded the hood up, slipped it into his cloak, and then dragged Conté up a few steps.

'Calo.' Locke coughed. 'My disguise – damaged?'

'Not that I can see. Looks like he didn't do anything that shows, provided you can walk without a slouch. Stay here a moment.'

Calo slipped down to the foot of the stairs and took a peek around the darkened solar; soft city light fell through the barred windows, faintly illuminating a long table and a number of glass cases on the walls holding plates and unidentifiable knick-knacks. Not another soul was in sight, and not a sound could be heard from below.

When Calo returned, Locke had pushed himself up on his knees and hands; Conté slumbered beside him with a look of comical bliss on his craggy face.

'Oh, he's not going to keep that expression when he wakes up.' Calo waved a pair of thin, leather-padded brass knuckles at Locke, then made them vanish up his sleeves with a graceful flourish. 'I had my footpad's little friends on when I knocked him around that last time.'

'Well, I for one have no expressions of sympathy to spare, since he kicked my balls hard enough to make them permanent residents of my lungs.' Locke tried to push himself up off his hands and failed; Calo caught him under his right arm and eased him up until he was kneeling, shakily, on his knees alone.

'You've got your breath back, at least. Can you actually walk?'

'I can stumble, I think. I'll be hunched over for a while. Give me a few minutes and I think I can pretend nothing's wrong. At least until we're out of here.'

Calo assisted Locke back up the stairs to the third floor. Leaving him there to keep watch, he then began quietly, slowly to drag Conté up the same way. The Don's man didn't actually weigh all that much.

Embarrassed and eager to make himself useful again, Locke pulled two lengths of tough cord out of his own cloak and bound Conté's feet and hands with them; he folded a handkerchief three times and used it as a gag. Locke pulled Conté's knives out of their sheaths and passed them to Calo, who stashed them within his cloak.

The Don's study door still hung open, shedding warm light into the passage; the bedchamber door remained locked tight.

'I pray you both may be gifted with a demand and an endurance well beyond your usual expectations, m'lord and lady,' whispered Calo. 'Your household thieves would appreciate a short break before continuing with their duties for the evening.'

Calo grasped Conté beneath his arms, and Locke, slouched in obvious pain, nonetheless grabbed the man's feet when Calo began to drag him all by himself. With tedious stealth, they retraced their steps and deposited the unconscious bodyguard around the far bend in the corridor, just beside the stairs leading back up to the fourth-floor laboratories.

The Don's study was a most welcome sight when they finally stole in a few minutes later. Locke settled into a deeply cushioned leather armchair on the left-hand wall, while Calo took up a standing guard position. More laughter could be heard, faintly, from across the hall.

'We could be here quite a while,' said Calo.

'The gods are merciful.' Locke stared at the Don's tall glass-fronted liquor cabinet, even more impressive than the one his pleasure barge carried. 'I'd pour us a draught or six, but I don't think it would be in character.'

They waited ten minutes, fifteen, twenty. Locke breathed steadily and deeply, and concentrated on ignoring the throbbing ache that seemed to fill his guts from top to bottom. Yet when the two thieves heard the door across the hallway unbolting, Locke leapt to his feet, standing tall, pretending that his balls didn't feel like clay jugs dropped onto cobblestones from a great height. He cinched his black mask back on and willed a wave of perfect arrogance to claim him from the inside out.

As Father Chains had once said, the best disguises were those that were poured out of the heart rather than painted on the face.

Calo kissed the back of his left hand through his own mask and winked.

Don Lorenzo Salvara walked into his study whistling, lightly dressed and completely unarmed.

'Close the door,' said Locke, and his voice was steady, rich with the absolute presumption of command. 'Have a seat, m'lord, and don't bother calling for your man. Your man is indisposed.'

7

An hour past midnight, two men left the Alcegrante district via the Eldren Arch. They wore black cloaks and had black horses; one of them rode with a leisurely air, while the other led his horse on foot, walking in a curiously bow-legged fashion.

'Un-fucking believable,' said Calo. 'It really did work out just as you planned. It's a pity we can't brag about this to anyone. Our biggest score ever, and all we had to do was tell our mark exactly what we were doing to him.'

'And get kicked around a bit,' muttered Locke.

'Yeah, sorry about that. What a beast that man was, eh? Take comfort that he'll feel the same way when he opens his eyes again.'

'How very comforting. If reassurances could dull pain, nobody would ever go to the trouble of pressing grapes.'

'By the Crooked Warden, I never heard such self-pity dripping from the mouth of a wealthy man. Cheer up! Richer and cleverer than everyone else, right?'

'Richer and cleverer and walking very funny, yes.'

The pair of thieves made their way south through Twosilver Green, towards the first of the stops where they would gradually lose their horses and shed their black clothes, until they were finally heading back to the Temple District dressed as common labourers. They nodded companionably at patrols of yellowjackets stomping about in the mist with lanterns swaying on pike-poles to light their way. Not once were they given any reason to glance up.

The fluttering shadow that trailed them on their way through the streets and alleys was quieter than a small child's breath; swift and graceful, it swooped from rooftop to rooftop in their wake, following their actions with absolute single-mindedness. When they slipped back into the Temple District, it beat its wings and rose into the darkness in a lazy spiralling circle until it was up above the mists of Camorr and lost against the grey haze of the low-hanging clouds.

INTERLUDE:
The Last Mistake

I

Locke's first experience with the mirror wine of Tal Verrar had even more of an effect on the boy's malnourished body than Chains had expected. Locke spent most of the next day tossing and turning on his cot, his head pounding and his eyes unable to bear anything but the most gentle spark of light.

'It's a fever,' Locke muttered into his sweat-soaked blanket.

'It's a hangover.' Chains ran a hand through the boy's hair and patted his back. 'My fault, really. The Sanza twins are natural liquor sponges. I shouldn't have let you live up to their standard on your first night with us. No work for you today.'

'Liquor does this? Even after you're sober?'

'A cruel joke, isn't it? The gods put a price tag on everything, it seems. Unless you're drinking Austershalin brandy.'

'Auffershallow?'

'Austershalin. From Emberlain. Among its many other virtues, it doesn't cause a hangover. Some sort of alchemical component in the vineyard soil. Expensive stuff.'

Falselight came after many hours of half-sleep, and Locke found himself able to walk once again, though the brain within his skull felt like it was attempting to dig a hole down through his neck and escape. Chains insisted that they would still be visiting Capa Barsavi ('The only people who break appointments with him are the ones that live in glass towers and have their pictures on coins, and even they think twice.') though he consented to allow Locke a more comfortable means of transportation.

It turned out that the House of Perelandro had a small stable tucked around the back, and in this smelly little stall there lived a Gentled goat. 'He's got no name,' Chains said as he set Locke atop the creature's back. 'I just couldn't bring myself to give him one, since he wouldn't answer to it anyway.'

Locke had never developed the instinctive revulsion most boys and girls felt for Gentled animals; he'd already seen too much ugliness in his life to care about the occasional empty stare from a docile, milky-eyed creature.

There is a substance called Wraithstone, a chalky white material found in certain remote mountain caverns. The stuff doesn't occur naturally; it is found only in conjunction with glass-lined tunnels presumably abandoned by the Eldren, the same unsettling race that built Camorr, ages past. In its solid state, Wraithstone is tasteless, nearly odourless, and inert. It must be burned to activate its unique properties.

Physikers have begun to identify the various means and channels by which poisons attack the bodies of the living; *this* one stills the heart, while *this* one thins the blood, and still others damage the

133

stomach or the intestines. Wraithstone smoke poisons nothing physical; what it does is burn out personality itself. Ambition, stubbornness, pluck, spirit, drive – all of these things fade with just a few breaths of the arcane haze. Accidental exposure to small amounts can leave a man listless for weeks; anything more than that and the effect will be permanent. Victims remain alive but entirely unconcerned by anything – they don't respond to their names, or to their friends, or to mortal danger. They can be prodded into eating or excreting or carrying something, and little else. The pale white cataracts that grow to fill their eyes are an outward expression of the emptiness that takes hold in their hearts and their minds.

Once, in the time of the Therin Throne, the process was used to punish criminals, but it has been centuries since any civilised Therin city-state allowed the use of Wraithstone on men and women. A society that still hangs children for petty theft and feeds prisoners to sea creatures finds the results too disquieting to bear.

Gentling, therefore, is reserved for animals – mostly beasts of burden intended for urban service. The cramped confines of a hazard-rich city like Camorr are ideally suited to the process; Gentled ponies may be trusted never to throw the children of the wealthy. Gentled horses and mules may be trusted never to kick their handlers or dump expensive cargoes into a canal. A burlap sack with a bit of the white stone and a slow-smouldering match is placed over an animal's muzzle, and the human handlers retreat to fresh air. A few minutes later the creature's eyes are the colour of new milk, and it will never do anything on its own initiative again.

But Locke had a throbbing headache, and he was just getting used to the idea that he was a murderer *and* a resident of a private glass fairyland, and the eerily mechanical behaviour of his goat didn't bother him at all.

'This temple will be exactly where I left it when I return later this evening,' said Father Chains as he finished dressing for his venture outside; the Eyeless Priest had vanished entirely, to be replaced by a hale man of middle years and moderate means. His beard and his hair had been touched up with some sort of brown dye; his vest and cheap cotton-lined half-cloak hung loosely over a cream-coloured shirt with no ties or cravats.

'Exactly where you left it,' said one of the Sanzas.

134

'And not burned down or *anything*,' said the other.

'If you boys can burn down stone and Elderglass, the gods have higher aspirations for you than a place as my apprentices. Do behave. I'm taking Locke to get his, ahh . . .'

Chains glanced sideways at the Lamora boy. He then mimed taking a drink, and held his jaw afterwards as though in pain.

'Ohhhhhhhhhhhh,' said Calo and Galdo in pitch-perfect unison.

'Indeed.' Chains settled a little round leather cap on his head and took the reins of Locke's goat. 'Wait up for us. This should be interesting, to say the least.'

2

'This Capa Barsavi,' Locke said as Chains led the nameless goat across one of the narrow glass arches between the Fauria and Coin-Kisser's Row, 'my old master told me about him, I think.'

'You're quite right. That time you got the Elderglass Vine burned down, I believe.'

'Ah. You know about that.'

'Well, once your old master started telling me about you, he just sort of . . . didn't shut up for several hours.'

'If I'm your *pezon*, are you Barsavi's *pezon*?'

'That's a plain neat description of our relationship, yes. All the Right People are Barsavi's soldiers. His eyes, his ears, his agents, his subjects. His *pezon*. Barsavi is . . . a particular sort of friend. I did some things for him, back when he was coming to power. We rose together, you might say – I got special consideration and he got the, ah, entire city.'

'Special consideration?'

It was as pleasant a night for a stroll as Camorr ever produced during the summer. A hard rain had fallen not an hour before, and the fresh mist that spread its tendrils around buildings like the grasping hands of spectral giants was slightly cooler than usual, and its odour wasn't yet saturated with the redolence of silt and dead fish and human waste. Other people were few and far between on Coin-Kisser's Row after Falselight, so Locke and Chains spoke fairly freely.

'Special consideration. I've got *the distance*. Which means . . .

Well, there are a hundred gangs in Camorr, Locke. A hundred and more. Certainly I can't remember them all. Some of them are too new or too unruly for Capa Barsavi to trust as well as he might. So he keeps a close eye on them – insists on frequent reports, plants men in them, reins their actions in tightly. Those of us that don't suffer such scrutiny' – Chains pointed to himself, then to Locke – 'are sort of presumed to be doing things honestly until proven otherwise. We follow his rules and pay him a cut of our take and he thinks he can more or less trust us to get it right. No audits, no spies, no bullshit. "The distance." It's a privilege worth paying for.'

Chains stuck a hand in one of his cloak pockets; there was the pleasing jingle of coins. 'I've got a little show of respect for him right here, in fact. Four tenths of this week's take from the charity kettle of Perelandro.'

'More than a hundred gangs, you said?'

'This city has more gangs than it has foul odours, boy. Some of them are older than many families on the Alcegrante, and some of them have stricter rituals than some of the priestly orders. Hell, at one point there were nearly thirty Capas, and each one had four or five gangs under his thumb.'

'Thirty Capas? All like Capa Barsavi?'

'Yes and no. Yes, that they ran gangs and gave orders and cut men open from cock to eyeballs when they got angry; no, that they were anything like Barsavi otherwise. Five years ago there were the thirty bosses I talked about. Thirty little kingdoms, all fighting and thieving and spilling each other's guts in the street. All at war with the yellowjackets, who used to kill twenty men a week. In slow weeks.

'Then Capa Barsavi walked in from Tal Verrar. Used to be a scholar at the Therin Collegium, if you can believe it. Taught *rhetoric*. He got a few gangs under his thumb and he started cutting. Not like a back-alley slasher, but more like a physiker cutting out a chancre. When Barsavi took out another Capa, he took their gangs, too. But he didn't lean on them if he didn't have to. He gave them full territories and let them choose their own *garristas* and he cut them in on his take.

'So – five years ago, there were thirty. Four years ago there were ten. Three years ago there was one. Capa Barsavi and his hundred gangs. The whole city, all the Right People, present company included, in his pocket. No more open war across the bloody canals. No more platoons of thieves getting strung up all at once at the Palace of Patience – nowadays they have to do them two or three at a time.'

'Because of the Secret Peace? The one I broke?'

'The one you broke, yes. Good guess, presuming I'd know about that. Yes, my boy, it's the key to Barsavi's peculiar success. What it comes down to is, he has a standing agreement with the Duke, handled through one of the Duke's agents. The gangs of Camorr don't touch the nobles; we don't lay a finger on ships or drays or crates that have a legitimate coat of arms on them. In exchange, Barsavi is the actual ruler of a few of the city's more charming points: Catchfire, the Narrows, the Dregs, the Wooden Waste, the Snare, and parts of the docks. Plus the city watch are much more . . . relaxed than they ought to be.'

'So we can rob anyone who isn't a noble?'

'Or a yellowjacket, yes. We can have the merchants and the money changers and the incoming and the outgoing. There's more money passing through Camorr than any other city on this coast, boy. Hundreds of ships a week; thousands of sailors and officers. We don't have any problem laying off the nobility.'

'Doesn't that make the merchants and the money changers and the other people angry?'

'It might if they knew about it. That's why there's that word "Secret" in front of "Peace". And that's why Camorr's such a lovely, fine, safe place to live; you really only need to worry about losing your money if you don't have much of it in the first place.'

'Oh,' said Locke, fingering his little shark's-tooth necklace. 'Okay. But now I wonder . . . you said my old master bought and paid for, um, killing me. Will you get in trouble with Barsavi for not . . . killing me?'

Chains laughed. 'Why would I be taking you to see him if that'd get me in trouble, boy? No, the death-mark's mine to use, or not, as I see fit. I bought it. Don't you see? The Capa doesn't care if we actually use 'em, only that we acknowledge that the *power* of granting life or death is his. Sort of like a tax only he can collect. You see?'

Locke allowed himself to be trundled along silently for a few minutes, absorbing all of this. His aching head made the scale of what was going on a bit difficult to grasp.

'Let me tell you a story,' said Father Chains after a while. 'A story that will let you know just what sort of man you're going to meet and swear fealty to this evening. Once upon a time, when Capa Barsavi's hold on the city was very new and very delicate, it was an open secret that a pack of his *garristas* was plotting to get rid of him just as soon as the chance presented itself. And they were very alert for his counter-moves, see; they'd helped him take over the city, and they knew how he worked.

'So they made sure he couldn't get all of them at once; if he tried to cut some throats the gangs would scatter and warn each other and it'd be a bloody mess, a long war. He made no open move. And the rumours of their disloyalty intensified.

'Capa Barsavi would receive visitors in his hall – it's still out there in the Wooden Waste; it used to be a big Verrari hulk, one of those fat wide galleons they used for hauling troops. It's just anchored there now, a sort of makeshift palace. He calls it the Floating Grave. Well, at the Floating Grave, he made a big show of putting down this one large carpet from Ashmere, a really lovely thing, the sort of cloth the Duke would hang on a wall for safe keeping. And he made sure that everyone around him knew how much he liked that carpet.

'It got so his court could tell what he was going to do to a visitor by watching that carpet; if there was going to be blood, that carpet would be rolled up and packed away safe. Without exception. Months went by. Carpet up, carpet down. Carpet up, carpet down. Sometimes men who got called to see him would try to run the moment they saw bare floor beneath his feet, which of course was as good as admitting wrongdoing out loud.

'Anyhow. Back to his problem *garristas*. Not one of them was stupid enough to enter the Floating Grave without a gang at his back, or to be caught alone with Barsavi. His rule was still too uncertain at this point for him to just throw a tantrum about it. So he waited . . . and then one night he invited nine of his trouble-some *garristas* to dinner. Not all the troublemakers, of course, but the cleverest and the toughest, and the ones with the biggest gangs. And their spies brought back word that that lovely embroidered carpet, the Capa's prize possession, was rolled out on the floor for everyone to see, with a banquet table on top of it and more food than the gods themselves had ever seen.

'So those stupid bastards, they figured Barsavi was serious, that he really wanted to talk. They thought he was scared and they expected negotiations in good faith, so they didn't bring their gangs or make alternative plans. They thought they'd won.

'You can imagine,' said Chains, 'just how surprised they were when they sat down at their chairs on that beautiful carpet, and fifty of Barsavi's men piled into the room with crossbows and shot those poor idiots so full of bolts that a porcupine in heat would have taken any one of them home and fucked him. If there was a drop of blood that wasn't on the carpet, it was on the *ceiling*. You get my meaning?'

'Yeah – so the carpet was ruined?'

'And then some. Barsavi knew how to *create* expectations, Locke, and how to use those expectations to mislead those who would harm him. They figured his strange obsession was a guarantee of their lives. Turns out there are just some enemies numerous enough and powerful enough to be worth losing a damn carpet over.'

Chains pointed ahead of them and to the south.

'That's the man waiting to talk to you about half a mile that way. I would strongly recommend cultivating a civil tongue.'

3

The Last Mistake was a place where the underworld of Camorr bubbled to the surface; a flat-out crooks' tavern where Right People of every sort could drink and speak freely of their business, where respectable citizens stood out like serpents in a nursery and were quickly escorted out the door by mean-looking, thick-armed men with very small imaginations.

Here entire gangs would come to drink and arrange jobs and just show themselves off. In their cups, men would argue loudly about the best way to strangle someone from behind, and the best sorts of poisons to use in wine or food. They would openly proclaim the folly of the Duke's court, or his taxation schemes, or his diplomatic arrangements with the other cities of the Iron Sea. They would refight entire battles with dice and fragments of chicken bones as their armies, loudly announcing how *they* would have turned left when Duke Nicovante had gone right, how *they* would have stood fast when the five thousand blackened iron spears of the Mad Count's rebellion had come surging down Godsgate Hill towards them.

Not one of them, no matter how far doused in liquor or Gaze or the strange narcotic powders of Jerem, no matter what feats of generalship or statecraft he credited himself with the foresight to bring off, would dare suggest to Capa Vencarlo Barsavi that he should ever change so much as a single button on his waistcoat.

4

The Broken Tower is a landmark of Camorr, jutting ninety feet skyward at the very northern tip of the Snare, that low and crowded district where sailors from a hundred ports of call are passed from bar to alehouse to gaming den and back again on a nightly basis. They are shaken through a sieve of tavern keepers, whores, muggers, dicers, cobble-cogs and other low tricksters until their pockets are as empty as their heads are heavy, and they can be dumped on ship to nurse their new hangovers and diseases. They come in like the tide and go out like the tide, leaving nothing but a residue of copper and silver (and occasionally blood) to mark their passing.

Although human arts are inadequate to the task of cracking Elderglass, the Broken Tower was found in its current state when humans first settled Camorr, stealing in among the ruins of an older civilisation. Great gashes mar the alien glass and stone of the tower's upper storeys; these discontinuities have been somewhat covered over with wood and paint and other human materials. The sturdiness of the whole affair is hardly in question, but the repairs are not beautiful, and the rooms for let on the upper six floors are some of the least desirable in the city, as they are accessible only by rank upon rank of narrow, twisting exterior stairs, a spindly wooden frame that sways nauseatingly in high winds. Most of the residents are young bravos from various gangs to whom the insane accommodation is a strange badge of honour.

The Last Mistake fills the ground floor at the wide base of the Broken Tower, and after the fall of Falselight it rarely has less than a hundred patrons in it at any given time. Locke clung tightly to the back of Father Chains' half-cloak as the older man elbowed his way past the crowd at the door. The outward rush of the bar's air was full of smells Locke knew quite well: a hundred kinds of liquor and the breath of the men and women drinking them, sweat both stale and fresh, piss and vomit, spiced pomanders and wet wool, the sharp bite of ginger and the acrid fog of tobacco.

'Can we trust that boy to watch our goat?' Locke cried above the din.

'Of course, of course.' Chains made some elaborate hand-sign in greeting to a group of men arm-wrestling just inside the bar's main room; those not locked in bitter struggles grinned and waved back. 'First, it's his job. Second, I paid well. Third, only a crazy person would want to steal a Gentled goat.'

The Last Mistake was a sort of monument to the failure of human artifice at critical moments; its walls were covered in a bewildering variety of souvenirs, each one telling a visual tale that ended with the verdict 'Not quite good enough.' Above the bar was a full suit of armour, a square hole punched through at the left breast by a crossbow quarrel. Broken swords and split helmets covered the walls, along with fragments of oars, masts, spars, and tatters of sails. One of the bar's proudest claims was that it had secured a memento of every ship that had foundered within sight of Camorr in the past seventy years.

Into this mess Father Chains dragged Locke Lamora, like a launch being towed at the stern of a huge galleon. On the south wall of the bar was an elevated alcove, given privacy by partially drawn curtains. Men and women stood at attention here, their hard eyes constantly sweeping across the crowd, their hands never far from the weapons they carried openly and ostentatiously – daggers, darts, brass and wooden clubs, short swords, hatchets, and even crossbows, ranging from slender alleypieces to big horse-murderers that looked (to Locke's wide eyes) as though they could knock holes in stone.

One of these guards stopped Father Chains and the two exchanged a few whispered words; another guard was dispatched into the curtained alcove while the first eyed Chains warily. A few moments later the second guard reappeared and beckoned; thus it was that Locke was led for the first time into the presence of Vencarlo Barsavi, Capa of Camorr, who sat in a plain chair beside a plain table. Several minions stood against the wall behind him, close enough to respond to a summons but far enough to be out of earshot for quiet conversation.

Barsavi was a big man, as wide as Chains but obviously a bit younger; his oiled black hair was pulled tight behind his neck, and his beards curved off his chin like three braided whipcords of hair, one atop the other, neatly layered. These beards flew about when Barsavi turned his round head, and they looked quite thick enough to sting if they struck bare skin.

Barsavi was dressed in a coat, vest, breeches and boots of some odd dark leather that seemed unusually thick and stiff even to Locke's untrained eyes; after a moment, the boy realised it must be shark hide. The strangely uneven white buttons that dotted his vest and his cuffs and held his layered red silk cravats in place . . . they were human teeth.

Sitting on Barsavi's lap, staring intently at Locke, was a girl about his own age with short tangled dark hair and a heart-shaped face. She too wore a curious outfit; her dress was white embroidered silk, fit for any noble's daughter, while the little boots that dangled beneath her hem were black leather, shod with iron, bearing sharpened steel kicking-spikes at the heels and the toes.

'So this is the boy,' said Barsavi in a deep, slightly nasal voice with the pleasant hint of a Verrari accent. 'The industrious little boy who so confounded our dear Thiefmaker.'

'The very one, your honour, now happily confounding myself and my other wards.' Chains reached behind himself and pushed Locke out from behind his legs. 'May I present Locke Lamora, late of Shades' Hill, now an initiate of Perelandro?'

'Or *some* god, anyway, eh?' Barsavi chuckled and held out a small wooden box that had been resting on the table near his arm. 'It's always nice to see you when your sight miraculously returns, Chains. Have a smoke. They're Jeremite blackroot, extra fine, just rolled this week.'

'I can't say no to that, Ven.' Chains accepted a tightly rolled sheaf of tobacco in red paper. While the two men bent over a flickering taper to light up (Chains dropped his little bag of coins on the table at the same time), the girl seemed to come to some sort of decision about Locke.

'He's a very ugly little boy, Father. He looks like a skeleton.'

Capa Barsavi coughed out his first few puffs of smoke, the corners of his mouth crinkling upward. 'And you're a very inconsiderate little girl, my dear!' The Capa drew on his sheaf once more and exhaled a straight stream of translucent smoke; the stuff was pleasantly mellow and carried the slightest hint of burnt vanilla. 'You must forgive my daughter Nazca; I am helpless to deny her indulgences, and she has acquired the manners of a pirate princess. Particularly now that we are all afraid to come near her deadly new boots.'

'I am *never* unarmed,' said the little girl, kicking up her heels a few times to emphasise the point.

'And poor Locke most certainly is not ugly, my darling; what he bears is clearly the mark of Shades' Hill. A month in Chains' keeping and he'll be as round and fit as a catapult stone.'

'Hmmph.' The girl continued to stare down at him for a few seconds, then suddenly looked up at her father, absently toying with one of his braided beards while she did so. 'Are you making him a *pezon*, Father?'

'Chains and I did have that in mind, sweetling, yes.'

'Hmmph. Then I want another brandy while you're doing the ceremony.'

Capa Barsavi's eyes narrowed; seams deepened by habitual suspicion drew in around his flinty grey stare. 'You've already had your two brandies for the night, darling; your mother will murder me if I let you have another. Ask one of the men to get you a beer.'

'But I prefer—'

'What you prefer, little tyrant, has nothing to do with what I am *telling* you. For the rest of the night, you can drink beer or air; the choice is entirely yours.'

'Hmmph. I'll have beer, then.' Barsavi reached out to lift her down, but she hopped off his lap just ahead of his thick-fingered, heavily calloused hands. Her heels went *clack-clack-clack* on the hardwood floor of the alcove as she ran to some minion of preference to give her order.

'And if just one more of my men gets kicked in the shin, darling, you're going to wear reed sandals for a month, I promise,' Barsavi shouted after her, then took another drag of tobacco and turned back to Locke and Chains. 'She's a keg of fire-oil, that one. Last week she refused to sleep at all unless we let her keep a little garrotte under her pillows. "Just like daddy's bodyguards", she said. I don't think her brothers yet realise that the next Capa Barsavi might wear summer dresses and bonnets.'

'I can see why you might have been amused by the Thiefmaker's stories about our boy here,' Chains said, clasping both of Locke's shoulders as he spoke.

'Of course. I have become very hard to shock since my children grew above the tops of my knees. But you're not here to discuss them – you've brought me this little man so he can take his last oath as a *pezon*. A few years early, it seems. Come here, Locke.'

Capa Barsavi reached out with his right hand and turned Locke's head slightly upward by the chin, staring down into Locke's eyes as he spoke. 'How old are you, Locke Lamora? Six? Seven? Already responsible for a breach of the Peace, a burnt-down tavern, and six or seven deaths.' The Capa smirked. 'I have assassins five times your age who should be so bold. Has Chains told you the way it is, with my city and my laws?'

Locke nodded.

'You know that once you take this oath I can't go easy on you, ever again. You've had your time to be reckless. If Chains needs to put you down, he will. If I tell him to put you down, he will.'

Again, Locke nodded. Nazca returned to her father's side, sipping from a tarred leather ale-jack; she stared at Locke over the rim of this drinking vessel, which she had to clutch in both hands.

Capa Barsavi snapped his fingers; one of the toadies in the background vanished through a curtain. 'Then I'm not going to bore you with any more threats, Locke. This night, you're a man. You will do a man's work and suffer a man's fate if you cross your brothers and sisters. You will be one of us, one of the Right People; you'll receive the words and the signs and you'll use them discreetly. As Chains, your *garrista*, is sworn to me, so you are sworn to me, through him. I am your *garrista* above all *garristas*. I am the only Duke of Camorr you will ever acknowledge. Bend your knee.'

Locke knelt before Barsavi; the Capa held out his left hand, palm down. He wore an ornate ring of black pearl in a white iron setting;

144

nestled inside the pearl by some arcane process was a speck of red that had to be blood.

'Kiss the ring of the Capa of Camorr.'

Locke did so; the pearl was cool beneath his dry lips.

'Speak the name of the man to whom you have sworn your oath.'

'Capa Barsavi,' Locke whispered. At that moment, the Capa's underling returned to the alcove, and handed his master a small crystal tumbler filled with dull brown liquid.

'Now,' said Barsavi. 'As has every one of my *pezon*, you will drink my toast.' From one of the pockets of his waistcoat the Capa drew a shark's tooth slightly larger than the death-mark Locke wore around his neck. Barsavi dropped the tooth into the tumbler and swirled it around a few times. He then handed the tumbler to Locke. 'It's dark-sugar rum from the Sea of Brass. Drink the entire thing, including the tooth. But don't swallow the tooth, whatever you do. Keep it in your mouth. Draw it out after all the liquor is gone. And try not to cut yourself.'

Locke's nose smarted from the stinging aroma of hard liquor that wafted from the tumbler, and his stomach lurched, but he ground his jaws together and stared down at the slightly distorted shape of the tooth within the rum. Silently praying to his new Benefactor to save him from embarrassment, he dashed the contents of the glass into his mouth, tooth and all.

Swallowing was not as easy as he'd hoped – he held the tooth against the roof of his mouth with his tongue, gingerly, feeling its sharp points scrape against the back of his upper front teeth. The liquor burned; he began to swallow in small gulps that soon turned into wheezing coughs. After a few interminable seconds, he shuddered and sucked down the last of the rum, relieved that he had held the tooth carefully in place—

It twisted in his mouth. Twisted physically, as though wrenched by an unseen hand, and scored a burning slash across the inside of his left cheek. Locke cried out, coughed, and spat out the tooth – it lay there in his open palm, flecked with spit and blood.

'Ahhhhh,' said Capa Barsavi as he plucked the tooth up and slipped it back into his waistcoat, blood and all. 'So you see – you are bound by an oath of blood to my service. My tooth has tasted of your life, and your life is mine. So let us not be strangers, Locke

Lamora. Let us be Capa and *pezon*, as the Crooked Warden intended.'

At a gesture from Barsavi, Locke stumbled to his feet, already inwardly cursing the now-familiar sensation of liquor rapidly going to his head. His stomach was empty from the day's hangover; the room was already swaying a bit around him. When he set eyes on Nazca once again, he saw that she was smiling at him above her ale-jack with the air of smarmy tolerance the older children in Shades' Hill had once shown to him and his compatriots in Streets.

Before he knew what he was doing, Locke bent his knee to her as well.

'If you're the next Capa Barsavi,' he said rapidly, 'I should swear to serve you, too. I do. Madam. Madam Nazca. I mean Madam Barsavi.'

The girl took a step back. 'I already have servants, boy. I have *assassins*. My father has a hundred gangs and two thousand knives!'

'Nazca Belonna Jenavais Angeliza de Barsavi!' her father thundered. 'Now it seems you only grasp the value of *strong* men as servants. In time, you will come to see the value of *gracious* ones as well. You shame me.'

Nonplussed, the girl glanced back and forth between Locke and her father several times. Her cheeks slowly turned red. After a few more moments of pouting consideration, she stiffly held out her ale-jack to Locke.

'You may have some of my beer.'

Locke responded as though this were the deepest honour ever conferred upon him, realising (though hardly in so many words) all the while that the liquor was somehow running a sort of rump parliament in his brain that had overruled his usual cautious social interactions – especially with girls. Her beer was bitter dark stuff, slightly salted. She drank like a Verrari. Locke took two sips to be polite, then handed it back to her, bowing in a rather noodle-necked fashion as he did so. She was too flustered to say anything in return, so she merely nodded.

'Ha! Excellent!' Capa Barsavi chomped on his slender cigar in mirth. 'Your first *pezon*! Of course, both of your brothers are going to want some just as soon as they hear about this.'

The trip home was a muggy, misty blur to Locke; he clung to the neck of his Gentled goat while Chains led them back north towards the Temple District, frequently cackling to himself.

'Oh, my boy,' he muttered. 'My dear, dear charming sot of a boy. It was all bullshit, you realise.'

'What?'

'The shark's tooth. Capa Barsavi had a Bondsmage enchant that thing for him in Karthain years ago. Nobody can swallow it without cutting themselves. He's been carrying it around ever since; all those years he spent studying Throne Therin theatre have given him a substantial fetish for the dramatic.'

'So it wasn't . . . like, fate, or the gods, or anything like that.'

'No, it was just a shark's tooth with a tiny bit of sorcery. A good trick, I have to admit.' Chains rubbed his own cheek in sympathy and remembrance. 'No, Locke, you don't belong to Barsavi. He's good enough for what he is, a good ally to have on your side, and a man that you must appear to obey at all times. But he certainly doesn't own you. In the end, neither do I.'

'So I don't have to—'

'Obey the Secret Peace? Be a good little *pezon*? Only for pretend, Locke. Only to keep the wolves from the door. Unless your eyes and ears have been stitched shut with rawhide these past two days, by now you must have realised that I intend you and Calo and Galdo and Sabetha to be nothing less,' Chains confided through a feral grin, 'than a fucking ballista bolt right through the heart of Vencarlo's precious Secret Peace.'

BOOK II
COMPLICATION

I can add colours to the chameleon,
Change shapes with Proteus for advantages,
And set the murderous Machiavel to school

Shakespeare, *Henry VI, Part 3*

CHAPTER FOUR

At the Court of Capa Barsavi

I

'Nineteen thousand,' said Bug, 'nine hundred and twenty. That's all of it. Can I please *kill* myself now?'

'What? I'd have thought you'd be enthusiastic about helping us tally the loot, Bug.' Jean sat cross-legged in the middle of the dining area in the glass cellar beneath the House of Perelandro; the table and chairs had been moved away to make room for a vast quantity of gold coins, stacked into little glittering mounds that circled Jean and Bug, nearly walling them in completely.

'You didn't tell me you'd be hauling it home in tyrins.'

'Well, white iron is dear. Nobody's going to hand out five thousand crowns in it, and nobody's going to be dumb enough to carry it around like that. Meraggio's makes all of its big payouts in tyrins.'

There was a rattling noise from the entrance passage to the cellar, and then Locke appeared around the corner, dressed as Lukas Fehrwight. He whipped his false optics off, loosened his cravats, and shrugged out of his wool coat, letting it fall unceremoniously to the floor. His face was flushed, and he was waving a piece of folded parchment affixed with a blue wax seal.

'Seventy-five hundred more, my boys! I told him we'd found four likely galleons, but that we were already having cash-flow problems – bribes to be paid, crews to be called back and sobered up, officers to be placated, other cargo-shippers to be chased off – and he just handed it right over, smiling all the while. Gods. I should've thought this scam up two years ago. We don't even have to bother setting up fake ships and paperwork and so forth, because Salvara *knows* the Fehrwight part of the game is a lie. There's nothing for us to do except relax and count the money.'

'If it's so relaxing, why don't *you* count it, then?' Bug jumped to his feet and leaned backwards until his back and his neck made a series of little popping noises.

'I'd be happy to, Bug!' Locke took a bottle of red wine out of a wooden cupboard and poured himself half a glass, then watered it from a brass pitcher of lukewarm rainwater until it was a soft pink. 'And tomorrow you can play Lukas Fehrwight. I'm sure Don Salvara would never notice any difference. Is it all here?'

'Five thousand crowns in the form of twenty thousand tyrins,' said Jean, 'less eighty for clerking fees and guards and a rented dray to haul it from Meraggio's.'

The Gentlemen Bastards used a simple substitution scheme for hauling large quantities of valuables to their hideout at the House of Perelandro: at a series of quick stops, strongboxes of coins would vanish from one wagon and barrels marked as common food or drink would roll away on another. Even a decrepit little temple needed a steady infusion of basic supplies.

'Well,' said Locke, 'let me get rid of poor Master Fehrwight's clothes and I'll give you a hand dumping it all in the vault.'

There were actually three vaults tucked away at the rear of the cellar, behind the sleeping quarters. Two of them were wide Elderglass-coated shafts that went down about ten feet; their original purpose was unknown. With simple wooden doors mounted on hinges set atop them, they resembled nothing so much as miniature grain-storage towers sunk into the earth and filled to a substantial depth with coins of every sort.

Silver and gold in large quantities went into the shafts; narrow wooden shelves around the periphery of the vault room held small bags or piles of more readily useful currency. There were cheap purses of copper barons, fine leather wallets with tight rolls of silver solons, and small bowls of clipped half-copper bits, all of them set out for the rapid taking for any scam or need one of the gang might face. There were even little stacks of foreign coinage – marks from the Kingdom of the Seven Marrows, solari from Tal Verrar, and so forth.

Even back in the days of Father Chains there had been no locks on the shafts or on the room that held them. This was not merely because the Gentlemen Bastards trusted one another (and they did), nor because the existence of their luxurious cellar was a closely-guarded secret (and it certainly was). The primary reason was one of practicality – not one of them, Calo or Galdo or Locke or Jean or Bug, had anything they could conceivably do with their steadily growing pile of precious metal.

Outside of Capa Barsavi, they had to be the wealthiest thieves in Camorr; the little parchment ledger on one of the shelves would list more than forty-three *thousand* full crowns when Don Salvara's second note was turned into cold coin. They were as wealthy as the man they were currently robbing, and far wealthier than most of his peers, and some of the most famous merchant houses and combines in the entire city.

Yet as far as anyone knew, the Gentlemen Bastards were an unassuming gang of ordinary sneak thieves; competent and discreet enough, steady earners but hardly shooting stars. They could live comfortably for ten crowns apiece each year, and to spend much more than that would invite the most unwelcome scrutiny imaginable, from every authority in Camorr, legal or otherwise.

In four years they'd brought off three huge scores and were currently working on their fourth; for four years the vast majority of the money had simply been counted and thrown down into the darkness of the vaults.

The truth was, Chains had trained them superbly for the task of relieving Camorr's nobility of the burden of some of its accumulated wealth, but had perhaps neglected to discuss possible uses for the sums involved. Other than financing further theft, the Gentlemen Bastards really had no idea what they were eventually going to do with it all.

Their tithe to Capa Barsavi averaged about a crown a week.

2

'Rejoice!' cried Calo as he appeared in the kitchen, just as Locke and Jean were moving the dining table back to its customary position. 'The Sanza brothers are returned!'

'I do wonder,' said Jean, 'if that particular combination of words has ever been uttered by anyone before now.'

'Only in the chambers of unattached young ladies across the city,' said Galdo, as he set a small burlap sack down on the table. Locke shook it open and perused the contents – a few lockets set with semi-precious stones, a set of moderately well-crafted silver forks and knives, and an assortment of rings ranging from cheap engraved copper to one made of threaded gold and platinum, set with flecks of obsidian and diamond.

'Oh, very nice,' said Locke. 'Very likely. Jean, would you pick out a few more bits from the Bullshit Box, and get me . . . twenty solons, right?'

'Twenty's good and proper.'

While Locke gestured for Calo and Galdo to help him set chairs back in place around the dining table, Jean walked back to the vault room, where there was a tall, narrow wooden chest tucked against the left-hand wall. He threw back the lid on its creaky hinges, and began rummaging inside, a thoughtful expression on his face.

The Bullshit Box was filled to a depth of about two feet with a glittering pile of jewellery, knick-knacks, household items and decorative gewgaws. There were crystal statues, mirrors in carved ivory frames, necklaces and rings, candle-holders in five kinds of precious metal. There were even a few bottles of drugs and alchemical draughts, wrapped in felt to cushion them and marked with little paper labels.

Since the Gentlemen Bastards could hardly tell the Capa about the true nature of their operations, and since they had neither the time nor the inclination to actually break houses and clamber down chimneys, the Bullshit Box was one of the pillars of their ongoing deception. They topped it off once or twice a year, going on buying sprees in the pawnshops and markets of Talisham or Ashmere, where they could get whatever they needed openly. They supplemented it only slightly and carefully with goods picked up in Camorr, usually things stolen on a whim by the Sanzas or secured by Bug as part of his continuing education.

Jean selected a pair of silver wine goblets, a pair of gold-framed optics inside a fine leather case and one of the little wrapped bottles. Clutching all of this carefully in one hand, he then counted twenty small silver coins off a shelf, kicked the Bullshit Box shut, and hurried back out to the dining room. Bug had rejoined the group and was ostentatiously walking a solon across the knuckles of his right hand; he'd mastered the trick only weeks previously, after long months of watching the Sanzas, who could each do both hands at once, reversing directions in perfect unison.

'Let us say,' said Jean, 'that we have had a somewhat slothful week. Nobody expects much from second-storey men when the nights are wet like this anyway; we might look out of place if we hauled in too much. Surely His Honour will understand.'

'Of course,' said Locke. 'Quite a reasonable thought.' He reached out and took the felt-wrapped bottle for close examination; his handwritten label identified it as sugared milk of opium, a rich ladies' vice made from dried Jeremite poppies. He removed the label and the felt, then tucked the faceted glass bottle with its brass stopper into the burlap sack. The rest of the loot followed.

'Right! Now, is there any speck of Lukas Fehrwight still clinging to me? Any make-up or mummery?' He stuck out his arms and twirled several times; Jean and the Sanzas assured him that he was entirely Locke Lamora for the moment.

'Well, then, if we're all our proper selves, let's go pay our taxes.' Locke lifted the sack of 'stolen' items and tossed it casually to Bug; the boy yelped, dropped his coin, and caught the sack with a muffled clatter of shaken metal.

'Good for my moral education, I suppose?'

'No,' said Locke, 'this time I really am just being a lazy old bastard. At least you won't have to work the bargepole.'

3

It was the third hour of the afternoon when they set out from the Temple of Perelandro, via their assorted escape tunnels and side entrances. A warm drizzle was falling from the sky, which was neatly divided as though by some ruler and stylus of the gods – low dark clouds filled the north, while the sun was just starting downward in the bright, clear south-west. The pleasant scent of fresh rain on hot stone welled up everywhere, briefly washing the usual city miasmas from the air. The Gentlemen Bastards gathered once again at the south-western docks of the Temple District, where they hailed a gondola-for-hire.

The boat was long and shallow and heavily weathered, with a freshly killed rat lashed to the bow spar just beneath a small wooden idol of Iono; this was allegedly a peerless ward against capsizing and other misfortunes. The poleman perched at the stern like a parrot in his red-and-orange-striped cotton jacket, protected from the rain by a broad-brimmed straw hat that drooped out past his skinny shoulders. He turned out to be a canal-jumper and purse-cutter of their acquaintance, Nervous Vitale Vento of the Grey Faces gang.

Vitale rigged a mildewy leather umbrella to keep some of the drizzle off his passengers, and then began to pole them smoothly east between the high stone banks of the Temple District and the overgrown lushness of the Mara Camorrazza. The Mara had once been a garden maze for a rich governor of the Therin Throne era; now it was largely abandoned by the city watch and haunted by cutpurses. The only reason honest folk even ventured into its dangerous green passages was that it was the heart of a network of footbridges connecting eight other islands.

Jean settled in to read from a very small volume of verse he'd tucked into his belt, while Bug continued practising his coin manipulation, albeit with a copper-piece that would look much less incongruous in public. Locke and the Sanza brothers talked shop with Vitale, whose job, in part, was to mark particularly lightly guarded or heavily loaded cargo barges for the attention of his fellows. On several occasions he made hand-signals to concealed watchers on shore while the Gentlemen Bastards politely pretended not to notice.

They drew close to Shades' Hill; even by day those heights were steeped in gloom. By chance the rain stiffened and the old kingdom of tombs grew blurred behind a haze of mist. Vitale swung the boat to the right. Soon he was pushing them southward between Shades' Hill and the Narrows, aided by the current of the seaward-flowing canal, now alive with the spreading ripples of raindrops.

Traffic grew steadily thinner and less reputable on the canal as they sped south; they were passing from the open rule of the Duke of Camorr to the private dominion of Capa Barsavi. On the left the forges of the Coalsmoke district were sending up columns of blackness, mushrooming and thinning out beneath the press of the rain. The Duke's Wind would push it all down over Ashfall, the most ill-looking island in the city, where gangs and squatters contended for space in the mouldering, smoke-darkened villas of an opulent age now centuries past.

A northbound barge moved past on their left, wafting forth the stench of old shit and new death. What looked to be an entire team of dead horses was lying in the barge, attended by half a dozen knackers; some were slicing at the corpses with arm-length serrated blades while others were frantically unrolling and adjusting blood-stained tarps beneath the rain.

A more appropriate match for the sight and stink of the Cauldron, no Camorri could have asked for. If the Dregs were poverty-wracked, the Snare disreputable, the Mara Camorrazza openly dangerous and Ashfall dirty and falling apart, the Cauldron was all of these things with a compound interest of human desperation. It smelled something like a keg of bad beer overturned in a mortician's storage room on a hot summer day; most of this district's dead never made it as far as the paupers' holes dug by convicts on the hills of the Beggars' Barrow. They were tipped into canals or simply burned. No yellowjackets had dared enter the Cauldron save in platoons even before the Secret Peace; no temples had been maintained here for fifty years or more. Barsavi's least sophisticated and restrained gangs ruled the Cauldron's blocks; brawlers' taverns and Gaze dens and itinerant gambling circles were packed wall to wall with families crammed into ratholes.

It was commonly held that one in three of Camorr's Right People were crammed into the Cauldron, a thousand wasters and cut-throats bickering endlessly and terrorising their neighbours, accomplishing nothing and going nowhere. Locke had come out of Catchfire, Jean from the comfortable North Corner. Calo and Galdo had been Dregs boys prior to their stay in Shades' Hill. Only Bug had come out of the Cauldron, and he had never once spoken of it, not in the several years he'd been a Gentleman Bastard.

He was staring at it now, at the sagging docks and layered tenements, at the clothes flapping on washlines, soaking up water. The streets were brown with the unhealthy haze of sodden cookfires. Its flood walls were crumbling, its Elderglass mostly buried in grime and piles of stone. Bug's coin had ceased to flow across his knuckles and stood still on the back of his left hand.

A few minutes later, Locke was privately relieved to slip past the heart of the Cauldron and reach the high, thin breakwater that marked the eastern edge of the Wooden Waste. Camorr's maritime graveyard seemed positively cheerful by comparison once the boat had put the Cauldron to its stern.

A graveyard it was; a wide sheltered bay, larger than the Shifting Market, filled with the bobbing, undulating wrecks of hundreds of ships and boats. They floated hull up and hull down, anchored as well as drifting freely, some merely rotting while others were torn open from collisions or catapult stones. A layer of smaller wooden debris floated on the water between the wrecks like scum on cold soup, ebbing and resurging with the tide. When Falselight fell this junk would sometimes ripple with the unseen passage of creatures drawn in from Camorr Bay. While tall iron gates shuttered every major canal against intrusion, the Wooden Waste was open to the sea on its south side.

At the heart of the Waste floated a fat, dismasted hulk, sixty yards long and nearly half as wide, anchored firmly in place by chains leading down into the water, two at the bow and two at the stern. Camorr had never built anything so heavy and ungainly; that vessel was one of the more optimistic products of the arsenals of distant Tal Verrar, just as Chains had told Locke many years before. Wide silk awnings now covered its high, flat castle decks; beneath those canopies parties could be thrown that rivalled the pleasure pavilions of Jerem for their decadence, but at the moment the decks were clear of everything but the cloaked shapes of armed men, peering out through the rain – Locke could see at least a dozen of them, standing in groups of two or three with longbows and crossbows at hand.

There was human movement here and there throughout the Waste. Some of the less damaged vessels housed families of squatters, and some of them were being openly used as observation points by more teams of hard-looking men. Vitale navigated through the twisting channels between larger wrecks, carefully making obvious hand gestures at the men on guard whenever the gondola passed them.

'Grey King got another one last night,' he muttered, straining against his pole. 'Lots of twitchy boys with big murder-pieces keeping an eye on us right now, that's for damn sure.'

'Another one?' Calo narrowed his eyes. 'We hadn't heard yet. Who got it?'

'Tall Tesso, from the Full Crowns. They found him up in Rustwater, hanging in an old shop. Strung up, balls cut off. His blood ran out, is what it looked like.'

Locke and Jean exchanged a glance and Nervous Vitale grunted. 'Acquainted, were you?'

'After a fashion,' said Locke, 'and some time ago.'

Locke pondered. Tesso was – had been – *garrista* of the Full Crowns, one of Barsavi's big earners and a close friend of the Capa's younger son, Pachero. Nobody in Camorr should have been able to touch him (save only Barsavi and the Spider), yet that damned invisible lunatic calling himself the Grey King had touched him in no uncertain terms.

'That's six,' said Jean, 'isn't it?'

'Seven,' said Locke. 'There haven't been this many dead gods-damned *garristas* since you and I were five years old.'

'Heh,' said Vitale, 'and to think I once envied you, Lamora, even with this tiny little gang of yours.'

Locke glared at him, willing the puzzle to come together in his head and not quite succeeding. Seven gang leaders in two months; all of them given the distance, but otherwise having little in common. Locke had long taken comfort in his own lack of importance to the Capa's affairs, but now he began to wonder. Might he be on someone's list? Did he have some unguessed value to Barsavi that the Grey King might want to end with a crossbow bolt? How many others were between him and that bolt?

'Damn,' said Jean. 'As if things needed to get more complicated.'

'Maybe we should take care of . . . current business.' Galdo had shifted against the side of the gondola and was looking around as he spoke. 'And then maybe we should get lost for a while. See Tal Verrar or Talisham . . . or at least get *you* out, Locke.'

'Nonsense.' Locke spat over the side of the boat. 'Sorry, Galdo. I know it seems like wisdom, but do the sums. The Capa would never forgive our running out in his desperate hour. He'd rescind the distance and put us under the thumb of the most graceless pig-hearted motherfucker he could find. We can't run as long as he stays. Hell, Nazca would break my knees with a mallet before anyone else did anything.'

'You have my sympathy, boys.' Vitale shifted his pole from hand to hand, using precise shoves to warp the gondola around a chunk of debris too large to ignore. 'Canal work ain't easy, but at least nobody wants me dead for more'n the usual reasons. Did you want me to leave you at the Grave or at the quay?'

'We need to see Harza,' said Locke.

'Oh, he's sure to be in a rare mood today.' Vitale began poling hard for the northern edge of the Waste, where a few stone docks jutted out before a row of shops and rooming houses. 'The quay it is, then.'

4

The pawnshop of No-Hope Harza was one of the major landmarks of the domain of Capa Barsavi; while there were many shops that paid slightly more and a great many with less surly proprietors, there were no others located a bare stone's throw from the very seat of the Capa's power. Right People cashing in their creatively acquired loot with Harza could be sure that their presence would be reported to Barsavi. It never hurt to reinforce the impression that one was an active, responsible thief.

'Oh, of course,' said the old Vadran as Jean held the barred and armoured door open for the other four Gentlemen Bastards. 'Figures only the least important *garristas* would dare show their faces on a day like this. Come in, my ill-looking sons of Camorri bitches. Rub your oily Therin fingers on my lovely merchandise. Drip water on my beautiful floors.'

Harza's shop was always closed up like a coffin, rain or shine; dusty canvas sheets were drawn over the narrow, barred windows and the place smelled of silver polish, mildew, stale incense, and old sweat. Harza himself was a snow-skinned old man with wide, watery eyes; every seam and wrinkle on his face seemed to be steadily sliding towards the ground, as though he'd been shaped by a slightly drunk god who'd pressed the mortal clay just a little too far down. No-Hope had earned his moniker with his firm policy against extending credit or loaning coin; Calo had once remarked that if he ever took an arrow in the skull he'd sit around and wait for it to fall out on its own before he'd pay a physiker for so much as a gauze scrap.

In the right-hand corner of the shop a burly, bored-looking

young man with cheap brass on all of his fingers and greasy ringlets hanging in his eyes shifted his position on the tall wooden stool he occupied. An iron-studded club swung from a loop at his belt, and he nodded slowly at the visitors, unsmiling, as though they were too stupid to comprehend his function.

'Locke Lamora,' said Harza. 'Perfume bottles and ladies' small-clothes. Tableware and drinking goblets. Scraped and dented metal I can't sell to anyone with any class ever again. You breakers and second-storey boys think you're so clever. You'd steal shit from a dog's arsehole if you had the right sort of bag to bring it home with you.'

'Funny you should say that, Harza, because this bag here' – Locke plucked the burlap sack from Bug's hands and held it up – 'happens to contain—'

'Something other than dogshit; I can hear it jingling. Give over and let's see if you accidentally brought in anything worth buying.'

Harza's nostrils flared as he opened the sack and slid it along a leather pad atop his shop counter, gently spilling the contents. The appraisal of stolen goods seemed to be the only form of sensual gratification left to the old man, and he dived into the task with enthusiasm, long crooked fingers wiggling.

'Crap.' He lifted the three lockets secured by Calo and Galdo. 'Fucking alchemical paste and river agates. Not fit for goat feed. Two coppers apiece.'

'Harsh,' said Locke.

'Fair,' said Harza. 'Yes or no?'

'Seven coppers for all three.'

'Two times three is six,' said Harza. 'Say yes or go twist a shark's balls, for all I care.'

'I suppose I'll say yes, then.'

'Hmmm.' Harza perused the silver goblets Jean had selected from the Bullshit Box. 'Dented, of course. You idiots never see a pretty silver thing you don't want to stuff inside a scratchy fucking bag. I suppose I can polish them and send them upriver. One solon three coppers apiece.'

'One solon four per,' said Locke.

'Three solons one copper total.'

'Fine.'

'And this.' Harza picked up the bottle of opium milk, unscrewed

161

the cap, sniffed, grunted to himself, and sealed the vial once again. 'Worth more than your life, but I can't hardly do much with it. Fussy bitches like to make their own or get an alchemist to do it for them; they never buy premixed from strangers. Maybe I can pass it off on some poor fucker that needs a vacation from grapes or Gaze. Three solons three barons.'

'Four solons two.'

'The gods wouldn't get four and two from me. Morgante himself with a flaming sword and ten naked virgins yanking at my breeches might get four solons one. You get three and four and that's final.'

'Fine. And only because we're in a hurry.'

Harza was keeping a running total with a goose quill and a scrap of parchment; he ran his fingers over the small pile of cheap rings from Calo and Galdo and laughed. 'You can't be serious. This crap is as welcome as a pile of severed dog cocks.'

'Oh come on . . .'

'I could sell the dog cocks to the knackers, at least.' Harza flung the brass and copper rings at the Gentlemen Bastards one by one. 'I'm serious. Don't bring that crap around; I've got boxes on boxes of the fucking things I won't sell this side of death.'

He came to the threaded gold and platinum ring with the diamond and obsidian chips. 'Mmmm. This one signifies, at least. Five solons flat. Gold's real but the platinum's cheap Verrari shit, genuine as a glass eye. And I crap bigger diamonds five or six times weekly.'

'Seven and three,' said Locke. 'I went to pains to get that particular piece.'

'I have to pay extra because your arse and your brains switched places at birth? I think not; if that were the case I'd have heard about it before. Take your five and consider yourself lucky.'

'I can assure you, Harza, that nobody who comes to this shop considers himself particularly . . .'

And so it went – the apparently summary judgement, the two-way flow of abuse, the grudging assent from Locke, and the gnashing of the old man's remaining teeth when he took each item and set it down behind the counter. In short order Harza was sweeping the last few things he had no interest in back into the burlap sack.

'Well, sweetmeats, looks as though we're quits at sixteen solons five. I suppose it beats driving a shit-wagon, doesn't it?'

'Or running a pawnshop, yes,' said Locke.

'Very amusing!' cried the old man as he counted out sixteen tarnished silver coins and five smaller copper discs. 'I give you the legendary lost treasure of Camorr. Grab your things and fuck off until next week. Assuming the Grey King doesn't get you first.'

5

The rain had faded back to a drizzle when they emerged from Harza's shop, giggling to themselves. 'Chains used to claim that there's no freedom quite like the freedom of being constantly underestimated,' said Locke.

'Gods, yes.' Calo rolled his eyes and stuck out his tongue. 'If we were any freer we'd float away into the sky and fly like the birds.'

From the northern edge of the Wooden Waste, a long, high wooden bridge, wide enough for two people, ran straight out to the Capa's waterbound fortress. There were four men on guard at the shore, standing around in the open with weapons clearly visible under their lightweight oilcloaks. Locke surmised there would be at least as many concealed nearby, within easy crossbow shot. He made the month's proper hand signs as he approached with his gang behind him; everyone here knew each other, but the formalities were non-negotiable, especially at a time like this.

'Hello, Lamora.' The oldest man in the guard detail, a wiry fellow with faded shark tattoos running up his neck and his cheeks all the way to his temples, reached out and shook; they grasped left forearms. 'Heard about Tesso?'

'Yeah, hello yourself, Bernell. One of the Grey Faces told us on the way down. So it's true? Strung up, balls, the whole bit?'

'Balls, the whole bit. You can imagine how the boss feels about it. Speaking of which, Nazca left orders. Just this morning – next time you came by she wanted to see you. Said not to let you pay your taxes until she'd had a word. You are here for taxes, right?'

Locke shook a little grey purse; Jean's twenty solons plus Harza's sixteen and change. 'Here to do our civic duty, indeed.'

'Good. Not passing many folks for any other reason. Look, I

163

know you've got the distance and Nazca's a friend and all, but maybe you want to take it *real* easy today, right? Lots of *pezon* around, obvious and not so obvious. Tight as it's ever been. Capa's making inquiries with some of the Full Crowns right now, as regards their whereabouts last night.'

'Inquiries?'

'In the grand old fashion. So mind your manners and don't make any sudden moves, right?'

'Savvy,' said Locke. 'Thanks for the warning.'

'No trouble. Crossbow bolts cost money. Shame to waste them on the likes of you.'

Bernell waved them through and they strolled down the wooden walkway, which was about a hundred yards long. It led to the stern of the wide, motionless vessel, where the timbers of the outer hull had been cut away and replaced with a pair of iron-reinforced witchwood doors. Another pair of guards stood here, one male and one female, the dark circles under their eyes evident. The woman knocked four times at their approach, and the doors swung inward just a few seconds later. Stifling a yawn, the female guard leaned back against the outer wall and pulled the hood of her oilcloak up over her head. The dark clouds were sweeping in from the north, and the heat of the sun was starting to fade.

The reception hall of the Floating Grave was nearly four times Locke's height, as the cramped horizontal decks of the old galleon had been torn out long ago, save for the upper castle and waist decks, which now served as roofs. The floor and walls were coffee-coloured hardwood; the bulkheads were hung with black and red tapestries on which sharks'-teeth border patterns were embroidered in gold and silver thread.

A half-dozen bravos stood facing the Gentlemen Bastards, crossbows levelled. These men and women wore leather bracers and doublets over silk tunics reinforced with light metal bands; their necks were girded with stiff leather collars. A more genteel foyer would have been decorated with glow-lamps and flower arrangements; the walls of this one held wicker baskets of crossbow quarrels and racks of spare blades.

'Ease up,' said a young woman standing behind the gaggle of guards, 'I know they're suspicious as hell, but I don't see a Grey King among 'em.'

She wore men's breeches and a loose black silk blouse with billowing sleeves under a ribbed leather duelling harness that looked to have seen more use than storage. Her iron-shod boots (a taste she had never lost) clicked against the floor as she stepped between the sentries. Her welcoming smile didn't quite reach all the way to her eyes, which darted nervously behind the lenses of her plain, black-rimmed optics.

'My apologies for the reception, loves,' said Nazca Barsavi, addressing all the Bastards but placing a hand on Locke's left shoulder. She was a full two inches taller than he was. 'And I know it's cramped in here, but I need the four of you to wait around. *Garristas* only. Papa's in a mood.'

There was a muffled scream from behind the doors that led to the inner chambers of the Floating Grave, followed by the faint murmur of raised voices – shouts, cursing, another scream.

Nazca rubbed her temples, pushed back a few stray curls of her black hair, and sighed. 'He's making a vigorous case for . . . full disclosure from some of the Full Crowns. He's got Sage Kindness in there with him.'

'Thirteen gods,' said Calo. 'We're happy to wait.'

'Indeed.' Galdo reached into his coat and pulled out a slightly soggy deck of playing cards. 'We can certainly keep ourselves entertained out here. Indefinitely, if need be.'

At the sight of a Sanza brother offering cards, every guard in the room took a step back; some of them visibly struggled against the idea of raising their crossbows again.

'Oh, not you fuckers too,' said Galdo, 'look, those stories are all bullshit. Everyone else at that table was just having a very unlucky night . . .'

Past the wide, heavy doors was a short passage, unguarded and empty. Nazca slid the foyer doors closed behind herself and Locke, then turned to him. She reached and slicked back his wet hair. The corners of her mouth were turned down. 'Hello, *pezon*. I see you haven't been eating.'

'I eat regular meals.'

'You should try eating for quantity as well as consistency. I believe I once mentioned that you looked like a skeleton.'

'And I believe I'd never before seen a seven-year-old girl pushy-drunk in public.'

'Well. Perhaps I was pushy-drunk then, but today I'm just pushy. Papa's in a bad way, Locke. I wanted to see you before you saw him – he has some . . . things he wishes to discuss with you. I want you to know that whatever he asks, I don't want you to . . . for my sake . . . Well, please just agree. Please him, do you understand?'

'No *garrista* who loves life has ever tried to do otherwise. You think I'm inclined to walk in on a day like today and deliberately twist his breeches? If your father says "Bark like a dog," I say "What breed, your honour?"'

'I know. Forgive me. But my point is this. He's not himself. He's afraid now, Locke. Absolutely, genuinely afraid. He was morose when mother died, but damn, now he's . . . he's crying out in his sleep. Taking wine and laudanum every day to keep his temper in check. Used to be I was the only one not allowed to leave the Grave, but now he wants Anjais and Pachero to stay here, too. Fifty guards on duty at all times. The Duke's life is more carefree. Papa and my brothers were up shouting about it all night.'

'Well, ah . . . look, I'm sorry, but I don't think I can help you with that. But just what is it you think he's going to ask me?'

Nazca stared at him, mouth half-open as though she were preparing to speak. She seemed to think better of it, and her lips compressed back into a frown.

'Dammit, Nazca, I'd jump in the bay and try to blackjack a shark for you if you wanted it, really, but you'd have to tell me how big it was and how hungry it was first. Savvy?'

'Yes, look, I just . . . It'll be less awkward if he does it himself. Just remember what I said. Hear him. Please him, and you and I can sort things out later. If we get a later.'

' "If we get a later?" Nazca, you're worrying me.'

'This is it, Locke. This is the bad one. The Grey King is finally getting to Papa. Tesso had sixty knives, any ten of which were with him all the time. Tesso was deep into Papa's good graces; there were big plans for him in the near future. But Papa's had things his way for so long I . . . I can't rightly say if he knows what to do about this. So he just wants to fold everything up and hide us here. Siege mentality.'

'Hmmmm.' Locke sighed. 'I can't say that what he's done so far is imprudent, Nazca. He's—'

166

'Papa's mad if he thinks he can just keep us all here, locked up in this fortress forever! He used to be at the Last Mistake half the nights of the week. He used to walk the docks, walk the Mara, walk the Narrows any time he pleased. He used to throw out coppers at the Procession of the Shades. The Duke of Camorr can lock himself in his privy and rule legitimately; the Capa of Camorr cannot. He needs to be seen.'

'And risk assassination by the Grey King.'

'Locke, I've been stuck inside this fucking wooden tub for two months, and I tell you, we're no safer here than we would be bathing naked at the dirtiest fountain in the darkest courtyard in the Cauldron.' Nazca had folded her arms beneath her breasts so tightly that her leather cuirass creaked. 'How can we be? Who is this Grey King, and where is he, and who are his men? We don't have a *single* idea – and yet this man reaches out and kills our people at leisure, at random, however he sees fit. Something is wrong. He has resources we don't understand.'

'He's clever and he's lucky. Neither of those things lasts forever; trust me.'

'Not just clever and lucky, Locke. I agree there are limits to both. So what does he have up his sleeves? What does he know? Or who? If we are not betrayed, then it must be that we are overmatched. And I am reasonably certain that we are not yet betrayed.'

'Not yet?'

'Don't play stupid with me, Locke. Business could go on after a fashion with Papa and myself cooped up here. But if he won't let Anjais and Pachero out to run the city, the whole regime will go to hell. The *garristas* might think it prudent for some of the Barsavis to stay here; they'll think it cowardice for *all* of us to hide. And they won't just talk behind our backs, they'll actively court another Capa. Maybe a pack of new Capas. Or maybe the Grey King.'

'So, naturally, your brothers will never let him trap them here.'

'Depends on how mad and crazy the old man gets, Locke. But even if they stay free to roam, that's only the lesser part of the problem solved. We are, again, overmatched. Three thousand knives at our command and the ghost still has the twist on us.'

'What do you suspect? Sorcery?'

'I suspect everything. They say the Grey King can kill a man with just a touch. They say that blades won't cut him. I suspect the gods themselves. And so my brothers think I'm crazy.

'When they look at the situation all they see is a regular war. They think we can just outlast it, lock the old man and the baby sister up and wait until we know where to hit back. But I don't see that. I see a cat with his paw over a mouse's tail. And if the cat's claws haven't come out yet, it's not because of anything the mouse has done. Don't you get it?'

'Nazca, I know . . . Look, you're agitated. I'll listen. I'm a stone. You can yell at me all you like. But what can I do for you? I'm just a thief. I'm your father's littlest thief; if there's a gang smaller than mine I'll go play cards in a wolf shark's mouth, I—'

'I need you to start helping me calm Papa down, Locke. I need him back to something resembling his normal self so I can get him to take my points seriously. That's why I'm asking you to go in there and take pains to please him. *Especially* please him. Show him a loyal *garrista* who does whatever he's told, the moment he's told. When he starts to lay reasonable plans for the future again, I'll know he's coming back to a state of mind I can deal with.'

At the end of the short passage was another set of heavy wooden doors, nearly identical to the ones that led back to the reception hall. These doors, however, were barred and locked with an elaborate Verrari clockwork device attached to crossbars of polished iron. A dozen keyholes were visible in the lock-box at the centre of the doors. Nazca withdrew two keys that hung on a chain around her neck and briefly put her body between Locke and the doors so he couldn't see the apertures she chose. There was a cascading series of clicks and the noise of machinery within the doors; one by one the hidden bolts un-shot themselves and the gleaming crossbars slid open until the doors finally cracked open in the middle.

Another scream, loud and vivid without the closed door to muffle it, sounded from the room beyond.

'It's worse than it sounds,' said Nazca.

'I know what the Sage does for your father, Nazca.'

'Knowing's one thing. Usually Sage just does one or two at a time. Papa's got the bastard working wholesale today.'

6

'I've made it clear that I don't enjoy this,' said Capa Barsavi, 'so why do you force me to persist?'

The dark-haired young man was secured to a wooden rack. He hung upside down with metal shackles around his legs, with his arms tied down at their maximum extension. The Capa's heavy fist slammed into the prisoner's side just beneath his armpit; the sound was like a hammer slapping meat. Droplets of sweat flew and the prisoner screamed, writhing against his restraints.

'Why do you insult me like this, Federico?' Another punch to the same spot, with the heavy old man's first two knuckles cruelly extended. 'Why don't you even have the courtesy to give me a convincing lie?' Capa Barsavi lashed Federico's throat with the flat of one hand; the prisoner gasped for breath, snorting wetly as blood and spit and sweat ran down into his nose.

The heart of the Floating Grave was something like an opulent ballroom with curving sides; warm amber light came from glass globes suspended on silver chains. Stairs ran to overhead galleries, and from these galleries to the silk-canopied deck of the old hulk. A small raised platform against the far wall held the broad wooden chair from which Barsavi usually received visitors. The room was tastefully decorated in a restrained and regal fashion, but today it stank of fear and sweat and soiled breeches.

The frame that held Federico folded down from the ceiling; an entire semicircle of the things could be pulled down at need for Barsavi occasionally did this sort of business in a volume that rewarded the standardisation of his procedures. Six were now empty and spattered with blood; only two still held prisoners.

The Capa looked up as Locke and Nazca entered; he nodded slightly and gestured for them to wait against the wall. Old Barsavi remained bullish, but he wore his years in plain view. He was rounder and softer now, his three braided grey beards backed by three wobbly chins. Dark circles cupped his eyes, and his cheeks were the unhealthy sort of red that came out of a bottle. Flushed with exertion, he had thrown off his overcoat and was working in his silk undertunic.

Standing nearby with folded arms were Anjais and Pachero Barsavi, Nazca's older brothers. Anjais was like a miniature version of the Capa, minus thirty years and two beards, while Pachero was of a kind with Nazca, tall and slender and curly-haired. Both of the brothers wore optics, for whatever eye trouble the old Madam Barsavi had borne had been passed to all three of her surviving children.

Leaning against the far wall were two women. They were not slender; their bare, tanned arms were corded with muscle and criss-crossed with scars, and while they radiated an air of almost feral good health they were well past the girlishness of early youth. Cheryn and Raiza Berangias, identical twins, were the greatest *contrarequialla* the city of Camorr had ever known. Performing only as a pair, they had given the Shifting Revel nearly a hundred performances against sharks, devilfish, death-lanterns, and other predators of the Iron Sea.

For nearly five years they had been Capa Barsavi's personal bodyguards and executioners. Their long, wild manes of smoke-black hair were tied back under nets of silver that jangled pleasantly with sharks' teeth. One tooth, it was said, for every man or woman the Berangias twins had killed in Barsavi's service.

Last but certainly not least alarming in this exclusive gathering was Sage Kindness, a round-headed man of moderate height and middle years. His short-cropped hair was the butter-yellow of certain Therin families from the westerly cities of Karthain and Lashain; his eyes always seemed to be wet with emotion, though his expression never changed. He was perhaps the most even-tempered man in Camorr; he could pull fingernails with the mellow disinterest of a man polishing boots. Capa Barsavi was a very capable torturer, but when he found himself stymied the Sage never disappointed him.

'He doesn't know anything!' The last prisoner, as yet untouched, hollered at the top of his voice as Barsavi slapped Federico around some more. 'Capa, your honour, please, none of us knows anything! Gods! None of us remembers!'

Barsavi stalked across the wooden floor and shut the second prisoner up by giving his windpipe a long, cruel squeeze. 'Were the questions addressed to you? Are you eager to get involved in the proceedings? You were quiet enough when I sent your other six friends down into the water. Why do you cry for this one?'

'Please,' the man sobbed, sucking in air as Barsavi lightened his

170

grip just enough to permit speech, 'please, there's no point. You must believe us, Capa Barsavi, please. We'd have told you anything you wanted if only we know. We don't remember! We just don't—'

The Capa silenced him with a vicious cuff across the face. For a moment the only sound in the room was the frightened sobbing and gasping of the two prisoners.

'I must believe you? I must do *nothing*, Julien. You serve me bullshit, and tell me it's steamed beef? So many of you, and you can't even come up with a decent story. A serious attempt to lie would still piss me off, but I could *understand* it. Instead you cry that you *don't remember*. You, the eight most powerful men in the Full Crowns, after Tesso himself. His chosen. His friends, his bodyguards, his loyal *pezon*. And you cry like babies to me about how you don't remember where any of you were last night, when Tesso just happened to *die*.'

'But that's just how it is, Capa Barsavi. Please, it's—'

'I ask you again, were you drinking last night?'

'No, not at all!'

'Were you smoking anything? All of you, together?'

'No, nothing like that. Certainly not . . . not together.'

'Gaze, then? A little something from Jerem's pervert alchemists? A little bliss from a powder?'

'Tesso never permitted—'

'Well then.' Barsavi drove a fist into Julien's solar plexus, almost casually. While the man gasped in pain, Barsavi turned away and held up his arms with theatrical joviality. 'Since we've eliminated every possible earthly explanation for such dereliction of duty, short of sorcery or divine intervention . . . oh, forgive me. You weren't enchanted by the gods themselves, were you? They're hard to miss.'

Julien writhed against his bonds, red-faced, shaking his head. 'Please . . . please . . .'

'No gods, then. Didn't think so. I was saying . . . well, I was saying that your little game is boring the hell out of me. Kindness.'

The round-headed man lowered his chin to his chest and stood with his palms out, facing upward, as though he were about to receive a gift.

'I want something creative. If Federico won't talk, let's give Julien one last chance to find his tongue.'

Federico began screaming before Barsavi had even finished speaking – the high, sobbing wail of the conscious damned. Locke found himself clenching his teeth to keep himself from shaking. So many meetings with slaughter as a backdrop . . . the gods could be perverse.

Sage Kindness moved to a small table at the side of the room on which there was a pile of small glasses and a heavy cloth sack with a drawstring. Kindness threw several glasses into the sack and began banging it against the table; the sound of breaking, jangling glass wasn't audible beneath Federico's wild hollering, but Locke could imagine it easily enough. After a few moments Kindness seemed satisfied, and he walked slowly over to Federico.

'Don't, don't, no, don't don't please no no . . .'

With one hand holding the desperate young man's head still, Kindness rapidly drew the bag up over the top of his head, over his face, all the way to Federico's neck, where he cinched the drawstring tight. The bag muffled Federico's screams, which had become high and wordless again. Kindness then began to knead the bag, gently at first, almost tenderly; the torturer's long fingers pushed the jagged contents of the sack up and around Federico's face. Red stains began to appear on the surface of the bag; Kindness manipulated the contents of the sack like a sculptor giving form to his clay. Federico's throat mercifully gave out just then, and for the next few moments the man choked out nothing more than a few hoarse moans; Locke prayed silently that he had already fled beyond pain to the temporary refuge of madness.

Kindness increased the vigour with which he massaged the cloth. He pressed now where Federico's eyes would be, and on the nose, and the mouth, and the chin. The bag grew wetter and redder until at last Federico's twitching stopped altogether. When Kindness took his hands off the bag they looked as though he'd been pulping tomatoes. Smiling sadly, he let his red hands drip red trails on the wood, and he walked over to Julien, staring intently, saying nothing.

'Surely,' said Capa Barsavi, 'if I've convinced you of anything by this point, it must be the depth of my resolve. Will you not speak?'

'Please, Capa Barsavi,' whispered Julien. 'Please, there's no need for this. I have nothing I can tell you. Ask me anything else, anything at all. What happened last night is a blank. I don't remember. I would tell you, please, gods, please believe me, I would tell you anything. We are loyal *pezon*, the most loyal you have.'

'I sincerely hope not.' Barsavi seemed to come to a decision; he gestured to the Berangias sisters and pointed at Julien. The dark-haired ladies worked quickly and silently, undoing the knots and shackles that held him to the wooden frame while leaving the cords that bound him from ankles to neck. They cradled the shivering man effortlessly, one at his shoulders and one at his feet.

'Loyal? Please. We are grown men, Julien. Refusing to tell me the truth of what happened last night is hardly a loyal act. You let me down, so I return like for like.' On the far left side of the great hall a man-sized wooden panel had been slid aside; barely a yard down was the dark surface of the water beneath the Grave. The floor around the opening was wet with blood. 'I shall let *you* down.'

Julien screamed one last time as the Berangias sisters heaved him into the opening, head first; he hit the water with a splash and didn't come back up. It was the Capa's habit to keep something nasty beneath the Grave at all times, constrained there by heavy nets of wire-reinforced rope that surrounded the underside of the galleon like a sieve.

'Kindness, you are dismissed. Boys, when I call you back you can get some people in here to clean up, but for now go wait on deck. Raiza, Cheryn – please go with them.'

Moving slowly, Capa Barsavi walked to his plain, comfortable old chair and settled into it. He was breathing heavily and quivering all the more for his effort not to show it. A brass wine goblet with the capacity of a large soup tureen was set out on the little table beside his chair; the Capa took a deep draught and seemed to brood over the fumes for a few moments, his eyes closed. At last he came back to life and beckoned for Locke and Nazca to step forward.

'Well. My dear Master Lamora. How much money have you brought me this week?'

'Thirty-six solons, five coppers, your honour.'

'Mmm. A slender week's work, it seems.'

'Yes, with all apologies, Capa Barsavi. The rain, well . . . sometimes it's murder on those of us doing second-storey work.'

'Mmmm.' Barsavi set the goblet down and folded his right hand inside his left, caressing the reddened knuckles. 'You've brought me more, of course. Many times. Better weeks.'

'Ah . . . yes.'

'There are some that don't, you know. They try to bring me the exact same amount, week after week after week, until I finally lose patience and correct them. Do you know what that sort of *garrista* must have, Locke?'

'Ah. A . . . very boring life?'

'Ha! Yes, exactly. How very *stable* of them to have the exact same income every single week, so they might give me the exact same percentage as a cut. As though I were an infant who would not notice. And then there are *garristas* such as yourself. I know you bring me the honest percentage, because you're not afraid to walk in here and apologise for having less than last week.'

'I, ah, do hope I'm not considered shy about sharing when the balance tilts the other way . . .'

'Not at all.' Barsavi smiled and settled back in his chair. Ominous splashing and muffled banging was coming from beneath the floor in the vicinity of the hatch that Julien had vanished down. 'You are, if anything, the most reliably correct *garrista* in my service. Like Verrari clockwork. You deliver my cut yourself, promptly and without a summons. For four years, week in and week out. Unfailing, since Chains died. Never once did you suggest that anything took precedence over your personal appearance before me, with that bag in your hand.'

Capa Barsavi pointed at the small leather bag Locke held in his left hand, and gestured to Nazca. Her formal role in the Barsavi organization was to act as *finnicker*, or record-keeper. She could rattle off the running total of the payments made by any gang in the city, itemised week by week and year by year, without error. Locke knew she updated records on parchment for her father's private use, but as far as the Capa's subjects in general knew, every coin of his fabled treasure was catalogued solely behind her cold and lovely eyes. Locke tossed the leather purse to her and she plucked it out of the air.

'Never,' said Capa Barsavi, 'did you think to send a *pezon* to do a *garrista*'s job.'

'Well, ah, you're most kind, your honour. But you made that very easy today, since only *garristas* are allowed past the door.'

'Don't dissemble. You know of what I speak. Nazca, love, Locke and I must now be alone.'

Nazca gave her father a deep nod, and then gave a much quicker, shallower one to Locke. She turned and walked back towards the doors to the entrance hall, iron heels echoing on the wood.

'I have many *garristas*,' Barsavi said when she was gone, 'tougher than yourself. Many more popular, many more charming, many with larger and more profitable gangs. But I have very few who are constantly at pains to be so courteous, so careful.'

Locke said nothing.

'My young man, while I take offence at many things, rest assured that courtesy is not one of them. Come, stand easy. I'm not fitting you for a noose.'

'Sorry, Capa. It's just . . . you've been known to begin expressing your displeasure in a very . . . ahhh . . .'

'Roundabout fashion?'

'Chains told me enough about scholars of the Therin Collegium,' said Locke, 'to understand that their primary habit of speech is the, ah, booby trap.'

'Ha! Yes. When anyone tells you habits die hard, Locke, they're lying – it seems they never die at all.' Barsavi chuckled and sipped from his wine before continuing. 'These are . . . alarming times, Locke. This damn Grey King has finally begun to get under my skin. The loss of Tesso is particularly . . . Well, I had plans for him. Now I am forced to begin bringing other plans forward sooner than intended. Tell me, *pezon* . . . what do you think of Anjais and Pachero?'

'Uh. Ha. Well . . . my honest opinion, your honour?'

'Full and honest, *pezon*. By my command.'

'Ah. They're very respected, very good at their jobs. Nobody jokes about them behind their backs. Jean says they really know how to handle themselves in a fight. The Sanzas are nervous about playing fair card games with them, which is saying something.'

'This I could hear from two dozen spies any time I wanted to. This I know. What is *your* personal opinion of my sons?'

'Ah . . .' Locke swallowed and looked Capa Barsavi straight in the eyes. 'Well, they are worthy of respect. They are good at their jobs, and they know their business in a fight. They're fairly hard workers and they're bright enough . . . but . . . your honour, begging your pardon, they tease Nazca when they should be heeding her warnings and taking her advice. She has the patience and the subtlety that . . . that . . .'

'Eludes them?'

'You knew what I was going to say, didn't you?'

'I said you were a careful and considerate *garrista*, Locke. Those are your distinguishing characteristics, though they imply many other qualities. Since the time of your prodigious early cock-ups, you have been the very picture of a careful thief, firmly in control of his own greed. You *would* be very sensitive to any opposing lack of caution in others. My sons . . . have lived all their lives in a city that fears them because of their last name. They expect deference in an aristocratic fashion. They are incautious, a bit brazen. I need to make arrangements to ensure that they receive good counsel in the months and years to come. I can't live forever, even after I deal with the Grey King.'

The jovial certainty that filled Capa Barsavi's voice when he said this made the hair on the back of Locke's neck stand up. The Capa was sitting in a fortress he hadn't left in more than two months, drinking wine in air still rank with the blood of eight members of one of his most powerful and loyal gangs.

Was Locke speaking to a man with a far-ranging and subtle scheme? Or had Barsavi finally cracked, like window glass in a fire?

'I should very much like,' said the Capa, 'to have you in a position to give Anjais and Pachero the counsel they'll require.'

'Ah . . . your honour, that's extremely . . . flattering, but . . . I get along well enough with Anjais and Pachero, but I'm not exactly what you'd call a close friend. We play some cards every now and then, but . . . let's be honest. I'm just not a very important *garrista*.'

'As I said. Even with the Grey King at work in my city, I still have many who are tougher than you, more daring than you, more

176

popular. I don't say this to strike a blow, because I've already discussed your own qualities. And it is *those* qualities they sorely need. Not toughness, daring or charm, but cold and steady caution. Prudence. You are my most prudent *garrista*; you only think of yourself as the least important because you make the least noise. Tell me, now – what do you think of Nazca?'

'Nazca?' Locke was suddenly even warier than before. 'She's . . . brilliant, your honour. She can recite conversations we had ten years ago and get every word right, especially if it embarrasses me. You think I'm prudent? Compared to her I'm as reckless as a bear in an alchemist's lab.'

'Yes,' said the Capa. 'Yes. She should be the next Capa Barsavi when I'm gone, but that won't happen. It's nothing to do with her being a woman, you know. Her older brothers would never stand to have their little sister lording it over them. And I should prefer not to have my children murdering one another for scraps of the legacy I intend to leave them, so I cannot push them aside in her favour.

'What I can do, and what I must do, is ensure that when the time comes, they will have a voice of sobriety in such a place that they cannot get rid of it. You and Nazca are old friends, yes? I remember the first time you met, so many years ago . . . when she used to sit on my knee and pretend to order my men around. In all the years since, you have always stopped to see her, always given her kind words? Always been her good *pezon*?'

'Ah . . . I certainly hope so, your honour.'

'I know you have.' Barsavi took a deep draught from his wine goblet, then set it back down firmly, a magnanimous smile on his round, wrinkled face. 'And so I give you my permission to court my daughter.'

Let's start wobbling, shall we? said Locke's knees, but this offer was met by a counter-proposal from his better judgement to simply freeze up and do nothing, like a man treading water who sees a tall black fin coming straight at him. 'Oh,' he finally said, 'I don't . . . I didn't expect . . .'

'Of course not,' said Barsavi. 'But in this our purposes are complementary. I know you and Nazca have feelings for one another. A union between the two of you would bring you into the Barsavi family. You would become Anjais and Pachero's responsibility . . . and they yours. Don't you see? A brother-by-bonding would be much harder for them to ignore than even their most powerful *garrista*.' Barsavi set his left fist inside his right and smiled broadly once again, like a red-faced god dispensing benevolence from a celestial throne.

Locke took a deep breath. There was nothing else for it; the situation required absolute acquiescence, as surely as if the Capa were holding a crossbow to his temple. Men died for refusing Barsavi far less; to refuse the Capa's own daughter would be messy suicide. Probably not here, and not now, but if Locke baulked at the Capa's plan he wouldn't live out the night.

'I . . . I'm honoured, Capa Barsavi. So deeply honoured. I hope not to disappoint you.'

'Disappoint me? Certainly not. Now, I know that several of my other *garristas* have had their eyes on Nazca for some time. But if one of them was going to catch her eye, he'd have done it by now, eh? What a surprise, when they hear the news. They'll never see this coming!'

And for a wedding present, thought Locke, *the angry jealousy of an unknown number of jilted suitors!*

'How, then . . . how and when should I begin, your honour?'

'Well,' said Barsavi, 'why don't I give you a few days to think it over? I'll speak to her, in the interim. Of course, for the time being, she's not to leave the Floating Grave. Once the Grey King is dealt with – well, I would expect you to begin courting her in a more colourful and public fashion.'

'You're telling me,' Locke said, very carefully, 'I should start stealing more, then.'

'Consider it my challenge to you, to go hand-in-hand with my blessing.' Barsavi smirked. 'Let's see if you can stay prudent while becoming more productive. I suspect you can – and I know that you wouldn't want to disappoint me *or* my daughter.'

'Certainly not, your honour. I'll . . . I'll do my very best.'

Capa Barsavi beckoned Locke forward and held his left hand out, fingers outstretched, palm down. Locke knelt before Barsavi's chair, took that hand with both of his own, and kissed the Capa's ring, that familiar black pearl with the blood-red heart. 'Capa Barsavi,' he said with his eyes to the ground. The Capa pulled him up again, by the shoulders.

'I give you my blessing, Locke Lamora, the blessing of an old man who worries for his children. I set you above many dangerous people by doing this for you. Surely it has occurred to you that my sons will inherit a dangerous office. And if they're not careful enough, or hard enough for the task . . . well, stranger things have happened. Some day this city could be ruled by Capa Lamora. Have you ever dreamed of this?'

'Truthfully,' whispered Locke, 'I have never desired a Capa's power, because I would never want a Capa's problems.'

'Well, there's that prudence again.' The Capa smiled and gestured towards the far doors, giving Locke permission to withdraw. 'A Capa's problems are very real. But you've helped me put one of them to rest.'

Locke walked back towards the entrance hall, thoughts racing. The Capa sat on his chair behind him, staring at nothing, saying no more. The only sounds after that were Locke's own footsteps and the steady drip of blood from the gore-soaked bag around Federico's head.

8

'Well, Nazca, if I were a thousand years old and had already seen everything there is to see six times over, that still would have been about the *last damn thing* I'd have ever expected . . .'

She was waiting for him in the passage leading to the reception hall; once the clockwork mechanisms had sealed the door to the main hall behind them, she gave him a wry and apologetic look.

'But don't you see that it would have been even stranger if I'd explained it beforehand?'

'The whole mess would be hard-pressed to get any gods-damned weirder, Nazca. Look, please, don't take any of this the wrong way. I—'

'I don't take any of it the wrong way, Locke—'

'You're a good friend, and—'

'I feel the same way, and yet—'

'It's hard to put this right—'

'No it isn't. Look.' She grabbed him by the shoulders and bent down slightly to look right into his eyes. 'You are a good friend,

Locke. Probably the best I have. My loyal *pezon*. I am extremely fond of you, but not . . . as a possible husband. And I know that you . . .'

'I . . . ah . . .'

'Locke,' said Nazca, 'I know that the only woman with the key to that peculiar heart of yours is a thousand miles away. And I know you'd rather be miserable for her than happy with anyone else.'

'Really?' Locke balled his fists. 'Seems like it's pretty common fucking knowledge. I bet the Duke gets regular reports. Seems as though your father is the only person who *doesn't* know.'

'Or doesn't care.' Nazca raised her eyebrows. 'Locke, it's Capa-to-*pezon*. It's not personal. He gives the orders and you carry them out. In most cases.'

'But not this one? I thought you'd be happy. At least he's making plans for the future again.'

'I said *reasonable* plans.' Nazca smiled, a real smile this time. 'Come on, *pezon*. Play along for a few days. We can go through the motions and put our heads together to come up with a way out of this. It's you and me we're talking about, right? The old man can't win, and he won't even know he's lost.'

'Right. If you say so.'

'Yes, I say so. Come back the day after tomorrow. We'll scheme. We'll slip this noose. Now go tend to your boys. And be *careful*.'

Locke stepped back out into the entrance hall and Nazca pushed the doors shut behind him; he stared back at her as the space between the black doors narrowed, gradually sealing her off from view until they slammed shut with the click of tumbling locks. He could have sworn she winked just before the heavy doors closed between them.

'. . . and this is the card you picked. The six of spires,' said Calo, holding up a card and displaying it for the entrance-hall guards.

'Fuck me,' said one of them, 'that's sorcery.'

'Nah, it's just the old Sanza touch.' Calo re-shuffled his deck one-handed and held it out toward Locke. 'Care to give it a go, boss?'

'No thanks, Calo. Pack up, lads. Our business here is finished for the day, so let's stop bothering the folks with the crossbows.' He punctuated this with hand gestures – *Major complications; discuss elsewhere.*

'Damn, I'm hungry,' said Jean, picking up the cue. 'Why don't we get something at the Last Mistake and take it up to our rooms?'

'Yeah,' said Bug. 'Beer and apricot tarts!'

'A combination so disgusting I feel oddly compelled to actually try it.' Jean swatted the smallest Gentleman Bastard on the back of his head, then led the way as the gang made for the slender wooden path that tied the Floating Grave to the rest of the world.

9

Save Capa Barsavi (who imagined that Locke's gang merely continued sitting the steps a few days of the week even with Chains in his grave), no Right People of Camorr knew that the Gentlemen Bastards still worked out of the House of Perelandro. Calo and Galdo and Bug rented rooms at various points in and around the Snare, moving every few months. Locke and Jean had maintained the fiction of rooming together for several years. By a great stroke of luck (though whether it was good or ill had really yet to be determined) Jean had managed to get them the rooms on the seventh floor of the Broken Tower.

The night was dark and full of rain, and none of the gang was particularly eager to make his way back onto the creaking exterior stairs that staggered down the north side of the Broken Tower. Hissing rain rattled the window shutters and the wind made an eerie rising-and-falling sigh as it passed over the gaps and crevices in the old tower. The Gentlemen Bastards sat on floor cushions in the light of paper lanterns and nursed the last of their beer, the pale sweet sort that most Camorr natives preferred to the bitter Verrari dark. The air was stuffy, but at least tolerably dry.

Locke had given them the whole story over dinner.

'Well,' said Galdo, 'this is the damnedest damn thing that ever dammed things up for us.'

'I say again,' said Jean, 'that we should pull an early blow-off on the Don Salvara game and get ready to ride out a storm. This Grey King business is getting scary and we can't have our attention diverted if Locke's going to be mixed up at the middle of things.'

'Where do we cut ourselves off?' asked Calo.

'We cut ourselves off now,' said Jean. 'Now, or after we get one more note out of the Don. No later.'

'Mmmm.' Locke stared down at the dregs in the bottom of his tin cup. 'We've worked hard for this one. I'm confident we can run it for another five or ten thousand crowns, at least. Maybe not the twenty-five thousand we were hoping to squeeze out of Salvara, but enough to make ourselves proud. I got the crap kicked out of me, and Bug jumped off a building for this money, you know.'

'And got rolled two miles inside a bloody barrel!'

'Now, Bug,' said Galdo, 'it's not as though the nasty old barrel jumped you in an alley and forced you to crawl inside it. And I concur with Jean. I said it this afternoon, Locke. Even if you won't seriously consider using them, can we at least make some arrangements to get you under cover in a hurry? Maybe even out of town.'

'I still can't believe I'm hearing a Sanza counsel caution,' Locke said with a grin. 'I thought we were richer and cleverer than everyone else.'

'You'll hear it again and again when there's a chance you'll get your throat slit, Locke.' Calo picked up his brother's argument. 'I've changed my mind about the Grey King, that's for damn sure. Maybe the lone lunatic *does* have it over the three thousand of us. You might be one of his targets. And if Barsavi wants you even tighter with his inner circle, it invites further trouble.'

'Can we set aside talk of slitting throats, just for a moment?' Locke rose and turned toward the shuttered seaward window. He pretended to stare out of it with his hands folded behind his back. 'Who are we, after all? I admit I was almost ready to jump into the gods-damned bay when the Capa sprang this on me. But I've had time to think, so get this straight – we've got the old fox dead to rights. We've got him in the palms of our hands. Honestly, boys. We're so good at what we do that he's asking the Thorn of fucking Camorr to *marry his daughter*. We're so far in the clear it's comical.'

'Nonetheless,' said Jean, 'it's a complication that could mess up our arrangements *forever*, not an accomplishment we can crow about.'

'Of course we can crow about it, Jean. I'm going to crow about it right now. Don't you see? This is nothing we don't do every day.

It's a plain old Gentlemen Bastards sort of job – only we'll have Nazca working with me to pull it off as well. We can't lose. I'm no more likely to marry her than I am to be named Duke Nicovante's heir tomorrow morning.'

'Do you have a plan?' Jean's eyes said he was curious but wary.

'Not even remotely. I don't have the first damned clue what we're going to do. All my best plans start just like this.' Locke tipped the last of his beer down his throat and tossed the tin cup against the wall. 'I've had my beer and I've had my apricot tarts, and I say the hell with them both, Grey King *and* Capa Barsavi. Nobody's going to scare us out of our Don Salvara game, and nobody's going to hitch me and Nazca against our will. We'll do what we always do – wait for an opening, take it, and fucking well win.'

'Uh . . . well.' Jean sighed. 'Will you at least let us take a few precautions? And will you watch yourself, coming and going?'

'Naturally, Jean, naturally. You grab us some places on likely ships; spend whatever you have to. I don't care where they're going as long as it's not Jerem. We can lose ourselves anywhere for a few weeks and creep back when we please. Calo, Galdo, you get out to the Viscount's Gate tomorrow. Leave some considerations for the boys in yellow so we can get out of the city at an awkward hour if we need to. Don't be shy with the silver and gold.'

'What can I do?' asked Bug.

'You can watch our backs. Keep your eyes wide open. Skulk around the temple. Spot me anyone out of place, anyone who lingers too long. If anyone is trying to keep an eye on us, I promise, I *guarantee*, we will go to ground and vanish like piss into the ocean. Until then, trust me. I promise to do most of my moving around as Lukas Fehrwight for the next few days; I can swap in some cheaper disguises, too.'

'Then I suppose that's that,' Jean said quietly.

'Jean, I can be your *garrista* or I can just be the fellow who buys beer and tarts when everyone else mysteriously misplaces their purses.' Locke eyed the gathering with an exaggerated scowl. 'I can't be both; it's one or the other.'

'I'm nervous,' said Jean, 'because I don't like having as little information as I fear we do. I share Nazca's suspicions. The Grey King has something up his sleeve, something we don't understand. Our game is very delicate and our situation is very . . . fluid.'

'I know. But I follow my gut, and my gut says that we meet this one head on with smiles on our faces. Look,' said Locke. 'The more we do this, the more I learn about what I think Chains was really training us for. And this is it. He wasn't training us for a calm and orderly world where we could pick and choose when we needed to be clever. He was training us for a situation that was *fucked up on all sides*. Well, we're in it, and I say we're equal to it. I don't need to be reminded that we're up to our heads in dark water. I just want you boys to remember that we're the gods-damned sharks.'

'Hell yes,' cried Bug. 'I knew there was a reason I let you lead this gang!'

'Well, I can't argue with the manifest wisdom of the boy that jumps off temple roofs. But I trust my points are noted,' said Jean.

'Very noted,' said Locke. 'Received, recognised, and duly considered with the utmost gravity. Sealed, notarised, and firmly imprinted upon my rational essence.'

'Gods, you really are cheerful about this, aren't you? You only play vocabulary games when you feel genuinely sunny about the world.' Jean sighed, but couldn't keep the slightest hint of a smile from tugging at the corners of his lips.

'If you do end up in danger, Locke,' said Calo, 'you must understand that we will ignore the orders of our *garrista*, and we'll bludgeon our *friend* on the back of his thick skull and smuggle him out of Camorr in a box. I have just the bludgeon for the job.'

'And I have a box,' said Galdo. 'Been hoping for an excuse to use it for years, really.'

'Also noted,' said Locke, 'with thanks. But by the grace of the Crooked Warden, I choose to trust *us*. I choose to trust Chains' judgement. I choose to keep doing what we do best. Tomorrow, I've got some work to do as Fehrwight, and then I'll go see Nazca again the day after. The Capa will be expecting it, and I'm sure she'll have some ideas of her own by then.'

Locke thought once again of his last glimpse of her, that wink as the two great doors of dark wood slammed shut between them.

Maintaining her father's secrets was Nazca's entire life. Did it mean something for her, to have one of her own that she could keep from him?

INTERLUDE:
The Boy Who Cried For a Corpse

I

Father Chains gave Locke no respite from his education on the day after the visit to the Last Mistake; with his head still pounding from a brown-sugar rum headache, Locke began to learn about the priesthood of Perelandro and the priesthood of the Benefactor. There were hand-signs and ritual intonations, methods of greeting and meanings behind robe decorations. On his fourth day in Chains' care, Locke began to sit the steps as one of the 'initiates of Perelandro', clad in white and trying to look suitably humble and pathetic.

As the weeks passed, the breadth of Chains' instruction expanded. Locke did two hours of reading and scribing each day; his pen-scratchings grew smoother step by halting step until the Sanza brothers announced that he no longer wrote 'like a dog with an arrow in its brain'. Locke was moved enough by their praise to dust their sleeping pallets with red pepper. The Sanzas were distraught when their attempted retaliation was foiled by the utter paranoia Locke still carried with him from his experiences in Shades' Hill and the Catchfire plague; it was simply impossible to sneak up on him or catch him sleeping.

'The brothers have never before met their match in mischief,' said Chains as he and Locke sat the steps one particularly slow day. 'Now they're wary of you. When they start coming to you for *advice*, well . . . that's when you'll know that you have them tamed.'

Locke had smiled and said nothing; just that morning Calo had offered to give Locke extra help with his sums if the smallest Gentleman Bastard would only tell the twins how he kept spotting their little booby traps and rendering them harmless.

Locke revealed precious few of his survival tricks, but he did accept the help of both Sanzas in his study of arithmetic. His only reward for each accomplishment was a more complex problem from Chains. At the same time, he began his education in spoken Vadran; Chains would issue simple commands in the language, and once Locke was reasonably familiar with the tongue Chains often forbade the three boys to speak anything else for hours at a time. Even their dinner conversation was conducted in the harsh and illogical language of the north; to Locke it often seemed impossible to say anything in Vadran that didn't sound angry.

'You won't hear this among the Right People, much, but you'll hear it on the docks and among the merchants, that's for damn sure,' said Chains. 'And when you hear someone speaking it, don't ever let on that you know it unless you absolutely have to. You'd be surprised how arrogant some of those northern types are when it comes to their speech. Just play dumb, and you never know what they might let slip.'

There was more instruction in the culinary arts; Chains had Locke slaving away at the cooking hearth every other night, with Calo and Galdo vigorously henpecking him in tandem. 'This is *vicce alo apona*, the fifth Beautiful Art of Camorr,' said Chains. 'Guild chefs learn all eight styles better than they learn the uses of their own cocks, but you'll just get the basics for now. Mind you, our basics piss on everyone else's best. Only Karthain and Emberlain come close; most Vadrans wouldn't know fine cuisine from rat shit in lamp oil. Now, this is pinch-of-gold pepper, and this is Jereshti olive oil, and just behind them I keep dried cinnamon-lemon rind . . .'

Locke stewed octopus and boiled potatoes; he sliced pears and apples and alchemical hybrid fruit that oozed honey-scented liquor. He spiced and seasoned and bit his tongue in furious concentration. He was frequently the architect of gruesome messes that were hauled out behind the temple and fed to the goat. But as he improved at everything else required of him, he improved steadily at the hearth; soon the Sanzas ceased to tease him and began to trust him as an assistant with their own delicate creations.

One night about half a year after his arrival at the House of Perelandro, Locke and the Sanzas collaborated on a stuffed platter of infant sharks; this was *vicce enta merre*, the first Beautiful Art, the cuisine of sea-creatures. Calo gutted the soft-skinned little sharks and stuffed them with red and yellow peppers, which had in turn been stuffed with sausage and blood-cheese by Locke; the tiny staring eyes of the creatures were replaced with black olives. Once the little teeth were plucked out, their mouths were stuffed with glazed carrots and rice, and their fins and tails cut off to be boiled in soup. 'Ahhh,' said Chains when the elaborate meal was settling in four appreciative gullets, 'now that was genuinely excellent, boys. But while you're cleaning up and scouring the dishes, I only want to hear you speaking Vadran . . .'

And so it went; Locke was schooled further in the art of setting a table and waiting on individuals of high station. He learned how to hold out a chair and how to pour tea and wine; he and the Sanzas conducted elaborate dinner-table rituals with the gravity of physikers cutting open a patient. There were lessons in clothing: the tying of cravats, the buckling of shoes, the wearing of expensive affectations such as hose. In fact, there was a dizzying variety of instruction in virtually every sphere of human accomplishment except thievery.

As the first anniversary of Locke's arrival at the temple loomed, that changed.

'I owe some favours, boys,' said Chains one night as they all hunkered down in the lifeless rooftop garden. This was where he preferred to discuss all the weightier matters of their life together, at least when it wasn't raining. 'Favours I can't put off when certain people come calling.'

'Like the Capa?' asked Locke.

'Not this time.' Chains took a long drag on his habitual after-dinner smoke. 'This time I owe the black alchemists. You know about them, right?'

Calo and Galdo nodded, but hesitantly; Locke shook his head.

'Well,' said Chains, 'there's a right and proper Guild of Alchemists, but they're very choosy about the sort of person they let in, and the sort of work they let them do. Black alchemists are sort of the reason the Guild has such strict rules. They do business in false shopfronts, with people like us. Drugs, poisons, what have you. The Capa owns them, same as he owns us, but nobody really leans on them directly. They're, ah, not the sort of people you want to upset.

'Jessaline d'Aubart is probably the best of the lot. I, uh, I had occasion to get poisoned once. She took care of it for me. So I owe

187

her, and she's finally called in the favour. What she wants is a corpse.'

'Beggars' Barrow,' said Calo.

'And a shovel,' said Galdo.

'No, she needs a fresh corpse. Still warm and juicy, as it were. See, the Guilds of Alchemists and Physikers are entitled to a certain number of fresh corpses each year by ducal charter. Straight off the gallows, for cutting open and poking around. The black alchemists don't receive any such courtesy, and Jessaline has some theories she wants to put to the test. So I've decided you boys are going to work together on your first real job. I want you to find a corpse, fresher than morning bread. Get your hands on it without attracting undue attention, and bring it here so I can hand it off to Jessaline.'

'Steal a corpse? This won't be any fun,' said Galdo.

'Think of it as a valuable test of your skills,' said Chains.

'Are we likely to steal many corpses in the future?' asked Calo.

'It's not a test of your corpse-plucking abilities, you cheeky little nitwit,' Chains said amiably. 'I mean to see how you all *work together* on something more serious than our dinner. I'll consider setting you up with anything you ask for, but I'm not giving you hints. You get to figure this one out on your own.'

'Anything we ask for?' said Locke.

'Within reason,' said Chains. 'And let me emphasise that you can't make the corpse yourself. You have to find it honestly dead by someone else's doing.'

So forceful was Chains' voice when he said this that the Sanza brothers stared warily at Locke for a few seconds, then gave each other a look with eyebrows arched.

'When,' said Locke, 'does this lady want it by?'

'She'd be very pleased to have it in the next week or two.'

Locke nodded, then stared down at his hands for a few seconds. 'Calo, Galdo,' he said, 'will you sit the steps tomorrow so I can think about this?'

'Yes,' they said without hesitation, and Father Chains didn't miss the note of hope in their voices. He would remember that moment ever after; the night the Sanzas conceded that Locke would be the brains of their operation. The night they were *relieved* to have him as the brains of their operation.

'Honestly dead,' said Locke, 'and not killed by us and not even stiff yet. Right. I know we can do it. It'll be easy, I just don't know why or how yet.'

'Your confidence heartens me,' said Chains, 'but I want you to remember that you're on a very short leash. If a tavern should happen to burn down or a riot should happen to break out around you, I'll throw you off this roof with lead ingots tied around your neck.'

Calo and Galdo stared at Locke once again.

'Short leash. Right. But don't worry,' said Locke. 'I'm not as reckless as I was. You know, when I was little.'

2

The next day Locke walked the length of the Temple District on his own for the very first time, hooded in a clean white robe of Perelandro's order with silver embroidery on the sleeves, waist-high to virtually everyone around him. He was astonished at the courtesy given to the robe (a courtesy, he clearly understood, that in many cases only partially devolved on the poor fool wearing the robe).

Most Camorri regarded the Order of Perelandro with a mixture of cynicism and guilty pity; the unabashed charity of the god and his priesthood just didn't speak to the rough heart of the city's character. Yet the reputation of Father Chains as a colourful freak of piety paid certain dividends; men who surely joked about the simpering of the Beggar God's white-robed priests with their friends nonetheless threw coins into Chains' kettle, eyes averted, when they passed his temple. It turned out they also let a little robed initiate pass on the street without harassment; groups parted fluidly and merchants nodded almost politely as Locke went on his way.

For the first time he learned what a powerful thrill it was to go about in public in an effective disguise.

The sun was creeping up towards noon, the crowds were thick and the city was alive with the echoes and murmurs of its masses. Locke padded intently to the south-west corner of the Temple District where a glass catbridge arched across the canal to the island of the Old Citadel.

Catbridges were another legacy of the Eldren who'd ruled before the coming of men; narrow glass arches no wider than an ordinary man's hips, arranged in pairs over most of Camorr's canals and at several places along the Angevine River. Although they looked smooth, their glimmering surfaces were as rough as shark's-hide leather; for those with a reasonable measure of agility and confidence, they provided a convenient means of crossing the canals at many points. Traffic was always one-directional over each catbridge; ducal decree clearly stated that anyone going the wrong direction on a catbridge could be shoved off by those with the right of way.

As he scuttled across this bridge, pondering furiously, Locke recalled some of the history lessons Chains had drilled into him. The Old Citadel district had once been the home of the Dukes of Camorr, centuries earlier, when all the city-states claimed by the Therin people had knelt to a single Throne in the imperial city of Therim Pel. That line of Camorri nobility, in superstitious dread of the perfectly good glass towers left behind by the Eldren, had erected a massive stone palace in the heart of southern Camorr.

When one of Nicovante's great-great-predecessors (on finer points of city lore such as this, Locke's otherwise prodigious knowledge dissolved in a haze of total indifference) took up residence in the silver glass tower called Raven's Reach, the old family fortress had become the Palace of Patience – the heart of Camorr's municipal justice, such as it was. The yellowjackets and their officers were headquartered there, as were the Duke's Magistrates, twelve men and women who presided over their cases in scarlet robes and velvet masks, their true identities never to be revealed to the general public. Each was named for one of the months of the year – Justice Parthis, Justice Festal, Justice Aurim, and so forth – though each one passed judgement year-round.

And there were dungeons, and there were the gallows on the Black Bridge that led to the palace gates, and there were *other things*. While the Secret Peace had greatly reduced the number of people who took the short, sharp drop off the Black Bridge (and didn't Duke Nicovante love to publicly pin that on his own magnanimity), the Duke's servants had devised other punishments that were spectacular in their cruel cleverness, if technically non-lethal.

The palace was a great square heap of pitted black and grey stone, ten storeys high; the huge bricks that formed its walls had been arranged to form simple mosaics that had weathered to a ghostly state. The rows of high arched windows decorating every other level of the tower were stained glass, with black and red designs predominating. At night a light would burn ominously behind each one, dim red eyes in the darkness, staring out in all directions. Those windows were never dark; the intended message was clear.

There were four open-topped circular towers, one jutting from each corner of the palace, seemingly hanging in air from the eighth or ninth level up. On the sides of these hung black iron crow cages, in which prisoners singled out for special mistreatment would be aired for a few hours or even a few days, with their feet dangling. Yet even these were seats in paradise compared to the spider cages, a spectacle that became visible to Locke (between the backs and shoulders of adults) as he stepped off the catbridge and into the crowds of the Old Citadel.

From the south-eastern tower of the Palace of Patience there dangled a half-dozen cages on long steel chains, swaying gently in the wind like little spiders on cords of silk. Two of these were moving, one slowly heading up and the other rapidly descending. Prisoners condemned to the spider cages were not to be allowed a moment's peace, so other prisoners condemned to hard labour would toil at the huge capstans atop the tower, working in shifts around the clock until the occupant of a cage was deemed to be sufficiently unhinged and contrite. Lurching and creaking and open to the elements on all sides, the cages would go up and down ceaselessly. At night one could frequently hear the occupants pleading and screaming, even from a district or two away.

The Old Citadel wasn't a very cosmopolitan district. Outside the Palace of Patience there were canal docks and stables reserved for the yellowjackets, offices for the Duke's tax collectors and scribes and other functionaries, and seedy little coffee houses where freelance solicitors and lawscribes would try to drum up work from the families and friends of those being held in the palace. A few pawnshops and other businesses clung tenaciously to the northern part of the island, but for the most part they were crowded out by the grimmer business of the Duke's government.

The district's other major landmark was the Black Bridge that spanned the wide canal between Old Citadel and the Mara Camorrazza, a tall arch of black human-set stone adorned with red lamps fixed up with ceremonial black shrouds that could be lowered with a few tugs on a rope. The hangings were conducted from a wooden platform that jutted off the bridge's south side; supposedly, the unquiet shades of the condemned would be carried out to sea if they died over running water. Some thought that they would then be incarnated in the bodies of sharks, which explained why Camorr Bay had such a problem with the creatures, and the idea was not entirely scoffed at. As far as most Camorri were concerned, turnabout was fair play.

Locke stared at the Black Bridge for a good long while, exercising that capacity for conniving which Chains had so forcefully repressed for many long months. He was far too young for much self-analysis, but the process of scheming gave him real pleasure, like a little ball of tingling warmth in the pit of his stomach. He had no name for what he was doing, but in the collision of his whirling thoughts a plan began to form, and the more he thought on it the more pleased he became with himself. It was a fine thing that his white hood concealed his face from most passersby, lest anyone should see an initiate of Perelandro staring fixedly at a gallows and grinning wildly.

3

'I need the names of any people who are going to hang in the next week or two,' said Locke, as he and Chains sat the temple steps the next day.

'If you were enterprising,' said Chains, 'and you most certainly are, you could get them yourself, and leave your poor fat old master in peace.'

'I would, but I need someone else to do it. It won't work if I'm seen around the Palace of Patience before the hangings.'

'What won't work?'

'The plan.'

'Oh-ho! Nervy little Shades' Hill purse-clutcher, thinking you can keep me in the dark. What plan?'

'The plan to steal a corpse.'

'Ahem. Anything else you'd like to tell me about it?'

'It's brilliant.'

A passerby tossed something into the kettle. Locke bowed and Chains waved his hands in the man's general direction, his restraints clattering, and he yelled, 'Fifty years of health to you and your children, and the blessings of the Lord of the Overlooked!'

'It would've been a hundred years,' muttered Chains when the man had passed, 'but that sounded like a clipped half-copper. Now, your brilliant plan. I know you've had audacious plans, but I'm not entirely sure you've had a *brilliant* one yet.'

'This is the one, then. Honest. But I need those names.'

'If it's so, it's so.' Chains leaned back and stretched, grunting in satisfaction as his back creaked and popped. 'I'll get them for you tonight.'

'And I'll need some money.'

'Ah. Well, I expected that. Take what you need from the vault and mark it on the ledger. Screw around with it, though . . .'

'I know. Lead ingots, screaming, death.'

'Something like that. You're a little on the small side, but I suppose Jessaline might learn a thing or two from your corpse anyway.'

4

Penance Day was the traditional day for hangings in Camorr; each week a sullen lot of prisoners would be trotted out from the Palace of Patience, priests and guards surrounding them. Noon was the hour of the drop.

At the eighth hour of the morning, when the functionaries in the courtyard of the palace threw open their wooden shutters and settled in for a long day of saying 'Fuck off in the name of the Duke' to all comers, three robed initiates of Perelandro wheeled a narrow wooden pull-cart into the courtyard. The smallest of the three made his way over to the first available clerk; his thin little face barely topped the forward edge of the clerk's booth.

'Well, this is odd,' said the clerk, a woman of late-middle years, shaped something like a bag of potatoes but perhaps not quite as warm or sympathetic. 'Help you with something?'

'There's a man being hanged,' said Locke. 'Noon today.'

'You don't say. Here I thought it was a state secret.'

'His name's Antrim. Antrim One-Hand, they call him. He's got—'

'One hand. Yes, he drops today. Fire-setting, theft, dealing with slavers. Charming man.'

'I was going to say that he had a wife,' said Locke. 'She has business. About him.'

'Look, the time for appeals is past. Saris, Festal and Tathris sealed the death-warrant. Antrim One-Hand belongs to Morgante now, and then to Aza Guilla. Not even one of the Beggar God's cute little sprats can help him at this point.'

'I know,' said Locke. 'I don't want him spared. His wife doesn't care if he gets hanged. I'm here about the body.'

'Really?' Genuine curiosity flickered in the clerk's eyes for the first time. 'Now that *is* odd. What about the body?'

'His wife knows he deserves to get hanged, but she wants him to get a fairer chance. You know, with the Lady of the Long Silence. So she's paid for us to take the body and put it in our temple. So we can burn candles and pray for intercession in Perelandro's name for three days and nights. We'll bury him after that.'

'Well now,' said the clerk. 'The corpses usually get cut down after an hour and tossed into holes on the Beggars' Barrow. More than they deserve, but it's tidy. We don't usually just go handing them out to anyone who wants one.'

'I know. My master cannot see, or leave our temple, or else he'd be here to explain himself. But we're all he has. I'm supposed to say that he knows this is making trouble for you.' Locke's little hand appeared over the edge of the booth, and when it withdrew a small leather purse was sitting on the clerk's counting-board.

'That's very considerate of him. We all know how devoted old Father Chains is.' The clerk swept the purse behind her counter and gave it a shake; it jingled, and she grunted. 'Still a bit of a problem, though.'

'My master would be grateful for any help you could give us.' Another purse appeared on the counter, and the clerk actually broke into a smile.

'It's within the realm of possibility,' she said. 'Not quite certain yet, of course.'

Locke conjured a third purse, and the clerk nodded. 'I'll speak to the Masters of the Ropes, little one.'

'We even brought our own cart,' said Locke. 'We don't want to be any trouble.'

'I'm sure you won't be.' Her demeanour softened for just a moment. 'I didn't mean ill by what I said about the Beggar God, boy.'

'I didn't take it ill, madam. After all, it's what we do.' He favoured her with what he thought was his most endearing little grin. 'Did you not give me what I asked for because I begged, simply out of the goodness of your own heart, with no coin involved?'

'Why, of course I did.' She actually winked at him.

'Twenty years of health to you and your children,' Locke said, bowing and briefly disappearing beneath the lip of her counter, 'and the blessings of the Lord of the Overlooked.'

5

It was a short, neat hanging; the Duke's Masters of the Ropes were nothing if not well practised at their trade. It wasn't the first execution Locke had ever seen, nor would it be the last. He and the Sanza brothers even had a chance to make all the proper reverential gestures when one of the condemned begged for Perelandro's blessings at the last minute.

Traffic across the Black Bridge was halted for executions; a small crowd of guards, spectators and priests milled about afterwards as the requisite hour passed. The corpses twisted in the breeze beneath them, ropes creaking; Locke and the Sanzas stood off to the side respectfully with their little cart.

Eventually, yellowjackets began to haul the bodies up one by one under the watchful eyes of several priests of Aza Guilla; the corpses were carefully set down in an open dray pulled by two black horses draped in the black and silver of the Death Goddess's order. The last corpse to be drawn up was that of a wiry man with a long beard and a shaved head; his left hand ended in a puckered red stump.

Four yellowjackets carried this body over to the cart where the boys waited; a priestess of Aza Guilla accompanied them. Locke felt a chill run up and down his spine when that inscrutable silver-mesh mask tilted down towards him.

'Little brothers of Perelandro,' said the priestess, 'what intercession would you plead for on behalf of this man?' Her voice was that of a very young woman, perhaps no more than fifteen or sixteen. If anything, that only enhanced her eeriness in Locke's eyes, and he found his throat suddenly dry.

'We plead for whatever will be given,' said Calo.

'The will of the Twelve is not ours to presume,' continued Galdo.

The priestess inclined her head very slightly. 'I'm told this man's widow requested an interment in the House of Perelandro before burial.'

'Apparently she thought he might need it, begging pardon,' said Calo.

'It's not without precedent. But it is far more usual for the grieving to seek our intercession with the Lady.'

'Our master,' managed Locke, 'made, ah, a solemn promise to the poor woman that we would give our care. Surely, we, we mean no ill towards you or the Lady Most Fair, but we must keep our word.'

'Of course. I did not mean to suggest that you had done anything wrong; the Lady will weigh him in the end, whatever is said and done before the vessel is entombed.' She gestured, and the yellowjackets set the corpse down on the cart. One of them unfurled a cheap cotton shroud and swung it over Antrim's body, leaving only the top of his head uncovered. 'Blessings of the Lady of the Long Silence to you and your master.'

'Blessings of the Lord of the Overlooked,' said Locke as he and the Sanzas bowed in unison from the waist; a braided silver cord around the priestess's neck marked her as more than a simple initiate like themselves. 'To you and your brothers and sisters.'

The Sanza brothers each took one pole at the front of the cart, and Locke took up the rear, to push and to keep the load balanced. He was instantly sorry that he'd taken this spot; the hanging had filled the man's breeches with his own shit, and the smell was rising. Gritting his teeth, he called out, 'To the House of Perelandro, with all dignity.'

Plodding slowly, the Sanzas pulled the cart down the western side of the Black Bridge, and then turned north to head for the wide, low bridge that led to the Shifting Market's eastern district. It was a slightly roundabout way home, but not at all suspicious – at least until the three white-robed boys were well away from anyone who'd seen them leave the hanging. Moving with a bit more haste (and enjoying the added deference the dead man was bringing them, save only for Locke, who was still effectively downwind of the poor fellow's last futile act in life), they turned left and headed for the bridges to the Fauria.

Once there, they pressed south and crossed into the Videnza district; a relatively clean and spacious island well-patrolled by yellowjackets. At the heart of the Videnza was a market square of merchant-artisans, recognised names who disdained the churning chaos of the Shifting Market. They operated from the ground floors of their fine old sagging houses, which were always freshly mortared and whitewashed over their post-and-timber frames. The district's tiled roofs, by tradition, were glazed in bright, irregular colours; blue and purple and red and green, they teased the eyes and gleamed like glass in the bright, hot sun.

At the northern entrance to this square Calo darted away from the cart and vanished into the crowd; Locke came up from the rear (muttering prayers of gratitude) to take his place. So arrayed, they hauled their odd cargo towards the shop of Ambrosine Strollo, first lady of Camorr's chandlers, furnisher to the Duke himself.

'If there's a niggardly speck of genuine fellowship in Camorr,' Chains had once said, 'one little place where Perelandro's name isn't spoken with a sort of sorry contempt, it's the Videnza. Merchants are a miserly lot and craftsfolk are pressed by cares. However, those that turn a very pretty profit plying their chosen trade *are* likely to be somewhat happy. They get the best of all worlds, for common folk. Assuming our lot doesn't fuck with them.'

Locke was impressed with the response he and Galdo received as they drew the cart up in front of Madam Strollo's four-storey home. Here, merchants and customers alike bowed their heads as the corpse passed; many of them even made the worldless gesture of benediction in the name of the Twelve, touching first their eyes with both hands, and then their lips, and finally their hearts.

'My dears,' said Madam Strollo, 'what an honour, and what an *unusual* errand you must be on.' She was a slender woman getting well on in years, a sort of cosmic opposite to the clerk Locke had dealt with that morning. Strollo exuded attentive deference; she behaved as though the two little red-faced initiates, sweating heavily under their robes, were full priests of a more powerful order. If she could smell the mess in Antrim's breeches, she refrained from saying so.

She sat at the streetside window of her shop, under a heavy wooden awning that folded down at night to seal the place tight against mischief. The window was perhaps ten feet wide and half as high, and Madam Strollo was surrounded by candles, stacked layer upon layer, tier upon tier, like the houses and towers of a fantastical wax city. Alchemical globes had largely replaced the cheap taper as the light source of choice for nobility and lowbility alike; the few remaining master chandlers fought back by mingling ever-more-lovely scents in their creations. Additionally, there were the ceremonial needs of Camorr's temples and believers, needs that cold glass light was universally considered inadequate to meet.

'We're interring this man,' said Locke, 'for three days and nights before his burial. My master needs new candles for the ceremony.'

'Old Chains, you mean? Poor dear man. Let's see . . . You'll want lavender for cleanliness, and autumn bloodflower for the blessing, and sulfur roses for the Lady Most Fair?'

'Please,' said Locke, pulling out a humble leather purse that jingled with silver, 'and some votives without scent. Half a dozen of all four kinds.'

Madam Strollo carefully selected the candles and wrapped them in waxed burlap ('A gift of the house,' she muttered when Locke began to open his mouth, 'and perhaps I put a few more than half a dozen of each in the packet'). Locke tried to argue with her for form's sake, but the old woman grew conveniently deaf for a few crucial seconds as she finished wrapping her goods.

Locke paid three solons out of his purse (taking care to let her see that there were a dozen more nestled therein) and wished Madam Strollo a full hundred years of health for herself and her children in the name of the Lord of the Overlooked as he backed away. He set the package of candles on the cart, tucking it just under the blanket beside Antrim's glassy, staring eyes.

No sooner had he turned round to resume his place next to Galdo than a taller boy dressed in ragged, dirty clothes walked right into him, sending him tumbling onto his back.

'Oh!' said the boy, who happened to be Calo Sanza. 'A thousand pardons! I'm so clumsy; here, let me help you up . . .'

He grabbed Locke's outstretched hand and yanked the smaller boy back to his feet. 'Twelve gods! An initiate. Forgive me, forgive me. I simply did not see you standing there.' Clucking with concern, he brushed dirt from Locke's white robe. 'Are you well?'

'I am, I am.'

'Forgive my clumsiness; I meant no insult.'

'None is taken. Thank you for helping me back up.'

With that, Calo gave a mock bow and ran off into the crowd; in just a few seconds he was lost to sight. Locke made a show of dusting himself off while he slowly counted to thirty inside his head. At thirty-one, he sat down suddenly beside the cart, put his hooded head in his hands and began to sniffle. Just a few seconds later he was sobbing loudly. Responding to the cue, Galdo came over and knelt beside him, placing one hand on his shoulder.

'Boys,' said Ambrosine Strollo, 'boys! What's the matter? Are you hurt? Did that oaf jar something?'

Galdo made a show of muttering into Locke's ear; Locke muttered back, and Galdo fell back onto his own posterior. He reached up and tugged at his hood in an excellent imitation of frustration, and his eyes were wide. 'No, Madam Strollo,' he said, 'it's worse than that.'

'Worse? What do you mean? What's the trouble?'

'The silver,' Locke burbled, looking up to let her see the tears pouring down his cheeks and the artful curl of his lips. 'He took my purse. Picked my p-pocket.'

'It was payment,' said Galdo, 'from this man's widow. Not just for the candles, but for his interment, our blessings and his funeral. We were to bring it back to Father Chains along with the . . .'

'. . . with the b-body,' Locke burst out. 'I've failed him!'

'Twelve,' the old lady muttered, 'that incredible little bastard!' Leaning out over the counter of her shop window, she hollered in a voice of surprising strength, 'THIEF! STOP, THIEF!' As Locke buried his head in his hands once again, she turned her head upward and shouted, 'LUCREZIA!'

'Yes, gran'mama,' came a voice from an open window. 'What's this about a thief?'

'Rouse your brothers, child. Get them down here now and tell them to bring their sticks!' She turned to regard Locke and Galdo. 'Don't cry, my dear boys. Don't cry. We'll make this right somehow.'

'What's this about a thief?' A lanky sergeant of the watch ran up, truncheon out, mustard-yellow coat flapping behind him and two other yellowjackets at his heels.

'A fine constable you are, Vidrik, to let those little coat-charmer bastards from the Cauldron sneak in and rob customers right in front of my shop!'

'What? Here? Them?' The watch-sergeant took in the distraught boys, the furious old woman and the covered corpse; his eyebrows attempted to leap straight up off his forehead. 'Ah, that . . . I say, that man is *dead* . . .'

'Of course he's dead, thimblebrains; these boys are taking him to the House of Perelandro for blessings and a funeral! That little cutpurse just stole the bag with his widow's payment for it all!'

'Someone robbed the initiates of Perelandro? The boys who help that blind priest?' A florid man with an overachieving belly and an entire squad of spare chins wobbled up, with a walking stick in one hand and a wicked-looking hatchet in the other. 'Pissant ratfucker bastards! Such an infamy! In the Videnza, in broad light of day!'

'I'm sorry,' Locke sobbed. 'I'm so sorry, I didn't realise . . . I should have held it tighter, I just didn't realise . . . He was so quick . . .'

'Nonsense, boy, it was hardly your fault,' said Madam Strollo. The watch-sergeant began blowing his whistle; the fat man with the walking stick continued to spit vitriol, and a pair of young men appeared around the corner of the Strollo house, carrying curved truncheons shod with brass. There was more rapid shouting until they determined that their grandmother was unhurt; when they discovered the reason for her summons, they too began uttering threats and curses and promises of vengeance.

'Here,' said Madam Strollo. 'Here, boys. The candles will be my gift. This sort of thing doesn't happen in the Videnza. We won't stand for it.' She set the three solons Locke had given her back on her counter. 'How much was in the purse?'

'Fifteen solons before we paid you,' said Galdo, 'so twelve got stolen. Chains is going to throw us out of the order.'

'Don't be foolish,' said Madam Strollo. She added two more coins to the pile as the crowd around her shop began to swell.

'Hells yes,' cried the fat man. 'We can't let that little devil dishonour us like this! Madam Strollo, how much are you giving? I'll give more!'

'Gods take you, you selfish old pig, this isn't about showing me up—'

'I'll give you a basket of oranges,' said one of the women in the crowd, 'for you and for the Eyeless Priest.'

'I have a solon I can give,' said another merchant, pressing forward with the coin in his hand.

'Vidrik!' Madam Strollo turned from her argument with her florid neighbour. 'Vidrik, this is your fault! You owe these initiates some copper, at the very least!'

'My fault? Now look here—'

'No, *you* look here! When they speak of the Videnza now they'll say, "Ah, that's where they rob priests, isn't it? That's where they mug helpless initiates of Perelandro!" For the Twelve's sake! Just like Catchfire! Or worse!' She spat. 'You give something to make amends or I'll harp on your captain and you'll end up rowing a shitboat until your hair turns grey and your teeth come out at the roots!'

Grimacing, the watch-sergeant stepped forward and reached for his purse, but there was already a tight press around the two boys. They were helped to their feet, and Locke received too many comforting pats on the back to count. They were plied with coins, fruit and small gifts; one merchant tossed his more valuable coins into a coat pocket and handed over his purse. Locke and Galdo adopted convincing expressions of bewilderment and surprise. As each gift was handed over to them, they protested as best they could, for form's sake.

6

It was the fourth hour of the afternoon before the body of Antrim One-Hand was safely stashed in the damp sanctuary of the House of Perelandro. The three white-robed boys (for Calo had rejoined them safely at the edge of the Temple District) padded down the steps and took their seats beside Father Chains, who sat in his usual spot with one burly arm thrown over the rim of his copper kettle.

'So,' he said. 'Boys. Is Jessaline going to be sorry she saved my life?'

'Not at all,' said Locke.

'It's a great corpse,' said Calo.

'Smells a bit,' said Galdo.

'Other than that,' said Calo, 'it's a *fantastic* corpse.'

'Hanged at noon,' said Locke. 'Still fresh.'

'I'm very pleased. Very, very pleased. But I really must ask – why the hell have men and women been throwing money in my kettle for the past half-hour, telling me they're "sorry for what happened in the Videnza"?'

'It's because they're sorry for what happened in the Videnza,' said Galdo.

'It wasn't a burning tavern, Benefactor's own truth,' said Locke.

'What,' said Chains, speaking slowly as though to a misbehaving pet, 'did you boys do with the corpse before you stashed it in the temple?'

'Made money.' Locke tossed the merchant's donated purse into the kettle, where it hit with a heavy clang. 'Twenty-three solons three, to be precise.'

'And a basket of oranges,' said Calo.

'Packet of candles,' added Galdo, 'two loaves of black-pepper bread, a wax carton of small beer and some glow-globes.'

Chains was silent for a moment, and then he peeked down into the kettle, pretending to readjust his blindfold but actually raising it just a bit at the bottom. Calo and Galdo began to confide the roughest outline of the scheme Locke had prepared and executed with their help, giggling as they did so.

'Bugger me bloody with a boathook,' Chains said when they finished. 'I don't recall telling you that your leash was slipped enough for fucking street theatre, Lamora.'

'We had to get our money back somehow,' said Locke. 'Cost us fifteen silvers to get the body from the Palace of Patience. Now we're up some, plus candles and bread and beer.'

'Oranges,' said Calo.

'And glow-globes,' said Galdo. 'Don't forget those; they're pretty.'

'Crooked Warden,' said Chains, 'just this morning I was suffering from the delusion that *I* was handing out the education here.'

They sat in companionable silence for a few moments after that, while the sun settled into its downward arc in the west and long shadows began to creep across the face of the city.

'Well, what the hell.' Chains rattled his manacles a few times to keep up his circulation. 'I'll take back what I gave you to spend. Of the extra, Calo, you and Galdo can have a silver apiece to do as you please. Locke, you can have the rest to put towards your . . . dues. It was fairly stolen.'

At that moment a well-dressed man in a forest-green coat and a four-cornered hat walked up to the temple steps. He threw a handful of coins into the kettle; they sounded like mingled silver and copper as they clattered. The man tipped his hat to the three boys and said, 'I'm from the Videnza. I want you to know that I'm furious about what happened.'

'One hundred years of health for you and your children,' said Locke, 'and the blessings of the Lord of the Overlooked.'

CHAPTER FIVE

The Grey King

I

'You seem to be spending a great deal of our money very quickly, Lukas' said Doña Sofia Salvara.

'Circumstance has blessed us, Doña Sofia.' Locke gave a smile that was a measure of great triumph by Fehrwright standards, a tight-lipped little thing that might have been a grimace of pain from anyone else. 'Everything is proceeding with the most agreeable speed. Ships and men and cargo, and soon all we'll need to do is pack your wardrobe for a short voyage!'

'Indeed, indeed.' Were those dark circles under her eyes? Was there the slightest hint of wariness in her attitude towards him? She certainly wasn't at ease. Locke made a mental note to avoid pushing her too far, too fast. It was a delicate dance, playing straight lines and smiles with someone who knew he was a mummer but didn't know that *he* knew *she* knew.

With the slightest sigh, Doña Sofia pressed her personal sigil down into the warm blue wax at the bottom of the parchment she was contemplating. She added a few flowing lines of ink above the seal, her signature in the curving Therin script that had become something of a fad among literate nobles in the past few years. 'If you say you require another four thousand today, another four thousand it must be.'

'I am most sincerely grateful, my lady.'

'Well, you'll certainly pay for it soon enough,' she said. 'Many times over, if our hopes play out.' At that she smiled with genuine good humour that crinkled the edges of her eyes, and held out the fresh promissory note.

Oh-ho, thought Locke. *Much better. The more in control the mark thinks they are, the more easily they respond to real control.* Another one of Father Chains' old maxims, proven in Locke's experience too many times to count.

'Please give my warmest regards to your husband when he returns from his business in the city, my lady,' said Locke, taking the wax-sealed parchment in hand. 'Now, I fear, I must go see some men about . . . payments that will not appear on any official ledger.'

'Of course. I quite understand. Conté can show you out.'

The gruff, weathered man-at-arms was somewhat pale, and it seemed to Locke that there was a slight but obvious hitch in his stride. Yes – the poor fellow was clearly favouring a certain badly bruised portion of his anatomy. Locke's stomach turned in unconscious sympathy at his own memory of that night.

'I say, Conté,' he began politely, 'are you feeling quite well? You seem . . . forgive me for saying so . . . troubled this past day or two.'

'I'm well for the most part, Master Fehrwight.' There was slight hardening of the lines at the edges of the man's mouth. 'Perhaps a bit under the weather.'

'Nothing serious?'

'A minor ague, perhaps. They happen, this time of year.'

'Ah. One of the tricks of your climate. I've not yet felt such a thing, myself.'

'Well,' said Conté with an absolute lack of expression on his face, 'mind yourself then, Master Fehrwight. Camorr can be a very dangerous place in the most *unlooked-for* ways.'

Oh-ho-HO, Locke thought, so they'd let him in on the secret, as well. And the man had a proud streak at least as wide as Sofia's, to drop even the slightest hint of a threat. Worth noting, that.

'I'm the very soul of caution, my dear Conté.' Locke tucked the promissory note within his black waistcoat and adjusted his cascading cravats as they approached the front door of the Salvara manor. 'I keep my chambers very well illuminated, to ward off miasmas, and I wear copper rings after Falselight. Just the thing for your hot-and-cold fevers. I would wager that a few days at sea will put you right.'

'No doubt,' said Conté. 'The voyage. I do look forward to the . . . voyage.'

'Then we are of one mind!' Locke waited for the Don's man to open the wide glass-and-iron door for him, and as he stepped out into the moist air of Falselight, he nodded stiffly but affably. 'I shall pray for your health tomorrow, my good fellow.'

'Too kind, Master Fehrwight.' The ex-soldier had set one hand on the hilt of one of his knives, perhaps unconsciously. 'I shall most assuredly offer prayers concerning *yours*.'

2

Locke began walking south at a leisurely pace, crossing from the Isla Durona to Twosilver Green as he and Calo had just a few nights previously. The Hangman's Wind was stronger than usual, and as he walked through the park in the washed-out light of the city's glowing Elderglass, the hiss and rustle of leaves was like the sighing of vast creatures, hiding in the greenery all around him.

Just under seventeen thousand crowns in half a week; the Don Salvara game was well ahead of their original plans, which had called for a two-week span between first touch and final blow-off. Locke was certain he could get one more touch out of the Don in perfect safety . . . push the total up over twenty-two or maybe twenty-three thousand, and then pull a vanish. Go to ground, take it easy for a few weeks, stay alert and let the Grey King mess sort itself out.

And then, as a bonus miracle, somehow convince Capa Barsavi to dis-engage him from Nazca, and do so without twisting the old man's breeches. Locke sighed.

When Falselight died and true night fell, the glow never seemed to simply fade so much as recede, as though it were being drawn back within the glass, a loan reclaimed by a jealous creditor. Shadows widened and blackened until finally the whole park was swallowed by them from below. Emerald lanterns flickered to life here and there in the trees, their light soft and eerie and strangely relaxing. They offered just enough illumination to see the crushed-stone paths that wound their way through the walls of trees and hedges. Locke felt as though the spring of tension within him was unwinding itself ever so slightly; he listened to the muted *crunch* of his footsteps on gravel and for a few moments he was surprised to find himself possessed by something perilously close to contentment.

He was alive; he was rich; he had made the decision not to skulk and cringe from the troubles that gnawed at his Gentlemen Bastards. And for one brief moment, in the middle of eighty-eight thousand people and all the heaving, stinking, ever-flowing noise and commerce and machinery of their city, he was alone with the gently swaying trees of Twosilver Green.

Alone.

The hairs on the back of his neck stood up, and the old cold fear, the constant companion of anyone raised on the streets, was suddenly alive within him. It was a summer night in Twosilver Green, the safest open park in the city, patrolled at any given time by two or three squads of yellowjackets with their night-lanterns waving on poles. Filled, sometimes to the point of comedy, with the strolling sons and daughters of the moneyed classes, holding hands and swatting insects and seeking the privacy of nooks and shadows.

Locke gazed quickly up and down the curving paths around him; he was *truly* alone. There was no sound in the park but the sighing of the leaves and the buzzing of the insects; no voices or footsteps that he could hear. He twisted his right forearm, and a thin stiletto of blackened steel fell from his coat sleeve into his palm, pommel down. He carried it straight against his arm, rendering it invisible from any distance, and hurried towards the southern gate of the park.

A mist was rising, seeping up as though the grass were pouring grey vapours into the night; Locke shivered despite the warm, heavy air. A mist was perfectly natural, wasn't it? The whole city was blanketed in the stuff two nights out of three; a man could lose track of the end of his own nose in it sometimes. But why—

The southern gate of the park. He was standing before the southern gate of the park, staring out across an empty cobbled lane at a mist-shrouded bridge. That bridge was the Eldren Arch, its red lanterns soft and ominous in the fog.

The Eldren Arch leading north to the Isla Durona.

He'd somehow turned round. How was that possible? His heart was beating so fast, and then – *Doña Sofia*. That cunning, cunning bitch. She'd done something to him . . . slipped him some alchemical mischief on the parchment. The ink? The wax? Was it a poison, drawing some cloud around his senses before it did its work? Was it some other drug, intended to make him ill? Petty, perfectly deniable revenge to sate her for the time being? He fumbled for the parchment, missing his inner coat pocket, aware that he was moving a bit too slowly and clumsily for the confusion to be entirely in his imagination.

There were men moving under the trees.

One to his left, another to his right . . . The Eldren Arch was gone; he was back at the heart of the curving paths, staring out into a darkness cut only by the emerald light of the lanterns. He gasped, crouched, brought up the stiletto, head swimming. The men were cloaked; they were on either side. There was the sound of footsteps on gravel, not his own. The dark shape of crossbows, the backlit shapes of the men . . . His head whirled.

'Master Thorn,' said a man's voice, muffled and distant, 'we require an hour of your attention.'

'Crooked Warden,' Locke gasped, and then even the faint colours of the trees seemed to drain from his vision, and the whole night went black.

3

When he came to, he was already sitting up. It was a curious sensation. He'd awoken before from blackness brought on by injuries and by drugs, but this was different. It was as though someone had simply set the mechanisms of his consciousness moving again, like a scholar opening the spigot on a Verrari water-clock.

He was in the common room of a tavern, seated on a chair at his own table. He could see the bar, and the hearth, and the other tables, but the place was dank and empty, smelling of mould and dust. A flickering orange light came from behind him – an oil lantern. The windows were greasy and misted over, turning the light back upon itself; he couldn't see anything of the outside through them.

'There's a crossbow at your back,' said a voice just a few feet behind him – a pleasantly cultured man's voice, definitely Camorri but somewhat off in a few of the pronunciations. A native who'd spent time elsewhere? The voice was entirely unknown to him. 'Master Thorn.'

Icicles seemed to grow in Locke's spine. He racked his brains furiously for recall of those last few seconds in the park – hadn't one of the men there called him that, as well? He gulped. 'Why do you call me that? My name is Lukas Fehrwight. I'm a citizen of Emberlain working for the House of bel Auster.'

'I could believe that, Master Thorn. Your accent is convincing, and your willingness to suffer that black wool is nothing short of heroic. Don Lorenzo and Doña Sofia certainly believed in Lukas Fehrwight, until you yourself disabused them of the notion.'

It isn't Barsavi, Locke thought desperately. It couldn't be . . . Barsavi would be conducting this conversation himself, if he knew. He would be conducting it at the heart of the Floating Grave, with every Gentleman Bastard tied to a post and every knife in Sage Kindness's bag sharpened and gleaming.

'My name *is* Lukas Fehrwight,' Locke insisted. 'I don't understand what you want or what I'm doing here. Have you done anything to Graumann? Is he safe?'

'Jean Tannen is perfectly safe,' said the man. 'As you well know. How I would have loved to see it up close, when you strolled into Don Salvara's office with that silly sigil-wallet under your black cloak. Destroying his confidence in Lukas Fehrwight just as a father gently tells his children there's really no such thing as the Blessed Bringer! You're an artist, Master Thorn.'

'I have already told you, my name is *Lukas*, Lukas Fehrwight, and . . .'

'If you tell me that your name is Lukas Fehrwight one more time, I'm going to put a bolt through the back of your upper left arm. I wouldn't mean to kill you, just to complicate your life. A nice big hole, maybe a broken bone. Ruin that fine suit of yours, perhaps get blood all over that lovely parchment. Wouldn't the clerks at Meraggio's *love* to hear an explanation for that? Promissory notes are so much more attention-getting when they're covered in gore.'

Locke said nothing for quite a long while.

'Now that won't do either, Locke. Surely you must have realised I can't be one of Barsavi's men.'

Thirteen, Locke thought. *Where the hell did I make a mistake?* If the man was speaking truthfully, if he didn't work for Capa Barsavi, there was only one other possibility. The real Spider. The real Midnighters. Had Locke's use of the pretend sigil-wallet been reported? Had that counterfeiter in Talisham decided to try for a bit of extra profit by dropping a word to the Duke's secret constables? It seemed the likeliest explanation.

'Turn around. Slowly.'

Locke stood up and did so, and bit his tongue to avoid crying out in surprise.

The man seated at the table before him could have been anywhere between thirty and fifty; he was lean and rangy and grey at the temples. The mark of Camorr was upon his face; he bore the sun-darkened olive skin, the high temples and cheekbones, the sharp nose.

He wore a grey leather doublet over a grey silk tunic; his cloak and mantle were grey, as was the hood that was swept back behind his head. His hands, folded neatly before him, were covered with thin grey swordsman's gloves, kid leather that was weathered and creased with use. The man had hunter's eyes, cold and steady and measuring. The orange light of the lantern was reflected in their dark pupils. For a second it seemed to Locke that he was seeing not a reflection but a revelation; that the dark fire burned *behind* the man's eyes. He shivered despite himself.

'*You*,' he whispered, dropping the accent of Lukas Fehrwright.

'None other,' said the Grey King. 'I disdain these clothes as something of a theatrical touch, but it's a necessary one. Of all the men in Camorr, surely *you* understand these things, Master Thorn.'

'I have no idea why you keep calling me that,' said Locke, shifting his footing as unobtrusively as he could, feeling the comforting weight of his second stiletto in the other sleeve of his coat, 'and I don't see this crossbow you mentioned.'

'I said it was at your back.' The Grey King gestured at the far wall with a thin, bemused smile. Warily, Locke turned his head.

There was a man standing against the wall of the tavern, right in the spot Locke had been staring at until the previous moment. A cloaked and hooded man, broad-shouldered, leaning lazily against the wall with a loaded alleypiece in the crook of his arm, the quarrel pointed casually at Locke's chest.

'I . . .' Locke turned back, but the Grey King was no longer seated at the table. He was standing a dozen feet away, to Locke's left, behind the disused bar. The lantern on the table hadn't moved, and Locke could see that the man was grinning. 'This isn't possible.'

'Of course it is, Master Thorn. Think it through. The number of possibilities is actually *vanishingly* small.'

The Grey King waved his left hand in an arc, as though wiping a window; Locke glanced back at the wall and saw that the cross-bowman had disappeared once again.

'Well, fuck me,' said Locke. 'You're a Bondsmage.'

'No,' said the Grey King, 'I'm a man without that advantage, no different than yourself. But I employ a Bondsmage.' He pointed to the table where he'd previously been sitting.

There, without any sudden movement or jump in Locke's perception, sat a slender man surely not yet out of his twenties. His chin and cheeks were peach-fuzzed, and his hairline was already in rapid retreat to the back of his head. His eyes were alight with amusement and Locke immediately saw in him the sort of casual presumption of authority that most congenital bluebloods wore like a second skin.

He was dressed in an extremely well-tailored grey coat with flaring red silk cuffs; the bare skin of his left wrist bore three tattooed black lines. On his right hand was a heavy leather gauntlet, and perched atop this, staring at Locke as though he were nothing more than a field mouse with delusions of grandeur, was the fiercest hunting hawk Locke had ever seen. The bird of prey stared directly at him, its eyes pinpoints of black within gold on either side of a curved beak that looked dagger-sharp. Its brown and grey wings were folded back sleekly, and its talons – what was wrong with its talons? Its rear claws were huge, distended, oddly lengthened.

'My associate, the Falconer,' said the Grey King. 'A Bondsmage of Karthain. My Bondsmage. The key to a great many things. And now that we've been introduced, let us speak of what I expect you to do for me.'

4

'They are not to be fucked with,' Chains had told him once, many years before.

'Why not?' Locke was twelve or thirteen at the time, about as cocksure as he'd ever be in life, which was saying something.

'I see you've been neglecting your history again. I'll assign you more reading shortly.' Chains sighed. 'The Bondsmagi of Karthain are the only sorcerers on the continent because they permit no one else to study their art.'

'And none resist? Nobody fights back or hides from them?'

'Of course they do, here and there. But what can two or five or ten sorcerers in hiding do against four hundred with a city-state at their command? What the Bondsmagi do to outsiders and renegades . . . they make Capa Barsavi look like a priest of Perelandro. They are utterly jealous, utterly ruthless and utterly without competition. They have achieved their desired monopoly. No one will shelter sorcerers against the will of the Bondsmagi, no one. Not even the King of the Seven Marrows.'

'Curious,' said Locke, 'that they still call themselves Bondsmagi, then.'

'It's false modesty. I think it amuses them. They set such ridiculous prices for their services, it's less like mercenary work to them and more like a cruel joke at the expense of their clients.'

'Ridiculous prices?'

'A novice would cost you five hundred crowns a day. A journeyman might cost you a thousand. They mark their rank with tattoos around their wrists. The more black circles you see, the more polite you become.'

'A thousand crowns a *day*?'

'You see now why they're not everywhere, on retainer to every court and noble and pissant warlord with a treasury to waste. Even in times of war and other extreme crises, they can be secured for a very limited duration. When you do cross paths with one, you can be sure that the client is paying them for serious, active work.'

'Where did they come from?'

'Karthain.'

'Ha ha. I mean their guild. Their monopoly.'

'That's easy. One night a powerful sorcerer knocks on the door of a less powerful sorcerer. "I'm starting an exclusive guild," he says. "Join me now or I'll blast you out of your fucking boots right where you stand." So naturally the second mage says . . .'

'You know, I've always wanted to join a guild!'

'Right. Those two go bother a third sorcerer. "Join the guild," they say, "or fight both of us, two on one, right here and right now." Repeat as necessary, until three or four hundred guild members are knocking on the door of the last independent mage around, and everyone who said "No" is dead.'

'They must have weaknesses,' said Locke.

'Of course they've got weaknesses, boy. They're mortal men and women, same as us. They eat, they shit, they age, they die. But they're like gods-damned hornets; mess with one and the rest show up to punch you full of holes. Thirteen help anyone who kills a Bondsmage, purposely or otherwise.'

'Why?'

'It's the oldest rule of their guild, a rule without exceptions. Kill a Bondsmage, and the whole guild drops whatever it's doing to come after you. They seek you out by any means they need to use. They kill your friends, your family, your associates. They burn your home. They destroy everything you've ever built. Before they finally let you die, they make sure you know that your line has been wiped from the earth, root and branch.'

'So nobody is allowed to oppose them at all?'

'Oh, you can oppose them, all right. You can try to fight back, for what it's worth when one of them is against you. But if you go as far as killing one, well, it's just not worth it. Suicide would be preferable; at least then they won't kill everyone you ever loved or trusted.'

'Wow.'

'Yes.' Chains shook his head. 'Sorcery's impressive enough, but it's their fucking attitude that makes them such a pain. And that's why, when you find yourself face to face with one, you bow and scrape and mind your "sirs" and "madams". '

213

5

'Nice bird, arsehole,' said Locke.

The Bondsmage stared coldly at him, nonplussed.

'So *you* must be the reason nobody can find your boss. The reason none of the Full Crowns could remember what they were doing when Tall Tesso got nailed to a wall.'

The falcon screeched, and Locke flinched backward; the creature's anger was extremely expressive. It was more than the cry of an agitated animal . . . it was somehow personal. Locke raised his eyebrows.

'My familiar mislikes your tone of voice,' said the Falconer. 'I for one have always found her judgement to be impeccable. I would mind your tongue.'

'Your boss expects me to do something for him,' said Locke, 'which means I have to remain functional. Which means the manner in which I address his fucking Karthani lackeys is immaterial. Some of the *garristas* you killed were friends of mine. I'm looking at an arranged fucking marriage because of you! So eat hemp and shit rope, Bondsmage.'

The falcon exploded, screeching, from its perch on its master's hand. Locke raised his left arm in front of his face and the bird slammed against it, talons clutching with edges that sliced through the fabric of Locke's coat sleeve. The bird fastened itself on Locke's arm, excruciatingly, and beat its wings to steady itself. Locke hollered and raised his right hand to punch the bird.

'Do that,' said the Falconer, 'and die. Look closely at my familiar's talons.'

Biting the insides of his cheeks against the pain, Locke did just that. The creature's rear talons weren't talons at all, but more like smooth curved hooks that narrowed to needle points at their tips. There were strange pulsating sacs on its legs just above them, and even with Locke's limited knowledge of hunting birds this seemed very wrong.

'Vestris,' said the Grey King, 'is a scorpion hawk. A hybrid, facilitated by alchemy and sorcery. One of many that the Bondsmagi amuse themselves with. She carries not just talons, but a sting. If she were to cease being tolerant of you, you might make it ten steps before you fell dead in your tracks.'

Blood began to drip from Locke's arm; he groaned. The bird snapped at him with its beak, clearly enjoying itself.

'Now,' said the Grey King, 'are we not all grown men and birds here? Functional is such a relative state of affairs, Locke. I would hate to have to give you another demonstration of just *how* relative.'

'I apologise,' said Locke between gritted teeth. 'Vestris is a fine and persuasive little bird.'

The Falconer said nothing, but Vestris released her grip on Locke's left arm, unleashing new spikes of pain. Locke clutched his blooded wool sleeve, massaging the wounds within it. Vestris fluttered back to her perch on her master's glove, and resumed staring at Locke.

'Isn't it just as I said, Falconer?' The Grey King beamed at Locke. 'Our Thorn knows how to recover his equilibrium. Two minutes ago he was too scared to think. Now he's already insulting us and no doubt scheming for a way out of this situation.'

'I don't understand,' said Locke, 'why you keep calling me Thorn.'

'Of course you do,' said the Grey King. 'I'm only going to go over this once, Locke. I know about your little burrow beneath the House of Perelandro. Your vault. Your fortune. I know you don't spend any of your nights sneak-thieving, as you claim to all the other Right People. I know you breach the Secret Peace to spring elaborate confidence schemes on nobles who don't know any better, and I know you're good at it. I know *you* didn't start these ridiculous rumours about the Thorn of Camorr, but you and I both know they refer to your exploits, indirectly. Lastly, I understand that Capa Barsavi would do some very interesting things to you and all of your Gentlemen Bastards if the things I know were to be confided to him.'

'Oh, please,' said Locke. 'You're not exactly in any position to whisper politely in his ear and be taken seriously.'

'*I'm* not the one who would be whispering in his ear,' said the Grey King, smiling, 'if you failed at the task I have for you. I have others close enough to him to whisper for me. I trust I have made myself very clear.'

Locke glared for a few seconds, then sat down with a sigh,

turning his chair around and leaning his injured arm against the back. 'I see your point. And in exchange?'

'In exchange for the task I require, I would promise you that Capa Barsavi won't hear about your very cleverly arranged double life, nor that of your closest companions.'

'So,' said Locke slowly, 'that's how it is.'

'My Bondsmage excepted, I'm a thrifty man, Locke.' The Grey King stepped out from behind the bar and folded his arms. 'You get paid in life, not coin.'

'What's the task?'

'A straightforward beguilement,' said the Grey King. 'I want *you* to become *me*.'

'I, ah, I don't understand.'

'The time has come for me to quit this game of shadows. Barsavi and I need to speak face to face. I will very shortly arrange a clandestine conference with the Capa, one that will bring him forth from the Floating Grave.'

'Fat chance.'

'In this you must trust me. I'm the architect of his current troubles; I assure you, I know what can bring him out from that soggy fortress of his. But it won't be me that he'll speak to. It will be you. The Thorn of Camorr. The greatest mummer this city has ever produced. You, cast in the role of me. Just for one night. A virtuoso performance.'

'A command performance. Why?'

'I will be required elsewhere at that time. The conference is one part of a wider concern.'

'I am personally known to Capa Barsavi and his entire family!'

'You have already convinced the Salvaras that you are two different men. In the same day, no less. I'll coach you in what I wish you to say and provide you with a suitable wardrobe. Between your skills and my current anonymity, no one will ever be aware that you are even involved, or that you are not the real Grey King.'

'An amusing plan. It has balls, and that appeals to me. But you do realise that I'm going to look like quite the ass,' said Locke, 'when the Capa opens our conversation with a dozen crossbow bolts to my chest.'

'Hardly an issue. You'll be quite well protected against routine foolishness on the Capa's part. I'll be sending the Falconer with you.'

Locke flicked his gaze back to the Bondsmage, who smiled with mock magnanimity.

'Do you really think,' continued the Grey King, 'that I would have let you keep that other stiletto in your coat sleeve if any weapon in your hands could touch me? Try to cut me. I'll let you borrow a crossbow or two, if you like. A quarrel will do no better. The same protection will be yours when you meet the Capa.'

'Then it's true,' said Locke. 'Those stories aren't just stories. Your pet mage gives you more than just the ability to make my head lock up like I've been drinking all night.'

'Yes. And it was my men who started spreading those stories, for one purpose – I wanted Barsavi's gangs to so dread my presence that they wouldn't dare to get close to you when the time came for you to speak to him. After all, I have the power to kill men with a touch.' The Grey King smiled. 'And when you're me, so will you.'

Locke frowned. That smile, that face . . . there was something damned familiar about the Grey King. Nothing immediately obvious – just a nagging sensation that Locke had been in his presence before. He cleared his throat. 'That's very thoughtful of you. And what happens when I've finished this task for you?'

'A parting of the ways,' said the Grey King. 'You to your business, and me to my own.'

'I find that somewhat difficult to believe.'

'You'll leave your meeting with Barsavi alive, Locke. Fear not for what happens after that; I assure you it won't be as bad as you think. If I merely wanted to assassinate him, can you deny that I could have done it long ago?'

'You've killed seven of his *garristas*. You've kept him locked away on the Floating Grave for months. Not as bad as I think? He killed eight of his own Full Crowns after Tesso died. He won't accept less than blood from *you*.'

'Barsavi has kept himself locked away on the Floating Grave, Locke. And as I said, you must trust me to deal with that end of the situation. The Capa *will* acquiesce to what I have to offer him. We'll settle the question of Camorr once and for all, to everyone's satisfaction.'

'I grant that you're dangerous,' said Locke, 'but you must be mad.'

'Suit whatever meaning you wish to my actions, Locke, provided that you perform as required.'

'It would appear,' Locke said sourly, 'that I have no choice.'

'This is no accident. Are we agreed? You'll perform this task for me?'

'I'll receive instruction in what you wish me to say to Capa Barsavi?'

'Yes.'

'There will be one other condition.'

'Really?'

'If I'm going to do this for you,' said Locke, 'I need to have a way to speak to you, or at least get a message to you, at my own will. Something may come up which can't wait for you to prance around appearing out of nowhere.'

'It's unlikely,' said the Grey King.

'It's a necessity. Do you want me to be successful in this task or not?'

'Very well.' The Grey King nodded. 'Falconer.'

The Falconer rose from his seat; Vestris never took her eyes from Locke's. The hawk's master reached inside his coat with his free hand and withdrew a candle, a tiny cylinder of white wax with an odd smear of crimson swirling through it. 'Light this,' said the Bondsmage, 'in a place of solitude. You must be absolutely alone. Speak my name, and I will hear and come, soon enough.'

'Thank you.' Locke took the candle with his right hand and slipped it into his own coat. 'Falconer. Easy to remember, that.'

Vestris opened her beak but made no noise. It snapped shut, and the bird blinked. A yawn? Her version of a chuckle at Locke's expense?

'I'll be keeping an eye on you,' said the Bondsmage. 'Just as Vestris feels what I feel, I see what she sees.'

'That explains quite a bit,' said Locke.

'If we are agreed,' said the Grey King, 'our business here is finished. I have something else to do, and it must be done tonight. Thank you, Master Thorn, for seeing reason.'

'Said the man with the crossbow to the man with the money purse.' Locke stood up and slipped his left hand into a coat pocket;

the forearm was still throbbing with pain. 'So when is this meeting supposed to take place?'

'Three nights hence,' said the Grey King. 'No interruption at all to your Don Salvara game, I trust.'

'I don't think you really care, but no.'

'All for the better, then. Let us return you to your own affairs.'

'You're not going to—'

But it was too late; the Falconer had already begun to gesture with his free hand and move his lips, forming words but not quite vocalising them. The room spun; the orange lantern light became a fading streak of colour against the darkness of the room, and then there was only darkness.

6

When Locke's senses returned he found himself standing on the bridge between the Snare and Coin-Kisser's Row; not a moment had passed by his own personal reckoning, but when he looked up he saw that the clouds were gone, the stars had whirled in the dark sky, and the moons were low in the west.

'Son of a *bitch*,' he hissed. 'It's been hours! Jean's got to be having fits.'

He thought quickly. Calo and Galdo had planned to spend the evening making their rounds in the Snare, with Bug in tow. They would probably have ended up at the Last Mistake, dicing and drinking and trying not to get thrown out for card-sharping. Jean had intended to spend the night feigning occupancy in the Broken Tower rooms, at least until Locke returned. That would be the closest place to begin hunting for them. Just then, Locke remembered that he was still dressed as Lukas Fehrwight. He slapped his forehead.

He pulled his coat and cravats off, yanked the false optics from the bridge of his nose and stuffed them in a pocket. He gingerly felt the cuts on his left arm; they were deep and still painful, but the blood had crusted on them, so at least he wasn't dripping all over the place. *Gods damn the Grey King*, thought Locke, *and gods grant I get the chance to balance this night out in the ledger*.

He ruffled his hair, unbuttoned his vest, untucked his shirt and reached down to fold and conceal the ridiculous ribbon tongues of his shoes. His cravats and his decorative belts went into the coat, which Locke then folded up and tied by the sleeves. In the darkness it bore an excellent resemblance to a plain old cloth sack. With the outward flourishes of Lukas Fehrwight broken down, he could at least pass without notice for a reasonably short period of time. Satisfied, he turned and began to walk quickly down the south side of the bridge, towards the still-lively lights and noises of the Snare.

Jean Tannen actually appeared from an alley and took him by the arm as he turned onto the street on the north side of the Broken Tower, where the main entrance to the Last Mistake opened onto the cobbles. 'Locke! Where the hell have you been all night? Are you well?'

'Jean, gods, am I ever glad to see you. I'm not well, and as it turns out neither are you. Where are the others?'

'When you didn't return,' Jean said, speaking in a low voice close to Locke's ear, 'I found them in the Last Mistake and sent them up to our rooms, with Bug. I've been pacing the alleys down here, trying to keep out of sight. I didn't want us all getting scattered across the city by night. I – we feared—'

'I was taken, Jean. But then I was let go. Let's get up to the rooms. We have a new problem, fresh from the oven and hot as hell.'

7

They let the windows in their rooms stay open this time, with thin sheets of translucent mesh drawn down to keep out biting insects. The sky was turning grey, with lines of red visible just beneath the eastern window sills, when Locke finished relating the events of the night. His listeners had shadows beneath their bleary eyes, but none showed any indication of sleepiness just then.

'At least we know now,' Locke finished, 'that he won't be trying to kill me like he did the other *garristas*.'

'Not until three nights hence, anyway,' said Galdo.

'Bastard simply can't be trusted,' said Bug.

'But for the time being,' said Locke, 'he must be *obeyed*.'

Locke had changed his clothes; he now looked much more

suitably lower class. Jean had insisted on washing his arm with reinforced wine, heated to near-boiling on an alchemical hearth-stone. Locke now had a compress of brandy-soaked cloth pressed to it, and he bathed it in the light of a small white glow-globe. It was common knowledge among the physikers of Camorr that light drove back malodorous air and helped prevent lingering infections.

'Must he?' Calo scratched a stubbly chin. 'How far do you figure we can get if we run like hell?'

'From the Grey King, who knows?' Locke sighed. 'From the Bondsmage, not far enough, ever.'

'So we just sit back,' said Jean, 'and let him pull your strings, like a marionette on stage.'

'I was rather taken,' said Locke, 'with the whole idea of him not telling Capa Barsavi about our confidence games, yes.'

'This whole thing is mad,' said Galdo. 'You said you saw three rings on this Falconer's wrist?'

'The one that didn't have the damn scorpion hawk, yes.'

'Three rings.' Jean muttered. 'It *is* mad. To keep one of those people in service . . . It must be two months now since the first stories of the Grey King appeared. Since the first garrista got it . . . Who was it, again?'

'Gil the Cutter, from the Rum Hounds,' said Calo.

'The coin involved has to be . . . ludicrous. I doubt the *Duke* could keep a Bondsmage of rank on for this long. So who the fuck is this Grey King, and how is he paying for this?'

'Immaterial,' said Locke. 'Three nights hence, or two and a half now that the sun's coming up, there'll be two Grey Kings, and I'll be one of them.'

'Thirteen,' said Jean. He put his head in his hands and rubbed his eyes with his palms.

'So that's the bad news. Capa Barsavi wants me to marry his daughter and now the Grey King wants me to impersonate him at a secret meeting with Barsavi.' Locke grinned. 'The good news is I didn't get any blood on that new promissory note for four thousand crowns.'

'I'll kill him,' said Bug. 'Get me poisoned quarrels and an alleypiece and I'll drill him in the eyes.'

'Bug,' said Locke, 'that makes leaping off a temple roof sound reasonable by comparison.'

'But who would ever expect it?' Bug, sitting beneath one of the room's eastern windows, turned his head to stare out it for a few moments, as he had been intermittently doing all night. 'Look, everyone knows that one of you four could kill him. But nobody would expect me! Total surprise, one shot in the face, no more Grey King!'

'Assuming the Falconer allowed your quarrel to hit his client,' said Locke, 'he would probably cook us where we stood right after that. Also, I very much doubt that fucking bird is going to be fluttering around this tower where we can easily see it and avoid it.'

'You never know,' said Bug. 'I think I saw it before, when we made first touch on Don Salvara.'

'I'm pretty sure I did, too.' Calo was knuckle-walking a solon on his left hand without looking at it. 'While I was strangling you, Locke. Something flew overhead. Damn big and fast for a wren or a sparrow.'

'So,' said Jean, 'he really has been watching us and he really knows all there is to know about us. Knuckling under might be wiser for the time being, but we've got to have some contingencies we can cook up.'

'Should we call off the Don Salvara game now?' asked Bug, meekly.

'Hmmm? No.' Locke shook his head vigorously. 'There's absolutely no reason, for the time being.'

'How,' said Galdo, 'do you figure that?'

'The reason we discussed shortening the game was to keep our heads down and try to avoid getting killed by the Grey King. Now we can be pretty damn sure that won't happen, at least not for three days. So the Salvara game stays in play.'

'For three days, yes. Until the Grey King has no further use for you.' Jean spat. 'Next step in whatever the plans are – thanks for your cooperation, here's a complimentary knife in the back for all of you.'

'It's a possibility,' said Locke. 'So what we do is this. Jean, you scuttle around today after you've had some sleep. Cancel those arrangements for sea travel. If we need to run, waiting for a ship to put out will take too long. Likewise, drop more gold at the Viscount's Gate. If we go out, we go out by land, and I want that gate swinging wider and faster than a whorehouse door.'

'Calo, Galdo, you find us a wagon. Stash it behind the temple; set it up with tarps and rope for fast packing. Get us food and drink for the road. Simple stuff, sturdy stuff. Spare cloaks. Plain clothing. You know what to do. If any Right People spot you at work, maybe drop a hint that we're after a fat score in the next few days. Barsavi would like that, if it gets back to him.

'Bug, tomorrow you and I are going to go through the vault. We'll bring up every coin in there and pack them in canvas sacks for easy transport. If we have to run, I want to be able to throw the whole mess on the back of our wagon in just a few minutes.'

'Makes sense,' said Bug.

'So, Sanzas, you stick together,' said Locke. 'Bug, you're with me. Nobody goes it alone for any length of time except Jean. You're the least likely to get troubled, if the Grey King's got anything less than an army hidden in the city.'

'Oh, you know me.' Jean reached behind his neck, down behind the loose leather vest he wore over his simple cotton tunic. He withdrew a pair of matching hatchets, each a foot and a half in length, with leather-wrapped handles and straight black blades that narrowed like scalpels. These were balanced with balls of blackened steel, each as wide around as a silver solon. The Wicked Sisters – Jean's weapons of choice. 'I never travel alone. It's always the three of us.'

'Right, then.' Locke yawned. 'If we need any other bright ideas, we can conjure them when we wake up. Let's set something heavy against the door, shut the windows and start snoring.'

The Gentlemen Bastards had just stumbled to their feet to begin putting this sensible plan into action when Jean held up one hand for silence. The stairs outside the door on the north wall of the chamber were creaking under the weight of many feet. A moment later, someone was banging on the door itself.

'Lamora,' came a loud male voice, 'open up! Capa's business!'

Jean slipped his hatchets into one hand and put that hand behind his back, then stood against the north wall a few feet to the right of the door. Calo and Galdo reached under their shirts for their daggers, Galdo pushing Bug back behind him as they did so. Locke stood in the centre of the room, remembering that his stilettos were still wrapped up in his Fehrwight coat.

'What's the price of a loaf,' he shouted, 'at the Shifting Market?'

'One copper flat, but the loaves ain't dry,' came the response. Locke un-tensed just a bit – that was this week's proper greeting and counter-sign, and if they were coming to haul him off for anything bloody, well, they'd have simply kicked in the door. Signalling with his hands for everyone to stay calm, he drew back the bolt and slid the front door open just wide enough to peek out.

There were four men on the platform outside his door, seventy feet in the air above the Last Mistake. The sky was the colour of murky canal water behind them, with just a few twinkling stars vanishing slowly here and there. They were hard-looking men, standing easy and ready like trained fighters, wearing leather tunics, leather collars and red bandannas under black leather caps. Red Hands – the gang Barsavi turned to when he needed muscle work and he needed it fast.

'Begging your pardon, brother.' The apparent leader of the Red Hands put one arm up against the door. 'Big man wants to see Locke Lamora right this very moment, and he don't care what state he's in, and he won't let us take no for an answer.'

INTERLUDE:
Jean Tannen

I

In the year that followed, Locke grew, but not as much as he would have liked; although it was difficult to guess his true age with any accuracy, it was obvious that he was more than a little runty for it.

'You missed a few meals in your very early years,' Chains told him. 'You've done much better since you came here, to be sure, but I suspect you'll always be a bit on the . . . medium side.'

'Always?'

'Don't be too upset.' Chains put his hands on his own round belly and chuckled. 'A little man can slip out of a pinch that a greater man might find inescapable.'

There was further schooling, always schooling. More sums, more history, more maps, more languages. Once Locke and the Sanzas had a firm grasp of conversational Vadran, Chains began having them instructed in the art of accents. A few hours each week were spent in the company of an old Vadran sail-mender, who would chide them for their 'fumble-mouthed mangling' of the northern tongue while he drove his long, wicked needles through yard upon yard of folded canvas. They would chat about any subject on the old man's mind, and he would fastidiously correct every consonant that was too short and every vowel that was too long. He would also get steadily more red-faced and belligerent as each session went on, for Chains paid him in wine for his services.

There were trials, some trivial and some quite harsh. Chains tested his boys constantly, almost ruthlessly, but when he was finished with each new conundrum he always took them to the temple roof to explain what he'd wanted, what the hardships signified. His openness after the fact made his games easier to bear, and they had the added effect of uniting Locke, Calo, and Galdo against the world around them. The more Chains tightened the screws, the closer the boys grew, the more smoothly they worked together, the less they had to say out loud to set a plan in motion.

The coming of Jean Tannen changed all that.

It was the month of Saris in the Seventy-Seventh year of Iono, the end of an unusually dry and cool autumn. Storms had lashed the Iron Sea but spared Camorr, by some trick of the winds or the gods, and the nights were finer than any in Locke's living memory. He was sitting the steps with Father Chains, flexing his fingers, eagerly awaiting the rise of Falselight, when he spotted the Thiefmaker walking across the square towards the House of Perelandro.

Two years had lessened the dread Locke had once felt towards his former master, but there was no denying that the skinny old fellow retained a certain grotesque magnetism. The Thiefmaker's spindly fingers spread as he bowed from the waist, and his eyes lit up when they seized on Locke.

'My dear, bedevilling little boy, what a pleasure it is to see you leading a productive life in the order of Perelandro.'

'He owes his success to your early discipline, of course.' Chains' smile spread beneath his blindfold. 'It's what helped to make him the resolute and morally upright youth he is today.'

'Upright?' The Thiefmaker squinted at Locke, feigning concentration. 'Heh. I'd be hard-pressed to say he's grown an inch.

225

But no matter. I've brought you the boy we discussed, the one from the North Corner. Step forward, Jean. You can't hide behind me any more than you could hide under a copper coin.'

There was indeed a boy standing behind the Thiefmaker; when the old man shooed him out into plain view, Locke saw that he was about his own age, perhaps ten, and in every other respect his opposite. The new boy was fat, red-faced, shaped like a dirty pear with a greasy mop of black hair atop his head. His eyes were wide and nervous; he clenched and unclenched his soft hands continually.

'Ahhh,' said Chains. 'Ahhh. I can't see him, but then, the qualities the Lord of the Overlooked desires in his servants cannot be seen by any man. Are you penitent, my boy? Are you sincere? Are you as upright as those our charitable celestial master has already taken into his fold?'

He gave Locke a pat on the back, manacles and chains rattling. Locke, for his part, stared at the newcomer and said nothing.

'I hope so, sir,' said Jean, in a voice that was soft and haunted.

'Well,' said the Thiefmaker, 'hope is what we all build lives for ourselves upon, is it not? The good Father Chains is your master now, boy. I leave you to his care.'

'Not mine, but that of the higher power I serve,' said Chains. 'Oh, before you leave, I just happened to find this purse sitting on my temple steps earlier today.' He held out a fat little leather bag, stuffed with coins, and waved it in the Thiefmaker's general direction. 'Is it yours, by chance?'

'Why, so it is! So it is!' The Thiefmaker plucked the purse from Chains' hands and made it vanish into the pockets of his weather-beaten coat. 'What a fortunate coincidence that is!' He bowed once more, turned, and began to walk back in the direction of Shades' Hill, whistling tunelessly.

Chains arose, rubbed his legs and clapped his hands. 'Let us call an end to our public duties for the day. Jean, this is Locke Lamora, one of my initiates. Please help him carry this kettle into the sanctuary. Careful, it's heavy.'

The thin boy and the fat boy heaved the kettle up the steps and into the damp sanctuary; the Eyeless Priest groped along his chains, gathering the slack and dragging it with him until he was safely inside. Locke worked the wall-mechanism to slide the temple doors shut, and Chains settled himself down in the middle of the sanctuary floor.

'The kindly gentleman,' said Chains, 'who delivered you into my care said that you could speak, read and write in three languages.'

'Yes, sir,' said Jean, gazing around him in trepidation. 'Therin, Vadran and Issavrai.'

'Very good. And you can do complex sums? Ledger-balancing?'

'Yes.'

'Excellent. Then you can help me count the day's takings. But first, come over here and give me your hand. That's it. Let us see if you have any of the gifts necessary to become an initiate of this temple, Jean Tannen.'

'What . . . what must I do?'

'Simply place your hands on my blindfold . . . No, stand easy. Close your eyes. Concentrate. Let whatever virtuous thoughts you have within you bubble to the surface . . .'

2

'I don't like him,' said Locke. 'I don't like him at all.'

He and Chains were preparing breakfast early the next morning; Locke was simmering up a soup from sliced onions and irregular little brown cubes of reduced beef stock, while Chains was attempting to crack the wax seal on a honey-crock. His bare fingers and nails having failed, he was hacking at it with a stiletto and muttering to himself.

'Don't like him at all? That's rather silly,' said Chains, his voice distant, 'since he's not yet been here a single day.'

'He's fat. He's soft. He's not one of *us*.'

'He most certainly is. We showed him the temple and the burrow; he took oath as my *pezon*. I'll go see the Capa with him in just a day or two.'

'I don't mean one of us, Gentleman Bastards, I mean one of *us*, us. He's not a thief. He's a soft fat—'

'Merchant. Son of merchant parents is what he is. But he's a thief now.'

'He didn't steal things! He didn't charm or tease! He said he was in the hill for a few days before he got brought here. So he's not one of *us*.'

'Locke.' Chains turned from the business of the honey-crock and stared down at him, frowning. 'Jean Tannen is a thief because I'm going to train him as a thief. You do recall, that's what I train here, thieves of a very particular sort. This hasn't slipped your mind?'

'But he's—'

'He's better-learned than any of you. Scribes in a clean, smooth hand. Understands business, ledgers, money-shifts and a great many other things. Your former master knew I'd want him right away.'

'He's fat.'

'So am I. And you're ugly. Calo and Galdo have noses like siege engines. Sabetha had spots breaking out last we saw her. Did you have a point?'

'He kept us up all night. He was *crying*, and he wouldn't shut up.'

'I'm sorry,' said a soft voice from behind them. Locke and Chains turned (the latter much more slowly than the former); Jean Tannen was standing by the door to the sleeping quarters, red-eyed. 'I didn't mean to. I couldn't help it.'

'Ha!' Chains turned back to his stiletto and his honey-crock. 'Looks as though boys who live in glass burrows shouldn't speak so loudly of those in the next room.'

'Well, don't do it again, Jean,' said Locke, hopping down from the wooden step he still used to reach the top of the cooking hearth. He crossed to one of the spice cabinets and began shuffling jars, looking for something. 'Shut up and let us sleep. Calo and Galdo and I don't blubber.'

'I'm sorry,' said Jean, sounding close to tears again. 'I'm sorry, it's just . . . my mother. My father. I . . . I'm an orphan.'

'So *what*?' Locke took down a little glass bottle of pickled radishes, sealed with a stone stopper like an alchemical potion. '*I'm* an orphan. We're *all* orphans here. Shut up about it and let the rest of us *sleep*. Whining won't make them live again.'

Locke turned and took two steps back towards the cooking hearth, so he didn't see Jean cross the space between them. He *did* feel Jean's arm wrap around his neck from behind; it might have been soft but it was damned heavy, for a ten-year-old. Locke lost his grip on the pickled radishes; Jean picked him off the ground by main force, whirled, and *heaved* him.

Locke's feet left the ground at the same instant the radish jar shattered against it; a confused second later the back of Locke's head bounced off the heavy witchwood dining table and he fell to the ground, landing painfully on his rather bony posterior.

'You shut up!' There was nothing subdued about Jean now; he was screaming, red-faced, with tears pouring out of his eyes. 'You shut up! You shut your filthy mouth! You *never* talk about my mother and father!'

Locke put up his hands and tried to stand; one of Jean's fists grew in his field of vision until it seemed to blot out half the world. The blow knocked all the light out of his eyes and folded him over like a pretzel. When he recovered something resembling his senses he was hugging a table leg; the room was dancing a minuet around him.

'Wrrblg,' he said, his mouth full of salt and pain.

'Now, Jean,' said Chains, pulling the heavyset boy away from Locke. 'I think your message is rather thoroughly delivered.'

'Ugh. That really hurt,' said Locke.

'It's only fair.' Chains released Jean, who balled his fists and stood glaring at Locke, shuddering. 'You really deserved it.'

'Huh . . . wha?'

'Sure we're all orphans here. My parents were long dead before you were even born. Your parents are years gone. Same for Calo and Galdo and Sabetha. But Jean,' said Chains, 'lost his only five nights ago.'

'Oh.' Locke sat up, groaning. 'I didn't . . . I didn't know.'

'Well, then.' Chains finally succeeded in prying open the honey-crock; the wax seal split with an audible crack. 'When you don't know everything you could know, it's a fine time to shut your fucking noisemaker and be polite.'

'It was a fire.' Jean took a few deep breaths, still staring at Locke. 'They burned to death. The whole shop. Everything gone.' He turned and walked back to the sleeping quarters, head down, rubbing at his eyes.

Chains turned his back on Locke and began stirring the honey, breaking up the little patches of crystallisation.

There was an echoing clang from the fall of the secret door that led down from the temple above; a moment later Calo and Galdo appeared in the kitchen, each twin dressed in his white Initiate's robe, each one balancing a long, soft loaf of bread on his head.

'We have returned,' said Calo.

'With bread!'

'Which is obvious!'

'No, *you're* obvious!'

The twins stopped short when they saw Locke pulling himself up by the edge of the table, lips swollen, blood trickling from the corners of his mouth.

'What did we miss?' asked Galdo.

'Boys,' said Chains, 'I might have forgotten to tell you something when I introduced you to Jean and showed him around last night. Your old master from Shades' Hill warned me that while Jean is mostly soft-spoken, the boy has one hell of a colourful temper.'

Shaking his head, Chains stepped over to Locke and helped him stand upright. 'When the world stops spinning,' he said, 'don't forget that you've got broken glass and radishes to clean up, too.'

3

Locke and Jean maintained a healthy distance from one another at the dinner table that night, saying nothing. Calo and Galdo exchanged exasperated looks approximately several hundred times per minute, but made no attempts at conversation themselves. Preparations for the meal were conducted in near-silence, with Chains apparently happy to oblige his sullen crew.

Once Locke and Jean had seated themselves at the table, Chains set a carved ivory box down before each of them. The boxes were about a foot long and a foot wide, with hinged covers. Locke immediately recognised them as Determiners' Boxes, delicate Verrari devices that used clockwork, sliding tiles and rotating wooden knobs to enable a trained user to rapidly conduct certain mathematical operations. He'd been taught the basics of the device, but it had been months since he'd last used one.

'Locke and Jean,' said Father Chains. 'If you would be so kind. I have nine hundred and ninety-five Camorri solons, and I am taking ship for Tal Verrar. I should very much like to have them converted to solari when I arrive, the solari currently being worth, ah, four-fifths of one Camorri full crown. How many solari will the changers owe me before their fee is deducted?'

Jean immediately flipped open the lid on his box and set to work, fiddling knobs, flicking tiles and sliding little wooden rods back and forth. Locke, flustered, followed suit. His nervous fiddlings with the machine were nowhere near fast enough, for Jean shortly announced, 'Thirty-one full solari, with about one-tenth of one left over.' He stuck out the tip of his tongue and calculated for a few more seconds. 'Four silver volani and two coppers.'

'Marvellous,' said Chains. 'Jean, you can eat this evening. Locke, I'm afraid you're out of luck. Thank you for trying, nonetheless. You may spend dinner in your quarters, if you wish.'

'What?' Locke felt the blood rushing to his cheeks. 'But that's not how it worked before! You always gave us individual problems! And I haven't used this box for—'

'Would you like another problem, then?'

'Yes!'

'Very well. Jean, would you indulge us by doing it as well? Now . . . a Jereshti galleon sails the Iron Sea, and her captain is quite the penitent fellow. Every hour on the hour he has a sailor throw a loaf of ship's biscuit into the sea as an offering to Iono. Each loaf weighs fourteen ounces. The captain is a remarkably neat fellow as well; he keeps his biscuit in casks, a quarter-ton apiece. He sails for one week even. How many casks does he open? And how much biscuit does the Lord of the Grasping Waters get?'

Again the boys worked their boxes, and again Jean looked up while Locke was still working with little beads of sweat clearly visible on his little forehead. 'He only opens one cask,' Jean said, 'and he uses one hundred and forty-seven pounds of biscuit.'

Father Chains clapped softly. 'Very good, Jean. You'll still be eating with us tonight. As for you, Locke, well . . . I shall call you when the clearing-up needs to be done.'

'This is ridiculous,' Locke huffed. 'He works the box better than I do! You set this up for me to lose!'

'Ridiculous, is it? You've been putting on airs recently, my dear boy. You've reached a certain age when many boys seem to just sort of fold up their better judgement and set it aside for a few years. Hell, Sabetha's done it too. Part of the reason I sent her off to where she is at the moment. Anyhow, it seems to me that your nose is tilting a little high in the air for someone with a death-mark around his throat.'

Locke's blush deepened. Jean sneaked a furtive glance at him; Calo and Galdo, who already knew about the shark's tooth, stared fixedly at their empty plates and glasses.

'The world is full of conundrums that will tax your skills. Do you presume that you will always get to choose the ones that best suit your strengths? If I wanted to send a boy to impersonate a money changer's apprentice, who do you think I'd give the job to, if I had to choose between yourself and Jean? It's no choice at all.'

'I . . . suppose.'

'You suppose too much. You deride your new brother because his figure aspires to the noble girth of my own.' Chains rubbed his stomach and grinned. 'Didn't it ever occur to you that he fits in some places even better than you do, because of it? Jean looks like a merchant's son, like a well-fed noble, like a plump little scholar. His appearance could be as much an asset to him as yours is to you.'

'I guess . . .'

'And if you needed any further demonstration that he can do things you cannot, well, why don't I instruct him to wallop the shit out of you one more time?'

Locke attempted to spontaneously shrink down inside his tunic and vanish into thin air. Failing, he hung his head.

'I'm sorry,' said Jean. 'I hope I didn't hurt you badly.'

'You don't need to be sorry,' Locke mumbled. 'I suppose I really did deserve it.'

'The threat of an empty stomach soon rekindles wisdom.' Chains smirked. 'Hardships are arbitrary, Locke. You never know which particular quality in yourself or a fellow is going to get you past them. For example, raise your hand if your surname happens to be Sanza.'

Calo and Galdo did so, a bit hesitantly.

'Anyone with the surname Sanza,' said Chains, 'may join our new brother Jean Tannen in dining this evening.'

'I love being used as an example!' said Galdo.

'Anyone with the surname Lamora,' said Chains, 'may eat, but first he will serve all the courses, and attend on Jean Tannen.'

So Locke scuttled about, embarrassment and relief mingled on his face. The meal was roasted capon stuffed with garlic and onions, with grapes and figs scalded in a hot wine sauce on the side. Father Chains poured all of his usual prayer toasts, dedicating the last to 'Jean Tannen, who lost one family but came to another soon enough.'

At that Jean's eyes watered, and the boy lost whatever good cheer the food had brought to him. Noticing this, Calo and Galdo took action to salvage his mood.

'That was really good, what you did with the box,' said Calo.

'None of us can work it that fast,' said Galdo.

'And we're good with sums!'

'Or at least,' said Galdo, 'we thought we were, until we met you.'

'It was nothing,' said Jean. 'I can be even faster. I am . . . I meant to say . . .'

He looked nervously at Father Chains before continuing.

'I need optics. Reading optics, for things up close. I can't see right without them. I, um, I could work a box even faster if I had them. But . . . I lost mine. One of the boys in Shades' Hill . . .'

'You shall have new ones,' said Chains. 'Tomorrow or the next day. Don't wear them in public; it might contravene our air of poverty. But you can certainly wear them in here.'

'You couldn't even see straight,' asked Locke, 'when you beat me?'

'I could see a little bit,' said Jean. 'It's all sort of blurry. That's why I was leaning back so far.'

'A mathematical terror,' mused Father Chains, 'and a capable little brawler. What an interesting combination the Benefactor has given the Gentlemen Bastards in young Master Tannen. And he *is* a Gentleman Bastard, isn't he, Locke?'

'Yes,' said Locke, trying to keep a sullen tone out of his voice. 'I suppose he is.'

4

The next night was clear and dry; all the moons were up, shining like sovereigns in the blackness with the stars for their court. Jean Tannen sat beneath one parapet wall on the temple roof, a book held out before him at arm's length. Two oil lamps in glass boxes sat beside him, outlining him in warm yellow light.

'I don't mean to bother you,' said Locke, and Jean looked up, startled.

'Gods! You're quiet!'

'Not all the time.' Locke stepped to within a few feet of the larger boy. 'I can be very loud, when I'm being stupid.'

'I . . . um . . .'

'Can I sit?'

Jean nodded, and Locke plopped down beside him. He folded his legs and wrapped his arms around his knees.

'I am sorry,' said Locke. 'I guess I really can be a shit sometimes.'

'I'm sorry, too. I didn't mean . . . When I hit you, it just . . . I'm not myself. When I'm angry.'

'You did right. I didn't know about your mother and your father. I'm sorry. I should . . . I shouldn't have presumed. I've had a long time . . . to get used to it, you know.'

The two boys said nothing for a few moments after that; Jean closed his book and stared up at the sky.

'You know, I might not even be one after all. A real orphan, I mean,' said Locke.

'How so?'

'Well, my . . . my mother's dead. I saw that. I know that. But my father . . . he, um, he went away when I was very little; I don't remember him, never knew him.'

'I'm sorry,' said Jean.

'We're both sorry a lot, aren't we? I think he might have been a sailor or something. Maybe a mercenary, you know? Mother never wanted to talk about him. I don't know. I could be wrong.'

'My father was a good man,' said Jean. 'He was . . . They both had a shop in North Corner. They shipped leathers and silks and some gems. All over the Iron Sea, some trips inland. I helped them. Not shipping, of course, but record-keeping. Counting. And I took care of the cats. We had nine. Mama used to say . . . she used to say that I was her only child who didn't go about on all fours.'

He sniffled a bit and wiped his eyes.

'I seem to have used up all my tears,' he said. 'I don't know what to feel about all this any more. My parents taught me to be honest, that the laws and the gods abhor thieving. But now I find out thieving has its very own god. And I can either starve on the street or be comfortable here.'

'It's not so bad,' said Locke. 'I've never done anything else, as long as I can remember. Thieving is an honest trade, when you look at it like we do. We can work really hard at it, sometimes.' Locke reached inside his tunic and brought out a soft cloth bag. 'Here,' he said, handing it over to Jean.

'What . . . what's this?'

'You said you needed optics.' Locke smiled. 'There's a lens grinder over in the Videnza who's older than the gods. He doesn't watch his shop window like he ought to. I lifted some pairs for you.'

Jean shook the bag open and found himself looking down at three pairs of optics; there were two circular sets of lenses in gilt wire frames, and a half-moon set in silver rims.

'I . . . thank you, Locke!' He held each pair up to his eyes and squinted through them in turn, frowning slightly. 'I don't . . . quite know . . . Um, I'm not ungrateful, not at all, but none of these will work.' He pointed at his eyes and smiled sheepishly. 'Lenses need to be made for the wearer's problem. There's some for people who can't see long ways, and I think that's what these pairs are for. But I'm what they call close-blind, not far-blind.'

'Oh. Damn.' Locke scratched the back of his neck and smiled sheepishly. 'I don't wear them; I didn't know. I really am an idiot.'

'Not at all. I can keep the rims and do something with them, maybe. Rims break. I can just set proper lenses in them. They'll be spares. Thank you again.'

The boys sat in silence for a short while after that, but this time it was a companionable silence. Jean leaned back against the wall and closed his eyes. Locke stared up at the moons, straining to see the little blue and green specks Chains had once told him were the forests of the gods. Eventually, Jean cleared his throat.

'So you're really good at . . . stealing things?'

'I have to be good at something. It's not fighting and it's not mathematics, I guess.'

'You, um . . . Father Chains told me about this thing you can do, if you pray to the Benefactor. He called it a death-offering. Do you know about that?'

'Oh,' said Locke, 'I know all about it, truth of all thirteen gods, cross my heart and pray to die.'

'I'd like to do that. For my mother and my father. But I . . . I've never stolen anything. Can you maybe help me?'

'Teach you how to steal so you can do a proper offering?'

'Yes.' Jean sighed. 'I guess if this is where the gods have put me I should bend to local custom.'

'Can you teach me how to use a numbers box so I look less like a halfwit next time?'

'I think so,' said Jean.

'Then it's settled!' Locke jumped back up to his feet and spread his hands wide. 'Tomorrow, Calo and Galdo can plant their arses on the temple steps. You and I will go out and plunder!'

'That sounds dangerous,' said Jean.

'For anyone else, maybe. For Gentlemen Bastards, well, it's just what we do.'

'We?'

'We.'

CHAPTER SIX

Limitations

I

The Red Hands led Locke up the long gangway to the Floating Grave just as the scarlet sun broke above the dark silhouettes of the buildings of the Ashfall district. The whole Wooden Waste turned to blood in that light, and when Locke blinked to clear the brightness from his eyes, even the darkness flashed with red.

Locke struggled to keep his head clear, as the combination of nervous excitement and fatigue made him feel as though he was sliding along an inch or two above the ground, his feet not quite reaching all the way down. There were sentries on the quay, sentries at the doors, sentries in the foyer . . . more than there had been before. They were all grim-faced and silent as the Red Hands led Locke deeper into the Capa's floating fortress. The inner clockwork doors weren't locked.

Capa Barsavi stood in the middle of his great audience chamber, facing away from Locke, his head bowed and his hands behind his back. Curtains had been drawn away from the high glass windows on the eastern side of the galleon's hull. Red fingers of light fell on Barsavi, his sons, a large wooden cask and a long object that lay covered on a portable wooden bier.

'Father,' said Anjais, 'it's Lamora.'

Capa Barsavi grunted and turned. He stared at Locke for a few seconds, his eyes glassy and dead. He waved his left hand. 'Leave us,' he said. 'Leave us now.'

Heads down, Anjais and Pachero hurried out of the room, dragging the Red Hands with them as they went. A moment later the hall echoed with the sound of the doors slamming shut and the clockwork locks tumbling into position.

'Your honour,' said Locke, 'what's going on?'

'He killed her. The son of a bitch killed her, Locke.'

'What?'

'He killed Nazca. Last night. Left us . . . the body, just a few hours ago.'

Locke stared at Barsavi, dumbfounded, aware that his mouth was hanging open.

'But . . . but she was here, wasn't she?'

'She left.' Barsavi was clenching and unclenching his fists. 'She sneaked off, near as we can tell. Second or third hour of the morning. She . . . she was returned at half past the fourth hour of the morning.'

'Returned? By who? *What happened?*'

'Come. See.'

Vencarlo Barsavi drew back the cloth that covered the bier, and there lay Nazca – her skin waxy, her eyes closed, her hair damp. Two livid purple bruises marred the otherwise smooth skin on the left side of her neck. Locke felt his eyes stinging, and he found himself biting down hard on the first knuckle of his right index finger.

'See what the bastard has done,' Barsavi said softly. 'She was the living memory of her mother. My only daughter. I would rather be dead than see this.' Tears began sliding down the old man's cheeks. 'She has been . . . washed.'

'Washed? What do you mean?'

'She was returned,' said the Capa, 'in that.' He gestured to the cask, which stood upright a few feet to the side of the bier.

'In a barrel?'

'Look inside.'

Locke slid the barrel's lid back and recoiled as the full stench of the barrel's contents wafted out at him.

It was full of urine. Horse urine, dark and cloudy.

Locke whirled away from the cask and clapped both hands over his mouth, his stomach spasming.

'Not just killed,' said Barsavi. 'But drowned. Drowned in *horse piss.*'

Locke growled, fighting tears. 'I can't believe this,' he said. 'I just can't believe it. This doesn't make any fucking sense.'

He moved back beside the bier and took another look at Nazca's neck. The purple bruises were actually raised bumps; straight red scratches were visible just in front of them. Locke stared at them, thinking back to the feel of talons in his own skin. The injury on his forearm still burned.

'Your Honour,' he said, 'maybe she was . . . returned in that thing. But I'm pretty sure she didn't drown in it.'

'What can you possibly mean?'

'The marks on her neck, the little scratches beside them.' Locke extemporised, keeping his voice level and his face neutral. *What would sound plausible?* 'I've seen them before, several years ago in Talisham. I saw a man murdered by a scorpion hawk. Have you ever heard of such a thing?'

'Yes,' said the Capa, 'an unnatural hybrid, some sort of creature dreamed up by the sorcerers of Karthain. Is that . . . the marks on her neck? Can you be sure?'

'She was stung by a scorpion hawk,' Locke said. 'The talon marks beside the wounds are clear. She would have been dead almost instantly.'

'So he merely . . . he merely *pickled* her, afterwards' Barsavi whispered, 'to increase the insult. To cut me more cruelly.'

'I'm sorry,' said Locke. 'I know it . . . it can't be much comfort.'

'If you're right, it was a much quicker death.' Barsavi pulled the cloth back up over her head, running his fingers through her hair one last time before he covered her completely. 'If that is the only comfort I can pray that my little girl received, I will pray for it. That grey bastard . . . he will receive no such comfort when the time comes.'

'Why would he do this?' Locke ran both of his hands through his hair, wide-eyed with agitation. 'It doesn't make any sense. Why her, why now?'

'He can tell you himself,' said Barsavi.

'What? I don't understand.'

Capa Barsavi reached into his vest and drew out a folded piece of parchment. He passed it over to Locke, who opened the fold and saw that a note was scribed there in a clean, even hand:

BARSAVI

> *For the necessity of what was done, We apologise, though it was done to facilitate your understanding of our power, and therefore your*

cooperation. We earnestly desire a meeting with yourself, man to man in all courtesy, to settle once and for all between us this matter of Camorr. We shall be in attendance at the Echo Hole, at the eleventh hour of the evening, on the Duke's Day, three nights hence. We shall be alone and unarmed, though you for your part may bring as many counsellors as you wish, and you may arm them as you wish. Man to man we may discuss our situation, and with the kind favour of the gods, perhaps abjure the need for you to lose any more of your loyal subjects, or any more of your own flesh and blood.

'I don't believe it,' said Locke. 'Meet in good faith, after this?'

'He cannot be Camorri,' said Barsavi. 'I have become Camorri, in my years here. I am more of this place than many who were born here. But this man?' Barsavi shook his head vigorously. 'He cannot understand what an infamy he has done to "get my attention", what an insult my sons and I must bear if we negotiate with him. He wastes his time with his letter – and look, the royal "we". What an affectation!'

'Your honour . . . what if he *does* understand what he's done?'

'The possibility is very remote, Locke.' The Capa chuckled sadly. 'Or else he would not have done it.'

'Not if you presume that the meeting at the Echo Hole is an ambush. That he wants to get you off the Floating Grave and into a place where he has prepared some real harm for you.'

'Your prudence again.' Barsavi smiled without humour. 'The thought has occurred to me, Locke. But I do not believe so . . . I believe he genuinely thinks that if he frightens me enough, I will negotiate in good faith. I am indeed going to the Echo Hole. We shall have our meeting. And for my counsellors, I will bring my sons, my Berangias sisters, a hundred of my best and my cruellest. And I will bring you and your friend Jean.'

Locke's heart beat against the inside of his chest like a trapped bird. He wanted to scream.

'Of course,' he said. 'Of course! Jean and I will do anything you ask. I'm . . . grateful for the opportunity.'

'Good. Because the only negotiation we'll be doing is with bolt, blade and fist. I've got a surprise for that grey piece of shit, if he thinks to dictate terms to *me* over the body of my only daughter.'

Locke ground his teeth together. *I know what can bring him out from that soggy fortress of his*, the Grey King had said.

'Capa Barsavi,' said Locke, 'have you considered . . . well, the things they say about the Grey King. He can kill men with a touch; he can walk through walls; he can't be harmed by blades or by arrows.'

'Stories told in wine. He does as I did, when I first took this city: he hides himself well and he chooses his targets wisely.' The Capa sighed. 'I admit that he is good at it, perhaps as good as I was. But he's not a ghost.'

'There is another possibility,' said Locke, licking his lips. *How much of what was said here might reach the Grey King's ears? He'd unravelled the secrets of the Gentlemen Bastards thoroughly enough. To hell with him.* 'The possibility of a . . . Bondsmage.'

'Aiding the Grey King?'

'Yes.'

'He's been vexing my city for months, Locke. It might explain some things, yes, but the price . . . the price. Even I could not pay a Bondsmage for that length of time.'

'Scorpion hawks,' said Locke, 'aren't just created by the Bonds-magi. As far as I know, only Bondsmagi themselves keep them. Could an ordinary . . . falconer train a bird that could kill him with one accidental sting?' *Bullshit well*, he thought, *bullshit very well*. 'The Grey King wouldn't need to have kept one this whole time. What if the Bondsmage is newly arrived? What if the Bondsmage has only been hired for the next few days, the critical point of whatever the Grey King's scheme is? The rumours about the Grey King's powers . . . could have been spread to prepare for all of this.'

'Fantastical,' said Barsavi, 'and yet it would explain some things.'

'It would explain why the Grey King is willing to meet you alone and unarmed . . . with a Bondsmage to shield him, he could appear both yet be neither.'

'Then my response is unchanged.' Barsavi squeezed one fist inside the other. 'If one Bondsmage can best a hundred knives, can best you and I, my sons, my Berangias sisters, your friend Jean and his hatchets . . . then the Grey King has chosen his weapons better than I. But for my part, I do not imagine that he has.'

'You will keep the possibility in mind?' Locke persisted.

'Yes. I shall.' Barsavi placed a hand on Locke's shoulder. 'You must forgive me, my boy. For what has happened.'

'There's nothing to forgive, your honour.' *When the Capa changes the subject*, thought Locke, *the subject is finished*. 'It wasn't your fault . . . what happened.'

'It is my war. It's me the Grey King truly wishes to cut.'

'You offered me a great deal, sir.' Locke licked his lips, which had gone dry. 'I'd very much like to help you kill the bastard.'

'So we shall. At the ninth hour of the evening, on the Duke's Day, we begin to gather. Anjais will come to fetch you and Tannen at the Last Mistake.'

'What of the Sanzas? They're good with knives.'

'And with cards, or so I hear. I like them well enough, Locke, but they're fiddlers. Amusers. I'm taking serious folk for serious business.'

'As you say.'

'Now.' Barsavi took a silk handkerchief from his vest pocket and slowly mopped his brow and cheeks with it. 'Leave me, please. Come back tomorrow night, as a priest. I'll have all my other priests of the Benefactor. We'll give her . . . a proper ritual.'

Despite himself, Locke was flattered. The Capa had known that all of Father Chains' boys were initiates of the Benefactor, and Locke a full priest, but he'd never before asked for Locke's blessing in any official sense.

'Of course,' he said quietly.

He withdrew then, leaving the Capa standing in the bloody morning light, leaving him all alone at the heart of his fortress, for the second time, with nothing but a corpse for company.

2

'Gentlemen,' said Locke as he closed the door to the seventh-floor rooms behind him, huffing and puffing, 'we have done our bit for appearances this week; let's all work out of the temple until further notice.'

Jean was sitting in a chair facing the door, hatchets resting on his thigh, with his battered old volume of the *The Korish Romances* in his hands. Bug was snoring on a sleeping pallet, sprawled in one of those utterly careless positions that give instant arthritis to all save the very young and foolish. The Sanzas were sitting against the far wall, playing a desultory hand of cards; they looked up as Locke entered.

'We are released from one complication,' said Locke, 'and flung headlong into another, and this bitch has teeth.'

'What news?' said Jean.

'The worst sort.' Locke dropped into a chair, threw back his head, and closed his eyes. 'Nazca's dead.'

'What?' Calo leapt to his feet; Galdo wasn't far behind. 'How did that happen?'

'The Grey King happened. It must have been the "something else" he referred to when I was his guest. He sent the body back to her father in a vat of horse piss.'

'Gods,' said Jean. 'I'm so sorry, Locke.'

'And now,' continued Locke, 'you and I are expected to accompany the Capa when he avenges her, at the "clandestine conference" three nights hence. Which will be at the Echo Hole, by the way. And the Capa's idea of "clandestine" is a hundred knives charging in to cut the Grey King to bloody pieces.'

'Cut *you* to bloody pieces, you mean,' said Galdo.

'I'm well aware of who's supposed to be strutting around wearing the Grey King's clothes, thanks very much. I'm just debating whether or not I should hang an archery butt around my neck. Oh, and wondering if I can learn to split myself in two before Duke's Day.'

'This entire situation is insane.' Jean slammed his book shut in disgust.

'It was insane before; now it's become malicious.'

'Why would the Grey King kill Nazca?'

'To get the Capa's attention.' Locke sighed. 'Either to frighten him, which it certainly hasn't accomplished, or to piss him off beyond all mortal measure, which it has.'

'There will never be peace, now. The Capa will kill the Grey King or get himself killed trying.' Calo paced furiously. 'Surely the Grey King must realise this. He hasn't facilitated negotiations; he's made them impossible. Forever.'

'The thought had crossed my mind,' said Locke, 'that the Grey

King may not be telling us everything, concerning this scheme of his.'

'Out the Viscount's Gate, then,' said Galdo. 'We can spend the afternoon securing transportation and goods. We can pack up our fortune; we can vanish onto the road. Fuck, if we can't find somewhere to build another life with forty-odd thousand crowns at our fingertips, we don't deserve to live. We could buy titles in Lashain; make Bug a count and set ourselves up as his household.'

'Or make ourselves counts,' said Calo, 'and set Bug up as our household. Run him back and forth. It'd be good for his moral education.'

'We can't,' said Locke. 'We have to presume the Grey King can follow us wherever we go, or, perhaps more accurately, that his Bondsmage can. As long as the Falconer serves him, we can't run. At least not as a first option.'

'What about as a second?' asked Jean.

'That's still in play, as far as I'm concerned. We can stick with the earlier plan; get things ready, and if we absolutely, positively must run for the road, well, we'll put ourselves in harness and pull with the horses if we have to.'

'Which leaves only the conundrum,' said Jean, 'of which commitment to slip you out of, the night of this meeting at the Echo Hole.'

'No conundrum,' said Locke. 'The Grey King has it over us; Barsavi we know we can fool. So I'll play the Grey King and figure out some way to ease us out of our commitment to the Capa without getting executed for it.'

'That would be a good trick,' said Jean.

'But what if it's not necessary?' Calo pointed at his brother. 'One of us can play the Grey King, and you and Jean can stand beside Barsavi as required.'

'Yes,' said Galdo, 'an excellent idea.'

'No,' said Locke. 'For one thing, I'm a better false-facer than either of you, and you know it. You two are just slightly too conspicuous. It can't be risked. For another, while I'm playing the Grey King, you two should be forgotten by everyone. You'll be free to move around as you like. I'd rather have you waiting with transportation at one of our meeting spots, in case things go sour and we do need to flee.'

'And what about Bug?'

'Bug,' said Bug, 'has been faking snoring for the past few minutes. And I know the Echo Hole; I used to hide there sometimes when I was with the Shades' Hill gang. I'll be down there under the floor, beside the waterfall, watching for trouble.'

'Bug,' said Locke, 'you'll—'

'If you don't like it, you'll have to lock me in a box to stop me. You need a spotter, and the Grey King didn't say you couldn't have friends lurking. That's what I do. I lurk. And none of you can do it like I can, because you're all bigger and slower and creakier and—'

'Gods,' said Locke. 'My days as *garrista* are numbered; Duke Bug is dictating the terms of his service. Very well, Your Grace. I'll give you a role that will keep you close at hand – but you lurk where I tell you to lurk, right?'

'Bloody right!'

'Then it's settled,' said Locke, 'and if no one else has a pressing need for me to imitate the great and powerful, or a friend of mine they'd like to murder, I could use some sleep.'

'It's too gods-damned bad about Nazca,' said Galdo. 'The son of a *bitch*.'

'Yes,' said Locke. 'In fact, I'm going to speak to him about it this very evening. Him or his pet sorcerer, whichever thinks to come.'

'The candle,' said Jean.

'Yeah. After you and I finish our business, and after Falselight. You can wait down in the Last Mistake. I'll sit up here, light it, and wait for them to show.' Locke grinned. 'Let *those* fuckers enjoy the walk up our stairs.'

3

The day turned out clear and pleasant, the evening as fresh as they ever came in Camorr; Locke sat in the seventh-floor rooms with the windows open and the mesh screens down as the purple sky lit up with rising streamers of ghostly light.

The Falconer's candle smouldered on the table beside the remains of Locke's small dinner and a half-empty bottle of wine. The other half of that bottle was warming Locke's stomach as he sat, facing the door, massaging the fresh dressing Jean had insisted on wrapping around his arm before taking up his post in the Last Mistake.

'Crooked Warden,' said Locke to thin air, 'if I'm pissing you off for some reason, you don't need to go to such elaborate lengths to chastise me. And if I'm not pissing you off, well, I pray that you still find me amusing.' He flexed the fingers of his injured arm, wincing, then took up his wine glass and the bottle one more time.

'A glass poured to air for an absent friend,' he said as he filled it with dark red wine, a *Nacozza* retsina that had actually come from Don Salvara's upriver vineyards. A gift to Lukas Fehrwight as he stepped off the Don's pleasure barge so many days earlier . . . or not so many days earlier. It felt like a lifetime.

'We miss Nazca Barsavi already, and we wish her well. She was a fair *garrista* and she tried to help her *pezon* out of an untenable situation for them both. She deserved better. Piss on me all you like, but do what you can for her. I beg this as your servant.'

'If you wish to measure a man's true penitence,' said the Falconer, 'observe him when he believes himself to be dining alone.'

The front door was just closing behind the Bondsmage; Locke had not seen or heard it open. For that matter, it had been bolted. The Falconer was without his bird, and dressed in the same wide-skirted grey coat with silver-buttoned scarlet cuffs Locke had seen the night before. A grey velvet cap was tilted back atop his head, adorned with a silver pin securing a single feather, easily identified as having come from Vestris.

'I for one have never been a very penitent man,' he continued. 'Nor have I ever been overly fond of stairs.'

'My heart is overcome with sorrow for your hardship,' said Locke. 'Where's your hawk?'

'Circling.'

Locke was suddenly acutely aware of the open windows, such a comfort just a moment earlier. The mesh wouldn't keep Vestris out if the hawk became agitated.

'I'd hoped that perhaps your master might come along with you.'

'My *client*,' said the Bondsmage, 'is otherwise occupied. I speak for him, and I will bear your words to him. Assuming you have any worth hearing.'

'I always have words,' said Locke. 'Words like "complete lunatic". And "fucking idiot". Did it ever occur to you or your *client* that the one certain way to ensure that a Camorri would never negotiate with you with any good faith would be to kill someone of his blood?'

'Heavens,' said the Falconer. 'This is ill news indeed. And the Grey King was *so certain* Barsavi would interpret his daughter's murder as a friendly gesture.' The sorcerer's eyebrows rose. 'I say, did you want to tell him yourself, or shall I rush off right now with your revelation?'

'Very funny, you half-copper cocksucker. While I agreed under duress to prance around dressed as your master, you must admit that sending his only daughter back to him in a vat of piss does complicate my fucking job.'

'A pity,' said the Bondsmage. 'But the task remains, as does the duress.'

'Barsavi wants me by his side at this meeting, Falconer. He made the request this morning. Maybe I might have slipped out if it before, but now? Nazca's murder has put me in a hell of a squeeze.'

'You're the Thorn of Camorr. I would be, personally, very disappointed if you couldn't find a way past this difficulty. Barsavi's summons is a request; my client's is a requirement.'

'Your client isn't telling me everything he should.'

'You may safely presume that he knows his own business better than you do.' The Falconer began to idly wind a slender thread back and forth between the fingers of his right hand; it had an odd silver sheen.

'Gods dammit,' Locke hissed. 'Maybe I don't care what happens to the Capa, but Nazca was my friend. Duress I can accept; gleeful malice I cannot. You fuckers didn't *need* to do what you did to her.'

The Falconer splayed his fingers, and the thread gleamed, woven into a sort of cat's cradle; he began to move his fingers slowly, tightening some threads and loosening others, as deftly as the Sanzas moved coins across the backs of their hands.

'I cannot tell you,' said the sorcerer, 'what a weight it is upon my conscience to learn that we might lose your gracious acceptance.'

Then the Falconer hissed a word; a single syllable in a language Locke didn't understand. The very sound was awry and unnerving; it echoed in the room as though heard from a distance.

The wooden shutters behind Locke slammed shut, and he jumped out of his chair.

One by one, the other windows banged closed and their little clasps clicked, moved by an unseen hand. The Falconer shifted his fingers yet again, light gleamed on the web within his hands, and Locke gasped – his knees suddenly ached as though they'd been kicked from the sides, sharply.

'This is the second time,' said the Bondsmage, 'that you have been flippant with me. I fail to find it amusing, so I shall reinforce my client's instructions, and I shall take my time doing so.'

Locke gritted his teeth; unbidden tears came to his eyes as the pain in his legs intensified, throbbed, spread. It now felt as though a cold flame were playing against his knee sockets from the inside; unable to support his own weight, he tottered forward. One hand clutched helplessly at his legs while the other tried to hold him up against the table. He glared at the Bondsmage and tried to speak, but found that the muscles of his neck began spasming as he did.

'You are *property*, Lamora. You belong to the Grey King. He cares not that Nazca Barsavi was your friend; it was her ill fortune to be born to the father the gods gave her.'

The spasming spread down Locke's spine, across his arms and down his legs, where it met the freezing, gnawing pain already at work there in a hideous fusion. He fell onto his back, gasping and shuddering, his face a rictus mask, his hands curved in the air above his head like claws.

'You look like an insect thrown into a fire. And this is the merest exercise of my Art. The things I could *do* to you if I were to stitch your true name into cloth or scribe it on parchment . . . "Lamora" is obviously not your given name; it's Throne Therin for "shadow". But your first name, now that . . . that would be just enough, if I wished to make use of it.'

The Falconer's fingers flew back and forth, blurring in Locke's vision, shifting and stretching those silver threads, and the tempo of Locke's torment rose in direct proportion to the motion of that gleaming design. His heels were slapping against the floor; his teeth were rattling in his jaw; it seemed to him that someone was trying to cut the bones out of his thighs with icicles. Again and again he tried to suck in enough air to scream, but his lungs would not move, his throat was packed with thorns, and the world was growing black and red at the edges . . .

Release itself was a shock; he lay on the ground, bonelessly, still feeling the ghosts of pain throbbing across his body. Warm tears slid down his cheeks.

'You're not a particularly intelligent man, Lamora. An intelligent man would never deliberately waste my time. An intelligent man would grasp the nuances of the situation without the need for . . . repetition.'

Another motion of blurred silver in the corner of Locke's vision, and new pain erupted in his chest, like a blossom of fire surrounding his heart. He could feel it there, burning the very core of his being; it seemed to him that he could actually smell the crisping flesh, and feel the air in his lungs warming until it was as hot as that of a bread-oven. Locke groaned, writhed, threw his head back and finally screamed.

'I need you,' said the Falconer, 'but I will have you meek and grateful for my forbearance. Your friends are another matter. Shall I do this to Bug, while you watch? Shall I do it to the Sanzas?'

'No . . . please, no,' Locke cried out, curled in agony, his hands clutching at his left breast. He found himself tearing at his tunic, mad like an animal with pain. 'Not them!'

'Why not? They are immaterial to my client. They are expendable.'

The burning pain abated, once again shocking Locke with its absence. He huddled on his side, breathing raggedly, unable to believe that heat so fierce could vanish so swiftly.

'One more sharp word,' said the Bondsmage, 'one more flippant remark, one more demand, one more scrap of anything less than *total abjection*, and they will pay the price for your pride.' He lifted the glass of retsina from the table and sipped at it. He then snapped the fingers of his other hand and the liquid in the glass vanished in an instant, boiled away without a speck of flame. 'Are we now free from misunderstanding?'

'Yes,' said Locke, 'perfectly. Yes. Please don't harm them. I'll do whatever I must.'

'Of course you will. Now, I've brought the components of the costume you'll be wearing at the Echo Hole. You'll find them just outside your door. They're appropriately theatrical. I won't presume to tell you how to make ready with your mummery; be in position across from the Echo Hole at half past ten on the night of the meeting. I shall guide you from there, and direct you in what to say.'

'Barsavi,' Locke coughed out. 'Barsavi . . . will mean to kill me.'

'Do you doubt that I could continue punishing you here, at my leisure, until you were mad with pain?'

'No . . . no.'

'Then do not doubt that I can protect you from whatever nonsense the Capa might wish to employ.'

'Direct me . . . how?'

I do not need the air, came the voice of the Bondsmage, echoing in Locke's head with shocking force, *to carry forth my instructions. When you require prompting in your meeting with Barsavi, I shall supply it. When you must make a demand or accept a demand, I shall let you know how to proceed. Is this clear?*

'Yes . . . yes. Perfectly clear. Thank you.'

'You should be grateful for what my client and I have done on your behalf. Many men wait years for a chance to ingratiate themselves with Capa Barsavi. Your chance has been served forth to you like a fine meal. Are we not generous?'

'Yes . . . certainly.'

'Just so. I suggest you now find some means to extricate yourself from the duty he asks of you. This will leave you free to concentrate on the duty we require. We wouldn't want your attention divided at a critical moment; it would certainly cause you *distress*.'

4

The Last Mistake was half-empty, a phenomenon Locke had never before witnessed. Conversation was muted, eyes were cold and hard, entire gangs were conspicuous in their absence. Men and women alike wore heavier clothing than the season required; more half-cloaks and coats and layered vests. It was easier to conceal weapons that way.

'So what the hell happened to you?'

Jean rose to help Locke sit down; he'd got them a small table in a side cranny of the tavern with a clear view of the doors. Locke settled into his chair, a slight echo of the Falconer's phantom pains still haunting his joints and his neck muscles.

'The Falconer,' Locke said in a low voice, 'had several opinions he wished to express, and apparently I'm not as charming as I think I am.' He idly fingered his torn tunic and sighed. 'Beer now, bitch later.'

Jean slid over a clay mug of warm Camorri ale and Locke drank half of it down in two gulps. 'Well,' he said after wiping his mouth, 'I suppose it was worth it just to say what I said to him. I don't believe Bondsmagi are used to being insulted.'

'Did you accomplish anything?'

'Nothing.' Locke drank the remaining half of his ale and turned the mug upside down before setting it on the tabletop. 'Not a gods-damned thing. I did get the shit tortured out of myself, which was informational, from a certain point of view.'

'That fucker.' Jean's hands balled into fists. 'I could do so much to him, without killing him. I very much hope I get to try.'

'Save it for the Grey King,' muttered Locke. 'My thoughts are that if we survive what's coming on Duke's Day night, he won't be able to keep the Falconer on retainer forever. When the Bondsmage leaves . . .'

'We talk to the Grey King again. With knives.'

'Too right. We follow him if we have to. We've been needing something to do with all of our money . . . well, here's something. Whatever that bastard's got planned, when he can't pay his mage any more, we'll show him just how much we like being knocked around like handballs. Even if we have to follow him down the Iron Sea and around the Cape of Nessek and all the way to Balinel on the Sea of Brass.'

'Now there's a plan. And what are you going to do tonight?'

'Tonight?' Locke grunted. 'I'm going to take Calo's advice. I'm going to stroll over to the Guilded Lilies and get my brains wenched out. They can put them back in in the morning when they're through with me; I understand there's an extra fee involved, but I'll pay it.'

'I must be going mad,' said Jean. 'It's been four years, and all this time you've been—'

'I'm frustrated and I need a break and she's a thousand miles away and I guess I'm human after all, gods damn it. Don't wait up.'

'I'll walk with you,' said Jean. 'It's not wise to be out alone, on a night like this. The city's in a mood, now that word of Nazca's got around.'

'Not wise?' Locke laughed. 'I'm the safest man in Camorr, Jean. I know for a fact I'm the only one that absolutely nobody out there wants to kill yet. Not until they finish pulling my strings.'

5

'This isn't working,' he said, less than two hours later. 'I'm sorry, it's . . . not your fault.'

The room was warm and dark and exceedingly pleasant, ventilated by the soft *swish-swish-swish* of a wooden fan flapping back and forth in a concealed shaft. Waterwheels churned outside the ornate House of the Guilded Lilies at the northern tip of the Snare, driving belts and chains to operate its many mechanisms of comfort.

Locke lay on a wide bed with soft feather mattresses, covered in silk sheets, overhung with a silk canopy. He sprawled naked in the soft red light of a misted alchemical globe, little stronger than scarlet moonlight, and he admired the soft curves of the woman who was running her hands along the insides of his thighs. She smelled like mulled apple wine and cinnamon musk. Yet he was nothing resembling aroused.

'Felice, please,' he said. 'This was a bad idea.'

'You're tense,' whispered Felice. 'You've obviously got something on your mind, and that cut on your arm – it can't be helping at all. Let me try a few things more. I'm always up for a . . . professional challenge.'

'I can't imagine anything would help.'

'Hmmm.' Locke could hear the pout in her voice, though her face was little more than soft slashes of shadow in the red half-light. 'There's wines, you know. Alchemical ones, from Tal Verrar. Aphrodisiacs. Not cheap, but they do work.' She rubbed his stomach, toying with the slender line of hair that ran down its centre. 'They can work *miracles*.'

'I don't need wine,' he said distantly, grabbing her hand and moving it away from his skin. 'Gods, I don't know what I need.'

'Allow me to make a suggestion, then.' She moved herself up on the bed until she was crouched beside his chest, on her knees. With one confident motion (for there was real muscle under those curves) she flipped him over onto his stomach and began kneading the muscles of his neck and back, alternating gentle caresses and firm pressure.

'Suggestion . . . ow . . . accepted . . .'

'Locke,' Felice said, losing the breathy, anything-to-please-you bedroom voice that was one of the cherished illusions of her trade, 'you do know that the attendants in the waiting chambers tell us exactly what each client requests, when they give us assignments?'

'So I've heard.'

'Well, I know you specifically asked for a redhead.'

'Which . . . ow, lower please . . . which means . . . ?'

'There's only two of us in the Lilies,' she said, 'and we get that request every now and again. But the thing is, some men want any redhead in *general*, and some men want one redhead in *particular*.'

'Oh . . .'

'Those that want a redhead in general have their fun and go their way. But you . . . you want one redhead in particular. And I'm not her.'

'I'm sorry . . . I said it's not your fault.'

'I know. That's ever so gracious of you.'

'I'm happy paying anyway.'

'And that's also sweet.' She chuckled. 'But you'd be taking it up with the room full of burly men with clubs if you didn't, not just worrying about hurting my poor feelings.'

'You know,' Locke said, 'I think I prefer you like this to all that how-may-I-please-you-master bullshit earlier.'

'Some men like a straightforward whore. Some don't want to hear anything but how wonderful they are.' She worked at his neck muscles with the heels of her palms. 'It's all business. But like I said, you seem to be pining for someone. And now you've remembered yourself.'

'Sorry.'

'No need to keep apologising to me. You're the one whose lady-love ran halfway across the continent.'

'Gods.' Locke groaned. 'Find me a single person in Camorr who doesn't know and I'll give you a hundred crowns, I swear.'

'It's just something I heard from one of the Sanzas.'

'One of the Sanzas? Which one?'

'Couldn't say. They're so hard to tell apart in the dark.'

'I'm going to cut their gods-damned tongues out.'

'Oh, tsk.' She ruffled his hair. 'Please don't. Us girls have a use for those, at least.'

'Hmmmph.'

'You poor, sweet idiot. You do have it bad for her. Well, what can I say, Locke? You're fucked.' Felice laughed softly. 'Just not by me.'

INTERLUDE:
Brat Masterpieces

I

The summer after Jean came to the Gentlemen Bastards, Father Chains took him and Locke up to the temple roof one night after dinner. Chains smoked a paper-wrapped sheaf of Jeremite tobacco while the sunlight sank beneath the horizon and the caught fire of the city's Elderglass rose glimmering in its place.

That night, he wanted to talk about the eventual necessity of cutting throats.

'I had this talk with Calo and Galdo and Sabetha last year,' he began. 'You boys are investments, in time and treasure both.' He exhaled ragged crescents of pale smoke, failing as usual to conjure full rings. 'Big investments. My life's work, maybe. A pair of brat masterpieces. So I want you to remember that you can't always smile your way around a fight. If someone pulls steel on you, I expect you to survive. Sometimes that means giving back in kind. Sometimes it means running like your arse is on fire. Always it means knowing which is the right choice – and that's why we've got to talk about your inclinations.'

Chains fixed Locke with a stare while he took a long, deliberate drag on his sheaf; the final breath of a man treading unpleasant water, preparing to go under the surface.

'You and I both know that you have multiple talents, Locke, genuine gifts for a great many things. So I have to give this to you straight – if it comes down to hard talk with a real foe, you're nothing but a pair of pissed breeches and a bloodstain. You can kill, all right, that's the gods' own truth, but you're just not made for stand-up, face-to-face bruising. And you know it, right?'

Locke's red-cheeked silence was an answer in itself. Suddenly unable to look Father Chains in the eyes, he tried to pretend that his feet were fascinating objects that he'd never seen before.

'Locke, Locke, we can't all be mad dogs with a blade in our hands, and it's nothing to sob about, so let's not see that lip of yours quivering like an old whore's tits, right? You will learn steel, and you'll learn rope, and you'll learn the alleypiece. But you'll learn them sneak style. In the back, from the side, from above, in the dark.' Chains grabbed an imaginary opponent from behind, left hand round the throat, right hand thrusting at kidney level with his half-smoked sheaf for a dagger. 'All the twists, because fighting wisely will keep you from getting cut to shit-mince.'

Chains pretended to wipe the blood from his ember-tipped 'blade', then took another drag. 'That's that. Put it in your hat and wear it to town, Locke. We need to face our shortcomings head on. The old saying for a gang is, "Lies go out, but the truth stays home".' He forced twin streams of smoke from his nostrils, and cheered up visibly as the tails of grey vapour swirled around his head. 'Now stop acting like there's a fucking naked woman on your shoes, will you?'

Locke did grin at that, weakly, but he also looked up and nodded.

'Now, you,' Chains said, turning to regard Jean, 'we all know you've got the sort of temper that cracks skulls when it's off the leash. We've got a properly evil brain in Locke here, a fantastic liar. Calo and Galdo are silver at all trades, gold at none. Sabetha's the born queen of all the charmers that ever lived. But what we *don't* have yet is a plain old bruiser. I think it could be you, a stand-up brawler to keep your friends out of trouble. A real rabid-dog bastard with steel in your hand. Care to give it a go?'

Jean's eyes were immediately drawn down to the fascinating spectacle of his own feet. 'Um, well, if you think that would be good, I can try . . .'

'Jean, I've seen you angry.'

'I've felt you angry,' said Locke, grinning.

'Give me some credit for being four times your fucking age,

255

Jean. You don't smoulder and you don't make threats; you just go cold, and then you make things happen. Some folks are made for hard situations.' He drew smoke from his sheaf once again, and flicked white ashes to the stones beneath his feet. 'I think you have the knack for smacking brains out of heads. That's neither good nor bad in itself, but it's something we can use.'

Jean seemed to think this over for a few moments, but Locke and Chains could both see the decision already made in his eyes. They had gone hard and hungry under his black tangle of hair, and his nod was just a formality.

'Good, good! Thought you'd like the idea, so I took the liberty of making arrangements.' He produced a black leather wallet from one of the pockets of his laze-coat and handed it over to Jean. 'Half past noon tomorrow, you're expected at the House of Glass Roses.'

Locke and Jean both widened their eyes at the mention of Camorr's best-known and most exclusive school of arms. Jean flipped the sigil-wallet open. Inside was a flat token, a stylised rose in frosted glass, fused directly onto the inner surface of the leather. With this, Jean could pass north over the Angevine and past the guard-posts at the foot of the Alcegrante hills; it placed him under the direct protection of Don Tomsa Maranzalla, Master of the House of Glass Roses.

'That rose will get you over the river and up among the swells, but don't fuck around once you're up there. Do what you're told, go straight there and come straight back. You go four times a week from now on. And for all our sakes, tame that mess on top of your head. Use fire and a poleaxe if you have to.' Chains took a final drag of evergreen-scented smoke from his rapidly disappearing sheaf, then flicked the butt up and over the roof wall. His last exhalation of the night sailed over the heads of the two boys, a wobbly but otherwise fully formed ring.

'Fuck me! An omen!' Chains reached after the drifting ring as though he could pluck it back for examination. 'Either this scheme is fated to work out, or the gods are pleased with me for engineering your demise, Jean Tannen. I love a win-win proposition. Now don't you two have work to do?'

In the House of Glass Roses, there was a hungry garden.

The place was Camorr in microcosm; a thing of the Eldren left behind for men to puzzle over, a dangerous treasure discarded like a toy. The Elderglass that mortared its stones rendered it proof against all human arts, much like the Five Towers and a dozen other structures scattered over the islands of the city. The men and women who lived in these places were squatters in glory, and the House of Glass Roses was the most glorious, dangerous place on the Alcegrante slopes. That Don Maranzalla held it was a sign of his high and lasting favour with the Duke.

Just before the midpoint of the noon hour the next day, Jean Tannen stood at the door of Don Maranzalla's tower: five cylindrical storeys of grey stone and silver glass, a hulking fastness that made the lovely villas around it look like an architect's scale models. Great waves of white heat beat down from the cloudless sky, and the air was heavy with the slightly beery breath of a city river boiling under long hours of sun. A frosted-glass window was set into the stone beside the tower's huge lacquered oak doors, behind which the vague outline of a face could be discerned. Jean's approach had been noted.

He'd gone north over the Angevine on a glass catbridge no wider than his hips, clinging to the guide ropes with sweaty hands for all six hundred feet of the crossing. There were no large bridges to the south bank of the Isla Zantara, second most easterly of the Alcegrante isles. Ferry rides were a copper half-baron; for those too poor to ride, that left the ecstatic terror of the catbridges. Jean had never been aloft on one before, and the sight of more experienced men and women ignoring the ropes as they crossed at speed had turned his bowels to ice water. The feel of hard pavement beneath his shoes had been a blessed relief when it came again.

The sweat-soaked yellowjackets on duty at the Isla Zantara gatehouse had let Jean pass far more quickly than he'd thought possible, and he'd seen the mirth drain from their ruddy faces the moment they recognised the sigil he carried in his little black wallet. Their directions after that had been terse; was it pity that tinged their voices, or fear?

'We'll look for you, boy,' one of them suddenly called after him as he started up the clean white stones of the street, 'if you come back down the hill again!'

Mingled pity *and* fear, then. Had Jean really been enthusiastic for this adventure as recently as the night before?

The creak and rattle of counterweights heralded the appearance of a dark crack between the twin doors before him. A second later, the portals swung wide with slow majesty, muscled outward by a pair of men in blood-red waistcoats and sashes, and Jean saw that each door was half a foot of solid wood backed with iron bands. A wave of scents washed out over him: humid stone and old sweat, roasting meat and cinnamon incense. Smells of prosperity and security, of life within walls.

Jean held his wallet up to the men who'd opened the door and one of them waved a hand impatiently. 'You're expected. Enter as a guest of Don Maranzalla and respect his house as you would your own.'

Against the left-hand wall of the opulent foyer a pair of curlicue staircases in black iron wound upward; Jean followed the man around and up one set of narrow steps, self-consciously trying to keep his sweating and gasping under control. The tower doors were pulled shut beneath them with an echoing slam.

They wound their way up past three floors of glittering glass and ancient stone, decorated with thick red carpets and innumerable stained tapestries that Jean recognised as battle flags. Don Maranzalla had served as the Duke's personal swordmaster and the commander of his blackjackets for a quarter of a century. These bloody scraps of cloth were all that remained of countless companies of men fate had thrown against Nicovante and Maranzalla in fights that were now legend: the Iron Sea Wars, the Mad Count's Rebellion, the Thousand-Day War against Tal Verrar.

At last, the winding stair brought them up into a small dim room, barely larger than a closet, lit by the gentle red glow of a paper lantern. The man placed one hand on a brass knob and turned to look down at Jean.

'This is the Garden Without Fragrance,' he said, 'Step with care and touch nothing, as you love life.' Then he pushed the door to the roof open, letting in a sight so bright and astounding that Jean rocked back on his heels.

The House of Glass Roses was more than twice as wide as it was tall, so the roof must have been at least one hundred feet in diameter, walled in on all sides. For a frightful moment Jean thought he stood before a blazing, hundred-hued alchemical fire. All the stories and rumours had done nothing to prepare him for the sight of this place beneath the full light of a white summer sun; it seemed as though liquid diamond pulsed through a million delicate veins and scintillated on a million facets and edges. Here was an entire rose garden, wall after wall of perfect petals and stems and thorns, silent and scentless and alive with reflected fire, for it was all carved from Elderglass, a hundred thousand blossoms perfect down to the tiniest thorn. Dazzled, Jean stumbled forward and stretched out a hand to steady himself; when he forced his eyes closed the darkness was alive with after-images like flashes of heat lightning.

Don Maranzalla's man caught him by the shoulders, gently but firmly.

'It can be overwhelming at first. Your eyes will adjust in a few moments, but mark my words well and, by the gods, touch *nothing*.'

As Jean's eyes recovered from the initial shock of the garden, he began to see past the dazzling glare. Each wall of roses was actually transparent; the nearest was just two paces away. And it was flawless, as flawless as the rumours claimed, as though the Eldren had frozen every blossom and every bush in an instant of summer's fullest perfection. Yet there were patches of genuine colour here and there in the hearts of the sculptures, swirled masses of reddish-brown translucence like clouds of rust-coloured smoke frozen in ice.

These clouds were human blood.

Every petal, leaf and thorn was sharper than any razor; the merest touch would open human skin like paper, and the roses would drink blood, just as the stories said, siphoning it deep inside the network of glass stems and vines. Presumably, if enough lives were fed to the garden, every blossom and every wall would some day turn a rich, rusty red. Some rumours had it that the garden merely drank what was spilled upon it, others claimed that the roses would actually draw blood forth from a wound, and could drain a man white from any cut, no matter how small.

It would take intense concentration to walk through these garden paths; most were only two or three paces wide, and a moment of distraction could be deadly. It said much about Don Maranzalla that he thought of his garden as the ideal place to teach young people how to fight. For the first time, Jean felt a sense of dreadful awe at the creatures who'd vanished from Camorr a thousand years before his birth; how many other alien surprises had they left behind for men to stumble over? What could drive away beings powerful enough to craft something like this? The answer did not bear thinking of.

Maranzalla's man released his grip on Jean's shoulders and re-entered the dim room at the apex of the stairs; the room, as Jean now saw, jutted out of the tower's wall like a gardener's shack. 'The Don will be waiting at the centre of the garden,' he said.

Then he pulled the door shut after him, and Jean seemed alone on the roof, with the naked sun overhead and the walls of thirsty glass before him.

Yet he wasn't alone; there was noise coming from the heart of the glass garden, the whickering skirl of steel against steel, low grunts of exertion, a few terse commands in a deep voice rich with authority. Just a few minutes earlier, Jean would have sworn that the catbridge crossing was the most frightening thing he'd ever done, but now that he faced the Garden Without Fragrance, he would have gladly gone back to the midpoint of that slender arch fifty feet above the Angevine and danced on it without guide ropes.

Still, the black wallet clutched in his right hand drew his mind to the fact that Father Chains had thought him right for whatever awaited him in this garden. Despite their scintillating danger, the roses were inanimate and unthinking; how could he have the heart of a killer if he feared to walk among them? Shame drove him forward, step by sliding step, and he threaded the twisting paths of the garden with exquisite care, sweat sliding down his face and stinging his eyes.

'I am a Gentleman Bastard,' he muttered to himself.

It was the longest thirty feet of his brief life, that passage between the cold and waiting walls of roses.

He didn't allow them a single taste of him.

At the centre of the garden was a circular courtyard about thirty feet wide; here, two boys roughly Jean's age were circling one another, rapiers flicking and darting between them. Another half-dozen boys watched uneasily, along with a tall man of late-middle age. This man had shoulder-length hair and drooping moustaches the colour of cold campfire ashes; his face was like sanded leather, and though he wore a gentleman's doublet in the same vivid red as the attendants downstairs, he wore it over weather-stained soldier's breeches and tattered field boots.

There wasn't a boy at the lesson that didn't put his master's clothes to shame. These were sons of the *quality*, in brocade jackets and tailored breeches, silk tunics and polished imitations of swordsman's boots; each one also wore a white leather buff coat and silver-studded bracers of the same material; just the thing for warding off thrusts from training weapons. Jean felt naked the instant he stepped into the clearing, and only the threat of the glass roses kept him from leaping back into concealment.

One of the duellists was surprised to see Jean emerge from the garden, and his opponent made good use of that split second of inattention; he deftly thrust his rapier into the meat of the first boy's upper arm, punching through the leather. The skewered boy let out an unbecoming howl and dropped his own blade.

'My lord Maranzalla.' One of the boys in the crowd spoke up, and there was more oil in his voice than there was on a blade put away for storage. 'Lorenzo was clearly distracted by the boy who just came out of the garden! That was not a fair strike.'

Every boy in the clearing turned to regard Jean, and it was impossible to guess what soonest ignited their naked disdain: his labourer's clothing, his pear-like physique, his lack of weapons and armour? Only the boy with a spreading circle of blood on his tunic sleeve failed to stare at him with open loathing; he had other problems. The grey-haired man cleared his throat, then spoke in the deep voice Jean had heard earlier. He seemed amused.

'You were a fool to take your eyes from your opponent, Lorenzo, so in a sense you earned that sting. But it is true, all things being equal, that a young gentleman should not exploit an outside distraction to score a touch. You will both try to do better next time.' He pointed a hand toward Jean without looking at him, and his voice lost its warmth. 'And you, boy, lose yourself in the garden until we've finished here; I don't want to see you again until these young gentlemen have left.'

Certain that the fire rising in his cheeks could outshine the sun itself, Jean rapidly scuttled out of sight; several seconds passed before he realised with horror that he had leapt back into the maze of sculpted glass walls without hesitation. Positioning himself a few bends back from the clearing, he stood in mingled fear and self-loathing, and tried to hold himself rigid as the sun's heat cooked great rivers of sweat out of him.

Fortunately, he hadn't long to wait; the sound of steel on steel faded, and Don Maranzalla dismissed his class. They filed past Jean with their coats off and their jackets open, each boy seemingly at ease with the lethal labyrinth of transparent blossoms. Not one said anything to Jean, for this was Don Maranzalla's house, and it would be presumptuous of them to chastise a commoner within his domain. The fact that each boy had sweated his silk tunic to near-translucency, and that several were red-faced and wobbly with sun-sickness, did little to leaven Jean's misery.

'Boy,' called the Don after the troop of young gentlemen had passed out of the garden and down the stairs, 'attend me now.'

Summoning as much dignity as he could, but realising that most of it was pure imagination, Jean sucked in his wobbling belly and went out into the courtyard once again. Don Maranzalla wasn't facing him; the Don held the undersized training rapier that had recently stung a careless boy's bicep. In his hands it looked like a toy, but the blood that glistened on its tip was quite real.

'I, uh, I'm sorry, sir, my lord Maranzalla; I must have come early. I, ah, didn't mean to distract from the lesson . . .'

The Don turned on his heel, smooth as Tal Verrar clockwork, every muscle in his upper body ominously statue-still. He stared down at Jean now, and the cold scrutiny of those black, squinting eyes gave Jean his third great scare of the young afternoon.

He suddenly remembered that he was alone on the roof with a man who had butchered his way into the position he currently held.

'Does it amuse you, lowborn,' the Don asked in a serpentine whisper, 'to speak before you are spoken to, in a place such as this, to a man such as myself? To a *Don*, such as myself?'

Jean's blubbered apology died in his throat with an unmanly choke; the sort of wet noise a clam might make if you broke its shell and squeezed it out through the cracks.

'Because, if you're merely being careless, I'll beat that habit out of your butter-fat ass before you can blink.' The Don strode over to the nearest wall of glass roses, and with evident care he slid the tip of the bloodied rapier into one of the blossoms. Jean watched in horrified fascination as the red stain quickly vanished from the blade and was drawn into the glass, where it diffused into a mist-like pink tendril and was carried into the heart of the sculpture. The Don tossed the clean sword to the ground. 'Is that it? Are you a careless little fat boy sent up here to pretend at arms? You're a dirty little urchin from the Cauldron, no doubt; some whore's gods-damned droppings.'

At first the paralysis of Jean's tongue refused to lift, then he heard the blood pounding in his ears like the crashing of waves on a shore. His fists clenched on some impulse of their own.

'I was born in the *North Corner*,' he yelled, 'and my mother and father were folk of *business*!'

Almost as soon as he'd finished spitting this out, his heart seemed to stop; mortified, he put his arms behind his back, bowed his head and took a step backwards.

After a moment of weighted silence, Maranzalla laughed loudly and cracked his knuckles with a sound like pine logs popping in a fire.

'Forgive me, Jean,' he said. 'But I wanted to see if Chains was telling the truth. By the gods, you do have balls. And a temper.'

'You . . .' Jean stared at the Don, comprehension dawning. 'You *wanted* to make me angry, my lord.'

'I know you're sensitive about your parents, boy. Chains told me quite a bit about you.' The Don knelt on one knee before Jean, bringing them eye to eye, and put a hand on Jean's shoulder.

'Chains isn't blind,' said Jean. 'I'm not an initiate. And you're not really . . . not really . . .'

'A mean old son-of-a-bitch?'

Jean giggled despite himself. 'I, uh . . . I wonder if I'll ever meet anyone who is what they seem to be, ever again, my lord.'

'You have. They walked out of my garden a few minutes ago. And I *am* a mean old son-of-a-bitch, Jean. You're going to hate my miserable guts before this summer's out. You're going to curse me at Falselight and curse me at dawn.'

'Oh,' said Jean. 'But . . . that's just business.'

'Very true,' said Don Maranzalla. 'Can I confide something to you, Jean? I wasn't born to this place; it was had as a gift for services rendered. And don't think that I don't value it . . . but my mother and father weren't even from the North Corner. I was actually born on a farm.'

'Wow,' said Jean.

'Yes,' said the Don. 'Up here in this garden it won't matter who your parents were; I'll make you work until you sweat blood and plead for mercy. I'll thrash you until you're inventing new gods to pray to. The only thing this garden respects is concentration. Can you concentrate, every moment you're up here? Can you distill your attention, drive it down to the narrowest focus, live absolutely in the now, and shut out all other concerns?'

'I . . . I shall have to try, my lord. I already walked through the gardens once. I can do it again.'

'You'll do it again. You'll do it a thousand times. You'll run through my roses. You'll sleep among them. And you'll learn to concentrate. I warn you, some men could not.'

The Don arose and swept a hand in a semicircle before him.

'You can find what they left behind, here and there. In the glass.'

Jean swallowed nervously and nodded.

'Now, you tried to apologize before for coming early. Truth is, you didn't. I let my previous lesson run long because I tend to indulge those wretched little shits when they want to cut each other up a bit. In future, come at the stroke of one to make sure they're long gone. They cannot be allowed to see me actually teaching you.'

Once, Jean had been the son of substantial wealth, and he had worn clothes as fine as any just seen on this rooftop. What he felt now was the old sting of his loss, he told himself, and no mere shame for anything as stupid as his hair or his clothes or even his hanging belly. This thought was just self-importantly noble enough to keep his eyes dry and his face composed.

'I understand, my lord. I . . . don't wish to embarrass you again.'

'Embarrass me? Jean, you misunderstand.' Maranzalla kicked idly at the toy rapier and it clattered across the tiles of the rooftop. 'Those prancing little pants-wetters come here to learn the colourful and gentlemanly art of fencing, with its many sporting limitations and its proscriptions against *dishonourable* engagements.

264

'You, on the other hand,' he said as he turned to give Jean a firm but friendly poke in the centre of his forehead, '*you* are going to learn how to *kill men with a sword*.'

Chapter Seven

Out the Window

I

Locke outlined his plan over a long, nervous lunch.

The Gentlemen Bastards sat at the dining table in their glass burrow, just after noon on the Duke's Day. Outside, the sun was pouring down its usual afternoon punishment, but in the burrow it was cool, perhaps unnaturally so, even for an underground cellar. Chains had often speculated that the Elderglass did tricks with more than just light.

They had laid on a feast more befitting a festival than a midday meeting; there was stewed mutton with onions and ginger, stuffed eels in spiced wine sauce, and green-apple tarts baked by Jean (with a liberal dose of Austershalin brandy poured over the fruit). 'I'll bet even the Duke's own cook would have his balls skinned if he did this,' he'd said. 'Makes each tart worth two or three crowns, by my reckoning.'

'What'll they be worth,' said Bug, 'once they're eaten, and they come out the other end?'

'You're welcome to take measurements,' said Calo. 'Grab a scale.'

'And a scoop,' added Galdo.

The Sanzas spent the meal picking at seasoned omelettes topped with minced sheep's kidneys, usually a favourite with the whole table. But today, though they all agreed it was their best effort in weeks, topping even the celebration of their first success in the Salvara game, the savour seemed to have evaporated. Only Bug ate with real vigour, and his attention was largely concentrated on Jean's plate of tarts.

'Look at me,' he said with his mouth half full, 'I'm worth more with every bite!'

Quiet half-smiles met his clowning, and nothing more; the boy 'harrumphed' in annoyance and banged his fists on the table. 'Well, if none of you wants to eat,' he said, 'why don't we get on with planning how we're going to dodge the axe tonight?'

'Indeed,' said Jean.

'Too right,' added Calo.

'Yes,' said Galdo. 'What's the game and how do we play it?'

'Well.' Locke pushed his plate away, crumpled his cloth napkin, and threw it into the centre of the table. 'For starters, we need to use the damn Broken Tower rooms again. It seems the stairs aren't through with us just yet.'

Jean nodded. 'What will we do with the place?'

'That's where you and I will be when Anjais comes looking to collect us, at the ninth hour. And that's where we'll stay, after he's thoroughly convinced that we have a very honest reason for not going with him.'

'What reason would that be?' asked Calo.

'A very colourful one,' said Locke. 'I need you and Galdo to pay a quick visit to Jessaline d'Aubart this afternoon. I need help from a black alchemist for this. Here's what you tell her . . .'

2

The illicit apothecary shop of Jessaline d'Aubart and her daughter Janellaine was located above a scribes' collective in the respectable Fountain Bend neighbourhood. Calo and Galdo stepped onto the scribing floor at just past the second hour of the afternoon; here, a dozen men and women were hunched over wide wooden boards, working quills and salt and charcoal sticks and drying sponges back and forth like automatons. A clever arrangement of mirrors and skylights let the natural light of day in to illuminate their work. There were few tradesfolk in Camorr more penny-conscious than journeymen scriveners.

At the rear of the first floor was a winding staircase guarded by a tough-looking young woman who feigned boredom while fingering weapons beneath her brocaded brown coat. The Sanza twins established their bona-fides with a combination of hand-gestures and copper barons that made their way into the young woman's coat pockets. She tugged on a bell-rope beside the stairs, then waved them up.

On the second floor there was a reception room, windowless, panelled walls and floor alike with a golden hardwood that retained a faint aroma of pine lacquer. A tall counter divided the room in half; there were no chairs on the customers' side, and nothing at all on display on the merchants' side, just a single locked door.

Jessaline stood behind the counter, a striking woman in her mid-fifties with a tumbling cascade of charcoal-coloured hair and dark, wary eyes nestled in laugh-lines. Janellaine, half her age, stood to her mother's right with a crossbow pointed just over Calo and Galdo's heads. It was an indoor murder-piece, lightweight and low-powered, which almost certainly meant some hideous poison on the quarrel. Neither Sanza was particularly bothered; this was business as usual for a black alchemist.

'Madam d'Aubart and Miss d'Aubart,' said Calo, bowing from the waist, 'your servants.'

'Not to mention,' said Galdo, 'still very much available.'

'Master Sanza and Master Sanza,' said the elder d'Aubart, 'pleased to see you.'

'Although we are,' said Janellaine, 'still very much disinclined.'

'Perhaps you'd care to buy something, though?' Jessaline folded her hands on the counter and raised one eyebrow.

'As it happens, a friend of ours needs something special.' Calo fished a coin-purse from under his waistcoat and held it in plain view without opening it.

'Special?'

'Or perhaps not so much special as specific. He's got to get sick. Very sick.'

'Far be it from me to drive away business, my dears,' said the elder d'Aubart, 'but three or four bottles of rum would do the trick at a fraction of the price for anything I could give you.'

'Ah, not that sort of sick,' said Galdo. 'He's got to be in a bad way, like to knocking on the Death Goddess's bedchamber and asking if he can come in. And then he's got to be able to recover his strength after playing ill for a while. A sort of mummer's sick, if you will.'

'Hmmm,' said Janellaine, 'I don't know if we have anything that works quite like that, at least not on hand.'

'When,' said Jessaline, 'would your friend require a solution by?'

'We were sort of hoping to walk out of here with one,' said Calo.

'We don't brew miracles here, my dears.' Jessaline drummed her fingers on her countertop. 'Contrary to all common belief. We do prefer a bit of notice for something like this. Messing about with someone's insides, fit to ill and then fit again in the span of a few hours . . . well, that's delicate.'

'We're not Bondsmagi,' added Janellaine.

'Praise the gods,' said Galdo, 'but it's very pressing.'

'Well.' Jessaline sighed. 'Perhaps we can bang something together, a bit on the crude side, but it might do the trick.'

'Barrow-robber's blossom,' said her daughter.

'Yes.' Jessaline nodded. 'And Somnay pine, after.'

'I believe we've both in the shop,' Jannelaine said. 'Shall I check?'

'Do, and hand over that alley-piece while you're back there.'

Janellaine passed the crossbow to her mother, then unlocked the door at the rear of the room and disappeared, closing it behind her once again. Jessaline set the weapon gently down on the counter, keeping one long-fingered hand on the padded stock.

'You wound us, madam,' said Calo. 'We're harmless as kittens.'

'More so,' said Galdo. 'Kittens have claws and piss on things indiscriminately.'

'It's not you, boys. It's the city. Whole place is like to boil, what with Nazca getting clipped. Old Barsavi's got to have some retribution in the works. Gods know who this Grey King is or what he wants, but I'm more worried by the day for what might come up my stairs.'

'It *is* a messy time,' said Calo.

Janellaine returned with two small pouches in her hands. She locked the door behind her, passed the pouches to her mother, and picked up the crossbow once again.

'Well,' said the elder d'Aubart, 'here's what it is, then. Your friend takes this, the red pouch. It's barrow-robber's blossom, a sort of purple powder. In the red pouch, remember. Put it in water. It's an emetic, if the word means anything to you.'

'Nothing pleasant,' said Galdo.

'Five minutes after he drinks it, he gets an ache in the belly. Ten minutes and he gets wobbly at the knees. Fifteen minutes and he starts vomiting up every meal he's had for the past week. Won't be pretty. Have buckets close at hand.'

'And it'll look absolutely real?' asked Calo.

'Look? Sweetmeat, it'll be as real as it gets. You ever see anyone feign vomiting?'

'Yes,' said the Sanzas in perfect unison.

'He does this thing with chewed-up oranges,' added Galdo.

'Well, he won't be feigning *this*. Any physiker in Camorr would swear it was a real and natural distress. You can't even see the barrow-robber's blossom once it comes up; it dissolves quickly.'

'And then,' said Calo, 'what about the other pouch?'

'This is Somnay pine bark. Crumble it and steep it in a tea. It's the perfect counter for the purple blossom; it'll cancel it right out. But the blossom will already have done its work; keep that in mind. The bark won't put food back in your friend's belly, nor give back the vigour he loses while he's retching his guts out. He's going to be weak and sore for at least an evening or two.'

'Sounds wonderful,' said Calo, 'for our own peculiar definition of wonderful. What do we owe you?'

'Three crowns, twenty solons,' said Jessaline. 'And that's only because you were old Chains' boys. This isn't much by way of alchemy, just refined and purified, but the powders are hard to get hold of.'

Calo counted out twenty gold tyrins from his purse and set them on the counter in a vertical stack. 'Here's five crowns, then. With the understanding that this transaction is best forgotten by everyone involved.'

'Sanza,' said Jessaline d'Aubart without humour, 'every purchase at my shop is forgotten, as far as the outside world is concerned.'

'Then this one,' said Calo, adding four more tyrins to the pile, 'needs to stay *extra* forgotten.'

'Well, if you really want to reinforce the point . . .' She pulled a wooden scraper from beneath the counter and used it to pull the coins over the back edge into what sounded like a leather bag. She was careful not to touch the coins themselves; black alchemists rarely got to be her age if they relaxed their paranoia towards all things touched, tasted or smelled.

'You have our thanks,' said Galdo. 'And that of our friend as well.'

'Oh, don't count on that.' Jessaline d'Aubart chuckled. 'Give him the red pouch first, then see what a grateful frame of mind it puts him in.'

3

'Get me a glass of water, Jean.' Locke stared out the canal-side window of the seventh-floor room as the buildings of southern Camorr grew long black shadows toward the east. 'It's time to take my medicine. I'm guessing it's close on twenty minutes to nine.'

'Already set,' said Jean, passing over a tin cup with a cloudy lavender residue swirling in it. 'That stuff did dissolve in a blink, just like the Sanzas said.'

'Well,' he said, 'here's to deep pockets poorly guarded. Here's to true alchemists, a strong stomach, a clumsy Grey King and the luck of the Crooked Warden.'

'Here's to living out the night,' said Jean, miming the clink of a cup against Locke's own.

'Mmm.' Locke sipped hesitantly, then tilted the cup back and poured it down his throat in one smooth series of gulps. 'Actually not bad at all. Tastes minty, very refreshing.'

'A worthy epitaph,' said Jean, taking the cup.

Locke stared out the window a while longer; the mesh was up, as the Duke's Wind was still blowing in strongly from the sea and the insects weren't yet biting. Across the Via Camorrazza the Arsenal District was mostly silent and motionless; with the Iron Sea city-states at relative peace, all the great saw-yards and warehouses and wet docks had little business. In times of need they could build or service two dozen ships at once; now Locke could see only one skeletal hull rising within the yards.

Beyond that, the sea broke white against the base of the South Needle, an Elderglass-mortared stone breakwater nearly three quarters of a mile in length. At its southernmost tip a human-built watchtower stood out against the darkening sea; beyond that, the white blurs of sails could be seen beneath the red tendrils of clouds in the sky.

'Oh,' he said, 'I do believe something's happening.'

'Take a seat,' said Jean. 'You're supposed to get wobbly in just a bit.'

'Already happening. In fact . . . gods, I think I'm going to—'

So it began; a great wave of nausea bubbled up in Locke's throat, and with it came everything he'd eaten for the past day. For a few long minutes he crouched on his knees, clutching a wooden bucket, as devoutly as any man had ever prayed over an altar for intercession from the gods.

'Jean,' he gasped out during a brief lull between spasms of retching, 'next time I conceive a plan like this, consider planting a hatchet in my skull.'

'Hardly efficacious.' Jean swapped a full bucket for an empty one and gave Locke a friendly pat on the back. 'Dulling my nice sharp blades on a skull as thick as yours . . .'

One by one, Jean shuttered the windows. Falselight was just rising outside. 'Ghastly as it is,' he said, 'we need the smell to make an impression when Anjais shows up.'

Even once Locke's stomach was thoroughly emptied, the dry heaving continued; he shuddered and shook and moaned, clutching at his guts. Jean hauled him bodily over to a sleeping pallet, where he looked down in genuine worry. 'You're pale and clammy,' he muttered. 'Not bad at all. Very realistic.'

'Pretty, isn't it? Gods,' whispered Locke, 'how much longer?'

'Can't rightly say,' said Jean. 'They should be arriving down there right about now; give them a few minutes to get impatient with waiting around for us and come storming up here.'

During those few minutes Locke became intimately acquainted with the idea of 'a short eternity'. Finally, there came the creak of footsteps on the stairs, and a loud banging on the door.

'Lamora!' Anjais Barsavi's voice. 'Tannen! Open up or I'll kick the fucking door in!'

'Thank the gods,' croaked Locke as Jean rose to unbolt the door.

'We've been waiting in front of the Last Mistake! Are you coming or— gods, what the hell happened in here?'

Anjais threw one arm up over his face as he stepped into the apartment and the smell of sickness. Jean pointed to Locke, writhing on the bed, moaning, half-wrapped in a thin blanket despite the moist heat of the evening.

272

'He took ill just half an hour ago, maybe,' said Jean. 'Losing his stomach all over the damn place. I don't know what's the matter.'

'Gods, he's turning green.' Anjais took a few steps closer to Locke, staring in horrified sympathy. Anjais was dressed for a fight, in a boiled-leather cuirass, an unbuckled leather collar and a pair of studded leather bracers tied over his ham-like forearms. Several men had accompanied him up the stairs, but none of them seemed in any hurry to follow him into the rooms.

'I had capon for lunch,' said Jean, 'and he had fish rolls. That's the last thing either of us ate, and I'm fine.'

'Iono's piss. Fish rolls. Fresher than he bargained for, I'd wager.'

'Anjais,' Locke croaked, reaching out towards him with a shaking hand, 'don't . . . don't leave me. I can still go. I can still fight.'

'Gods, no.' Anjais shook his head emphatically. 'You're in a bad way, Lamora. I think you'd best see a physiker. Have you summoned one, Tannen?'

'I haven't had a chance. I fetched out the buckets and I've been looking after him since it started.'

'Well, keep it up. Both of you stay. No, don't get angry, Jean, he clearly can't be left on his own. Stay and tend him. Fetch a physiker when you can.'

Anjais gave Locke two brief pats on his exposed shoulder.

'We'll get the fucker tonight, Locke. No worries. We'll do him for good, and I'll send someone to look in on you when we're done. I'll square this with Papa; he'll understand.'

'Please . . . please. Jean can help me stand. I can still . . .'

'End of discussion. You can't fucking stand up; you're sick as a fish dropped in a wine bottle.' Anjais backed towards the door and gave Locke a brief, sympathetic wave before he ducked out. 'If I get my hands on the bastard personally, I'll deck him once for you, Locke. Rest easy.'

Then the door slammed, and Locke and Jean were alone once again.

4

Long minutes passed; Jean unshuttered the canal-side window and stared out into the glimmer of Falselight. He watched as Anjais and his men broke loose from the crowds below, then hurried across a Via Camorrazza catbridge and into the Arsenal District. Anjais didn't look back even once, and soon enough he was swallowed up by shadows and distance.

'Long gone. Can I help you out of—' Jean said, turning away from the window. Locke had already stumbled out of bed and was splashing water on the alchemical hearthstone, looking ten years older and twenty pounds thinner. That was alarming; Locke didn't have twenty pounds to spare.

'Lovely. The least complicated, least important job of the night is done. Carry on, Gentlemen Bastards,' said Locke. His face was alight in the reflected glow of the simmering stone as he set a glazed jug of water atop it. Ten years older? More like twenty. 'Now for the tea, gods bless it, and it had better be as good as the purple powder.'

Jean grimaced and grabbed two vomit buckets, then moved back to the window. Falselight was dying down now; the Hangman's Wind was blowing up warm and strong, bringing a low ceiling of dark clouds with it, visible just past the Five Towers. The moons would be swallowed by those clouds tonight, at least for a few hours. Pinpricks of firelight were appearing across the city as though an unseen jeweller were setting his wares out on a field of black cloth.

'Jessaline's little potion seems to have brought up every meal I've had in the past five years,' said Locke. 'Nothing left to spit up but my naked soul. Make sure it isn't floating around in one of those before you toss them, right?' His hands shook as he crumbled the dry Somnay pine bark into the jug of water; he didn't feel like messing about with proper tea-brewing.

'I think I see it,' Jean said. 'Nasty, crooked little thing it is, too; you're better off with it floating out to sea.'

Jean took a quick glance out the window to ensure that there were no canal boats drifting below in the path of a truly foul surprise, then simply flung the buckets, one after the other. They hit the grey water seventy-odd feet below with loud splashes, but Jean was certain nobody noticed or cared. Camorri were always throwing disgusting things into the Via Camorrazza.

Satisfied with his aim, Jean then slid a hidden closet open and pulled out their disguises – cheap traveller's cloaks and a pair of

274

broad-brimmed Tal Verrar caps fashioned from some ignoble leather with the greasy texture of sausage casings. He flung one brownish-grey cloak over Locke's shoulders; Locke clutched at it gratefully and shivered.

'You've got that motherly concern in your eyes, Jean. I must look like hammered shit.'

'Actually, you look like you were executed last week. I hate to ask, but are you sure you're going to be up for this?'

'Whatever I am, it has to be sufficient.' Locke wrapped one end of his cloak around his right hand and picked up the jug of half-boiled tea. He sipped and swallowed, bark and all, reasoning that the best place for the stuff would be his empty stomach. 'Ugh. It tastes like a kick in the gut feels. Have I pissed Jessaline off recently, too?'

His expression was picturesque, as though the skin of his face were trying to peel itself back and leap off his bones, but he continued to choke the near-tea down anyway, mustering his will against the urge to spit up the wet, gritty fragments of bark as they slid down his throat. Jean steadied him by placing both hands on his shoulders, privately afraid that another bout of vomiting might be more than Locke could handle.

After a few minutes Locke set the empty jug down and sighed deeply.

'I can't wait to have words with the Grey King when this shit is all finished,' Locke whispered. 'There's a few things I want to ask him. Philosophical questions. Like, "How does it feel to be dangled out a window by a rope tied around your balls, motherfucker?"'

'Sounds more like physik than philosophy. And as you said, we have to wait for the Falconer to leave first,' said Jean, his voice steady and totally empty of emotion, the voice he always used when discussing a plan only loosely tethered to prudence and sanity. 'Pity we can't just blind-side the bastard from an alley.'

'Couldn't give him as much as a second to think, or we'd lose.'

'Anything less than twenty yards,' mused Jean. 'One good throw with one Sister; wouldn't take but half a second.'

'But you and I both know,' Locke replied slowly, 'that we can't kill a Bondsmage. We wouldn't live out the week. Karthain would make examples of us, plus Calo, Galdo and Bug as well. Not very clever at all, that way out. A drawn-out suicide.'

Locke stared down at the fading glow of the hearthstone and rubbed his hands together.

'I wonder, Jean. I really wonder. Is this what other people feel like when we're through with them? After we get the goods and pull the vanish and there's nothing they can *do* about it?'

The light from the hearthstone sank several stages further before Jean answered.

'I thought we'd agreed long ago that they get what they deserve, Locke. Nothing more. This is a fantastically silly moment to start giving a shit.'

'Giving a shit?' Locke started, blinking as though he had just woken up. 'No, don't get me wrong. It's just this sewn-up feeling. "No way out" is for other people, not for the Gentlemen Bastards. I don't like being trapped.'

At a sudden gesture from Locke, Jean pulled him to his feet. Jean wasn't sure if the tea was any more responsible than the cloak, but Locke was no longer shivering.

'Too right,' Locke continued, his voice gaining strength. 'Too right it's not for the Gentlemen Bastards. Let's get this shit job over with; we can have a good ponder on the subject of our favourite grey rat-fucker and his pet mage after I've danced to his little tune.'

Jean grinned and cracked his knuckles; then ran a hand down the small of his back. The old familiar gesture, making sure that the Wicked Sisters were ready for a night out.

'You sure,' he said, 'that you're ready for the Vine Highway?'

'Ready as I can be, Jean. Hell, I weigh considerably less than I did before I drank that potion. Climbing down'll be the easiest thing I do all night.'

5

The trellis ran up the full height of the Broken Tower on the westward face of the structure from a narrow alley. The lattice of wood was threaded with tough old vines and built around the windows on each floor. Though something of a bitch to climb, it was the perfect way to avoid the few dozen familiar faces that were sure to be in the Last Mistake on any given night. The Gentlemen Bastards used the Vine Highway frequently.

The alley-side shutters banged open on the top floor of the Broken Tower; all the light inside Locke and Jean's suite of rooms had been extinguished. A large dark shape slid out into the mass of trellised vines, shortly followed by a smaller shape. Clinging with white-knuckled determination, Locke gently eased the shutters closed above him, then willed his queasy stomach to stop complaining for the duration of the descent. The Hangman's Wind, on its way out to the salty blackness of the Iron Sea, caught at his cap and cloak with invisible fingers that smelled of marshes and farmers' fields.

Jean kept himself two or three feet under Locke, and they descended steadily, one foothold or handhold at a time. The windows on the sixth floor were shuttered and dark.

Thin slivers of amber light could be seen around the shutters on the fifth floor; both climbers slowed without the need for words and willed themselves to be as quiet as possible; to be patches of grey invisible against deeper darkness, nothing more. They continued down.

The fifth-floor shutters flew outward as Jean was abreast with them on their left.

One hinged panel rebounded off his back, almost startling him out of his hold on the trellis. He curled his fingers tightly around wood and vine, and looked to his right. Locke stepped on his head in surprise, but quickly pulled himself back up.

'I know there's no other way out, you miserable bitch!' hissed a man's voice.

There was a loud thump, and then a shudder ran up and down the trellis; someone had climbed out the window, and was scrabbling in the vines beside and just below them. A black-haired woman stuck her head out of the window, intent on yelling something in return, but when she caught sight of Jean through the cracks in her swinging shutter, she gasped. This in turn drew the attention of the man clinging just beneath her, a larger man even than Jean.

'What the hell is this shit,' he gasped. 'What are *you* doing outside this window?'

'Amusing the gods, arsehole,' Jean kicked out and tried to nudge the newcomer further down the trellis, to no avail. 'Kindly heave yourself down!'

'What are you doing outside this window, huh? You like to sneak a peek? You can sneak a peek of my fist, cocksucker!'

Grunting with exertion, he began to climb back up, grabbing at Jean's legs. Jean yanked himself just out of the way, and the world reeled around him as he regained his balance. Black wall, black sky, wet black cobblestones fifty feet below. That was a bad fall, the kind that cracked men like eggs.

'All of you, get off my damned window NOW! Ferenz, for Morgante's sake, leave them be and get *down*!' the woman hollered.

'Shit,' Locke muttered from a few feet above and to her left, his eloquence temporarily frightened into submission. 'Madam, you're complicating our night, so before we come in and complicate yours, kindly cork your bullshit bottle and close the gods-damned window!'

She looked up, aghast. 'Two of you? All of you, get down, get down, get DOWN!'

'Close your window, close your window, close your fucking *WINDOW*!'

'I'll kill both you shitsuckers,' huffed Ferenz, 'drop you both off this fucking—'

There was a marrow-chillingly loud cracking noise, and the trellis shuddered beneath the hands of the three men clinging to it.

'Ah,' said Locke. 'Ah, that figures. Thanks ever so much, Ferenz.'

Then there was a torrent of polysyllabic blasphemy from four mouths; exactly who said what would never be clearly recalled. Two careful men were apparently the trellis's limit; under the weight of three careless flailers, it began to tear free of the stone wall with a series of creaks and pops.

Ferenz surrendered to gravity and common sense and began sliding downward at prodigious speed, burning his hands as he went, all but peeling the trellis off the wall above him. It finally gave way when he was about twenty feet above the ground, flipping over and dashing him down into the darkened alley, where he was promptly covered in falling vines and wood. His descent had snapped off a section of trellis at least thirty feet long, starting just beneath Jean's dangling feet.

Wasting no time, Locke shimmied to his right and dropped down onto the window ledge, shoving the screaming woman back with the tip of one boot. Jean scrambled upward, for the shutter still blocked his direct access to the window, and as the section of trellis under his hands began to pull out of the wall, he gracelessly swung himself over the shutter and in through the window, taking Locke with him.

They wound up in a heap on the hardwood floor, tangled in cloaks.

'Get back out the fucking window, *now*!' the woman screamed, punctuating each word with a swift kick to Jean's back and ribs. Fortunately, she wasn't wearing shoes.

'That would be stupid,' Locke said, from somewhere under his larger friend.

'Hey,' Jean said. 'Hey! Hey!' He caught the woman's foot and propelled her backwards. She landed on her bed; it was the sort commonly called a 'dangler', a two-person hammock of strong but lightweight demi-silk, anchored to the ceiling at four points. She went sprawling across it, and both Locke and Jean suddenly noticed that she wasn't wearing anything but her smallclothes. In the summer, a Camorri woman's smallclothes are small indeed.

'Out, you bastards! Out, OUT! I—'

As Locke and Jean stumbled to their feet, the door in the wall opposite the window slammed open, and in stepped a broad-shouldered man with the slab-like muscles of a stevedore or a smith. Vengeful satisfaction gleamed in his eyes, and the smell of hard liquor rolled off him, sour and acute even from ten paces away.

Locke wasted half a second wondering how Ferenz had got back upstairs so quickly, and another half second realising that the man in the doorway wasn't Ferenz.

He giggled, briefly but uncontrollably.

The night wind slammed the shutter against the open window behind him.

The woman made a noise somewhere in the back of her throat, a noise not unlike a cat falling down a deep, dark well.

'You filthy bitch,' the man said, his speech a thick slow

drawl. 'Filthy, filthy bitch. I jus' knew it. Knew you weren' alone.' He spat, then shook his head at Locke and Jean. 'Two guys at once, too. Damn. Go figure. Guess it takes that many t' replace me.

'Hope you boys had y'rselves a fun time with 'nother man's woman,' he continued, drawing nine inches of blackened-steel stiletto from his left boot, ' 'cause now I'm gonna *make* you women.'

Jean spread his feet and moved his left hand under his cloak, ready to draw the Sisters. With his right hand he nudged Locke a pace behind him.

'Hold it!' Locke cried, waving both of his hands. 'Whoa! I know what this looks like, but you've got the wrong idea, friend.' He pointed at the petrified woman clinging to the hanging bed. 'She came *before* we came!'

'Gathis,' hissed the woman. 'Gathis, these men attacked me! Get them! Save me!'

Gathis charged at Jean, growling. He held his knife out before him in the grip of an experienced fighter, but he was still drunk and he was still angry. Locke dodged out of the way as Jean caught Gathis by his wrist, stepped inside his reach, and sent him sprawling to the floor with a quick sweep of the legs.

There was an unappetising snapping noise, and the blade fell from Gathis' grip; Jean had retained a firm hold on his wrist, and then twisted as the man went down on his back. For a moment Gathis was too bewildered to cry out; then the pain broke through to his dulled senses and he roared.

Jean hoisted him up off the ground with one quick yank by the front of his tunic, and then he shoved Gathis with all his might into the stone wall to the left of the window. The big man's head bounced off the hard surface and he stumbled forward; the blurred arc of Jean's right fist met his jaw with a *crack*, abruptly cancelling his forward momentum. He flopped to the ground, boneless as a sack of dough.

'Yes! Yes,' cried the woman, 'Yes! Now throw him out the window!'

'For the love of the gods, madam,' snapped Locke, 'can you please pick one man in your bedroom to cheer for and stick with him?'

'If he's found dead in the alley beneath your window,' said Jean, 'I'll come back and give you the same.'

'If you tell anyone that we came through here,' added Locke, 'you'll only *wish* my friend had come back and given you the same.'

'Gathis will remember,' she screeched. 'He'll certainly remember!'

'A big man like him? Please.' Jean made a show of arranging his cloak and re-donning his hat. 'He'll say it was eight men and they all had clubs.'

Locke and Jean hurried out the door through which Gathis had entered, which led to the landing of the fifth-floor steps on the north side of the tower. With the trellis damaged, there was nothing else for it but to proceed quickly down on foot and pray to the Crooked Warden. Locke drew the door closed behind them, leaving the bewildered woman sprawled on her hanging bed with the unconscious Gathis curled up beside her window.

'The luck of the gods must certainly be with us,' said Locke as they hurried down the creaking steps. 'At least we didn't lose these stupid fucking hats.'

A small dark shape hissed past them, wings fluttering, a sleek shadow visible as it swooped between them and the lights of the city.

'Well,' said Locke, 'for better or worse, from this point on I suppose we're under the Falconer's wing.'

INTERLUDE:
Up the River

I

Jean was away at the House of Glass Roses the afternoon that Locke found out he was going to be sent up the Angevine to live on a farm for several months.

Hard rains were pounding Camorr that Idler's Day, so Chains had taken Locke, Calo and Galdo down into the dining room to teach them how to play Rich-Man, Beggar-Man, Soldier-Man, Duke – a card game that revolved around attempting to cheat one's neighbour out of every last bent copper at his disposal. Naturally, the boys took to it quickly.

'Two, three, and five of spires,' said Calo, 'plus the sigil of the twelve.'

'Die screaming, halfwit,' said Galdo. 'I've got a run of chalices and the sigil of the sun.'

'Won't do you any good, quarter-wit. Hand over your coins.'

'Actually,' said Father Chains, 'A sigil run beats a sigil stand, Calo. Galdo would have you. Except . . .'

'Doesn't anyone care what I've got in my hand?' asked Locke.

'Not particularly,' said Chains, 'since nothing in the game tops a full Duke's hand.' He set his cards on the table and cracked his knuckles with great satisfaction.

'That's cheating,' said Locke. 'That's six times in a row, and you've had the Duke's hand for two of them.'

'Of course I'm cheating,' said Chains. 'Game's no fun unless you cheat. When you figure out *how* I'm cheating, then I'll know you're starting to improve.'

'You shouldn't have told us that,' said Calo.

'We'll practise all week,' said Galdo.

'We'll be robbing you blind,' said Locke, 'by next Idler's Day.'

'I don't think so,' said Chains, chuckling, 'since I'm sending you off on a three-month apprenticeship on Penance Day.'

'You're what?'

'Remember last year, when I sent Calo off to Lashain to pretend to be an initiate in the Order of Gandolo? And Galdo went to Ashmere to slip into the Order of Sendovani? Well, your turn's come around. You'll be going up the river to be a farmer for a few months.'

'A *farmer*?'

'Yes, you might have heard of them.' Chains gathered the cards from around the table and shuffled them. 'They're where our food comes from.'

'Yes, but . . . I don't know anything about farming.'

'Of course not. You didn't know how to cook, serve, dress like a gentleman or speak Vadran when I bought you, either. So now you're going to learn something else new.'

'Where?'

'Up the Angevine, seven or eight miles. Little place called Villa Senziano. It's tenant farmers, mostly beholden to the Duke or some of the minor swells from the Alcegrante. I'll dress as a priest

282

of Dama Elliza, and you'll be my initiate, being sent off to work the earth as part of your service to the goddess. It's what they do.'

'But I don't know anything about the order of Dama Elliza.'

'You won't need to. The man you'll be staying with understands that you're one of my little bastards. The story's just for everyone else.'

'What,' said Calo, 'are we going to do in the meantime?'

'You'll mind the temple. I'll only be gone two days; the Eyeless Priest can be sick and locked away in his chambers. Don't sit the steps while I'm away; people always get sympathetic if I'm out of sight for a bit, especially if I cough and hack when I return. You two and Jean can amuse yourselves as you see fit, as long as you don't make a bloody mess of the place.'

'But by the time I get back,' said Locke, 'I'll be the worst card-player in the temple.'

'Yes. Best wishes for a safe journey, Locke,' said Calo.

'Savour the country air,' said Galdo. 'Stay as long as you like.'

2

The Five Towers loomed over Camorr like the upstretched hand of a god; five irregular, soaring Elderglass cylinders, dotted with turrets and spires and walkways, and much curious evidence that the creatures that had designed them did not quite share the aesthetic sense of the humans who'd appropriated them.

Easternmost was Dawncatcher, four hundred feet high, its natural colour a shimmery silver-red, like the reflection of a sunset sky in a still body of water. Behind it was Blackspear, slightly taller, in obsidian glass that shone with broken rainbows like a pool of oil. At the far side – as one might reckon by looking across the Five with Dawncatcher in the middle of one's vision – was Westwatch, which shone with the soft violet of a tourmaline, shot through with veins of snow-white pearl. Beside it was stately Amberglass, with its elaborate flutings from which the wind would pull eerie melodies. In the middle, tallest and grandest of all, was Raven's Reach, the palace of Duke Nicovante, which gleamed like molten silver and was crowned with the famous Sky Garden, whose lowest-hanging vine trailed in the air some six hundred feet above the ground.

A network of glassine cables (miles and miles of spun Elderglass cords had been found in the tunnels beneath Camorr centuries before) threaded the roofs and turret-tops of the Five Towers. Hanging baskets passed back and forth on these cables, drawn by servants at huge clacking capstans. These baskets carried both passengers and cargo. Although many of the residents of lower Camorr proclaimed them mad, the nobles of the Five Families regarded the lurching, bobbing passages across the yawning empty spaces as tests of honour and courage.

Here and there, large cargo-cages were being drawn up or lowered from jutting platforms on several of the towers. They reminded Locke, who stared up at all this with eyes that were not yet sated with such wonders, of the spider cages at the Palace of Patience.

He and Chains sat in a two-wheeled cart with a little walled space behind the seat where Chains had stashed several parcels of goods under an old canvas tarp. Chains wore the loose brown robes with green and silver trim that marked a priest of Dama Elliza, Mother of Rains and Reaping; Locke wore a plain tunic and breeches, without shoes.

Chains had their two horses (un-Gentled, for Chains misliked using the white-eyed creatures outside the city walls) trotting at a gentle pace up the winding cobbles of the Street of Seven Wheels, the heart of the Millfalls district. In truth, there were more than seven wheels spinning in the white froth of the Angevine; there were more in sight than Locke could count.

The Five Towers had been built on a plateau some sixty feet above the lower city; the Alcegrante islands sloped up towards the base of this plateau. The Angevine came into Camorr at that height, just to the east of the Five, and fell down a crashing six-storey waterfall nearly two hundred yards across. Wheels turned at the top of these falls, within a long glass and stone bridge topped with wooden millhouses.

Wheels turned beneath the falls as well, jutting out into the river on both sides, making use of the rushing white flow to work everything from grinding-stones to the bellows that blew air across the fires beneath brewers' vats. It was a district choked with businessfolk and labourers alike, with escorted nobles in gilded carriages rolling here and there to inspect their holdings or place orders.

They turned east at the tip of the Millfalls, and crossed a wide low bridge into the Cenza Gate district, the means by which most northbound land traffic left the city. Here was a great mess, barely controlled by a small army of yellowjackets. Caravans of wagons were rolling into the city, their drivers at the mercy of the Duke's tax and customs agents, men and women marked by their tall black brimless caps and commonly referred to (out of earshot) as 'vexationers'.

Petty merchants were pitching everything from warm beer to cooked carrots; beggars were pleading countless improbable reasons for impoverishment and claiming lingering wounds from wars that had obviously ended long before they were born. Yellowjackets were driving the most persistent or malodorous off with their black-lacquered sticks. It was not yet the tenth hour of the morning.

'You should see this place around noon,' said Chains, 'especially during harvest-time. And when it rains. Gods.'

Chains' clerical vestments (and a silver solon passed over in a handshake) got them out of the city with little more than a 'Good day, your holiness.' The Cenza Gate was fifteen yards wide, with huge ironwood doors almost as tall. The guardhouses on the wall were occupied not just by the city watch but by blackjackets, Camorr's regular soldiers. They could be seen pacing here and there atop the wall, which was a good twenty feet thick.

North of Camorr proper was neighbourhood after neighbour-hood of lightly-built stone and wooden buildings, arranged in courts and squares more airy than those found on the islands of the city itself. Along the riverbank there were the beginnings of a marsh; to the north and the east were terraced hills, criss-crossed by the white lines of boundary stones set out to mark the property of the families that farmed them. The air took on divergent qualities depending on which way the chance breezes blew; it would smell of sea salt and woodsmoke one minute, of manure and olive groves the next.

'Here beyond the walls,' said Chains, 'are what many folks living outside the great cities would think of as cities; these little scatterings of wood and stone that probably don't look like much to someone like you. Just as you haven't really seen the country, they haven't truly seen the city, most of them. So keep your eyes open and your mouth shut, and be mindful of differences until you've had a few days to acclimatise yourself.'

'What's the point of this trip, Chains, really?'

'You might one day have to pretend to be a person of very lowly station, Locke. If you learn something about being a farmer, you'll probably learn something about being a teamster, a barge-poleman, a village smith, a horse-physiker and maybe even a country bandit.'

The road north from Camorr was an old Therin Throne road, a raised stone expanse with shallow ditches at the sides. It was covered with a gravel of pebbles and iron filings, waste from the forges of the Coalsmoke district. Here and there the rains had fused or rusted the gravel into a reddish cement; the wheels clattered as they slid over these hard patches.

'A lot of blackjackets,' Chains said slowly, 'come from the farms and villages north of Camorr proper. It's where the Dukes of Camorr go, when they need more men, and they need them better trained than a general levy of the lowborn. It's good wages, and there's the promise of land for those that stay in service a full twenty-five years. Assuming they don't get killed, of course. They come from the north and they go back to the north.'

'Is that why the blackjackets and the yellowjackets don't like each other?'

'Heh.' Chains' eyes twinkled. 'Good guess; there's some truth to it. Most of the yellowjackets are city boys that want to stay city boys. But on top of that, soldiers can be some of the cattiest, most clannish damn folk you'll ever find outside of a highborn lady's wardrobe. They'll fight over anything; they'll brawl over the colours of their hats and the shapes of their shoes. I know, believe me.'

'You pretended to be one once?'

'Thirteen gods, no. I *was* one.'

'A blackjacket?'

'Yes.' Chains sighed and settled back against the hard wooden seat of the cart. 'Thirty years past, now. More than thirty. I was a pikeman for the old Duke Nicovante. Most of us from the village my age went; it was a bad time for wars. Duke needed fodder; we needed food and coin.'

'Which village?'

286

Chains favoured him with a crooked smile. 'Villa Senziano.'

'Oh.'

'Gods, it was a whole pile of us that went.' The horses and the cart rattled down the road for a few long moments before Chains continued. 'There were three of us that came back. Or at least got out of it.'

'Only three?'

'Three that I know of.' Chains scratched at his beard. 'One of them is the man I'm going to be leaving you with. Vandros. A good fellow; not book-smart but very wise in the everyday sense. He did his twenty-five years and the Duke gave him a spot of land as a tenancy.'

'Tenancy?'

'Most common folk outside the city don't own their own land any more than city renters own their buildings. An old soldier with a tenancy gets a nice spot of land to farm until he dies; it's a sort of allowance from the Duke.' Chains chuckled. 'Given in exchange for one's youth and health.'

'You didn't do the twenty-five, I'm guessing.'

'No.' Chains fiddled with his beard a bit more, an old nervous gesture. 'Damn, I wish I could have a smoke. It's a very frowned-on thing in the order of the Dama, mind you. No, I took sick after a battle. Something more than just the usual shits and sore feet. A wasting fever. I couldn't march and I was like to die, so they left me behind . . . myself and many others. In the care of some itinerant priests of Perelandro.'

'But you didn't die.'

'Clever lad,' said Chains, 'to deduce that from such slender evidence after living with me for just three years.'

'And what happened?'

'A great many things,' said Chains, 'and you know how it ends. I wound up in this cart, riding north and entertaining you.'

'Well, what happened to the third man from your village?'

'Him? Well,' said Chains, 'he always had his head on right. He made banneret-sergeant not long after I got laid up with the fever. At the Battle of Nessek he helped young Nicovante hold the line together when old Nicovante took an arrow right between his eyes. He lived, got elevated and served Nicovante in the next few wars that came their way.'

'And where is he?'

'At this very moment? How should I know? But,' said Chains, 'later this afternoon he'll be giving Jean Tannen his usual afternoon weapons lesson at the House of Glass Roses.'

'Oh,' said Locke.

'Funny old world,' said Chains. 'Three farmers became three soldiers; three soldiers became one farmer, one baron and one thieving priest.'

'And now I'm to become a farmer, for a while.'

'Yes. Useful training indeed. But not just that.'

'What else?'

'Another test, my boy. Just another test.'

'Which is?'

'All these years you've had me looking over you. You've had Calo and Galdo, and Jean, and Sabetha from time to time. You've got used to the temple as a home. But time's a river, Locke, and we've always drifted farther down it than we think.' He smiled down at Locke with real affection. 'I can't stand watch on you forever, boy. Now we need to see what you can do when you're off in a strange new place, all on your own.'

CHAPER EIGHT

The Funeral Cask

I

It began with the slow, steady beat of mourning drums and the slow cadence of marchers moving north from the Floating Grave, red torches smouldering in their hands, a double line of blood-red light stretching out beneath the low, dark clouds.

At its heart, Vencarlo Barsavi, Capa of Camorr, with a son at either hand. Before him a covered casket, draped in black silk and cloth of gold, carried at either side by six pall-bearers in black cloaks and black masks, one for each of the twelve Therin gods. At Barsavi's back, a huge wooden cask on a cart pulled by another six men, with a black-shrouded priestess of the Nameless Thirteenth close behind.

The drums echoed against stone walls, against stone streets and bridges and canals; the torches cast reflections of fire in every window and shred of Elderglass they passed. Folk looked on in apprehension, if they looked on at all; some bolted their doors and drew shutters over their windows as the funeral procession passed. This is how things are done in Camorr for the rich and the powerful: the slow mournful march to the Hill of Whispers, the interment, the ceremony, and then the wild tearful celebration afterwards. A toast on behalf of the departed; a bittersweet revel for those not yet taken for judgement by Aza Guilla, Lady of the Long Silence. The funeral cask is what fuels this tradition.

The lines of marchers left the Wooden Waste just after the tenth hour of the evening and marched into the Cauldron, where no urchin or drunkard dared to get in their way, where gangs of cut-throats and Gaze addicts stood in silent attention as their master and his court walked past.

Through Coalsmoke they marched, and then north into the Quiet, as silvery mist rose warm and clinging from the canals around them. Not a single yellowjacket crossed their path; not one constable even caught sight of the procession, for arrangements had been made to keep them busy elsewhere that night, to keep their attention firmly fixed on the western part of the city. The east belonged to Barsavi and his long lines of torches, and the farther north they went the more honest families bolted their doors and doused their lights and prayed that the business of the marchers lay far away from them.

Had there been many staring eyes, they might have noticed that the procession had already failed to turn towards the Hill of Whispers; that it had instead gone north and snaked towards the western tip of the Rustwater district, where the great abandoned structure called the Echo Hole loomed in the darkness and the fog.

A curious observer might have wondered at the sheer size of the procession, more than a hundred men and women, and at their accoutrements. Only the pall-bearers were dressed for a funeral; the torch-bearers were dressed for war, in armour of boiled leather with blackened studs, in collars and helmets and bracers and gloves, with knives and clubs and axes and bucklers at their belts. They were the cream of Barsavi's gangs, the hardest of the Right People, cold-eyed men and women with murders to their names. They were from all of his districts and all of his gangs – the Red Hands and the Rum Hounds, the Grey Faces and the Arsenal Boys, the Canal Jumpers and the Black Twists, the Catchfire Barons and a dozen others.

The most interesting thing about the procession, however, was something no casual observer could know.

The fact was, Nazca Barsavi's body still lay in her old chambers in the Floating Grave, sealed away under silk sheets alchemically impregnated to keep the rot of death from setting in too quickly. Locke Lamora and a dozen other priests of the Nameless Thirteenth, the Crooked Warden, had said prayers for her the previous night and placed her within a circle of sacred candles, there to lie until her father finished his business this evening, which had nothing to do with the Hill of Whispers. The coffin that was draped in funeral silks was empty.

'I am the Grey King,' said Locke Lamora. 'I am the Grey King, gods damn his eyes, I *am* the Grey King.'

'A little lower,' said Jean Tannen, struggling with one of the grey cuffs of Locke's coat, 'and a little scratchier. Give it a hint of Tal Verrar. You said he had an accent.'

'I am the Grey King,' said Locke, 'and I'll be smiling out the other side of my head when the Gentlemen Bastards are through with me.'

'Oh, that's good,' said Calo, who was streaking Locke's hair with a foul-scented alchemical paste that was steadily turning it charcoal grey. 'I like that one. Just different enough to be noticed.'

Locke stood stock-still as a tailor's mannequin, surrounded by Calo, Galdo and Jean, who worked on him with clothes, cosmetics and threaded needles. Bug leaned up against one wall of their little enclosure, keeping his eyes and ears alert for interlopers.

The Gentlemen Bastards were hidden away in an abandoned storefront in the fog-choked Rustwater district, just a few blocks north of the Echo Hole. Rustwater was a dead island, ill-favoured and barely inhabited. A city that had thrown off its old prejudices about the structures of the Eldren still held Rustwater in unequivocal dread. It was said that the black shapes that moved in the Rustwater lagoon were nothing as pleasant as mere man-eating sharks but something worse, something *older*. Whatever the truth of those rumours, it was a conveniently deserted place for Barsavi and the Grey King to play out their strange affair. Locke privately suspected that he'd been taken somewhere in this neighbourhood on the night the Grey King had first interrupted his life.

They were working every trick of their masquerade art to fashion Locke into the Grey King; already his hair was grey, his clothes were grey, he was dressed in heavy padded boots that added two inches to his height, and he had a drooping grey moustache firmly affixed above his lips.

'It looks good,' said Bug, an approving note in his voice.

'Damn showy, but Bug's right,' said Jean. 'Now that I've got this stupid coat cinched in to your proper size, you do look rather striking.'

'Pity this isn't one of our games,' said Galdo. 'I'd be enjoying myself. Lean forward for some wrinkles, Locke.'

Working very carefully, Galdo painted Locke's face with a warm, waxy substance that pinched his skin as it went on; in seconds it dried and tightened, and in just a few moments Locke had a complete network of crow's feet, laugh-lines, and forehead wrinkles. He looked to be in his mid-forties, at the very least. The disguise would have done very well in the bright light of day; at night it would be impenetrable.

'Virtuoso,' said Jean, 'relatively speaking, for such short notice and the conditions we have in which to put it all together.'

Locke flipped his hood up and pulled on his grey leather gloves. 'I am the Grey King,' he said, his voice low, mimicking the odd accent of the real Grey King.

'I bloody well believe it,' said Bug.

'Well, let's get on with everything, then.' Locke moved his jaw up and down, feeling the false wrinkle-skin stretch back and forth as he did so. 'Galdo, hand me my stilettos, would you? I think I'll want one in my boot and one in my sleeve.'

Lamora, came a cold whisper, the Falconer's voice. Locke tensed, then realised that the noise hadn't come from the air.

'What is it?' asked Jean.

'It's the Falconer,' said Locke. 'He's . . . he's doing that damn thing . . .'

Barsavi will soon be at hand. You and your friends must be in place, ere long.

'We have an impatient Bondsmage,' said Locke. 'Quickly now. Bug, you know the game, and you know where to put yourself?'

'I've got it down cold,' said Bug, grinning. 'Don't even have a temple roof to jump off this time, so don't worry about anything.'

'Jean, you're comfortable with your place?'

'Not really, but there's none better.' Jean cracked his knuckles. 'I'll be in sight of Bug, down beneath the floor. If the whole thing goes to shit, you just remember to throw yourself down the damn waterfall. I'll cover your back, the sharp and bloody way.'

'Calo, Galdo.' Locke whirled to face the twins, who had hurriedly packed away all the tools and substances used to dress Locke up for the evening. 'Are we good to move at the temple?'

'It'll be smoother than a Guilded Lily's backside if we do,' said

Galdo. 'A sweet fat fortune wrapped up in sacks, two carts with horses, provisions for a nice long trip on the road.'

'And there's men at the Viscount's Gate who'll slip us out so fast it'll be like we'd never even set foot in Camorr in the first place,' added Calo.

'Good. Well. Shit.' Locke rubbed his gloved hands together. 'I guess that's that. I'm all out of rhetorical flourishes; let's just go get the bastards and pray for a straight deal.'

Bug stepped forward and cleared his throat.

'I'm only doing this,' he said, 'because I really love hiding in haunted Eldren buildings on dark and creepy nights.'

'You're a liar,' said Jean, slowly. 'I'm only doing this because I've always wanted to see Bug get eaten by an Eldren ghost.'

'Liar,' said Calo. 'I'm only doing this because I fucking *love* hauling half a ton of bloody coins up out of a vault and packing them away on a cart.'

'Liar!' Galdo chuckled. 'I'm only doing this because while you're all busy elsewhere, I'm going to go pawn all the furniture in the burrow at No-Hope Harza's.'

'You're all liars,' said Locke as their eyes turned expectantly to him. 'We're only doing this because nobody else in Camorr is good enough to pull this off, and nobody else is dumb enough to get stuck doing it in the first place.'

'*Bastard!*' They shouted in unison, forgetting their surroundings for a bare moment.

I can hear you shouting, came the ghostly voice of the Falconer. *Have you all gone completely mad?*

Locke sighed.

'Uncle doesn't like us keeping him up all night with our carrying-on,' he said. 'Let's get to it, and by the grace of the Crooked Warden, we'll all see each other back at the temple when this mess is over.'

3

The Echo Hole is a cube of grey stone mortared with a dull sort of Elderglass; it never gleams at Falselight. In fact, it never returns the reflection of any light passed before it. It is perhaps one

293

hundred feet on a side, with one dignified entrance, a man-sized door about twenty feet above the street at the top of a wide staircase.

A single aqueduct cuts from the upper Angevine, past the Millfalls, south at an angle and into Rustwater, where it spills its water into a corner of the Echo Hole. Like the stone cube itself, this aqueduct is thought to be touched by some ancient ill, and no use has ever been made of it. A small waterfall plunges through a hole in the floor, down into the catacombs beneath the Echo Hole, where dark water can be heard rushing. Some of these passages empty into the canal on the south-western side of Rustwater; some empty into no place known to living men.

Locke Lamora stood in darkness at the centre of the Echo Hole, listening to the rush of water down the break in the floor, staring fixedly at the patch of greyness that marked the door to the street. His only consolation was that Jean and Bug, crouched unseen in the wet darkness beneath the floor, would probably be even more apprehensive. At least until the proceedings started.

Near, came the voice of the Falconer, *very near. Stand ready.*

Locke heard the Capa's procession before he saw it; the sound of funeral drums came through the open door to the street, muffled and nearly drowned out by the falling water. Steadily, it grew louder; a red glow seemed to kindle beyond the door, and by that light Locke saw that the grey mist had thickened. Torches flickered softly, as though glimpsed from underwater. The red aura rose; the barest outline of the room around him became visible, etched in faint carmine. The beating of the drums ceased, and once again Locke was alone with the sound of the waterfall. He threw back his head, placed one hand behind his back, and stared at the door, his blood pounding in his ears.

Two small red fires appeared in the doorway like the eyes of a dragon from one of Jean's stories; black shadows moved behind them, and as Locke's eyes adjusted to the influx of scarlet light he saw the faces of two men, tall men, cloaked and armoured. He could see enough of their features and posture to note that they were almost surprised to spot him; they hesitated, then continued forward, one moving to his left and the other to his right. For his part, he did nothing, moving not a muscle.

Two more torches followed, and then two more; Barsavi was

294

sending his men up the stairs in pairs. Soon a loose semicircle of men faced Locke, and their torches cast the interior of the Echo Hole into red-shaded relief. There were carvings on the walls, strange old symbols – the tongue of the Eldren, which men had never deciphered.

A dozen men, two dozen; the crowd of armoured shapes grew, and Locke saw faces that he recognised. Throat-slitters, leg-breakers, maulers. Assassins. A hard lot. Exactly what Barsavi had promised him, when they'd stood looking down at the body of Nazca together.

Moments passed; still, Locke said nothing. Still, men and women filed in. The Berangias sisters – even in a dimmer light, Locke would have recognised their swagger. They stood at the front centre of the gathering crowd, saying nothing, arms folded and eyes gleaming in the torchlight. By some unspoken command, none of Barsavi's people moved behind Locke. He continued to stand alone as the great press of Right People continued spreading before him.

At last, the crowd of cut-throats began to part; Locke could hear the echoes of their breathing and murmuring and the creaking of their leathers, bouncing from wall to wall and mingling with the sound of falling water. Some of those on the edges of the crowd extinguished their torches with wet leather pouches; gradually the smell of smoke seeped into the air, and gradually the light sank, until perhaps only one in five of the Capa's folk was still holding a lit torch.

There was more than enough light to see Capa Barsavi as he turned the corner and stepped through the door; his grey hair was pulled back in oiled rows, his three beards were freshly brushed. He wore his coat of sharkskin, and a black cloak of velvet lined with cloth of gold, thrown back from one shoulder. Anjais was on his right and Pachero on his left as the Capa strode forward, and in the reflected fires of their eyes Locke saw nothing but death.

But nothing is as it seems, came the voice of the Falconer. *Stand resolute.*

At the front of the crowd Barsavi halted, and for a long moment he only stared at Locke, stared at the apparition before him, at the cool orange eyes within a shadowed hood, at the cloak and mantle and coat and gloves of grey.

'King,' he finally said.

'Capa,' Locke replied, willing himself to feel the hauteur, conjuring it forth from nothing. The sort of man who would stand in front of a hundred killers with a smile on his face; the sort of man who would summon Vencarlo Barsavi with a trail of corpses, the last of them his only daughter. That was the man Locke needed to be, not Nazca's friend but her murderer; not the Capa's mischievous subject, but his equal. His *superior*.

Locke grinned, wolfishly, then swept his cloak back from his left shoulder. With his left hand he beckoned the Capa, a taunting gesture, like a bully in an alley daring his opponent to step forward and take the first swing.

'Oblige him,' said the Capa, and a dozen men and women raised crossbows.

Crooked Warden, thought Locke, *give me strength*. He ground his teeth in expectation. He could hear his jaw muscles creaking.

The snap-hiss of release echoed throughout the hall; a dozen taut strings twanged. The bolts were too fast to follow, dark afterimages that blurred the air, and then – a dozen narrow black shapes rebounded off nothing right before his face, and fell clattering to the floor, scattered in an arc like dead birds at his feet.

Locke laughed, a high and genuine sound of pleasure. For one brief moment he would have kissed the Falconer if the Bondsmage had stood before him.

'Please,' he said. 'I thought you'd listened to the stories.'

'Just establishing your bona fides,' said Capa Barsavi, 'Your *Majesty*.' The last word was sneered; Locke had at least expected a certain wariness following the blunting of the crossbow attack, but Barsavi stepped forward without apparent fear.

'I'm pleased that you've answered my summons,' Locke replied.

'The blood of my daughter is the only thing that's summoned me,' said Barsavi.

'Dwell on it if you must,' said Locke, praying silently as he extemporised. *Nazca, gods, please forgive me*. 'Were you any gentler when you took this city for yourself, twenty-two years ago?'

'Is that what you think you're doing?' Barsavi stopped and stared at him; they were about forty feet apart. 'Taking my city from me?'

'I summoned you to discuss the matter of Camorr,' said Locke.

'To settle it to our mutual satisfaction.' The Falconer hadn't interrupted him yet; he presumed he was doing well.

'The satisfaction,' said Barsavi, 'will not be mutual.' He raised his left hand, and one man stepped forth from the crowd.

Locke peered at this man carefully; he seemed to be an older fellow, slight and balding, and he wasn't wearing armour. Very curious. He also appeared to be shivering.

'Do as we discussed, Eymon,' said the Capa. 'I'll hold true to my bargain, truer than any I've ever made.'

The unarmoured man began to walk forward, slowly, hesitantly, staring at Locke with obvious fear. But still he kept coming, straight towards Locke, while a hundred armed men and women waited behind him, doing nothing.

'I pray,' said Locke, with a bantering tone, 'that man isn't contemplating what I suspect.'

'We'll all see what his business is soon enough,' said the Capa.

'I cannot be cut or pierced,' said Locke, 'and this man will die at my touch.'

'So it's been said,' replied the Capa. Eymon continued to move forward; he was thirty feet from Locke, then twenty.

'Eymon,' said Locke, 'you are being ill-used. Stop now.'

Gods, he thought. *Don't do what I think you're going to do. Don't make the Falconer kill you.*

Eymon continued to shamble forward; his jowls were quivering, he was breathing in short sharp gasps. His hands were out before him, shaking, like a man about to reach into a fire.

Crooked Warden, Locke thought, *please, let him be scared. Please let him stop. Falconer, Falconer, please, put a fright into him, do anything else but kill him*. A river of sweat ran down his spine; he bent his head slightly and fixed Eymon with a stare. Ten feet now between them.

'Eymon,' he said, striving for a casual tone, not entirely succeeding, 'you have been warned. You are in mortal peril.'

'Oh yeah,' said the man, his voice quavering. 'Yeah, that I know.' And then he closed the distance between them, and he reached out for Locke's right arm with both of his hands . . .

Fuck, thought Locke, and although he knew deep down that it would be the Falconer killing the man and not himself . . .

He flinched back from Eymon's touch.

Eymon's eyes lit up; he gasped, and then, to Locke's horror, he leapt forward and grabbed Locke's arm with both of his hands, like a scavenger bird clutching at a long-delayed meal. 'Haaaaaaaaaaaa!' he cried, and for one brief second Locke thought something terrible was happening to him.

But no; Eymon still lived, and he had a very firm grip.

'Double fuck,' Locke mumbled, bringing up his left fist to clout the poor fellow, but he was off balance, and Eymon had him at a disadvantage; the slender man gave Locke a shove back, screaming once again, 'HAAAAAAAAAAAAAAA!' A cry of absolute triumph; Locke puzzled over it as he fell flat on his arse.

And then there were booted feet slapping the stones behind Eymon, and dark shapes rushing round him to grab at Locke, and in the dancing light cast by two dozen moving torches Locke found himself hauled back up to his feet, pinned by strong hands that clutched at his arms and his shoulders and his neck.

Capa Barsavi pushed through his eager crowd of men and women, forced Eymon more gently to the side, and then he was face to face with Locke, his fat ruddy features alight with anticipation.

'Well, Your Majesty,' he said, 'I'll bet you're one confused son of a bitch right about now.'

And then Barsavi's people were laughing, cheering. And then the Capa's ham-hock fist planted itself in Locke's stomach, and the air rushed out of his lungs, and black pain exploded in his chest. And then he knew just how deeply in the shit he truly was.

4

'Yes, I'll bet you're pretty *gods-damned curious* at this point,' said Barsavi, strutting back and forth in front of Locke, who remained pinioned by half a dozen men, any one of them half again his size. 'And so am I. Let's throw that hood back, boys.'

Rough hands yanked at Locke's hood and mantle, and the Capa stared coldly at him, running one hand up and down his beards. 'Grey, grey, grey. You look like you belong on a stage.' He laughed. 'And such a skinny fellow, too. What a weak little man we've caught ourselves tonight – the Grey King, sovereign of fog and shadows and precious little else.'

The Capa backhanded him, grinning; the stinging pain had just registered when he did it again, from the other direction. Locke's head lolled; he was grabbed from behind by his hair and made to look the Capa right in the face. Locke's thoughts whirled. Had the Capa's men somehow located the Falconer? Had they distracted him? Was the Capa mad enough to actually kill a Bondsmage, if he had the chance?

'Oh, we know you can't be cut,' continued Barsavi, 'and we know you can't be pierced, more's the pity. But bruised? It's a curious thing about the spells of a Bondsmage, they're so damn *specific*, aren't they?'

And then he punched Locke in the stomach again, to a murmur of widespread amusement. Locke's knees buckled beneath him, and his attendants hoisted him again, holding him upright, as bolts of pain radiated from his abdomen.

'One of your men,' said Barsavi, 'strolled into my Floating Grave this very morning.'

A little chill crept down Locke's spine.

'Seems I'm not the only one you pissed off when you sent my Nazca back to me the way you did,' said Barsavi, leering. 'Seems that some of your men didn't sign on with your merry little crew for that sort of gods-damned *desecration*. So your man and I, we had ourselves a talk. And we fixed a price. And then he told me all sorts of *fascinating* things about that spell of yours. And that story about you being able to kill men with a touch? Oh, he told me it was bullshit.'

Sewn up, said a little voice at the back of Locke's head that most certainly was not the Falconer. *Sewn up, sewn up*. Of course the Falconer hadn't been distracted, or taken by any of Barsavi's men. *Neat as a gods-damned hanging*.

'But I was only willing to trust the fellow so far,' Barsavi said. 'I made a deal with Eymon, whom I'm sure you don't recognise. Eymon is dying. He has the cold consumption, tumours in his stomach and his back. The sort no physiker can cure. He's got maybe two months, maybe less.' The Capa clapped Eymon on the back as proudly as if the skinny man were his own flesh and blood.

'So I said, "Why don't you step up and grab the filthy little bastard, Eymon? If he really can kill with a touch, well, you'll go quick and easy. And if he can't . . ." ' Barsavi grinned, his red cheeks wrinkling grotesquely. 'Well, then.'

'A thousand full crowns,' said Eymon, giggling.

'For starters,' added Barsavi. 'A promise I intend to keep. A promise I intend to *expand*. I told Eymon he'd die in his own villa, with gems and silks and half a dozen ladies of his choice from the Guilded Lilies to keep him company. I will *invent* pleasures for him. He'll die like a fucking *Duke*, because tonight I name him the bravest man in Camorr.'

There was a general roar of approval; men and women applauded, and fists banged on armour and shields.

'Quite the opposite,' Barsavi whispered, 'of a sneaking, cowardly piece of shit who would murder my only daughter. Who wouldn' even do it with his own hands. Who'd let some fucking hireling work a twisted magic on her. A *poisoner*.' Barsavi spat in Locke's face; the warm spittle trickled down his cheek. 'Your man told me, of course, that your Bondsmage had set his spell and left your service last night; that you were so very confident, you didn't want to keep paying him. Well, I for one applaud your sense of economy.'

Barsavi gestured to Anjais and Pachero; grim-faced, the two men stepped forward. They slipped their optics off and put them in vest pockets, an ominous gesture conducted in unconscious unison. Locke opened his mouth to say something – and then the realisation of exactly how sewn up he was struck him cold.

He could proclaim his true identity – have the Capa tear off his false moustache and rub away the wrinkles, spill the entire story – and what would it gain him? He would never be believed. *He'd already displayed a Bondsmage's protection*. If he confessed to being Locke Lamora, the hundred men and women here would be after Jean and Bug and the Sanzas next. All the Gentlemen Bastards would be hunted in the streets; all their lives would be forfeit.

If he was going to save them, he had to play the Grey King until the Capa was finished with him, and then he would pray for a quick and easy death. Let Locke Lamora just vanish one night; let his friends slip away to whatever better fate awaited them. Blinking back hot tears, he summoned up a grin, looked at the two Barsavi sons, and said, 'By all means, you fucking curs, let's see if you can do any better than your father.'

Anjais and Pachero knew how to strike a man to kill, but just now they had no such intent. They bruised his ribs, knuckle-punched his arms, kicked his thighs, slapped his head from side to side, and punched him in the neck until every breath was a chore. At last, Anjais had him hoisted back up, and took hold of his chin so that the two of them were looking eye to eye.

'By the way,' said Anjais, 'this is from Locke Lamora.'

Anjais balanced Locke's chin on one finger and walloped him with his other hand; white-hot pain shot through Locke's neck, and in the red-tinted darkness around him he saw stars. He spat blood, coughed, and licked his sore, swollen lips.

'Now,' said Barsavi, 'I'll have a father's justice for Nazca's death.' He clapped his hands three times.

Behind him, there was the sound of men cursing, and heavy footfalls banging against the stone steps. Through the door came a half-dozen more men, carrying a large wooden cask, a cask the size of the one Nazca Barsavi had been returned to her father in. The funeral cask. The crowd around Barsavi and his sons parted eagerly to let the cask-haulers through. They set it on the ground beside the Capa, and Locke heard the slosh of liquid.

Oh, thirteen gods, he thought.

'Can't be cut, can't be pierced,' said the Capa, as though he were musing out loud. 'But you can certainly be bruised. And you certainly need to breathe.'

Two of the Capa's men popped the lid on the cask open, and Locke was dragged over to it. The eye-watering stench of horse urine spilled out into the air, and he gagged, coughing.

'Look at the Grey King cry,' whispered Barsavi. 'Look at the Grey King sob. A sight I will treasure to the last hour of my dying day.' His voice rose. 'Did Nazca sob? Did Nazca cry, as you gave her her death? Somehow I don't think so.'

The Capa was shouting now. 'Take a last look! He gets what Nazca got; he dies as she died, but by *my hand*!'

Barsavi seized Locke by the hair and tilted his face towards the barrel; for one brief irrational moment Locke was grateful that there was nothing in his stomach to throw up. The dry retching brought spasms of pain to his much-abused stomach muscles.

'With one small touch,' said the Capa, actually gulping back sobs. 'With one small touch, you son of a bitch. No poison for you. No quick way out before I put you in. You get to taste it, the whole time. All the while as you *drown* in it.'

And then he hefted Locke by the mantle, grunting. His men joined in, and together they hoisted him up over the rim, and then down he plunged face first, down into thick, lukewarm filth that blotted out the noise of the world around him, down into darkness that burned his eyes and his cuts and swallowed him whole.

Barsavi's men slammed the lid back onto the barrel. Several of them hammered it down with mallets and axe-butts until it was tight. The Capa gave the top of the barrel a thump with his fist, and smiled broadly. Tears were still running down his cheeks.

'Somehow I don't think the poor fucker did as well as he hoped with our negotiations!'

The men and women around him whooped and hollered, arms in the air, torches waving and casting wild shadows on the walls.

'Take this bastard and send him out to sea,' said the Capa, gesturing towards the waterfall.

A dozen pairs of eager hands grabbed at the barrel; laughing and joking, a crowd of the Capa's men hoisted it and carried it over to the north-western corner of the Echo Hole, where water poured in from the ceiling and vanished into blackness through a fissure about eight feet wide. 'One,' said the leader, 'two . . .' and on the cusp of 'three' the men flung the barrel down into darkness. It struck water somewhere beneath them with a splash; then they threw up their arms and began cheering once again.

'Tonight,' cried Barsavi, 'Duke Nicovante sleeps safe in his bed, locked away in his glass tower! Tonight the Grey King sleeps in *piss*, in a tomb that I have made for him! Tonight is my night! Who rules Camorr?'

'BARSAVI!' came the response from every throat in the Echo Hole, reverberating around the alien-set stones of the structure, and the Capa was surrounded by a sea of noise, laughter, applause.

'Tonight,' he yelled, 'send messengers to every corner of MY domains! Send runners to the Last Mistake! Send runners to Catchfire! Wake the Cauldron and the Narrows and the Dregs and all the Snare! Tonight, I throw open my doors! The Right People of Camorr will come to the Floating Grave as my guests!

Tonight, we'll have such a revel that the honest folk will bar their doors, that the yellowjackets will cringe in their barracks, that the gods themselves will look down and cry, "what *is* that fucking racket?"'

'BARSAVI! BARSAVI! BARSAVI!' his people chanted.

'Tonight,' he said at last, 'we will celebrate. Tonight Camorr has seen the last of kings.'

INTERLUDE:
The Half-Crown War

I

As time went by, Locke and the other Gentlemen Bastards were occasionally set free to roam at leisure, dressed in ordinary clothing. Locke and Jean were getting on near twelve; the Sanzas were visibly slightly older. It was more difficult to keep them cooped up beneath the house of Perelandro all the time, when they weren't sitting the steps or away on Father Chains' 'apprenticeships'.

Slowly but steadily, Chains was sending his boys out to be initiated at all the great temples of the other eleven Therin gods. One of them would enter a temple under a false name, sped along by whatever strings Chains could pull and whatever palms he could slip coins into. Once there, the young Gentleman Bastard would inevitably please his superiors with his scribing, his theological knowledge, his discipline and his sincerity. Advancement came quickly, as fast as it could be had; soon the newcomer would receive training in what was called 'interior ritual', the phrases and activities that priests only shared among themselves and their initiates.

They were not quite secrets, these things, for to any priest of a Therin order, the thought of someone being audacious enough to offend the gods by falsely seeking initiation was utterly alien. Even those that knew of the slightly heretical idea of the Thirteenth, and even the minority that actually believed in him, failed to imagine that anyone would *want* to do what Chains and his boys were doing.

Invariably, after several months of excellent accomplishments, each sterling young initiate would die in a sudden accident. Calo favoured 'drowning', for he could hold his breath a very long time, and he enjoyed swimming underwater. Galdo preferred to simply disappear, preferably during a storm or some other dramatic event. Locke constructed elaborate little mummeries that took weeks to plan. On one occasion, he vanished from the Order of Nara (Plague Mistress, Lady of Ubiquitous Maladies) by leaving his initiate's robe, torn apart and splashed with rabbit's blood, wrapped around his copy-work and a few letters in an alley behind the temple.

Thus enlightened, each boy would return and teach the others what he had seen and heard. 'The point,' said Chains, 'is not to make you all candidates for the High Conclave of the Twelve, but to allow you to throw on whatever robes and masks are required and pass as a priest for any short period of need. When you're a priest, people tend to see the robe rather than the man.'

But there was no apprenticeship underway at the moment; Jean was drilling at the House of Glass Roses, and the other boys waited for him on the southern edge of the Shifting Market, at a crumbling stone pier at the end of a short alley. It was a warm spring day, breezy and fresh, with the sky half-occluded by crescents of grey and white clouds sweeping in from the north-west, heralding storms.

Locke and Calo and Galdo were watching the results of a collision between a chicken-seller's boat and a transporter of cats. Several cages had flown open when the small boats cracked against one another, and now agitated merchants were stepping warily back and forth as the battle between birds and felines progressed. A few chickens had escaped into the water and were flapping uselessly in little circles, squawking, for nature had conspired to make them even worse at swimming than they were at flying.

'Well,' said a voice behind them, 'have a look at this. These little wasters look very likely.'

Locke and the Sanzas turned around as one to see a half-dozen boys and girls their own age standing behind them, spread out across the alley. They were dressed much as the Gentlemen Bastards were, in unassuming clothes of common cut. Their apparent leader had a thick mane of curly black hair, pulled back and tied with a black silk ribbon, quite a mark of distinction for an urchin.

'Are you friends of the friends, lads? Are you the right sort of people?' The leader of the newcomers stood with his hands on his hips; behind him, a short girl made several hand-gestures used for common identification by Capa Barsavi's subjects.

'We are friends of the friends,' said Locke.

'The rightest sort of right,' added Galdo, making the appropriate counter-gestures.

'Good lads. We're the seconds to the Full Crowns, in the Narrows. Call ourselves Half-Crowns. What's your allegiance?'

'Gentlemen Bastards,' said Locke, 'Temple District.'

'Who're you seconds to?'

'We're not seconds to anyone,' said Galdo. 'It's just the Gentlemen Bastards, one and all.'

'Savvy,' said the leader of the Half-Crowns, with a friendly grin. 'I'm Tesso Volanti. This is my crew. We're here to take your coin. Unless you want to kneel and give us your preference.'

Locke scowled. 'Preference' in the parlance of the Right People meant that the Gentlemen Bastards would proclaim the Half-Crowns the better, tougher gang; make way for them on the street and tolerate whatever abuse the Half-Crowns saw fit to heap upon them.

'I'm Locke Lamora,' said Locke as he rose slowly to his feet, 'and, excepting the Capa, the Gentlemen Bastards bend the knee to nobody.'

'Really?' Tesso feigned shock. 'Even with six on three? It's soft talk, if no's your answer.'

'You must not hear very well,' said Calo, as he and his brother stood up in unison. 'He said you get our preference when you pick the peas out of our shit and suck on 'em for dinner.'

'Now that was uncalled for,' said Tesso. 'So I'm gonna make some noise with your skulls.'

Even before he'd finished speaking, the Half-Crowns were moving forward. Locke was the smallest child involved, even counting the girls, and while he went into the melee with his little fists swinging, he caught mostly air and was quickly knocked down. One older girl sat on his back, while another kicked alley-grit into his face.

The first boy to reach for Calo got a knee in the groin and went down moaning; right behind him came Tesso, with a hard right that sent Calo backwards. Galdo tackled Tesso around the waist, howling, and they hit the ground scrabbling for leverage. 'Soft talk' meant no weapons, and no blows that could kill or cripple; just about anything else was on the table. The Sanzas were capable brawlers, but even if Locke had been able to hold up his end of the fight the numbers would have told against them. In the end, after a few minutes of wrestling and swearing and kicking, the three Gentlemen Bastards were dumped in the middle of the alley, dusty and battered.

'Right, lads. Preferences, is it? Let's hear 'em.'

'Go fold yourself in half,' said Locke, 'and lick your arse.'

'Oh, that's the wrong answer, short-wit,' said Tesso, and while one of his boys pinned Locke's arms, the leader of the Half-Crowns patted Locke down for coins. 'Hmm. Nothing. Well then, sweetmeats, we'll be looking for you again tomorrow. And the next day. And the next. Until you bend the knee, we'll watch you and we'll make your lives miserable. Mark my words, Locke Lamora.'

The Half-Crowns strolled off laughing, a few nursing bruises and sprains, but not nearly as many as they'd inflicted. The Sanzas rose groaning and helped Locke to his feet. Warily, they limped back to the House of Perelandro together and slipped into the glass burrow through a drainage culvert equipped with a secret door.

'You're not going to believe what happened,' said Locke, as he and the Sanzas entered the dining room. Chains sat at the witch-wood table, peering down at a collection of parchments, carefully scribing on one with a fine-cut quill. Forging customs papers was a sort of hobby, one he practised the way some men kept gardens or bred hounds. He had a leather portfolio full of them and occasionally made good silver selling them.

'Mmmm,' said Chains, 'you got your arses walloped by a pack of Half-Crowns.'

'How did you know?'

'Stopped by the Last Mistake last night. Heard about it from the Full Crowns. Told me their seconds might be sweeping the neighbourhoods, looking for other juvies to push around.'

'Why didn't you tell us?'

'I figured if you were being adequately cautious, they'd never be

306

able to get the better of you. Looks like your attention was somewhere else.'

'They said they wanted our preference.'

'Yeah,' said Chains. 'It's a juvie game. Most of the seconds don't get to pull real jobs, so they train themselves up by pushing other seconds around. You should be proud of yourselves; you finally got noticed. Now you've got a little war until one of you cries mercy. Soft talk only, mind you.'

'So,' Locke said slowly, 'what should we do?'

Chains reached over and grabbed Locke's fist, then mimed swinging it into Calo's jaw. 'Repeat as necessary,' said Chains, 'until your problems are spitting up teeth.'

'We tried that. And they jumped us while Jean was away. And you know I'm not much good at that sort of thing.'

'Sure I do. So next time make sure you've got Jean with you. And use that devious little brain of yours.' Chains began melting a cylinder of sealing wax over a small candle. 'But I don't want to see anything too elaborate, Locke. Don't pull the watch or the temples or the Duke's army or anyone else into it. Try and make it look like you're just the pack of ordinary sneak-thieves I tell everyone you are.'

'Oh, great.' Locke folded his arms while Calo and Galdo washed one another's bruised faces with wet cloths. 'So it's just another bloody test.'

'What a clever boy,' muttered Chains, pouring liquid wax into a tiny silver vessel. 'Of course it is. And I'll be personally very upset if those little shits aren't begging and pleading to give you *their* preference before midsummer.'

2

The next day Locke and the Sanza brothers sat on the very same pier at the very same time. All over the Shifting Market merchants were hauling down canvas tarps and furling canopies, for the rains that had drenched the city all night and half the morning were long gone.

'I must be seeing things,' came the voice of Tesso Volanti, 'because I can't imagine that you shit-wits would really be sitting there right where we beat the trouser gravy out of you just yesterday.'

'Why not,' said Locke, 'since we're closer to our turf than yours, and you're going to be using your balls for tonsils in about two minutes?'

The three Gentlemen Bastards arose; facing them were the same half-dozen Half-Crowns, with eager smiles on their faces.

'I see you're none better at sums than you were when we left you,' said Tesso, cracking his knuckles.

'Funny you should say that,' said Locke, 'since the sums have changed.' He pointed past the Half-Crowns; Tesso warily shifted his head to look behind him, but when he saw Jean Tannen standing in the alley behind his gang, he laughed.

'Still in our favour, I'd say.' He strolled towards Jean, who simply looked at him with a bland smile on his round face. 'And what's this? A fat red bastard. I can see your glass eyes in your vest pocket. What do you think you're doing, fatty?'

'My name's Jean Tannen, and I'm the ambush.'

Long months of training with Don Maranzalla had left Jean looking little different than when he'd first begun, but Locke and the Sanzas well knew that a sort of alchemy had taken place beneath his soft exterior. Tesso stepped within his reach, grinning, and Jean's arms lashed out like the brass pistons in a Verrari water-engine.

Tesso reeled back, arms and legs wobbling like the limbs of a marionette caught in a high wind. His head bowed forward, then he simply collapsed in a heap, his eyes rolling back in their sockets.

A minor sort of hell broke loose in the alley. Three Half-Crown boys charged Locke and the Sanzas; the two girls approached Jean warily. One of them tried to dash a handful of alley gravel in his face; he sidestepped, caught her arm, and swung her easily into one of the alley's stone walls. One of Don Maranzalla's lessons – let walls and streets do the work for you when you fight with empty hands. As she bounced back, out of control, Jean caught her with a swift right hook and sent her face first to the gravel.

'It's not polite to hit girls,' said her companion, circling him.

'It's even less polite to hit my friends,' said Jean.

She replied by pivoting on her left heel and snapping a swift kick at his throat; he recognised the art called *chasson*, a sort of foot-boxing imported from Tal Verrar. He deflected the kick with the palm of his right hand and she whirled into a second, using the momentum from her first to send her left leg whirling up and round. But Jean was moving past it before she struck; her thigh rather than her foot slapped into his side, and he snaked his left arm round it. While she flailed for balance, he let her have a vicious kidney punch, and then he hooked her right leg out from beneath her, sending her to the gravel on her back, where she lay writhing in pain.

'Ladies,' said Jean, 'you must accept my deepest apologies.'

Locke, as usual, was getting the worst of his encounter, until Jean grabbed his opponent by the shoulder and spun him around. Jean wrapped his heavy arms round the boy's waist and planted a head-butt in the boy's solar plexus; no sooner did the Half-Crown gasp in pain than Jean straightened up, cracking the boy's chin against the back of his head. The boy fell back, dazed, and at that point the issue was decided. Calo and Galdo had been evenly matched with their opponents; when Jean suddenly loomed before them (with Locke at his side doing his best to look dangerous), the Half-Crowns scrambled back and put their hands in the air.

'Well, Tesso,' said Locke when the curly-haired boy rose a few minutes later, bloody-nosed and wobbly, 'will you be giving over your preference now or shall I let Jean beat you some more?'

'I admit it was well done,' said Tesso as his gang limped into a semi-circle behind him, 'but I'd call us even at one and one. You'll see us again soon.'

3

So the battle went, as the days lengthened and spring turned into summer. Chains excused the boys from sitting the steps with him after the first hour of the afternoon, and they began roaming the north of Camorr, hunting Half-Crowns with vigour.

Tesso responded by unleashing the full strength of his band; the Full Crowns were the largest real gang in Camorr, and their seconds had a comparable pool of recruits, some of them fresh from Shades' Hill. Even with their numbers, however, the prowess of Jean Tannen was hard to answer, and so the nature of the battle changed.

The Half-Crowns split into smaller groups, attempting to isolate and ambush the Gentlemen Bastards when they weren't together. For the most part Locke kept his gang close at hand, but sometimes individual errands were unavoidable. Locke was beaten fairly badly on several occasions; he came to Jean one afternoon nursing a split lip and a pair of bruised shins.

'Look,' he said, 'it's been a few days since we had any piece of Tesso. So here's what we're going to do. I'm going to lurk just south of the market tomorrow and look like I'm up to something. You're going to hide a long way off, two or three hundred yards maybe. Somewhere they can't possibly spot you.'

'I'll never get to you in time,' said Jean.

'The point isn't to get to me before I get beaten,' said Locke. 'The point is, when you *do* get there tomorrow, you pound the crap out of him. You beat him so hard they'll hear the screaming in Talisham. Smack him around like you've never smacked him before.'

'With pleasure,' said Jean, 'but it won't happen; they'll only run away when they see me coming, as always. The one thing I can't do is keep up with them on foot.'

'Just you leave that to me,' said Locke, 'and fetch your sewing kit. There's something I need you to do for me.'

So it was that Locke Lamora lurked in an alley on an overcast day, very near to the place where the whole affair with the Half-Crowns had started. The Shifting Market was doing brisk business, as folk attempted to get their shopping done before the sky started pouring down rain. Out there somewhere, watching Locke with comfortable anonymity from a little cockleshell boat, was Jean Tannen.

Locke only had to lurk conspicuously for half an hour before Tesso found him.

'Lamora,' he said, 'I thought you'd know better by now. I don't see any of your friends in the neighbourhood.'

'Tesso. Hello.' Locke yawned. 'I think today's the day you'll be giving over your preference to me.'

'In a pig's fucking eye,' said the older boy. 'What I think I'm

310

going to do is take your clothes when I'm done and throw them in a canal. That'll be right humorous. Hell, the longer you put off bending the knee, the more fun I can have with you.'

He advanced confidently to the attack, knowing that Locke had never once so much as kept up with him in a fight. Locke met him head-on, shaking the left sleeve of his coat strangely. That sleeve was actually five feet longer than usual, courtesy of Jean Tannen's alterations; Locke had cleverly kept it folded against his side to conceal its true nature as Tesso had approached.

Although Locke had few gifts as a fighter, he could be startlingly fast; the cuff of his unusual sleeve had a small lead weight sewn into it to aid him in casting it. He flung it forth, wrapping it around Tesso's chest beneath the taller boy's arms. The lead weight carried it around as it stretched taut, and Locke caught it in his left hand.

'What,' huffed Tesso, 'the hell do you think you're doing?' He clouted Locke just above his right eye; Locke flinched but ignored the pain. He slipped the extended sleeve into a loop of cloth that hung out of his coat's left pocket, folded it back over itself, and pulled another cord just below it. The network of knotted cords that Jean had sewn inside his coat's lining cinched tight; now the boys were chest to chest, and nothing short of a knife could free Tesso from the loop of thick cloth that tied them together.

Locke wrapped his arms round Tesso's abdomen for good measure, and then curled his spindly legs round Tesso's legs, just above the taller boy's knees. Tesso shoved and slapped at Locke, struggling to part the two of them. Failing, he began punching Locke in the teeth and on the top of his head, heavy blows that left Locke seeing flashes of light.

'What the hell *is* this, Lamora?' Tesso grunted with the effort of supporting Locke's weight in addition to his own; finally, as Locke had hoped and expected, he threw himself forward. Locke landed on his back in the gravel, with Tesso on top of him; the air burst out of Locke's lungs and the whole world seemed to shudder. 'This is ridiculous. You can't fight me. And now you can't run! Give up, Lamora!'

Locke spat blood into Tesso's face. 'I don't have to fight you and I don't have to run.' He grinned wildly. 'I just have to keep you here . . . until Jean gets back.'

Tesso gasped and looked around; out on the Shifting Market one small cockleshell boat was heading straight towards them. The plump shape of Jean Tannen was clearly visible within it, hauling rapidly on the oars.

'Oh, shit. You little *bastard*. Let me go, let me go, let me go!'

Tesso punctuated this with a series of punches; Locke was pummelled in the eyes and on the nose and on the scalp. Soon enough he was bleeding from his nose, his lips, his ears, and somewhere under his hair; Tesso was pounding him but good, yet he continued to cling madly to the older boy. His head was whirling with the combination of pain and triumph; Locke actually started laughing, high and gleeful and perhaps a little bit mad.

'I don't have to fight or run,' he cackled. 'I changed the rules of the game. I just have to keep you here . . . asshole. Here . . . until . . . Jean gets back.'

'Gods *dammit*,' Tesso hissed, and he redoubled his assault on Locke, punching and spitting and biting, heaping terrible punishment onto the head and face of the defenceless younger boy.

'Keep hitting,' Locke spluttered. 'You just keep hitting. I can take it all day. You just keep . . . hitting me . . . until . . . *Jean gets back*!'

BOOK III
REVELATION

'Nature never deceives us; it is always we who deceive ourselves.'

Jean-Jacques Rousseau,
from *Émile, ou Traité de l'éducation*

Chapter Nine

A Curious Tale for Countess Amberglass

I

At half past the tenth hour of the evening on the Duke's Day, as low dark clouds fell in above Camorr, blotting out the stars and the moons, Doña Sofia Salvara was being hoisted up into the sky to have a late tea with Doña Angiavesta Vorchenza, Dowager Countess of Amberglass, at the top of the great lady's Elderglass tower.

The passenger cage rattled and swayed, and Sofia clung to the black iron bars for support. The sweaty Hangman's Wind fluttered at her hooded coat as she stared south. All of the city lay spread beneath her, black and grey from horizon to horizon, suffused with the glow of fire and alchemy. This was a point of quiet pride for her every time she had the chance to take in this view from one of the Five Towers. The Eldren had built glass wonders for men to claim; engineers had crafted buildings of stone and wood in the Eldren ruins to make the cities their own; Bondsmagi pretended to the powers the Eldren must have once held. But it was alchemy that drove back the darkness every evening, alchemy that lit the commonest home and the tallest tower alike, cleaner and safer than natural fire. It was her Art that tamed the night.

At last her long ascent ended; the cage rattled to a halt beside an embarkation platform four-fifths of the way up Amberglass's full height. The wind sighed mournfully in the strange fluted arches at the peak of the tower. Two footmen in cream-white waistcoats and immaculate white gloves and breeches helped her out of the cage, as they might have assisted her from a carriage down on the ground. Once she was safely on the platform, the two men bowed from the waist.

'M'lady Salvara,' said the one on the left, 'my mistress bids you welcome to Amberglass.'

'Most kind,' said Doña Sofia.

'If it would please you to wait on the terrace, she will join you momentarily.'

The same footman led the way past a half-dozen servants in similar livery, who stood panting beside the elaborate arrangement of gears, levers and chains they worked to haul the cage up and down. They, too, bowed as she passed; she favoured them with a smile and an acknowledging wave. It never hurt to be pleasant to the servants in charge of that particular operation.

Doña Vorchenza's terrace was a wide crescent of transparent Elderglass jutting out from the north face of her tower, surrounded by brass safety rails. Doña Sofia looked straight down, as she had always been warned not to do, and as she always did. It seemed that she and the footman walked on thin air forty storeys above the stone courtyards and storage buildings at the base of the tower; alchemical lamps were specks of light and carriages were black squares smaller than one of her nails.

On her left, visible through a series of tall arched windows whose sills were on a level with her waist, were dimly lit apartments and parlours within the tower itself. Doña Vorchenza had very few living relatives and no children; she was effectively the last of a once-powerful clan and there was little doubt (among the grasping, ambitious nobles of the Alcegrante slopes, at least) that Amberglass would pass to some new family upon her death. Most of her tower was dark and quiet, most of its opulence packed away in closets and chests.

The old lady still knew how to host a late-night tea, however. At the far north-western corner of her transparent terrace, with a commanding view of the lightless countryside to the north of the city, a silk awning fluttered in the Hangman's Wind. Tall alchemical lanterns in cages of gilded brass hung from the four corners of the awning, shedding warm light on the little table and the two high-backed chairs arranged thereunder.

The footman placed a thin black cushion upon the right-hand chair and pulled it out for her; with a swish of skirts she settled into it and nodded her thanks. The man bowed and strolled away, taking up a position politely out of earshot but within easy beckoning distance.

Sofia did not have long to wait for her hostess; a few minutes after her arrival old Doña Vorchenza appeared out of a wooden door in the tower's north wall.

Age has a way of exaggerating the physical traits of those who live to feel its strains; the round tend to grow rounder and the slim tend to waste away. Time had narrowed Angiavesta Vorchenza; she was not so much withered as collapsed, a spindly living caricature like a wooden idol animated by the sorcery of sheer willpower. Seventy was a fading memory for her, yet she still moved about without an escort on her arm or a cane in her hands. She dressed eccentrically in a black velvet frock coat with fur collar and cuffs. Eschewing the cascading petticoats the ladies of her era had favoured, she actually wore black pantaloons and silver slippers. Her white hair was pulled back and fixed with lacquered pins; her dark eyes were bright behind her half-moon optics.

'Sofia,' she said as she stepped daintily beneath the awning, 'what a pleasure it is to have you up here again! It's been months, my dear girl, months. No, do sit, pulling out my own chair holds no terrors for me. Ah. Tell me, how is Lorenzo? And surely we must speak of your garden.'

'Lorenzo and I are well, considered solely in ourselves. And the garden thrives, Doña Vorchenza. Thank you for asking.'

'Considered solely in yourselves? Then there is something else? Something, dare I pry, external?'

Night tea in Camorr was a womanly tradition when one wished to seek the advice of another, or simply make use of a sympathetic ear while expressing regrets or complaints – most frequently concerning men.

'You may pry, Doña Vorchenza, by all means. And yes, yes, "external" is a very proper term for it.'

'But it's not Lorenzo?'

'Oh, no. Lorenzo is satisfactory in every possible respect.' Sofia sighed and glanced down at the illusion of empty air beneath her feet and her chair. 'It's . . . both of us that may be in need of advice.'

'Advice,' Doña Vorchenza chuckled. 'Advice. The years play a sort of alchemical trick, transmuting one's mutterings to a state of respectability. Give advice at forty and you're a nag. Give it at seventy and you're a sage.'

'Doña Vorchenza,' said Sofia, 'you have been of great help to me before. I couldn't think . . . Well, there was no one else I was comfortable speaking to about this matter, for the time being.'

'Indeed? Well, dear girl, I'm eager to be of whatever help I can. But here's our tea – come, let us indulge ourselves for a few moments.'

One of Doña Vorchenza's jacketed attendants wheeled a silver-domed cart towards them and slid it into place beside the little table. When he whisked the dome away, Sofia saw that the cart held a gleaming silver tea-service and a subtlety – a perfect culinary replica of Amberglass Tower, barely nine inches high, complete with minuscule specks of alchemical light dotting its turrets. The little glass globes were not much larger than raisins.

'You see how little real work I give to my poor chef,' said Doña Vorchenza, cackling. 'He suffers in the service of such a plain and simple palate; he takes his revenge with these surprises. I cannot order a soft-boiled egg but that he finds a dancing chicken to lay it directly on my plate. Tell me, Gilles, is that edifice truly edible?'

'So I am assured, my lady Vorchenza, save for the tiny lights. The tower itself is spice cake; the turrets and terraces are jellied fruit. The buildings and carriages at the base of the tower are mostly chocolate; the heart of the tower is an apple brandy cream, and the windows—'

'Thank you, Gilles, that will do for an architectural synopsis. But spit out the lights when we're finished, you say?'

'It would be more decorous, m'lady,' said the servant, a round, delicate-featured man with shoulder-length black ringlets, 'to let me remove them for you prior to consumption . . .'

'Decorous? Gilles, you would deny us the fun of spitting them over the side of the terrace like little girls. I'll thank you not to touch them. The tea?'

'Your will, Doña Vorchenza,' he said smoothly. 'Tea of Light.' He lifted a silver tea pot and poured a steaming line of pale brownish liquid into a tea glass; Doña Vorchenza's etched glasses were shaped like large tulip buds with silver bases. As the tea settled into the container, it began to glow faintly, shedding an inviting orange radiance.

'Oh, very pretty,' said Doña Sofia. 'I've heard of it . . . Verrari, is it?'

'Lashani.' Doña Vorchenza took the glass from Gilles and

cradled it in both hands. 'Quite the latest thing. Their tea-masters are mad with the competitive spirit. This time next year we'll have something even stranger to one-up one another with. But forgive me, my dear; I do hope you're not averse to drinking the products of your art as well as working with them in your garden?'

'Not at all,' Sofia replied as the servant set her own glass before her and bowed. She took the cup into her hands and took a deep breath; the tea smelled of vanilla and orange blossom. When she sipped, the flavours ran warmly on her tongue and the scented steam rose into her nostrils. Gilles vanished back into the tower itself while the ladies commenced to drinking; for a few moments they enjoyed their tea in appreciative silence, and for a few moments Sofia was almost content.

'Now we shall see,' said Doña Vorchenza as she set her half-empty glass down before her, 'if it continues to glow when it comes out the other side.'

Doña Sofia giggled despite herself, and the lines on her hostess's lean face drew upwards as she smiled. 'What did you want to ask me about, my dear?'

'Doña Vorchenza,' she began, and then hesitated. 'It is . . . it is commonly thought that you have some, ah, means to communicate with the . . . the Duke's secret constabulary.'

'The Duke has a secret constabulary?' Doña Vorchenza placed a hand against her breast in an expression of polite disbelief.

'The Midnighters, Doña Vorchenza, the Midnighters and their leader . . .'

'The Duke's Spider. Yes, yes. Forgive me, dear girl; I do know of what you speak. But this idea you have . . . "commonly thought", you say. Many things are commonly thought, but perhaps not commonly thought *all the way through*.'

'It is very curious,' said Sofia Salvara, 'that when the Doñas come to you with problems, on more than one occasion, their problems have . . . reached the ear of the Spider. Or seemed to. And . . . the Duke's men have become involved in assisting with those problems.'

'Oh, my dear Sofia. When gossip comes to me I pass it on in packets and parcels; I drop a word or two in the right ear and the gossip acquires a life of its own. Sooner or later it must reach the notice of someone who will take action.'

'Doña Vorchenza,' said Sofia, 'I hope I can say without intending or giving offence that you are dissembling.'

'I hope I can say without disappointing you, dear girl, that you have a very slender basis for making that suggestion.'

'Doña Vorchenza.' Sofia clutched at her edge of the table so hard that several of her finger joints popped. 'Lorenzo and I are being robbed.'

'Robbed? Whatever do you mean?'

'And we have Midnighters involved. They've . . . made the most extraordinary claims, and made requests of us. But something is . . . Doña Vorchenza, there must be some way to confirm that they are what they say they are.'

'You say *Midnighters* are robbing you?'

'No,' said Sofia, biting her upper lip. 'No, it's not the Midnighters themselves. They are . . . supposedly watching the situation and waiting for a chance to act. But something is almost certainly wrong. Or they are not telling us everything they perhaps should.'

'My dear Sofia,' said Doña Vorchenza, 'my poor troubled girl, you must tell me exactly what has happened, and leave out not one detail.'

'It is . . . difficult, Doña Vorchenza. The situation is rather . . . embarrassing. And complicated.'

'We are all alone up here on my terrace, my dear. You have done all the hard work already, in coming over to see me. Now you must tell me everything – *everything*. Then I'll see to it that this particular bit of gossip speeds on its way to the right ear.'

Sofia took another small sip of tea, cleared her throat, and hunched down in her seat to look Doña Vorchenza directly in the eyes.

'Surely,' she began, 'you've heard of Austershalin brandy, Doña Vorchenza?'

'More than heard of, my dear. I may even have a few bottles hidden away in my wine cabinets.'

'And you know how it is made? The secrets surrounding it?'

'Oh, I believe I understand the essence of the Austershalin mystique. The fussy black-coated vintners of Emberlain are well served by the stories surrounding their wares.'

'Then you can understand, Doña Vorchenza, how Lorenzo and I reacted as we did when the following opportunity supposedly fell into our laps by an act of the gods . . .'

2

The cage containing Doña Salvara creaked and rattled towards the ground, growing ever-smaller and fading into the background grey of the courtyard. Doña Vorchenza stood by the brass rail of the embarkation platform, staring into the night for many minutes while her team of attendants pulled at the machinery of the capstan. Gilles wheeled the silver cart with the near-empty pot of tea and the half-eaten cake Amberglass past her, and she turned to him.

'No,' she said. 'Send the cake up to the solarium. That's where we'll be.'

'Who, m'lady?'

'Reynart.' She was already striding back towards the door to her terrace-side apartments; her slippered feet made an echoing *slap-slap-slap* against the walkway. 'Find Reynart. I don't care what he's doing. Find him and send him up to me, the moment you've seen to the cake.'

Inside the suite of apartments, through a locked door, up a curving stairway . . . Doña Vorchenza cursed under her breath. Her knees, her feet, her ankles. 'Damn venerability,' she muttered. 'I piss on the gods for the gift of rheumatism.' Her breathing was ragged; she undid the buttons on the front of her fur-trimmed coat as she continued to drive herself up the steps.

At the top, the very peak of the inner tower, there was a heavy oak door reinforced with iron joints and bands. She pulled forth a key that hung around her right wrist on a silk cord. This she inserted into the silver lock-box above the crystal knob, while carefully pressing a certain decorative brass plate in a wall sconce. A series of clicks echoed within the walls and the door fell open, inwards.

Forgetting the brass plate would be a poor idea; she'd specified a rather excessive pull for the concealed crossbow trap when she'd had it installed three decades earlier.

This was the solarium, then, another eight storeys up from the level of the terrace. The room took up the full diameter of the tower at its apex, fifty feet from edge to edge. The floor was thickly carpeted; a long curving brass-railed gallery, with stairs at either end, spread across the northern half of the space. This gallery held a row of tall witchwood shelves, divided into thousands upon thousands of cubbyholes and compartments. The transparent hemispherical ceiling dome revealed the low clouds like a bubbling lake of smoke. Doña Vorchenza tapped alchemical globes to bring them to life as she mounted the stairs to her file gallery.

There she worked, engrossed, heedless of the passage of time as her narrow fingers flicked from compartment to compartment. She pulled out some piles of parchment and set them aside, half-considered others and pushed them back in, muttering remembrances and conjecture under her breath. She snapped out of her fugue only when the solarium door clicked open once more.

The man who entered was tall and broad-shouldered; he had an angular Vadran face and ice-blond hair pulled back in a ribbon-bound tail. He wore a ribbed leather doublet over slashed black sleeves, with black breeches and tall black boots. The little silver pins at his collar gave him the rank of captain in the Nightglass Company, the blackjackets. The Duke's Own. A rapier with straight quillions hung at his right hip.

'Stephen,' said Doña Vorchenza without preamble, 'have any of your boys or girls paid a recent visit to Don and Doña Salvara, on the Isla Durona?'

'The Salvaras? No, certainly not, m'lady.'

'You're sure? Absolutely sure?' Parchments in hand, eyebrows arched, she stalked down the steps, barely keeping her balance. 'I need certain truth from you right now as badly as I ever have.'

'I know the Salvaras, m'lady. I met them both at last year's Day of Changes feast; I rode up to the Sky Garden in the same cage with them.'

'And you haven't sent any of the Midnighters to pay them a visit?'

'Twelve gods, no. Not one. Not for any reason.'

'Then someone is abusing our good name, Stephen. And I think we may finally have the Thorn of Camorr.'

322

Reynart stared at her, then grinned. 'You're joking. You're not? Pinch me, I must be dreaming. What's the situation?'

'First things first; I know you think fastest when we nurse that damned sweet tooth of yours. Peek inside the dumb waiter; I'm going to have a seat.'

'Oh my,' said Reynart, peering into the chain-hoist shaft that held the dumb waiter, 'looks as though someone's already made a merry work of this poor spice cake. I'll put it out of its misery. There's wine and glasses, too – looks like one of your sweet whites.'

'Gods bless Gilles; I'd forgotten to ask him for that, I was in such haste to get to my files. Be a dear dutiful subordinate and pour us a glass.'

' "Dear dutiful subordinate", indeed. For the cake, I'd polish your slippers as well.'

'I'll hold that promise in reserve for the next time you vex me, Stephen. Oh, fill the glass – I'm not thirteen years old. Now, take your seat and listen to this. If everything signifies, as I believe it shall, the bastard has just been delivered to us right in the middle of one of his schemes.'

'How so?'

'I'll answer a question with a question, Stephen.' She took a deep draught of her white wine and settled back into her chair. 'Tell me, how much do you know of the body of lore surrounding Austershalin brandy?'

3

'Posing as one of us,' Reynart mused after she'd finished her tale. 'The sheer fucking cheek. But are you sure it's the Thorn?'

'If it isn't, then we could only presume that we now have *another* equally skilled and audacious thief picking the pockets of my peers. And I think that's presuming a bit much. Even for a city crammed as full of ghosts as this one.'

'Mightn't it be the Grey King? He's the right sort of slippery, by all reports.'

'Mmmm. No, the Grey King's been murdering Barsavi's men. The Thorn's mode of operation is plain trickery; not a drop of real blood shed yet, as near as I can tell. And I don't think that's a coincidence.'

Reynart set aside his empty cake plate and took a sip from his glass of wine. 'So if we can trust Doña Salvara's story, we're looking at a gang of at least four men. The Thorn himself – let's call him Lukas Fehrwight, for the sake of argument. His servant Graumann. And the two men who broke into the Salvara manor.'

'That's a beginning, Stephen. But I'd say the gang is more probably five or six.'

'How do you figure?'

'I believe the false Midnighter was telling the truth when he told Don Salvara that the attack near the Temple of Fortunate Waters was staged; it would have to be, for a scheme this complex. So we have two more accomplices – the masked attackers.'

'Assuming they weren't just hired for the task.'

'I doubt it. Consider the total paucity of information we've had previous to this . . . Not one report, one boast, one slender whisper from anyone, anywhere. Not a speck of information pointing to anyone who even claimed to *work* with the Thorn of Camorr. Yet on any given day thieves will boast loudly for hours about who among them can piss the farthest. Most unusual.'

'Well,' said Reynart, 'if you just slit a hireling's throat when he's done his job, you don't have to pay him, either.'

'But we're still dealing with the Thorn, and I hold that such an act would be outside his pattern of operations.'

'So his gang runs a closed shop; that would make sense. But it still might not be six. The two in the alley could also be the two who entered the manor dressed as Midnighters.'

'Oh, my dear Stephen. An interesting conjecture. Let us say four minimum, six maximum as our first guess, or we'll be here all night drawing diagrams for one another. I suspect anything larger would be difficult to hide as well as they have.'

'So be it, then.' Reynart thought for a moment. 'I can give you fifteen or sixteen swords right this very hour; some of my lads are mumming it up tonight down in the Snare and the Cauldron, since we got those reports of Nazca Barsavi's funeral. I can't pull them on short notice. But give me until the dark of the morning and I can have everyone else, kitted up and ready for a scrap. We've got the Nightglass to back us; no need to even bring the yellowjackets in on it. We know they might be compromised anyway.'

'That would be well, Stephen, if I wanted them snatched up right now. But I don't . . . I think we have a few days, at least, to draw the web tight around this man. Sofia said they'd discussed an initial outlay of about twenty-five thousand crowns; I suspect the Thorn will wait around to collect the other seven or eight he's due.'

'At least let me hold a squad ready, then. I'll keep them at the Palace of Patience; tuck them in among the yellowjackets. They can be ready to dash off with five minutes' notice.'

'Very prudent; do so. Now, as for how we move on the Thorn himself, send someone down to Meraggio's tomorrow, the subtlest you have. See if Fehrwight holds an account there, and when it was begun.'

'Calviro. I'll send Maraliza Calviro.'

'An excellent choice. As far as I'm concerned, anyone else this Fehrwight has introduced the Salvaras to is suspect. Have her check up on the lawscribe she said her husband met just after the staged attack behind the temple.'

'Eccari, wasn't it? Evante Eccari?'

'Yes. And then I want you to check out the Temple of Fortunate Waters.'

'Me? M'lady, you of all people know I don't keep the faith, I just inherited the looks.'

'But you can fake the faith, and it's the looks I need. They'll keep you from being too suspicious. Case the place; look for anyone out of sorts. Look for gangs or goings-on. It's remotely possible someone at the temple was in on the staged attack. Even if it's not the case, we need to eliminate it as a possibility.'

'It's as good as done, then. And what about their inn?'

'The Tumblehome, yes. Send one person and one person only. I have a pair of old informants on the staff; one of them thinks he's reporting to the yellowjackets and one thinks she's working for the Capa. I'll pass the names along. For now, I just want to find out if they're still there, at the Bowsprit Suite. If they are, you can place a few of your men there dressed as staff. Observation only, for the time being.'

'Very well.' Reynart rose from his chair and brushed crumbs

from his breeches. 'And the noose? Assuming you get your wish, where and when would you like to draw it tight?'

'Going after the Thorn has always been like trying to grab fish with bare hands,' she replied. 'I'll want him sewn up somewhere, some place where escape will be impossible, cut off from *his* friends, and entirely surrounded by ours.'

'By ours? How . . . *Oh*. Raven's Reach!'

'Yes. Very good, Stephen. The Day of Changes, just a week and a half from now. The Duke's own feast. Five hundred feet in the air, surrounded by the peers of Camorr and a hundred guards. I'll instruct Doña Sofia to invite this Lukas Fehrwight to dine with the Duke, as a guest of the Salvaras.'

'Assuming he doesn't suspect a trap . . .'

'I think it's just the sort of gesture he'd appreciate. I think our mysterious friend's audacity is going to be what finally arranges our direct introduction. I shall have Sofia feign financial distress; she can tell Fehrwight that the last few thousand crowns won't be forthcoming until after the festival. A double-baited hook, his greed hand in hand with his vanity. I daresay he'll relish the temptation.'

'Shall I pull everyone in for it?'

'Of course.' Doña Vorchenza sipped her wine and smiled slowly. 'I want a Midnighter to take his coat; I want Midnighters serving him before the meal. If he uses a chamber pot, I want a Midnighter to close it for him afterwards. We'll take him in Raven's Reach; then we'll watch the ground to see who runs, and where they run to.'

'Anything else?'

'No. Get to it, Stephen. Come back and let me have your report in a few hours. I'll still be up – I'm expecting messages from the Floating Grave once Barsavi's funeral procession gets back. In the meantime, I'll send old Nicovante a note about what we suspect.'

'Your servant, m'lady.' Reynart bowed briefly and then departed the solarium, his strides long and rapid.

Before the heavy door had even slammed shut, Doña Vorchenza was up and moving towards a small scrivener's desk tucked into an alcove to the left of the door. There she withdrew a half-sheet of parchment, scribbled a few hasty lines, folded it, and closed the fold with a small dollop of blue wax from a paper tube. The stuff was alchemical, hardening after a few moments of exposure to air. She preferred to allow no sources of open flame into this room, with its many decades of carefully collected and indexed records.

Within the desk was a signet ring that Doña Vorchenza never wore outside her solarium; on that ring was a sigil that appeared nowhere on the crest of the Vorchenza family. She pressed the ring into the stiffening blue wax and then withdrew it with a slight popping noise.

When she passed it down the dumb-waiter, one of her night attendants would immediately run to the north-eastern cage platform of her tower and have himself cranked over to Raven's Reach via cable-car. There, he would place the message directly into the old Duke's hands, even if Nicovante had retired to his bedchamber.

Such was the custom with every note that was sealed in blue with nothing but the stylised sigil of a spider for its credentials.

INTERLUDE:
The Schoolmaster of Roses

I

'No, this is my heart. Strike. Strike. Now here. *Strike*.'

Cold grey water poured down on the House of Glass Roses; Camorr's winter rain pooled an inch deep beneath the feet of Jean Tannen and Don Maranzalla. Water ran in rivulets and threads down the face of every rose in the garden; it ran in small rivers into Jean Tannen's eyes as he struck out with his rapier again and again at the stuffed leather target little larger than a big man's fist the Don held on the end of a stick.

'Strike here. And here. No, too low. That's the liver. Kill me now, not a minute from now. I might have another thrust left in me. Up! Up at the heart, under the ribs. Better.'

Grey-white light exploded within the swirling clouds overhead, rippling like fire glimpsed through smoke. The thunder came a moment later, booming and reverberating, the sound of the gods throwing a tantrum. Jean could barely imagine what it must be like atop the Five Towers, now just a series of hazy grey columns lost in the sky behind Don Maranzalla's right shoulder.

'Enough, Jean, enough. You're passing fair with a pig-sticker; I want you to be familiar with it at need. But it's time to see what else you have a flair for.' Don Maranzalla, who was wrapped up inside a much-abused brown oilcloak, splashed through the water to a large wooden box. 'You won't be able to haul a long blade around in your circles. Fetch me the woundman.'

Jean hurried through the twisting glass maze towards the small room that led back down into the tower. He respected the roses still, only a fool would not, but he was quite used to their presence now. They no longer seemed to loom and flash at him like hungry things; they were just an obstacle to keep one's fingers away from.

The woundman, stashed in the little dry room at the top of the staircase, was a padded leather dummy in the shape of a man's head, torso and arms, standing upon an iron pole. Bearing this awkwardly over his right shoulder, Jean stepped back out in the driving rain and returned to the centre of the Garden Without Fragrance. The woundman scraped the glass walls several times, but the roses had no taste for empty leather flesh.

Don Maranzalla had opened the wooden chest and was rummaging around in it; Jean set the woundman up in the centre of the courtyard. The metal rod slid into a hole bored down through the stone and locked there with a twist, briefly pushing up a little fountain of water.

'Here's something ugly,' said the Don, swinging a four-foot length of chain wrapped in very fine leather, likely kid. 'It's called a bailiff's lash; wrapped up so it doesn't rattle. If you look close, it's got little hooks at either end, so you can hitch it round your waist like a belt. Easy to conceal under heavier clothes . . . though you might eventually need one a bit longer, to fit round yourself.' The Don stepped forward confidently and let one end of the padded chain whip towards the woundman's head; it rebounded off the leather with a loud, wet *whack*.

Jean amused himself for a few minutes by laying into the woundman with the lash, while Don Maranzalla watched. Mumbling to himself, the Don then took the padded chain away and offered Jean a pair of matched blades. They were about a foot long, one-sided, with broad and curving cutting edges. The hilts were attached to heavy hand-guards, studded with small brass spikes.

'Nasty little bitches, these things. Generally known as thieves' teeth. No subtlety to them; you can stab, hack or just plain punch. Those little brass nubs can scrape a man's face off, and those guards'll stop most anything short of a charging bull. Have at it.'

Jean's showing with the blades was even better than his outing with the lash; Maranzalla clapped approvingly. 'That's right, up through the stomach, under the ribs. Put a foot of steel there and tickle a man's heart with it, and you've just won the argument, son.'

As he took the matched blades back from Jean, he chuckled. 'How's that for teeth lessons, eh, boy? Eh?'

Jean stared at him, puzzled.

'Haven't you heard that one before? Your Capa Barsavi, he's not from Camorr, originally. Taught at the Therin Collegium. So, when he drags someone in for a talking-to, that's "etiquette lessons". And when he ties them up and makes them talk, that's "singing lessons". And when he cuts their throats and throws them in the bay for the sharks . . .'

'Oh,' said Jean, 'I guess that'd be "teeth lessons". I get it.'

'Right. I didn't make that one up, mind you. That's your kind. I'd lay odds the big man knows about it, but nobody says anything like that to his face. That's how it always is, be it cut-throats or soldiers. So . . . next lovely toy . . .'

Maranzalla handed Jean a pair of wooden-handled hatchets; these had curved metal blades on one side and round counterweights on the other.

'No fancy name for these skull-crackers. I wager you've seen a hatchet before. Your choice to use the blade or the ball; it's possible to avoid killing a man with the ball, but if you hit hard enough it's just as bad as the blade, so judge carefully when you're not attacking a woundman.'

Almost immediately, Jean realised that he liked the feel of the hatchets in his hands; they were long enough to be more effective than pocket weapons, like the gimp steel or the blackjacks most Right People carried as a matter of habit. Yet they were small enough to move swiftly and use in tight spaces, and it seemed to him they could hide themselves rather neatly under a coat or vest.

He crouched; the knife-fighter's crouch seemed natural with these things in his hands. Springing forward, he chopped at the woundman from both sides at once, embedding the hatchet blades in the dummy's ribs. With an overhand slash to the woundman's right arm, he made the whole thing shudder. He followed that cut with a back-handed stroke against the head, using a ball rather than a blade. For several minutes, he chopped and slashed at the woundman, his arms pistoning, a smile growing on his face.

'Hmmm. Not bad,' said Don Maranzalla. 'Not bad at all for a total novice, I'll grant you that. You seem very comfortable with them.'

On a whim, Jean turned and ran to one side of the courtyard, putting fifteen feet between himself and the woundman. The driving rain thrust fingers of grey down between him and the target, so he concentrated very hard – and then he lined up and threw, whipping one hatchet through the air with the full twisting force of his arm, hips, and upper body. The hatchet sank home in the woundman's head, where it held fast in the layers of leather without as much as a quiver.

'Oh, my,' said Don Maranzalla. Lightning roiled the heavens yet again, and thunder echoed across the rooftop. 'My, yes. Now *there's* a foundation we can build upon.'

Chapter Ten

Teeth Lessons

I

In the darkness beneath the Echo Hole, Jean Tannen was moving even before the cask, lit faintly from above by the red glow of Barsavi's torches, came crashing down into the black water.

Beneath the ancient stone cube there was a network of hanging rafters, built from black witchwood and lashed with Elderglass cords; the rafters were slimy with age and unmentionable growths, but they had held sure as long as the stones above had, and they retained their strength.

The waterfall that cascaded in from the roof terminated here in one of the swirling channels beneath the rafters. There was a veritable maze of channels; some were as smooth as glass, while others were as turbulent as white-water rapids. A few wheels and even stranger devices turned slowly in the corners beneath the under-rafters; Jean had briefly appraised them by the light of a tiny alchemical ball when he'd settled himself in for his long wait. Bug, understandably unwilling to move too far from Jean's company, had crouched on a rafter of his own about twenty feet to Jean's left.

There were little shafts in the stone floor of the Echo Hole, square cuts about two inches wide, irregularly spaced and serving some unguessable function. Jean had positioned himself between two of these, knowing it would be impossible to hear any of the activities above with the noise of the waterfall right in his ear.

His understanding of the situation above was imperfect, but as the long minutes rolled by and the red light grew, and Capa Barsavi and Locke began speaking to one another, Jean's uneasiness deepened into dread. There was shouting, cursing, the tramp of booted feet on stone – cheers. Locke was taken. Where was the gods-damned Bondsmage?

Jean scuttled along his rafter, looking for the best way to cross to the waterfall. It would be a good five or six feet up from the rafters to the lip of the stone gash through which the waterfall poured, but if he stayed out of the falling water he could make that – it was the quickest way up, the only way up from within here. In the thin red light pouring down through the little holes in the floor, Jean signalled for Bug to stay put.

There was another outburst of cheering above, and then the Capa's voice, loud and clear through one of the holes: 'Take this bastard and send him out to sea.'

Send him out to sea? Jean's heart pounded; had they already cut Locke's throat? His eyes stung at the thought that the next thing he'd see was a limp body falling in the white stream of gushing water, a limp body dressed all in grey.

Then came the cask, a heavy dark object that plunged into the black canal at the base of the waterfall with a loud splash and a geyser of water; Jean blinked twice before he realised what he'd just seen. 'Oh, gods,' he muttered. 'Like for like! Barsavi had to be fucking poetic.'

Overhead there was more cheering, more stomping of feet. Barsavi was yelling something; his people were yelling in response. Then the faint lines of red light began to flicker; shadows passed before them, and they began to recede in the direction of the street door. Barsavi was moving; Jean decided to take a risk and go for the cask.

There was another splash, audible even over the hiss and rumble of the waterfall. What the hell was that? Jean reached beneath his vest, drew out his light-globe, and shook it. A faint white star blossomed in the darkness. Clinging tightly to the wet rafter with his other hand, Jean tossed the globe down towards the channel in which the cask would have fallen, about forty feet to his right. It hit the water and settled, giving Jean enough light to discern the situation.

The little channel was about eight feet wide, stone-bordered, and the cask was bobbing heavily in it, three-quarters submerged.

Bug was thrashing about in the canal, visible only from the arms up. Jean's light-globe had struck the water about three feet to the right of his head; Bug had jumped down into the water on his own.

Damn, but the boy seemed to be constitutionally incapable of remaining in high places for any length of time.

Jean looked around frantically; it would take him a few moments to work his way over to a point where he could splash down into the right channel without cracking his legs against one of the stone dividers.

'Bug,' Jean cried, judging that the ruckus above would cover his own voice, 'Bug! Your light! Slip it out, now! Locke's in that cask!'

Bug fumbled within his tunic, drew out a light-globe and shook it; by the sudden flare of added white light Jean could clearly see the outline of the bobbing black cask. He judged the distance between himself and it, came to a decision, and reached for one of his hatchets with his free hand.

'Bug,' he yelled, 'don't try to get through the sides. Attack the flat top of the cask!'

'How?'

'Stay right where you are.' Jean leaned to his right, clinging to the rafter with his left arm; he raised the hatchet in his right hand, whispered a single 'Please' to the Benefactor, and let fly. The hatchet struck, quivering, in the dark wood of the cask. Bug flinched back, then splashed through the water to pry at the weapon.

Jean began sliding his bulk along the rafter, but more dark motion in the corner of his eye brought him up short. He peered down into the shadows on his left; something was moving across the surface of one of the other waterways in the damned maze. Several somethings – black scuttling shapes the size of dogs. Their bristling legs spread wide when they slipped just beneath the surface of the dark water, then drew in to propel them up and over stone just as easily . . .

'Fuck me,' he muttered. 'Fuck me, that's not possible.'

Salt devils, despite their horrific size and aspect, were timid creatures. The huge spiders crouched in crevices on the rocky coasts to the south-west of Camorr, preying on fish and gulls, occasionally falling prey to sharks or devilfish if they ventured too far from shore. Sailors flung stones and arrows at them with superstitious dread.

Only a fool would approach one, with their fangs the length of a grown man's fingers and their venom, which might not always bring death but could make a man fervently pray for it. Yet salt devils were quite content to flee from humans; they were ambush hunters, solitary, incapable of tolerating one another at close quarters. Jean had scared himself witless in his early years reading the observations of scholars and naturalists concerning the creatures.

Yet here was an entire pack of the damn things, leg-to-leg like hounds, scrabbling across stone and water alike towards Bug and the cask.

'Bug,' Jean screamed, 'Bug!'

2

Bug had heard even less of the goings-on upstairs then Jean, yet when the cask had splashed down into the darkness, he'd realised immediately that it hadn't been dropped down idly. Having placed himself directly over the canal that flowed from the waterfall, he'd simply let himself drop the fifteen feet down into the rushing water.

He'd tucked his legs and hit like a catapult stone, arse-first; although his head had plunged under with the momentum of his drop, he quickly found that he could plant his feet; the canal was only about four feet deep.

Now, with Jean's hatchet gripped in one hand, he chopped frantically at the flat barrel-top before him. He'd set his own light-glass on the stone walkway beside the canal, as there was enough working light coming from Jean's beneath the surface of the water.

'Bug,' the big man yelled, his voice suddenly loud with real alarm. 'Bug!'

The boy turned to his right and caught a glimpse of what was moving out of the far shadows towards him; a shudder of pure revulsion passed up and down his spine, and he looked around frantically to make sure the threat was approaching from only one direction.

'Bug, get out of the water! Get up on the stones!'

'What about Locke?'

'He doesn't want to come out of that cask right this fucking second,' Jean hollered. 'Trust me!'

As Bug scrambled up out of the rippling, alchemically lit water, the cask began once again bobbing towards the south end of the building, where the canal exited to gods knew where. Too desperate to think clearly about his own safety, Jean scrambled out along the crossbeam, feet sliding in the muck of the ages, and he ran in the direction of the waterfall, arms windmilling crazily for balance. A few seconds later he arrested his forward momentum by wrapping his arms around a vertical beam; his feet slipped briefly out from beneath him but he clung tightly to his perch. His mad dash had brought him to a point beside the waterfall; now he flung himself forward into the air, carefully drawing his legs into his chest; he hit the water with a splash as great as that caused by the cask and bumped the channel-bottom.

He came up spluttering, second hatchet already in hand. Bug was crouched on the stone lip beside the canal, waving his alchemical globe at the spiders. Jean saw that the salt devils were about fifteen feet away from the boy, across the water and moving more warily, but still approaching. Their carapaces were mottled black and grey, their multiple eyes the colour of deepest night, starred with eerie reflections of Bug's light. Their hairy pedipalps waved in the air before their faces, and their hard black fangs twitched.

Four of the damn things. Jean heaved his bulk up out of the canal on Bug's side, spitting water; he fancied that he saw some of those inhuman black eyes turn to regard him.

'Jean,' Bug moaned. 'Jean, those things look pissed off.'

'It's not natural,' said Jean, as he ran to Bug's side; the boy tossed him his other hatchet. The spiders had closed to ten feet, just across the water; he and Bug seemed hemmed in by thirty-two unblinking black eyes, thirty-two twitching legs with jagged dark hairs. 'Not natural at all; salt devils don't act like this.'

'Oh, good.' Bug held the alchemical globe out at arm's length as though he could conceal himself entirely behind it. 'You discuss it with them.'

'I suspect the only language they'll understand is hatchet.'

No sooner were these words out of Jean's mouth than the spiders moved in eerie unison, forward into the water with four splashes. The cask had drifted now a few feet to Jean and Bug's right; one black shape actually passed beneath it. Multiple black legs speared up out of the water, flailing for purchase; Bug cried out in mingled disgust and horror. Jean lunged forward, striking

335

out with each hatchet in rapid downward strokes; two spider limbs opened with stomach-turning cracking noises, spurting dark blue blood. Jean leapt back.

The two uninjured spiders pulled themselves up out of the water a few seconds ahead of their wounded brethren and rushed Jean, their barbed feet clacking against the wet stone blocks beneath them. Realising he would be dangerously overbalanced if he attempted to swing at both at once, Jean opted for a more disgusting plan of action.

The Wicked Sister in his right hand arced down viciously, splitting the rightmost salt devil's head between its symmetrical rows of black eyes; its legs spasmed in its death reflex and Bug actually dropped his alchemical globe, so quickly did he leap back. Jean used the momentum of his right-hand swing to raise his left leg up off the ground; the left-hand spider reared up with its fangs spread just as he brought his boot-heel down on what he supposed was its face. Its eyes cracked like jellied fruit; Jean shoved down with all his might, feeling as though he was stomping on a sack of wet leathers.

Warm blood soaked his boot as he pulled it free, and now the wounded spiders were scuttling up right behind their fallen counterparts, hissing and clicking in anger.

One shoved its way in front of the other and lunged at Jean, legs wide, head up to bare its curving fangs. Jean brought both the Sisters down in a hammer-blow, blades reversed, smashing the spider's head down into the wet stones and stopping it in its tracks. Ichor spurted; Jean felt it spattering his neck and forehead, and he did his best to ignore it.

One damn monster left; incensed at the delay they'd caused him, Jean bellowed and leapt into the air. Arms spread, he landed with both of his feet in the middle of the last creature's carapace. It exploded wetly beneath him, folding its flailing legs up at an unnatural angle. They beat their last few pulses of life against his legs as he ground in his heels, growling.

'Gah!' cried Bug, who'd got a good soaking from something blue and previously circulating through a salt devil; Jean didn't waste a second in tossing the boy one of his gore-soaked Sisters before jumping down into the water once again. The cask had floated about ten feet farther south; Jean splashed frantically towards it and secured it with his left hand. Then he began to piston his right arm up and down, hacking at the wood of the barrel's lid with his hatchet.

'Bug,' he cried, 'kindly make sure there aren't any more of those damn things creeping up on us!'

There was a splash behind Jean as Bug hopped back into the waterway; a few seconds later the boy came up beside the cask and steadied it with his thin arms. 'None that I can see, Jean. Hurry.'

'I am' – *crack, crack, crack* – 'fucking hurrying.' His hatchet blade bit through the wood at last; horse urine poured out into the water and Bug gagged. Working furiously, Jean widened the hole, then managed to pry off the end of the cask entirely. A wave of the foul yellow-slick stuff swept out across his chest; tossing his hatchet away without a further thought, he reached inside and tugged out the motionless body of Locke Lamora.

Jean checked him frantically for cuts, slashes or raised purple welts; his neck seemed to be quite intact.

Heaving Locke rather ungently up onto the stone walkway beside the dead spiders, some parts of which were still twitching, Jean then pushed himself up out of the water to crouch beside Locke. He wrenched off Locke's mantle and cloak; Bug appeared at his side just in time to yank them away and toss them in the water. Jean tore open Locke's grey vest and began thumping on his chest.

'Bug,' he gasped, 'get up here and push his legs in for me. His warm humours are all snuffed out. Let's get a rhythm going and maybe we can rekindle them. Gods, if he lives I swear I'll get ten books on physik and memorise every single one.'

Bug clambered out of the water and began pumping Locke's legs, moving them in and out one at a time, while Jean alternately pressed on Locke's stomach, pounded on his chest and slapped him on the cheeks. 'Come on, gods damn it,' Jean muttered, 'be stubborn, you skinny little—'

Locke's back arched convulsively and harsh wet coughing noises exploded out of his throat; his hands scrabbled weakly at the stone and he rolled over onto his left side. Jean sat back and sighed with relief, oblivious to the puddle of spider blood he'd settled into.

Locke vomited into the water, retched and shuddered, then vomited again. Bug knelt beside him, steadying him by the

337

shoulders. For several minutes, Locke lay there shaking, breathing heavily and coughing wetly.

'Oh, gods,' Locke said at last in a small hoarse voice. 'Oh, gods. My eyes. I can barely see. Is that water?'

'Yes, running water.' Jean reached over and took one of Locke's arms.

'Then get me in there. Thirteen gods, get this foulness *off* me.'

Locke rolled into the canal with a splash before Jean or Bug could even move to assist him; he dunked his head beneath the dark stream several times, then began tearing off his remaining clothes, until he was wearing nothing but a white undertunic and his grey breeches.

'Better?' asked Jean.

'I suppose I must be.' Locke retched again. 'My eyes sting, my nose and throat burn, my chest hurts, I've got a pounding black headache the size of Therim Pel, I got slapped around by the entire Barsavi family, I'm covered in horse piss, and it looks like the Grey King just did something pretty clever at our expense.' He set his head against the edge of the stone pathway and coughed a few more times; when he raised his head again, he noticed the spider carcasses for the first time and jerked back. 'Ugh. Gods. Looks like there's things I've missed, too.'

'Salt devils,' said Jean. 'A whole pack of them, working together. They came on looking for a fight, ravenous. Suicidal, like.'

'That doesn't make any sense,' said Locke.

'One thing could explain it,' Jean replied.

'A conspiracy of the gods,' Locke muttered. 'Oh. *Sorcery*.'

'Yes. That bloody Bondsmage. If he can tame a scorpion hawk, he could—'

'But what if it's just this place?' interrupted Bug. 'You've heard the stories.'

'No need to fret about stories,' said Locke, 'when there's a live mage known to have it in for us. Jean's right. I didn't get stuffed in that barrel as a criticism of my play-acting, and those biting bitches weren't here for a rest holiday. You were both meant to be dead as well, or if not dead—'

'Scared off,' said Jean. 'Distracted. The better for you to drown.'

'Seems plausible.' Locke rubbed at his stinging eyes once again.

'Amazing how every time I think my tolerance for this affair has reached a final low, I find something new to hate about the situation. Calo and Galdo . . . we need to get to them.'

'They could be in a world of shit,' agreed Jean.

'They already are, but we'll face it better once we're back together.'

Locke attempted to heave himself up out of the water and failed. Jean reached down and pulled him up by the collar of his tunic. Locke nodded his thanks and slowly stood up, shaking. 'I'm afraid my strength seems to have fled. I'm sorry, Jean.'

'Don't be. You've taken a hell of a lot of abuse tonight. I'm just pleased we broke you out of that thing before it was too late.'

'I'm indebted to the pair of you, believe me. That was . . . It would have been . . .' Locke shook his head. 'It was pretty gods-damned awful.'

'I can only suppose,' said Jean. 'Shall we go?'

'With all haste. Back out the way you two came in, quietly. Barsavi's crowd may still be in the area. And keep your eyes open for, ah, birds.'

'Too right. We came in through a sort of crawlway, western canal-side.' Jean slapped his forehead and looked around. 'Damn me, I've mislaid the Sisters.'

'Never fear,' said Bug, holding them up. 'I figured you'd want them back, so I kept an eye on them.'

'Much obliged, Bug,' said Jean. 'I'm of a mind to use them on some people before this night is done.'

3

Rustwater was as dead as ever when they sneaked out the crawlway and scrambled up onto the canal bank just to the west of the Echo Hole. Barsavi's procession had vanished; although the three Gentlemen Bastards crouched low and scanned the occluded sky for any hint of a swooping hawk, they caught not a glimpse.

'Let's make for Coalsmoke,' said Locke. 'Past Beggars' Barrow. We can steal a boat and slip home through the culvert.' The drainage culvert on the south side of the Temple District, just beneath the House of Perelandro, had a concealed slide mechanism within the cage that covered it from the outside. The Gentlemen Bastards could open it at will to come and go quietly.

'Good idea,' said Jean. 'I'm not comfortable being about on the streets and bridges.'

They crept south, grateful for the low, warm mists that swirled around them. Jean had his hatchets out and was moving his head from side to side, watchful as a cat on a swaying clothesline. He led them over a bridge, with Locke constantly stumbling and falling behind, then down the south-eastern shore of the Quiet. Here the lightless black heap of Beggars' Barrow loomed in the mists to their left, and the wet stink of paupers' graves filled the air.

'Not a watchman,' whispered Locke. 'Not a Shades' Hill boy or girl. Not a soul. Even for this neighbourhood, that's damn peculiar.'

'Has anything about tonight been right yet?' Jean set as rapid a pace as he could, and they soon crossed another bridge, south into Coalsmoke. Locke laboured to keep up, clutching his aching stomach and ribs. Bug brought up their rear, constantly peering over his shoulder.

On the north-eastern edge of Coalsmoke there was a line of weathered docks, sagging stairs and crumbling stone quays. All the larger, nicer boats and barges were locked and chained, but a few cockleshells bobbed here and there, secured by nothing more than rope. In a city full of such little boats, no sane thief would bother stealing one – most of the time.

They clambered into the first one that chanced to have an oar; Locke collapsed at the stern, while Bug took up the oar and Jean cast off the rope.

'Thank you, Bug.' Jean squeezed himself down into the wet bottom of the little wooden craft; all three of them made for a tight fit. 'I'll swap with you in just a bit.'

'What, no crack about my moral education?'

'Your moral education's over.' Jean stared up into the sky as the dockside receded and Bug took them out into the canal's heart. 'Now you're going to learn a thing or two about war.'

4

Unseen, undisturbed, Jean quietly paddled them up against the north bank of the canal just south of their temple; the House of Perelandro was nothing more than a dark impression of mass, lightless in the silver fog above their heads.

'Smartly, smartly,' the big man muttered to himself as he brought them abreast of the drainage culvert; it was about a yard up from the water, with an opening five feet in diameter. It led more or less directly to a concealed passage just behind the ladder that led down from the temple itself. Bug slipped a hand past the iron bars at the end of the culvert and tripped the hidden locking mechanism; he then drew a little stiletto from his tunic and prepared to climb in.

'I'll go first,' he said, just before Jean grabbed him by the collar.

'I think not. The Wicked Sisters will go first. You sit down and keep the boat steady.'

Bug did so, pouting, and Locke smiled. Jean pulled himself up into the culvert and began crawling into the darkness.

'You can have the honour of going second, Bug,' said Locke. 'I might need a hand pulling me up.'

When all three of them were wedged safely into the pipe, Locke turned and nudged the little boat back out into mid-canal with his feet. The current would carry it to the Via Camorrazza, lost in the mists, until someone ran into it with a larger boat or claimed it as a windfall. Locke then slid the bars closed and locked them once again; the Gentlemen Bastards actually oiled the hinges on the grate to keep their comings and goings quiet.

They crawled forward into blackness, surrounded by the gentle echoes of their own breathing and the soft noise of scuffing cloth. There was a quiet click as Jean operated the hidden entrance into the burrow, then a line of pale silver light spilled in on them.

Jean stepped out onto the wooden floor of the dim passage; just to his right, the rungs ran up to the entrance beneath what had once been Father Chains' sleeping pallet. Despite Jean's best efforts to move quietly, the floor creaked slightly as he moved forward. Locke slipped out into the passage behind him, his heart pounding.

The illumination was too dim. The walls had been golden for as long as he'd known the place.

Jean crept forward, hatchets bobbing in his fists. At the far end of the passage, he whirled round the corner, crouched low – and then stood straight up, growling, '*Shit.*'

The kitchen had been thoroughly trashed.

The spice cabinets were overturned; broken glass and shattered crockery littered the floor. The storage cupboards hung open, empty; the water barrel had been dumped on the tiles. The gilded chairs were torn apart, thrown into a heap in one corner. The beautiful chandelier that had swung above their heads for as long as any of them had lived within the glass burrow was a total ruin. It dangled now by a few wires; its planets and constellations were smashed, its armillary paths bent beyond all possible repair. The sun that had burned at the heart of it all was cracked like an egg; the alchemical oils that had lit it from within had seeped onto the table.

Locke and Jean stood at the opening to the entrance passage, staring in shock. Bug rounded the corner, hot for action against unseen foes, and came up short between them. 'I . . . Gods. *Gods!*'

'Calo?' Locke abandoned all thoughts of sneaking about. 'Galdo! Calo! Are you here?'

Jean swept aside the heavy curtain over the door that led to the Wardrobe. He didn't say anything or make any noise, but the Wicked Sisters fell out of his hands and clattered to the floor.

The Wardrobe, too, had been ransacked. All the rows of fine clothing and costume garments, all the hats and cravats and breeches and hose, all the waistcoats and vests and thousands of crowns' worth of accessories – all of it was gone. The mirrors were smashed; the masque box was overturned, its contents strewn and broken across the floor.

Calo and Galdo lay beside it, on their backs, staring up in the semi-darkness. Their throats were slashed from ear to ear, a pair of smooth gashes – identical twin wounds.

5

Jean fell forward onto his knees.

Bug tried to squeeze past Locke, who shoved him back into the kitchen with all the feeble strength he could muster, saying, 'No, Bug, don't . . .' But it was already too late. The boy sat down hard against the witchwood table and broke into sobs.

Gods, Locke thought as he stumbled past Jean into the Wardrobe, *gods, I have been a fool. We should have packed up and run.*

'Locke . . .' Jean whispered, and then he sprawled forward onto the ground, fingers grasping, shaking and shuddering as though he were having some sort of fit.

'Jean! Gods, what now . . .' Locke crouched beside the bigger man and placed a hand beneath his round, heavy chin. Jean's pulse was racing . . . He looked up at Locke with wide eyes, his mouth opening and closing, failing to spit out words. Locke's mind raced.

Poison? A trap of some sort? An alchemical trick left behind in the room? Why wasn't he affected – did he feel so miserable already that the symptoms hadn't caught his attention yet? He glanced frantically around the room and his eyes seized on a dark object that lay between the sprawled Sanza twins.

A hand – a severed human hand, grey and dried and leathery. It lay with its palm towards the ceiling and its fingers curled tightly inward. A black thread had been used to sew a name into the dead skin of the palm; the script was crude but nonetheless clear, for it was outlined with the faintest hint of pale blue fire:

JEAN TANNEN

The things I could do to you if I were to stitch your true name. The words of the Falconer returned unbidden to Locke's memory; Jean groaned again, his back arched in pain, and Locke reached down towards the severed hand. A dozen plans whirled in his head – chop it to bits with a hatchet, scald it on the alchemical hearthslab, throw it in the river . . . He had little knowledge of practical sorcery, but surely something was better than nothing.

New footsteps crunched on the broken glass in the kitchen.

'Don't move, boy. I don't think your fat friend can help you at the moment. That's it, just sit right there.'

Locke slid one of Jean's hatchets off the ground, placed it in his left hand, and stepped to the Wardrobe door.

A man was standing at the opening to the entrance hall, a complete stranger to Locke's eyes. He wore a brownish-red oilcloak with the hood thrown back, revealing long stringy black hair and drooping black moustaches. He held a crossbow in his right hand almost casually, pointed at Bug. His eyes widened when Locke appeared in the Wardrobe doorway.

'This ain't right,' he said. 'You're not supposed to be here.'

'You're the Grey King's man,' said Locke. His left hand was up against the back of the wall beside the door, as though he were holding himself up, concealing the hatchet.

'*A* Grey King's man. He's got a few.'

'I will give you any price you name,' said Locke. 'Tell me where he is, what he's doing and how I can avoid the Bondsmage.'

'You can't. I'll give you that one for free. And any price I name? You got no such pull.'

'I have forty-five thousand full crowns.'

'You did,' said the crossbowman, amiably enough. 'You don't any more.'

'One bolt,' said Locke, 'two of us.' Jean groaned from the floor behind him. 'The situation bears thinking on.'

'You don't look so well, and the boy don't look like much. I said *don't move*, boy.'

'One bolt won't be enough,' said Bug, his eyes cold with an anger Locke had never before seen in him. 'You have no idea who you're fucking with.'

'One bolt,' repeated Locke. 'It was for Bug, wasn't it? If I weren't here, you'd have shot him down first thing. Then done for Jean. A commendable arrangement. But now there's two of us, and you're still armed for one.'

'Easy, gents,' said the Grey King's man. 'I don't see either of you eager for a hole in the face.'

'You don't know what you're up against. What we've done.' Bug flicked his wrist slightly, and something fell into his hand from his sleeve. Locke only barely caught the motion – what was that thing? An Orphan's Twist? Oh, gods . . . that wouldn't do any good against a crossbow quarrel . . .

'Bug . . .' he muttered.

344

'Tell him, Locke. Tell him he doesn't know who he's *fucking* with. Tell him he doesn't know what he's going to get! We can take him.'

'First one of you moves an inch, I let fly.' The crossbowman backed off a stride, braced his weapon with his left arm, and swung his aim back and forth between Locke and Bug.

'Bug, don't . . .'

'We can take him, Locke. You and I. He can't stop both of us. Hell, I bet he can't stop *either* of us.'

'Bug, listen . . .'

'Listen to your friend, boy.' The intruder was sweating behind his weapon.

'I'm a Gentleman Bastard,' said Bug, slowly and angrily. 'Nobody messes with us. Nobody gets the best of us. You're going to *pay*!'

Bug sprang up from the floor, raising the hand that held the Orphan's Twist, a look of absolute burning determination on his slender face. The crossbow snapped, and the *whip-crack* of its unleashed cord echoed, impossibly loud, from the enclosed glass walls of the kitchen.

The bolt that was meant to catch Bug between the eyes took him in the neck instead.

He jerked back as though stung by an insect; his knees buckled only halfway into his leap, and he spun back, his useless little Orphan's Twist arcing out of his hands as he fell.

The Grey King's man threw down his crossbow and reached for a blade at his belt, but Locke was preceded out the doorway by the hatchet he'd concealed, flung with all of his rage. Jean could have split the man's head with the blade; Locke barely managed to crack him hard with the ball side of the weapon. But it was enough – the ball caught him just beneath his right eye and he flinched, crying out in pain.

Locke scooped up the crossbow and fell upon the intruder, howling. He swung the stock of the weapon into the man's face, and his nose broke with a spray of blood. He fell, his head cracking against the Elderglass of the passage wall. As he slid down he raised his hands before him in an attempt to ward off Locke's next blow. Locke smashed his fingers with the crossbow; the screams of the two men mingled and echoed in the enclosed space.

345

Locke ended the affair by slamming one curved end of the bow into the man's temple. His head spun, blood spattered against the glass, and he sagged into the passage corner, motionless.

Locke threw down the crossbow, turned on his heel, and ran to Bug.

The bolt had pierced the boy's neck to the right of his windpipe, where it was buried up to its rounded feathers in a spreading cascade of dark blood. Locke knelt and cradled Bug's head in his hands, feeling the tip of the crossbow quarrel protruding from the back of the boy's neck. Slick warmth poured out over Locke's hands; he could feel it coursing out with every ragged breath the boy took. Bug's eyes were wide, and they fixed on him.

'Forgive me,' Locke mumbled through his tears. 'Gods damn me, Bug, this is my fault. We could have run. We should have. My pride . . . you and Calo and Galdo. That bolt should have been for me.'

'Your pride,' the boy whispered. 'Justified. Gentleman . . . Bastard.'

Locke pressed his fingers against Bug's wound, imagining he could somehow dam the flow of blood, but the boy cried out, and Locke withdrew his shaking fingers.

'Justified,' Bug spat. Blood ran out of the corner of his mouth. 'Am I . . . not a second? Not . . . apprentice. Real Gentleman Bastard?'

'You were never a second, Bug. You were never an apprentice.' Locke sobbed, tried to brush the boy's hair back, and was aghast at the bloody handprint he left on Bug's pale forehead. 'You brave little idiot. You brave, stupid little bastard. This is my fault, Bug, please . . . please say this is all my fault.'

'No,' whispered Bug. 'Oh gods . . . hurts . . . hurts so much . . .'

The boy's breathing stopped while Locke held him. He said nothing more.

Locke stared upward. It seemed to him that the alien glass ceiling that had shed warm light on his life for so many long years now took a knowing pleasure in showing him nothing but dark red: the reflection of the floor on which he sat with the motionless body of Bug, still bleeding in his arms.

He might have stayed there, locked in a reverie of grief all night – but Jean groaned loudly in the next room.

Locke remembered himself, shuddered, and set Bug's head down as gently as he could. He stumbled to his feet and lifted Jean's hatchet up off the ground once more. His motions were slow and unsteady as he walked back into the Wardrobe, raised the hatchet above his head, and brought it down with all the force he could muster on the sorcerous hand that lay between the bodies of Calo and Galdo.

The faint blue fire dimmed as the hatchet blade bit down into the desiccated flesh; Jean gasped loudly behind him, which Locke took as an encouraging sign. Methodically, maliciously, he hacked the hand into smaller pieces. He chopped at leathery skin and brittle bones until the black threads that had spelled Jean's name were separated and the blue glow faded entirely.

He stood staring down at the Sanzas until he heard Jean moving behind him.

'Oh, Bug. Oh, gods damn it.' The big man stumbled to his feet and groaned. 'Forgive me, Locke. I just couldn't . . . couldn't move.'

'There's nothing to forgive.' Locke spoke as though the sound of his own voice pained him. 'It was a trap. It had your name on it, that thing the mage left for us. They guessed you'd be coming back.'

'A . . . a severed hand? A human hand, with my name stitched into it?'

'Yes.'

'A Hanged Man's Grasp,' said Jean, staring at the fragments of flesh and at the bodies of the Sanzas. 'I . . . read about them, when I was younger. Gods.'

'Neatly removing you from the situation,' said Locke, coldly. 'So one assassin hiding up above could come down, kill Bug and finish you.'

'Just one?'

'Just one.' Locke sighed. 'Jean. In the temple rooms up above. Our lamp oil . . . please fetch it down.'

'Lamp oil?'

'All of it,' said Locke. 'Hurry.'

Jean paused in the kitchen, knelt, and slid Bug's eyes closed with his left hand. Then he stumbled back to his feet, wiping away tears, and ran off to carry out Locke's request.

Locke walked slowly back into the kitchen, dragging the body of Calo Sanza with him. He placed the corpse beside the table, folded its arms across its chest, knelt and kissed its forehead.

The man in the corner moaned and moved his head. Locke rose, kicked him once in the face, then returned to the Wardrobe for Galdo's body. In short order, he had the Sanzas laid out neatly in the middle of the ransacked kitchen, with Bug beside them. Unable to bear the glassy stare of the twins' eyes, Locke covered all the bodies with silk tablecloths from a smashed cabinet.

'I promise you a death-offering, brothers,' Locke whispered when he'd finished. 'I promise you an offering that will make the gods take notice. An offering that will make the shades of all the Dukes and Capas of Camorr feel like paupers. An offering in blood and gold and fire. This I swear by Aza Guilla who gathers us, and by Perelandro who sheltered us, and by the Crooked Warden who places his finger on the scale when our souls are weighed. This I swear to Chains, who kept us safe. I beg forgiveness that I failed to do the same.'

Locke forced himself to stand up and return to work.

A few old garments had been thrown into the Wardrobe corners; Locke gathered them up, along with a few components from the spilled masque box; a handful of false moustaches, a bit of false beard, some stage adhesive. These he threw into the entrance corridor to the burrow, and then he peeked into the vault. As he'd suspected, it was utterly empty. Not a single coin remained in either well or on any shelf. No doubt the sacks loaded onto the wagon earlier had vanished as well.

From the sleeping quarters at the back of the burrow he gathered sheets and blankets, then parchment, books and scrolls; he threw these into a heap on the dining room table. At last, he stood over the Grey King's assassin, his hands and clothes covered in blood, and he waited for Jean to return.

6

'Wake up,' said Locke. 'I know you can hear me.'

The Grey King's assassin blinked, spat blood, and tried to push himself further back into the corner with his feet.

Locke stared down at him, a curious reversal of the natural way of things; the assassin was well muscled, a head taller than Locke, and Locke was particularly unimposing after the events of this night. But everything frightening about him was concentrated in his eyes, and they bore down on the assassin with a bright, hard hatred.

Jean stood a few paces behind him, a bag over his shoulder, his hatchets tucked into his belt.

'Do you want to live?' asked Locke.

The assassin said nothing.

'It was a simple question, and I won't repeat it again. Do you want to live?'

'I . . . yes,' the man said, softly.

'Then it pleases me to deny you your preference.' Locke knelt beside him, reached beneath his own undertunic, and drew forth a little leather pouch that hung by a cord around his neck.

'Once,' said Locke, 'when I was old enough to understand what I'd done, I was ashamed to be a murderer. Even after I'd paid the debt, I wore this. All these years, to remind me.'

He pulled the pouch away from himself, snapping the cord. He opened it, and removed a single small white shark's tooth. He grabbed the assassin's right hand, placed the pouch and the tooth on his palm, and then squeezed the man's broken fingers together around them. The assassin writhed and screamed. Locke punched him.

'But now,' he said, 'now I'll be a murderer once again. I will set myself to slay until every last Grey King's man is gone. You hear me, cocksucker? I will have the Bondsmage and I will have the Grey King, and if all the powers of Camorr and Karthain and Hell itself oppose me, it will be *nothing* – nothing but a longer trail of corpses between me and your master.'

'You're mad,' the assassin whispered. 'You'll never beat the Grey King.'

'I'll do more than that. Whatever he's planning, I will *unmake* it. Whatever he desires, I will *destroy* it. Every reason you came down here to murder my friends will evaporate. Every Grey King's man will die for nothing, starting with you.'

Jean Tannen stepped forward and grabbed the assassin with one hand, hauling him to his knees. Jean dragged him into the kitchen, oblivious to the man's pleas for mercy. The assassin was flung against the table, beside the three covered bodies and the pile of cloth and paper, and he became aware of the cloying smell of lamp oil.

Without a word, Jean brought the ball of one of his hatchets down on the assassin's right knee; the man howled. Another swift crack shattered his left kneecap, and the assassin rolled over to shield himself from further blows – but none fell.

'When you see the Crooked Warden,' said Locke, twisting something in his hands, 'tell him that Locke Lamora learns slowly, but he learns well. And when you see my friends, you tell them that there are more of you on the way.'

He opened his hands and let an object fall to the ground; it was a piece of knotted cord, charcoal-grey, with white filaments jutting out from one end. Alchemical twist-match – when the white threads were exposed to air for several moments, they would spark, igniting the heavier, longer-burning grey cord they were wrapped in. It splashed into the edge of a pool of lamp oil.

Locke and Jean went up through the concealed hatch into the old stone temple, letting the ladder cover fall shut with a bang behind them.

In the glass burrow beneath their feet, the flames began to rise.

First the flames, and then the screams.

INTERLUDE:
The Tale of the Old Handball Players

I

Handball is a Therin pastime, as cherished by the people of the southern city-states as it is scorned by the Vadrans in their kingdom to the north (although Vadrans in the south seem to love it well enough). Scholars belittle the idea that the game had its origin in the era of the Therin Throne, when the mad emperor Sartirana would amuse himself by bowling with the severed heads of his executed victims. They do not, however, deny it out of hand, for it is rarely wise to underestimate the Therin Throne's excesses without the very firmest sort of proof.

Handball is a rough sport for the rough classes, played between two teams on any reasonably flat surface that can be found. The ball itself is a rubbery mass of tree latex and leather about six inches in diameter; the field is somewhere between twenty and thirty yards long, with straight lines marked (usually with chalk) at either end. Each team tries to move the ball across the other side's goal line; the ball must be held in both hands of a player as he runs, steps or dives across the end of the field.

The ball may be passed freely from player to player, but it must not be touched with any part of the body below the waist, and it must not be allowed to touch the ground, or possession will revert to the other team. A neutral adjudicator, referred to as the Justice, attempts to enforce the rules at any given match, with varying degrees of success.

Matches are sometimes played between teams representing entire neighbourhoods or islands in Camorr, and the drinking, wagering and brawling surrounding these affairs always starts several days beforehand and ends when the match is but a memory. Indeed, the match is frequently an island of relative calm and goodwill in a sea of chaos.

It is said that once, in the reign of the first Duke Andrakana, a match was arranged between the Cauldron and Catchfire. One young fisherman, Markos, was reckoned the finest handballer in the Cauldron, while his closest friend Gervain was thought of as the best and fairest handball Justice in the city. Naturally, the adjudication of the match was given over to Gervain.

The match was held in one of the dusty, abandoned public squares of the Ashfall district with a thousand screaming, barely sober spectators from each side crowding the wrecked houses and alleys that surrounded the open space. It was a bitter contest, close-fought all the way. At the very end the Cauldron was behind by one point, with the final sands trickling out of the hourglass that kept the time.

Markos, bellowing madly, took the ball in hand and bashed his way through an entire line of Catchfire defenders. With one eye blackened, with his hands bruised purple, with blood streaming from his elbows and knees, he flung himself desperately for the goal line as the very last second of the game fell away.

Markos lay upon the stones, his arms at full extension, with the ball touching but not quite crossing the chalked line. Gervain pushed aside the crowding players, stared down at Markos for a few seconds, and then said; 'Not across the line. No point.'

The riot and the celebration that broke out afterwards were indistinguishable from one another; some say the yellowjackets killed a dozen men while quelling it, others say it was closer to a hundred. At least three of the city's Capas died in a little war that broke out over reneged bets, and Markos vowed never to speak to Gervain again. The two had fished together on the same boat since boyhood; now the Cauldron as a whole warned Gervain's entire family that their lives wouldn't be worth sausage casings if any one of them set foot in that district ever again.

Twenty years passed, thirty, thirty-five. Old Andrakana died and the first Duke Nicovante rose to eminence in the city. Markos and Gervain saw nothing of one another during this time; Gervain travelled to Jeresh for many years, where he rowed galleys and hunted devilfish for pay. Eventually, homesick, he took passage for Camorr. At the dockside he was astounded to see a man stepping off a little fishing boat, a man weathered and grey and bearded just like himself, but certainly none other than his old friend Markos.

'Markos,' he cried. 'Markos, from the Cauldron! Markos! The gods are kind! Surely you remember me?'

Markos turned to regard the traveller who stood before him; he stared for a few seconds. Then, without warning, he drew a long-bladed fisherman's knife from his belt and buried it, up to the hilt, in Gervain's stomach. As Gervain stared down in shock, Markos gave him a shove sideways, and the former handball Justice fell into the water of Camorr Bay, never to surface again.

'Not across the line, my *arse*,' Markos spat.

Verrari, Karthani and Lashani nod knowingly when they hear this story. They assume it to be apocryphal, but it confirms something they claim to know in their hearts – that Camorri are all gods-damned crazy.

Camorri, on the other hand, regard it as a valuable warning against procrastinating in matters of revenge – or, if one cannot get satisfaction immediately, on the merits of having a long memory.

Chapter Eleven

At the Court of Capa Raza

I

They had to steal another boat, Locke having so profligately disposed of their first. On any other night he would have had a good laugh about that.

And so would Bug and Calo and Galdo, he told himself.

Locke and Jean drifted south between the Narrows and the Mara Camorrazza, hunched over in old cloaks from the floor of the Wardrobe, locked away from the rest of the city in the mist. The soft flickering lights and murmuring voices in the distance seemed to Locke artefacts of an alien life he'd left long ago, not elements of the city he'd lived in for as long as he could remember.

'I am such a fool,' he muttered. He was lay along a gunwale, head swimming, feeling the dry heaves rise up again from the battered pit of his stomach.

'If you say that one more time,' said Jean, 'I will throw you into the water and row the boat over your head.'

'I should have let us run.'

'Perhaps,' said Jean. 'But perhaps not everything miserable that happens to us stems directly from one of your choices, brother. Perhaps bad tidings come regardless of what we do. Perhaps if we'd run, that Bondsmage would have hunted us down upon the road, and scattered our bones somewhere between here and Talisham.'

'And yet—'

'We live,' said Jean forcefully. 'We live and we may avenge them. You had the right idea when you did for that Grey King's man back in the burrow. The questions now are *Why*, and *What next?* Quit acting like you've been breathing Wraithstone smoke. I need your wits, Locke. I need the Thorn of Camorr.'

'Let me know when you find him. He's a fucking fairy tale.'

'He's sitting here in this boat with me. If you're not him now,

354

you must become him. The Thorn is the man who can beat the Grey King. I can't do it alone; I know that much. Why would the Grey King do this to us? What does it bring him? Think, damn it!'

'Too much to guess at,' said Locke. His voice regained a bit of its vigour as he pondered. 'But . . . narrow the question. Let's consider the means. We saw one of his men beneath the temple; I saw another man when I was taken for the first time. So we know he had at least two working for him, in addition to the Bondsmage.'

'Does he strike you as a sloppy operator?'

'No.' Locke rubbed his hands together. 'No, everything he did seemed to me to be as intricate as Verrari clockwork.'

'Yet he sent only one man down into the burrow.'

'Yes – the Sanzas were already dead; I was thought to be dead, you would walk into another trap set by the Bondsmage, and it would have been a crossbow quarrel for Bug. Deftly done. Quick and cruel.'

'But why not send two men? Why not three? Why not be *absolutely* sure of the issue?' Jean gave the water a few gentle strokes to hold their position against the current. 'I cannot believe he suddenly became lazy, at the very culmination of his scheme.'

'Perhaps,' said Locke, 'perhaps . . . he needed what other men he had elsewhere, very badly. Perhaps one was all he could spare.' Locke gasped and slammed his right fist down into the open palm of his left hand. 'Perhaps we weren't the culmination of his scheme after all.'

'What, then?'

'Not what, *who*. Who has he been attacking all these months? Jean, Barsavi believes the Grey King to be dead. What will he do tonight?'

'He . . . he'll throw a revel. Just like he used to do on the Day of Changes. He'll celebrate.'

'At the Floating Grave,' said Locke. 'He'll throw the doors open, haul in casks – gods, real ones this time. He'll summon his whole court. All the Right People, drunk three deep along the causeway and the wharfs of the Wooden Waste. Just like the good old days.'

'So the Grey King faked his own death to lure Barsavi into throwing a revel?'

'It's not the revel,' said Locke. 'It's the people. All the Right

355

People. That's it, gods, that's it! Barsavi will appear before his people tonight for the first time in months. Do you understand? All the gangs, all the *garristas* will witness anything that happens there.'

'Which does what for the Grey King?'

'The fucker has a flair for the dramatic. I'd say Barsavi's in a heap of shit. Row, Jean. Get me down to the Cauldron right now. I can cross to the Waste myself. I need to be at the Floating Grave, with haste.'

'Have you lost your mind? If the Grey King and his men are still prowling, they'll kill you for sure. And if Barsavi sees you, you're supposed to be nearly dead of a stomach flux! You *are* nearly dead, of more than that!'

'They won't see Locke Lamora,' said Locke, fumbling with some of the items he'd managed to salvage from the masque box. He held a false beard up to his chin and grinned, sending twinges of pain along his jaw. 'My hair's going to be grey for a few days, since the removal salve is burning up as we speak. I'll throw on some soot and put up the hood, and I'll be just another skinny nobody with bruises all over his face, come looking for some free wine from the Capa.'

'You should rest; you've had your life damn near pounded out of you. You're a complete mess. I didn't mean you should go running off right this instant.'

'I do ache in places I didn't previously realise I owned,' said Locke, applying adhesive paste to his chin with his fingers. 'But it can't be helped. This is all the disguise gear we have left; we've got no money, no wardrobe, no more temple, no more friends. And you only have a few hours, at best, to go to ground and find us a place to stay before the Grey King's men realise one of their number is missing.'

'But still—'

'I'm half your size, Jean. You can't pamper me on this one. I can go unseen; you'll be obvious as the rising sun. My suggestion is that you find a hovel in Ashfall, clear out the rats and leave some of our signs in the area. Just scrawl soot on the walls. I'll find you when I'm done.'

'But—'

'Jean, you wanted the Thorn of Camorr. You've got him.' Locke jammed the false beard onto his chin and pressed until the adhesive ceased tingling, letting him know that it was dry. 'Take me to the Cauldron and let me off. Something's about to happen at the Floating Grave, and I need to see what it is. Everything that bastard has done to us comes down to the next few hours – if it isn't happening already.'

2

It could be said, on several levels of truthful meaning, that Vencarlo Barsavi outdid himself with the celebrations for his victory over the murderer of his daughter.

The Floating Grave was thrown open; the guards remained at their posts, but discipline slackened agreeably. Huge alchemical lanterns were hauled up under the silk awnings on the topmost decks of the harbour-locked galleon; they lit up the Wooden Waste beneath the dark sky and shone like beacons through the fog.

Runners were sent out to the Last Mistake for food and wine; the tavern was rapidly emptied of all its edibles, most of its casks and every single one of its patrons. They streamed towards the Wooden Waste, drunk or sober, united in curiosity and expectation.

The guards on the quay eyed the guests pouring in but did little else; men and women without obvious weapons were passed through without so much as a cursory search. Flush with victory, the Capa had decided to be magnanimous in more ways than one. This was to Locke's benefit; hooded and bearded and thoroughly begrimed, he slipped in with a huge crowd of Cauldron cut-throats making their rowdy way across the walkway to Barsavi's galleon, which was lit like a pleasure-galley from some romantic tale of the pashas of the Bronze Sea.

The Floating Grave was packed with men and women; Capa Barsavi sat on his raised chair, surrounded by his inner circle: his red-faced, shouting sons, his most powerful surviving *garristas*, his quiet, watchful Berangias twins. Locke had to push and shove and curse to make his way into the heart of the fortress; he wedged himself into a corner near the main doors to the ballroom and watched, aching and uncomfortable but grateful just to be able to claim a vantage point.

The balconies were spilling over with toughs from all the gangs in Camorr – the rowdiness was growing by the minute. The heat was incredible, and the smell; Locke felt pressed against the wall by the weight of odours. Wet wool and sweated-through cotton, wine and wine-breath, hair oils and leather.

It was just past the first hour of the morning when Barsavi suddenly rose from his chair and held up a single hand.

Attentiveness spread outwards like a wave; Right People nudged one another into silence and pointed to the Capa. It took less than a minute for the echoing chaos of the celebration to subside to a soft murmur. Barsavi nodded appreciatively.

'I trust we're enjoying ourselves?'

There was a general outburst of cheers, applause, and foot-stomping. Locke privately wondered how wise that really was in a ship of any sort. He was careful to applaud along with the crowd.

'Feels marvellous to be out from under a cloud, doesn't it?'

Another cheer. Locke itched under his temporary beard, now damp with sweat. There was a sudden sharp pain in his stomach, right where one of the younger Barsavis had given him particular consideration with a fist. The heat and the smells were triggering strange tickly feelings of nausea in the back of his throat, and he'd had enough of that particular sensation to last for the rest of his life. Sourly, he coughed into his hands and prayed for just a few more hours of strength.

One of the Berangias sisters stepped over beside the Capa, her sharks' teeth bangles shining in the light of the hall's chandeliers, and whispered into his ear. He listened for a few seconds and then he smiled.

'Cheryn,' he shouted, 'proposes that I allow her and her sister to entertain us. Shall I?'

The answering cheer was twice as forceful (and twice as genuine, to Locke's ears) as anything yet heard. The wooden walls reverberated with it; Locke flinched.

'Let's have a Teeth Show, then!'

All was chaos for the next few minutes; dozens of Barsavi's men pushed revellers back, clearing a square area at the centre of the floor about ten yards across. Revellers were pressed up the stairs until the balconies creaked beneath their weight; observation holes were cranked open so those on the top deck could peer down at the proceedings. Locke was pushed back into his corner more firmly than ever.

Men with hooked poles drew up wooden panels in the floor, revealing the dark water of Camorr Bay; a thrill of anticipation and alarm passed through the crowd at the thought of what might be swimming down there. *The unquiet spirits of eight Full Crowns, for one thing*, thought Locke.

As the final panels in the centre of the opening were removed, almost everyone present could see the little support platforms on which they'd rested, not one inch wider than a man's hand-spread. They were spaced about five feet apart. Barsavi's arena for his own private Teeth Shows; a challenge for any *contrarequialla*, even a pair as experienced as the Berangias sisters.

Cheryn and Raiza, old hands at teasing a crowd, were stripping out of their leather doublets, bracers and collars. They took their graceful time while the Capa's subjects hooted approval, hoisted cups and glasses, and in some cases even shouted unlikely propositions at them.

Anjais hurried forward with a little packet of alchemical powder in his hands; he dumped this into the water, then took a prudent step back. This was the 'summons', a potent mix of substances that would rouse a shark's ire and maintain it for the duration of the contest. Blood in the water could attract and enrage a shark, but the summons would make it utterly drunk with the urge to attack – to leap, thrash and roll at the women jumping back and forth between their little platforms.

The Berangias sisters stepped forward to nearly the edge of the artificial pool, holding the traditional weapons, the pick-head axes and the short javelins. Anjais and Pachero stood behind them and just to their left; the Capa remained standing by his chair, clapping his hands and grinning broadly.

A black fin broke the surface of the pool; a tail thrashed and the electric atmosphere in the crowd intensified. Locke could feel it washing over him – lust and fear entwined, a powerful, animalistic sensation. The spectators had backed off about two yards from the edges of the pool, but some in the front ranks were still nervous, and a few were trying to push their way back through the crowd, to the delight and derision of those around them.

In truth, the shark couldn't have been longer than five or six feet; some of those at the Shifting Revel reached twice that length. Nothing that large could be used for the Capa's private pool. Still, a fish like that could easily maim on the leap, and if it dragged a person down into the water with it, raw size would mean little in such an uneven contest.

The Berangias sisters threw up their arms, then turned as one to the Capa. The sister on the right (Raiza? Cheryn? Locke had never learned the trick of telling them apart, and at the thought his heart ached for the Sanzas) beckoned to him. Playing deftly to the crowd, Barsavi put up his hands and looked around at his court; when they cheered him on, he stepped down between the ladies and received a kiss on the cheek from each of them.

The water stirred just before the three of them; a sleek black shadow swept past the edge of the pool, then dived down into the lightless depths. Locke could feel five hundred hearts skip a beat, and the breath in five hundred throats catch; his own concentration seemed to peak, and he caught every detail of that moment as though it were frozen before him, from the eager smile on Barsavi's round red face to the rippling reflection of chandelier light on the water.

'Camorr!' cried the Berangias sister to the Capa's right. Again, the noise of the crowd died, this time as though one gigantic windpipe had been slit. Five hundred pairs of eyes were fixed on the Capa and his bodyguards.

'We dedicate this death,' she continued, 'to Capa Vencarlo Barsavi, our lord and patron!'

'Well does he deserve it,' said the other.

The shark exploded out of the pool immediately before them, a sleek dark devilish thing, with black lidless eyes and white teeth gaping; a ten-foot fountain of water rose up with it, and it half-somersaulted in mid-air, falling forward, falling . . .

Directly onto Capa Barsavi.

Barsavi put up his arms to shield himself; the shark came down with its mouth wide open around one of them. The fish's muscle-heavy body slammed hard against the wood floor, yanking Barsavi down with it. Those implacable jaws squeezed tight, and the Capa

360

screamed as blood gushed from just beneath his right shoulder, running out across the floor and down the shark's blunt snout.

His sons dashed forward to his aid. The Berangias sister to the right looked down at the shark, shifted her weight fluidly to a fighting stance, raised her gleaming axe, and whirled with all the strength of her upper body behind the blow.

Her blade smashed Pachero Barsavi's head just above his left ear; the tall man's optics flew off and he staggered forward, his skull caved in, dead before his knees hit the deck.

The crowd screamed and surged, and Locke prayed to the Benefactor to preserve him long enough to make sense of whatever happened next.

Anjais gaped at his struggling father and his falling brother. Before he could utter a single word the other Berangias stepped up behind him, reached around to press her javelin shaft up beneath his chin, and buried the spike of her axe in the back of his head. He spat blood and toppled forward, unmoving.

The shark writhed and tore at the Capa's right arm, while he screamed and beat at its snout until his left hand was scraped bloody by the creature's abrasive skin. With a final sickening wrench, the shark tore the arm completely off and slid backwards into the water, leaving a broad streak of blood on the wooden deck behind it. Barsavi rolled away, spraying blood from the stump of his arm, staring at the bodies of his sons in uncomprehending terror. He tried to stumble up.

One of the Berangias sisters kicked him back to the deck.

There was a tumult behind the fallen Capa; several Red Hands rushed forward, weapons drawn, hollering incoherently at the Berangias sisters. What happened next was a blurry, violent mystery to Locke's eyes, but the half-clothed Berangias sisters dealt with half a dozen armoured men with a brutality the shark would have envied. Javelins flew, axes whirled, throats opened and blood spurted. The last Red Hand was slumping to the deck, his face a jagged scarlet ruin, perhaps five seconds after the first had charged forward.

There was fighting on the balconies, now – Locke could see people pushing their way through the crowds, people in heavy grey oilcloaks armed with crossbows and long knives. Some of Barsavi's guards stood back and did nothing, some attempted to flee, others were taken from behind by their cloaked assailants and killed out of hand. Crossbow strings sang; bolts whirred through the air. There was a resounding *bang* to Locke's left; the great doors to the ballroom had slammed shut, seemingly of their own accord, and the clockwork mechanisms within were whirring and clicking. People battered at them uselessly.

One of Barsavi's men pushed his way out of a crowd of panicking, shoving Right People and raised a crossbow at the Berangias sisters, who stood over the wounded Capa like lionesses guarding a kill. A dark streak fell on him from out of the shadowy corners of the ceiling; there was an inhuman screech, and the shot went far awry, hissing above the sisters' heads to strike the far wall. The guard batted furiously at the brown shape, which flapped back into the air on long curving wings – then he put a hand to his neck, staggered, and fell flat on his face.

'Remain where you are,' boomed a voice with an air of assured authority. 'Remain where you are and attend.'

The command had a greater effect than Locke would have expected; he even felt his own fear dimming, his own urge to flee vanishing. The wailing and screaming of the crowd quietened and an eerie calm rapidly fell on what had been not two minutes earlier the exultant court of Capa Barsavi.

The hairs on the back of Locke's neck stood up; the change in the crowd was not natural. He might have missed it but he'd been under its influence before – there was sorcery in the air. He shivered despite himself. *Gods, I hope coming to see this was as wise an idea as it seemed.*

The Grey King was suddenly there with them.

It was as though he'd stepped out of a door that opened from thin air, just beside the Capa's chair. He wore his cloak and mantle, he stepped with a hunter's easy assurance across the bodies of the Red Hands, and at his side strode the Falconer, with a gauntletted fist held up to the air. Vestris settled upon it, pulled in her wings and screeched triumphantly. There were gasps and murmurs in the crowd.

'No harm will come to you,' said the Grey King. 'I've done what harm I came to do tonight.' He stepped up between the Berangias sisters, and he looked down at Capa Barsavi, who was writhing and moaning on the deck at his feet.

'Hello, Vencarlo. Gods, but you've looked better.'

Then the Grey King swept back his hood, and once again Locke saw those intense eyes, the hard lines of the face, the dark hair with streaks of grey, the lean rugged countenance. And he gasped, because he finally realised what had nagged him during his first meeting with the Grey King – that odd familiarity.

All the pieces of that particular puzzle were before him. The Grey King stood between the Berangias sisters, and it was now plain to Locke's eyes that they were siblings – very nearly triplets.

3

'Camorr,' shouted the Grey King, 'the reign of the Barsavi family is at an end!'

His people had taken firm control of the crowd; there were perhaps two dozen of them, in addition to the Berangias sisters and the Falconer. The fingers of the mage's left hand curled and twisted and flexed, and he muttered under his breath as he gazed around the room. Whatever spell he was weaving did its part to calm the crowd, but no doubt the three black rings visible on his exposed wrist arrested the attention of the revellers as well.

'In fact,' said the Grey King, 'the Barsavi family is at an end. No more sons or daughters, Vencarlo. I wanted you to know, before you died, that I had wiped the disease of your loins from the face of the world.

'In the past,' he shouted, 'you have known me as the Grey King. Well, now I am out of the shadows. That name is not to be spoken again. Henceforth, you may call me . . . *Capa Raza*.'

Raza, thought Locke. *Throne Therin for 'vengeance'. Not subtle.*

Very little about the Grey King, he was learning to his sorrow, actually was.

Capa Raza, as he now styled himself, bent over Barsavi, who was weak with blood loss, whimpering. Raza reached down and pried the Capa's signet ring from his pale remaining hand; he held this up for all the crowd to behold, then slid it onto the fourth finger of his own left hand.

'Vencarlo,' said Capa Raza, 'I have waited so many years to see you like this. Now your children are dead, and your office is passed to me, along with your fortress and your treasure. Every legacy you thought to leave to someone of your name is in my hands. I have erased you from history itself. Does that suit your fancy, scholar? Like an errant chalk-mark upon a slate, I have wiped you clean away.

'Do you remember the slow death of your wife? How she trusted your Berangias sisters so? How they would bring her meals to her? She didn't die of stomach tumours. It was black alchemy. I merely wanted a little something to whet my appetite during the long years I spent building this death for you.' Capa Raza grinned with demonic mirth. 'Lingered, didn't she? I heard it was very painful. Well, it wasn't an act of the gods, Vencarlo. Like everyone else you loved – she died because of you.'

'Why?' Barsavi's voice was weak and small.

Capa Raza knelt beside him, cradled his head almost tenderly, and whispered in his ear for several long moments. Barsavi stared up at him when he was finished, jaw slack, eyes wide with disbelief, and Raza nodded slowly.

He yanked Barsavi's head up and backward by his beards. A stiletto fell into his other hand from within his sleeve, and he rammed it into the underside of Vencarlo Barsavi's exposed chins, all the way to the hilt. Barsavi kicked weakly, just once.

Capa Raza stood up, withdrawing the blade. The Berangias sisters grabbed their former master by his lapels and slid him into the dark water of the bay, which received his body as readily as it had taken his victims and his enemies, over all the long years of his rule.

'One Capa rules Camorr,' said Raza, 'and now it is me. Now it is me!' He raised the bloody stiletto over his head and gazed around the room, as though inviting disagreement. When none came forth, he continued.

'It is not my intention merely to remove Barsavi, but to replace him. My reasons are my own. So now there is business between myself and all the rest of you, all the Right People.' He looked slowly around, his arms folded before him, his chin thrust out like a conquering general in an old bronze sculpture.

'You must hear my words, and then come to a decision.'

'Nothing that you have achieved shall be taken from you,' he continued. 'Nothing that you have worked or suffered for will be revoked. I admire the arrangements Barsavi built, as much as I hated the man who built them. So this is my word.

'All remains as it was. All *garristas* and their gangs will control the same territories; they will pay the same tribute, on the same day, once a week. The Secret Peace remains; as it was death to breach under Barsavi's rule, so shall it be death under mine.

'I claim all of Barsavi's offices and powers. I claim all of his dues. In justice, I must therefore claim his debts and his responsibilities. If any man can show that he was owed by Barsavi, he will now be owed the same by Capa Raza. First among them is Eymon Danzier . . . Step forward, Eymon.'

There was a murmur and a ripple in the crowd to Capa Raza's right; after a few moments the skinny man Locke remembered very well from the Echo Hole was pushed forward, obviously terrified. His bony knees all but knocked together.

'Eymon, be at ease.' Raza held out his left hand, palm down, fingers splayed, as Barsavi had once done to every single person watching. 'Kneel to me and name me your Capa.'

Shaking, Eymon dropped to one knee, took Raza's hand and kissed the ring. His lips came away wet with Barsavi's blood. 'Capa Raza,' he said, in an almost pleading tone.

'You did a very brave thing at the Echo Hole, Eymon. A thing few men would have done in your place. Barsavi was right to promise you much for it – I will make good on that promise. You will have a thousand crowns and a suite of rooms, and such comforts that men with many long years of life ahead of them will pray to the gods to put them in your place.'

'I . . . I . . .' Tears were actually pouring out of the man's eyes. 'I wasn't sure what you would . . . Thank you, Capa Raza. Thank you.'

'I wish you much pleasure, for the service you have given me.'

'Then . . . it wasn't . . . it wasn't you, at the Echo Hole, if I may ask, Capa Raza.'

'Oh, no, Eymon.' Raza laughed, a deep and pleasant sound. 'No, that was but an illusion.'

In the far corner of the Floating Grave's ballroom, that particular illusion fumed silently to himself, clenching and unclenching his fists.

'Tonight you have seen me with blood on my hands,' Raza shouted, 'and you have seen them open in what I hope will be seen as true generosity. I am not a difficult man to get along with; I want us to prosper together. Serve me as you served Barsavi, and I know it will be so. I ask you, *garristas*, who will bend the knee and kiss my ring as your Capa?'

'The Rum Hounds,' shouted a short, slender woman at the front of the crowd on the ballroom floor.

'The Falselight Cutters,' cried another man, 'the Falselight Cutters say aye!'

That doesn't make any gods-damned sense, thought Locke. *The Grey King murdered their old garristas. Are they playing some sort of game with him?*

'The Wise Mongrels!'

'The Catchfire Barons.'

'The Black Eyes.'

'The Full Crowns,' came another voice, and an echoing chorus of affirmations. 'The Full Crowns stand with Capa Raza!'

Suddenly Locke wanted to laugh out loud. He put a fist to his mouth and turned the noise into a stifled cough. It was suddenly obvious – the Grey King hadn't just been knocking off Barsavi's most loyal *garristas*. He must have been cutting deals with their subordinates, beforehand. Gods, there had been more Grey King's men in the room out of costume than in . . . waiting for the evening's real show to commence.

The half-dozen men and women stepped forward and knelt before Raza at the edge of the pool, wherein the shark hadn't shown as much as a fin since forcibly relieving Barsavi of his arm. *The damned Bondsmage certainly has a way with animals*, Locke thought, with mixed anger and jealousy. He found himself feeling very small indeed before each new display of the Falconer's arts.

One by one the *garristas* knelt and made their obeisance to the Capa, kissing his ring and saying 'Capa Raza' with real enthusiasm. Five more stepped forward to kneel directly after them, apparently giving in to the direction they felt events to be slipping. Locke calculated rapidly; with just the pledges he'd already received, Raza

366

could now call five or six hundred Right People his own. His overt powers of enforcement had increased substantially.

'Then we are introduced,' said Raza to the entire crowd. 'We are met, and you know my intentions. You are free to return to your business.'

The Falconer made a few gestures with his free hand; the clockwork mechanisms within the doors to the hall clattered in reverse, and the doors clicked open.

'I give the undecided three nights,' Capa Raza shouted. 'Three nights to come to me here and bend the knee, and swear to me as they did to Barsavi. I devoutly wish to be lenient – but I warn you now is not the time to anger me. You have seen my work. You know I have resources Barsavi lacked. You know I can be merciless when I am moved to displeasure. If you are not content serving beneath me, if you think it might be wiser or more exciting to oppose me, I will make one suggestion. Pack what fortune you have and leave the city by the landward gates. If you wish to part ways, no harm will come to you from my people. For three nights, I give you my leave and my parole.

'After that,' he said, lowering his voice, 'after that, I will make what examples I must. Go now, and speak to your *pezon*. Speak to your friends, and to other *garristas*. Tell them what I have said; tell them I wait to receive their pledges.'

Some of the crowd began to disperse out the doors; others, wiser perhaps, began to line up before Capa Raza. The former Grey King took each pledge at the heart of a circle of corpses; the Red Hands and the Barsavi sons still lay bleeding on the deck where they'd fallen.

Locke waited for several minutes until the press had lessened, until the solid torrent of hot, smelly humanity had decreased to a few thick streams, and then he moved towards the entrance. His feet felt as heavy as his head; fatigue seemed to be gaining on him rapidly.

There were corpses here and there on the floor – Barsavi's guards, the loyal ones. Locke could see them now as the crowds continued to thin. Just beside the tall doors to the hall lay Bernell, who'd grown old in Capa Barsavi's service. His throat was slashed; he lay in a pool of his own blood, and his fighting knives remained in their sheaths. He'd not had time to pull them.

Locke sighed. He paused for a moment in the doorway and stared back at Capa Raza and the Falconer. The Bondsmage seemed to stare right back at him, and for the tiniest instant Locke's heart raced, but the sorcerer said nothing and did nothing. He merely continued to stand watch over the ritual as Capa Raza's new subjects kissed his ring. Vestris yawned, snapping her beak briefly open as though the affairs of the un-winged bored her terribly. Locke hurried out.

All the guards that watched the revellers as they left the galleon and filed up the walkway to the quay were Raza's men; they hadn't bothered to move the bodies that lay on the ground at their feet. Some merely watched coldly; others nodded companionably. Locke recognized more than a few of them.

'Three nights, ladies and gents, three nights,' said one. 'Tell your friends. You're Capa Raza's now. No need to be alarmed; just do as you've always done.'

So now we have some answers, thought Locke. *Forgive me again, Nazca. I couldn't have done anything even if I'd had the courage to try.*

He clutched his aching stomach as he shambled along, head down. No guard spared a second glance for the skinny, bearded, dirty old beggar; there were a thousand in Camorr just like him, a thousand interchangeable losers, hopeless and penniless at the very bottom of the many levels of misery the underworld had to offer.

Now to hide. And to plan.

'Please yourself with what you've stolen tonight, you son of a bitch,' Locke whispered to himself when he'd made his way past the last of Raza's guards. 'Please yourself very well – the better to see the loss in your eyes when I put the fucking dagger in your heart.'

5

But one can only get so far on thoughts of vengeance alone. The sharp pains in his stomach started up again about halfway through his slow, lonely walk to the Ashfall district.

His stomach ached and churned and growled; the night seemed to turn darker around him, and the narrow, fog-softened city horizons tilted strangely, as though he were drunk. Locke staggered and clutched at his chest, sweating and mumbling.

'Damned Gazer,' said a voice from the darkness. 'Probably chasing dragons and rainbows and the lost treasure of Camorr.' Laughter followed this, and Locke stumbled on, anxious to avoid becoming a target for mischief. He'd never felt such weariness. It was as though his vigour had burned down to a pile of embers within him, fading and cooling and greying with every passing second.

Ashfall, never hospitable, was a hellish conglomeration of shadow-shapes to Locke's decreasing concentration – he was breathing heavily and sweating rivers. It felt as though someone was steadily packing more and more dry cotton in behind his eyeballs. His feet grew heavier and heavier; he urged them forward, one scraping step after another, on into the darkness and the jagged looming shadows of collapsed buildings. Unseen things skittered in the night; unseen watchers murmured at his passing.

'What the . . . Gods, I . . . must . . . Jean,' he mumbled, as he tripped against a man-sized chunk of fallen masonry and sprawled in the dusty shadows behind it; the place smelled of limestone and cookfires and urine. He lacked the strength to push himself back up.

'Jean,' he gasped, one last time, then he fell forward onto his face, unconscious even before his head struck the ground.

6

The lights became visible in the third hour of the morning, perhaps a mile out to sea due south of the Dregs, where a nucleus of greater darkness slid low against the water, tacking slowly and gracelessly. The ship's ghostly white sails flapped in the breezes as it made its way towards the Old Harbour; the bored watch in the three-storey tower at the tip of the South Needle were the first to spot it.

'Right sloppy sailor, that one,' said the younger watchman, spy-glass in hand.

'Probably Verrari,' muttered the senior, who was methodically torturing a piece of ivory with a slender carving knife. He wanted it to come out like a sculpted terrace he'd seen at the Temple of Iono, alive with lovely relief and fantastical representations of drowned men taken by the Lord of the Grasping Waters. What he seemed to be producing more closely resembled a lump of white dogshit, life-size. 'Sooner trust a sailing ship to a blind drunkard with no hands than a Verrari.'

Nothing else the vessel did warranted much attention, until the lights suddenly appeared, and their deep yellow glow could be seen rippling on the dark surface of the water.

'Yellow lights, sergeant,' said the younger watchman. 'Yellow lights.'

'What?' The older man set down his piece of ivory, plucked the spy-glass from the younger man's hands, and gave the incoming ship a good long stare. 'Shit. Yellow it is.'

'A plague ship,' whispered the other watchman. 'I've never seen one.'

'Either it's a plague ship, or some bum-fancier from Jerem who don't know proper colours for harbour lights.' He slid the glass shut and stepped over to a brass cylinder, mounted sideways on the rim of the watch station's western wall, pointed towards the softly lit towers on the shore of the Arsenal District. 'Ring the bell, boy. Ring the damn bell.'

The younger watchman reached over the other side of the little tower's parapet to grasp a rope that dangled there. He began ringing the station's heavy brass bell, a steady repetition of two pulls, *ding-ding, ding-ding, ding-ding*.

Flickering blue light flashed out from one of the Arsenal towers; the watch-sergeant worked the knob on the brass cylinder, turning the shutters that concealed the light of the unusually powerful alchemical globe within. There was a list of simple messages he could flash to the Arsenal stations; they would flash it in turn to other ready sets of eyes. With luck, it might reach the Palace of Patience, or even Raven's Reach, within two minutes.

Some time did pass; the plague ship grew larger and more distinct.

'Come on, halfwits,' muttered the watch-sergeant. 'Rouse yourselves. Stop pulling that damn bell, boy. I think we've been heard.'

Echoing across the mist-shrouded city came the high whistles of the Quarantine Guard; this noise was joined in short order by the rattle of drums – a night-muster of yellowjackets. Bright white lights flared to life in the towers of the Arsenal, and the watch-sergeant could see the tiny black shapes of people running along the waterfront.

'Oh, now we'll see something,' he muttered. More lights appeared to the north-east; little towers dotted the South Needle and the Dregs, overlooking the Old Harbour, where Camorr set its plague anchorage by law and custom. Each little tower held a stone-throwing engine that could reach out across the water with fifty-pound loads of rock or fire-oil. The plague anchorage was one hundred and fifty yards south of the Dregs, directly over sixty fathoms of water, within the throwing arc of a dozen engines that could sink or burn anything afloat in minutes.

A galley was sliding out of the Arsenal gate between the brightly lit towers, one of the swift little patrol vessels called 'gulls', for the winglike sweep of their oars. A gull carried twenty oars on each side and was rowed by eighty paid men; on its deck it carried forty swordsmen, forty archers and a pair of the heavy bolt-throwers called *scorpia*. It had no provisions for cargo and only one mast with a simple, furled sail. It was meant to do just one thing – close with any ship that threatened the city of Camorr and kill everyone aboard, if its warnings were not heeded.

Smaller boats with red and white lanterns blazing at their prows were putting out from the northern edge of the South Needle, carrying harbour pilots and crews of yellowjackets.

On the opposite side of the long breakwater, the gull was just getting up to speed; the rows of graceful oars dipped and cut white froth in the black sea. A rippling wake grew behind the galley; a drumbeat could be heard echoing across the water, along with the shouts of orders.

'Close, close,' muttered the watch-sergeant. 'Going to be close. That poor bastard don't sail well; might have to get a stone across the bows before she slows up.'

A few small, dark shapes could be seen moving against the pale billow of the plague ship's sails – too few, it seemed, to work them properly. Yet as the vessel slid into the Old Harbour, it began to show signs of slowing down. Its topsails were drawn up, albeit in a laggardly and lubberly fashion, the remaining sails were braced so as to spill the ship's wind. They slackened, and with the creak of pulleys and the muted shouts of orders, they too began to draw up towards the yards.

'Oh, she's got fine lines,' mused the watch-sergeant. 'Fine lines.'

'That's not a galleon,' said the younger watchman.

'Looks like one of those flush-deckers they were supposed to be building up in Emberlain; frigate-fashion, I think they call it.'

The plague ship wasn't black from the darkness alone; it was lacquered black, and ornamented from bow to stern with witchwood filigree. There were no weapons to be seen.

'Crazy northerners. Even their ships have to be black. But she does look damn fine. Fast, I'll bet. What a heap of shit to fall into; now she'll be stuck at quarantine for weeks. Poor bastards'll be lucky to live.'

The gull rounded the point of the South Needle, oars biting hard into the water. By the galley's running-lamps, the two watchmen could see that the *scorpia* were loaded and fully manned; that the archers stood on their raised platforms with longbows in hand, fidgeting.

A few minutes later the gull pulled abreast of the black ship, which had drifted in to a point about four hundred yards offshore. An officer strode out onto the gull's long bow-spur and put a speaking trumpet to her mouth.

'What vessel?'

'*Satisfaction*; Emberlain,' came a return shout.

'Last port of call?'

'Jerem!'

'Ain't that pretty,' muttered the watch-sergeant. 'Poor bastards might have anything.'

'What is your cargo?' asked the officer on the gull.

'Ships's provisions only; we were to take cargo in Ashmere.'

'Complement?'

'Sixty-eight! Twenty now dead.'

'You fly the plague lights in real need, then?'

'Yes, for the love of the gods. We don't know what it is . . . The men are burning with fever. The captain is dead; the physiker died yesterday. We beg assistance.'

'You may have a plague anchorage,' shouted the Camorri officer.

372

'You must not approach our shore closer than one hundred and fifty yards, or you will be sunk. Any boats put out will be sunk or burned. Anyone who attempts to swim to shore will be shot down – assuming he makes it past the sharks.'

'Please, send us a physiker. Send us alchemists, for the love of the gods.'

'You may not throw corpses overboard,' continued the officer. 'You must keep them on board. Any packages or objects somehow conveyed to shore from your vessel will be burnt without examination. Any attempt to make such conveyance will be grounds for burning or sinking. Do you understand?'

'Yes, but, please, is there nothing else you can do?'

'You may have priests on shore, and you may have fresh water and charitable provisions sent forth by rope from the dockside – these ropes to be sent out by boat from shore, and to be cut after use if necessary.'

'And nothing else?'

'You may not approach our shore, on pain of attack, but you may turn and leave at will. May Aza Guilla and Iono aid you in your time of need; I pray mercy for you, and wish you a swift deliverance in the name of Duke Nicovante of Camorr.'

A few minutes later the sleek black ship settled into its plague anchorage with furled sails, yellow lights gleaming above the black water of the Old Harbour, and there it rocked, gently, as the city slept in silver mists.

INTERLUDE:
The Lady of the Long Silence

I

Jean Tannen entered the service of the Death Goddess about half a year after Locke returned from his sojourn with the priesthood of Dame Eliza, to which he had gone with the usual instructions to learn what he could and then return home in five or six months. Jean used the assumed name Tavrin Callas, and he travelled south from Camorr for more than a week to reach the great temple of Aza Guilla known as Revelation House.

Unlike the other eleven (or twelve) orders of Therin clergy, the servants of Aza Guilla began their initiation in only one place. The coastal highlands that rose south of Talisham ended at vast, straight white cliffs that fell three or four hundred feet to the crashing waves of the Iron Sea. Revelation House was carved from one of these cliffs, facing out to sea, on a scale that recalled the work of the Eldren but was accomplished – gradually and painstakingly, in an ongoing process – solely with human arts.

Picture a number of deep rectangular galleries, dug straight back into the cliff, connected only by exterior means. To get anywhere in Revelation House, one had to venture outside, onto the walkways, stairs and carved stone ladders, regardless of the weather or the time of day. Safety rails were unknown at Revelation House; initiates and teachers alike scuttled along in light or darkness, in rain or bright clear skies, with no barrier between themselves and a plunge to the sea save their own confidence and good fortune.

Twelve tall excised columns to the west of Revelation House each held a brass bell at the top; these open-faced rock tubes, about six feet across and seventy feet high, had slender hand and foot holds carved into their rear walls. At dawn and dusk initiates were expected to climb them and ensure that each bell was rung twelve times, once for each god in the pantheon. The carillon was always somewhat ragged; when Jean thought he could get away with it, he rang his own bell thirteen times.

Three initiates plunged to their deaths attempting to perform this ritual before Jean had passed his first month at the temple. This number struck him as surprisingly low, given how many of the devotional duties of Aza Guilla's new servants (not to mention the architecture of their home) were clearly designed to encourage premature meetings with the Death Goddess.

'We are concerned here with death considered in two aspects – Death the Transition and Death Everlasting,' said one of their lecturers, an elderly priestess with three braided silver collars at the neck of her black robe. 'Death Everlasting is the realm of the Lady Most Kind; it is a mystery not intended for penetration or comprehension from our side of the Lady's shroud. Death the Transition, therefore, is the sole means by which we may achieve a greater understanding of her dark majesty.

'Your time here in Revelation House will bring you close to

Death the Transition on many occasions, and it is a certainty that some of you will pass beyond before you finish your initiation. This may be achieved through inattentiveness, lassitude, ill fortune or the inscrutable will of the Lady Most Kind herself. As initiates of the Lady, you will be exposed to Death the Transition and its consequences for the rest of your lives. You must grow accustomed to it. It is natural for living flesh to recoil from the presence of death, and from thoughts of death. Your discipline must overcome what is natural.'

2

As with most Therin temples, initiates of the First Inner Mystery were expected to train their scribing, sums and rhetoric to the point that they could enter higher levels of study without distracting more advanced initiates. Jean, with his advantages in age and training over all of the temple's other new initiates, was inducted into the Second Inner Mystery a bare month and a half after arrival.

'Henceforth,' said the priest conducting the ceremony, 'you will conceal your faces; you will have no features of boy or girl, man or woman. The priesthood of the Lady Most Kind has only one face, and that face is inscrutable. We must not be seen as individuals, as fellow men and women. The office of the Death Goddess's servants must disquiet if those we minister to are to compose their thoughts to her properly.'

The Sorrowful Visage was the silver mask of the order of Aza Guilla; for initiates, it bore a crude resemblance to a human face, with a rough representation of the nose and holes for the eyes and mouth. For full priests, it was a slightly ovoid hemisphere of fine silver mesh. Jean donned his Sorrowful Visage, eager to get to work cataloguing more secrets of the order, only to discover that his duties were little changed from his month as an initiate of the First Inner Mystery. He still carried messages and scribed scrolls, swept floors and scoured the kitchens, and still scurried up and down the precarious rock ladders beneath the Bells of the Twelve, with the unfriendly sea crashing far below and the wind tugging at his robes.

Only now he had the honour of doing all these things in his silver mask, with his peripheral vision partly blocked. Two initiates of the Second Inner Mystery fell to a first-hand acquaintance with Death the Transition shortly after Jean's elevation.

About a month after that, Jean was poisoned for the first time.

3

'Closer and closer,' said the priestess, whose voice seemed muffled and distant. 'Closer and closer, to Death the Transition, to the very edge of the mystery. Feel your limbs growing cold. Feel your thoughts slowing. Feel the beating of your heart growing sluggish. The warm humours are banking down; the fire of life is fading.'

She had given them some sort of green wine, a poison that Jean could not identify; each of the dozen initiates of the Second Inner Mystery in his morning class lay prostrate and twitching feebly, their silver masks staring fixedly up, as they could no longer move their necks.

Their instructor hadn't quite managed to explain what the wine would do before she ordered them to drink it; Jean suspected that the willingness of the initiates around him to dance gaily on the edge of Death the Transition was still more theory than actuality.

Of course, look who knows so much better, he thought to himself as he marvelled at how tingly and distant his legs had become. *Crooked Warden . . . this priesthood is crazy. Give me strength to live, and I'll return to the Gentlemen Bastards . . . where life makes sense.*

Yes, where he lived in a secret Elderglass cellar beneath a rotting temple, pretending to be a priest of Perelandro while taking weapons lessons from the Duke's personal swordmaster. Perhaps a bit drunk on whatever drug was having its way with him, Jean giggled.

The sound seemed to echo and reverberate in the low-ceilinged study hall; the priestess turned slowly. The Sorrowful Visage concealed her true expression, but in his drug-hazed mind Jean was certain he could feel her burning stare.

'An insight, Tavrin?'

He couldn't help himself; he giggled again. The poison seemed to be making merry with the inhibitions he'd feigned since arriving

376

at the temple. 'I saw my parents burn to death,' he said. 'I saw my cats burn to death. Do you know the noise a cat makes, when it burns?' Another damn giggle; he almost choked on his own spit in surprise. 'I watched and could do nothing. Do you know where to stab a man, to bring death now, or death in a minute, or death in an hour? I do.' He would have been rolling with laughter, if he had been able be move his limbs; as it was, he shuddered and twitched his fingers. 'Lingering death? Two or three days of pain? I can give that, too. Ha! Death the Transition? We're old friends!'

The priestess's mask fixed directly on him; she stared for several drug-lengthened moments while Jean thought, *oh, gods damn this stuff, I've really done it now.*

'Tavrin,' said the priestess, 'when the effects of the emerald wine have passed, remain here. The High Proctor will speak to you then.'

Jean lay in mingled bemusement and dread for the rest of the morning; the giggles still came, interspersed with bouts of drunken self-loathing. *So much for a full season of work. Some false-facer I turned out to be.*

That night, much to his surprise, he was confirmed as having passed into the Third Inner Mystery of Aza Guilla.

'I knew we could expect exceptional things from you, Callas,' said the High Proctor, a bent old man whose voice wheezed behind his Sorrowful Visage. 'First the extraordinary diligence you showed in your mundane studies and your rapid mastery of the exterior rituals. Now, a vision . . . a vision during your very first Anguishment. You are marked, marked! An orphan who witnessed the death of his mother and father . . . You were fated to serve the Lady Most Kind.'

'What, ah, are the additional duties of an initiate of the Third Inner Mystery?'

'Why, Anguishment,' said the High Proctor. 'A month of Anguishment, a month of exploration into Death the Transition. You shall take the emerald wine once again, and then you shall experience other means of closeness to the precipitous moment of the Lady's embrace. You shall hang from silk until nearly dead; you shall be exsanguinated. You shall take up serpents, and you shall swim in the night ocean, wherein dwell many servants of the Lady. I envy you, little brother. I envy you, newly born to our mysteries.'

Jean fled Revelation House that very night.

He packed his meagre bag of belongings and raided the kitchens for food. Before entering Revelation House, he'd buried a small bag of coins beneath a certain landmark about a mile inland from the cliffs, near the village of Sorrow's Ease, which supplied the cliffside temple's material wants. That money should suffice to get him back to Camorr.

He scrawled a note and left it on his sleeping pallet in the fresh new solitary chamber accorded to him for his advanced rank:

> *GRATEFUL FOR OPPORTUNITIES, BUT COULD NOT*
> *WAIT. HAVE ELECTED TO SEEK THE STATE OF*
> *DEATH EVERLASTING; CANNOT BE CONTENT WITH*
> *THE LESSER MYSTERIES OF DEATH THE*
> *TRANSITION. THE LADY CALLS.*
>
> *– TAVRIN CALLAS*

He climbed the stone stairs for the last time, as the waves crashed in the darkness below; the soft red glow of alchemical storm-lamps guided him to the top of Revelation House, and thence to the top of the cliffs, where he vanished into the night.

4

'Damn,' said Galdo, when Jean had finished his tale. 'I'm glad I got sent to the Order of Sendovani.'

The night of Jean's return, after Father Chains had grilled Jean in depth on his experiences at Revelation House, he'd let the four boys head up to the roof with clay mugs of warm Camorri ale. They sat out beneath the stars and the scattered silver clouds, sipping their ale with much-exaggerated casualness. They savoured the illusion that they were men, gathered of their own accord, with the hours of the night theirs to spend entirely at their own whim.

'No shit,' said Calo. 'In the Order of Gandolo, we got pastries and ale every second week, and a copper piece every Idler's Day, to spend as we wished. You know, for the Lord of Coin and Commerce.'

'I'm particularly fond of our priesthood of the Benefactor,' said

Locke, 'since our main duties seem to be sitting around and pretending that the Benefactor doesn't exist – when we're not stealing things.'

'Too right,' said Galdo. 'Death-priesting is for morons.'

'But still,' asked Calo, 'didn't you wonder if they might not be right?' He sipped his ale before continuing. 'That you might really be fated to serve the Lady Most Kind?'

'I had a long time to think about it, on the way back to Camorr,' said Jean. 'And I think they were right. Just maybe not the way they thought.'

'How do you mean?' The Sanzas spoke in unison, as they often did when true curiosity seized the pair of them at once.

In reply, Jean reached behind his back, and from out of his tunic he drew a single hatchet, a gift from Don Maranzalla. It was plain and unadorned, but well maintained and ideally balanced for someone who'd not yet come into his full growth. Jean set it on the stones of the temple roof and smiled.

'Oh,' said Calo and Galdo.

BOOK IV
DESPERATE IMPROVISATION

'I pitch like my hair's on fire.'

Mitch Williams

Chapter Twelve

The Fat Priest from Tal Verrar

I

When Locke awoke, he was lying on his back and looking up at a fading, grime-covered mural painted on a plaster ceiling. The mural depicted carefree men and women in the robes of the Therin Throne era, gathered around a cask of wine with cups in their hands and smiles on their rosy faces. Locke groaned and closed his eyes again.

'And here he is,' said an unfamiliar voice, 'it is as I said, just as I said. It was the poultice that answered for him; most uncommonly good physik for the enervation of the bodily channels.'

'Who the hell might you be?' Locke found himself in a profoundly undiplomatic temper. 'And where am I?'

'You're safe, though I wouldn't go so far as to say comfortable.' Jean Tannen rested a hand on Locke's left shoulder and smiled down at him. Usually rather fastidious, he was now several days unshaven, and his face was streaked with dirt. 'And some former patients of the renowned Master Ibelius might also take issue with my pronouncement of safety.'

Jean made a quick pair of hand-gestures to Locke: *We're safe; speak freely.*

'Tut, Jean, your little cuts are fine repayment for the work of the past few days.' The unfamiliar voice, it seemed, came from a wrinkled, bird-like man with skin like a weathered brown tabletop; his nervous dark eyes peeped out from behind thick optics, thicker than any Locke had ever seen. He wore a disreputable cotton tunic, spattered with what might have been dried sauces or dried blood, under a mustard-yellow waistjacket in the style of twenty years before. His coils of curly grey hair seemed to sprout straight out from the back of his head, where they were pulled into a queue. 'I have navigated your friend back to the shores of consciousness.'

'Oh, for Perelandro's sake, Ibelius, he didn't have a crossbow quarrel in his brain, he just needed to rest.'

'His warm humours were at a singularly low ebb; the channels of his frame were entirely evacuated of vim. He was pale, unresponsive, bruised, desiccated and malnourished.'

'Ibelius?' Locke attempted to sit up and was partially successful; Jean caught him by the back of his shoulders and helped him the rest of the way. The room spun. 'Ibelius the dog-leech from the Redwater district?'

Dog-leeches were the medical counterparts of the black alchemists; without credentials or a place in the Conclave of Physikers, they treated the injuries and maladies of the Right People of Camorr. A genuine physiker might look askance at treating a patient for an axe wound at half past the second hour of the morning, and summon the city watch. A dog-leech would ask no questions, provided his fee was paid in advance.

The trouble with dog-leeches, of course, was that one took one's chances with their abilities. Some really were trained healers, fallen on hard times or banished from the profession for crimes such as grave-robbing. Others were merely improvisers, applying years' worth of practical knowledge acquired tending to the results of bar fights and muggings. A few were entirely mad, or homicidal, or – charmingly – both.

'My colleagues are dog-leeches.' Ibelius sniffed. 'I am a physiker, Collegium-trained. Your own recovery is a testament to that.'

Locke glanced around the room; he was lying (wearing nothing but a loincloth) on a pallet in a corner of what must have been an abandoned Ashfall villa. A canvas curtain hung over the room's only door; two orange-white alchemical lanterns filled the space with light. Locke's throat was dry, his body still ached, and he smelled rather unpleasant; not all of it was the natural odour of an unwashed man. A strange translucent residue flaked off his stomach and sternum. He poked at it with his fingers.

'What,' said Locke, 'is this crap on my chest?'

'The poultice, sir, the poultice. Varagnelli's Poultice, to be precise, though I hardly presume your familiarity with the subject. I employed it to concentrate the waning energy of your bodily channels; to confine the motion of your warm humours in the

384

region where it would do you the most good – to wit, your abdomen. We did not want your energy to dissipate.'

'What was in it?'

'The poultice is a proprietary conglomeration, but the essence of its function is provided by the admixture of the gardener's assistant and turpentine.'

'Gardener's assistant?'

'Earthworms,' said Jean. 'He means earthworms ground in turpentine.'

'And you let him smear it all over me?' Locke groaned and sank back down onto the pallet.

'Only your abdomen, sir, your much-abused abdomen.'

'He's the physiker,' said Jean. 'I'm only good at breaking people; I don't put them back together.'

'What happened to me, anyway?'

'Enervation – absolute enervation, as thorough as I've ever seen it.' Ibelius lifted Locke's left wrist while he spoke and felt for a pulse. 'Jean told me that you took an emetic, the evening of the Duke's Day.'

'Did I ever.'

'And that you ate and drank nothing afterwards. That you were then seized and severely beaten, and nearly slain by immersion in a cask of horse urine – how fantastically vile! You have my sympathies. And that you had received a deep wound to your left forearm, a wound that is now scabbing over nicely, no thanks to your ordeals. That you remained active all evening despite your injuries and your exhaustion. That you pursued your course with the utmost dispatch, taking no rest.'

'Sounds vaguely familiar.'

'You simply collapsed, sir. In layman's terms, your body revoked its permission for you to continue heaping abuse upon it.' Ibelius chuckled.

'How long have I been here?'

'Two days and two nights,' said Jean.

'What? Gods damn me. Out cold the whole time?'

'Quite,' said Jean. 'I watched you fall over; I wasn't thirty yards away, crouched in hiding. Took me a few minutes to realise why the bearded old beggar looked familiar.'

385

'I have kept you somewhat sedated,' said Ibelius. 'For your own good.'

'Gods damn it!'

'Clearly, my judgement was sound, for you would have had no will to rest otherwise. And it made it easier to use a series of fairly unpleasant poultices to reduce the swelling and bruising of your face. Had you been awake, you surely would have complained of the smell.'

'Argh,' said Locke. 'Tell me you have something at hand I can drink.'

Jean passed him a skin of red wine; it was warm and sour and watered to the point that it was more pink than red, but Locke drank half of it down in a rapid series of undignified gulps.

'Have a care, Master Lamora, have a care,' said Ibelius. 'I fear you have little conception of your own natural limitations. Make him take the soup, Jean. He needs to recover his animal strength, or his humours will fade again. He is far too thin for his own good; he is fast approaching anaemia.'

Locke devoured the proffered soup (boiled shark in a milk and potato stew; bland, congealed, many hours past freshness, and positively the most splendid thing he could recall ever having tasted) and then stretched. 'Two days, gods. I don't suppose we've been lucky enough to have Capa Raza fall down some stairs and break his neck?'

'Hardly,' said Jean. 'He's still with us. Him and his Bondsmage. They've been very busy, those two. It might interest you to know that the Gentlemen Bastards are formally outcast, and I'm the only one presumed at large. I'm worth five hundred crowns to the man that brings me in, preferably after I stop breathing.'

'Hmmm,' said Locke. 'Dare I ask, Master Ibelius, what keeps you here smearing earthworms on my behalf when either of us is your key to Capa Raza's monetary favour?'

'I can explain that,' said Jean. 'Seems there was another Ibelius, who worked for Barsavi as one of his Floating Grave guards. A *loyal* Barsavi man, I should say.'

'Oh,' said Locke. 'My condolences, Master Ibelius. A brother?'

'My younger brother. The poor idiot; I kept telling him to find another line of work. It seems we have a great deal of common sorrow, courtesy of Capa Raza.'

'Yes,' said Locke. 'Yes, Master Ibelius. I'm going to put that fucker in the dirt as deeply as any man who's ever been murdered, ever since the world began.'

'Ahhh,' said Ibelius. 'So Jean says. And that's why I'm not even charging for my services. I cannot say I think highly of your chances, but any enemy of Capa Raza is most welcome to my care, and to my discretion.'

'Too kind,' said Locke. 'I suppose if I must have earthworms and turpentine smeared on my chest, I'm very happy to have you . . . overseeing the affair.'

'Your servant, sir,' said Ibelius.

'Well, Jean.' said Locke, 'we seem to have a hiding place, a physiker and the two of us. What are our other assets?'

'Ten crowns, fifteen solons, five coppers,' said Jean. 'That cot you're lying on. You ate the wine and drank the soup. I've got the Wicked Sisters, of course. A few cloaks, some boots, your clothes. All the rotting plaster and broken masonry a man could dream of.'

'And that's it?'

'Yes, except for one small thing.' Jean held up the silver mesh mask of a priest of Aza Guilla. 'The aid and comfort of the Lady of the Long Silence.'

'How the hell did you arrange that?'

'Right after I dropped you off at the edge of the Cauldron,' said Jean, 'I decided to row back to the Temple District and make myself useful.'

2

The fire within the House of Perelandro had yet to burn itself out when Jean Tannen threw himself down, half-dressed, at the service entrance to the House of Aza Guilla, two squares north-east of the temple the Gentlemen Bastards had called their home.

Elderglass and stone could not burn, of course, but the contents of the House of Perelandro were another matter. With the Elderglass reflecting and concentrating the heat of the flames, everything within the burrow would be scorched to white ash, and the rising heat would certainly do for the contents of the actual temple. A bucket brigade of yellowjackets milled around the temple, with little to do but wait for the heat and the hideous death-scented smoke to cease boiling out from the doors of the upper temple.

Jean banged a fist on the latched wooden door behind the Death Goddess's temple and prayed for the Crooked Warden's aid in maintaining the Verrari accent he had too rarely practised in recent months. He knelt down, to make himself seem more pathetic.

After a few minutes, there was a click, and the door slid open a fraction of an inch. An initiate, in unadorned black robes and a simple silver mask, so familiar to Jean, stared down at him.

'My name is Tavrin Callas,' said Jean. 'I require your aid.'

'Are you dying?' asked the initiate. 'We can do little for those still in good health; if you require food and succour, I would suggest the House of Perelandro, although there seem to be . . . difficulties, this evening.'

'I'm not dying, and I *do* require food and succour. I am a bound servant of the Lady Most Kind, an initiate of the Fifth Inner Mystery.'

Jean had judged this lie carefully; the fourth rank of the order of Aza Guilla was full priesthood. The fifth would be a realistic level for someone assigned to courier important business from city to city. Any higher rank, and he would be forced to deal with senior priests and priestesses who should have heard of him.

'I was dispatched from Tal Verrar to Jeresh on the business of our order, but along the way my ship was taken by Jeremite raiders. They took my robes, my seals of office, my papers and my Sorrowful Visage.'

'What?' The initiate, a girl, bent down to help Jean up; she was a quarter of his weight, and the effort was slightly comical. 'They dared interfere with an envoy of the Lady?'

'The Jeremites do not keep the faith of the Twelve, little sister,' said Jean, who allowed himself to be dragged up to his knees. 'They delight in tormenting the pious. I was chained to an oar for many long days. Last night, the galley that captured me weighed anchor in Camorr Bay; I was assigned to dumping chamber pots over the side while the officers went ashore to debauch themselves. I saw the fins of our Dark Brothers in the water; I prayed to the Lady and seized my opportunity.'

388

One thing the brothers and sisters of Aza Guilla rarely advertised to outsiders (especially in Camorr) was their belief that sharks were beloved of the Goddess of Death; that their mysterious comings and goings and their sudden brutal attacks were a perfect encapsulation of the nature of the Lady Most Kind. Sharks were powerful omens to the silver-masked priesthood; the High Proctor had not been joking with his suggestion that Jean feel free to swim in the ocean after dark. Only the faithless, it was said, would be attacked in the waters beneath Revelation House.

'The Dark Brothers,' said the initiate with rising excitement, 'and did they aid you in your escape?'

'You mustn't think of it as aid,' said Jean. 'The Lady does not aid, she *allows*. And so it is with the Dark Brothers. I dived into the water and felt their presence around me; I felt them swimming beneath my feet and I saw their fins cutting the surface of the water. My captors screamed that I was mad; when they saw the Brothers, they assumed that I was soon to be devoured, and they laughed. I laughed, too – when I crawled up onto the shore, unharmed.'

'Praise the Lady, brother.'

'I do, I have and I shall,' said Jean. 'She has delivered me from our enemies; she has given me a second chance to fulfil my mission. I pray, take me to the steward of your temple. Let me meet with your Father or Mother Divine. I need only a Visage and robes, and a room for several nights while I put my affairs in order.'

3

'Wasn't that the name you apprenticed under,' said Locke, 'all those years ago?'

'It was indeed.'

'Well, won't they send messages? Won't they make inquiries and find out that Tavrin Callas was moved by divine curiosity to fling himself off a cliff?'

'Of course they will,' said Jean. 'But it'll take weeks to send one and get a reply . . . and I don't mean to keep the disguise for quite that long. Besides, it'll be a bit of fun for them. When they eventually discover Callas is supposed to be dead, they can proclaim all sorts of visions and miracles. A manifestation from beyond the shadelands, as it were.'

'A manifestation straight from the arse of a magnificent liar,' said Locke. 'Well done, Jean.'

'I suppose I just know how to talk to death-priests. We all have our little gifts.'

'I say,' interrupted Ibelius. 'Is this wise? This . . . flaunting of the robes of office of the priests of the Death Goddess herself? Tweaking the nose of . . . of the Lady Most Kind?' Ibelius touched his eyes with both hands, then his lips, and then entwined his fingers over his heart.

'If the Lady Most Kind wished to take offence,' said Jean, 'she has had ample opportunity to crush me flatter than gold leaf for my presumptions.'

'Furthermore,' said Locke, 'Jean and I are sworn into the divine service of the Benefactor, Father of Necessary Pretexts. Do you hold with the Crooked Warden, Master Ibelius?'

'It never hurts to have a care, in my experience. Perhaps I do not light hearth-candles or give coin, but . . . I do not speak unkindly of the Benefactor.'

'Well,' said Locke, 'our mentor once told us that the initiates of the Benefactor are strangely immune to consequences when they find they must pass as members of other priesthoods.'

'Made to feel strangely welcome, I'd say,' added Jean. 'And, in the present circumstances, there are precious few practical disguises for a man of my size.'

'Ah. I do see your point, Jean.'

'It seems that the Death Goddess has been very busy of late,' said Locke, 'with a great many people other than ourselves. I'm quite awake now, Jean, and very comfortable, Master Ibelius. No need to get up – I'm quite positive my pulse is right where I left it, safe inside my wrist. What else can you tell me, Jean?'

'The situation is tense and bloody, but I'd say Capa Raza's carried it. Word's out that all of us are dead, except myself, with that pretty price on my head. Supposedly, we refused to swear allegiance to Raza and tried to fight back on Barsavi's behalf, and were justly slain in the process. All the other *garristas* are sworn; Raza didn't wait three days before he hit. The most recalcitrant got their throats slit tonight, five or six of them. Happened a few hours ago.'

'Gods. Where do you hear this from?'

'Some from Ibelius, who can get around a bit provided he keeps his head down. Some from ministering; I happened to be in the Wooden Waste when a lot of people suddenly turned up needing death-prayers.'

'The Right People are in Raza's pockets, then.'

'I'd say so. They're getting used to the situation. Everyone's like to pull knives at the drop of a pin or the bite of a mosquito, but he's got them coming round. He's operating out of the Floating Grave, same as Barsavi did. He's keeping most of his promises. It's hard to argue with stability.'

'And what about our . . . other concern?' Locke made the hand-gesture for *Thorn of Camorr*. 'Heard anything about that? Any, ah, cracks in the façade?'

'No,' whispered Jean. 'Seems like Raza was content to kill us off as sneak-thieves and leave us that way.'

Locke sighed in relief.

'But there's other strangeness afoot,' said Jean. 'Raza hauled in about half a dozen men and women last night, from different gangs and different districts. Publicly named them as agents of the Spider.'

'Really? You think they were, or is it another damn scheme of some sort?'

'I think it's likely they were,' said Jean. 'I got the names from Ibelius, and I had a good long ponder, and there's just nothing linking them all. Nothing that signifies to me, anyway. Raza spared their lives, but exiled them – said they had a day to put their affairs in order and leave Camorr for good.'

'Interesting. I wish I knew what it meant.'

'Maybe nothing, for once.'

'That would certainly be pleasant.'

'And the plague ship, Master Lamora!' Ibelius spoke up eagerly. 'A singular vessel! Jean has neglected to speak of it so far.'

'Plague ship, Jean?'

'A black-hulled vessel from Emberlain, a sleek little piece of business. Beautiful as all hell, and you know I barely know which part of a ship goes in the water.' Jean scratched his stubble-shadowed chin before continuing. 'It pulled into plague anchorage the very night that Capa Raza gave Capa Barsavi his own teeth lessons.'

'That's a . . . a very interesting coincidence.'

'Isn't it? The gods do love their omens. Supposedly, there's twenty or thirty dead already. But here's the *very* odd part: Capa Raza has assumed responsibility for the charitable provisioning.'

'What?'

'Yes. His men escort the proceedings down to the docks; he's giving coin to the Order of Sendovani for bread and meat. They're filling in for the Order of Perelandro since, well, you know.'

'Why the hell would his men escort food and water down to the docks?'

'I was curious about that myself,' said Jean. 'So last night I tried to poke around a bit, in my official priestly capacity, you see. It's not just food and water they're sending out.'

4

The softest rain was falling, little more than a warm wet kiss from the sky, on the night of Throne's Day – the night following the ascension of Capa Raza. An unusually stocky priest of Aza Guilla, with his wet robes fluttering in the breeze, stood staring out at the plague ship moored in Camorr Bay. By the yellow glow of the ship's lamps the priest's mask glowed golden-bronze.

A decrepit little boat was bobbing in the gentle water beside the very longest dock that jutted out from the Dregs; the boat, in turn, had a rope leading out to the plague ship. The *Satisfaction*, anchored out at extreme bowshot, looked strangely skeletal with its sails tightly furled. A few shadowy men could be seen here and there on the ship's deck.

On the dock a small team of burly stevedores was unloading the contents of a donkey-cart into the little boat, under the watch of half a dozen cloaked men and women, obviously armed. No doubt the entire operation could be seen by spy-glass from any of the guard stations surrounding the Old Harbour; while most of those stations were still manned (and would stay that way as long as the plague ship remained), not one of them would much care what was sent out to the ship, provided nothing at all was sent *back*.

Jean, on the other hand, was very curious about Capa

Raza's sudden interest in the welfare of the poor seafarers from Emberlain.

'Look, best just turn right around and get your arse back— Oh. Beg pardon, your holiness.'

Jean took a moment to savour the obvious disquiet on the faces of the men and women who turned at his approach to the end of the dock; they seemed like tough lads and lasses, proper bruisers, seasoned in giving and taking pain. Yet the sight of his Sorrowful Visage made them look as guilty as children caught hovering too close to the honey-crock.

He didn't recognise any of them; that meant they were almost certainly part of Raza's private gang. He tried to size them up with a glance, looking for anything incongruous or unusual that might shed light on their origins, but there was very little. They wore a great deal of jewellery: earrings, mostly – seven or eight of them per ear in one young woman's case. That was a fashion more nautical than criminal, but it still might not mean anything.

'I merely came to pray,' said Jean, 'for the intercession of the Lady Most Kind for those unfortunates out there on the water. Pay me no heed; do continue with your labours.'

Jean encouraged them by turning his back to the gang of labourers; he stood staring out at the ship, listening very carefully to the sounds of the work going on behind him. There were grunts of lifting and the tread of footfalls, the creaking of weathered, water-eaten boards. The donkey-cart had looked to be full of little sacks, each about the size of a one-gallon wineskin. For the most part, the crew handled them gingerly, but after a few minutes . . .

'Gods damn it, Mazzik!' There was a strange clattering, clinking noise as one of the sacks hit the dock. The overseer of the labour gang immediately wrung his hands and looked over at Jean. 'I, uh . . . Begging your pardon, your holiness. We, uh, we swore . . . We promised we would see these supplies safely to the plague ship.'

Jean turned slowly and let the man have the full, drawn-out effect of his faceless regard. Then he nodded, ever so slightly. 'It is a penitent thing you do. Your master is most charitable to undertake the work that would ordinarily fall to the Order of Perelandro.'

'Yeah, uh . . . that really was too bad. Quite the, uh, tragedy.'

'The Lady Most Kind tends the mortal garden as she will,' said Jean, 'and plucks what blossoms she will. Don't be angry with your man. It's only natural to be discomfited in the presence of something . . . so unusual.'

'Oh, the plague ship,' said the man. 'Yeah, it gives us all the creeps.'

'I shall leave you to your work,' said Jean. 'Call for us at the House of Aza Guilla, if the men aboard that ship should chance to need us.'

'Uh . . . sure. Th-thank you, your holiness.'

As Jean walked slowly along the dock, back towards shore, the crew finished loading the small boat, which was then unlashed from its mooring.

'Haul away,' bellowed one of the men at the end of the dock.

Slowly the rope tautened, and then as the little black silhouettes aboard the *Satisfaction* picked up the rhythm of their work, the boat began to draw across the Old Harbour towards the frigate at good speed, leaving a wavering silver wake on the dark water.

Jean strolled north into the Dregs, using the dignified pace of a priest to give himself time to roll one question over and over in his mind.

What could a ship full of dead and dying men reasonably do with bags of coins?

5

'Bags of coins? You're absolutely sure?'

'It was good cold spending-metal, Locke. You may recall we had a whole vault full of it until recently. I'd say we both have a pretty keen ear for the sound of coins on coins.'

'Hmmm. So unless the Duke's started minting full crowns in bread since I fell ill, those provisions are as charitable as my gods-damned mood.'

'I'll keep nosing about and see if I can turn anything else up, Locke.'

'You will . . . Good, good. Now we need to haul me out of this bed and get *me* working on something.'

'Master Lamora,' cried Ibelius, 'you are in no shape to be out of bed and moving around under your own volition! It is your own volition that has brought you here, to this enervated state!'

'Master Ibelius, with all due respect, now that I am conscious, if I have to crawl about the city on my hands and my knees to do something useful against Capa Raza, I will. I start my war from here.'

He heaved himself up off the sleeping pallet and tried to stand; once again, his head swam, his knees buckled and he toppled to the ground.

'From there?' said Jean. 'Looks damned uncomfortable.'

'Ibelius,' said Locke, 'this is intolerable. I must be able to move about. I require my strength back.'

'My dear Master Lamora,' said Ibelius, reaching down to help pick Locke up. Jean took Locke's other side, and the two of them soon had him back on the pallet. 'You are learning that what you require and what your frame may endure can be two very different things. If only I could have a solon for every patient who came to me speaking as you do! "Ibelius, I have smoked Jeremite powders for twenty years and now my throat bleeds; make me well!", "Ibelius, I have been drunk and brawling all night, and now my eye has been cut out! Restore my vision, damn you!" Why, let us not speak of solons, let us instead say a copper baron per such outburst . . . I could still retire to Lashain a gentleman!'

'I can do precious little harm to Capa Raza with my face planted in the dust of this hovel,' said Locke, his temper flaring once again.

'Then rest, sir, *rest*,' snapped Ibelius, his own colour rising. 'Have the grace not to lash your tongue at me for failing to carry the power of the gods about in my fingertips! Rest, and recover your strength. Tomorrow, when it is safe to move about, I shall bring you more food; a restored appetite will be a welcome sign. With food and rest, you may achieve an acceptable level of vigour in but a day or two. Only recently you fell insensible in your very tracks! You cannot expect to skip lightly away from nervous enervation, smiling and laughing. Rest and have patience.'

Locke sighed. 'Very well. I just . . . I ache to be about the business of keeping Capa Raza's reign short.'

'And I yearn to have you about it as well, Master Lamora.' Ibelius removed his optics and polished them against his tunic. 'If

I thought you could slay him now, with little more strength in you than a half-drowned kitten, why, I'd put you in a basket and carry you to him myself. But that is not the case, and no poultice in my books of physik could make it so.'

'Listen to Master Ibelius, Locke, and stop sulking.' Jean gave him a pat on the shoulder. 'Look on this as a chance to exercise your mind. I'll gather what further information I can, and I'll be your strong arm. You give me a plan to trip that fucker up and send him to hell. For Calo, Galdo, and Bug.'

6

By the next night Locke had recovered enough of his strength to pace about the room under his own power. His muscles felt like jelly, and his limbs moved as though they were being controlled from a very great distance – the messages transmitted by heliograph, perhaps, before being translated into movements of joint and sinew. But he no longer fell on his face when he got up off the sleeping pallet, and he'd eaten an entire pound of roast sausages, along with half a loaf of bread slathered in honey since Ibelius had brought the food in the late afternoon.

'Master Ibelius,' said Locke as the physiker counted off Locke's pulse for what Locke suspected must be the thirteen-thousandth time. 'We are of a like size, you and I. Do you by chance have any coats in good care? With suitably matching breeches, vests and gentlemen's trifles?'

'Ah,' said Ibelius, 'I did have such things, after a fashion, but I fear . . . I fear Jean did not tell you . . .'

'Ibelius is living with us here for the time being,' said Jean. 'Around the corner, in one of the villa's other rooms.'

'My chambers, from which I conducted my business, well . . .' Ibelius scowled, and it seemed to Locke that a very fine fog actually formed behind his optics. 'They were burned, the morning after Raza's ascension. Those of us with blood ties to Barsavi's slain men . . . we have not been encouraged to remain in Camorr. Quite the contrary. There have already been several murders. I can still come and go, if I'm careful, but . . . I have lost most of my finer things, such as they were. And my patients. And my books! Yet another reason for me to earnestly desire that some harm should befall Raza.'

'Damnation,' said Locke. 'Master Ibelius, might I beg just a few minutes alone with Jean? What we have to discuss is . . . well, it is of the utmost privacy, and for very good reason. You have my apologies.'

'Hardly necessary, sir, hardly necessary.' Ibelius rose from his seat and brushed plaster dust from his waistjacket. 'I shall conceal myself outside until required. The night air will be invigorating for the actions of the capillaries; it will quite restore the full flush of my balanced humours.'

When he had gone, Locke ran his fingers through his greasy hair and groaned. 'Gods, I could do with a bath. Right now I'd even take standing in the rain for half an hour. Jean, we need resources to hit out at Raza. The fucker took forty-five thousand crowns from us; here we sit with ten. I need to kick the Don Salvara game back into life, but I'm deathly afraid it's in tatters, with me being out of it for these past few days.'

'I doubt it,' said Jean. 'I spent some coin the day before you woke up on a bit of stationery and some ink. I sent a note to the Salvaras by courier, from Graumann, stating that you'd be handling some very delicate business for a few days and might not be around.'

'You did?' Locke stared at him like a man who'd gone to the gallows only to have a pardon and a sack of gold coins handed to him at the last minute. 'You *did*? Gods bless your heart, Jean. I could kiss you, but you're as covered in muck as I am.'

Locke circled the room furiously, or as close to furiously as he could manage, still jerky and stumbling. Hiding in this damned hovel, suddenly torn from the advantages he'd taken for granted for many years – no cellar, no vault full of coins, no Wardrobe, no masque box . . . no gang. Raza had taken everything.

Packed up with the coins from the vault had been a packet of papers and keys, wrapped in oilcloth. Those papers were documents of account at Meraggio's counting house, for Lukas Fehrwright, Evante Eccari and all the other false identities the Gentlemen Bastards had planted over the years. There were hundreds upon hundreds of crowns in those accounts, but without the documents they were beyond mortal reach. In that packet as well were the keys to the Bowsprit Suite at the Tumblehome Inn, where extra clothing suitable to Lukas Fehrwight was neatly set out in a cedar-lined closet – locked away behind a clockwork box that no lock-charmer with ten times the skill Locke had ever possessed could tease open.

'Damn,' said Locke. 'We can't get to *anything*. We need money, and we can get that from the Salvaras, but I can't go to them like this. I need gentleman's clothes, rose-oil, trifles . . . Fehrwight has to look like Fehrwight. I can't conjure him for ten crowns.'

Indeed, the clothes and accessories he'd worn when dressed as the Vadran merchant (not even counting the ornate false optics) had easily come to forty full crowns . . . not the sort of sum he could simply tease out of pockets on the street – and the few tailors that catered to appropriately rarefied tastes had shops like fortresses, in the better parts of the city, where the yellowjackets prowled not in squads but in battalions.

'Son of a bitch,' said Locke, 'but I am *displeased*. It all comes down to clothes. Clothes, clothes, clothes. What a ridiculous thing to be restrained by.'

'You can have the ten crowns, for what it's worth,' said Jean. 'We can eat off the silver for a long time.'

'Well,' said Locke, 'that's something.' He heaved himself back down onto the sleeping pallet and sat with his chin resting on both of his hands. His eyebrows and his mouth were turned down in the same expression of aggrieved concentration Jean remembered from their years as boys. After a few minutes, Locke sighed and looked up at Jean.

'If I'm fit to move, I suppose I'll take seven or eight crowns and go out on the town tomorrow, then.'

'Out on the town? You have a plan?'

'No,' said Locke. 'Not even a speck of one. Not the damnedest idea. But don't all of my better schemes start like this? I'll find an opening, somehow . . . and then I suppose I'll be rash.'

INTERLUDE:
The White Iron Conjurers

It is said in Camorr that the difference between honest and dishonest commerce is that when an honest man or woman of business ruins someone, they don't have the courtesy to cut their throat to finish the affair.

This is, in some respects, a disservice to the traders, speculators and moneylenders of Coin-Kisser's Row, whose exertions over the centuries have helped to draw the Therin city-states (all of them, not merely Camorr) up out of the ashes of the collapse of the Therin Throne and into something resembling energetic prosperity . . . for certain fortunate segments of the Therin population.

The scale of operations on Coin-Kisser's Row would set the minds of most small shopkeepers spinning. A merchant might move two stones on a counting-board in Camorr; sealed documents are then dispatched to Lashain, where four galleons crewed by three hundred souls make sail for the far northern port of Emberlain, their holds laden with goods that beggar description. Hundreds of merchant caravans are embarking and arriving across the continent on any given morning, on any given day, all of them underwritten and itemised by well-dressed men and women who weave webs of commerce across thousands of miles while sipping tea in the back rooms of counting houses.

But there are also bandits, warned to be in certain places at certain times, to ensure that a caravan flying a certain merchant's colours will vanish. There are whispered conversations, recorded in no formal minutes, and money that changes hands with no formal entry in any ledger. There are assassins, and black alchemy, and quiet arrangements made with gangs. There is usury and fraud and insider speculation; there are hundreds of financial practices so clever and so arcane that they do not yet have common names – manipulations of coin and paper that would have Bondsmagi bowing at the waist in recognition of their devious subtlety.

Trade is all of these things, and in Camorr, when one speaks of business practices fair or foul, when one speaks of commerce on the grandest scale, one name leaps to mind above and before all others – *the Meraggio*.

Giancana Meraggio is the seventh in his line; his family has owned and operated its counting house for nearly two and a half centuries. But in a sense the first name isn't important; it is always simply *the* Meraggio at Meraggio's. 'The Meraggio' has become an office.

The Meraggio family made its original fortune from the sudden death of the popular Duke Stravoli of Camorr, who died of an ague while on a state visit to Tal Verrar. Nicola Meraggio, trader-captain of a relatively fast brig, outraced all other news of the Duke's death back to Camorr, where she expended every last half-copper at her command to purchase and control the city's full stock of black mourning crêpe. When this was resold at extortionate prices so the state funeral could take place in proper dignity, she sank some of the profits into a small coffee house on the canalside avenue that would eventually be called (thanks largely to her family) Coin-Kisser's Row.

As though it were an outward manifestation of the family's ambitions, the building has never remained one size for very long. It expands suddenly at irregular intervals, consuming nearby structures, adding lodges and storeys and galleries, spreading its walls like a baby bird slowly pushing its unhatched rivals from the nest.

The early Meraggios made their names as active traders and speculators; they were men and women who loudly proclaimed their ability to squeeze more profit from investors' funds than any of their rivals could. The third Meraggio of note, Ostavo Meraggio, famously sent out a gaily decorated boat each morning to throw fifty gold tyrins into the deepest part of Camorr Bay; he did this every day without fail for a complete year. 'I can do this and still have more fresh profit at the end of any given day than any one of my peers,' he boasted.

The later Meraggios shifted the emphasis from investing coin to hoarding, counting, guarding and loaning it; they were among the first to recognise the stable fortunes that could be made by becoming facilitators of commerce rather than direct participants. And so the Meraggio now sits at the heart of a centuries-old financial network that has effectively become the blood and sinews of the Therin city-states; his signature on a piece of parchment can carry as much weight as an army in the field or a squadron of warships on the seas.

Not without reason is it sometimes said that in Camorr there are two Dukes – Nicovante, the Duke of Glass, and Meraggio, the Duke of White Iron.

Chapter Thirteen

Orchids and Assassins

I

Locke Lamora stood before the steps of Meraggio's counting house the next day, just as the huge Verrari water-clock inside the building's foyer chimed out the tenth hour of the morning. A sun shower was falling, gentle hot rain blown in beneath a sky that was mostly blue-white and clear. Traffic on the Via Camorrazza was at a high ebb, with cargo barges and passenger boats duelling for water space with the sort of enthusiasm usually reserved for battlefield manoeuvres.

One of Jean's crowns had been broken to furnish Locke (who still wore his grey hair and a false beard, trimmed down now to a modest goatee) with acceptably clean clothing in the fashion of a courier or scribe; while he certainly didn't look like a man of funds, he was the very picture of a respectable employee.

Meraggio's counting house was a four-storey hybrid of two hundred years of architectural fads; it had columns, arched windows, façades of stone and lacquered wood alike, and external sitting-galleries both decorative and functional. These galleries were covered with silk awnings in the colours of Camorr's coins – brownish copper, yellowish gold, silver-grey and milky white. There were a hundred Lukas Fehrwights in sight even outside the place, a hundred men of business in lavishly tailored coats. Any one of their ensembles was worth several years' pay for a common labourer.

And if Locke set an unkind finger on as much as a coat sleeve, Meraggio's house guards would boil out the doors like bees from a shaken hive. It would be a race between them and the several squads of city watchmen pacing this side of the canal – the winner would get the honour of knocking his brains out through his ears with their truncheons.

Seven white iron crowns, eight gold tyrins, and a few silver solons jingled in Locke's coin-purse. He was completely unarmed. He had only the vaguest idea of what he would do or say if his very tentative plan went awry.

'Crooked Warden,' he whispered, 'I'm going into this counting house and I'm going to come out with what I need. I'd like your aid. And if I don't get it, well, to hell with you. I'll come out with what I need anyway.'

Head high, chin out, he began to mount the steps.

2

'Private message for Koreander Previn,' he told the guards on duty just inside the foyer as he ran a hand through his hair to sweep some of the water out of it. There were three of them, dressed in maroon velvet coats, black breeches and black silk shirts; their gilded buttons gleamed, but the grips on the long fighting knives and clubs sheathed at their belts were worn from practice.

'Previn, Previn . . .' muttered one of the guards as he consulted a leather-bound directory. 'Hmmm. Public gallery, fifty-five. I don't see anything about him not receiving walk-ins. You know where you're going?'

'Been here before,' said Locke.

'Right.' The guard set down the directory and picked up a slate which served as a writing board for the parchment atop it; the guard then plucked a quill from an inkwell on a little table. 'Name and district?'

'Tavrin Callas,' said Locke. 'North Corner.'

'You write?'

'No, sir.'

'Just make your mark there, then.'

The guard held out the slate while Locke scratched a big black 'X' next to 'TEVRIN KALLUS'. The guard's handwriting was better than his spelling.

'In with you, then,' said the guard.

The main floor of Meraggio's counting house – the public gallery – was a field of desks and counters, eight across and eight deep. Each heavy desk had a merchant, a money-changer, a lawscribe, a clerk or some other functionary seated behind it; the vast majority also had clients sitting before them, talking earnestly or waiting patiently or arguing heatedly. The men and women behind those desks rented them from Meraggio's; some took them every working day of the week, while others could only afford to alternate days with partners. Sunlight poured down on the room through long clear skylights; the gentle patter of rain could be heard mingled with the furious babble of business.

On either side, four levels of brass-railed galleries rose up to the ceiling. Within the pleasantly darkened confines of these galleries, the more powerful, wealthy, and established businessfolk lounged. They were referred to as members of Meraggio's, though the Meraggio shared no actual power with them, but merely granted them a long list of privileges that set them above (both literally and figuratively) the men and women at work on the public floor.

There were guards in every corner of the building, relaxed but vigilant; dashing about here and there were waiters in black jackets, black breeches and long maroon waist-aprons. There was a large kitchen at the rear of Meraggio's, and a wine cellar that would have done any tavern proud. The affairs of the men and women at the counting house were often too pressing to waste time going out or sending out for food. Some of the private members lived at the place, to all intents and purposes, returning to their homes only to sleep and change clothes, and then only because Meraggio's closed its doors shortly after Falselight.

Moving with calm self-assurance, Locke found his way to public gallery desk 55. Koreander Previn was a lawscribe who'd helped the Sanzas set up the perfectly legitimate accounts of Evante Eccari several years previously. Locke remembered him as having been a near-match for his own size; he prayed to himself that the man hadn't developed a taste for rich food in the time since.

'Yes,' said Previn, who thankfully remained as trim as ever, 'how can I help you?'

Locke considered the man's loosely tailored, open-front coat; it was pine green with yellow-gold trimmings on the flaring purple cuffs. The man had a good eye for fashionable cuts and was apparently as blind as a brass statue when it came to colours.

'Master Previn,' said Locke, 'my name is Tavrin Callas, and I find myself possessed of a very singular problem, one that you may

403

well be able to lay to rest, though I must warn you it is somewhat outside the purview of your ordinary duties.'

'I'm a lawscribe,' said Previn, 'and my time is usually measured, when I am sitting with a client. Do you propose becoming one?'

'What I propose,' said Locke, 'would put no fewer than five full crowns in your pocket, perhaps as early as this afternoon.' He passed a hand over the edge of Previn's desk and caused a white iron crown to appear there by legerdemain; his technique might have been a little bit shaky, but Previn was apparently unacquainted with the skill, for his eyebrows rose.

'I see . . . You *do* have my attention, Master Callas,' said Previn.

'Good, good. I hope that I shall shortly have your earnest cooperation as well. Master Previn, I am the representative of a trade combine that I would, in all honour, prefer not to name. Although I am Camorri-born, I live and work out of Talisham. I am scheduled tonight to dine with several very important contacts, one of them a Don, to discuss the business matter I have been sent to Camorr to see through. I, ah . . . This is most embarrassing, but I fear I have been the victim of a rather substantial theft.'

'A theft, Master Callas? What do you mean?'

'My wardrobe,' said Locke. 'All of my clothing and all of my belongings were stolen while I slept. The tavern-master, confound the bastard, claims that he can bear no responsibility for the crime, and he insists I must have left my own door unlocked.'

'I can recommend a solicitor that would suit, for such a case.' Previn opened a desk drawer and began hunting through the parchments that lay within. 'You could bring the tavern-master before the Common Claims Court at the Palace of Patience; it might take as little as five or six days, if you can get an officer of the watch to corroborate your story. And I can draw up all the documents necessary to—'

'Master Previn, forgive me. That is a wise course of action; in most other circumstances I would gladly pursue it and ask you to draw up whatever forms were required. But I don't have five or six days; I fear I have only hours. The dinner, sir, the dinner is this evening, as I said.'

'Hmmm,' said Previn, 'could you not reschedule the dinner? Surely your associates would understand, in such extremity – such an unfortunate turn of events.'

'Oh, if only I could. But, Master Previn, how am I to appear before them, asking them to entrust tens of thousands of crowns to the ventures of my combine, when I cannot even be entrusted to keep safe my own wardrobe? I am . . . I am most embarrassed. I fear I shall lose this affair, let it slip entirely through my fingers. The Don in question, he is . . . he is something of an eccentric. I fear he would not tolerate an irregularity such as my situation presents; I fear, if put off once, he would not desire to meet again.'

'Interesting, Master Callas. Your concerns may be . . . valid. I shall trust you to best judge the character of your associates. But how may I be of assistance?'

'We are of a like size, Master Previn,' said Locke. 'We are of a like size, and I very much appreciate your subtle eye for cuts and colours – you have singular taste. What I propose is the loan of a suitable set of clothing, with the necessary trifles and accoutrements. I shall give you five crowns as an assurance for their care, and when I am finished with them and have returned them, you may keep the assurance.'

'You, ah . . . you wish me to *lend* you some of my clothes?'

'Yes, Master Previn, with all thanks for your consideration. The assistance would be immeasurable. My combine would not be ungrateful, I daresay.'

'Hmmm.' Previn closed the drawer of his desk and steepled his fingers beneath his chin, frowning. 'You propose to pay me an assurance worth about one sixth of the clothing I would be loaning you, were you to dress for a dinner party with a Don. One sixth, at a minimum.'

'I, ah, assure you, Master Previn, that with the sole exception of this unfortunate theft, I have always thought of myself as the soul of caution. I would look after your clothing as though my life depended upon it – indeed, it *does*. If these negotiations go amiss, I am likely to be out of a job.'

'This is . . . this is quite unusual, Master Callas. Quite an irregular thing to ask. What combine do you work for?'

'I . . . I am embarrassed to say, Master Previn. For fear that my situation should reflect poorly on them. I am only trying to do my duty by them, you understand.'

'I do, I do, and yet it must be plain to you that no man can call himself wise who would give a stranger thirty crowns in exchange

405

for five, without . . . something more than earnest assurances. I do beg your pardon, but that's the way it must be.'

'Very well,' said Locke. 'I am employed by the West Iron Sea Mercantile Combine, registered out of Tal Verrar.'

'West Iron Sea Mercantile . . . hmmm.' Previn opened another desk drawer and flipped through a small sheaf of papers. 'I have Meraggio's directory for the current year, Seventy-Eighth Year of Aza Guilla, and yet . . . Tal Verrar . . . there is no listing for a West Iron Sea Mercantile Combine.'

'Ah, damn that old problem,' said Locke. 'We were incorporated in the second month of the year; we are too new to be listed yet. It has been such a bother, believe me.'

'Master Callas,' said Previn, 'I sympathise with you, I truly do, but this situation is – you must forgive me, sir – this situation is entirely too irregular for my comfort. I fear that I cannot help you, but I pray you find some means of placating your business associates.'

'Master Previn, I beg of you, please—'

'Sir, this interview is at an end.'

'Then I am doomed,' said Locke. 'I am entirely without hope. I do beseech you, sir, to reconsider—'

'I am a lawscribe, Master Callas, not a clothier. This interview is over; I wish you good fortune, and a good *day*.'

'Is there nothing I can say that would at least raise the possibility of—'

Previn picked up a small brass bell that sat on one edge of his desk; he rang it three times, and guards began to appear out of the nearby crowd. Locke palmed his white iron piece from the desktop and sighed.

'This man is to be escorted from the premises,' said Previn, when one of Meraggio's guards set a gauntletted hand on Locke's shoulder. 'Please show him every courtesy.'

'Certainly, Master Previn. As for you, right this way, sir,' said the guard, as Locke was helped from his seat by no fewer than three stocky men, and then enthusiastically assisted down the main corridor of the public gallery, out the foyer and back to the steps. The rain had ceased to fall, and the city had the freshly washed scent of steam rising from warm stones.

'It'd be best if we didn't see you again,' said one of the guards.

Three of them stood there, staring down at him, while men and women of business made their way up the steps around him, patently ignoring him. The same could not be said for some of the yellowjackets, who were staring interestedly.

'Shit,' he muttered to himself, and he set off to the south-west at a brisk walk. He would cross one of the bridges to the Videnza, he told himself, and find one of the tailors there . . .

3

The water-clock was chiming the noon hour when Locke returned to the foot of Meraggio's steps. The light-coloured clothing of 'Tavrin Callas' had vanished; Locke now wore a dark cotton doublet, cheap black breeches and black hose; his hair was concealed under a black velvet cap, and in place of his goatee (which had come off rather painfully – some day he would learn to carry adhesive-dissolving salve with him as a matter of habit) he now wore a thick moustache. His cheeks were red, and his clothing was already sweated through in several places. In his hands he clutched a rolled parchment (blank), and he gave himself a hint of a Talishani accent when he stepped into the foyer and addressed the guards.

'I require a lawscribe,' said Locke. 'I have no appointment and no associates here; I am content to wait for the first available.'

'Lawscribe, right.' The familiar directory guard consulted his lists. 'You might try Daniella Montagu, public gallery, desk sixteen. Or maybe . . . Etienne Acalo, desk thirty-six. Anyhow, there's a railed area for waiting.'

'You are most kind,' said Locke.

'Name and district?'

'Galdo Avrillaigne,' said Locke. 'I am from Talisham.'

'You write?'

'Why, all the time,' said Locke, 'except of course when I'm wrong.'

The directory guard stared at him for several seconds until one of the guards standing behind Locke sniggered; the symptoms of belated enlightenment appeared on the directory guard's face, but he didn't look very amused. 'Just sign or make your mark here, Master Avrillaigne.'

Locke accepted the proffered quill and scribed a fluid, elaborate signature beside the guard's 'GALLDO AVRILLANE', then strolled into the counting house with a friendly nod.

Locke rapidly cased the public gallery once again while he feigned good-natured befuddlement; rather than settling into the waiting area, which was marked off with brass rails, he walked straight towards the well-dressed young man behind desk 22, who was scribbling furiously on a piece of parchment and currently had no client to distract him. Locke settled into the chair before his desk and cleared his throat.

The man looked up; he was a slender Camorri with slicked-back brown hair and optics over his wide, sensitive eyes. He wore a cream-coloured coat with plum-purple lining visible within the cuffs; the lining matched his tunic and his vest. The man's ruffled silk cravats were composed of layers of cream upon dark purple. Somewhat dandified, perhaps, and the man was a few inches taller than Locke, but that was a difficulty relatively easily dealt with.

'I say,' said Locke in his brightest, most conversational I'm-not-from-your-city tone of voice, 'how would you like to find your pockets laden down with five white iron crowns before the afternoon is done?'

'I . . . that . . . five . . . Sir, you seem to have me at a disadvantage. What can I do for you, and, indeed, who are you?'

'My name is Galdo Avrillaigne,' said Locke. 'I'm from Talisham.'

'You don't say,' said the man. 'Five crowns, you mentioned? I usually don't charge that much for my services, but I'd like to hear what you have in mind.'

'Your services,' said Locke, 'your professional services, that is, are not what I'll be requiring, Master . . . ?'

'Magris, Armand Magris,' said the man. 'But you, you don't know who I am and you don't want my—'

'White iron, I said.' Locke conjured the same piece he'd set down on Koreander Previn's desk two hours before. He made it appear to pop up out of his closed knuckles and settle there; he'd never developed the skill for knuckle-walking that the Sanzas had. 'Five white iron crowns for a trifling service, if somewhat unusual.'

'Unusual how?'

'I have had a streak of rather ill fortune, Master Magris,' said Locke. 'I am a commercial representative of Strollo and Sons, the foremost confectioner in all of Talisham, purveyor of subtleties and sweets. I took ship from Talisham for a meeting with several potential clients in Camorr – clients of rank, I confide in you. Two Dons and their wives, looking to my employers to liven up their tables with new gustatory experiences.'

'Do you wish me to draw up documents for a potential partnership, or some sale?'

'Nothing so mundane, Master Magris, nothing so mundane. Pray hear the full extent of my misfortune. I was dispatched to Camorr by sea with a number of packages in my possession. These packages contained spun sugar confections of surpassing excellence and delicacy, subtleties the likes of which even your famed Camorri chefs have never conceived: hollow sweetmeats with alchemical cream centres . . . cinnamon tarts with the Austershalin brandy of Emberlain for a glaze . . . Wonders. I was to dine with our potential clients, and see that they were suitably overcome with enthusiasm for my employer's arts. The sums involved for furnishing festival feasts alone, well . . . The engagement is a very important one.'

'I don't doubt it,' said Magris. 'Sounds like very pleasant work.'

'It would be, save for one unfortunate fact,' said Locke. 'The ship that brought me here, while as fast as had been promised, was badly infested with rats.'

'Oh dear . . . surely not your—'

'Yes,' said Locke. 'My wares. My very excellent wares were stored in rather lightweight packages. I kept them out of the hold; unfortunately, this seems to have given the rats an easier time of it. They fell upon my confections quite ravenously; everything I carried was destroyed.'

'It pains me to hear of your loss,' said Magris. 'How can I be of aid?'

'My wares,' said Locke, 'were stored with my clothes. And that is the final embarrassment of my situation. Between the depredations of teeth and of, ah, droppings, if I may be so indelicate . . . my wardrobe is entirely destroyed. I dressed plainly for the voyage, and now this is the only complete set of clothes to my name.'

'Twelve gods, that is a pretty pickle. Does your employer have an account here at Meraggio's? Do you have credit you might draw against for the price of clothes?'

'Sadly, no,' said Locke. 'We have been considering it; I have long argued for it. But we have no such account to help me now, and my dinner engagement this evening is most pressing, most pressing indeed. Although I cannot present the confections, I can at least present myself in apology – I do not wish to give offence. One of our potential clients is, ah, a very particular and picky man. *Very* particular and picky. It would not do to stand him up entirely. He would no doubt spread word in his circles that Strollo and Sons was not a name to be trusted. There would be imputations not just against our goods, but against our very civility, you see.'

'Yes, some of the Dons are . . . very firmly set in their customs. As yet I fail to see, however, where my assistance enters the picture.'

'We are of a similar size, sir, of a fortuitously similar size. And your taste, why, it is superlative, Master Magris; we could be long-lost brothers, so alike are we in our sense for cuts and colours. You are slightly taller than I am, but surely I can bear that for the few hours necessary. I would ask, sir, I would *beg* – aid me by lending me a suitable set of clothing. I must dine with Dons this evening; help me to look the part, so that my employers might salvage their good name from this affair.'

'You desire . . . you desire the loan of a coat and breeches, and hose and shoes, and all the fiddle-faddle and necessaries?'

'Indeed,' said Locke, 'with a heartfelt promise to look after every single stitch as though it were the last in the world. What's more, I propose to leave you an assurance of five white iron crowns. Keep it until I have returned every thread of your clothing, and then keep it thereafter. Surely it is a month or two of pay, for so little work.'

'It is, it is . . . it is a very handsome sum. However,' said Magris, looking as though he were trying to stifle a grin, 'this is . . . as I'm sure you know, rather odd.'

'I am only too aware, sir, only too aware. Can I not inspire you to have some pity for me? I am not too proud to beg, Master Magris. It is more than just my job at stake; it is the reputation of my employers.'

'No doubt,' said Magris. 'No doubt. A pity that rats cannot speak Therin; I wager they'd offer a very fine testimony.'

'Six white iron crowns,' said Locke. 'I can stretch my purse that far. I implore you, sir—'

'Squeak-squeak,' said Magris, 'squeak-squeak, they would say. And what fat little rats they would be after all that; what round little miscreants. They would give their testimony and then beg to be put back on a ship for Talisham, to continue their feasting. Your Strollo and Sons could have loyal employees for life; though rather small ones, of course.'

'Master Magris, this is quite—'

'You're not really from Talisham, are you?'

'Master Magris, *please*.'

'You're one of Meraggio's little tests, aren't you? Just like poor Willa got caught up in last month.' Magris could no longer contain his mirth; he was obviously very pleased with himself indeed. 'You may inform the good Master Meraggio that my dignity doesn't flee at the sight of a little white iron; I would never dishonour his establishment by participating in such a prank. You will, of course, give him my very best regards?'

Locke had known frustration on many occasions before, so it was easy enough to stifle the urge to leap over Magris's desk and strangle him. Sighing inwardly, he let his gaze wander around the room for a split second – and there, staring out across the floor from one of the second-level galleries, stood Meraggio himself.

Giancana Meraggio wore a frock coat in the present high fashion, loose and open, with flaring cuffs and polished silver buttons in unnecessary places. His coat, breeches and cravats were of a singularly pleasing dark blue, the colour of the sky just before Falselight – there was little surface ostentation, but the clothes were fine, rich and subtle in a way that made their expense clear without offending the senses. It had to be Meraggio, for there was an orchid pinned at the right breast of his coat – that was his sole affectation, a fresh orchid picked every single day to adorn his clothes.

Judging by the advisers and attendants who stood close behind the man, Locke estimated that Meraggio was very close in height and build to himself.

The plan seemed to come up out of nowhere; it swept into his thoughts like a boarding party rushing onto a ship – in the blink of an eye he was in its power, and it was set out before him, plain as walking in a straight line. He dropped his Talishani accent and smiled back at Magris.

'Oh, you're too clever for me, Master Magris. Too clever by half. My congratulations; you were only too right to refuse. And never fear – I shall report to Meraggio himself, quite presently and directly. Your perspicacity will not escape his notice. Now, if you will excuse me . . .'

4

At the rear of Meraggio's was a service entrance in a wide alley, where deliveries came in to the storage rooms and kitchens. This was also where the waiters took their breaks, newcomers to the counting house received scant minutes, while senior members of the staff might have as long as half an hour to lounge and eat between shifts on the floor. A single bored guard leaned on the wall beside the service door, arms folded; he came to life as Locke approached.

'What business?'

'Nothing, really,' said Locke. 'I just wanted to talk to some of the waiters, maybe one of the kitchen stewards.'

'This isn't a public park. Best you took your stroll elsewhere.'

'Be a friend,' said Locke. A solon appeared in one of his hands, conveniently held up within the guard's reach. 'I'm looking for a job, that's all. I just want to talk to some of the waiters and stewards, right? The ones that are off duty. I'll stay out of everyone else's way.'

'Well, mind that you do.' The guard made the silver coin vanish into his pocket. 'And don't take too long.'

Just inside the service entrance, the receiving room was un-adorned, low-ceilinged and smelly. Half a dozen silent waiters stood against the walls or paced; one or two sipped tea, while the rest seemed to be savouring the simple pleasure of doing nothing at all. Locke appraised them rapidly, selected the one closest to his own height and build, and quickly stepped over to the man.

'I need your help,' said Locke. 'It's worth five crowns, and it won't take but a few minutes.'

'Who the hell are you?'

Locke reached down, grabbed one of the waiter's hands, and slapped a white iron crown into it. The man jerked his hand away, then looked down at what was sitting on his palm. His eyes did a credible imitation of attempting to jump out of their sockets.

'The alley,' said Locke. 'We need to talk.'

'Gods, we certainly do,' said the waiter, a bulldog-faced, balding man somewhere in his thirties.

Locke led him out the service door and down the alley, until they were about forty feet from the guard, safely out of earshot. 'I work for the Duke,' said Locke. 'I need to get this message to Meraggio, but I can't be seen in the counting house dressed as myself. There are . . . complications.' Locke waved his blank parchment pages at the waiter; they were rolled into a tight cylinder.

'I, ah, I can deliver that for you,' said the waiter.

'I have orders,' said Locke. 'Personal delivery, and nothing less. I need to get on that floor and I need to be inconspicuous; it just needs to be for five minutes. Like I said, it's worth five crowns. Cold spending metal, this very afternoon. I need to look like a waiter.'

'Shit,' said the waiter. 'Usually, we have some spare togs lying around . . . black coats and a few aprons. We could fix you up with those, but it's laundry day. There's nothing in the whole place.'

'Of course there is,' said Locke. 'You're wearing exactly what I need.'

'Now, wait just a minute. That's not really possible . . .'

Locke grabbed the waiter's hand again and slid another four white iron crowns into it.

'Have you ever held that much money before in your life?'

'Twelve gods, no,' the man whispered. He licked his lips, stared at Locke for a second or two, and then gave a brief nod. 'What do I do?'

'Just follow me,' said Locke. 'We'll make this easy and quick.'

'I have about twenty minutes,' said the waiter. 'And then I need to be back on the floor.'

'When I'm finished,' said Locke, 'that won't matter. I'll let Meraggio know you've helped us both; you'll be off the hook.'

'Uh, okay. Where are we going?'

'Just around the corner here – we need an inn.'

The Welcoming Shade was just around the block from Meraggio's counting house; it was tolerably clean, cheap and devoid of luxuries – the sort of place that hosted couriers, scholars, scribes, attendants and lesser functionaries rather than the better classes of businessfolk. The place was a two-storey square, built around an open central space in the fashion of a Therin Throne villa. At the centre of this courtyard was a tall olive tree with leaves that rustled pleasantly in the sunlight.

'One room,' said Locke, 'with a window, just for the day.' He set coins down on the counter. The innkeeper scurried out, key in hand, to show Locke and the waiter to a second-storey room with '9' on the door.

Chamber 9 had a pair of folding cots, an oiled-paper window, a small closet and nothing else. The master of the Welcoming Shade bowed as he left, and kept his mouth shut. Like most Camorri innkeepers, any questions he might have had about his customers or their business tended to vanish when silver hit the counter.

'What's your name?' Locke drew the door closed and shot the bolt.

'Benjavier,' said the waiter. 'You're, ah, sure . . . this is going to work out like you say it is?'

In response, Locke drew out his coin-purse and set it in Benjavier's hand. 'There's two more full crowns in there, above and beyond what you'll receive. Plus quite a bit of gold and silver. My word's as good as my money – and you can keep that purse, here, as an assurance until I return.'

'Gods,' said Benjavier. 'This is . . . this is all so very odd. I wonder what I've done to deserve such incredible fortune?'

'Most men do nothing to deserve what the gods throw their way,' said Locke. 'Shall we be about our business?'

'Yes, yes.' Benjavier untied his apron and tossed it to Locke; he then began to work on his jacket and breeches. Locke slipped off his velvet cap.

'I say, grey hair. You don't look your age – in the face, I mean.'

'I've always been blessed with youthful lines,' said Locke. 'It's been of some benefit in the Duke's service. I'll need your shoes, as well – mine would look rather out of place beneath that finery.'

Working quickly, the two men removed their clothing and Locke dressed until he stood in the centre of the room, fully garbed as a Meraggio's waiter, with the maroon apron tied at his waist. Benjavier lounged on one of the sleeping pallets in his undertunic and breechclout, tossing the bag of jingling coins from hand to hand.

'Well? How do I look?'

'You look right smart,' said Benjavier. 'You'll blend right in.'

'Good. You, for your part, look right wealthy. Just wait here with the door locked; I'll be back soon enough. I'll knock exactly five times, savvy?'

'Sounds fine.'

Locke closed the door behind him, hurried down the stairs, across the courtyard, and back out into the street. He took the long way round to return to Meraggio's, so he could enter via the front and avoid the guard at the service entrance.

'You're not supposed to come and go this way,' said the directory guard when Locke burst into the foyer, red-cheeked and sweating.

'I know, sorry.' Locke waved his blank roll of parchment at the man. 'I was sent out to fetch this for one of the lawscribes – one of the private gallery members, I should say.'

'Oh, sorry. Don't let us keep you; go right through.'

Locke entered the crowd on the floor of Meraggio's for the third time, gratified by how few looks he received as he hurried on his way. He wove deftly between well-dressed men and women and ducked out of the path of waiters bearing covered silver trays; he was careful to give these men a friendly, familiar nod as they passed. In moments, he found what he was looking for – two guards lounging against a back wall, their heads bent together in conversation.

'Look lively, gentlemen,' said Locke as he stepped up before them; either one of them had to outweigh him by at least five stone. 'Either of you lads know a man named Benjavier? He's one of my fellow waiters.'

'I know him by sight,' said one of the guards.

'He's in a heap of shit,' said Locke. 'He's over at the Welcoming Shade, and he's just fucked up one of Meraggio's tests. I'm to fetch him back; I'm supposed to grab you two for help.'

'One of Meraggio's tests?'

'You know,' said Locke. 'Like he did to Willa.'

'Oh, her. That clerk in the public section. Benjavier, you say? What's he done?'

'Sold the old man out, and Meraggio's not pleased. We really should do this sooner rather than later.'

'Uh . . . sure, sure.'

'Out the side, through the service entrance.'

Locke positioned himself very carefully to make it seem as though he were confidently walking along beside the guards when in fact he was following their lead through the kitchens, the service corridors and finally the receiving room. He slipped into the lead, and the two guards were at his heels as he stepped out into the alley, waving casually at the lounging guard. The man showed no signs of recognising him; Locke had seen dozens of waiters already with his own eyes. No doubt a stranger could pass as one for quite some time, and he didn't even need quite some time.

A few minutes later, he rapped sharply on the door of chamber 9 at the Welcoming Shade, five times. Benjavier opened the door a crack, only to have it shoved open all the way by Locke, who called up some of the manner he'd used when he'd lectured Don Salvara as a Midnighter.

'It was a loyalty test, Benjavier,' said Locke as he stalked into the room, his eyes cold. 'A *loyalty* test. And you fucked it up. Take him and hold him, lads.'

The two guards moved to restrain the half-naked waiter, who stared at them in shock. 'But . . . but I didn't . . . But you said . . .'

'Your job is to serve Meraggio's customers and sustain Meraggio's trust. My job is to find and deal with men who *aren't* worthy of his trust. You sold me your gods-damned uniform.' Locke swept white irons crowns and the coin-purse up from the bed; he dropped the loose coins into the leather bag as he spoke. 'I could have been a thief. I could have been an assassin. And you would have let me walk right up to Master Meraggio, with the perfect disguise.'

'But you . . . Oh gods, you can't be serious; this can't be happening!'

'Do these men look less than serious? I'm sorry, Benjavier. It's nothing personal – you made a very poor decision.' Locke held the door open. 'Right, out with him. Back to Meraggio's, quick as you can.'

Benjavier kicked out, snarling and crying, 'No, no, you can't, I've been loyal all my—'

Locke grabbed him by the chin and stared into his eyes. 'If you fight back,' he said, 'if you kick or scream or continue to raise a gods-damned fuss, this matter will go beyond Meraggio's, do you understand? We will bring in the watch. We will have you hauled to the Palace of Patience in irons. Master Meraggio has many friends at the Palace of Patience . . . Your case might fall between the cracks for a few months. You might get to sit in a spider cage and ponder your wrongdoing until the rains of winter start to fall. Do I make myself clear?'

'Yes,' sobbed Benjavier. 'Oh gods, I'm sorry, I'm sorry . . .'

'It's not me you need to apologise to. Now, like I said, let's get him back quickly. Master Meraggio's going to want a word with him.'

Locke led the way back to the counting house, with Benjavier sobbing but quiescent. Locke strolled into the receiving room, right past the startled service-door guard, and bellowed, 'Clear this room. *Now.*'

A few of the lounging waiters looked as though they might offer argument, but the sight of Benjavier, half-dressed and firmly held by the two guards, seemed to convince them that something was deeply amiss. They scuttled from the room, and Locke turned to the guards.

'Hold him here,' said Locke. 'I'm going to fetch Master Meraggio; we'll return in a few moments. This room is to stay clear until we return. Let the waiters take their ease somewhere else.'

'Hey, what's going on?' The service-door guard poked his head into the receiving room.

'If you value your job,' said Locke, 'keep your eyes out there in that alley, and don't let anyone else in. Meraggio's going to be down here soon, and he's going to be in a mood. It'd be best not to catch his attention.'

'I think he's right, Laval,' said one of the guards holding Benjavier.

'Uh . . . sure, sure.' The service-door guard vanished.

'As for you,' said Locke, stepping close to Benjavier, 'like I said, it's nothing personal. Can I give you a bit of advice? Don't play games. Don't bullshit; you can't lie to Meraggio. None of us could, on our best day. Just confess straight out. Be totally honest. Do you understand?'

'Yes,' Benjavier sniffed, 'yes, please, I'll do anything . . .'

'You don't need to do *anything*. But if you want Master Meraggio to be at all lenient or sympathetic, then by the gods you fucking confess and you do it in a hurry. No games, remember?'

'O-okay, yes – anything . . .'

'I shall return very shortly,' said Locke, and he spun on his heel and made for the door. As he left the receiving room, he allowed himself a brief smirk of pleasure; the two guards now looked almost as frightened of him as the waiter did. It was strange how readily authority could be conjured from nothing but a bit of strutting jackassery. He made his way through the service passages and kitchens, and back out onto the public floor.

'I say,' said Locke to the first guard he came across, 'is Master Meraggio in the members' galleries?' Locke waved his blank rolled parchment as though it were pressing business.

'Far as I know,' said the guard, 'I think he's up on the third level, taking reports.'

'Many thanks.'

Nodding to the pair of guards at its base, Locke climbed the wide black iron staircase that led up to the first member's gallery. His uniform seemed to be sufficient guarantee of gallery privileges, but he kept the parchment clutched visibly in both hands, as an added assurance. He scanned the first-floor gallery, found no sign of his quarry, and continued upward.

He found Giancana Meraggio on the third floor, just as the guard had indicated. Meraggio stood staring out at the public gallery, abstracted, as he listened to a pair of finnickers behind him read figures from wax tablets that meant very little to Locke. Meraggio didn't seem to keep a bodyguard near his person; apparently he felt safe enough within the bounds of his commercial kingdom. So much the better. Locke stepped right up beside him, relishing the arrogance of the gesture, and stood waiting to be noticed.

The finnickers and several nearby gallery members started muttering to themselves; after a few seconds Meraggio turned and let the full power of his storm-lantern glare rest on Locke. It took only a moment for that glare to shift from irritation to suspicion.

'You,' said Meraggio, 'do *not* work for me.'

'I bring greetings from Capa Raza of Camorr,' said Locke, in a quiet and respectful voice. 'I have a very serious matter to bring to your attention, Master Meraggio.'

The master of the counting house stared at him, then removed his optics and tucked them in a coat pocket. 'So it's true, then. I'd heard Barsavi had gone the way of all flesh . . . and now your master sends a lackey. How kind of him. What's his business?'

'His business is rather congruent with yours, Master Meraggio. I'm here to save your life.'

Meraggio snorted. 'My life is hardly in danger, my improperly dressed friend. This is my house, and any guard here would cut your balls off with two words from me. If I were you, I'd start explaining where you got that uniform.'

'I purchased it,' said Locke, 'from one of your waiters, a man by the name of Benjavier. I knew he was tractable, because he's already in on the plot against your life.'

'Ben? Gods damn it – what proof have you?'

'I have several of your guards holding him down by your service entrance, half dressed.'

'What do you mean *you* have several of *my* guards holding him down? Who the hell do you think you are?'

'Capa Raza has given me the job of saving your life, Master Meraggio. I mean exactly what I said. And as for who I am, I happen to be your *saviour*.'

'My guards and my waiters . . .'

'Are not reliable,' hissed Locke. 'Are you blind? I didn't purchase this at a second-hand clothier's; I walked right in through your service entrance, offered a few crowns, and your man Benjavier was out of his uniform like that.' Locke snapped his fingers. 'Your guard at the service door slipped me in for much less – just a solon. Your men are not made of stone, Master Meraggio; you presume much concerning their fidelity.'

Meraggio stared at him, colour rising in his cheeks; he looked as though he were about to strike Locke. Instead, he coughed, and held out his hands, palms up.

'Tell me what you came to tell me,' said Meraggio. 'I'll take my own counsel from there.'

'Your finnickers are crowding me. Dismiss them and give us a bit of privacy.'

'Don't tell me what to do in my own—'

'I *will* tell you what to do, gods damn it,' Locke spat. 'I am your fucking bodyguard, Master Meraggio. You are in deadly danger; minutes count. You already know of at least one compromised waiter and one lax guard; how much longer are you going to prevent me from keeping you alive?'

'Why is Capa Raza so concerned for my safety?'

'Your personal comfort likely means nothing to him,' said Locke. 'The safety of *the* Meraggio, however, is of paramount importance. An assassination contract has been taken out against you by Verrari commercial interests who wish to see Camorr's fortunes diminished. Raza has been in power for four days; your assassination would shake the city to its foundations. The Spider and the city watch would tear Raza's people apart looking for answers; he simply cannot allow harm to come to you. He must keep this city stable, as surely as the Duke must.'

'And how does your master know all of this?'

'A gift from the gods,' said Locke. 'Letters were intercepted, while my master's agents were pursuing an unrelated matter. Please dismiss your finnickers.'

Meraggio pondered for a few seconds, then grunted and waved his attendants away with an irritated wrist-flick. They backed off, wide-eyed.

'Someone very nasty is after you,' said Locke. 'It's a crossbow job; the assassin is Lashani. Supposedly, his weapons have been altered by a Karthani Bondsmage; he's slippery as all hell and he almost always hits the mark. Be flattered; we believe his fee is ten thousand crowns.'

'This is a great deal to swallow, Master . . .'

'My name isn't important,' said Locke. 'Come with me down to the receiving room behind the kitchens. You can talk to Benjavier yourself.'

'The receiving room behind the kitchens?' Meraggio frowned deeply. 'As yet I have no reason to believe that you yourself might not be trying to lure me there for mischief.'

'Master Meraggio,' said Locke, 'you are wearing silk and cotton, not chain mail. I have had you within dagger-reach for several minutes now; if my master wished you dead, your entrails would be staining the carpet. You don't have to thank me, you don't even have to like me, but for the love of the gods please accept that I have been ordered to guard you, and one does not refuse the orders of the Capa of Camorr.'

'Hmmm. A point. Is he as formidable a man as Barsavi was, this Capa Raza?'

'Barsavi died weeping at his feet,' said Locke, 'Barsavi and all of his children. Draw your own conclusions.'

Meraggio slipped his optics back onto his nose, adjusted his orchid and put his hands behind his back.

'We shall go to the receiving room,' he said. 'You lead the way.'

5

Benjavier and the guards alike looked terrified when Meraggio stormed into the receiving room behind Locke. They were clearly more attuned to their boss's moods than Locke was, and what they saw on his face must have been something truly unpleasant.

'Benjavier,' said Meraggio, 'Benjavier, I simply cannot believe it. After all I did for you – after I took you in and cleared up that mess with your old ship's captain . . . I haven't the words!'

'I'm sorry, Master Meraggio,' said the waiter, whose cheeks were wetter than the roof of a house in a storm. 'I'm so sorry. I didn't mean anything by it—'

'Didn't *mean* anything by it? Is it true, what this man has been telling me?'

'Oh yes, gods forgive me, Master Meraggio, it's true! It's all true. I'm sorry, I'm so sorry . . . Please believe me . . .'

'Be silent, gods damn your eyes!'

Meraggio stood, jaw agape, like a man who'd just been slapped. He looked around him as though seeing the receiving room for the first time, as though the liveried guards were alien beings. He seemed ready to stagger and fall backwards; instead he whirled on Locke with his fists clenched.

'Tell me everything you know,' he growled. 'By the gods,

everyone involved in this affair is going to learn the length of my reach, I swear it.'

'First things first,' said Locke. 'You must live out the afternoon. You have private apartments above the fourth-floor gallery, right?'

'Of course.'

'Let us go there immediately,' said Locke. 'Have this poor bastard thrown into a storeroom; surely you have one that would suffice. You can deal with him when this affair is over. For now, time is not our friend.'

Benjavier burst into loud sobs once again, and Meraggio nodded, looking disgusted. 'Put Benjavier in dry storage and bolt the door. You two, stand watch. And *you* . . .'

The service-door guard had been poking his head round the corner again. He flushed red.

'Let another unauthorised person, so much as a small child, in through that door this afternoon, and I'll have your balls cut out and hot coals put in their place. Is that clear?'

'P-perfectly clear, M-master Meraggio, sir.'

Meraggio turned and swept out of the room, and this time it was Locke hurrying to keep up.

6

Giancana Meraggio's fortified private apartments were of a kind with his clothing, richly furnished in the most subtle fashion; the man seemed content to let materials and craftsmanship serve as his primary ornaments.

The steel-reinforced door clicked shut behind them, and the Verrari lock-box rattled as its teeth slid home within the wood. Meraggio and Locke were alone. The elegant miniature water-clock on Meraggio's lacquered desk was just filling the bowl that marked the first hour of the afternoon.

'Now,' said Locke, 'Master Meraggio, you cannot be out on the floor again until our assassin is sewn up. It is not safe; we expect the attack to come between the first and fourth hours of the afternoon.'

'That will cause problems,' said Meraggio. 'I have business to look after; my absence from the floor will be noticed.'

'Not necessarily,' said Locke. 'Has it not occurred to you that we are of a very similar build? And that one man, in the shadows of one of the upper-level galleries, might look very much like another?'

'You . . . you propose to masquerade as me?'

'In the letters we intercepted,' said Locke, 'we received one piece of information that is very much to our advantage. The assassin did not receive a detailed description of your appearance – rather, he was instructed to put his bolt into the only man in the counting house wearing a *rather large orchid* at the breast of his coat. If I were to be dressed as you, in your customary place in the gallery, with an orchid pinned to my coat – well, that bolt would be coming at me, rather than you.'

'I find it hard to believe that you're saintly enough to be willing to put yourself in my place, if this assassin is as deadly as you say.'

'Master Meraggio,' said Locke, 'begging you pardon, but I plainly haven't made myself clear. If I don't do this on your behalf, my master will kill me anyway. Furthermore, I am perhaps more adept at ducking the embrace of the Lady of the Long Silence than you might imagine. Lastly, the reward I have been promised for bringing this affair to a satisfactory close – well, if you were in my shoes, you'd be willing to face a bolt as well.'

'What would you have me do, in the meantime?'

'Take your ease in these apartments,' said Locke. 'Keep the doors tightly shut. Amuse yourself for a few hours; I suspect we won't have long to wait.'

'And what happens when the assassin lets fly his bolt?'

'I am ashamed to have to admit,' said Locke, 'that my master has at least a half-dozen other men out on the floor of your counting house. Some of your clients are not clients; they're the sharpest, roughest lads Capa Raza has, old hands at fast, quiet work. When our assassin takes his shot, they'll move on him. Between them and your own guards, he'll never know what hit him.'

'And if you aren't as fast as you think you are? And that bolt hits home?'

'Then I'll be dead, and you'll still be alive, and my master will be satisfied,' said Locke. 'We swear oaths in my line of work as well, Master Meraggio. I serve Raza even unto death. So what's it going to be?'

Locke Lamora stepped out of Meraggio's apartments at half past one, dressed in the most excellent coat, vest and breeches he had ever worn; they were the dark blue of the sky just before Falselight, and he thought the colour suited him remarkably well. The white silk tunic was as cool as autumn river-water against his skin; it was fresh from Meraggio's closet, as were the hose, shoes, cravats and gloves. His hair was slicked back with rose oil; a little bottle of the stuff rested in his pocket, along with a purse of gold tyrins he'd lifted from Meraggio's Wardrobe drawers. Meraggio's orchid was pinned at his right breast, still crisply fragrant; it smelled pleasantly like raspberries.

Meraggio's finnickers had been appraised of the masquerade, along with a select few of his guards. They nodded at Locke as he strolled out into the fourth-floor members' gallery, sliding Meraggio's optics over his eyes. That was a mistake; the world went blurry. Locke cursed his own absent-mindedness as he slipped them back into his coat – his old Fehrwight optics had been clear fakes, but of course Meraggio's actually functioned for Meraggio's eyes. A point to remember.

Casually, as though it were all part of his plan, Locke stepped onto the black iron stairs and headed downward. From a distance he certainly resembled Meraggio well enough to cause no comment; when he reached the floor of the public gallery, he strolled through rapidly enough to gather only a few odd looks in his wake. He plucked the orchid from his breast and shoved it into a pocket as he entered the kitchen.

At the entrance to the dry-storage room, he waved to the two guards and jerked a thumb over his shoulder. 'Master Meraggio wants you two watching the back door. Give Laval a hand. Nobody comes in, just as he said. On pain of, ah, hot coals. You heard the old man. I need a word with Benjavier.'

The guards looked at one another and nodded; Locke's authority over them now seemed so solid that he supposed he could have strolled back here in ladies' smallclothes and gotten the same response. Meraggio had probably used a few special agents in the past to whip his operations into shape; no doubt Locke was now riding on the coat-tails of their reputations.

Benjavier looked up as Locke entered the storeroom and slid the door shut behind him. Sheer bewilderment registered on his face; he was so surprised when Locke threw a coin-purse at him that the little leather bag struck him in the eye. Benjavier cried out and fell back against the wall, both hands over his face.

'Shit,' said Locke. 'Beg pardon; you were meant to catch that.'

'What do you want now?'

'I came to apologise. I don't have time to explain; I'm sorry I dragged you into this, but I have my reasons, and I have needs that must be met.'

'Sorry you dragged me into this?' Benjavier's voice broke; he sniffed once and spat. 'What the fuck are you talking about? What's going on? What does Master Meraggio think I did?'

'I don't have time to sing you a tale. I put six crowns in that bag; some of it's in tyrins, so you can break it down easier. Your life won't be worth shit if you stay in Camorr; get out through the landward gates. Get my old clothes from the Welcoming Shade; here's the key.'

This time Benjavier caught what was thrown at him.

'Now,' said Locke, 'no more gods-damned questions; I'm going to grab you by the ear and haul you out into the alley; you make like you're scared shitless. When we're round the corner and out of sight, I'm going to let you go. If you have any love for life, you fucking run to the Welcoming Shade, get dressed, and get the hell out of the city. Make for Talisham or Ashmere; you've got more than a year's pay there in that purse. You should be able to do something with it.'

'I don't . . .'

'We go now,' said Locke, 'or I leave you here to die. Understanding is a luxury; you don't get to have it. Sorry.'

A moment later, Locke was hauling the waiter into the receiving room by the earlobe; this particular come-along was a painful hold well known to any guard or watchman in the city. Benjavier did a very acceptable job of wailing and sobbing and pleading for his life; the three guards at the service door looked on without sympathy as Locke hauled the waiter past them.

'Back in a few minutes,' said Locke. 'Master Meraggio wants me to have a few more words with this poor bastard in private.'

'Oh, gods,' cried Benjavier, 'don't let him take me away! He's going to hurt me . . . Please!'

The guards chuckled at that, although the one who'd originally taken Locke's solon didn't seem quite as mirthful as the other two. Locke dragged Benjavier down the alley and round the corner; the moment they were out of sight of the three guards, Locke pushed him away. 'Go,' he said. 'Run like hell. I give them maybe twenty minutes before they all figure out what a pack of asses they've been, and then you'll have hard men after you in squads. Don't just stand there, fucking *go*.'

Benjavier stared at him, then shook his head and stumbled off towards the Welcoming Shade. Locke toyed with one of the ends of his false moustache as he watched the waiter go, and then he turned around and lost himself in the crowds. The sun was pouring down light and heat with its usual intensity, and Locke was sweating hard inside his fine new clothes, but for a few moments he let a satisfied smirk creep onto his face.

He strolled north towards Twosilver Green; there was a gentlemen's trifles shop very near to the southern gate of the park, and black alchemists in various districts that didn't know him by sight. A bit of adhesive dissolver to get rid of the moustache and something to restore his hair to its natural shade; with those things accomplished, he'd be Lukas Fehrwright once again, fit to visit the Salvaras and relieve them of a few thousand more crowns.

CHAPTER FOURTEEN

Three Invitations

I

'Oh, Lukas!' Doña Sofia's smile lit up her face when she met him at the door to the Salvara manor. Yellow light spilled out past him into the night; it was just past the eleventh hour of the evening. Locke had hidden himself away for most of the day following the affair at Meraggio's and dispatched a note by courier to let the Don and the Doña know that Fehrwight would pay them a late visit. 'It's been days! We received Graumann's note, but we were beginning to worry for our affairs – and for you, of course. Are you well?'

'My lady Salvara, it is a pleasure to see you once again. Yes, yes, I am very well, thank you for enquiring. I have met with some disreputable characters over the past week, but all will be for the best; one ship is secured, with cargo, and we may begin our voyage as early as next week in it. Another is very nearly in our grasp.'

'Well, don't stand there like a courier on the stair; do come in. Conté! We would have refreshment. I know – fetch out some of my oranges, the new ones. We'll be in the close chamber.'

'Of course, m'lady.' Conté stared at Locke with narrowed eyes and a grudging half-smile. 'Master Fehrwight. I do hope the night finds you in good health.'

'Quite good, Conté.'

'How splendid. I shall return very shortly.'

Almost all Camorri manors had two sitting rooms near their entrance hall; one was referred to as the 'duty chamber', where meetings with strangers and other formal affairs would be held. It would be kept coldly, immaculately and expensively furnished; even the carpets would be clean enough to eat off. The 'close chamber', in contrast, was for intimate and trusted acquaintances and was traditionally furnished for sheer comfort in a manner that reflected the personality of the lord and lady of the manor.

427

Doña Sofia led Locke to the Salvaras' close chamber, which held four deeply padded leather armchairs with tall backs like caricatures of thrones. Where most sitting rooms had little tables beside the chairs, this one had four potted trees, each just slightly taller than the chair it stood beside. The trees smelled of cardamon, a scent that suffused the room.

Locke looked closely at the trees; they were not saplings, as he had first thought. They were miniatures, somehow; they had leaves barely larger than his thumbnail; their trunks were no thicker than a man's forearms and their branches narrowed to the width of fingers. Within the twisting confines of its branches, each tree supported a small wooden shelf and a hanging alchemical lantern. Sofia tapped these to bring them to life, filling the room with amber light and green-tinted shadows; the patterns cast by the leaves onto the walls were at once fantastical and relaxing. Locke ran a finger through the soft, thin leaves of the nearest tree.

'Your handiwork, Doña Sofia?' he said. 'Even for those of us well acquainted with the work of our Planting Masters, it's striking . . . we are all business, all soils and grape yields. You, on the other hand, possess flair in abundance.'

'Thank you, Lukas. Do be seated. Alchemically reducing the frame of larger botanicals is an old art, but one I happen to particularly enjoy, as a sort of hobby. And, as you can see, these are functional pieces as well. But these are hardly the greatest wonders in the room – I see you've taken up our Camorri fashions.'

'This? Well, one of your clothiers seemed to believe he was taking pity on me; he offered such a bargain I could not in good conscience refuse. This is by far the longest I've ever been in Camorr; I decided I might as well attempt to blend in.'

'How splendid!'

'Yes, it is,' said Don Salvara, who strolled in fastening the buttons of his own coat cuffs. 'Much better than your black Vadran prisoners' outfits. Don't get me wrong, they're quite the thing for a northern clime, but down here they look like they're trying to strangle the wearer. Now, Lukas, what's the status of all the money we've been spending?'

'One galleon is definitely ours,' said Locke. 'I have a crew and a suitable cargo; I'll supervise the loading myself over the next few days. It will be ready to depart next week; I have a promising lead on a second to accompany it, ready within the same time frame.'

'A "promising lead",' said Doña Sofia, 'is not quite the same as "definitely ours", unless I am very much mistaken.'

'You are not, Doña Sofia.' Locke sighed and attempted to look as though he were ashamed to bring up the issue once again. 'There is some question . . . That is, the captain of the second vessel is being tempted by an offer to carry a special cargo to Balinel, a relatively long voyage but for a very decent price. He has, as yet, to commit to my offers.'

'And I suppose,' said Don Lorenzo as he took a seat beside his wife, 'that a few thousand more crowns might need to be thrown at his feet to make him see reason.'

'I fear very much, my good Don Salvara, that shall be the case.'

'Hmmm. Well, we can speak of that in a moment. Here's Conté; I should quite like to show off what my lady has newly accomplished.'

Conté carried three silver bowls on a brass platter; each bowl held half an orange, already sliced so the segments of flesh within the fruit could be drawn out with a little two-pronged fork. Conté set a bowl, a fork and a linen napkin down on the tree-shelf to Locke's right. The Salvaras looked at him expectantly while their own orange halves were laid out.

Locke worked very hard to conceal any trepidation he might have felt; he took the bowl in one hand and fished out a wedge of orange flesh with the fork. When he set it on his tongue, he was surprised at the tingling warmth that spread throughout his mouth. The fruit was saturated with something alcoholic.

'Why, it's been suffused with liquor,' he said. 'Something very pleasant – an orange brandy? A hint of lemon?'

'Not suffused, Lukas,' said Don Lorenzo with a boyish grin that had to be quite genuine, 'these oranges have been served in their natural state. Sofia's tree manufactures its own liquor and mingles it in the fruit.'

'Sacred Marrows,' said Locke. 'What an intriguing hybrid! To the best of my knowledge, this has yet to be done with citrus . . .'

'I only arrived at the correct formulation a few months ago,' said Sofia, 'and some of the early growths were quite unfit for the table.

But this one seems to have gone well. Another few generations of tests, and I shall be very confident of its marketability.'

'I'd like to call it the Sofia,' said Don Lorenzo, 'the Sofia orange of Camorr, an alchemical wonder that will make the vintners of Tal Verrar cry for their mothers.'

'I, for my part, should like to call it something else,' said Sofia, playfully slapping her husband on his wrist.

'The Planting Masters,' said Locke, 'will find you quite as wondrous as your oranges, my lady. It is as I said . . . perhaps there is more opportunity in our partnership than any of us have foreseen. Your, ah, flair . . . the way you seem to make every green thing around you malleable . . . I daresay that the character of the House of bel Auster for the next century could be shaped more by your touch than by our old Emberlain traditions.'

'You flatter me, Master Fehrwight,' said the Doña, 'but let us not count our ships before they're in harbour.'

'Indeed,' said Don Lorenzo. 'And on that note, I shall return us to business . . . Lukas, I fear I have unfortunate news for you. Unfortunate and somewhat embarrassing. I have had . . . several setbacks in recent days. One of my upriver debtors has reneged on a large bill; several of my other projections have proven to be overly optimistic. We are, in short, not as fluid at the moment as any of us might hope. Our ability to throw a few thousand more crowns into our mutual project is very much in doubt.'

'Oh,' said Locke, 'that is . . . that is, as you say, unfortunate.'

He slid another orange slice into his mouth and sucked at the sweet liquor, using it as an artificial stimulus to tilt the corners of his lips upward, quite against his natural inclination.

2

On the waterfront of the Dregs a priest of Aza Guilla glided from shadow to shadow, moving with a slow and patient grace that belied his size.

The mist tonight was thin, the damp heat of the summer night especially oppressive. Streams of sweat ran down Jean's face behind the silver mesh of his Sorrowful Visage. Camorri lore held that the weeks before the midsummer mark and the Day of Changes were always the hottest of the year. Out on the water, the now-familiar yellow lamps glimmered; shouts and splashes could be heard as the men aboard the *Satisfaction* hauled out another boatful of 'charitable provisions'.

Jean doubted he could learn anything more about the items going out on those boats unless he did something more obvious, like attacking one of the loading crews – and that would hardly do. So tonight he'd decided to focus his attention on a certain warehouse about a block in from the docks.

The Dregs weren't quite as far gone as Ashfall, but the place was well on its way. Buildings were falling down or collapsing sideways in every direction; the entire area seemed to be sinking down into a sort of swamp of rotted wood and fallen brick. Every year the damp ate a little more of the mortar between the district's stones, and legitimate business fled elsewhere, and more bodies turned up loosely concealed under piles of debris – or not concealed at all.

While prowling in his black robes Jean had noticed gangs of Raza's men coming and going from the warehouse for several nights in a row; the structure was abandoned but not yet un-inhabitable, unlike its collapsed neighbours. Jean had observed lights burning behind its windows almost until dawn, parties of labourers coming and going with heavy bags over their shoulders and even a horse-cart or two.

But not tonight; the warehouse had previously been a hive of activity; now it was dark and silent. Tonight it seemed to invite his curiosity, and while Locke was off sipping tea with the quality, Jean aimed to pry into Capa Raza's business.

There were ways to do this sort of thing; they involved patience, vigilance and a great deal of slow walking. He'd been around the warehouse block several times, avoiding all contact with anyone on the street, throwing himself into whatever deep darkness was at hand. Given enough shadow, even a man Jean's size could be stealthy, and he was certainly light enough on his feet.

Circling and sweeping, circling and sweeping; he'd established to his satisfaction that none of the roofs of nearby buildings supported concealed watchers, and that there were no street-eyes either. *Of course*, he thought to himself as he pressed his back up against the southern wall of the warehouse, *they could just be better than I am*.

431

'Aza Guilla, have a care,' he mumbled as he edged towards one of the warehouse doors. 'If you don't favour me tonight, I'll never be able to return this fine robe and mask to your servants. Just a consideration, humbly submitted.'

There was no lock on the door; in fact, it hung slightly ajar. Jean slipped his hatchets into his right hand and pushed them up the sleeve of his robe; he'd want them ready for use but not quite visible, just in case he bumped into anyone who might still be awed by his vestments.

The door creaked slightly, and then he was into the warehouse, pressed up against the wall beside the door, watching and listening. The darkness was thick, criss-crossed by the mesh of his mask; there was a strange smell in the air above the expected smell of dirt and rotting wood – something like burnt metal.

He held his position, motionless, straining for several long minutes to catch any sound. There was nothing but the far-off creak and sigh of ships at anchor, and the sound of the Hangman's Wind blowing out to sea. He reached beneath his robe with his left hand and drew out an alchemical light-globe much like the one he'd carried beneath the Echo Hole. He gave it a series of rapid shakes, and it flared into incandescence.

By the pale white light of the globe he saw that the warehouse was one large open space; a pile of wrecked and rotted partitions against the far wall might have been an office at one time. The floor was hard-packed dirt, and here and there in corners or against walls were piles of debris, some under tarps.

Jean carefully adjusted the position of the globe, keeping it pressed close against his body so that it threw out light only in a forward arc. That would help to keep his activities unseen; he didn't intend to spend more than a few minutes poking around in this place.

As he slowly paced towards the northern end of the warehouse, he became aware of another odour, one that raised his hackles – something had been dumped in this place and left to rot. Meat, perhaps . . . but the odour was sickly-sweet. Jean was afraid he knew what it was even before he found the bodies.

There were four of them, thrown under a heavy tarp in the north-eastern corner of the building, three men and one woman. They were fairly muscular, dressed in undertunics and breeches, with heavy boots and leather gloves. This puzzled Jean until he peered at their arms and saw the tattoos. It was traditional in Camorr for journeymen artisans to mark their hands or arms with some symbol of their trade. Breathing through his mouth to avoid the stench, Jean shifted the bodies around until he could be sure of these symbols.

Someone had murdered a pair of glasswrights and a pair of goldsmiths. Three of the corpses had obvious stab wounds, and the fourth, the woman . . . she had a pair of raised purple welts on one cheek of her waxy, bloodless face.

Jean sighed and let the tarp settle back down on top of the bodies. As he did, his eye caught a glimmer of reflected light from the floor. He knelt down and picked up a speck of glass, a sort of flattened drop. It looked as though it had hit the ground in a molten state and cooled there. A brief flick of the light-globe showed him dozens of the little glass specks in the dirt around the tarp.

'Aza Guilla,' Jean whispered, 'I stole these robes, but don't hold it against these people. If I'm the only death-prayer they get, please judge them lightly, for the sorrow of their passing and the indignity of their resting place. Crooked Warden, if you could back that up somehow, I'd greatly appreciate it.'

There was a creak as the doors in the northern wall of the building were pushed open. Jean prepared to leap backwards, but thought better of it; his light was no doubt already seen, and it would be best to play the dignified priest of Aza Guilla. His hatchets remained up his right sleeve.

The last people he expected to walk through the north door of the warehouse were the Berangias sisters.

Cheryn and Raiza wore oilcloaks, but the hoods were thrown back and their sharks' teeth bangles gleamed by the light of Jean's globe. Each of the sisters held a light-globe as well; they shook them, and a powerful red glare rose up within the warehouse, as though each woman was cupping fire in the palms of her hands.

'Inquisitive priest,' said one of the sisters, 'a good evening to you.'

'Not the sort of place,' said the other, 'where your order usually prowls without invitation.'

'My order is concerned with death in every form, and in every

433

place.' Jean gestured towards the tarp with his light-globe. 'There has been a foul act committed here; I was saying a death-prayer, which is what every soul is due before it passes into the Long Silence.'

'Oh, a foul act. Shall we leave him to his business, Cheryn?'

'No,' said Raiza, 'for his business has been curiously concerned with ours these past few nights, hasn't it?'

'You're right, sister. Once or twice a-prowling, that we might excuse. But this priest has been persistent, hasn't he?'

'Unusually persistent.' The Berangias sisters were coming towards him, slowly, smiling like cats advancing on a crippled mouse. 'Aggravatingly persistent. On our docks and in our warehouse.'

'Do you dare suggest,' said Jean, his heart racing, 'that you intend to interfere with an envoy of the Lady of the Long Silence? Of Aza Guilla, the Goddess of Death itself?'

'Interfering's what we do professionally, I'm afraid,' said the sister on his right. 'We left the place open just in case you might want to stick your head in.'

'Hoped you wouldn't be able to resist.'

'And we know a thing or two about the Lady Most Kind ourselves.'

'Our service to her is a bit more direct than yours.'

With that, red light gleamed on naked steel; each sister had drawn a curved, arm-length blade – thieves' teeth, just like Maranzalla had shown him so many years earlier. The Berangias twins continued their steady approach.

'Well,' said Jean, 'if we're already past the pleasantries, ladies, allow me to quit this masquerade.' Jean tossed his light-globe on the ground, reached up, pulled back his black hood and slipped off his mask.

'*Tannen*,' said the sister on his right. 'Well, holy shit. So you didn't go out through the Viscount's Gate after all.' The Berangias sisters halted, staring at him. Then they began circling to his left, moving in graceful unison, giving themselves more space.

'You have some cheek,' said the other, 'impersonating a priest of Aza Guilla.'

'Beg pardon? You were going to *kill* a priest of Aza Guilla.'

'Yes, well, you seem to have saved us from that particular blasphemy, haven't you?'

434

'This is convenient,' said the other sister. 'I never dreamed it'd be this easy.'

'Whatever it is,' said Jean, 'I guarantee it won't be easy.'

'Did you like our work, in your little glass cellar?' The sister on the left spoke now. 'Your two friends, the Sanza twins. Twins done in by twins, same wounds to the throat, same pose on the floor. Seemed appropriate.'

'Appropriate?' Jean felt new anger building like pressure at the back of his skull. He ground his teeth together. 'Mark my words, bitch. I've been wondering how I'd feel when this moment finally came, and I have to say, I think I'm going to feel pretty fucking good.'

The Berangias sisters shrugged off their cloaks with nearly identical motions; as the oilcloth fluttered to the floor, they threw down their light-globes and drew out their other blades. Two sisters, four knives. They stared intently at Jean in the mingled red and white light and crouched, as they had a hundred times before crowds of screaming thousands at the Shifting Revel, as they had a hundred times before pleading victims in Capa Barsavi's court.

'Wicked sisters,' said Jean, as he let the hatchets fall out of his right robe sleeve and into his hand, 'I'd like you to meet the Wicked Sisters.'

3

'But don't take it too amiss, Lukas,' said Doña Sofia as she set her hollowed-out orange back down on her shelf. 'We have a few possible remedies.'

'We might only be out of the necessary funds for a few days,' said Don Lorenzo. 'I have other sources I can tap; I do have peers who would be good for the loan of a few thousand. I even have some old favours I can call in.'

'That . . . that is a relief, my lord and lady Salvara, quite a relief. I am pleased to hear that your . . . situation need not ruin our plan. And I wouldn't call it embarrassing, not at all – if anyone knows about financial hardship, why, it would be the House of bel Auster.'

'I shall speak to several of my likely sources of a loan next Idler's Day – which is, of course, the Day of Changes. Have you ever been to any formal celebration of the festival, Lukas?'

'I'm afraid not, Don Lorenzo. I have, previously, never been in Camorr at the midsummer mark.'

'Really?' Doña Sofia raised her eyebrows at her husband. 'Why don't we bring Lukas with us to the Duke's feast?'

'An excellent idea!' Don Lorenzo beamed at Locke. 'Lukas, since we can't leave until I've secured a few thousand more crowns anyway, why not be our guest? Every peer in Camorr will be there; every man and woman of importance from the lower city—'

'At least,' said Doña Sofia, 'the ones that currently have the Duke's favour.'

'Of course,' said Lorenzo. 'But come, do come with us. The feast will be held in Raven's Reach; the Duke opens his tower only on this one occasion every year.'

'My lord and lady Salvara, this is . . . quite an unexpected honour. But though I fear very much to refuse your hospitality, I also fear that it might . . . might possibly interfere with my ongoing work on our behalf.'

'Oh, come, Lukas,' said Lorenzo. 'It's five days hence; you said you'd be supervising loading the first galleon for the next few days. Take a rest from your labours – come and enjoy a very singular opportunity. Sofia can show you around while I press some of my peers for the loans I need. With that money in hand, we should be able to set out just a few days after that, correct? Assuming you've told us of every possible complication?'

'Yes, my lord Salvara, the matter of the second galleon is the only complication we face other than your, ah, loss of fluidity. And, at any rate, even its cargo for Balinel will not be in the city until next week . . . Fortune and the Marrows may be favouring us once again.'

'It's settled, then?' Doña Sofia linked hands with her husband and smiled. 'You'll be our guest at Raven's Reach?'

'It's accounted something of an honour,' confided the Don, 'to bring an unusual and interesting guest to the Duke's celebration. So we are eager to have you with us for several reasons.'

'If it would give you pleasure,' said Locke, 'why, I . . . I fear that

I am not much for celebrations, but I can set aside my work for a night to attend.'

'You won't be sorry, Lukas,' said Doña Sofia. 'I'm sure we'll all think back very fondly on the feast when we begin our voyage.'

4

In many ways, two was the worst possible number of opponents in a close-quarters fight; it was nearly impossible to lead them into crowding and interfering with one another, especially if they were experienced at working together. And if anyone in Camorr was any good at fighting in tandem, it was the Berangias sisters.

Jean counted his one advantage as he twirled his hatchets and waited for one of the sisters to make the first move: he'd seen them in action at least a dozen times, at the Shifting Revel and in the Floating Grave. It might not do him much good, since he didn't happen to be a shark, but it was something.

'We've heard that you're supposed to be good,' said the sister on his left, and just as she spoke, the one on the right exploded forward, one knife out in a guard position and the other held low to stab. Jean sidestepped her lunge, blocked the stabbing knife with his left hatchet, and whipped the other one towards her eyes. Her second blade was already there; the hatchet rebounded off the studded hand-guard. She was just as impossibly fast as he'd feared. So be it; he kicked out at her left knee, an easy trick he'd used to break a dozen kneecaps over the years.

Somehow, she sensed the blow coming and bent her leg to deflect it. It struck her calf, pushing her off balance but accomplishing little else. Jean disengaged his hatchets to swing at where she should have been falling, but she turned her sideways fall into a whirlwind kick; she swivelled on her left hip faster than his eyes could follow and her right leg whipped around in a blurred arc. That foot cracked against his forehead, right above his eyes, and the whole world shuddered.

Chasson. Of course. He could really learn to hate the art.

He stumbled back; drilled instinct alone saved him from her follow-up, a straight thrust that should have punched through his solar plexus and buried her blade to the hilt. He swung his hatchets down and inward, a manoeuvre Don Maranzalla had jokingly referred to as the 'crab's claws', he hooked her blade with his right-hand hatchet and yanked it sideways. That actually surprised her – Jean took advantage of her split-second hesitation to ram the tip of his other hatchet into the base of her neck; he didn't have time for an actual swing, but he could give a pretty forceful poke. She stumbled back coughing, and he suddenly had a few feet of space once again. He stepped back another yard; the wall of the warehouse was looming behind him. At a range of scant inches those knives were greatly superior to his own weapons. He needed reach to swing.

The left-hand Berangias dashed forward as the one on the right faded back, and Jean swore under his breath. With his back to the wall they couldn't try to take him from opposite sides, but nor could he run – they could alternate attacks, one falling back to recover while the other sister continued to wear him down, until he made a mistake.

His temper rose again; bellowing, he tossed both of his hatchets at his new opponent. That caught her by surprise; she sidestepped with speed that matched her sister's and the weapons whirled past on either side, one of them catching at her hair. He charged at her, hands outstretched – empty hands would do better against thieves' teeth when opponents were close enough to kiss. The sister before him spread her blades again, confident of a quick kill, yet it was easy to underestimate Jean's speed if one hadn't seen it up close. His hands clamped down on her forearms; he then used his mass and muscle to spread her arms forcefully. As expected, she raised one of her legs and prepared to kick out at him.

Digging his fingers into the hard muscle of her forearms to keep her blades firmly away from him, he yanked as hard as he could. She flew forward, and with a *smack* that echoed in the warehouse her nose met Jean's forehead. Hot blood spattered; it was on his robes, but he hoped Aza Guilla might eventually forgive him that little indignity. Before his opponent could recover, Jean let her arms go, cupped her entire face in one of his hands, and pushed from the hip with all of his might, like a shot-putter at the Therin Throne games of old. She flew into her sister, who barely got her blades out of the way in time to avoid skewering her sibling, and the Berangias twins toppled against the tarp-covered pile of corpses.

438

Jean ran to the centre of the warehouse floor, where his hatchets lay in the dirt. He picked them up, twirled them once, and quickly worked at the little clasp that held his robe together beneath the collar. While the sisters recovered themselves, Jean shrugged out of his robe and let it fall to the ground.

The Berangias twins advanced on him again, about ten feet apart, and now they looked distinctly upset. *Gods*, Jean thought, *most men would take a broken nose as a sign to run like hell*. But the sisters continued to bear down on him, malice gleaming in their dark eyes; the eerie red and white light was entirely at their backs, and it seemed to outline them in eldritch fire as they spread their blades for another pass at him.

At least he had room to manoeuvre.

Without a word between them, the Berangias sisters rushed at him, four knives gleaming. It was their professionalism that saved Jean this time; he knew before it happened that one would feint and one would strike home. The sister on his left, the one with the broken nose, attacked a split second before the one on his right. With his left-hand hatchet raised as a guard, he stepped directly into the path of the one on his left. The other sister, eyes wide in surprise, lunged at the space he'd just slipped out of, and Jean swung his right-hand hatchet in a backhand arc, ball first, that caught the crown of her skull. There was a wet crack, and she hit the floor hard, knives falling from her nerveless fingers.

The remaining sister screamed, and Jean's own mistake caught up with him at that moment; a feint can become a killing strike with very little effort. Her blades slashed out just as he was raising his right-hand weapon once again; he caught and deflected one with his raised hatchet but the other slid agonisingly across his ribs just beneath his right breast, laying open skin and fat and muscle. He gasped, and she kicked him in the stomach, staggering him. He toppled onto his back.

She was right on top of him, blood streaming down her face and neck, eyes full of white-hot hate; as she lunged down he kicked out with both of his legs. The air exploded out of her lungs and she flew back, but there was a sharp pain in his right bicep, and a line of fire seemed to erupt on his left thigh. Damn, she'd had her blades in him when he pushed her back – she'd slashed open a ragged line along the top of his thigh, with his help! He groaned; this had to

439

end quickly, or blood loss would do for him as surely as the blades of the surviving sister.

She was back on her feet already; gods, she was fast. Jean heaved himself up to his knees, feeling a tearing pain across his right ribs. He could feel warm wetness cascading down his stomach and his legs; that wetness was time running out. She was charging at him again; red light gleamed on steel, and Jean made his last move.

His right arm didn't feel strong enough for a proper throw, so he tossed his right-hand hatchet at her, underhand, directly into her face. It didn't have the speed to injure, let alone kill, but she flinched for a second, and that was long enough. Jean whipped his left-hand hatchet sideways into her right knee; it broke with the most satisfying noise Jean could recall hearing in his life. She staggered; a rapid yank and a backhand whirl, and his blade bit deep into the front of her other knee. Her blades came down at him then, and he threw himself sideways; steel whistled just past his ears as its wielder toppled forward, unable to bear weight on her legs any longer. She screamed once again.

Jean rolled several times to his right – a wise decision. When he stumbled up to his feet, clutching at his right side, he saw the surviving sister dragging herself towards him, one blade still held high.

'You're bleeding hard, Tannen. You won't live out the night, you fucking bastard.'

'That's Gentleman Bastard,' he said. 'And there's a chance I won't. But you know what? Calo and Galdo Sanza are *laughing* at you, bitch.'

He wound up his left arm and let his remaining hatchet fly, a true throw this time, with all the strength and hatred he could put behind it. The blade struck home right between the Berangias sister's eyes; with the most incredible expression of surprise on her face she fell forward, sprawled like a torn-apart rag doll.

Jean wasted no time in reflection. He knelt and checked the state of the first sister he'd struck down; the dark blood trickling out of her ears and nose told him that his swing had done its work. He then gathered his hatchets and threw on one of the sisters' oilcloaks, putting up the hood. His head was swimming; he recognised all the signs of blood loss, which he'd had the misfortune to experience before.

Leaving the bodies of the sisters in the light of the fallen glow-globes, he stumbled back out into the night. He would avoid the Cauldron, where some sort of trouble was sure to lurk, and make a straight run across the north of the Wooden Waste; if he could just make it to the Ashfall hovel, Ibelius would be there, and Ibelius would have some trick up his sleeves.

If the dog-leech attempted to use a poultice on him, however, Jean was likely to break his fingers.

5

In her solarium atop Amberglass Tower, Doña Vorchenza spent the midnight hour in her favourite chair, peering at the evening's notes. There were reports of the ongoing strife resulting from the Grey King's ascension to Barsavi's seat – more thieves found lying in abandoned buildings with their throats slashed. Vorchenza shook her head; this mess was really the last thing she needed with the affair of the Thorn finally coming to a head. Raza had identified and exiled half a dozen of her spies among the gangs; that in itself was deeply troubling. None of them had been aware of one another, as agents. So either all of her agents were clumsier than she'd suspected . . . or Raza was fantastically observant . . . or there was a breach in her security at some level above the spies on the street.

Damnation. And why had the man exiled them, rather than slaying them outright? Was he trying to avoid antagonising her? He'd certainly not succeeded. It was time to send him a very clear message of her own . . . summon this Capa Raza to a meeting with Stephen, with forty or fifty blackjackets to emphasise her points.

The elaborate locks to her solarium door clicked, and the door slid open. She hadn't been expecting Stephen to return this evening. A fortunate coincidence. She could give him her thoughts on the Raza situation . . .

The man that entered her solarium wasn't Stephen Reynart.

He was a rugged man, lean-cheeked and dark-eyed; his black hair was slashed with grey at his temples and he strolled into her most private chamber as though he belonged there. He wore a grey coat, grey breeches, grey hose and grey shoes; his gloves and vest were grey, and only the silk neckcloths tied casually above his chest had colour; they were blood-red.

Doña Vorchenza's heart hammered; she put a hand to her chest and stared in disbelief. Not only had the intruder managed to open the door, and do so without taking a crossbow bolt in the back, but there was another man behind him – a younger man, bright-eyed and balding, dressed in a similar grey fashion, with only the bright scarlet cuffs of his coat to set him apart.

'Who the hell are you?' she bellowed, and for a moment that age-weakened voice rose to something like its old crackling power. She rose from her seat, fists clenched. 'How did you get up here?'

'We are your servants, my lady Vorchenza, your servants come to pay you our proper respects at last. You must forgive us our previous discourtesy; things have been so busy of late in my little kingdom.'

'You speak as though I should know you, sir. I asked your name.'

'I have several,' said the older man, 'but now I am called Capa Raza. This is my associate, who styles himself the Falconer. And as for how we came to your truly lovely solarium . . .'

He gestured to the Falconer, who held up his left hand, palm spread towards Doña Vorchenza. The coat-sleeve fell away, revealing three thick black lines tattooed at his wrist.

'Gods,' Vorchenza whispered, 'a Bondsmage.'

'Indeed,' said Capa Raza. 'For which, forgive me, but his arts seemed the only way to ensure that your servants hauled us up here, and the only way to ensure we entered your sanctum without disturbing you beforehand.'

'I am disturbed now,' she spat. 'What is your meaning here?'

'It is past time,' said Raza, 'for my associate and I to have a conversation with the Duke's Spider.'

'What are you speaking of, by the gods? This is my tower; other than my servants, there is no one else here.'

'True,' said Capa Raza, 'and there is no need to maintain your little fiction before us, my lady.'

'You,' said Doña Vorchenza coldly and levelly, 'are greatly mistaken.'

'Those files behind you, what are they? Recipes? Those notes beside your chair, what are they? Does Stephen Reynart give you

442

regular reports on the cuts and colours of this year's new dresses, fresh off the docks? Come, my lady. I have very unusual means of gathering information, and I am no dullard. I would construe any further dissembling on your part as a deliberate insult.'

'I regard your uninvited presence here,' said Doña Vorchenza after a moment of consideration, 'as nothing less.'

'I have displeased you,' said Raza, 'and for that I apologise. But have you any means to back that displeasure with force? Your servants sleep peacefully; your Reynart and all of your Midnighters are elsewhere, prying into my affairs. You are alone with us, Doña Vorchenza, so why not speak civilly? I have come to be civil, and to speak in earnest.'

She stared coldly at him for several moments, and then waved a hand at one of the solarium's armchairs. 'Have a seat, Master Revenge. I fear there's no comfortable chair for your associate . . .'

'It will be well,' said the Falconer. 'I'm very fond of writing desks.' He settled himself behind the little desk near the door, while Raza crossed the room and sat down opposite Doña Vorchenza.

'Hmmm. Revenge, indeed. And have you had it?'

'I have,' said Capa Raza cheerfully. 'I find it's everything it's made out to be.'

'You bore Capa Barsavi some grudge?'

'Ha! Some grudge, yes. It could be said that's why I had his sons murdered while he watched, and then fed him to the sharks he so loved.'

'Old business between the two of you?'

'I have dreamed of Vencarlo Barsavi's ruin for twenty years,' said Raza. 'And now I've brought it about, and I've replaced him. I'm sorry if this affair has been . . . an inconvenience for you. But that is all that I am sorry for.'

'Barsavi was not a kind man,' said Vorchenza. 'He was a ruthless criminal. But he was perceptive; he understood many things the lesser Capas did not. The arrangement I made with him bore fruit on both sides.'

'And it would be a shame to lose it,' said Raza. 'I admire the Secret Peace very much, Doña Vorchenza. My admiration for it is quite distinct from my loathing for Barsavi; I should like to see the arrangement continued in full. I gave orders to that effect on the very night I took Barsavi's place.'

'So my agents tell me,' said Doña Vorchenza, 'but I must confess I had hoped to hear it in your own words before now.'

'My delay was unavoidable,' said Raza. 'There we are; I have terrible manners, to which I readily admit. Allow me to make it up to you.'

'How so?'

'I should greatly enjoy,' said Raza, 'a chance to attend the Duke's Day of Changes feast; I am capable of dressing and acting rather well. I could be introduced as a gentleman of independent means – I assure you, no one in Raven's Reach would recognise me. I gazed up at these towers as a boy in Camorr. I should like to pay my proper respects to the peers of Camorr just once. I would not come without gifts; I have something rather lavish in mind.'

'That,' said Doña Vorchenza slowly, 'may be too much to ask. Our worlds, Capa Raza, are not meant to meet; I do not come to your thieves' revels.'

'Yet your agents do,' he said cheerfully.

'No longer. Tell me, why did you order them exiled? The penalty for turncoating among your people is death, so why didn't they merit a knife across the throat?'

'Would you really prefer them dead, Doña Vorchenza?'

'Hardly,' she replied, 'but I am more curious about your motives.'

'I, for my part, thought they were transparent. I need to have a measure of security; I simply cannot leave your agents lying about underfoot, as Barsavi did. Of course, I didn't want to antagonise you more than necessary, so I presumed letting them live would be a friendly gesture.'

'Hmmm.'

'Doña Vorchenza,' said Raza, 'I have every confidence that you will begin the work of inserting new agents into the ranks of my people almost immediately. I welcome it; may the most subtle planner win. But we have set aside the main point of this conversation.'

'Capa Raza,' said the Doña, 'you do not seem to be a man who needs sentiments wrapped in delicacy to salve his feelings, so let me be plain. It is one thing entirely for the two of us to have a working relationship; to preserve the Secret Peace for the good of all Camorr. I am even content to meet you here, assuming you are

444

properly invited and escorted. But I simply cannot bring you before the Duke; I cannot bring a man of your station into his presence.'

'That is disappointing,' said Capa Raza. 'Yet he can have Giancana Meraggio as a guest, can he not? A man who utilised my predecessor's services on many occasions. And many other captains of shipping and finance who profited from arrangements with Barsavi's gangs. The Secret Peace enriches every peer of Camorr; I am, in effect, their servant. My forbearance keeps money in their pockets. Am I truly so base a creature that I cannot stand by the refreshment tables a while, keep to the background and merely enjoy the sights of the affair? Merely wander the Sky Garden and satisfy my curiosity?'

'Capa Raza,' said Doña Vorchenza, 'you are plucking at strings of conscience that will yield no sound; I am not the Duke's Spider because I have a soft heart. I mean you no insult, truly, but let me frame it in these terms. You have been Capa now for barely one week. I have only begun to form my opinion of you; you remain a stranger, sir. If you rule a year from now, and you maintain stability among the Right People and preserve the Secret Peace, well then . . . perhaps some consideration could be given to what you propose.'

'And that is how it must be?'

'That is how it must be, for now.'

'Alas,' said Capa Raza. 'This refusal pains me more than you could know; I have gifts that I simply cannot wait until next year to reveal to all the peers of this fair city. I must, with all apologies, refuse your refusal.'

'What on earth do you mean?'

'Falconer . . .'

The Bondsmage stood up at Doña Vorchenza's writing desk; he'd taken a quill in his hand and set one of her sheets of parchment out before him. 'Doña Vorchenza,' he said as he wrote in a bold looping script; 'Angiavesta Vorchenza, is it not? What a lovely name . . . what a very lovely, very true name . . .'

In his left hand the silver thread wove back and forth; his fingers flew, and on the page a strange silver-blue glow began to arise; ANGIAVESTA VORCHENZA was outlined in that fire, and across the room the Doña moaned and clutched her head.

445

'I am sorry to press my case by less than amiable means, Doña Vorchenza,' said Capa Raza, 'but can you not see that it would be to the Duke's very great advantage to have me as his guest? Surely you would not want to deny him those gifts which I would place at his feet, with all due respect.'

'I . . . I cannot say . . .'

'Yes,' said the Falconer. 'Oh yes, you would be very pleased to accept this idea; to ensure that Capa Raza was invited to the Day of Changes feast in the most cordial spirit of good fellowship.'

The words on the parchment in his hands glowed more brightly.

'Capa Raza,' said Doña Vorchenza slowly, 'you must . . . of course . . . accept the Duke's hospitality.'

'You will not be denied,' said the Falconer. 'Capa Raza *must* agree to accept your invitation; you simply will not settle for a refusal.'

'I will not . . . take no . . . for an answer.'

'And I will not give it,' said Raza. 'You are most kind, Doña Vorchenza. Most kind. And my gifts? I have four exquisite sculptures I should like to give to the Duke; I have no need to intrude on his affairs; my men can simply leave them somewhere at the feast, with your cooperation. We can bring them to his attention when he is less pressed for time.'

'How lovely,' said the Falconer. 'You are very fond of this suggestion.'

'Nothing . . . would please me more . . . Capa Raza. Very . . . proper of you.'

'Yes,' said Capa Raza, 'it is very proper of me. It is only just.' He chuckled, then rose from his seat and waved to the Falconer.

'Doña Vorchenza,' said the Bondsmage, 'this conversation has pleased you greatly. You will look forward to seeing Capa Raza at the Day of Changes, and to lending him every assistance in bringing his important gifts into Raven's Reach.' He folded the parchment and slipped it into a waistcoat pocket, then made a few more gestures with his silver thread.

Doña Vorchenza blinked several times, and breathed deeply. 'Capa Raza,' she said, 'must you really go? It has made for a pleasant diversion, speaking to you this evening.'

'And I, for my part, have found you the most charming of hostesses, my lady Vorchenza.' He bowed from the waist, right foot forward in perfect courtly style. 'But business is pressing everywhere; I must be about mine, and leave you to yours.'

'So be it, dear boy.' She began to rise, and he gestured for her to stay seated.

'No, no; don't trouble yourself on our account. We can find our way back down your lovely tower on our own; pray return to whatever you were doing before I interrupted you.'

'It was hardly an interruption,' said Doña Vorchenza. 'I shall see you, then, on the Day of Changes? You will accept the invitation?'

'Yes,' said Capa Raza. He turned and favoured her with a smile before he stepped out through the solarium door. 'I gladly accept your invitation. And I shall see you on the Day of Changes, at Raven's Reach.'

Interlude:
The Daughters of Camorr

The first true revolution in Camorr's criminal affairs came long before Capa Barsavi; it predated his rise by nearly fifty years, in fact, and it came about entirely as the result of a certain lack of self-control on the part of a pimp called Rude Trevor Vargas.

Rude Trevor had a great many other nicknames, most of them used privately among his little stable of whores; to say that he was an intemperate, murderous lunatic would wound the feelings of most intemperate, murderous lunatics. As is often the case, he was a greater danger to his whores than the marks they plied for coppers and silvers; the only protection he really offered them was from his own fists, which could be had by giving him all but a tiny fraction of the money they worked for.

One night, a particularly put-upon whore found herself unwilling to participate in his preferred evening diversion, which was to take his pleasure from her mouth while pulling on her hair until she screamed in pain. Her bodice-dagger was out before she realised it; she planted it just to the left of Trevor's manhood, in the very joint of his thigh, and slashed to his right. There was an awful lot of blood, not to mention screaming, but Trevor's attempts to first fight back and then to flee were greatly hampered by the speed with which his life was gushing out between his legs.

447

His (former) whore then pulled him to the ground and sat on his back to keep him from crawling out of the room; his strength ebbed, and he died in very short order, mourned by exactly no one.

The next night, Trevor's Capa sent another man round to take over his duties. The women in Trevor's old stable welcomed him with smiling faces, and offered him a chance to try out their services for free. Because he had a small pile of broken bricks where most people kept their brains, he accepted; when he was neatly undressed and separated from his weapons he was stabbed to death from several directions at once. That really caught the attention of Trevor's old Capa; the next night, he sent five or six men to straighten the situation out.

But a curious thing had happened: another two or three packs of whores had got rid of their pimps; and this growing nucleus of women claimed a warehouse in the northern Snare as their headquarters. The Capa's men found not six or seven frightened whores, as they'd been told, but nearly two dozen angry women who'd seen fit to buy arms with all the coin they could muster.

Crossbows are quite an equaliser, especially at close range and with the advantage of surprise. Those five or six men were never seen again.

So the war began in earnest; those Capas that had lost pimps and whores attempted to correct the situation, while with every passing day the number of women joining the rebellion grew. They hired several other gangs to serve as their own protection; they established houses of pleasure to their own standards, and began to work out of them. The service they offered, in comfortable and well-appointed chambers, was greatly superior to that which could be had from the gangs of whores still run by men, and prospective customers began to weigh in with their coin on the side of the ladies.

The whores of Camorr had effectively banded together into a guild; less than a year after Rude Trevor's death, the last few pimps clinging brutally to their livelihood were convinced (often convinced to death) to find new means of keeping body and soul together.

There was a great deal of blood; dozens of whores were brutally murdered, and several of their bordellos were burnt to the ground. But for every lady of the night that fell some Capa's man would get

448

the same; the ladies gave like for like as viciously as any Capa in Camorr's history. Eventually, an uneasy truce grew into a stable and mutually beneficial arrangement.

The whores of the city split amiably into two groups, defined by territory; the Docksies took the west side of Camorr while the Guilded Lilies ruled in the east, and both organisations mingled comfortably in the Snare, where business was most plentiful. They continued to prosper; they hired loyal muscle of their own and ceased renting cut-throats from other gangs. While their lives could not be deemed completely pleasant, in the light of their trade, at least they were now firmly in control of their own affairs and free to enforce certain rules of decorum on their customers.

They built and preserved a duopoly: in exchange for promising not to become involved in any other form of crime, they secured the right to mercilessly crush any attempt to pimp women outside their two gangs, and they exercised that right. Naturally, some men didn't pay close attention to the rules the women set; they attempted to slap their whores around, or renege on their payments for services, or ignore the standards the ladies set concerning cleanliness and drunkenness. Hard lessons were handed out; as many men learned to their sorrow, it's impossible to be intimidating when one angry woman has your cock between her teeth and another is holding a stiletto to your kidneys.

When Vencarlo Barsavi crushed his opponents and rose to prominence as the sole Capa of Camorr, even he dared not disturb the equilibrium established between the traditional gangs and the two guilds of whores. He met representatives from the Docksies and the Lilies with an air of great civility; he agreed to let them preserve their quasi-autonomous status and they agreed to regular payments for his assistance – payments, as a percentage of profits, significantly lower than any other dues paid to the Capa by the Right People of Camorr.

Barsavi realised something too many men in the city were slow to grasp, an idea that he reinforced years later when he adopted the Berangias sisters as his primary enforcers. He was wise enough to understand that the women of Camorr could be underestimated only at great peril to one's health.

CHAPTER FIFTEEN

Spiderbite

I

'Can you assure me,' said Ibelius, 'that you will take better care for yourself than you did previously, or that your friend Jean has taken for himself, this past week?'

'Master Ibelius,' said Locke, 'you are our physiker, not our mother, and as I have already told you a dozen times this afternoon, I am entirely prepared, body and mind, for this affair at Raven's Reach. I am the soul of caution.'

'La, sir, if that is the case, I should hope never to meet the soul of recklessness.'

'Ibelius,' groaned Jean, 'let him alone; you are henpecking him without having the decency to marry him first.'

Jean sat upon the sleeping pallet, haggard and rather scruffy; the darkness of the hairs thickening on his face only emphasised his unnatural pallor. His injuries had been a close thing; a great wad of cloth was tied around his naked chest, and similar bandages wrapped his leg beneath his breeches and his upper right arm.

'These physikers are handy things,' said Locke, adjusting his (formerly Meraggio's) coat cuffs, 'but I think next time we should pay a bit extra for the silent version, Jean.'

'And then you may dress your own wounds, sir, and apply your own poultices, though I daresay it would be quicker and easier for the pair of you to simply dig your own graves and take your ease in them until your inevitable transition to a more quiet state of affairs!'

'Master Ibelius,' said Locke, grasping the old man by the arms, 'Jean and I are more grateful than we can say for your aid; I suspect that we would both be dead without your intervention. I mean to repay you for the time you've endured with us here in this hovel; I expect to come into a few thousand crowns in very short order.

Some of it is yours; you shall have a new life far from here with very full pockets. And the rest will be used to put Capa Raza under the earth. Take heart; look what Jean has already done to his sisters.'

'A feat I'm in no condition to perform again,' said Jean. 'Take care of yourself, Locke; I won't be able to come running to the rescue if something goes awry tonight.'

'Though I have no doubt he would try,' said Ibelius.

'Don't worry, Jean. It'll be nothing but a routine evening with the Duke and his entire fucking court, assembled in a glass tower six hundred feet in the air. What could *possibly* go wrong?'

'That sarcasm sounds half-hearted,' said Jean. 'You're really looking forward to this, aren't you?'

'Of course I am, Jean. Chains would be beside himself with glee if he were alive; I'm going to play Lukas Fehrwight in front of the gods-damned Duke, not to mention all the other peers of our acquaintance; the de Marres, the Feluccias, old Javarriz . . . Glory to the Crooked Warden, it's going to be *a hell of a show*. Assuming I'm on top of my game. And then . . . money in our pockets. And then revenge.'

'When are you expected at the Salvara manor?'

'Third hour of the afternoon, which means I've no more time to dawdle. Jean, Ibelius . . . how do I look?'

'I would hardly recognise the man we laid on that sickbed not so many days ago,' said Ibelius. 'I'll confess you've a surprising degree of professional skill; I'd never conceived of such a thing as this false-facing of yours.'

'That's to our advantage, Master Ibelius,' said Jean. 'Very few have. You look ready for the evening, Master Fehrwight. Now, you're going to take the long way round to the Isla Durona, right?'

'Gods, yes,' said Locke. 'I'm only mad to a certain measure. I'll go north through the graveyards and up through the Quiet; I expect I won't see a soul once I'm out of Ashfall.'

As he spoke, he draped himself, despite the sweltering heat, with the oilcloak Jean had brought back from his encounter with the Berangias sisters. It would conceal his fine garments from sight until he reached the Hill of Whispers. A man dressed in evening best might attract too much attention from some of the lurkers in the dark places of Ashfall.

'I'm for Raven's Reach, then,' said Locke. 'Until much later.

Jean, rest up. Master Ibelius, favour Jean with your motherly attention; I hope to return with very good news.'

'I shall be grateful if you return at all,' said Ibelius.

2

Midsummer mark, the Day of Changes, the seventeenth of Parthis in the Seventy-Eighth Year of Aza Guilla, as the Therin calendar would have it. On the Day of Changes, the city of Camorr went mad.

A Shifting Revel commanded the wide circular pond of the market, but this one was smaller and more ragged than the formal monthly revels; the centrepiece was a floating handball court made from a number of flat-topped barges lashed together. Teams had selected colours from a barrel; now randomly matched, they were mauling one another drunkenly as a crowd composed entirely of commoners cheered. When a team scored, a small boat with a beer keg lashed midships would pull alongside the court and ladle out a drink for every man on that team. Naturally, the matches got wilder and dirtier as they progressed; quite a few players were flung into the water, there to be fished out by a crew of diligent yellowjackets who wouldn't otherwise have dreamed of interfering.

Commoners ruled the streets of lower Camorr on the Day of Changes; they held wandering picnics, hauling ale barrels and wine-bags around with them. Streams of celebrants would cross paths, jostle, join and split; a gods' eye view of the affair would have shown disorderly men and women circulating through the city streets like blood through the vessels of an inebriated man.

In the Snare business was bountiful; the celebration sucked in sailors and visitors from foreign shores like a filling tidal pool; a few hours of Camorri hospitality and the guest revellers were unlikely to be able to tell their arses from their eardrums. The rising tide of drinking and gambling and spending swept up over their heads; they drowned in debauchery, quite willingly. There would be few ships setting out from port the next day; few would have the able manpower necessary to raise so much as a pennant, let alone a sail.

In the Cauldron and the Narrows and the Dregs, Capa Raza's

people celebrated their new ruler's largesse; by his order, dozens upon dozens of casks of cheap red wine had been rolled out in dog-carts; those gangs that were too poor or too lazy to journey to the crossroads of wickedness that was the Snare drank themselves silly on their own doorsteps. Raza's *garristas* moved through the neighbourhoods he claimed as his own with baskets of bread, passing loaves out to anyone who asked for them; it turned out that each loaf had either a copper piece or a silver piece baked into it, and when these hidden gifts were revealed (by means of a few unlucky broken teeth), not a single loaf of bread was safe from depredation south of the Temple District.

Raza's Floating Grave was open for visitors; several of his *garristas* and their gangs amused themselves with a game of cards that grew to epic size; at its height, forty-five men and women were bickering and shuffling and drinking and screaming at one another on the floor above the dark waters of the Waste, the waters that had eaten Capa Barsavi and his entire family.

Raza was nowhere to be seen; he had business in the north that evening and had told none outside his close circle of original servants that he would be at the Duke's court, looking down on them from the tower of Raven's Reach.

In the Temple District the Day of Changes was celebrated in a more restrained fashion; each temple's full complement of priests and initiates traded places with another and then another in an ever-shifting cycle. The black robes of Aza Guilla conducted a stately ritual on the steps of Iono's temple; the servants of the Father of Grasping Waters did likewise at theirs. Dama Elliza and Azri, Morgante and Nara, Gandolo and Sendovani; all the delegations of the divine burned candles and sang to the sky before a different altar, then moved on a few minutes later. A few extra benedictions were offered at the burnt-out House of Perelandro, where a single old man in the white robes of the Lord of the Overlooked, recently summoned from Ashmere, pondered the mess of the temple that had been thrust into his care. He had no idea how to begin composing his report to the Chief Divine of Perelandro on the destruction he'd found in an Elderglass cellar – the existence of which he'd not been informed of before his journey.

In the North Corner and Fountain Bend well-to-do young

453

couples made for Twosilver Green, where it was thought to be good luck to make love on the eve of the midsummer mark. It was said that any union consummated there before Falselight would bring the couple whatever they most desired in a child; this was a pleasant bonus, if true, but for the time being most of the men and women hidden away among the crushed-stone paths and rustling walls of greenery desired only one another.

On the waters of the Old Harbour, the frigate *Satisfaction* floated at anchor, yellow flags flying from its masts, yellow lanterns shining even by day. A dozen figures moved on its deck, calmly, surreptitiously going about the business of preparing the ship for night action; crossbows were racked at the masts and canvas tarps flung over them. Anti-boarding nets were hauled out below the rails on the ship's upper deck, and set there for rapid rigging, out of sight. Buckets of sand were set out to smother flames; if the shore engines let fly, some of them would surely hurl alchemical fire against which water would be worse than useless.

In the darkened holds beneath the ship's upper deck, another three dozen men and women ate a large meal, to have their stomachs full when the time for action came. There wasn't an invalid among them – not so much as an ague fever.

At the foot of Raven's Reach, home and palace of Duke Nicovante of Camorr, a hundred carriages were parked in a spiralling pattern around the tower's base; four hundred liveried drivers and guards milled about, enjoying refreshments brought to them by scampering men and women in the Duke's colours. They would be there waiting all night for the descent of their lords and ladies – the Day of Changes was the only day of the year when nearly every peer of Camorr, every lesser noble from the Alcegrante islands and every last member of the Five Families in their glass towers would be crammed together in one place, to drink and feast and scheme and intrigue and offer compliments and insults, while the Duke gazed down on them with his rheumy eyes. Each year the coming generation of Camorr's rulers watched the old guard grey a bit more before their eyes; each year their bows and curtsies grew slightly more exaggerated; each year the whispers behind their hands grew more poisonous. Nicovante had, perhaps, ruled too long.

454

There were six chain-elevators serving Raven's Reach; they rose and fell, rose and fell. With each new cage that creaked open at the top of the tower, a new flurry of people in coloured coats and elaborate dresses was disgorged onto the embarkation terrace to mingle with the chattering flood of nobles and flatterers, power brokers and pretenders, merchants and idlers and drunkards and courtly predators. Flights of birds circled in lazy, fluttering clouds as the sun beat down on this gathering with all of its power; the lords and ladies of Camorr seemed to be standing on a lake of molten silver at the top of a pillar of white fire.

The air rippled with waves of heat as the iron cage holding Locke Lamora and the Salvaras swung, clattering, into the locking mechanisms at the edge of the Duke's terrace.

3

'Holy Marrows,' said Locke, 'but I have never seen the like. I have never been this high in the air; by the Hands Beneath the Waters, I have never been this high in *society*! My lord and lady Salvara, pardon me if I cling to you both like a drowning man.'

'Sofia and I have been coming here since we were children,' said Lorenzo, 'every year, on this day. It's only overwhelming the first ten or eleven times you see it, believe me.'

'I shall have to take you at your word, my lord!'

Attendants in black and silver livery, with rows of polished silver buttons gleaming in the sunlight, held the cage door open for them as Locke followed the Salvaras onto the embarkation terrace. A squad of blackjackets marched past in full ceremonial dress, with rapiers carried over their shoulders in silver-chased scabbards. The soldiers wore tall black fur hats with medallions bearing the crest of the Duchy of Camorr just above their eyes; Locke winced to think how they must feel, marching back and forth beneath the sun's merciless consideration for hours on end. In his own clothes he was working up a healthy sweat, but he and his hosts had the option of moving inside the tower.

'Don Lorenzo and Doña Sofia? My lord and lady Salvara?'

The man who approached from the edge of the crowd was very

tall and wide-shouldered; he stood a full head above most of the Camorri present, and his angular features and singularly fair hair were marks of the oldest, purest sort of Vadran blood. This man had roots in the far north-east, in Astrath or Vintila, the heartlands of the Kingdom of the Seven Marrows. Curiously, he was dressed in Nightglass Company black, with a captain's silver collar pips, and his voice was pure upper-class Camorr without the hint of any other accent.

'Why, yes,' said Don Lorenzo.

'Your servant, my lord and lady. My name is Stephen Reynart; Doña Vorchenza, I believe, should have mentioned me to you.'

'Oh, of course!' Doña Sofia held out her hand; Reynart bent at the waist with his right foot forward, took her hand, and kissed the air just above it. 'So pleased to make your acquaintance at last, Captain Reynart. And how is dear Doña Vorchenza this afternoon?'

'She is *knitting*, my lady,' said Reynart with a smirk that told of some private joke. 'She has commandeered one of the Duke's sitting rooms for herself; you know how she feels about large, noisy gatherings.'

'I must, of course, find her,' said Sofia. 'I should love to see her.'

'I'm sure the feeling will be mutual, my lady. But may I presume? Is this Master Fehrwight, the merchant of Emberlain I was told you would be bringing?' Reynart bowed again, just the neck this time, and in heavily accented Vadran he said; 'May the Marrows run sweet and the seas run calm, Master Fehrwight.'

'May the Hands Beneath the Waves carry you to good fortune,' Locke replied in his own much smoother Vadran, genuinely surprised. He switched back to Therin for the sake of politeness: 'One of my countrymen, Captain Reynart? In the service of the Duke of Camorr? How fascinating!'

'I am most definitely of the Vadran blood,' said Reynart, 'but my parents died when I was an infant, on a trading mission to this city. I was adopted and raised by Doña Vorchenza, the Countess of Amberglass, the bright golden tower over there. She had no children of her own; although I cannot inherit her title and her properties, I have been allowed to serve in the Duke's Nightglass Company.'

'Astonishing! I must say, you look exceedingly formidable – the

456

image of the Kings of the Marrows themselves. I'd wager the Duke is only too pleased to have you in his service.'

'I hope with all my heart for that to be true, Master Fehrwight. But come; I'm holding you up. I beg pardon, my lord and lady Salvara; I am hardly a worthy topic of conversation. Let me show you into the tower, by your leave.'

'By all means,' said Sofia. She leaned close to Locke's ear and whispered, 'Doña Vorchenza is a dear old thing, something like a grandmother to all us Alcegrante ladies; she is the arbiter of all our gossip, you might say. She is not well – she is more and more distant with every passing month – but she is still very close to us. I hope you will have the chance to make her acquaintance.'

'I shall look forward to it, my lady Salvara.'

Reynart ushered them into the tower of Raven's Reach itself, and the sight that met Locke's eyes drew an involuntary gasp from his mouth.

From the outside Raven's Reach was opaque silver; from the inside, at least on the levels he could see, it was nearly transparent. A smoky haze seemed to live within the glass, cutting out the glare of the sun, reducing it to a plain white circle overhead that the naked eye could easily bear to regard, but in all other ways it let in the view as though it were not there at all. The hilly countryside and the wide Angevine lay to the north, while all the islands of the lower city lay spread like illustrations on a map to the south. Locke stared hard; he could even make out the thin black shapes of ships' masts bobbing past the southern edge of the city. His stomach fluttered with the thrill of vertigo.

Just above them the Sky Garden began; there were said to be a hundred tons of rich earth in the pots and troughs atop that roof. Vines cascaded down the sides; well-tended bushes and full-sized trees sprouted from the apex of the tower, a little round forest in miniature. In the branches of one of those trees, facing south to the Iron Sea, was a wooden chair regarded as the very highest point in Camorr any sane person could reach. The Sky Garden would be full of children; it was where the youngest nobles were released to amuse themselves while their parents tended to the business of the court beneath their feet.

The floor they stood on did not cover the full hundred-foot width of the tower; it was a semi-circle occupying only the north half of the tower. Locke grasped a rail at the southern edge of the floor and looked down; there were four other semi-circular galleries beneath them, each about twenty feet below the one above, each full of men and women. The vertigo threatened to swallow him again; staring down at least eighty feet to the 'ground', with the transparent side of the tower and that mind-twisting southern view spread out before him, he felt almost as though the world were tilting on its axis. The hand of Don Salvara on his shoulder brought him back to the present moment.

'You've got Raven's Reach disease, Lukas.' The Don laughed. 'You're clutching that rail like a lover. Come have some refreshments; your eyes will sort out the views in time, and it will all come to seem perfectly normal.'

'Oh, my lord Salvara, if only that should prove to be the case. I would be glad to visit the banquet tables.'

The Don led him through the press of silks and cottons and cashmeres and rare furs, nodding here and waving there. Sofia had vanished, along with Reynart.

The banquet tables, fifty feet from end to end, (or perhaps these were merely the appetiser tables; the light afternoon refreshments at a feast like this could rival the main courses from any lesser occasion) were laid with silver-trimmed linen cloths. Guild chefs, the Masters of the Eight Beautiful Arts of Camorr, stood at attention in their cream-yellow ceremonial robes and black scholars' caps with hanging gold cords behind their ears. Each chef, male or female, had intricate black tattoos on each of the four fingers of each hand, every design representing mastery of one of the Eight Gourmet Forms.

At one end of the banquet table were desserts (the Fifth Beautiful Art) – cherry cream cakes encased in shells of gold leaf that were intended to be eaten; cinnamon tarts painstakingly assembled with honey-paste glue into the shape of sailing vessels, a whole fleet of little ships with white marzipan sails and raisins for crewmen. There were hollowed-out pears, their cores replaced with cylinders of river-melon pulp or brandy cream; there were shaved river-melons, their green exteriors scraped down to reveal the pink flesh inside. Every exposed pink face bore a relief sculpture of the crest of Camorr, and alchemical globes set within the melons made them glow with an inviting pink light.

At the other end of the table were meats; each one of the silver platters held a *phantasmavola* – an Impossible Dish, an imaginary animal formed by joining the halves of two different creatures during preparation and cooking. Locke saw a roast boar with the head of a salmon, resting on a pile of black caviar. Nearby there was a pig's head, complete with a marsh-apple in its mouth, with a roast capon for a body. The whole affair was covered in brown caramel sauce and figs, and Locke gave in to the growling sensation at the bottom of his stomach. He let one of the chefs slice him a fair portion of the pig/capon, which he ate from a silver dish with a little silver fork; it came apart in his mouth with the texture of butter, and the flavours set his head whirling. He hadn't tasted anything so magnificent in weeks; he knew that it would have taken all of his powers, with the help of the Sanza brothers at their peak, to prepare something so fine in his old glass cellar. The thought stole some of the savour from his meal, and he finished quickly.

The bullock's head with the body of a squid he was happy to avoid.

At the centre of the banquet tables was the crowning glory (of this particular level, at least). It was a massively unsubtle subtlety, eight feet in length: an edible sculpture of the city of Camorr. The islands were baked sweet-bread on little raised metal platforms; the channels between those platforms ran deep with some blue liquor that was being ladled into cups by a chef at the right side of the diorama. Each major bridge in the city was represented by a crystallised-sugar replica; each major Elderglass landmark was a tiny model, from the Broken Tower in the south to the House of Glass Roses to the Five Towers overlooking everything. Locke peered very closely; there was even a tiny frosted-chocolate galleon little bigger than an almond, floating on a brown-pudding Wooden Waste.

'How are you faring, Lukas?'

Don Salvara was beside him again, wine-glass in hand; a black-coated attendant plucked Locke's used dish from his fingers the moment he turned to speak to the Don.

'I am overwhelmed,' said Locke, without much exaggeration. 'I had no idea what to expect; by the Marrows, perhaps it is well that I had no preconceptions. The court of the King of the Marrows must be like this; I can think of nowhere else that would possibly compare.'

'You honour our city with your kind thoughts,' said Lorenzo. 'I'm very pleased you decided to join us. I've just been chatting with a few of my peers. I'll have a serious talk with one of them in about an hour; I think he'll be good for about three thousand crowns. I hate to say it, but he's rather malleable, and he's very fond of me.'

'Lukas,' cried Doña Sofia as she reappeared with Reynart at her heels, 'is Lorenzo showing you around properly?'

'My lady Salvara, I am quite astounded by the spectacle of this feast; I daresay your husband could leave me sitting in a corner with my thumb in my mouth, and I would be adequately entertained all evening.'

'I would do no such thing, of course.' Don Salvara laughed. 'I was just off speaking to Don Bellarigio, love; he's here with that sculptor he's been patronising these past few months, that Lashani fellow with the one eye.'

A team of liveried attendants walked past, four men carrying something heavy on a wooden bier between them. The object was a gold and glass sculpture of some sort, a gleaming pyramid crested with the arms of Camorr. It must have had alchemical lamps within it, for the glass glowed a lovely shade of orange. As Locke watched, the colour shifted to green, and then to blue, and then to white, and back to orange again.

'Oh my, how lovely!' Doña Sofia was clearly enamoured with all things alchemical. 'The shifting hues! Oh, those adjustments must be precise; how I would love to see inside! Tell me, can Don Bellarigio's Lashani sculpt me one of *those*?'

Three more teams of men hauled three more sculptures past; each one shifted through a slightly different pattern of changing colours.

'I don't know,' said Reynart. 'Those are gifts for the Duke from one of our . . . more unusual guests. They've been cleared with my superiors; they certainly do look lovely.'

Locke turned back to the banquet table and suddenly found himself six feet away from Giancana Meraggio, who had an orchid at his breast, a silver plate of fruit in one hand and a gorgeous young woman in a red gown on the other. Meraggio's gaze passed over Locke, then whirled back; those penetrating eyes fixed on him and on the clothes he wore. The master money-changer opened his mouth, seemed to think better of it, and then opened it again.

'Sir,' said Meraggio in a cold voice, 'I beg your pardon, but . . .'

'Why, Master Meraggio!' Don Salvara stepped up beside him; at the sight of a Don, Meraggio shut his mouth once again and bowed politely from the waist, though not very deeply.

'Don Salvara,' said Meraggio, 'and the lovely Doña Sofia. What a pleasure to see you both! Greetings to you as well, Captain Reynart.' He dismissed the tall Vadran from his consideration with a shift of his head and peered at Locke again.

'Master Meraggio,' said Locke, 'why, what a fortunate coincidence! It is a pleasure to meet you at last; I have looked for you at your counting house many times, but I am afraid I have never had a chance to pay my proper respects.'

'Indeed? Why, I was just about to ask . . . who might you be, sir?'

'Master Meraggio,' said Don Salvara, 'allow me to present Lukas Fehrwight, merchant of Emberlain, servant of the House of bel Auster. He has come down to discuss the import of a certain quantity of small beer; I'd like to see how those Emberlain ales fare against our native best. Lukas, this is the Honourable Giancana Meraggio, master of the counting house that bears his name, known by many as the Duke of White Iron, for very good reason. All finance whirls around him like the constellations in the sky.'

'Your servant, sir,' said Locke.

'Of Emberlain? Of the House of bel Auster?'

'Why yes,' said Doña Sofia. 'He's here at the feast as our special guest.'

'Master Meraggio,' said Locke, 'I hope I do not presume too much, but do you find the cut of my coat pleasing? And the fabric?'

'A singular question,' said Meraggio, scowling, 'for both seem strangely familiar.'

'And well they should,' said Locke. 'On the advice of the Salvaras, I secured for myself a single suit of clothes cut in your Camorri style; I requested of the tailor that he select a cut that was especially favoured by the best-known taste in the entire city. And who should he name but yourself, sir; this suit of clothes is fashioned after your *very own preferences*! I hope you will not find me forward if I say that I find it most excellently comfortable.'

'Oh no,' said Meraggio, looking terribly confused. 'Oh, no. Not too forward at all – very flattering, sir, very flattering. I, um . . . I do not feel entirely well; the heat, you see. I believe I shall avail myself of some of the punch from that subtlety. It was a pleasure to make your acquaintance, Master Fehrwight. If you will excuse me, Doña Sofia, Don Lorenzo.'

Meraggio moved off, peering back over his shoulder at Locke and then shaking his head. *Oh, Crooked Warden*, thought Locke, *you're one funny son of a bitch, aren't you?*

'Lukas,' said Doña Sofia, 'have you had enough food for the time being?'

'I believe I shall keep rather well, my lady Salvara.'

'Good! Why not hunt down Doña Vorchenza with me; she's hiding down on one of the other galleries, hunched over her knitting. If she's lucid today, you'll love her, I guarantee it.'

'Doña Vorchenza,' said Reynart, 'is in the northernmost apartment of the western gallery, two floors down. Do you know the place I speak of?'

'Oh, yes,' said Sofia. 'What do you say, Lukas? Let us pay our respects; Lorenzo can circulate and work on the important affairs he should be looking into.'

'The matter has not slipped my mind, darling,' said Don Lorenzo with mock irritation. 'Master Fehrwight, I for my part hope the old Doña is speaking Therin this evening; you may find yourself introduced to the equivalent of a stone statue. Or perhaps she merely behaves that way when I'm in the room.'

'I wish I could say that it was entirely an affectation, my lord Salvara,' said Reynart. 'I should circulate for a while and try to look as though I'm actually on duty. Give my affection to Doña Vorchenza, my lady Sofia.'

'Of course, Captain. Are you coming, Lukas?'

The Doña led him down one of the wide Elderglass staircases with lacquered wood banisters. Softly glowing alchemical lamps in ornate casings gleamed at the foot of the stairs; they would be lovely after dark. The layout of this floor was the same as that of the one above; there was another fifty-foot banquet table crowded with delicacies and wonders, and one of the strangely beautiful

462

glass and gold pyramids had been set down beside it. *Curious*, thought Locke.

'My lady Salvara,' he said, smiling and pointing, 'perhaps a few attendants could be convinced to borrow one of those sculptures for you when we leave, and you could have your peek inside?'

'Oh, Lukas, if only – but one does not repay the Duke's hospitality by borrowing his decorative fixtures on a whim. Come, we need to go down to the next level. Lukas? Lukas, what's the matter?'

Locke had frozen, looking straight at the staircase that led down to the level below. Someone was just coming up: a lean, fit-looking man in a grey coat, grey gloves and grey breeches; his vest and four-cornered hat were black, his neckcloths rich scarlet, and on his left hand he wore a very familiar ring over the leather of his glove – Barsavi's ring, the black pearl of the Capa of Camorr.

Locke Lamora matched gazes with Capa Raza, his heart beating like a war-galley's drum. The lord of Camorr's underworld halted, dumbfounded; sheer bewilderment fluttered across his face, a look that made mirth rise from the bottom of Locke's soul. Then for the briefest second there was hatred; Raza ground his teeth together and the lines of his face tautened. Finally he seemed to regain control of himself – he twirled a gold-capped swagger stick of lacquered black witchwood, stuck it beneath his left arm, and strolled casually towards Locke and Doña Sofia.

4

'Surely,' said Capa Raza, 'you must be a Doña of Camorr; I do not believe I have had the pleasure of your acquaintance, gracious lady.' He swept off his hat and bent from the waist at the ideal angle, right foot out before his left.

'I am Doña Sofia Salvara of the Isla Durona,' she said. She held out her hand; he took it and kissed the air above it.

'Your servant, my lady Salvara; I am Luciano Anatolius. Charmed, my lady, quite charmed. And your companion? Have we met?'

'I do not believe so, sir,' said Locke. 'You look strangely familiar, but I'm sure I would recall if we had met before.'

'Master Anatolius, this is Lukas Fehrwight, a merchant of Emberlain, of the House of bel Auster,' said Sofia. 'My personal guest here at the Duke's feast.'

'A merchant of Emberlain? Greetings to you, sir. Why, you must be very *resourceful*, to make it all the way up here into such rarefied circles.'

'I do what I must, sir, I do what I must. I have some unusually good friends in Camorr; they often bring me unexpected advantages.'

'I don't doubt it. The House of bel Auster, you say? The famous liquor merchants? How grand. I'm as fond of a good draught as the next man. In fact, I prefer to make all of my purchases by the cask.'

'Indeed, sir?' Locke smiled. 'Why, that is the speciality of my firm; a great many wonderful and surprising things come out of our casks. We pride ourselves on always giving satisfaction – on delivering full value for value received, like for like – if you take my meaning.'

'I do,' said Capa Raza, with a grim smile of his own. 'An admirable business practice, one near to my own heart.'

'But surely,' said Locke, 'I remember now why you are familiar, Master Anatolius. Do you not have a sister? Perhaps a pair of them? I seem to recall having met them at some occasion – the resemblance seems *very* striking.'

'No,' said Capa Raza, scowling, 'I'm afraid you're very much mistaken; I have no sisters. Doña Sofia, Master Fehrwight, it has been a distinct pleasure making your acquaintance, but I fear I have pressing business elsewhere. I wish you both much pleasure at the feast this evening.'

Locke held out his hand and put on an innocent friendly smile. 'It is always a pleasure to make new acquaintances, Master Anatolius. Perhaps we shall see each other again?'

Capa Raza glared down at Locke's outstretched hand, then seemed to remember himself; he could hardly refuse such a courtesy without causing a great stir. His strong hand clasped Locke's forearm, and Locke returned the gesture. The fingers of Locke's other hand twitched; if only his stiletto had not been inconveniently hidden in a boot, he would now be tempted beyond all rational thought. 'You are very good, Master Fehrwight,' said Capa Raza with a placid face, 'but I very much doubt it.'

'If I have learned anything about this city, Master Anatolius,' said Locke, 'I have learned that it is full of surprises. A very good evening to you.'

'And to you,' said Raza, 'merchant of Emberlain.'

He moved quickly away into the crowd; Locke watched him all the way. Raza turned once and their eyes locked yet again, and then the Capa was gone, up the stairs to the next level, grey coat fluttering in his wake.

'Lukas,' said Doña Sofia, 'did I miss something?'

'Miss something?' Locke gave her another innocent Fehrwright smile. 'I don't believe so, my lady. It is just that that man greatly resembled someone I once knew.'

'A friend from Emberlain?'

'Oh no,' said Locke. 'Not a friend. And the man in question is dead – he is very, very dead.' Aware that he was clenching his teeth, he let ease return to his countenance. 'Shall we go and find your Doña Vorchenza, my lady?'

'Why, yes,' said Sofia. 'Yes, let's be about it. Do follow me.'

She led him down the stairs Raza had come up, down to yet another gallery packed rim to rim with the quality – 'blue-bloods and gold-bloods', as Father Chains might have put it. Instead of a banquet table, this level held a bar: forty feet of polished witchwood staffed by two dozen men and women in the Duke's livery. Behind them, on tables and shelves, rose thousands upon thousands of bottles; alchemical lamps had been placed behind them, and they bathed the gallery in cascading ribbons of colour. Huge pyramids of wine and beer glasses were to the sides of the bar, cordoned off behind velvet ropes; one unprofessional gesture could send hundreds of crowns' worth of fine crystal crashing to the floor. Blackjackets stood at stiff attention beside the glass pyramids, as added insurance. And, speaking of pyramids, another one of the lovely pyramid sculptures had been set out here, a few feet to the right of the bar, behind one of the velvet ropes.

Doña Sofia led him to the west, past the bar and the long line of nobles waiting to take in the liquid courage of their choice; some of them were already obviously impaired in the fine art of standing up straight. On the western wall of the gallery there was a heavy witchwood door bearing the silver seal of Duke Nicovante's personal arms. Doña Sofia pushed this door open and led him into a curving hallway lit by the soft silver glow of alchemical lanterns. There were three doors in this hall, and Doña Sofia brought him to the one at the far end, near what Locke supposed was the northern wall of the tower.

'Now,' said Doña Sofia with a smirk, 'it will either be Doña Vorchenza, or it will be a pair of young people doing something they should not . . .'

She slid the door open and peeked inside, and then tugged on Locke's sleeve. 'It's quite all right,' she whispered. 'It's her.'

Locke and Sofia were looking into a nearly square chamber with a slightly curved outer wall; unlike in the public galleries, the Elderglass in this part of the tower was opaque. The single window was in the northern wall, its wooden shade cracked open to let in the sunlight and the warm air of the late afternoon.

There was a single tall-backed wooden chair in the room, and it held a single hunch-backed old lady; she was bent over a pair of glittering needles, utterly fixated on the unidentifiable knitted object flowing forth into her lap from her efforts. A few rolls of black wool yarn lay at her feet. She was eccentrically dressed in a man's black coat and a pair of dark purple pantaloons such as cavalry officers traditionally wore; her little black slippers curved up at the ends like something from a fairy story. Her eyes seemed to be clear behind her half-moon optics, but they didn't look up from her knitting when Doña Sofia led Locke into the centre of the room.

'Doña Vorchenza?' Sofia cleared her throat and raised her voice. 'Doña Vorchenza? It's Sofia, my lady . . . I've brought someone for you to meet.'

Snick-snick, went Doña Vorchenza's needles, *snick-snick*, but those eyes did not look up.

'Doña Angiavesta Vorchenza,' said Sofia to Locke, 'Dowager Countess of Amberglass. She, ah . . . she comes and goes.' Sofia sighed. 'Might I beg you to stay here with her for just a moment? I'm going to the bar; she often takes white wine. Perhaps a glass of it will bring her back to us.'

'Of course, Doña Sofia,' said Locke cheerfully. 'I would be very honoured to wait on the Countess. Fetch her whatever you feel proper.'

'Can I bring you anything, Lukas?'

466

'No, oh no; you are too kind, my lady Salvara. I shall have something later, perhaps.'

Sofia nodded and withdrew from the room, closing the door with a *click* behind her. Locke paced for a few moments, hands behind his back.

Snick-snick, went the needles, *snick-snick*. Locke raised an eyebrow; the object flowing from those needles remained a perfect mystery. Perhaps it wasn't yet near completion. He sighed, paced a bit more and turned to stare out the window.

The green and brown hills spread out to the curving horizon north of the city; Locke could see the lines of roads, the particoloured roofs of small buildings, and the grey-blue of the Angevine, all fading into heat haze and distance. The sun suffused everything in hot white light; there wasn't a cloud to be seen.

There was a sudden vicious stabbing pain at the back of his neck, on the left side.

Locke whirled and slapped a hand to the site of the pain; there was a bit of wetness beneath his fingers. Doña Angiavesta Vorchenza, Dowager Countess of Amberglass, stood before him, drawing back the knitting needle she had just plunged into the back of his neck. Now her eyes were lively behind those half-moon optics, and a smile broke out of the network of lines on her lean face.

'Gaaaaaaaaaaaaah-*owwwwww!*' He rubbed at the back of his neck and maintained his slight Vadran accent only with the greatest difficulty: 'What the *hell* was that?'

'Grief-willow, Master Thorn,' said Doña Vorchenza. 'The poison of the grief-willow tree, which I'm sure you've heard of. You have but a few minutes to live . . . and I should very much like to spend them speaking to you.'

5

'You . . . you . . .'

'Stabbed you in the neck. Yes, well, I must confess it gave me pleasure, dear boy. What can I say? You have led us on a trying chase.'

'But . . . but . . . Doña Vorchenza, I do not understand. How have I given offence?'

'You might as well drop the Vadran accent. It's excellent, but I'm afraid you won't be able to smile and bluff your way out of this one, Master Thorn.'

Locke sighed and rubbed his eyes. 'Doña Vorchenza, if that needle was really poisoned, why the hell should I bother telling you anything?'

'Now that's a sensible question.' She reached down the front of her tunic and drew out a little glass vial capped with silver. 'In exchange for your cooperation, I'm prepared to offer you the antidote. You will, of course, come peacefully with me. You're hundreds of feet in the air, and every one of my Midnighters is currently here, dressed as staff. You'd be rather ignominiously treated if you tried to run so much as ten feet past that hallway.'

'Your . . . Midnighters . . . You mean . . . You must be fucking kidding. *You're* the Spider?'

'Yes,' she said, 'and by the gods it feels good to finally fling that in the face of someone who can appreciate it.'

'But,' said Locke, 'the Spider is . . . or at least I thought the Spider was . . .'

'A man? You and all the rest of this city, Master Thorn. I have always found the presumptions of others to be the best possible disguise – haven't you?'

'Hmmm.' Locke actually chuckled. A tingling numbness was spreading around the wound; it definitely wasn't just his imagination. 'Hanged by my own rope, Doña Vorchenza.'

'You must be brilliant, Master Thorn,' said Doña Vorchenza. 'I shall give you that; to do what you've done, to keep my people guessing these past few years . . . Gods, I wish I didn't have to put you in a crow's cage. Perhaps a deal could be arranged, once you've had a few years to think it over. It must be very new, and very odd, to finally have someone spring such a trap on *you*.'

'Oh, no.' Locke sighed and put his face in his hands. 'Oh, Doña Vorchenza, I'm so sorry to disappoint you, but the list of people that haven't outsmarted me seems to be getting smaller all the fucking time.'

'Well,' said Doña Vorchenza, 'that can't be pleasant. But come, you must be feeling rather strange by now; you must be unsteady on your feet. Just say yes. Give me the location of the funds you've stolen, and perhaps those years in the Palace of Patience can be mitigated. Give me the names of your accomplices, and I'm sure an accommodation can be reached.'

'Doña Vorchenza,' said Locke forcefully, 'I have no accomplices, and even if I did, I certainly wouldn't tell you who they were.'

'What about Graumann?'

'Graumann is a hireling,' said Locke. 'He thinks I'm really a merchant of Emberlain.'

'And those so-called bandits in the alley beside the Temple of Fortunate Waters?'

'Hirelings, long since fled back to Talisham.'

'And the false Midnighters, the ones who visited the Salvaras?'

'Homunculi,' said Locke. 'They crawl out of my arse every full moon; they've been a problem for years.'

'Oh, Master Thorn . . . grief-willow will still that tongue of yours rather permanently. You don't have to speak your secrets now; just surrender so I can give you this vial, and we can continue this conversation in more pleasant surroundings.'

Locke stared at Doña Vorchenza for several long seconds; he locked his gaze with those ancient eyes of hers and saw the obvious satisfaction in them, and his right hand curled into a fist of its own accord. Perhaps Doña Vorchenza was so used to her privileged status that she had forgotten their disparity in ages; perhaps she'd simply never conceived that a man of apparent refinement, even a criminal, could do what Locke did next.

He punched her square in the teeth, a whirling right that would have been comical had he thrown it against a younger, fitter woman. But it snapped Doña Vorchenza's head back; her eyes rolled up and she buckled at the knees. Locke caught her as she toppled, carefully plucking the vial from her fingers as he did so. He heaved her back into her chair, then uncapped the vial and poured its contents down his throat. The warm fluid tasted like citrus; he gulped it eagerly and threw the vial aside. Then, working with the utmost haste, he took off his coat and used it to tie Doña Vorchenza into her chair, knotting the sleeves several times behind her back.

Her head lolled forward and she groaned; Locke gave her a pat on the shoulder. On an impulse, he ran his hands quickly (and as politely as possible) through her waistcoat; he grunted in satisfaction when he turned up a little silk purse, jingling with coins. 'Not what I was hoping for,' he said, 'but we'll call it fair payment for a gods-damned needle in the neck, hmmm?'

Locke stood up and paced for a few moments. He turned back to Doña Vorchenza, knelt before her, and said; 'My lady, it wounds me to have to treat someone such as yourself so crudely; the truth is, I admire you very much and at any other time I'd be very curious to hear just where I fucked up and tipped you off. But you must admit I'd have to be crazy to go with you; the Palace of Patience simply does not suit. Thank you for the very interesting afternoon; give my regards to Don and Doña Salvara.'

With that, he pushed the wooden shutter as wide as it would go and stepped out the window.

The exterior of Raven's Reach, considered up close, was actually covered with irregularities, with little indentations and ledges, circling the tower at virtually every level. Locke slipped out onto a slender ledge about six inches wide; he pressed his stomach up against the warm glass of the tower and waited for the pounding of the blood within his temples to cease sounding like a pummelling from a heavy man's fists. It didn't, and he sighed.

'I am the Idiot King,' he muttered, 'of all the world's fucking idiots.'

The warm wind pushed at his back as he inched to his right; the ledge grew wider a few moments later, and he found an indentation in which to place his hand. Confident that he was in no immediate danger of falling, Locke glanced down over his shoulder, and immediately regretted it.

The glass tower offered a layer of insulation between the viewer and the vista; out here, it seemed as though the whole world fell away in a vast arc; he wasn't six hundred feet in the air, he was a thousand, ten thousand, a million – some incomprehensible number of feet that only the gods were fit to dare. He squeezed his eyes shut and clutched at the glass wall as though he could pour himself into it, like mortar into stones. He shuddered. The pork and capon in his stomach made enthusiastic enquiries about coming up in a nauseous torrent; his throat seemed to be on the verge of granting the request.

Gods, he thought, *I wonder if I'm back on one of the transparent sections of the tower? I must look pretty fucking funny.*

There was a creaking noise from overhead; he looked up and gasped.

One of the elevator-cages was coming down towards him; it was in line with him, and it would pass by about three feet from the spot he was clinging to.

It was empty.

'Crooked Warden,' Locke whispered, 'I'll do this, but the only thing I ask, the *only* thing, is that when this is done, you make me fucking forget. Steal this memory out of my head. And I will never climb more than three feet off the ground as long as I draw breath. Praise be.'

The cage creaked down; it was ten feet above him, then five feet, and then its bottom was even with his eyes. Breathing in deep, ragged, panicky gasps, Locke turned himself round on the tower so that his back was against the glass. The sky and the world beneath his feet both seemed too big to fit into his eyes; gods, he didn't want to think about them. The cage was sliding past; its bars were right there, three feet away over fifty-some storeys of empty air.

He screamed, and pushed himself off the glass wall of the tower. When he hit the blackened iron of the cage, he clung with hands and feet as desperately as any cat ever clung to a tree branch. The cage swayed back and forth, and Locke did his best to ignore the incredible things that did to the sky and the horizon. The cage door – he had to slip the door. It closed tightly for safety, but didn't have elaborate locks.

Working with hands that shivered as though the air were freezing, Locke slipped the bolt on the cage door and let it fall open. He then stepped gingerly round from the exterior to the interior, and with one last burst of dreadful vertigo reached out and slammed the door shut behind him. He sat down on the floor of the cage, gasping in deep breaths, shaky with relief and the after-effects of the poison.

'Whew,' he muttered. 'Well. That was fucking hideous.'

A rising elevator-cage full of noble guests drew level with Locke, twenty feet to his right; the occupants of the cage looked at him very curiously, and he waved.

Dreading the cage would lurch to a halt before it reached the ground and start to draw back up, he decided if it did he would take his chances at the Palace of Patience. But the cage continued all the way down; Vorchenza must still have been tied to her chair, out of action. Locke was on his feet when the cage settled against the ground; the liveried men who opened the door peered in at him with wide eyes.

'Excuse me,' said one of them, 'but were you . . . did you . . . were you *in* this cage when it left the embarkation platform?'

'Of course,' said Locke. 'That shape you saw, darting out from the tower? Bird. Biggest gods-damned bird you ever saw. Scared the piss right out of me, let me tell you. I say, are any of these carriages for hire?'

'Go to the outer row,' said the footman. 'Look for the ones with the white flags and lanterns.'

'Much obliged.' Locke rapidly perused the contents of Doña Vorchenza's coin-purse; there was a very satisfactory quantity of gold and silver inside it. He tossed a solon apiece to the liveried men beside the cage as he stepped out. 'It was a bird, right?'

'Yes, sir,' said the other man with a tip of his black cap. 'Biggest gods-damned bird we ever saw.'

6

The hired carriage left him at the Hill of Whispers. He paid very well, the 'forget you made this run' sort of very well, and then walked south through Ashfall on his own. It was perhaps the sixth hour of the evening when he returned to the hovel, bursting through the curtained door, yelling as he came – 'Jean, we have one hell of a fucking problem . . .'

The Falconer stood in the centre of the little room, smirking at Locke, his hand folded before him. Locke took in the tableau in a split second: Ibelius slumped motionless against the far wall, and Jean at the Bondsmage's feet, writhing in pain.

Vestris perched upon her master's shoulder; she fixed him with those black and gold eyes, then opened her beak and screeched triumphantly. Locke winced.

'Oh yes, Master Lamora,' said the Falconer. 'Yes, I'd say you *do* have one hell of a fucking problem.'

INTERLUDE:
The Throne in Ashes

Therim Pel was once called the Jewel of the Eldren; it was the largest and grandest of the cities that the lost race of ancients left to the men who claimed their lands long after their disappearance.

Therim Pel sat at the headwaters of the Angevine River where they poured in a white torrent from the mountains; it sat beneath their craggy majesty and was surrounded by rich fields for two days' ride by fast horse in every other direction. In the autumn those fields would sway with stalks of amber grain; a bounty fit for the seat of an empire, which Therim Pel was.

All the cities of the south knelt before the Therin Throne; the engineers of the empire built tens of thousands of miles of roads to weave those cities together. The empire's generals manned them with patrols to put bandits down, and maintained garrisons in smaller towns and villages to ensure that commerce and letters could flow, without interruption, from one end of the empire to the other, from the Iron Sea to the Sea of Brass.

Karthain and Lashain, Nessek and Talisham, Espara and Ashmere, Iridain and Camorr, Balinel and Issara; all those mighty city-states were ruled by Dukes who took their crowns of silver from the hands of the emperor himself; the few Dukes who remain in present times may wield great power, but they are self-declared; the high lineages dating back to the time of the Therin Throne have long been severed.

The Therin Throne entered into decline when the Vadrans appeared from the north; a raiding sea-people, they took the Throne protectorates on the northern half of the continent; they named the seven great rivers that flowed to the northern sea their Seven Holy Marrows, and they frustrated the Throne's efforts to reclaim its territory by smashing every army it sent north. Weakened, the Therin Throne could not sustain the effort, and so it was diminished – diminished but not broken.

It took the Bondsmagi of Karthain to do that.

The Bondsmagi were newly formed in the city of Karthain; they were beginning to expand the reach of their unique and deadly guild to other cities, and they showed little sign of bowing to the angry demands of the emperor in Therim Pel. He insisted that they halt their activities, and they are said to have replied with a short letter listing the prices for which His August Majesty could hire their services. The emperor sent in his own royal circle of sorcerers; they were slain without exception. The emperor then raised his legions and marched on Karthain, vowing to slay every sorcerer who claimed the title of Bondsmage.

The emperor's declaration of war was a test of resolve for the new guild, which publicly vowed reprisals awful to behold against anyone who dared to harm one of their number.

During his march to Karthain, the emperor's soldiers managed to kill about a dozen.

Four hundred Bondsmagi met the emperor's legions just to the east of Karthain; the sorcerers condescended to offer a pitched battle. In less than two hours one third of the emperor's forces were slaughtered. Strange mists boiled up from the ground to mislead their manoeuvres; illusions and phantasms tormented them. Flights of arrows halted in the air and fell to the ground, or were hurled back upon the archers that had loosed them. Comrade turned upon comrade, maddened and misled by sorcery that could manipulate a man's actions as though he were a marionette. The emperor himself was hacked to pieces by his own personal guard; it is said that no piece larger than a finger remained to be burned on a pyre afterwards. With the emperor slain, his surviving generals scattered and his remaining soldiers scampered like rabbits for Therim Pel.

But the affair did not end there; the Bondsmagi in conclave decided to enforce their rules, to enforce them in such a fashion that the entire world would shudder at the thought of crossing them for as long as men might have memories.

They worked their retribution on the city of Therim Pel.

The firestorm they conjured was awesome and unnatural; four hundred magi, working in concert, kindled something at the heart of the empire that historians still fear to describe. It is said that the flames were as white as the hearts of the stars themselves; that the column of black smoke rose so high it could be seen from the deep Iron Sea, far east of Camorr, and as far north as Vintila, capital of the young Kingdom of the Seven Marrows.

Even this hideous conjuring could not touch Elderglass; those structures in the city built by Eldren art survived unscathed. But everything else the fire touched, it ate: wood and stone and metal, mortar and paper and living things, all the city's buildings and all the city's culture and all the city's population who could not flee before the magi began their work were burnt into a desert of grey ashes, a desert that settled a foot deep across a black scar baked into the ground.

Those ashes swirled in the hot wind at the foot of the one man-crafted object the magi preserved – the throne of the empire. That chair remains to this day in the haunted city of Therim Pel, surrounded by a field of ashes that time and rains have turned into a sort of black concrete. Nothing grows in Therim Pel; no sensible man or woman sets foot within that black monument to the resolve of the Bondsmagi of Karthain.

It was they who broke the Therin Throne with their unearthly fire; they who cast the city-states of the south into hundreds of years of warring and feuding while the Kingdom of the Seven Marrows grew powerful in the north.

It is that image that comes to mind when most men think to cross a Bondsmage – the image of an empty chair standing alone in a dry sea of desolation.

Chapter Sixteen

Justice is Red

I

The Falconer moved his fingers, and Locke Lamora fell to his knees, gripped by an all-too-familiar pain that burned within his bones. He toppled to the floor of the hovel, beside Jean.

'What a *pleasure*,' said the sorcerer, 'to see that you survived our little arrangement at the Echo Hole. I am impressed; despite your reputation; I had imagined we were too clever for you. And only this afternoon I thought it was Jean Tannen alone that I sought; but this is something finer by far.'

'You,' spat Locke, 'are a twisted fucking animal.'

'No,' said the Bondsmage, 'I obey the orders of my paying client. And my orders are to make sure the murderer of my client's sisters takes his time in dying.' The Falconer cracked his knuckles. 'You I regard as a windfall.'

Locke screamed and reached out towards the Bondsmage, willing himself forward through the pain, but the Falconer muttered under his breath and the wracking, stabbing sensations seemed to multiply tenfold. Locke arched his back and tried to breathe but the muscles behind and beneath his lungs were as solid as stones.

When the Bondsmage released him from this torment, he slumped down, gasping; the room spun.

'It's very strange,' said the Falconer, 'how the evidence of our victories can become the instruments of our downfall. Jean Tannen, for example – you must be a fantastic fighter to have taken my client's sisters, though I see you suffered in doing so. And now they've struck back at you from the shadelands. A great many divinations are possible when one of my kind gets his hands on the physical residue of another man – fingernail parings, for example. Locks of hair. *Blood on the edge of a knife.*'

Jean groaned, unable to speak.

'Oh, yes,' said the Falconer. 'I was certainly surprised to see who that blood led me to; in your shoes I'd have been in the first caravan to the other side of the continent. You might even have been left in peace.'

'Gentlemen Bastards,' hissed Locke, 'do not abandon one another, and we do not run when we owe vengeance.'

'That's right,' said the Bondsmage, 'and that's why they also die at my feet in filthy fucking hovels like this one.'

Vestris fluttered from his shoulder and settled onto a shelf high in a corner of the room, staring balefully down at Locke, twitching her head from side to side in excitement. The Falconer reached inside his coat and drew out a sheet of parchment, a quill and a small bottle of ink. He uncapped the bottle and set it down on the sleeping pallet; he dipped the quill and smiled down at Locke.

'Jean Tannen,' said the Falconer. 'What a simple name; easy to write, even easier than it was to stitch.'

His quill flew across the parchment; he wrote in great looping whorls and his smile grew with every letter. When he was finished, his silver thread snaked out around the fingers of his left hand and he moved them with an almost hypnotic rhythm. A pale silver glow rose from the page in his hands, outlining the curves of his face.

'Jean Tannen,' said the Falconer. 'Arise, Jean Tannen. Arise. I have a task for you.'

Shuddering, Jean rose first to his knees and then to his feet. He stood before the Falconer; Locke, for his part, still found it impossible to move.

'Jean Tannen,' said the Bondsmage, 'take up your hatchets. Nothing would please you more at this moment than to take up your hatchets.'

Jean reached beneath the sleeping pallet and took out the Wicked Sisters; he slipped one into either hand and the corners of his mouth drew up.

'You like to use those, don't you, Jean?' The Falconer shifted the silver threads in his left hand. 'You like to feel them biting into flesh . . . You like to see the blood spatter. Oh, yes . . . Don't worry; I have a task you can set them to.'

The Falconer gestured down at Locke with the sheet of paper in his right hand.

'Kill Locke Lamora,' he said.

477

Jean shuddered; he took a step towards Locke, then hesitated. He frowned and closed his eyes.

'I name your given name, Jean Tannen,' said the Bondsmage. 'I name your given name, the truthful name, the name of the spirit. I name your name. Kill Locke Lamora. Take your hatchets and *kill Locke Lamora*.'

Jean took another halting step towards Locke; his hatchets rose slowly; he seemed to be clenching his jaws. A tear rolled out of his right eye; he took a deep breath, and then another step. He sobbed, and raised the Wicked Sisters above his shoulders.

'No,' said the Falconer. 'Oh no. Wait. Step back.'

Jean obliged, backing off a full yard from Locke, who sent up silent prayers of relief mingled with dread for whatever might come next.

'Jean's rather soft-hearted,' said the Falconer, 'but you're the real weakling, aren't you? *You're* the one who begged me to do anything to you as long as I left your friends alone; you're the one who went into the barrel with his lips closed when he could have betrayed his friends and perhaps lived . . . Oh no. I know how to make this right. Jean Tannen, drop your hatchets.'

The Wicked Sisters hit the ground with a heavy thud just beside the Falconer's feet. A moment later the Bondsmage spoke in an eerie language, and shifted the threads in his left hand; Jean Tannen screamed and fell to the ground, shaking feebly.

'It would be much better, I think,' said the Falconer, 'if *you* were to kill *Jean*, Master Lamora.'

Vestris screeched down at Locke; the sound had a strange mocking undertone of laughter.

Oh, fuck, Locke thought. *Oh, gods.*

'Of course,' said the Falconer, 'we already know your last name is a sham. But I don't need a full name; even a fragment of a true name will be quite enough. You'll see, Locke. I promise that you'll see.' His silver threads disappeared; he dipped his quill once again and wrote briefly on the parchment.

'Yes,' he said. 'Yes. You may move again.' And as he spoke, it was so; the paralysis lifted, and Locke twitched his fingers experimentally. The Bondsmage wiggled his silver thread once more; Locke felt a strange *something* seem to form in the air around him, a sort of pressure, and the parchment glowed again.

'Now,' said the Falconer. 'I name your name, Locke. I name your given name, the truthful name, the name of the spirit. I name your name, Locke.' The Falconer kicked the Wicked Sisters along the ground towards Locke. 'Arise. Arise and take up Jean Tannen's hatchets. Arise and kill Jean Tannen.'

Locke pushed himself up to his knees and rested on his hands for a moment.

'*Kill Jean Tannen.*'

Shaking, he reached out for one of Jean's hatchets, slid it towards him, and crawled forward with it clutched in his right hand. His breathing was ragged; Jean Tannen lay at the Bondsmage's heels, just three or four feet away, on his face in the plaster dust of the hovel.

'*Kill Jean Tannen.*'

Locke paused at the Falconer's feet and turned his head slowly to stare at Jean. One of the big man's eyes was open, unblinking; there was real terror there. Jean's lips quivered uselessly, trying to form words.

Locke pushed himself up and raised the hatchet; he bellowed wordlessly.

He swung up with the heavy ball of the hatchet; the blow struck home right between the Falconer's legs. The silver thread and the parchment fluttered from the Bondsmage's hands as he gasped and fell forward, clutching at his groin.

Locke whirled to his right, expecting instant attack from the scorpion hawk, but to his surprise the bird had fallen from its perch and was writhing on the hovel floor, wings beating uselessly at the air; a series of choked half-screeches issued from its beak.

Locke smiled the cruellest smile he'd ever worn in his entire life as he rose to his feet.

'It's like that, is it?' He grinned fiercely at the Bondsmage as he slowly raised the hatchet, ball side down. 'You see what she sees; each of you feels what the other feels, right?'

The words brought him a warm sense of exultation, but they nearly cost him the fight; the Falconer managed to find concentration enough to utter one syllable and curl his fingers into claws. Locke gasped and staggered back, nearly dropping the hatchet. It felt as though a hot dagger had been shoved through both of his kidneys; the sizzling pain made it impossible to act, or even to think.

The Falconer attempted to stand up, but Jean Tannen suddenly rolled towards him and reached up, grabbing him by the lapels. The big man yanked hard, and the Falconer crashed back down, forehead-first, against the floor of the hovel. The pain in Locke's guts vanished, and Vestris screeched once again from the floor beside his feet. He wasted no further time.

He whipped the hatchet down in a hammer blow, breaking Vestris's left wing with a dry *crack*.

The Falconer screamed and writhed, flailing hard enough to briefly break free from Jean's grasp. He clutched at his left arm and hollered, his eyes wide with shock. Locke kicked him in the face, hard, and the Bondsmage rolled over in the dust, spitting up the blood that was suddenly running from his nose.

'Just one question, you arrogant fucking *cocksucker*,' said Locke. 'I'll grant the Lamora part is easy to spot; the truth is, I didn't know about the apt translation when I took the name. I borrowed it from this old sausage dealer, who was kind to me once, back in Catchfire before the plague. I just liked the way it sounded.

'But what the fuck,' he said slowly, 'ever gave you the fucking idea that *Locke* was the first name I was actually born with?'

He raised the hatchet again, reversed it so the blade side was towards the ground, and then brought it down with all of his strength, severing Vestris's head completely from her body.

The sound of the bird's suddenly-interrupted screech echoed and merged with the screams of the Falconer, who clutched at his head and kicked his legs wildly. His cries were pure madness, and it was a mercy to the ears of Locke and Jean when they died, and he fell sobbing into unconsciousness.

2

The Falconer of Karthain awoke to find himself lying spread-eagled, on the floor of the hovel. The smell of blood was in the air, Vestris's blood. He closed his eyes and began to weep.

'He is secure, Master Lamora,' said Ibelius. When the dog-leech had awoken from whatever spell the Bondsmage had flung at him, he'd been only too eager to help tie the Karthani down. He and Jean had scavenged some metal stakes from somewhere; these had been pounded into the floor, and the Bondsmage was lashed to them by long strips of bedding, tied tight around his wrists and ankles. Smaller strips had been tied around and between his fingers; he could barely wiggle them.

'Good,' said Locke.

Jean Tannen sat on the sleeping pallet, looking down at the Bondsmage with dull, deeply shadowed eyes. Locke stood at his feet, staring down at him with undisguised loathing.

A small oil fire burned in a glass jar; Ibelius crouched beside it, slowly heating a dagger. The thin brown smoke curled up to the ceiling.

'You are fools,' said the Falconer between sobs, 'if you think to kill me. My brethren will take satisfaction; think on the consequences.'

'I'm not going to kill you,' said Locke. 'I'm going to play a little game I like to call "Scream in pain until you answer my fucking questions."'

'Do what you will,' said the Falconer. 'The code of my order forbids me to betray my client.'

'Oh, you're not working for your client any more, arsehole,' said Locke. 'You're not working for your client ever again.'

'It's ready, Master Lamora,' said Ibelius.

The Bondsmage craned his neck to stare over at Ibelius; he swallowed and licked his lips, his eyes darting around the room.

'What's the matter?' Locke reached out and carefully took the dagger from the dog-leech's hand; its blade glowed red. 'Afraid of fire? Why ever should that be?' Locke grinned, an expression utterly without humour. 'Fire's the only thing that's going to keep you from *bleeding to death*.'

Jean rose from the sleeping pallet and knelt on the Falconer's left arm. He pressed it down at the wrist, and Locke slowly came over to stand beside him, hatchet in one hand and glowing knife in the other.

'I heartily approve in theory,' said Ibelius, 'but in practice I believe I shall . . . absent myself.'

'By all means, Master Ibelius,' said Locke.

The curtain swished and the dog-leech was gone.

'Now, said Locke, 'I can accept that it would be a bad idea to kill you. But when I finally let you slink back to Karthain, you're going as an object lesson. You're going to remind your pampered, twisted, arrogant fucking brethren about what might happen when they fuck with someone's friends in Camorr.'

The blade of Jean's hatchet whistled down, severing the Bondsmage's little finger of his left hand. The Falconer screamed.

'That's Nazca,' said Locke. 'Remember Nazca?'

He swung down again; the ring finger rolled in the dirt, and blood spurted.

'That's Calo,' said Locke.

Another swing, and the middle finger was gone. The Falconer writhed and pulled at his bonds, whipping his head from side to side in agony.

'Galdo, too. Are these names familiar, Master Bondsmage? These little *footnotes* to your fucking contract? They were awfully real to me. Now this finger coming up – this one's Bug. Actually, Bug probably should have been the little finger, but what the hell.' The hatchet fell again; the index finger of the Falconer's left hand joined its brethren in bloody exile.

'Now the rest,' said Locke, 'the rest of your fingers and both of your thumbs, those are for me and Jean.'

3

It was tedious work; they had to reheat the dagger several times to cauterise all the wounds. The Falconer was half-mad with pain by the time they'd finished; his eyes were closed and his teeth clenched. The air in the enclosed room stank of burnt flesh and scalded blood.

'Now,' said Locke, sitting on the Falconer's chest, 'it's time to talk.'

'I cannot,' said the Bondsmage. 'I cannot . . . betray my client's secrets.'

'You no longer have a client,' said Locke. 'You no longer serve Capa Raza; he hired a Bondsmage, not a fingerless freak with a dead bird for a best friend. When I removed your fingers, I removed your obligations to Raza – at least the way I see it.'

'Go to hell,' the Falconer spat.

'Oh, good. You've decided to do it the hard way.' Locke smiled again and tossed the dagger to Jean, who set it over the flame and began to heat it once more. 'If you were any other man, I'd threaten your balls next. I'd make all sorts of cracks about eunuchs, but I think you could bear that. You're *not* most men. I think the only thing I can take from you that would truly pain you to the depths of your soul would be your tongue.'

The Bondsmage stared at him, his lips quivering. 'Please,' he whispered at last, 'have pity, for the gods' sakes, have pity; my order exists to serve – I was carrying out a contract.'

'When that contract became my friends,' said Locke, 'you exceeded your mandate.'

'Please,' whispered the Falconer.

'No,' said Locke. 'I will cut it out; I will cauterise it while you lie there writhing. I will make you a mute – I'm guessing you might be able to conjure some magic without fingers, but without a tongue?'

'Please!'

'Speak,' said Locke. 'Tell me what I want to know.'

'Gods,' sobbed the Falconer. 'Gods forgive me. Ask. Ask your questions.'

'If I catch you in a lie,' said Locke, 'it's balls first, and then the tongue. Don't presume on my patience. Why did Capa Raza want us all dead?'

'Money,' said the Falconer. 'Coin. That vault of yours; I spied it out while I was first making my observations of you. He'd intended just to use you as a distraction for Capa Barsavi, but when we discovered how much money you'd already stolen, he wanted to have it – to pay for me. Almost another month of my services, to help him finish his tasks here in the city.'

'You murdered my fucking friends,' said Locke, 'and you tried to murder Jean and myself, for the metal in our vault?'

'You seemed the type to hold a grudge,' whispered the Falconer. 'Isn't that funny? We figured we'd be better off with all of you safely dead.'

'You figured right,' said Locke. 'Now, Capa Raza, the Grey King, whoever the fuck he is.'

'Anatolius.'

'That's his real name? Luciano Anatolius?'

'Yes. How did you know?'

'Fuck you, Falconer, answer *my* questions. Anatolius. What was his business with Barsavi?'

'The Secret Peace,' said the Bondsmage. 'The Secret Peace was not achieved without a great deal of bloodshed and difficulty. There was one rather powerful merchant, with the resources to discover what Barsavi and the Duke's Spider had put together; not being of noble blood, he was rather upset at being excluded.'

'Barsavi killed him,' said Locke.

'Yes. Avram Anatolius, a merchant of the Fountain Bend. Barsavi murdered him and his wife, and his three younger children – Lavin, Ariana and Maurin. But the three older children – they escaped with one of their master's maids. She protected them, pretending they were her own. She took them to safety in Talisham.'

'Luciano, Cheryn and Raiza.'

'Yes . . . the oldest son and the twin sisters. They have been rather consumed with the idea of vengeance, Master Lamora . . . your own amateur flirtation with the urge has nothing on them. They spent twenty-two *years* preparing for the events of the past two months. Cheryn and Raiza returned eight years ago under an assumed name; they built their reputations as *contrarequialla* and became Barsavi's most loyal servants.

'Luciano, on the other hand . . . Luciano went to sea, to train himself in the arts of war and command, and to amass a fortune. A fortune with which to purchase the services of a Bondsmage.'

'Capa Raza was a merchant captain?'

'No,' said the Falconer, 'a buccaneer. Not the ragged sort of idiot you find down on the Sea of Brass; but quiet, efficient, professional. He struck rarely and he struck well; he took good cargo from the galleons of Emberlain, sank the ships and left no one alive to speak his name.'

'Gods damn it,' said Jean. 'Gods *damn* it; he's the captain of the *Satisfaction*.'

'Yes, the so-called plague ship,' said the Falconer. 'Odd how easy it is to keep people away from your ship when you really want to, isn't it?'

'He's been sending his fortune out to it as "charitable

provisions"' said Jean. 'It must be all the money he stole from us, and everything he took from Capa Barsavi.'

'Yes,' said the Bondsmage sadly. 'It belongs to my order, for services rendered.'

'We'll just see about that. So what now? I saw your master Anatolius at Raven's Reach a few hours ago; what the fuck does he think he's doing next?'

'Hmmm.' The Bondsmage fell silent for several moments. Locke prodded him in the neck with Jean's hatchet, and he smiled strangely. 'Do you mean to kill him, Lamora?'

'*Ila justicca vei cala,*' said Locke.

'Your Throne Therin is passable,' said the Bondsmage, 'but your pronunciation is excrement. "Justice is red," indeed. So you want him, more than anything? You want him screaming under your knife?'

'That'd do for a start.'

Unexpectedly, the Falconer threw back his head and began to laugh – a high-pitched noise tinged with madness. His chest shook with mirth and fresh tears ran from his eyes.

'What?' Locke prodded him again with the hatchet. 'Stop being deliberately freakish and give me my fucking answer.'

'I'll give you two,' said the Falconer, 'and I'll give you a choice that's guaranteed to cause you pain. What hour of the evening is it?'

'What the hell does it matter to you?'

'I'll tell you everything; please, just tell me what the hour is.'

'I'd wager it's half past seven,' said Jean. The Bondsmage began laughing once again. A smile grew on his haggard face, impossibly beatific for a man who'd just lost his fingers and thumbs.

'What? What the fuck is it? Spit out a real answer or you lose something else.'

'Anatolius,' said the Falconer, 'will be at the Floating Grave. He'll have a boat behind the galleon; he can reach it through one of Barsavi's escape hatches. At Falselight the *Satisfaction* will turn on her anchor chain and put out to sea; she'll tack first to the east, sweeping past the south end of the Wooden Waste where it opens to the ocean. His crew in the city has been sneaking out to the ship, one or two at a time, in the provision boat. Like rats leaving a sinking vessel. He'll stay until the last; it's his style. Last out of danger. They'll pick him up south of the Waste.'

'His crew in the city,' said Locke, 'you mean the "Grey King's men," the ones who've been helping him all along?'

'Yes,' said the Bondsmage. 'Time your entrance properly . . . and you should have him to yourself, or very close, before he sets off in the boat.'

'That doesn't cause me pain,' said Locke. 'That thought brings me pleasure.'

'But here's the second point. The *Satisfaction* puts out to sea just as the greater part of Anatolius' plan goes into effect.'

'Greater part?'

'Think, Lamora; you can't truly be this dense. Barsavi slew Avram Anatolius, but who *allowed* it to happen? Who was complicit?'

'Vorchenza,' said Locke slowly. 'Doña Vorchenza, the Duke's Spider.'

'Yes,' said the Falconer. 'And behind her, the man who gave her the authority to make such decisions?'

'Duke Nicovante.'

'Oh yes,' whispered the sorcerer, genuinely warming to his subject. 'Oh, yes. But not just him, either. Who stood to benefit from the Secret Peace? Who did the arrangement shield, at the expense of men like Avram Anatolius?'

'The nobility.'

'Yes. The peers of Camorr. And Anatolius wants them.'

' "Them"? Which "them"?'

'Why, all of them, Master Lamora.'

'How the fuck is *that* possible?'

'Sculptures, Master Lamora, four unusual sculptures delivered as gifts to the Duke. Currently placed at various points within Raven's Reach.'

'Sculptures? I've seen them – gold and glass, with shifting alchemical lights. Your work?'

'Not my work,' said the Falconer. 'Not my sort of thing at all. The alchemical lights are just a bit of mummery – they are beautiful, I suppose. But there's a lot of room left inside those things for the real surprise.'

'What?'

486

'Alchemical fuses,' said the Falconer. 'Set for a certain time to ignite small clay pans of fire-oil.'

'But that can't be all.'

'Oh no, Master Lamora.' Now the sorcerer positively smirked. 'Before he hired me, Anatolius spent part of his considerable fortune on securing large amounts of a rare substance.'

'No more games, Falconer – what the hell is it?'

'Wraithstone.'

Locke was silent for a long moment; he shook his head as though to clear it. 'You can't be fucking serious.'

'Hundreds of pounds of it,' said the Falconer, 'distributed in the four sculptures. All the peers of Camorr will be crammed into those galleries at Falselight – the Duke and his Spider and all their relatives and friends and servants and heirs. Do you know anything about Wraithstone smoke, Master Lamora? It's slightly lighter than air. It will rise until it fills every level of the Duke's feast; it will pass out through the roof vents and it will fill the Sky Garden, where all the children of the nobility are playing as we speak. Those standing on the embarkation platform *might* escape,' he chuckled, 'but I very much doubt it.'

'At Falselight,' said Locke in a small voice. His hand was over his mouth.

'Yes,' hissed the sorcerer. 'At Falselight. So now you have your choice, Master Lamora. At Falselight, the man you want to kill more than anyone in the world will be briefly alone at the Floating Grave. At Falselight, six hundred people at the top of Raven's Reach will suffer a fate worse than death. Your friend Jean looks to be in very poor health; I doubt he can help you with either task. So the decision is yours. I wish you joy of it.'

Locke rose and tossed Jean his hatchet. 'It's no decision at all,' he said. 'Gods damn you, Falconer, it's no decision at all.'

'You're going to Raven's Reach,' said Jean.

'Of course I am.'

'Have a pleasant time,' said the Falconer, 'convincing the guards and the nobility of your sincerity; Doña Vorchenza herself is rather convinced that the sculptures are completely harmless.'

'Well,' said Locke, grinning wryly and scratching the back of his head, 'I'm kind of popular at Raven's Reach at the moment; they might be glad to see me.'

'How do you expect to get back out?' asked Jean.

'I don't know,' said Locke. 'I don't have the first fucking clue; it's a state of affairs that's served me well in the past. I need to run. Jean, for the love of the gods, hide near the Floating Grave if you must, but don't you dare go in there; you're in no condition to fight.' Locke turned to the Bondsmage. 'Capa Raza – how is he with a blade?'

'Deadly,' said the Falconer with a smile.

'Well, look, Jean. I'll do what I can at Raven's Reach and I'll try to get to the Floating Grave somehow. If I'm late, I'm late; we'll follow Raza and we'll find him somewhere else. But if I'm not late . . . If he's still there . . .'

'Locke, you can't be serious. At least let me come with you. If Raza has any skill with a blade at all, he'll kick the shit out of you.'

'No more arguments, Jean; you're hurt too badly to be of much use. I'm fit and I'm angry and I'm obviously crazy. Anything could happen. But I have to go, now.' Locke shook hands with Jean, stepped to the doorway, and turned back. 'Cut this bastard's fucking tongue out.'

'You promised,' yelled the Falconer. 'You *promised*!'

'I didn't promise you shit. My dead friends, on the other hand – I made them certain promises.'

Locke whirled and went out through the curtain; behind him, Jean was setting the knife over the oil flame once again. The Falconer's screams followed him down the debris-strewn street, and then faded into the distance as he turned north and began to jog towards the Hill of Whispers.

4

It was well past the eighth hour of the evening before Locke set foot on the flagstones beneath the Five Towers of Camorr once again; the journey north had been problematic. Between bands of drunken revellers with obliterated senses (and sensibilities) and the guards at the Alcegrante watch stations (Locke finally managed to convince them that he was a lawscribe heading north to meet an acquaintance leaving the Duke's feast; he also slipped them a 'midsummer mark gift' of gold tyrins from a little supply hidden up his sleeve), he felt himself fortunate to make it at all. Falselight would rise within the next hour and a quarter; the sky was already turning red in the west and dark blue in the east.

He made his way past the rows and rows of carriages in close array. Horses stamped and whinnied; a great many of them had relieved themselves onto the lovely stones of the largest courtyard in Camorr. Footmen and guards and attendants mingled in groups, sharing food and staring up at the Five Towers, where the glory of the coming sunset painted strange, fresh colours on their Elderglass walls.

Locke was so busy considering what to say to the men at the elevator hoists, he didn't even see Conté until the taller, stronger man had one hand around the back of his neck and one of his long knives jammed into Locke's back.

'Well, well,' he said, 'Master Fehrwight. The gods are kind. Don't say a fucking thing, just come with me.'

Conté half-led and half-hauled him to a nearby carriage; Locke recognised it as the one he'd ridden to the feast in with Sofia and Lorenzo. It was a black-lacquered box with a window on the side opposite the door; that window's curtains and shutters were drawn tightly shut.

Locke was thrown onto one of the padded benches within the carriage. Conté bolted the door behind him and sat down on the opposite bench with his knife held at the ready.

'Conté, please,' said Locke, not even bothering with his Fehrwight accent, 'I need to get back inside Raven's Reach; everyone inside is in terrible danger.'

Locke hadn't known that someone could kick hard from a sitting position; Conté braced himself against his seat with his free hand and showed him that it was possible. The bodyguard's heavy boot knocked him back into his corner of the carriage. Locke bit down hard on his tongue and tasted blood; his head rattled against the wooden walls.

'Where's the money, you little shit?'

'It's been taken from me.'

'Not fucking likely. Sixteen thousand five hundred full crowns?'

'Not quite; you're forgetting the additional cost of meals and entertainment at the Shifting—'

489

Conté's boot lashed out again and Locke went sprawling into the opposite corner of his side of the carriage.

'For fuck's sake, Conté! I don't have it! I don't have it! It's been taken from me! And it's not important at the moment!'

'Let me tell you something, Master Lukas-fucking-Fehrwight. I was at Godsgate Hill; I was younger then than you are now.'

'Good for you, but I don't give a sh—' Locke said, and for that he ate another boot.

'I was at Godsgate Hill,' continued Conté, 'too fucking young by far, the single most scared-shitless runt of a pikeman Duke Nicovante had in that mess. I was in it bad; my banneret was up to its neck in shit and Verrari and the Mad Count's cavalry. Our horse had withdrawn; my position was being overrun. Our peers of Camorr fell back and saw to their own safety – with one fucking exception.'

'This is the single most irrelevant thing I've ever—' said Locke, as he moved for the door; Conté brought up his knife and convinced him back into his seat.

'Baron Ilandro Salvara,' said Conté. 'He fought until his horse went down beneath him; he fought until he took four wounds and had to be hauled from the field by his legs. All the other peers treated us like garbage; Salvara nearly killed himself trying to save us. When I got out of the Duke's service, I tried the city watch for a few years; when that turned to shit, I begged for an audience with the old Don Salvara and I told him I'd seen him at Godsgate Hill; I told him he'd saved my fucking life, and that I'd serve him for the rest of his, if he'd have me. He took me in. When he passed away, I decided to stay on and serve Lorenzo. Fucking move for that door again and I will *bleed* some enthusiasm out of you.

'Now Lorenzo,' said Conté with undisguised pride, 'he's more a man of business than his father was. But he's made of the same stuff; he went into that alley with a blade in his hand when he didn't know you, when he thought you were being attacked for real, by real fucking bandits that meant you harm. Are you *proud*, you fucking pissant? Are you proud of what you've done to that man, who tried to save your fucking life?'

'I do what I do, Conté,' said Locke with a bitterness that surprised him. 'I do what I do. Is Lorenzo a saint of Perelandro?

He's a peer of Camorr; he profits from the Secret Peace. His great-great-grandfather probably slit someone's throat to claim a peerage; Lorenzo benefits from that every day. People make tea from ashes and piss in the Cauldron while Lorenzo and Sofia have you to peel their grapes and wipe their chins for them. Don't talk to me about what I've done. I need to get inside Raven's Reach *now*.'

'Get serious about telling me where that money is,' said Conté, 'or I'll kick your arse so hard every piece of shit that falls out of it for the rest of your life will have my gods-damned heel print on it.'

'Conté,' said Locke, 'everyone in Raven's Reach is in danger. I need to get back up there.'

'I don't believe you,' said Conté. 'I wouldn't fucking believe you if you told me my name was Conté. I wouldn't believe you if you told me fire was hot and water was wet! Whatever you want, you don't get it.'

'Conté, please, I can't fucking escape up there. Every gods-damned Midnighter in the city is up there; the Spider is up there; the Nightglass Company is up there; three hundred peers of Camorr are up there! I'm unarmed. Haul me up there yourself, but for the love of the fucking gods, get me up there. If I don't get up there before Falselight, it'll be too late.'

'Too late for what?'

'I don't have the time to explain; listen to me babble to Vorchenza and it'll all fall together.'

'Why the hell,' said Conté, 'do you need to talk to that fading old crone?'

'My mistake,' said Locke. 'I seem to have more of the pulse of things than you do. Look, I can't fuck around any more. Please, *please*, I'm begging you. I'm not Lukas Fehrwight; I'm a gods-damned thief. Tie my hands, put your knife to my back; I don't care what your terms are. Please take me back up into Raven's Reach; I don't care how. You tell me how we do it.'

'What's your real name?'

'How is that important?'

'Spit it up,' said Conté, 'and maybe I'll tie your hands and fetch some guards, and I'll try to get you up into Raven's Reach.'

'My name,' said Locke with a sigh of resignation, 'is Tavrin Callas.'

Conté looked hard at him for a moment, then grunted.

'Very well, Master Callas. Hold out your hands and don't move; I'm going to tie you up so tight I guarantee it'll fucking hurt. Then we'll take a walk.'

5

There were Nightglass soldiers near the chain-elevator landings who'd been given his description; naturally, they were delighted when Conté hauled him over with his hands tied in front of him. They ascended once again, Locke with Conté at his back and a blackjacket holding him by either arm.

'Please take me to Doña Vorchenza,' said Locke. 'If you can't find her, please find one of the Salvaras. Or even a captain in your company named Reynart.'

'Shut up, you,' said one of the blackjackets. 'You go where you go.'

The cage slid home into the locking mechanisms on the embarkation terrace; a milling crowd of nobles and their guests turned their attention to Locke as he was frogmarched forward between the three men. As they passed the threshold into the first gallery within the tower, Captain Reynart happened to be standing nearby with a plate of small confectionery ships in his hands. His eyes grew wide; he took a last bite of marzipan sail, wiped his mouth, and thrust his dish into the arms of a passing waiter, who nearly toppled over in surprise.

'By the gods,' he said, 'where did you find him?'

'We didn't, sir,' said one of the blackjackets. 'Man behind us says he's in the service of lord and lady Salvara.'

'I caught him by the carriages,' said Conté.

'Fantastic,' said Reynart. 'Take him down a level, to the eastern wing of suites. There's an empty storeroom with no windows. Search him, strip him down to his breechclout, and throw him in there. Two guards at all times. We'll pull him out after midnight, when the feast starts to break up.'

'Reynart, you can't,' cried Locke, struggling uselessly against the men that held him. 'I came back on my own. On my own, do you understand? Everyone here is in danger. Are you in on your adopted mother's business? I need to talk to Vorchenza!'

'I've been warned to develop selective hearing when it comes to you.' Reynart gestured to the blackjackets. 'Storeroom, now.'

'Reynart, no! The sculptures, Reynart! Look in the fucking sculptures!'

Locke was shouting; guests and nobles were taking an intense interest, and Reynart clapped a hand over his mouth. More blackjackets appeared out of the crowd.

'Keep making a fuss,' said Reynart. 'And these lords and ladies might just see blood.' He withdrew his hand.

'I know who she is, Reynart! I know who Vorchenza is. I'll shout it across all of these galleries. I'll go kicking and screaming, and before I'm in that room everyone will know. Look at the gods-damned sculptures, please.'

'What about the sculptures?'

'There's something in them, dammit. It's a plot. They're from Capa Raza.'

'They were a gift to the Duke,' said Reynart. 'My superiors cleared them personally.'

'Your superiors,' said Locke, 'have been interfered with. Capa Raza hired the services of a Bondsmage. I've seen what he can do to someone's mind.'

'This is ridiculous,' said Reynart. 'I can't believe I'm letting you conjure another fairy tale. Get him downstairs, but first let me gag him.' Reynart plucked a linen napkin from another nearby waiter's tray and began to wad it up.

'Reynart, please, please, take me to Vorchenza. Why the fuck would I come back if it wasn't important? Everyone here is going to fucking die if you throw me in that storeroom. *Please* take me to Vorchenza.'

Stephen stared coldly at him, then set the napkin down. He put his finger in Locke's face. 'I'll take you to see the Doña. If you utter so much as a single word while we're hauling you over to her, I will gag you, beat you senseless and put you in the storeroom. Is that clear?'

Locke nodded vigourously.

Reynart gestured for more blackjackets to join them; Locke was taken across the gallery and down two sets of stairs with six soldiers at his side and Conté scowling just behind. Reynart led him back to the very same hall and the very same chamber where he'd first met

Doña Vorchenza. She was sitting in her chair, knitting discarded at her feet, holding a wet cloth to her lips while Doña Salvara knelt beside her. Don Salvara stood staring out the window with his leg up on the sill; all three of them looked very surprised indeed when Reynart thrust Locke into the room before him.

'This room is closed,' said Reynart to his guards. 'Sorry, you too,' he said when Conté tried to pass.

'Let the Salvaras' man come in, Stephen,' said Doña Vorchenza. 'He already knows most of it; he might as well know the rest.'

Conté stepped in, bowed to Vorchenza, and grabbed Locke by the right arm while Reynart locked the door behind them. The Salvaras gave Locke a matching pair of undisguised scowls.

'Hello, Sofia. Hey, Lorenzo. Nice to see you two again,' said Locke in his natural voice.

Doña Vorchenza rose from her chair, closed the distance between herself and Locke with two steps, and hit him in the mouth, a straight-arm blow with the flat of her palm. His head whirled to the right and spikes of pain shot through his neck.

'Ow,' he said. 'What the fuck is it with you, anyway?'

'A debt to be repaid, Master Thorn.'

'You stuck a gods-damned poisoned needle in my neck!'

'You most certainly deserved it,' said Doña Vorchenza.

'Well, I for one would dis . . .'

Reynart grabbed him by his left shoulder, spun him round, and slammed his own fist into Locke's jaw. Vorchenza was rather impressive for someone of her age and build, but *Reynart* could really hit. The room seemed to go away for a few seconds; when it returned, Locke was sprawled in a corner, lying on his side. Small blacksmiths seemed to be pounding on anvils inconveniently located just above his eyes; Locke wondered how they'd got in there.

'I told you Doña Vorchenza was my adopted mother,' said Reynart.

'Oh my,' said Conté, chuckling. 'Now this is my sort of private party.'

'Has it occurred to any of you,' said Locke, crawling back to his feet, 'to ask why the fuck I came all the way back to Raven's Reach when I'd already made it clean away?'

'You jumped from one of the outside ledges,' said Doña

Vorchenza, 'and you grabbed one of the elevator-cages as it went past, didn't you?'

'Yes, as a matter of fact; all the other ways to the ground were too unhealthy to consider.'

'You see? I told you, Stephen.'

'Perhaps I thought it was possible,' said the Vadran, 'but I just didn't want to think it had actually been done.'

'Stephen is not fond of heights,' said Vorchenza.

'He's a very wise man,' said Locke, 'but please, please listen to me. I came back to warn you – those sculptures. Capa Raza gave you four of them. Everyone in this tower is in awful fucking danger from them.'

'Sculptures?' Doña Vorchenza stared down at him curiously. 'A gentleman left four gold and glass sculptures as a gift for the Duke.' She looked over at Stephen. 'I'm sure the Duke's security men have looked into them, and approved them. I wouldn't know; I'm just consulting in this affair as a favour to some of my peers.'

'So I've been told by my superiors,' said Reynart.

'Oh, stop that,' said Locke. 'You're the Spider. I'm the Thorn of Camorr. Did you meet Capa Raza? Did you meet a Bondsmage styling himself the Falconer? Did they speak to you about the sculptures?'

Don and Doña Salvara were staring at Doña Vorchenza; the old woman stuttered and coughed.

'Whoops,' said Locke. 'You hadn't told Sofia and Lorenzo, had you? Playing the old friend-of-a-friend angle. Sorry. But I need to talk to you as the Spider. When Falselight comes, everyone in Raven's Reach is fucked.'

'I knew it,' said Sofia. 'I knew it!' She grabbed her husband by the arm and squeezed hard enough to make him wince. 'Didn't I tell you?'

'I'm still not so sure,' said Lorenzo.

'No,' said Doña Vorchenza, sighing. 'Sofia has the truth of the matter, I *am* the Duke's Spider. There, I said it. If it gets beyond this room, throats will be cut.'

Conté looked at her with surprise and a strange sort of approval in his eyes; Locke stumbled back to his feet.

'As for the matter of the sculptures,' said Doña Vorchenza, 'I did clear them personally; they *are* a gift to the Duke.'

'They're a plot,' said Locke. 'They're a trap. Just open one up and you'll see! Capa Raza means to ruin every man, woman and child in this tower – it'll be worse than murder.'

'Capa Raza,' said Doña Vorchenza, 'was a perfect gentleman; he was almost too demure to accept my invitation to briefly join us this evening. This is another one of your fabulations, intended to bring you some advantage.'

'Oh, shit yes,' said Locke. 'I marched back here after escaping and had myself cleverly tied up and hauled in here by the whole gods-damned Nightglass Company on purpose. Now I've got you right where I fucking want you. Those sculptures are full of Wraithstone, Vorchenza! *Wraithstone.*'

'Wraithstone,' said Doña Sofia, aghast. 'How can you know?'

'He doesn't,' said Doña Vorchenza. 'He's lying. The sculptures are harmless.'

'Open one up,' said Locke. 'There's an easy remedy for this argument. Please, Falselight is coming. Open one up. They catch fire at Falselight.'

'Those sculptures,' said Vorchenza, 'are Ducal property worth thousands of crowns. They will not be damaged on some mad whim of a known criminal.'

'Thousands of crowns,' said Locke, 'versus hundreds of lives. Every peer in Camorr is going to be a drooling moron, do you understand? Can you imagine those children in that garden with white eyes like a Gentled horse? That's what we'll all be,' he shouted, '*Gentled.* That shit will *eat our fucking souls.*'

'Can it really hurt to check?'

Locke looked up at Reynart with gratitude on his face. 'No it can't, Reynart. Please. Please do.'

Doña Vorchenza massaged her temples. 'This is quite out of hand,' she said. 'Stephen, please throw this man somewhere secure until after the feast. A room without windows, please.'

'Doña Vorchenza,' said Locke, 'what does the name Avram Anatolius mean to you?'

Her eyes were cold. 'I couldn't begin to say,' she said. 'What do you imagine it means to you?'

'Capa Barsavi murdered Avram Anatolius twenty-two years ago,' said Locke. 'And you knew about it. You knew he was a threat to the Secret Peace.'

'I can't see what relevance this has to anything,' said Doña Vorchenza. 'You will be silent now, or I'll have you silenced.'

'Anatolius had a son,' said Locke with desperate haste, as Stephen took a step towards him. 'A surviving son, Doña Vorchenza. Luciano Anatolius. Luciano is Capa Raza. Luciano took revenge on Barsavi for the murder of his parents and his siblings, now he means to have revenge on you as well! You and all your peers.'

'No,' said Doña Vorchenza, touching her head again. 'No, that's not right. I enjoyed the time I spent with Capa Raza. I can't imagine he would do anything like this.'

'The Falconer,' said Locke. 'Do you recall the Falconer?'

'Raza's associate,' said Vorchenza distantly. 'I . . . I enjoyed my time with him, as well. A quiet and polite young man.'

'He did something to you, Doña Vorchenza,' said Locke. 'I've seen him do it, right before my eyes. Did he speak your true name? Did he write something on a piece of parchment?'

'I . . . I . . . cannot . . . This is . . .' Doña Vorchenza cringed; the wrinkles of her face bent inward, as though she were in pain. 'I must invite Capa Raza . . . It would be impolite not to invite him to the . . . to the feast . . .' She slumped against her chair and screamed.

Lorenzo and Sofia rushed to her aid; Reynart picked Locke up by the front of his vest and slammed him against the wall, hard. Locke's feet dangled a foot off the ground, as Reynart bellowed, 'What did you do to her?'

'Nothing,' gasped Locke. 'A Bondsmage cast a spell over her. Think, man – is she being rational about the sculptures? The bastard did something to her mind.'

'Stephen,' said Doña Vorchenza in a hoarse voice, 'put the Thorn down. He's right. He's right . . . Raza and the Falconer . . . It's like I'd forgotten, somehow. I wasn't going to accept Raza's request . . . The Falconer did something at the desk, and I . . . I . . .'

She stood up once more, assisted by Sofia. 'Luciano Anatolius, you said. Capa Raza is Avram Anatolius' son? How could you possibly know that?'

'Because I tied that Bondsmage to the floor just an hour or two ago,' said Locke, as Reynart let him slide back down the wall. 'I cut off his fingers to get him to talk, and when he'd confessed everything I wanted to hear, I had his fucking tongue cut out, and the stump cauterised.'

Everyone in the room stared at him.

'I called him an arsehole, too,' said Locke. 'He didn't like that.'

'It's worse than death to slay a Bondsmage,' said Doña Vorchenza.

'He's not dead; he's just very gods-damned sorry.'

Doña Vorchenza shook her head. 'Stephen, the sculptures. There's one on this floor, isn't there? Beside the bar.'

'Yes,' said Reynart, moving for the door. 'What else do you know about them, Thorn?'

'They've got alchemical fuses,' said Locke. 'And clay pots of fire-oil. At Falselight that fire-oil goes up; this whole tower fills with Wraithstone smoke. Anatolius sails away, laughing his head off.'

'This Luciano Anatolius,' said Sofia, 'is he the one we met on the stairs?'

'One and the same,' said Locke. 'Luciano Anatolius, also known as Capa Raza, also known as the Grey King.'

'If these things are alchemical,' said Sofia, 'I'd better be the one to have a look at them.'

'If it's going to be dangerous, I'm going as well,' said Lorenzo.

'And me,' said Conté.

'Great! We can all go! It'll be fun!' Locke waved his tied hands at the door. 'But hurry it up, for fuck's sake.'

Conté took him by the arm and pushed him along at the rear of the procession; Reynart and Vorchenza led the way out past the startled blackjackets. Reynart beckoned for them to follow. They left the hallway and returned to the main gallery.

The crowd of red-faced revellers parted as the strange procession swept through the gallery. Reynart strode up to the blackjacket standing beside the glittering pyramid of wine glasses. 'This end of the bar is temporarily closed. Make it so,' he said. Turning to his other soldiers, he said, 'Cordon this area off fifteen or twenty feet back. Don't let anyone else get close, in the name of the Duke.'

Doña Sofia ducked under the velvet rope and crouched beside the sculpted pyramid. The soft lights continued to flash and change behind the glass windows set into its faces; it was about two and a half feet on a side at its base, and three feet tall.

'Captain Reynart,' she said, 'You had a pair of gloves at your belt, I seem to recall. May I borrow them?'

Reynart passed her a pair of black leather gloves and she slipped them on. 'It's rarely wise to take too much for granted; contact poisons are child's play,' she said absently, and ran her fingers across the surface of the sculpture while peering at it closely. She shifted position several times, her frown deepening with each new examination.

'I can't see any opening in the casing,' she said, standing up again. 'Not so much as a seam; the workmanship is very good. If the device is intended to issue forth smoke, I can't imagine how the smoke would escape.' She tapped a gloved finger against one of the glass windows.

'Unless . . .' She tapped the window again. 'This is what we call ornamental glass; it's thin and fragile. It's not commonly used in sculpture, and we never use it in the laboratory, because it can't take heat . . .'

Her head whirled towards Locke; her almond-blonde ringlets spun like a halo. 'Did you say there were pots of fire-oil in this device?'

'So I heard,' he replied, 'from a man very eager not to lose his tongue.'

'That might be it,' she said. 'Fire-oil would generate a great deal of heat inside a metal enclosure. It would shatter the glass – shatter the glass and let out the smoke! Captain, draw your rapier, please. I should like to use it.'

Concealing any qualms he might have had, Reynart drew his rapier and carefully passed it to her, hilt first. She examined the silver butt of the weapon, nodded, and used it to smash in the glass. It broke with a high-pitched tinkle. She reversed the rapier and used the blade to sweep away the jagged fragments from around the edges of the window, then passed it back to Reynart. There were mutters and exclamations from the watching crowd, who were barely being kept in check by Reynart's thin arc of apologetic blackjackets.

'Careful, Sofia,' said Don Lorenzo.

'Don't teach a sailor to shit in the ocean,' she muttered as she peered into the window, which was about eight inches wide at its base, tapering slightly towards the top. She reached in with one gloved hand and touched one of the shifting alchemical lights; she twisted her wrist and drew it out.

'Not even attached to anything,' she said as she set it on the ground beside her. 'Oh, gods,' she whispered when she peeked back into the window without the light in her way. Her hand came up to her mouth and she stumbled back to her feet, shaking.

Doña Vorchenza stepped up directly beside her. 'Well?'

'It's Wraithstone,' said Doña Salvara with horror. 'The whole thing is full of it; I can see it in there, and I can smell the powder.' She shuddered as some people do when a large spider scuttles across their path. 'There's enough in just this one sculpture to do for the whole tower. It seems your Capa Raza wanted to be thorough.'

Doña Vorchenza stared out through the glass at the vista north of Camorr; the sky was noticeably darker than it had been even when Locke had been dragged past the bar for his second visit to her. 'Sofia,' said the Countess Amberglass, 'what can you do about these things? Can you prevent their ignition?'

'I don't believe so,' said Doña Salvara. 'I couldn't see the alchemical fuses; they must be under the Wraithstone. And it's also possible they might ignite if they're interfered with; I could easily craft a similar mechanism in my own lab. Trying to disable it might be as bad as letting it burn in the first place.'

'We need to get them out of the tower,' said Reynart.

'No,' said Sofia. 'Wraithstone smoke rises; it's lighter than the air around us. I doubt we can get them far enough away by Falselight; if they go off at the bottom of Raven's Reach, we'll still be standing in the column of smoke as it rose. The best thing to do would be to drown them; Wraithstone is rendered impotent by the admixture of water, after a few minutes. The fire-oil would still burn but the white smoke wouldn't rise. If only we could fling them into the Angevine!'

'We can't,' said Vorchenza, 'but we can drop them into the Sky Garden's cistern; it's ten feet deep and fifteen feet wide. Will that do?'

'Yes! Now we just need to get them up there.'

'Stephen—' said Doña Vorchenza, but Captain Reynart was already in motion.

'My lords and ladies,' Reynart bellowed at the top of his voice, 'your assistance is urgently required, in the name of Duke Nico-vante. Nightglass, to me. I require a clear path to the stairs, my lords and ladies. With all apologies, I will not be gentle with anyone in our way.

'We need to fetch these damn things off the galleries and haul them up to the Sky Garden,' said Reynart. He grabbed one of his men by the shoulder. 'Run up to the embarkation terrace and find Lieutenant Razelin. Tell him to clear the Sky Garden, on my authority. Tell him I don't want a single child up there five minutes from now. He'll know what to do. Act now, apologise later.'

'Free my hands,' said Locke. 'Those things are heavy; I'm not terribly strong, but I can help.'

Doña Vorchenza looked at him curiously. 'Why did you come back to warn us, Master Thorn? Why didn't you simply make good your escape?'

'I'm a thief, Doña Vorchenza,' he said quietly. 'I'm a thief, and maybe even a murderer, but this is too much. Besides, I mean to kill Raza. If he wanted it, I had to foil it. Simple as that.' He held out his hands, and she nodded slowly.

'You can help, but we must speak afterwards.'

'Yes, we must, hopefully without needles this time,' said Locke. 'Conté, be a friend and get rid of these ropes.'

The lean bodyguard slashed through Locke's bonds with one of his knives. 'If you try to fuck around,' he growled, 'I'll put you in the cistern and have them drop the sculptures on top of you.'

Locke, Conté, Reynart, Don Salvara and several blackjackets knelt to lift the sculpture; Sofia watched for a second or two, frowning, and then shoved her way in beside her husband to take part of his edge.

'I shall find the Duke,' said Vorchenza. 'I shall see that he's notified of what's going on.' She hurried away across the gallery.

'Well, this isn't so bad with eight of us,' said Reynart, 'but it's going to be awkward as all hell. We've got quite a few steps to go up.'

Stumbling along together, they hauled the sculpture up one flight of stairs. More blackjackets were waiting on that gallery floor. 'Find all of these sculptures,' Reynart yelled. 'Eight men to each of them! Find them and carry them up to the Sky Garden! In the Duke's name give a good shove to anyone who gets in your way! And by the gods don't drop them!'

Soon multiple parties of struggling, swearing soldiers were hauling sculptures up in the wake of Reynart's party. Locke was panting and sweating; the others around him weren't much better off.

'What if this thing goes off in our arms?' muttered one of the blackjackets.

'First, we'd burn our hands,' said Sofia, red-faced with exertion. 'Then we'd all fall over senseless before we could take six steps, and then we'd be Gentled. And then we'd feel very silly, wouldn't we?'

Up to the last gallery and beyond, they left the feast in their wake. Guards and servants leapt aside as they stumbled along service passages. At the very top of Raven's Reach a wide marble staircase wound its way up to the Sky Garden, spiralling along the inside of the smoky-transparent exterior walls. All of Camorr whirled around them as they went up spiral after spiral; the sun was just half a pale medallion sinking below the curved western horizon. Strange dark shapes hung down from above; Locke had to stare at them for several seconds before he realised they were the dangling vines of the Sky Garden, swaying in the wind outside.

Dozens of children were running down past them, shouting, chased by blackjackets and scolded by servants. The staircase opened onto the rooftop garden, which really was a forest in miniature; olive trees and orange trees and alchemical hybrids with rustling emerald leaves rippled in the warm wind beneath the cloudless purple sky.

'Where's the damn cistern?' asked Locke. 'I've never been up here.'

'On the eastern edge of the garden,' said Lorenzo. 'I used to play up here.'

Beneath the dangling tendrils of a weeping willow they found the cistern, a circular pond five yards across, as Doña Vorchenza had promised. Without preamble, they heaved the sculpture into the water; a great splash sprang up in its wake, dousing two of the blackjackets. It sank rapidly, trailing a milky white cloud in the water, and struck the bottom of the cistern with a heavy clank.

One by one the other three sculptures were tossed in on top of it, until all four were beneath the surface of the now-milky water and the Sky Garden was crowded with blackjackets.

'Now what?' Locke panted.

'Now we should clear the roof,' said Doña Sofia. 'That's still a great deal of Wraithstone; I wouldn't want anyone near it, even with it under water. Not until a few hours have passed.'

Everyone else on the roof was only too happy to comply with her suggestion.

6

Falselight was just beginning to rise when Doña Vorchenza met them once again on the top gallery of Raven's Reach. The scintillating streamers of ghostly colour from the Elderglass towers could just be seen through the tall door to the embarkation platform. The gathering was in an uproar around them; blackjackets were running to and fro, uttering apologies to Dons and Doñas as they stumbled against them.

'It's as good as war,' she said when the Salvaras, Locke, Conté and Reynart gathered around her. 'To try something like this, worse even than mass assassination. Gods! Nicovante's calling up the Nightglass, Stephen; you're going to have a busy night.'

'Midnighters?' he asked.

'Get them all out of here,' said Vorchenza, 'quickly and quietly. Assemble at the Palace of Patience; have them ready for a scrap. I'll throw them in wherever Nicovante decides they can do the most good.

'Master Thorn,' she said, 'we are grateful to you for what you've done; it will earn you a great deal of consideration. But now your part in this affair is over; I'll have you taken over to Amberglass under guard. You're a prisoner, but you've earned some comforts.'

'Bullshit,' said Locke. 'You owe me more than that. Raza's mine.'

'Raza,' said Doña Vorchenza, 'is now the most wanted man in all Camorr; the Duke intends to crush him like an insect. His domains will be invaded and the Floating Grave thrown open.'

'You *idiots*,' cried Locke. 'Raza isn't commanding the Right People, he's fucking using them! The Floating Grave is empty;

Raza's escaping as we speak. He didn't want to be Capa, he just wanted to use the position to get Barsavi and wipe out the peerage of Camorr.'

'How do you know so much about the affairs of Raza, Master Thorn?'

'Raza forced me to help him fox Capa Barsavi, back when Raza was still calling himself the Grey King. The deal was that he'd let me go after that, but it was a double-cross. He killed three of my friends and he took my money.'

'*Your* money?' said Don Lorenzo, curling one hand into a fist. 'I daresay you mean ours!'

'Yes,' said Locke. 'And everything I took from Doña de Marre and Don Javarriz and the Feluccias. More than forty thousand crowns – a fortune. Raza stole it from me. I wasn't lying when I said I didn't have it any more.'

'Then you've nothing of further value to bargain with,' said Doña Vorchenza.

'I said I didn't have it any more, not that I didn't know where it was,' said Locke. 'Raza's got it with Barsavi's fortune, ready to smuggle out of the city. It was meant to be used to pay for his Bondsmage.'

'Then tell us where it is,' said Doña Vorchenza.

'Raza's mine,' said Locke. 'I get sent back down to the ground and I go free. Raza killed three of my friends and I mean to cut out his fucking heart; I'd trade all the white iron in Camorr for the chance.'

'Men are hanged in this city for stealing a few pieces of silver,' said Doña Vorchenza, 'and you propose to go free after stealing tens of thousands of full crowns. I think not.'

'It's a moment of truth, Doña Vorchenza,' said Locke. 'Do you want the money back? I can tell you where it is; I'll tell you right where to find it, along with Barsavi's fortune, which has to be considerable. In exchange all I want is Raza. I go free and I kill the man who tried to wipe out you and all your peers. Be reasonable – now that you all know my face and my voice, I can hardly return to my old career, at least here in Camorr.'

'You presume too much.'

'Did the Spider of Camorr prevent Capa Raza from filling Raven's Reach with enough Wraithstone to Gentle the whole

504

fucking city? No, that was the *Thorn* of Camorr, thanks very much. Every man and woman and child here tonight is only well because *I* have a soft fucking heart; not because you were doing your job. You owe me, Vorchenza. You owe me, on your honour. Give me Raza and you can have the money, too.'

She gave him a stare that could have turned water to ice. 'On my honour, Master Thorn,' she said at last, 'for services rendered to the Duke and to my peers, you may go free, and if you beat us to Raza, you may have him, though if you do not, I shall not apologise. And should you resume your activities and our paths cross again, I will have you executed without trial.'

'Seems fair. I'm going to need a sword,' said Locke. 'I nearly forgot.'

To his surprise, Captain Reynart unbuckled his rapier belt and tossed it to Locke. 'Get it wet,' he said. 'With my compliments.'

'Well?' said Doña Vorchenza as Locke strapped the belt around his waist, over Meraggio's excellent blue breeches, 'Now the money. Where is it?'

'North of the Teeth of Camorr,' said Locke, 'there are three shit-barges at the private docks. You know the ones; they haul all the dreck and excrement out of the city and take it north to the fields.'

'Of course,' said Doña Vorchenza.

'Raza's been having his fortune hidden on one of them,' said Locke. 'In wooden chests sealed in layers of oilcloth, for obvious reasons. After he slipped out of Camorr his plan was to meet the barge up north and off load the treasure. It's all there, underneath those heaps of shit.'

'That's ridiculous,' said Doña Vorchenza.

'I didn't say my answer was going to be pleasant,' said Locke. 'Think about it. What's the last place anyone would *want* to look for a cache of coins?'

'Hmmm. Which barge?'

'I don't know,' said Locke. 'I just know that it's one of the three.'

Vorchenza looked over at Reynart.

'Well,' said the captain, 'there are reasons the gods saw fit to invent the enlisted man.'

'Oh, shit,' said Locke, swallowing a lump in his throat. *Make this good*, he thought. *Make this very good.* 'Doña Vorchenza, this isn't over.'

'What are you talking about?'

'Boats, barges, escape. I've been thinking. The Falconer made all sorts of strange jokes when he was under my knife. He was taunting me with something; I didn't have a chance to figure it out until now. That plague ship. The *Satisfaction*; you have to sink it.'

'And why would that be?'

'It belongs to Anatolius,' said Locke. 'According to the Falconer, Anatolius was a pirate on the White Iron Sea, building up his fortunes so he could hire a Bondsmage and return to Camorr for his revenge. The *Satisfaction* is his ship. But Anatolius isn't planning to escape on it – he's leaving the city to the north, going up the Angevine.'

'Meaning what?'

'The Falconer was dropping hints about a back-up plan,' said Locke. 'That plague ship is the back-up plan. It's not full of corpses, Doña Vorchenza. It has a token crew – men who've survived exposure to Black Whisper, like the Duke's Ghouls. A token crew and holds full of animals – goats, sheep, donkeys. I thought the Falconer was just trying to be irreverent . . . but think about it.'

'Animals can carry the Whisper,' said Reynart.

'Yes,' said Locke. 'It doesn't kill them, but they can sure as hell give it to us. Sink that fucking ship, Doña Vorchenza. It's Raza's other stroke. If he finds out he failed to wipe out the peers, he may attempt to take his revenge on the entire city. His last chance.'

'Madness,' Doña Vorchenza whispered, but she looked half-convinced.

'Anatolius already tried to wipe out every last peer of Camorr, down to the children. He *is* mad, Countess Amberglass. How well do you think he'll react to frustration? All his men have to do is run that ship up against the quay and let those animals out. Or maybe they'll just toss a few sheep into the city with a catapult. *Sink that fucking ship.*'

'Master Thorn,' said Doña Vorchenza, 'you have a curiously tender heart for a thief of your appetites.'

'I'm a sworn brother of the Nameless Thirteenth, the Crooked Warden, the Benefactor,' said Locke. 'I'm a *priest*. I didn't save the people in this tower just to see my entire city die. For propriety's sake, Doña Vorchenza, for propriety's sake, sink that gods-damned ship. I beg you.'

She stared at him over the edges of her half-moon optics, then turned to Reynart. 'Captain,' she said slowly, 'go to the lantern station on the embarkation platform. Flash messages to the Arsenal and the Dregs.'

She folded her hands over her stomach and sighed. 'On my authority, in the name of Duke Nicovante, sink the *Satisfaction* and shoot down any survivor who tries to reach shore.'

Locke sighed with relief. 'Thank you, Doña Vorchenza. Now, my elevator?'

'Your elevator, Master Thorn . . . On my honour, I'll have one made ready for you without delay. If the gods should give you Capa Raza before my men find him . . . may they give you strength.'

'I'm going to miss you, Doña Vorchenza,' said Locke. 'And you as well, my lord and lady Salvara – all apologies for getting most of your fortune buried under shit. I hope we can still be friends.'

'Set foot in our house again,' said Sofia, 'and you'll become a permanent fixture in my laboratory.'

7

Blue light flashed from the embarkation platform of Raven's Reach; even against the shifting glimmer of Falselight it stood out well enough to be seen at the relay station atop the Palace of Patience. In moments, shutters were falling rapidly open and closed over signal-lanterns; the message passed through the air over the heads of thousands of revellers and arrived at its destinations – the Arsenal, the South Needle, the Dregs.

'Holy mother of shit,' said the watch-sergeant in the tower at the very tip of the South Needle, blinking to clear his eyes, wondering if he'd counted the flashes right. He slipped his illicit Day of Changes wineskin beneath his chair with pangs of guilt.

'Watch-sergeant,' said his younger companion, 'that ship's up to something awful funny.'

Out on the water of the Old Harbour, the *Satisfaction* was slowly turning to larboard; sailors could just be seen on the yards of the main- and foremasts, preparing to unfurl topsails. Dozens of small dark shapes were moving on deck, doubly lit by the glow of yellow lamps and the glare of Falselight.

'She's casting, sir; she's going to make for sea. Where'd all those people come from?' said the younger watchman.

'I don't know,' said the sergeant, 'but the signal's just gone up. Merciful gods, they're going to sink that yellow-lit bitch.'

Pinpoints of bright orange light began to erupt around the periphery of the Dregs; each little engine-tower had emergency oil lamps that served to signal when they were manned and ready for action. Drums beat within the Arsenal; whistles sounded from across the city above the low echoing murmur of the Day of Changes crowds.

One of the engines on the shore loosed with an echoing crash. The stone was a blurred shadow in the air; it missed by yards and raised a white fountain on the frigate's starboard side.

The next engine to let fly hurled an arc of orange-white fire that seemed to hang in the sky, a hypnotic banner of burning light. The South Needle watchmen stared in awe as it crashed down onto the *Satisfaction*'s deck, spraying fiery tendrils in every direction. Men ran frantically about, some of them obviously on fire. One leapt from the vessel's side, plunging into the water like a burning cinder thrown into a puddle.

'Gods, that's fire-oil,' said the younger watchman. 'It won't stop burning even down there.'

'Well, even sharks like cooked meat,' said the sergeant with a chuckle. 'Poor bastards.'

A stone crashed into the side of the frigate, shattering wooden rails and sending splinters flying; men whirled and screamed and fell to the deck. The fire was rising into the sails and rigging, despite the frantic efforts of the crew to control it with sand. Another fire-barrel exploded on the quarterdeck; the men and women at the wheel were engulfed in a roaring nimbus of white flame. They didn't even have time to scream.

Stones battered the ship and tore through her few fluttering sails; fires burned out of control at her bow, her stern and mid-ships. Fingers of orange and red and white capered about the decks and rose into the sky, along with smoke in several colours. Within range of a dozen throwing-engines, the unarmed and nearly motionless frigate never had a chance. Five minutes after the signal had flashed forth from Raven's Reach, the *Satisfaction* was a pyre – a mountain of red and white flame reaching up from water that was a rippling red mirror beneath the dying ship's hull.

Archers took up position on the shore, ready to shoot down any survivors who tried to swim for it, but there were none. Between the fire and the water and the things that lurked in the harbour's depths, arrows were unnecessary.

8

Luciano Anatolius, the Grey King, the Capa of Camorr, the last living member of his family line, stood alone on the upper deck of the Floating Grave, beneath the silk awnings that fluttered in the Hangman's Wind, beneath the dark sky that reflected the eerie flicker of Falselight, and watched his ship burn.

He stared into the west with the red fire rippling in his eyes, and he did not blink; he stared north to the glowing tower of Raven's Reach, where flashing blue and red lights could be seen, where no cloud of pale smoke was rising against the sky.

He stood alone on the deck of the Floating Grave and he did not cry, though in his heart he desired nothing more at that moment.

Cheryn and Raiza would not have cried, he told himself. Mother and father would not have cried; they *had* not cried, when Barsavi's men kicked in their door in the middle of the night. When his father died trying to defend them all long enough for Gisella to bundle him and the little twins out the back door.

The *Satisfaction* burned before his eyes, but in his mind he was running through the darkness of the gardens once again, thirteen years old, stumbling over familiar paths with branches lashing his face and hot tears streaming down his cheeks. In the villa behind them knives were rising and falling, a small child was crying for her mother – and then that crying suddenly stopped.

'We'll never forget,' Raiza had said in the dark hold of the ship that had carried them to Talisham. 'We'll never forget, will we, Luciano?'

Her little hand curled tight inside his; Cheryn slept uneasily against his other side, murmuring and crying out in her sleep.

'We'll never forget,' he'd replied. 'And we'll go back. I promise you, some day we'll go back.'

He stood on the deck of Barsavi's fortress in Camorr, and he had the power to do exactly nothing as his ship turned the waters of the Old Harbour blood-red with its death.

'Capa Raza?'

There was a hesitant voice behind him; a man came up through the passage from the galleries below. One of the Rum Hounds from the extravagant gambling circle that had grown in his throne room. He turned slowly.

'Capa Raza, this just got brought in . . . One of the Falselight Cutters, your honour. Says a man in Ashfall gave him a tyrin and told him to get this to you right away.'

The man held out a burlap sack; 'RAZA' was scrawled on it in rough black letters. The ink still seemed to be wet.

Luciano took the bag and waved the man away; the Rum Hound ran for the passage and vanished down it, not at all pleased with what he'd seen in his master's eyes.

The Capa of Camorr opened the bag and found himself staring down at the body of a scorpion hawk – a headless scorpion hawk. He turned the bag upside down and let the contents fall to the deck; the head and the body of Vestris thudded against the wooden planks. A folded, bloodstained piece of parchment fluttered down after them. He grabbed at it and opened it.

WE'RE COMING.

Luciano stared down at the note for some time; it might have been five seconds, it might have been five minutes. He crumpled it in his hands and let it fall; it hit the deck and rolled to a rest beside Vestris's glassy, staring eyes.

If they were coming, they were coming. There would be time enough for escape when this last personal debt was discharged.

He went down the passage to the gallery below, into the light and the noise of the ongoing party. The smell of smoke and liquor hung in the air; his booted feet made the boards creak as he hurried down the stairs.

Men and women looked up from their cards and dice as he

stalked past; some waved and shouted greetings or honorifics; none of them received any response. Capa Raza threw open the door to his private suite of apartments (formerly Barsavi's) and vanished inside for several minutes.

When he emerged, he was dressed as the Grey King, in his old fog-grey leather vest and breeches, in his grey shark-skin boots with the tarnished silver buckles, in his grey swordsman's gloves creased at the knuckles from use, in his grey cloak and mantle with the hood raised. His cloak fluttered behind him as he moved forward; the lights of the Floating Grave gleamed on the naked steel of his drawn rapier.

The party died in an instant.

'Get out,' he said. 'Get out and stay away. Leave the doors open. No guards. Get out while I'll still give you the chance.'

Cards spiralled down to the deck; dice rattled across the wood. Men and women jumped to their feet, dragging drunk comrades with them; bottles rolled and wine pooled as the general retreat progressed. In less than a minute the Grey King stood alone at the heart of the Floating Grave.

He strolled slowly over to a bank of silver cords hanging down from the ceiling on the starboard side of the old galleon. He pulled on one and the white lights of the chandeliers died; he pulled another and the curtains over the room's tall windows were pulled back, opening the throne room to the night. A tug on a third cord, and red alchemical globes came to life in dark niches on the walls; the heart of the wooden fortress became a cave of carmine light.

He sat upon his throne with the rapier balanced across his legs, and the red light made fires of his eyes within the shadowed hood.

He sat upon his throne and waited for the last two Gentlemen Bastards to find him.

9

At half past the tenth hour of the evening, Locke Lamora entered that throne room and stood with one hand on his rapier, staring at the Grey King seated thirty yards away in the silent chamber. Locke was breathing hard, and not merely from his journey south; he'd covered most of the distance on a stolen horse.

The feel of the hilt of Reynart's blade beneath his hand was at once exhilarating and terrifying. He knew he was probably at a disadvantage in a straightforward fight, but his blood was up. He dared to imagine that anger and speed and hope could sustain him for what was coming. He cleared his throat.

'Grey King,' he said.

'Thorn of Camorr.'

'I'm pleased,' said Locke. 'I thought you might have left already. But I'm sorry . . . You needed that frigate, didn't you? I had my good friend the Countess Amberglass send it to the bottom of the fucking bay.'

'That deed,' said the Grey King in a weary voice, 'will lose its savour in a few minutes, I assure you. Where's Jean Tannen?'

'On his way,' said Locke. 'On his way.'

Locke walked forward slowly, cutting the distance between them in half.

'I warned the Falconer not to toy with Tannen,' said the Grey King. 'Apparently, my warning wasn't heeded. I congratulate you both on your improbable resilience, but now I fear I'll be doing you a favour by killing you before the Bondsmagi can take their revenge.'

'You're assuming the Falconer is dead,' said Locke. 'He's still breathing, but he'll, ah, never play any musical instruments again.'

'Interesting. How have you done all this, I wonder? Why does the Death Goddess scorn to snuff you like a candle? I wish I knew.'

'Fuck your wishes. Why did you do it the way you did, Luciano? Why didn't you try for an honest accommodation with us? One might have been reached.'

' "Might," ' said the Grey King, 'there was no room for "might," Master Lamora. There were only my needs. You had what I needed, and you were too dangerous to let live once I had it – as you've made only too clear.'

'But you could have settled for simple theft,' said Locke. 'I would have given it all to keep Calo and Galdo and Bug alive. I would have given it *all*, had you put it to me like that.'

'What thief does not fight to hold what he has?'

'One that has something better,' said Locke. 'The stealing was more the point for us than the keeping; if the keeping had been so fine, we would have found something to fucking do with it all.'

'Easy to say with hindsight.' The Grey King sighed. 'You would have said something different when they were still alive.'

'We stole from the *peers*, you arsehole. We stole from them exclusively. Of all the people to double-cross . . . You aided the nobility when you tried to take us out. You gave the people you hate a gods-damned gift.'

'So you relieved them of their money, Master Lamora, scrupulously refraining from taking lives in the process . . . Should I applaud? Name you a brother-in-arms? There's always more money. Theft alone would not teach them the lesson they had coming.'

'How could you do it, Luciano? How could a man who lost what you lost, who felt what you felt for Barsavi, do the same to me?'

'The same?' The Grey King stood up; the rapier was in his hand. 'The same? Were your parents murdered in their bed to protect a lie, Master Lamora? Were your infant siblings put under the knife so they could never grow old enough to take their revenge?'

'I lost three brothers at your hands,' said Locke. 'I almost lost four. You didn't need to do it. When you thought you were finished with me, you tried to kill hundreds. Children, Luciano, *children* – born years after Barsavi murdered your parents. It must be nice to be righteous; from where I'm standing it looks like fucking lunacy.'

'They were sheltered by the Secret Peace,' said the Grey King. 'They were parasites, guilty by birth. Save your arguments, priest. Don't you think I've had them with myself on too many nights to count over the past twenty-two *years*?'

The Grey King took a step forward, the tip of his blade rising in Locke's direction.

'If it were in my power,' he said, 'I would knock this city to the ground and write the names of my family in its ashes.'

'*Ila justicca vei cala*,' Locke whispered. He stepped forward once again until the men were separated by barely two yards. He slid Reynart's rapier out of its scabbard and stood at guard.

'Justice is red.' The Grey King faced Locke with his knees bent, the true edge of his rapier facing the ground, in the position Camorri fencers called 'the waiting wolf'. 'It is indeed.'

Locke struck out before the Grey King had finished speaking; for an eyeblink darting steel cut an after-image in the air between the two men. The King parried Locke's thrust, forte to foible, and riposted with speed more than equal to Locke's own. Lamora avoided a skewering only by an undignified backward leap; he landed in a crouch with his left hand splayed out to keep himself from going arse-over-elbows on the hard wood of the deck.

Warily, Locke circled in the direction the lunge had knocked him, barely rising from his crouch. A dagger appeared in his left hand as though by legerdemain; this he twirled several times.

'Hmm,' said the Grey King. 'Tell me you don't mean to fight Verrari-style. I find the school insipid.'

'Please yourself.' Locke wiggled his dagger suggestively. 'I'll try not to get too much blood on your cloak.'

Sighing theatrically, the Grey King plucked a narrow-hilted dagger from his own belt, which held two, and thrust it out so that his blades opened in the air before him like jaws. He then took two exaggerated hops forward.

Locke flicked his gaze down to the Grey King's feet for a fraction of a second, realising almost too late that he was intended to do just that. He whipped himself to his right and barely managed a parry with his dagger; the Grey King's thrust slid off and cut the air just an inch from his left shoulder. His own riposte met the King's dagger as though intended for it. Again, the King was too fast by half.

For a few desperate seconds the two men were fully engaged – their blades wove silver ghosts in the air, crossing and uncrossing, feint and false feint, thrust and parry. Locke remained just out of reach of the Grey King's longer, more muscular cuts while the King caught and turned Locke's every lunge with easy precision. At last they flew apart and stood panting, staring at one another with the resigned, implacable hatred of fighting dogs.

'Hmmm,' said the Grey King, 'an illuminating passage.'

He flicked out almost casually with his rapier; Locke darted back once again and parried feebly, tip to tip, like a boy in his first week of training. The Grey King's eyes glittered.

'Most illuminating.' Again a casual flick; again Locke jumped back. 'You're not actually very good at this, are you?'

'It would be to my advantage if you thought so, wouldn't it?'

At this the Grey King actually laughed. 'Oh no. No, no, *no*.' With one decisive gesture, he flung his cloak and mantle to the ground. A wild grin had etched deep furrows of anticipation into his lean face. 'No more bluffs. No more games.'

And then he fell on Locke, his footwork a blur, his brutality unmatched by anything in Locke's memory; behind his blade were twenty years of experience and twenty years of blackest hatred. Some tiny, detached part of Locke's mind coolly registered his own inadequacy as he desperately flailed parry after parry, chasing phantom thrusts with his eyes and hands even while the Grey King's steel was punching through cloth and flesh.

Once, twice, three times – in between breaths the Grey King's blade sang out and bit into Locke's left wrist, forearm and bicep.

Cold surprise hit Locke harder than the pain of the thrusts; then the warm blood began to flow across his sweat-slick skin, tickling devilishly, and a wave of nausea rose up from the pit of his stomach. The dagger dropped from his left hand, red with the wrong man's blood.

'At last we come to something you cannot *pretend* your way out of, Master Lamora.' The Grey King flicked Locke's blood from the tip of his rapier and watched it splash against the wooden deck in an arc. 'Goodbye.'

Then he was moving again, and in the wine-coloured light of the alchemical globes the full length of his blade was bright scarlet.

'Aza Guilla,' Locke whispered, 'give me justice for the death of my friends. Give me blood for the death of my brothers!'

His voice rising to a shout, he thrust, missed and thrust again, willing all of his desperate hatred and fear into each cut, driving the blade faster than he ever had in his life, and still the Grey King caught and turned his every thrust, still the Grey King displaced himself from the path of Locke's cuts as though fighting a child.

'It seems that the final difference between us, Master Lamora,' said the Grey King between passages, 'is that I knew what I was doing when I stayed here to meet you one last time.'

'No,' gasped Locke. 'The difference between us is that I am going to have my revenge.'

Cold pain exploded in Locke's left shoulder, and he stared down in horror at the Grey King's blade, sunk three inches into the flesh just above his heart. The King twisted savagely, scraping bone as he withdrew his blade, and the sensation sent Locke tumbling to his knees, his useless left arm thrown out instinctively to break his fall.

But instinct betrayed him here too; his hand struck the hard deck palm up, folded awkwardly under the full weight of his arm, and with a terrible snap his left wrist broke. He was too shocked to scream. A split second later the Grey King slammed a vicious kick into the side of Locke's head, and his world became a kaleidoscope of agony, tumbling end over end as stinging tears filled his eyes. Reynart's rapier clattered across the deck.

Locke was conscious of the wood pressing up against his back. He was conscious of the blood and the salt that misted his vision. He was conscious of the bright, hot rings of pain that radiated from his shattered wrist, and of the wet agony of the hole in his shoulder joint. But most of all he was conscious of his own shame, his terror of failure, and the great weight of three dead friends, lying unavenged, lying unquiet because Locke Lamora had *lost*.

He sucked in a great gasping breath, kindling new flickers of pain all across his chest and back, but now it was all one pain, all one red sensation that drove him up from the ground. Bellowing without an ounce of reason in his voice, he pulled his legs in and whipped himself up, attempting to tackle the Grey King around his stomach.

The killing thrust that had been falling towards Locke's heart struck his left arm instead; impelled with every ounce of the Grey King's ferocity, it punched fully through the meat of Locke's slender forearm and out the other side. Mad with pain, Locke threw this arm forward and up as the King struggled to withdraw; the edges of his rapier worked a terrible business on Locke's flesh, but stayed caught, sawing back and forth at the muscle as the two men struggled.

The Grey King's dagger loomed before Locke's eyes and animal instinct drove him to use the only weapon available. His teeth sank into the first three fingers of the King's hand around the hilt; he tasted blood and felt bone beneath the tips of his teeth. The Grey King cried out and the dagger fell, rebounding off Locke's left shoulder before clattering to the deck. The King jerked his hand free and Locke spat his own skin and blood at him.

'Give it up!' the Grey King screamed, punching Locke on the top of his skull, then across his nose. With his good right arm

Locke clutched for his opponent's sheathed dagger. The King slapped his hand away, laughing.

'You can't win! You can't win, Lamora!' With every shout, the Grey King rained blows on Locke, who clutched at him desperately, as a drowning man might hug a floating timber. The King laughed savagely as he pummelled Lamora's skull, his ears, his forehead and his shoulders, even driving his fist down into the seeping wound. 'You . . . cannot . . . beat me!'

'I don't have to beat you,' Locke whispered, grinning madly up at the Grey King, his face streaked with blood and tears, his nose broken and his lips cracked, his vision swimming and edged with blackness. 'I don't have to beat you, motherfucker. I just have to keep you here . . . until Jean shows up.'

At that, the Grey King became truly desperate and his blows fell like rain, but Locke was heedless of them, laughing the wet braying laugh of utter madness. 'I just have to keep you here . . . until Jean . . . shows up!'

Hissing with fury, the Grey King shook Locke off enough to make a grab for his sheathed dagger. As he tore his left hand from Locke's right, Lamora let a gold tyrin fall from his sleeve into his palm; a desperate flick of his wrist sent the coin caroming off the wall behind the Grey King, echoing loudly. 'There he is, motherfucker!' Locke yelled, spraying blood across the front of the King's shirt. 'Jean! Help me!'

And the Grey King whirled, dragging Locke halfway round with him; whirled in fear of Jean Tannen before he realised that Locke must be lying; whirled for just the half-second that Locke would have begged from any god that would hear his prayer; whirled for the half-second that was worth Locke's entire life.

He whirled just long enough for Locke Lamora to snake his right arm round the Grey King's waist, slide out the dagger sheathed there and bury it with a final scream of pain and triumph in the Grey King's back, just to the right of his spine.

The Grey King's back arched, and his mouth hung open, gasping in the icy thrall of shock; with both of his arms he pushed at Locke's head as though by prying the smaller man off him he could undo his wound, but Locke held fast and in an impossibly calm voice he whispered, 'Calo Sanza. My brother and my friend.'

Back, the Grey King toppled, and Locke slid the knife out of his back just before he struck the deck. Falling on top of him, Locke raised the dagger once again and brought it down in the middle of the Grey King's chest, just beneath his ribcage. Blood spurted and the King flailed like a beetle pinned inside a collection case. Locke's voice rose as he worked the knife further in: 'Galdo Sanza, my brother and my friend!'

With one last convulsive effort, the Grey King spat warm coppery blood into Locke's face and grabbed at the dagger that transfixed his chest; Locke countered by bearing down with his useless left side, batting the King's hands away. Sobbing, Locke wrenched the dagger out of the King's chest, raised it with a wildly shaking right arm, and brought it down in his throat. He sawed at the windpipe until the neck was half-severed and great rivers of blood were flowing on the deck beneath the men. The Grey King shuddered one last time and died, his wide white eyes still fixed on Locke's.

'Bug,' Locke whispered. 'His real name was Bertilion Gadek. My apprentice. My brother. And my friend.'

His strength failed, and he slid down over the Grey King's corpse.

'My friend.'

But the man beneath him said nothing, and Locke was acutely aware of the stillness of the chest beneath his ears, of the heart that should have been beating against his cheek, and he began to cry – long wild sobs that wracked his entire body, drawing new threads of agony from his tortured nerves and muscles. Mad with grief and triumph and the red haze of pain and a hundred other feelings he couldn't name, he lay atop the corpse of his greatest enemy and bawled like a baby, adding salt water to the warm blood that covered the body of the Grey King.

He lay there shaking in the light of the red lamps, in a silent hall, alone with his triumph, unable to move and bleeding to death.

10

Jean found him there just a minute or two later. The big man turned Locke over and slid him off the corpse, eliciting a sincere howl of pain from his half-conscious friend.

'Oh, gods,' Jean cried. 'Oh, gods, you fucking idiot, you miserable fucking bastard.' He pressed his hands against Locke's chest and neck as though he could simply will the blood back into his body. 'Why couldn't you wait? Why couldn't you wait for me?'

Locke stared drunkenly up at Jean, his mouth a little 'O' of concern.

'Jean,' Locke whispered gravely, 'you have . . . been running. You were in . . . no condition to fight. Grey King . . . so accommodating. Could not refuse.'

Jean snorted despite himself. 'Gods damn you, Locke Lamora. I sent him a message. I thought it might keep him around awhile.'

'Bless your heart. I did . . . get him, though. I got him and I burnt his ship.'

'So that's what happened,' Jean said, very gently. 'I saw. I was watching the fire from the other side of the Wooden Waste; I saw you walk into the Floating Grave like you owned the place and I came as fast as I could. But you didn't even need me.'

'Oh no.' Locke swallowed, grimacing at the taste of his own blood. 'I made excellent use . . . of your reputation.'

At this Jean said nothing, and the forlorn light in his eyes chilled Locke more than anything yet.

'So this is revenge,' Locke mumbled.

'It is,' whispered Jean.

After a few seconds new tears welled up in Locke's eyes and he closed them, shaking his head. 'It's a shit business.'

'It is.'

'You have to leave . . . me here.'

At this, Jean rocked back on his knees as though he'd been slapped. 'What?'

'Leave me, Jean. I'll be dead . . . just a few minutes. They won't get anything from me. You can still get away. Please . . . leave me.'

Jean's face turned bright red, a red that showed even by the light of the alchemical globes, and his eyebrows arched, and every line in his face drew so taut that Locke found the energy to be alarmed. Jean's jaw clenched; his teeth ground together, and the planes of his cheeks stood out like mountain ridges under his gilding of fat.

'That is a hell of a thing for you to say to me,' he finally hissed in the flattest, deadliest voice Locke had ever heard.

'I made a mistake, Jean!' Locke croaked in desperation. 'I couldn't really fight him. He did for me before I could cheat my way out of it. Just promise me . . . promise me that if you ever find Sabetha, you'll . . .'

'You can find her yourself, halfwit, after we both get the hell out of here!'

'Jean!' Locke clutched weakly at the lapels of Jean's coat with his good hand. 'I'm sorry; I fucked up. Please don't stay here and get caught; the blackjackets will be coming soon. I couldn't bear to have you taken. Please just leave me. I can't walk.'

'Idiot,' Jean whispered, brushing away hot tears with his good hand. 'You won't have to.'

Working awkwardly but rapidly, Jean took up the Grey King's cloak and tied it around his own neck, creating a makeshift sling for his right arm. This he slid beneath Locke's knees, and, straining mightily, he was able to pick the smaller man up and cradle him in front of his chest. Locke moaned.

'Stop sobbing, you damn baby,' Jean hissed as he began to lope back along the dock. 'You must have at least half a glass of blood left somewhere in there.' But Locke was now well and truly unconscious, whether from pain or blood loss Jean couldn't tell, though his skin was so pale it almost looked like glass. His eyes were open but unseeing, and his mouth hung open, trailing blood and spittle.

Panting and shuddering, ignoring the wrenching pains of his own wounds, Jean began to run as fast as he could.

The body of the Grey King lay forgotten on the deck behind him, and the red light shone on in the empty hall.

INTERLUDE:
A Minor Prophecy

Father Chains sat on the roof of the House of Perelandro, staring down at the astonishingly arrogant fourteen-year-old that the little orphan he'd purchased so many years before from the Thiefmaker of Shades' Hill had become.

'Some day, Locke Lamora,' he said, 'some day, you're going to fuck up so magnificently, so ambitiously, so *overwhelmingly* that the sky will light up and the moons will spin and the gods themselves will shit comets with glee. And I just hope I'm still around to see it.'

'Oh, please,' said Locke. 'It'll never happen.'

EPILOGUE

Falselight

I

The eighteenth of Parthis in the Seventy-Eighth Year of Aza Guilla; a wet Camorri summer. The whole city had a hangover and the sky did too.

Warm rain was falling in sheets, spattering and steaming. The water caught the Falselight glimmer like layers of shifting, translucent mirrors and formed split-second works of art in the air, but men cursed it anyway because it made their heads wet.

'Watch-sergeant! Watch-sergeant Vidrik!'

The man yelling outside Vidrik's station at the south end of the Narrows was another watchman. Vidrik stuck his lean, weathered face out through the window beside the shack door and was rewarded with a stream of run-off on his forehead. Thunder boomed overhead. 'What is it, son?'

The watchman approached out of the rain; it was Constanzo, the new lad just shifted in from the North Corner. He was leading a Gentled donkey; behind the donkey was an open-topped cart, with two more yellow-jacketed watchmen at its rear. They huddled in their oilcloaks and looked miserable, which meant they were sensible men.

'Found something, sergeant,' said Constanzo. 'Something pretty fucked.'

Teams of yellowjackets and blackjackets had been combing the south of Camorr since the previous night; rumours were swirling of some sort of assassination attempt at Raven's Reach. Gods only knew what the Spider thought his boys should be doing turning over stones in the Dregs and the Ashfall districts, but Vidrik was used to never hearing the whys and the wherefores.

'Define "pretty fucked",' he yelled as he slipped into his own oilcloak and threw up the hood. He stepped out into the rain and crossed to the donkey-cart, waving to the two men standing behind it. One of them owed him two barons from the previous week's dicing.

'Have a look,' said Constanzo, sweeping back the wet blanket that covered the load. It was a man, youngish and very pale, balding, with a fuzz of stubble on his cheeks. He was fairly well dressed, in a grey coat with red cuffs. It happened to be spattered with blood.

The man was alive, but he lay in the cart with his fingerless hands pressed against his cheeks, and he stared up at Vidrik without a speck of sane comprehension in his eyes. 'Mahhhhhh,' he moaned as the rain fell on his head. 'Mwaaaaaaaaah!'

His tongue had been cut out; a dark scar covered the stump at the bottom of his mouth, oozing blood.

'*MAAAAAAAAAAAAAAAAAAAAH!*'

'Sweet fucking Perelandro,' said Vidrik, 'tell me I don't see what I see on his wrists.'

'It's a Bondsmage, sergeant,' said Constanzo. 'It is, or was.'

He threw the soaked blanket back over the man's face and reached inside his oilcloak. 'There's more. Show it to you inside?'

Vidrik led Constanzo back into his shack. The two men swept their hoods back but didn't bother taking their cloaks off. Constanzo pulled out a piece of folded parchment.

'We found this fellow tied to a floor over in Ashfall,' he said. 'Pretty gods-damned weird. This parchment was on his chest.'

Vidrik took it and unfolded it to read,

*PERSONAL ATTENTION OF THE DUKE'S SPIDER
FOR RETURN TO KARTHAIN*

'Gods,' he said. 'A real Karthani Bondsmage. Looks like he won't be recommending Camorr to his friends.'

'What do we do with him, sergeant?'

Vidrik sighed, folded the letter and passed it back to Constanzo.

'We pass the coin, lad,' he said. 'We pass this fucking coin right up the chain of command and forget we ever saw it. Haul him to the Palace of Patience and let someone else give it a ponder.'

Falselight glimmered on the rain-rippled water of Camorr Bay as Doña Angiavesta Vorchenza, Dowager Countess of Amberglass, stood on the dock huddled in a fur-lined oilcloak while teams of men with wooden poles probed a barge full of rain-sodden shit beneath her. The smell was attention-grabbing.

'I'm sorry, my lady,' said the watch-sergeant at her left hand, 'We're positive there's nothing on the other two barges, and we've been at this one for six hours. I sincerely doubt that anything will turn up, although we will, of course, continue our efforts.'

Doña Vorchenza sighed deeply and turned to look at the carriage, drawn by four black stallions and framed with alchemical running lights in the Vorchenza colours, that stood on the dock behind her. Its door was open – Don and Doña Salvara sat inside peering out at her, along with Captain Reynart. She beckoned to them.

Reynart was the first to reach her side; as usual he wore no oilcloak and bore the heavy rain with stiff-necked stoicism. The Salvaras were sensibly covered up against the downpour; Lorenzo held up a silk parasol to shield his wife even further.

'Let me guess,' said Reynart. 'They're full of shit.'

'I'm afraid so,' said Doña Vorchenza. 'Thank you for your time, watch-sergeant; you are dismissed. You may call your men out of the barge as well. I don't believe we'll be needing them any more.'

As the greatly relieved yellowjackets filed away down the dock, wooden poles held very carefully on their shoulders, Doña Vorchenza seemed to shudder and gasp. She put her hands to her face and bent forward.

'Doña Vorchenza,' cried Sofia, rushing forward to support her. As they all bent close around her, she suddenly straightened up and cackled, gasping in air between bursts of dry-sounding laughter. She shook with it; her tiny fists punched the air before her.

'Oh gods,' she gasped, 'oh, this is too much.'

'What? Doña Vorchenza, what's the matter?' Reynart took her by the arm and peered at her.

'The money, Stephen.' She chuckled. 'The money was never

anywhere near this place. The little bastard had us digging through shit-barges purely for his own amusement. The money was on board the *Satisfaction.*'

'How do you figure that?'

'Isn't it plain? It's all striking me from so many directions at once. Gods bless and damn the clarity of hindsight. Capa Raza assisted with charitable contributions to the plague ship, yes?'

'He did.'

'Not from any sense of charitable duty. Because he needed a means to move his fortune out to the frigate!'

'Out to a plague ship?' said Doña Sofia. 'That wouldn't do him any good.'

'It would if there was no plague,' said Doña Vorchenza. 'The plague was a lie.'

'But,' said Don Lorenzo, 'why was Lukas so adamant about sinking that ship? Was it simple pique? If he couldn't have it, no one could?'

'His name was Callas, Lorenzo dear, Tavrin Callas.'

'Whichever, darling,' said Lorenzo. 'Forty-five thousand crowns, plus whatever Barsavi's fortune came to. That's a great deal of money to put out of *everyone's* grasp, forever.'

'Yes,' said Doña Vorchenza. 'And he told us why he was doing it while he stood there. Damn me for a fool.'

'I fear,' said Doña Sofia, 'I speak for the rest of us when I say we don't follow.'

'The Thorn said he was a priest of the Thirteenth,' she said. 'The heresy of the Nameless Thirteenth, the Crooked Warden, the god of thieves and malefactors. "For propriety's sake," he said, "for *propriety's* sake". He said that on purpose.'

She laughed again, biting down on her knuckles to contain herself.

'Oh gods. Anatolius killed three of his friends. So don't you see? There was no danger on that ship; he didn't want it sunk to save Camorr. It was a death-offering, Stephen, a *death-offering.*'

Reynart slapped one hand against his forehead; water flew.

'Yes,' said Doña Vorchenza. 'A death-offering. And I sank it for him, in sixty fathoms of shark-infested water, neat as you please.'

'So . . .' said Don Lorenzo. 'All of our money is three hundred and sixty feet down on the bottom of the Old Harbour?'

'I'm afraid so,' said Doña Vorchenza.

'Ah . . . what do we do now?'

Doña Vorchenza sighed and meditated for a few moments. 'First,' she said when she looked back up at the Salvaras, 'all the truths behind this affair will be declared state secrets of the Duchy of Camorr; I bind you all to silence concerning them. The Thorn of Camorr is a myth; the money he allegedly stole never existed; the Duke's Spider never took any formal interest in the matter.'

'But,' said Doña Sofia, 'they told Lorenzo that's how the Thorn guarantees his own secrecy – when they stole into our house dressed as Midnighters!'

'Yes,' said her husband. 'One of the false Midnighters specifically told me that the Thorn relied on the embarrassment of his victims to keep his thefts secret from other potential victims, and I don't think that part was a lie.'

'I'm sure it wasn't,' said Doña Vorchenza. 'But nonetheless that's just what we're going to do. In time, you'll come to understand that a state like ours cannot afford to show weakness for honesty's sake; Duke Nicovante charges me with guarding his security, not his conscience.'

The Salvaras stared at her, saying nothing.

'Oh, don't look so glum,' she said. 'Your real punishment for getting involved in this mess has not yet begun. Come back to Amberglass with me, and let's talk about the penalty.'

'Our punishment, Doña Vorchenza?' said Lorenzo hotly. 'Our punishment was nearly seventeen thousand crowns! Haven't we been punished enough?'

'Not nearly,' said Doña Vorchenza. 'I've decided who's to inherit the title of Countess Amberglass when it's my time to pass on.' She paused for just a moment before continuing. 'Or, should I say, Count and Countess Amberglass.'

'What?' Sofia squeaked like a girl of eight, a particularly squeaky girl of eight, much accustomed to squeaking loudly.

'It's no blessing,' said Doña Vorchenza. 'It comes with a job.'

'You can't be serious,' said Don Lorenzo. 'There are two dozen families on the Alcegrante with more rank and honour than ourselves; the Duke would never name us to Amberglass before them.'

'I believe I know Nicovante somewhat better than you do, young man,' said Doña Vorchenza. 'And I believe the inheritance is mine to dictate.'

'But . . . the job,' said Doña Salvara. 'You can't mean . . .'

'Of course I do, Sofia. I can't live forever. Each time something like this affair lands in my lap, I suddenly recall that I don't *want* to live forever. Let someone else play the Spider; we've deceived everyone for all these years letting them think the office was held by a man. Now let's deceive them further by passing it on to *two* individuals.'

She put her arm through Reynart's and allowed him to help her back towards the carriage.

'You'll have Stephen to help you and to run your operations; he'll serve as the link between you and the Midnighters. You both have acceptably malleable wits. Given just a few more years, I'm sure I can whip the two of you into something resembling the shape I require.'

'And then?' asked Doña Sofia.

'And then, my dear, all these gods-damned crises will be *yours* to deal with.' Doña Vorchenza sighed. 'Old sins will never be buried so deep that they cannot rise again when least expected. And so you'll pay for the good of Camorr with the coin of your own conscience, parcelled out year after year, until that purse is empty at last.'

3

'Master Lamora,' cried Ibelius, 'this is entirely unacceptable!'

The sea at Falselight was a surging field of grey and green; the waves rolled and crashed around the galleon *Golden Gain*, bound for Talisham and thence to Tal Verrar, one of only two vessels that had put out from Camorr that evening. The wind wailed in the shrouds and sails of the elderly vessel, and sailors in oilcloaks hurried here and there, muttering private prayers to Iono, Lord of the Grasping Waters.

Locke Lamora lay on a pile of tarp-covered crates on the

galleon's raised stern deck, bundled in blankets within oilcloths within tarps, like a sausage roll. Nothing of him was visible but his abnormally pale (and heavily bruised) face, poking out of the layers around him. Jean Tannen sat at his side, bundled against the rain but not to the point of immobility.

'Master Ibelius,' said Locke in a weak voice, made nasal by his broken nose, 'each time I have left Camorr, I have done so by land. This is something new . . . I wanted to see it, one last time.'

'You are very near death, Master Lamora,' said Ibelius, 'it is foolish for you to be larking about on deck in this weather.'

'Ibelius,' said Jean, 'if what Locke is doing were larking about, corpses could get jobs as acrobats. Can we have a moment's peace?'

'From the attentions that have sustained his life this past day? By all means, young masters . . . enjoy your sea-view, and on your heads be it!'

Ibelius stomped off across the rolling deck, sliding in this direction and that, quite unaccustomed to life at sea.

Camorr was diminishing behind them, fading gradually between shifting curtains of rain. Falselight rose up from the lower city like an aura above the waves; the Five Towers shone ghostly beneath the churning skies. The wake of the galleon seemed to gleam with phosphorescence, a roiling Falselight of its own.

They sat on the stern deck and watched the dark horizon swallow the city behind them.

'I'm sorry, Locke,' said Jean. 'I'm sorry I couldn't be more useful to you at the end.'

'What the hell are you talking about? You killed Cheryn and Raiza; I could never have done that. You pulled me out of the Floating Grave. You hauled me back to Ibelius and got another lovely fucking poultice smeared all over me. What do you have to apologise for, besides the poultice?'

'I'm a liability,' he said. 'My name. I've been using my real name all my life and I never thought it'd come to anything bad.'

'What, the Bondsmage? Oh gods, Jean. Take a false name wherever we end up. Tavrin Callas is good. Let the bastard pop up all over the place; the order of Aza Guilla will have a surfeit of miracles to cherish.'

'I tried to kill you, Locke. I'm sorry . . . I couldn't do anything about it.'

'You didn't try to kill me, Jean. The Falconer did. You *couldn't* do anything about it. Gods, I'm the one with his arm sliced open and his shoulder punched in and you're over there moping. Enough!'

Thunder rumbled in the clouds overhead, and there was the sound of shouted orders from the forward deck of the ship.

'Jean,' said Locke, 'you are a greater friend than I ever could have imagined before I met you; I owe you my life too many times over to count. I would rather be dead myself than lose you. Not just because you're all I have left.'

Jean said nothing for several minutes; they stared north across the Iron Sea as the whitecaps lashed one another in an increasing tempo.

'Sorry,' said Jean. 'Mouth sort of ran away with me. Thanks, Locke.'

'Well, cheer up. At least you've got more mobility than a fucking tadpole on dry land. Look at my little oilcloth castle.'

Locke sighed.

'So this is winning,' he said.

'It is,' replied Jean.

'It can go fuck itself,' said Locke.

They passed another few minutes in silence and rain.

'Locke,' said Jean at last, hesitantly.

'Yes?'

'If you don't mind my asking . . . what *is* your real name?'

'Oh gods.' Locke smiled weakly. 'Can't I have any secrets?'

'You know mine.'

'Yeah, but you've only got the one anyway.'

'Not a fair point.'

'Oh, fine,' said Locke. 'Get over here.'

Jean stumbled over to the pile of crates on which Locke was lying, and bent down. Locke whispered five syllables into his ear, and Jean's eyes widened.

'You know,' he said, 'I'd have gone with Locke myself in preference to that.'

'Tell me about it,' said Locke.

*

529

The galleon rode south before the winds of the storm, and the last few glimmers of Falselight faded behind them. The lights drew down into the darkness, and then they were gone for good, and the rain swept in like a wall above the surface of the sea.

ACKNOWLEDGEMENTS

A chunk of incredible good fortune fell right out of the sky and landed on my head when this novel was picked up for publication. I owe many thanks to Simon Spanton, Gillian Redfearn, Krystyna Kujawinska, Hannah Whitaker, and Susan Howe at Orion Books, not to mention Anne Groell at Bantam, and of course Deanna Hoak.

It takes a village to keep a first-time author's ego stoked (or in check, as necessary). I couldn't have asked for more patient or generous supporters than my parents, Jill and Tom Lynch, nor would anything have been the same without a certain energetic crew of online miscreant-savants: Gabe Chouinard, Matthew Woodring Stover, Kage Baker, Bob Urell, Summer Brooks, M. Lynn Booker, Chris Billett, Gabriel Mesa, Alex Berman, Clucky, Nate Blumenfeld, Ilya Popov, Ariel and all the rest – including the readers and players of the role-playing game *Deeds Not Words*.

Thanks also to friends near and far – Jason McCray, Darren Wieland, Cleo McAdams, Jayson Stevens, Peg Kerr, Philip Shill, Bradford Walker, J. H. Frank, Jason Sartin, Abra Staffin-Wiebe, Sammi and Louis, Mike and Becky, Bridget and Joe, Annie and Josiah, Erik and Aman, Mike and Laura, Paul, Adrian, Ben and Jenny Rose, Aaron, Jesse, Chris and Ren, Andy Nelson, and last but not least Rose Miller, who's not tall enough to ride the ride just yet, but we let her on anyway.

New Richmond, Wisconsin
September 16, 2005

THE GOLLANCZ 50 COLLECTION

Do Androids Dream of Electric Sheep *by Philip K. Dick*

Dune *by Frank Herbert*

Flowers for Algernon *by Daniel Keyes*

The Lies of Locke Lamora *by Scott Lynch*

I Am Legend *by Richard Matheson*

Eric *by Terry Pratchett*

The Name of the Wind *by Patrick Rothfuss*

Hyperion *by Dan Simmons*

The Time Machine *by H. G. Wells*

The Book of the New Sun *by Gene Wolfe*